Born in Melbour[...] teacher, a political journalist and an oral historian, but gave this up to pursue a literary career. Having won awards for her poetry and short stories, Patricia went on to write her first book, and *Brother Digger* was published in Australia in 1984. This was followed by *Pioneers of a Trackless Land, Valley of Lagoons, River of the Sun, The Feather and the Stone, Where the Willows Weep, Cry of the Rain Bird* and *Fires of Fortune*, which were warmly praised:

'Avoiding the obvious pitfalls and clichés, Shaw has crafted a solid, exciting, well-researched novel' *Publishers Weekly*

'An absorbing adventure . . . enjoyable by any standards . . . a rich literary lode' *Brisbane Courier Mail*

'Storyline as dramatic and colourful as the land itself' *Gold Coast Bulletin*

Apart from her writing, Patricia spends her time researching political history, reading and swimming. She lives on the beautiful Queensland Gold Coast of Australia and has a grown-up son and daughter. She is also a devoted fan of native birds and is concerned with animal welfare.

The Opal Seekers

Patricia Shaw

HEADLINE

First published in 1996
by HEADLINE BOOK PUBLISHING

10 9 8 7 6 5 4 3 2 1

ISBN 0 7472 5060 X

Typeset by Palimpsest Book Production Limited,
Polmont, Stirlingshire
Printed and bound in Great Britain by
Cox & Wyman Ltd, Reading, Berkshire

HEADLINE BOOK PUBLISHING
A division of Hodder Headline PLC
338 Euston Road
London NW1 3BH

On Opals:

I believe I admire them even more than the precious stones, for among them . . . we have only the four obvious colours, but here – why there's not a colour on land or sea but is imprisoned in one of these heavenly stones.

Oscar Wilde

Chapter One

1898

Trella Court was said to be a contrary woman.

'If black was white she'd say it was yellow,' her mother Maisie Grogan accorded, invoking her own brand of logic. She was still smarting from last week's episode when Trella had argued with the priest in the middle of his sermon. And not for the first time, God help us!

That was about young Mary Best, who'd got herself pregnant and sent away to the nuns in Dublin to hide her shame.

'Her absence is a lesson to all young women of the parish,' Father Daly had thundered, in a hellfire sermon that would have done a missionary proud, 'to keep themselves pure in body and mind! Fallen women are doomed in the eyes of God! The stain of their sinfulness can never be erased!'

He was going great guns, hammering away at the sin of lust that had driven Mary Best and others of her ilk from the holy portals of this church.

'Good people of Tullymore, beware the sin of Eve. Beware these women who revel in lust . . .'

Then it was that Trella had stood and Maisie had almost fainted.

The holy father stopped mid-blast. His eyes bulged and his pink cheeks flamed, and he dug under the white lace for his handkerchief to snuffle and fume.

But he didn't order her to sit down like last time. He waited for her to speak. And of course, she did.

'We've heard enough of poor little Mary Best, Father,' Trella called. 'No one gets themselves pregnant. It takes two. So what about that young feller over there in the second row? Have you nothing to say to him?'

Maisie was leaning over Garth, her grandson, frantically

poking at her daughter to sit down. She'd actually used the word 'pregnant' in a church, for God's sake! Had she gone mad altogether? Beside her, Brodie Court was grinning. He would, seeing this as nothing but a bit of entertainment! So she fixed her eyes on Michael, her son-in-law, trying to compel him to shut his wife up, but he had his eyes cast down, avoiding her. Avoiding everyone, probably not knowing what to do.

'Do you not have even a scold for him?' Trella was persisting. 'For the father of the child the young girl's about to bear? Or is it not a sin for men?'

The parishioners sat like statues, with never so much as a nudge for fear Father Daly would note their shocked delight at this sudden fracture of a pious morn.

Then at the rear of the tiny church, Sergeant Clemens lumbered to his feet and all eyes swung in his direction.

He tiptoed, as much as a man of his bulk could, down the aisle and, leaning across Michael, beckoned to Trella, who had resumed her seat, expecting a reply from the priest.

'Will ye come with me, Trella?' he whispered.

She blinked. 'Where to?'

'Outside.'

'Why?'

'I want a word with you.'

'Can't it wait?' Michael said, irritated.

'It cannot. You must come with me, Trella.'

'Why? What's wrong?' There was alarm in her voice. 'Is something wrong?'

You could have heard a pin drop in the church. The Sergeant shifted his weight from one foot to the other, his shoes creaking their complaint.

'It is an offence to interrupt divine service,' he hissed.

'Since when?' she retorted.

'Since always. Now will you come with me?'

Michael Court grasped his arm. 'What's this I'm hearing? Are you charging my wife?'

Clemens was now experiencing more discomfort than the priest, who stood in the pulpit in saintly pose, his eyes fixed on the circular stained-glass window over the front door.

The Sergeant faltered. Michael's tone was ominous, and further down the pew, Brodie, glaring at him, was no longer amused. The Court brothers were hard men, and even though the Sergeant knew they were often confused and irritated when Trella sounded off about something that irked her in the village, they'd balk at her arrest. Big, bearded Brodie never minded a fight, and the thought of a fight in the church was giving Clemens palpitations. He should never have agreed to this.

'It's Father Daly,' he whispered urgently to Michael, the quieter of the two. 'He's made a complaint. He can't have these disagreements in his church.'

'Is he the Pope then?' Michael asked, loyal to his wife. 'The man is infallible, is he?'

'I'm not about knowing these things. The complaint's been made and I have to act.' He appealed to Trella: 'Now be a good girl and come along with me. There'll be no charges. We'll just have a little talk outside.'

'We'll do no such thing,' she snapped.

He wondered what tribe of renegades had spawned this one. She was only a farm girl, married to a farmer. She'd never been further than Limerick in her life but she was a born nonconformist, full of peculiar ideas. Agin everything.

He looked at her beseechingly, still hoping she'd step out from the pew and come with him, quiet-like, but the stern face under her black bonnet told him no such luck.

'Father has to get on with the Mass,' he said.

'Then let him. It's time he did, since he has no answer for me. Let him think more of what he's saying in future.' She picked up her prayer book. 'Aren't we all sitting waiting here? If I leave now, before the bells, I'll be missing Sunday Mass, and that in itself is a sin, Rory Clemens, as well you know.'

The Sergeant heard Michael sigh, shaking his head at anyone foolish enough to take on his wife in an argument. He saw Brodie grin and move on to his knees as the altar bells intoned. Stunned, he looked up to see that the priest had left the pulpit and was continuing with the Mass, leaving him here floundering. Making a fool of him in front of everyone.

He genuflected and crept back to his pew, conspicuous still, head down then as if praying intensely, but with anger in his heart. Let the priest deal with Trella Court, he'd have no more of it. He mulled over what it was that she'd had to say in her outburst, and thought of little Mary Best. Her father had given her a belting when he'd found out she was in the family way, but he'd not dealt out the same punishment to her boyfriend. Nor had the priest blamed the lad, come to think of it.

Although he couldn't approve of her timing, Clemens was inclined to believe that Trella was right.

But her mother did not. Maisie was outraged, and more so the following week when she heard that Trella was demanding that the fair be held elsewhere.

She rounded on her daughter in the kitchen of their small thatched cottage. 'Who asked you to be telling the auctioneers where to hold the fair?'

'It's not a fair,' Trella said. ''Tis a cattle sale. I could understand it if we had a square but Tullymore village is but one narrow street, from the church at the top of the hill to the undertaker down the bottom. When they bring the cattle in, all the shops have to be shuttered and the streets are awash with cattle pee and dung! The place stinks.'

'Then keep out of it! 'Tis none of your business. I don't know how Michael puts up with you, always going on about something.'

'Then there's a lot you don't know,' Trella flared, storming outside.

Her mother loved to criticise her, especially in front of the men. Sometimes Trella thought it was Maisie's way of repaying them for taking her in when Dadda had passed on, because she fawned on them the whole time, running about after them like they were paralysed and could not pick up their own boots. Like she never had for Dadda even in his failing years. And the nagging and carping that Trella had to endure from her was all part of it. By belittling her daughter, Maisie felt she was showing herself in a better light.

'Ah, the poor woman,' Michael had said. 'She means well. Don't take it to heart.'

'But it's my home! She behaves as if I don't count. I fear she's trying to drive a wedge between us, Michael.'

He took her in his arms. 'And how could that be done? Aren't you still the love of my life?'

That was Michael. A good man. A loving husband. But not so Brodie. For all his outward charm he could be mean and unreasonable; you never knew which way he'd jump.

4

It was Maisie who'd started the row in the house after that business in the church, accusing her daughter of blasphemy.

'That's a bit strong,' Michael had said.

'Why is it?' Brodie asked. 'What do you call getting arrested in church? I couldn't believe my ears.'

Trella rounded on him. 'The cheek of you! I saw you grinning. 'Twas only the Sergeant wiped the smile off your face. There was nothing funny about what I had to say.'

Michael spoke quietly. 'Maybe it would have been better for you to wait, Trella. To see Father Daly afterwards and tell him your grievance.'

'What good would that do? Hiding in the vestry. It was him, up there blaming the girl and not the man, I had to stop. It wasn't as if I'd planned to say anything. I just got a shock listening to him.'

'You got a shock!' Maisie cried. 'You're as much a hussy as Mary Best, and you want the world to know it.'

'Don't speak like that to me in my house!'

Maisie drew herself up. She was inches taller than her daughter. 'So! It's your house, is it? And me a widow living on charity, never allowed to speak. I know my place. I'd be better off in the poorhouse the way you treat me.'

'There's no need for that, Maisie,' Michael said. 'You know you're welcome here. Trella feels keenly about things, you ought to understand that.' He smiled. 'Sometimes she gets a bit carried away, but her heart's in the right place.'

'Her heart'll be in jail,' Brodie snorted, 'if she pulls the same stunt next week. The priest's still mortified, they say, and in a fine old rage.'

'Pity about him,' Trella snapped. 'Anyway we'll all be in the poorhouse soon, the way we're going.'

'Where's Garth?' Michael asked, changing the subject.

'He's fishing,' Trella told him. 'Down at the deep hole.'

'Then let's me and you go for a walk and see what's doing.'

As they walked across the fields, Michael took her hand and kissed it. 'You worry too much, my darlin'.'

'Because I have to do the worrying for all of us. We've hardly a penny to our name, Michael. The spuds are poor, the maize is showing a blight already, I don't know how much longer we can hang on.'

'It's a bad year, that's all. Times will pick up.'

'That's what you said last year. I want you to speak to Brodie. He leaves you to work the farm and goes off doing odd jobs, but he doesn't bring the cash home.'

'He only makes a few quid here and there. He's a single man, he's entitled to have a life outside the house. When he settles down he'll be different.'

Will he? Trella thought. Michael meant marriage. She dreaded the day that Brodie brought a wife home to their already crowded cottage. For he'd nowhere else to go unless he married a rich girl and, not counting the Hadley-Jones family up on the hill, there weren't too many of them about. As it was, Brodie shared with Garth, she and Michael had the other room, and Maisie slept in the kitchen, on a bed that doubled as a couch in the daytime. She could already see what would happen. Her son would be pushed out to the shed, where visitors slept.

They slid down the grassy slope to the river bank, surprising the lad.

'Don't make a noise,' he told them. 'You'll frighten off the fish.'

'Have you caught any yet?' his father asked.

'Not yet, but they're there. I can see the varmints jumping. Maybe it's too cloudy for them to see the bait. I wish the sun would come out.'

Michael laughed. 'You'd have a wait, it'll be raining soon.'

As she watched them together Trella softened. If only there could be just the three of them, life would be perfect. Garth was twelve now, and Maisie was clamouring for him to leave school and find a job. Brodie backed her, encouraging the lad to keep asking to leave, but on this point Michael was adamant and Trella greatly relieved. He would stay at school for two more years. She wished they had the money to send him on to higher education, but there was little hope of that.

She smiled, remembering the ructions at Garth's christening, with everyone saying that 'Garth' was not a saint's name and Father Daly, even to the last minute, trying to make the change.

'What sort of a name is Garth anyway?' her mother had asked.

'It's the name Trella has chosen,' Michael said firmly. 'She had the babe, she's entitled to first go. I've given him the second name of James, so there's your saint and I'll hear no more of it.'

Garth, his mother thought fondly. It was deliberate. I wanted him to be different, to break out of this tiny village and be someone in his own right, not weighed down by blind prejudices. He was a stocky lad, with his father's brooding good looks and soft brown eyes. Some said he was more like Brodie, but Trella wouldn't have it. Brodie's dark hair was curly and his eyes were blue, a twinkling blue when he was in a good mood but ice-blue when he was not.

Trella and Michael were proud of their son, and they loved him dearly. More so, for they'd lost three babies since he was born; the little angel boy had died at only one month and then there'd been two miscarriages.

'You have to eat more,' the doctor had said. 'Feed yourself up, you're as skinny as a rake.'

Easy for him to say, Trella thought listlessly, since the pigs are gone and we're down to two cows for milking, and most of what the farm produces has to be sold. It can't support five people any more and that's the truth of it.

The rain brought with it cold winds that chilled them to the bone, and Michael came down with the bad cough again. But he would not go to bed until a steaming fever took hold and he was too weak to stand.

For days the women nursed him, until the fever broke, and with a little bit of sun glinting through the clouds, he was able to go outside and breathe the good air again.

'I think he's got consumption,' Trella whispered to her mother.

'It's you've got consumption on the brain,' Maisie retorted, 'every time someone sniffs.'

'They say it runs in families, and that's how his parents died.'

'Stop that talk. You'll put a hex on the poor man. It's the weather affects Michael, not your superstition. You make sure he wears the flannel in the cold and not be taking it off. Now that cold snap's passed, he'll be right as rain, you'll see.'

And sure enough he was back in the fields in no time,

working with Brodie to rescue the remnants of the potato crop from the mud.

With everything back to normal again, Trella took her basket and set off up the hill from the valley to deliver her preserves to the Hadley-Jones' kitchen. She was feeling better now too, able to enjoy the brisk walk with the worry of Michael lifted from her shoulders.

She strode over the bridge and on through the town, past the church, until, puffing a little, she climbed to the crest of the hill to look back at Tullymore, with the wind whipping at her skirts. From up here the village was just a row of stone buildings crouched either side of the cobbled street, a grey incision in the rolling green countryside. The scene was neat, ordered. Hard to believe that anyone lived there at all. And harder still to know that the familiar spectre of poverty lurked within those solid walls and under the brown roofs of farmhouses that speckled the valley far below.

For these people, true to their lights, poverty was a hidden thing, kept out of sight for shame, spoken of only as 'bad times' as if it were a shabby cloak that could be thrown off when it pleased them.

When Trella tried to speak of it they hushed her. 'Poverty!' the old 'uns said. 'You'd know poverty if you'd been alive in the great famine, with thousands starving to death in the streets, and little children dying in their mothers' arms.'

That was the awful thing about it. They used the famine as a yardstick: these might be bad times, but they could be worse, so count your blessings. Never mind Johnny Adair, who was trying to open a co-operative store, or his new idea of paying an expert to come from Dublin to inspect and advise on the problems with the crops. Never listen to him! But out with the silver to buy a statue for the church or build a monument to some old hurling player.

And there in Tullymore there was that other danger, the furtive, sinister fight for a free Ireland, further complicated by the arguments of the Fenians and Sinn Fein. Michael walked with a limp, thanks to a bullet in his leg attained when he was only eighteen as a courier for the freedom fighters. Then it was that his mother, a strong-willed woman, had made Brodie pledge to keep out of it. These days the fight seemed to have moved on, Tullymore forgotten, but the uneasiness lingered, noted by villagers but never spoken of; when men held secret meetings and disappeared for weeks on end without comment.

Trella feared for her son. The prisons were full of patriots. She was no dreamer of dreams, she had no great vision for the future. She was simply clear-headed, seeing things as they were. Her priority was the survival of the Court family. She had no patience with talk of the 'auld' days, when the Courts had owned half the valley, generations ago. The glory days were well gone. Their holdings had dwindled to the one-acre farm now owned by Michael and Brodie, and God alone knew how long that would last.

'We can get cash,' Brodie had said. 'I don't know what you're worrying about. We can raise a loan on the farm.'

'Never!' Michael had shouted. 'That's the road to ruin! I won't be beholden to anyone. Haven't we seen enough of mortgages in this valley? Farms sold up and families evicted.'

Trella agreed with her husband, but that left them in the same predicament, with barely enough to put food on the table.

'Like it or not,' she determined, 'there'll have to be some changes in our household.'

Angrily she pushed on over the hill towards the mansion owned by the Englishman, John Hadley-Jones, and occupied by more servants than family.

Trella admitted it had a grand view of the bay, but apart from that she found it an ugly business of a house. Everyone else saw it as a fine big place, boasting that it was designed by an architect from London, as if that made it right. 'Twas nothing but a two-storeyed square box, without even a portico to shelter a caller, and it was set in an ordered landscape of shrubs and lawns that looked as trim as if they'd been snipped with scissors. Inside, they said, were more rooms than a hotel, and all furnished grand, which Trella supposed made up for the cold grey exterior.

A man on horseback came trotting up the road, interrupting her musings, and when Trella saw who it was, in his tweedie coat and high hat, she jumped the ditch by the roadside and headed cross-country, avoiding the necessity of addressing him.

9

The villagers doffed their caps to Mr Hadley-Jones and called him 'your honour', which Trella steadfastly refused to do.

'He's nobody's honour,' she would say. 'He's just an ordinary man who happens to be a landlord and have a boodle of cash.'

She didn't envy him, or his folk, their money. That was their good fortune and it had nothing to do with her. She doubted that a man like him was interested in the village talk where some said he was hard on his tenants and others claimed he was fair. Everyone had to get on with their own lives as best they could.

Nevertheless it was a pleasure to cross the courtyard and pass by the stables with all those beautiful horses nodding and pouting from their stalls.

The cook came out of the kitchen, wiping her hands on her apron. 'Ah, Trella. What have you today?'

'Eggs. And potted eels. I thought you might take a jar or two.'

'I'll take the lot, eight jars, is it? They've got visitors and the little extras help. How much in all?'

'Three shillings,' Trella said hopefully, and the cook, being in a good mood today, probably too busy to haggle, paid up.

'Here,' she said, reaching into a nearby cupboard, 'take this end of bacon. I'll not be needing it.'

'Are you sure?' Trella asked nervously.

'I am. They just killed a porker, I've plenty.'

'Then I thank you. It will do us very well.'

Her spirits raised by this scrap of good fortune, she set off home with a definite plan in her head, and this time Michael would have to listen.

She found him bagging maize in the shed. 'Michael, I have to talk to you.'

He stood up, stretching his back. 'Here I am then. And aren't you looking pretty today. What have you been up to?'

'I sold some stuff up at the big house.'

'Good. What did you want to talk about?'

'Where's Brodie?' she asked, not wishing to be interrupted.

'He's gone over to Darcy's place to help with the ploughing

in exchange for spuds. We'll get good seeds from them and have a better crop next year.'

'If we can hang on that long. Michael, the way we're going we'll be living on turnips soon. We have to do something. The farm can't support us.'

'There you go worrying again. Things will get better, you'll see.'

'No, I don't see. We have to think of Garth. There are too many of us scraping by on the farm. Someone has to go.'

He looked at her, amazed, and then he laughed. 'If you're thinking of sending your mother away I'll be down at the pub when you tell her. But you couldn't be thinking of that. Where would she go?'

'I wasn't thinking of Maisie. It's Brodie I'm looking at. He's a full-grown man now, twenty-five he is. We can't feed him properly. For his own sake, as well as ours, he has to go. If he takes a wife we'll be further burdened.'

Michael threw the bag of cobs aside and turned on her. 'You'd throw out my own brother? Is this what you want? Throw him off a farm that's as much his as mine? Were he of a mind he could say the same thing to us. What's got into you?'

'Hush now, don't be cross. This is the only way. I'm not throwing him off, I'm just suggesting that he takes a real job somewhere, for a while, until things get better.'

'And where would he find a job? There are none here-abouts.'

'In Dublin. Garth and I can help in the fields while he's away. We could give him a few shillings to tide him over and find someone to give him a bed.'

'What if he can't find a job?'

'More chance there than here.' Trella shrugged. 'If not, he comes home again, no harm done. It's worth thinking about. And if he has a weekly paying job he could send you a little until the next harvest. Don't you see, Michael, it's worth the mentioning. If he doesn't agree, so be it. He stays and we struggle on.'

'Enough. Let me think about it. If anyone goes, I should. It's my side of the family taking up the most, remember. He has never complained about that.'

'You're not well enough, Michael, and you know it. But if

11

you go, we go too, and that hardly makes sense. It's now we have to decide, before things get worse.'

'I told you I'll think about it,' he said angrily.

She slipped a shilling into his hand. 'You could take him to the pub and have a talk on the quiet.'

Grudgingly he pocketed the money. Time was, years back, that the Court brothers could retire to the pub after work most days. Now they could only visit the Erin of a Saturday night when they had a few spare pence. Trella shivered, kissed him on the cheek and trudged over to the house.

This was a Friday. Not a good day for decisions. A bad omen. She hadn't thought of that in her rush to present her plan to Michael. But it was up to him now. The idea did sound cruel but Brodie wasn't a kid. He should have been looking for a decent job long ago. It was time he got moving.

Maisie was surprised when Michael said they were going to the pub, but she made no comment, allowing that men could do as they wished.

'This bacon,' she told Trella, 'will do for their supper.'

'No it won't. Put it in the stew, we'll share.' She retreated to her bedroom on the pretence of mending the quilt, but instead sat glumly staring out at the fog that was closing in on her. She felt like an outsider, as if she were standing outside the pub, staring in at the same old faces, intent on their talk in that shadowy interior. Weary men in their shabby coats and cloth caps, discussing the same old things over their pots, puffing and pointing with their pipes. Too early for the singing.

She worried that even if Michael had seen the sense of her idea, those men, so set in their ways, would talk him out of it. Sometimes, when she passed, she'd seen them peering at her, their grim faces disapproving of the Court woman and her habit of poking her nose into village affairs when no one needed her opinion. She'd fancied that she had a large brass key that she could turn in the heavy pub door to lock them all in. Then, a hundred years hence, she'd return to unlock the door and find them unchanged, still discussing and arguing and gossiping without noticing a century had passed.

In the back of her mind, where she didn't wish to rummage, was a small clutter of guilt that there was more to her wishing Brodie would take himself off. More than she'd dare mention to Michael. She knew she'd be glad to be rid of his noisy, boisterous presence; Brodie seemed to take up more room than the rest of them put together. And he was so damned single-minded, always having his own way, with Michael looking on, not minding, for he loved his brother and enjoyed to see him happy.

'The sooner he leaves, the better,' Trella muttered to herself. 'Even if he does own half the farm. Give us some elbow room for a change.'

Brodie didn't need a second telling to join Michael at the pub, nor did he enquire as to the source of the wherewithal to pay for the pints. A quick wash and a good combing of his thick hair and he was out the door with a tickle on the neck for Maisie Grogan as he passed.

She laughed, with more humour in her than her daughter. 'Get on with you, you young rascal.'

Rarely did the brothers drink together. They had their own pals and they saw enough of each other at home. But this time Michael called Brodie to the rear of the bar and stood the drinks.

Brodie was instantly suspicious. This was the spot Michael usually chose to give him one of his lectures about women, or spending, or missing Benediction too often, at the risk of his immortal soul. He grinned. There were times when his brother could deliver a better sermon than the priest. Making certain it wouldn't last too long, he gave one of the lads a wink to rescue him after a while.

He was fond of his brother. Proud of him, though he'd never say so. Michael was a fair fellow, always trying to do the best for everyone, and he was also a handy knuckle man when it came to a fight. It had been a long time since any man would take on either of the Courts, because the other one was never far away.

They'd downed two pints before Brodie twigged that this was not to be a lecture. He was being buttered up for a reason. He began to enjoy himself, even reaching for a pork pie, which Michael paid for without a blink and took only a bite himself.

On the third round, the crux of this meeting began to emerge.

'I was thinking,' Michael said quietly, 'with things so bad these days, of taking a job in Dublin.'

'What's this you're saying?' Brodie was stunned. 'You'd take your family to Dublin! Are you mad?'

'Not my family. Just me.'

Brodie gave this some thought. 'I could handle the farm without you, but would you leave the wife and kid? And what would she have to say about that?' He began to laugh. 'I can't imagine her letting you go off to that den of iniquity, a handsome gent like you! They say Dublin's full of pretty girls. And wanton widows.'

Michael frowned. 'We're up against it, Brodie. We need to draw in some cash money.'

Feeling mellow now, Brodie leaned against the counter. 'If that's the case, you can't be leavin'. You a family man and all. I'll have a go at it.'

If ever a man's face mirrored his soul, Michael was that man, and his brother could read it well. He saw the expression of relief on Michael's face, and realised he'd been taken for a ride.

'Do you want me to go?' he asked, giving away nothing.

And he listened as Michael went into a detailed explanation of their finances, which was not new, and talked hopefully of opportunities that could still be found in Dublin, on the wharves or with roadworks. ''Tis not that I want you to go,' he added. 'But one of us has to. I think maybe you're right. It would be best for me to stay to keep an eye on the family. Young Garth takes a bit of handling. Got a mind of his own, he has.'

It was too much for Brodie. He planted his pot on the counter and confronted Michael. 'Why don't you tell me straight up and stop beating about the bush. You had this planned from the start. You want to cut me loose.'

'I'm just trying to work out what's best, Brodie.'

'Sure you are. And it wasn't your idea, was it? That wife of yours is behind this. She wants the farm and the only way is to get rid of me!'

'Will you listen? The way we're going there'll be no farm. And I'll thank you not to speak of my wife like that. She's a good woman and she's only looking ahead. It would just be for a season, Brodie, until the next harvest.'

'I knew it! Her hand is heavy on this. The greedy bitch is

14

dead set on shoving me out. Good woman! She's a laughing stock and you too weak to put a stop to her . . .'

One minute Brodie was standing at the bar. The next he was on the floor, crashing among overturned tables, nursing his jaw.

'You shouldna' done that,' he shouted, climbing to his feet.

'And you shouldna' speak ill of my wife.'

'I'll speak the truth of her, the conniving bitch,' Brodie roared as he flung a punch at his brother.

The publican leapt the bar. 'Outside,' he yelled. 'Outside, the pair of you! I'll have no fighting in my house. And mind the lamps, lads! By Jesus! Mind the lamps!'

The other customers broke from their torpor to hustle the angry pair out into the yard, shifting barrels to give them room, for they were already hard at it without missing a beat.

It was a fight to be long remembered in the village. No one had seen the Court brothers fight since they'd scrapped as kids. Not each other, anyway. They were well matched, Michael with his bulk and Brodie, taller, with the arm length. Men ringed them, cheering, and bets were laid as they slugged it out for the best part of five minutes, until wearing down, faces and fists bloodied, it was suddenly over and they drew apart, still scowling and muttering threats.

'Who won?' disappointed villagers who had missed the fight wanted to know, but no one could say, although arguments ensued.

Brodie awoke in the morning, cold and shivering, at the back of the cowshed out on Darcy's farm. He vaguely remembered being shouted whiskeys after the night's entertainment, and he owned to that because he had the sort of hangover only Carmody's cheap whiskey could provide. And his face felt like a squashed melon, thanks to the battering he'd taken from Michael. His own brother!

It wasn't a rare thing for Brodie to have to struggle to his feet the morning after a drunken brawl, but he'd never woken lying in the mud and damp of a paddock. He remembered he had been on his way home after Carmody closed the pub, staggering across the fields, feeling no pain, until he'd realised he wasn't wanted at the farm. Michael had told him to leave.

In a rage he'd veered off towards Darcy's place and drunk some home-brew with him until he was once again turned out into the night.

Now the pain had arrived with a wallop. He felt his mouth, relieved that there were no loose teeth. Brodie was proud of his strong white teeth, rare in these parts. But the taste of blood was still foul in his mouth, blood from his nose and his sorely cut lip. He stumbled down to the stream and slopped freezing water on his face, wincing at the assault on his head and his aching jaw.

He wondered how Michael had fared. Not much better, he hoped. But then Michael would have gone straight home to have the women clucking over him and he'd have slept soundly in his own bed, not banished to the weather like this. Not pushed out of his own home. His own farm. Bitterly he blamed Trella. She'd been the cause of this. She'd come between the brothers, setting one against the other in a manner no one was likely to forget. The great friendship of the Court lads had been shattered by that bitch for all to see. Never before had Michael connived against him, it wasn't in his nature, but she'd made the bullets and left Michael to fire them in that insidious way of hers.

That thought roused Brodie to a rage.

And what was he to do now? Go home cap in hand? Creep in the door like a whipped dog begging for shelter? Knowing there'd be no real welcome.

Well now. They wanted him to go, so he'd bloody well go, this very day. And they'd better be looking over their shoulders from now on because there'd be no forgiving. The fight had settled it. But let them not be forgetting he still owned half that farm!

Brodie tramped across Darcy's fields until he came to the crossroads. And there he stood. Contemplating.

Turn right and you were on into Tullymore where everyone would have heard about the fight. And the reason for it. They'd be knowing by this that Brodie Court had been cast out from his family. It'd be all the talk this morning.

Abruptly he turned left, charging down the road to Limerick without a penny in his pocket, too angry to care.

'I'll be back one day,' he muttered. 'I'll make me bloody fortune on me own and then I'll be back to laugh at youse. I'll have more cash than even the Hadley-Jones skites, up there in their fine house. No one will make a fool of me again.'

He straightened his cap and turned his collar up against this grey and miserable day, and strode out, leaving Tullymore behind.

'Didn't you explain to him?' Trella wailed as she washed the blood from Michael's face and dabbed at the cut over his eye. 'Did you not tell him how bad things are?'

'He knows,' Michael mumbled. 'He just didn't take kindly to the idea.'

'Ah, the poor lad,' Maisie cried. 'You've gone and hurt his feelings.'

'He's hurt more than Michael's feelings!' Trella snapped. 'This cut by his eye will need stitching. Did you tell him, Michael, that we'll be giving him some cash to be going on with?'

'I didn't get a chance. Now leave me be! I'll talk to him tomorrow when he's cooled down.'

But Brodie didn't come home that night, nor the next day or the day after, and then someone mentioned in the pub that he'd seen Brodie Court riding on a brewery lorry leaving Limerick, and the news was conveyed to Michael.

'It's a sorry thing for a man to have to leave like that,' he lamented, 'making me feel as if I've driven him off.' He hadn't told his wife about the real cause of the fight, and never would. She was not to blame. He had tried to break the idea to Brodie as gently as he could and he'd made a mess of it.

Michael missed Brodie, he surely did. And he worried about him going off like that with nothing of his own. No money, not even the letters Michael had planned to arm him with, letters of reference from Father Daly and Sergeant Clemens to prove that Brodie was of good character, not just some footloose gypsy.

'When will Uncle Brodie be home again?' Garth asked.

'Soon,' Michael said, hoping that was not a lie.

God, how he hated Dublin! The bitterness he felt had now been extended to include this city and everyone in it. He'd tramped the streets until his boots were worn bare but he still couldn't find work. To Brodie, this was a personal insult, since he was a fit man and a willing worker, and he was vastly offended by all this rejection. And he was mortified to find that he was now, after all these weeks, thin as a rake, constantly hungry, and forced to live with filthy tramps in the squalor of an abandoned warehouse.

He'd made his way here by cadging rides on lorries and wagons, and, to his shame, cadging food from farmhouses, but he'd been confident that when he reached the big city he'd find work in no time.

Failure had him fearful that with no place to call his own, and his clothes threadbare, he was looking more like a dirty scarecrow every day. Not a fit person to be even asking for work, for hadn't he seen the bosses turn up their noses at him, waving him off as if he were a felon come to rob them?

Stuck in this filthy, stinking city, he was close to despair, but he would not go home. Damned if he would!

And then chance took a hand.

Footpads were rife in Dublin. Late at night they lurked in dark alleys off the main streets, waiting for unaccompanied gentlemen to pass by, and then they jumped them, bashing them senseless before robbing them so that the victim was unable to identify his assailants.

Brodie watched their activities with interest, sparing no compassion for their prey; this town, he'd learned, was dog eat dog. Rather he was out to learn how this was done. He had to get some cash somehow and the gents who fell foul of robbers could well afford the loss of a few quid for a good cause.

He grinned meanly at his own joke. Brodie considered he was a good cause if ever there was one. He had investigated the poor boxes at Dublin's great churches but always someone had been there before him, smashing and rifling. So he was even a dud at that.

Most of the footpads worked in pairs. And so they would, Brodie said to himself. City-bred rats with not a muscle between them. But Brodie Court won't be needing a partner. When he strikes, the gent will stay down. And there'll be no sharing.

All he needed was enough cash to buy some decent clothes and have a barber clean him up so that he could walk the streets presentable and begin again the search for a job.

Brodie was surprised at how easy it was. He'd chosen a lucrative spot near a row of fancy whorehouses, and after two attacks on lone gentlemen had slunk back to his hole, pleased with himself. He'd even scored a flat leather wallet which now held nine pounds and some coin.

But now he was wary. It wasn't enough. The cash would set him up for a while but what if he still couldn't find a job? Would the money dwindle away on bed and board and leave him back with the other derelicts who had accepted their lot? Brodie was determined not to fall into that trap. He resumed his new career as a footpad, finding two more victims and adding six pounds to his roll.

During the day he hung about waterfront pubs, grateful for their warmth and cheap meals, grudgingly shouting drinks here and there in an effort to find friends who might help him.

It was there, at last, that Brodie got his first break. He learned about emigration to America. Sailors were full of enthusiasm, spinning success stories until Brodie was dizzy with excitement. They even told which ships were the best and cheapest for emigrants bound for New York. Only a few weeks at sea and he'd be in a country a thousand times the size of Ireland where they were begging for workers.

This was the answer! He'd do it. He'd go to America. That'd be a slap in the eye to them back in Tullymore!

Now that he had a plan, Brodie decided he had to fix himself up proper. And then there was the fare to pay. A few more quid were needed; he couldn't step ashore in America stony broke, that wouldn't do at all.

Brodie knew that footpads were never foolish enough to pull off too many robberies from the same spot, but in his eagerness to have just one more go, he forgot. He forgot that the law would be on a sharp lookout in known danger areas for the protection of the gentry. He was too busy dreaming of his grand future.

One more go, he told himself as he took up his position in the dark alley. From this vantage point he could see over some crates by the entrance to the alley into the dimly lit street.

Shivering, on this freezing cold night, he clasped his arms about him and waited. Couples passed. Women with screechy voices. Several young fellows staggering about drunk. Too many to tackle. Wagons rolled by. Men on horseback. And then the street was quiet. Brodie realised he was a mite too early and was preparing himself for a long wait when a likely customer came out of one of the whorehouses and crossed the road. Coming this way, Brodie hoped, as the man disappeared from his line of vision.

If he turns left, I'll have him, Brodie said to himself. It would be just a few yards' sprint to grab this one as he passed the dark alley. Most of the footpads worked barefoot to cover the sound of their approach, but Brodie didn't need to. His boots were so worn and soft, insulated with newspaper, that they made less noise than slippers.

Glory be! There was his man. He'd turned left. Now let him go a few more paces and I'll grab him . . .

Suddenly, from behind the crates, two dark shadows leapt out and attacked the pedestrian. Brodie was beginning his run as it happened and he was outraged! Who were these villains grabbing his mark? His money? Blindly he charged on to enter the fray, punching at the footpads to get them out of his way. One punch sent the bigger one flying, and he turned to boot the other but only caught him in the rear as he fled. In seconds the two had disappeared.

The hapless victim was on the ground, sprawled out, defenceless. It was Brodie's intention to finish the job but the gentleman confused him, holding up his hand:

'Thank you, sir! Thank you. And thank God you came along! Would you kindly help me up?'

What else could he do? He took the hand and jerked the fellow to his feet. Even picked up his hat for him.

The gent leaned against the wall to steady himself. He was about forty. Well off, if the long cloak with its fur collar was any indication.

He grimaced in pain. 'I'm afraid I've twisted my ankle,' he said, gingerly testing a well-shod foot on the ground.

'Can you walk?' Brodie asked, thinking it was a stupid question because he didn't care whether he could or not, but he didn't know what else to say.

'I shall have to. Until I can find a hansom cab to get me home. But I do feel rather odd. Those wretches gave me such a wallop on the back of my head!' He looked at Brodie: 'I wonder if I could impose on you a little longer? I'm willing to pay you. Could you assist me down to the corner? It's busier out there and I could hail a cab.'

To add to Brodie's confusion there was a flurry of whistles and two policemen converged on them, wasting no time in grabbing Brodie. They were shouting at him, placing him under arrest and at the same time enquiring after the health of the victim.

Finally the gentleman shut them up. 'Let go of him, you fools! This man came to my rescue. I was attacked by two thieves and he drove them off!'

The policemen weren't so sure. They seemed to think that the tap on the head had addled the victim's brains, for their prisoner looked more like a footpad than a knight.

'He's a vagrant. We'll take him in,' they announced.

Brodie was insulted. 'I'm no vagrant! I have money. You can't arrest me!'

They spoke as if he weren't there. 'Look at him, sir. Look at the filth of him. You're lucky we came along.'

'By Jesus!' Brodie shouted. 'You'd not be looking so sharp either if you'd walked the distance I have. All the way from Tullymore, with my money saved to take me to America. I just got to Dublin this very day.'

'Show us the money.'

Brodie took out the wallet and the police were instantly suspicious. 'Where'd you get a purse so fine?'

'God help us!' Brodie cried. 'Is there no end to this? You're looking at a going-away present, given me by the good folk of Tullymore with the prayer that I not forget them.'

He gave them a glimpse of his money. 'First I have to pay me fare to America. Not knowing what it will cost me, I can't be spending on a travelling suit until I see what's left.'

'What's your name?'

'Court. Mr Brodie Court. Esquire.'

'That's enough!' the gentleman said sternly. 'Mr Court came to my aid, doing your duty for you. I won't have him harassed like this. Kindly step aside.'

Brodie was only too pleased to assist the injured man up to the corner, with the police, still suspicious, watching their progress.

When they were finally able to halt a cab, Brodie's new friend was cautious. 'You'd better hop in, lad, those two are keen to make an arrest, they could pounce on you again when I go.'

Brodie hung back, miserably aware of his appearance, but the gentleman didn't seem to care. 'Get in.'

'But I'm no vagrant!' Brodie had convinced himself by this that he was simply an innocent bystander. He glared back at the police. 'I own me own farm,' he said proudly.

'Are you carrying papers to prove it?'

'I am not.'

'Then get in, quickly.'

As the cab clattered away, Brodie was self-conscious, seated on the soft leather that smelled of fresh polish. He noticed that the gentleman opened the window on his side, despite the cold.

'Why did you leave your farm?' he was asked.

'It's going bad. Too many mouths to feed, so I said to me brother . . . we both own it, you see . . . I said I'd make myself scarce. He's got a family. I'm a single man. I wanted to give him a better chance.'

'Very commendable, Mr Court. Where can I drop you?'

'Anywheres. It doesn't matter. I'll get through the night and find the emigration place tomorrow.'

'And you're off to America?'

'Yes, sir.'

The gentleman called the cabbie to stop outside a large house with tall lamps shining a welcome from the gate to the porch.

'I was thinking, I have a job that might save you the passage money.'

'How's that?' Brodie asked.

'Here are five shillings for coming to my rescue. It will be well spent if you use it for decent board to avoid a vagrancy charge.'

Brodie knew it was a tactful way of telling him he stunk, but he pretended not to notice, to hide his shame. Never, he vowed, would he allow himself to sink this low again.

'I'll do that sir,' he agreed.

'Good. Now, about this job. I want you to come and see me in the morning before you make any arrangements to emigrate. I think I can assist you.'

He paid the cabbie and hobbled over to the gate. 'I can

cope from here. My name is Jack Delaney. I want you here at ten in the morning. No earlier. No later. That's if you're interested.'

'I am that, sir, indeed I am.'

'Very well. Off you go then. I'll see you in the morning.'

Chastened, Brodie installed himself in the first rooming house he could find, paying extra for the use of a rusting tin bath, and in the morning he was out early, searching for a barber shop.

Clean-shaven, his hair neatly trimmed and gleaming with brilliantine, he stared into the mirror.

'By Jesus,' he laughed, 'I look like someone else without me beard.'

The barber nodded sagely.

'I always say a man wears a beard to look older or more dignified, or to cover up an ugly face. You young bucks don't need to do that. Wear your good looks while you can.'

'Thank you. I'll remember that. Now, can you tell me where I can be buying some town clothes, good and cheap?'

'Sure I can. Round the corner to Abe Rosenstein's Allgoods Store. He'll look after you.'

Brodie found the store and marched in, staring about in bewilderment. It was more of a warehouse, packed to the rafters with all manner of goods. He had to push aside boxes and bundles to get himself in the door and down narrow aisles until he found the proprietor.

He was a short, dapper man with an embroidered pillbox cap on his bald head. More like something a Chinaman would wear, Brodie thought, but he made no comment.

'I need some clothes,' he said lamely, intimidated by the imposing variety massed about him.

'What sort of clothes?'

'I have to see a man about a job. The barber sent me here. Are you Mr Rosenstein?'

'At your service, sir. Now, let me see.' He rummaged in boxes, pulling out coats and shirts and trousers, insisting that Brodie try them there and then.

There was no arguing. Clothes were pulled on him, pulled off again, replaced, buttoned, unbuttoned, until at last Rosenstein was satisfied. He hurried Brodie to a long mirror.

'Did you say you were applying for a job? No man ever looked better. You can't fail.'

Brodie was astonished. And nervous. He certainly looked smart, in a striped shirt, bow tie, cord trousers and tan boots.

'How much is all this?'

'I won't charge you for socks. Gentlemen always wear socks with their boots.'

'How much?'

'You can have the lot for five and six.'

'What? That's daylight robbery!'

'Look again, sir. I've done you proud. And you can't be walking out in your shirtsleeves. Put this on.' He produced a black seaman's jacket. It was big and warm and comfortable, with deep pockets for cold hands, and Brodie loved it. He'd never owned a coat as good as this; all he'd ever had were hand-me-downs.

'Seven and six the lot,' Abe said. 'It's going cheap, believe me. You'll get the job. But you can't live in what you stand up in. You come back and buy more and I'll give you one of my best suitcases to carry so you don't look poor and get doors banged on you.'

That struck a nerve. He's right, Brodie thought as he took out his wallet. A man shouldn't look poor.

A maid bade him wait at the back door of Mr Delaney's house, and Brodie turned to admire the pleasant enclosed garden with its fountain and marble benches and neat shrubbery. He wondered if anyone sat there doing nothing, or if it was just for show.

'Is that you, Court?' Delaney was staring at him from the open doorway.

'That it is, sir,' Brodie grinned, preening himself.

'Well, I must say you shine up well. Come on in.'

Seated in a large room with a wide desk and leather chairs and carpet soft as down, Brodie heard that Delaney was a horse breeder and trainer.

'Do you know anything about horses?' he asked, and Brodie nodded enthusiastically, for hadn't he worked at Mr Hadley-Jones' stables often enough, when they were short-handed?

'Spent a lot of time with horses,' he said.

'Good. I'm shipping two of my thoroughbreds overseas, to a friend of mine. The groom who was to accompany them has fallen ill, which is very inconvenient. They're due to sail tomorrow and unless I can replace the groom I'll have to postpone all my arrangements. Would you be interested in travelling with them?'

'Yes, sir.'

'Let me tell you right now, if you take this on, you're not to leave them. You feed them, water them, care for them and keep them happy as if they're your own children. These horses are valuable, I wouldn't want anything to happen to them.'

'I'll look after them.'

'You sleep by them and you never take your eyes off them. Do I make myself clear?'

'Yes, sir.'

'To make certain, you'd be paid in halves. Ten pounds before you leave and ten pounds when the horses are delivered safe and sound to a Mr Vern Holloway. I'd need you to come out to my stables right away, so that my stable-master can give you your instructions and you can get to know the horses. There's little enough time, I know, but the travel will be hard on two young horses. I don't want them to go with a complete stranger. You'd have to stay at the stables tonight.'

'You can count on me.' Brodie hardly dared breathe. 'But I was wondering about my fare. On the ship, sir.'

'I'm coming to that. Your steerage fare will be paid. There's just one difficulty. The ship is not going to America. My friend lives in Australia. Does that make any difference to you?'

Brodie was deflated. What a disappointment! He'd had his heart set on America.

'It's a fine country,' Delaney said. 'Many an emigrant leaves Ireland for those shores. You wouldn't regret it.'

'I don't know anyone there,' Brodie protested. Easier than admitting he had no idea where this country was. Somewhere in the Far East, he was thinking, racking his brains for a hint.

'Do you have friends in America?'

'No,' he admitted.

'Well then!' Delaney was relieved. 'Don't forget you'll be making friends on the ship. It's bound for the town of

25

Brisbane, on the east coast, a warm and lovely place. New York has a cruel winter no better than here.'

Brodie had already made up his mind. This being the only job on offer, he didn't have any choice. And he supposed this other country would be much the same as America.

'Would I be able to get a job there?' he asked.

'Yes. I'll see to it. Mr Holloway will find you a job. On the condition, once again, that my horses are delivered in good shape. So, are you for it?'

'What will it cost me to live on the ship?' Brodie asked shrewdly.

'Nought. It's all in the fare. But I'll have extra provisions on board for you since shipboard food can be grim.'

'Then it looks like I'm going,' Brodie said. 'I'd need a little time to get me things,' he added, determined not to look poor.

Delaney stood and handed him ten crisp notes. 'I'm trusting you'll be back here in one hour, and we'll go straight to the stables.' He shook Brodie's hand. 'And you can trust me, Brodie, that you can do just as well in Australia as in America.'

Brodie was sure he would, with new cash in his pocket, another ten at the end, and a job already lined up. 'I'll be back in a flash, sir. You'll find no better protector for your fine horses than me. I'll see they get there safe and sound.'

Abe met him at the door. 'Ah, Mr Court! Don't tell me! You got the job already.'

'I did.' Brodie was thrilled to have someone to talk to. 'I'm to work as a groom, taking two fine horses on a ship all the way to Australia.'

'Good for you.'

'I had me heart set on going to America though; this other place is a bit of a come-down. But it was say yes or say no quick-smart, for the ship is leaving tomorrow, so I had to give him the nod.'

'You could be better off,' Abe said. 'Too many folks going to America. You could have more opportunities in the newer land.'

'I suppose so. What should I be taking? I think it's a lot further than America.'

26

Once again Abe went on a rummaging spree, unearthing clothing befitting a groom, as well as a blanket, a new cap and riding boots. Then from tea chests he produced toiletries and towels, brush and comb, razor and strop, hair oil, toothpaste, dumping them on his counter as Brodie watched in alarm.

'Do I need all this?'

'Cheaper to buy them here. And as a groom to a rich man you can't be making a fool of him. You have to keep yourself gussied up.' He added bottles of tonic to ward off various ailments.

'Don't forget my suitcase then.'

'Never.' A new brown suitcase was produced and Abe packed for him, laying everything out neatly until it was full.

'There you are, you'll be a credit to your boss.'

Brodie had never seen such a fine array for one man, and he felt very flash as he handed over three pounds.

'Would you do me one more favour, Mr Rosenstein?'

'Certainly. Call me Abe.'

'I need a pen and paper. I have to write to my family and tell them I'm off.'

'No trouble.'

Abe took him through to his narrow office, cleared a space on his cluttered desk and gave him the writing materials. 'Take your time.'

As he sat there, Brodie wasn't sure what to write, or even how to spell Australia, but he'd have a go. He could tell them that he'd found a good job with a rich employer and he was off overseas. That sounded impressive. And that he was going to Brisbane, Australia. A place with a fine warm climate.

But how could he write to Michael after what had happened to him? And with her leaning over Michael's shoulder crowing that she was right to send his brother away! They didn't deserve a letter of any sort. Nevertheless, he couldn't resist this chance to boast, imagining the surprise on their faces when they got his letter. By that time he'd be on the high seas.

Then he had a brilliant idea. He began writing: *Dear Father Daly* . . .

His letter would go to the priest, snubbing them, while he could depend on the holy father to race down the road with his news. And they could all sit around gaping!

'Leave it with me,' Abe said, as Brodie pasted the envelope

down and addressed it to Daly at the presbytery. 'I'll post it for you. But listen now. They say there are prospects in Australia. Opportunities, like. It being a new place and growing. If you get on to a good thing, something I can sell here for you, remember old Abe. Maybe we can do business. Or maybe I can send you things that are short out there. Keep your eyes open, lad. You never know. And I won't do you wrong.'

'I'll remember,' Brodie said, to be polite, but he couldn't see himself in the allgoods trade. He was a farmer.

Eager to be off now, he shook hands with Abe, picked up his suitcase with the blanket strapped to the outside, and strode out to his new life with cash in his pocket, new clothes on his back and a spring in his step. Luck was on his side at last. Fancy getting a free ride on a ship, and pay, to sit and watch a couple of nags. Money for jam.

The priest wasn't in the best of moods. His housekeeper had just brought him his mail, two letters. And a glass of brandy to settle his nerves because the top one, it was clear to see, was from the Bishop.

Opening it gave him no solace. His Grace was adamant.

'How in tarnation can I raise the money to rebuild the church in a community as poor as this?' Father Daly exploded. 'Has the man no sense at all?'

He threw the letter aside, deciding that his next move would be to ignore the directions from above, to cease replying so that his responses could not be interpreted as excuses. For that was what His Grace had written! He wanted no more excuses.

Then that was what he would get, no more excuses and no more replies. And if he sent an emissary Father Daly could find plenty of ways not to be found.

'And what's this?' he asked of the second letter, addressed to him in careful handwriting.

'Well I'll be! 'Tis from Brodie Court himself.'

Rumour had it that Brodie and Michael had fallen out over that woman, Trella Court. A wicked woman if ever there was one. And here was proof. His smile was smug as he reread the letter. Brodie was a good lad, he'd never go off with nary a word, and he'd shown respect by turning to his priest.

Father Daly had always known that Brodie was a cut above

the rest. He was disappointed that the lad had not entered the priesthood, but he'd always known he'd do well. And now here he was, having found a good job in Dublin and earned enough by dint of hard work to be travelling to Australia. Emigrating, no less. And not as a steerage passenger either but in style, with secure prospects for employment in Brisbane.

There was no message for his family, but reading between the lines, Daly knew he would be expected to pass on the news. This, he guessed, was Brodie's way of beginning to heal the rift with Michael, who would be overjoyed to hear from his brother.

He jumped up, pocketed Brodie's letter and buttoned his soutane, grabbing his umbrella as he pushed out into the cold drizzle of the day.

Brisbane! Father Daly had met priests from there who'd returned home for visits. They'd said it was a glorious sunny place with plenty of wealthy Catholics to keep troubles from the gate. Brodie had made a wise choice, bless him! There was no return address but that was understandable; he had no doubt that young Court would keep in touch with his parish priest.

She was in the field, working with the hoe, her skirts tucked up into her belt, bare legs showing like the hoyden she was. He gave her but a nod and passed on to young Garth, who was working back from the other direction.

'What's this you're doing, lad?' he asked.

'Planting corn, Father.'

'You won't earn much with that. It's potatoes that are in short supply.'

The boy looked at him with the same defiant eye the priest had seen many a time in his mother. 'It'll keep us fed though, me ma says.'

'Why aren't you in school?'

'Dadda's laid low with a bad cough and there's work to be done.'

'Schooling's just as important,' Father Daly retaliated, and left them to it.

Humility, that was what Garth needed, he mused as he made his way over to the farmhouse. Too much of the mother in him, even to a glint of red in his dark hair. Others remarked on Trella Court's rich red hair but Father Daly preferred to call women of that colouring gingerheads, so they didn't get carried away with pride. He decided to give a sermon on humility on Sunday. On the sin of pride. And he'd direct a few stares at young Garth since the mother was beyond redemption. The Lord would punish her in his own way.

Maisie Grogan was delighted to see him and rushed to put the kettle on. 'Kind of you to come, Father. Michael's poorly. It was a job making him stay in bed but you visiting will do him the world of good.'

He took off his cloak. 'Better than that. I've brought good news.'

'You have? What would that be?'

He placed a finger to his lips. 'Ah now. Be patient. Michael's the one to know first.'

Michael, he had to admit, looked poorly. His face was grey and thin and his hair lank against the pillow, but he raised a cheerful smile for his visitor. ''Tis good to see you, Father, but don't be thinking I'm ready for the Last Rites yet.'

'Indeed not,' the priest laughed. 'By the look of you I'd say you're shamming.'

'Ah, it's the bloody cough, it fair wears me out. But it's only a chill. I'll give it a rest today and be up tomorrow.'

'That's the way. Keep warm. Now, my lad, I have some news for you. Enough to gladden the heart.'

'What's this?' Michael wheezed.

'I had a letter from Brodie.'

'Is he all right?'

'He's in the pink!'

'Ah, thank God. It's been a terrible strain not hearing from him.'

'Then listen to this.' With a flourish Daly produced the letter and read it slowly to Michael, whose face now glowed with pleasure.

'I knew it!' he said. 'I knew he'd do well if he'd just give himself a chance. So he's off to Australia. That's grand! Brodie's smart. I'll miss him, by God I will, but sure now he's come round to see what's best.'

'And he's even got a job to go to! That's better than most, I have to say.'

'Does he have a word for us?'

'Not as you'd notice,' the priest said cautiously.

Michael grinned. 'Isn't that just like the rascal? He writes to you knowing full well you'd be down post-haste to tell us. This way he doesn't have to admit he cares for his family and at the same time he's talking to us through you.'

Another bout of coughing tired him, so eventually the priest retreated, feeling a little deflated by Michael's generous attitude towards his brother, but glad that the patient was resting happily now, cheered by news of Brodie.

He sat in the kitchen with Maisie to read her the letter, and she too was thrilled. 'That'll get Michael on his feet again,' she said. 'He was worried sick about Brodie.'

'Yes, it will surely help. But Michael there, he doesn't look too good.'

'He's strong. I've made him my cough mixture, it'll fix him in no time. I get that cough meself every so often, but do you think she'd want the doctor for me? Not on your life! Now when her husband gets a chill, she wants to go haring off and bring in the doctor.'

'Did he come?'

'No. Michael wouldn't have it. There's no need, and what's there to pay him with?'

For once Father Daly might have agreed with Trella Court, but then he supposed that Maisie Grogan had nursed many of the sick, young and old, in her day, so Michael was in good hands.

'May God be with you,' he said as he left, thinking he'd take a stroll back through the village for a word here and there. Several families from this district had emigrated to America but Brodie was the first to head for Australia. This would be big news in Tullymore.

Chapter Two

Vivien Holloway was not speaking to her husband. That man thought of nothing but damn horses. And his friends back up there on the Downs, with their sheep or cattle stations, were just as boring. They talked of nothing but the weather, the prices of their stock, the rise and fall of the markets, and, of course, about horses. And today, it was horses again.

Five years ago she'd been the envy of all her friends, with the handsome, wealthy Vern Holloway courting her and then proposing on New Year's Eve at the Governor's Ball in Brisbane. It had been a heavenly night! And Vern had been so romantic, presenting her with a magnificent diamond ring the very minute the clock struck twelve!

When he announced their engagement they were given the floor to waltz before the whole assembly, as people threw kisses and rose petals and called out to them, rejoicing in their happiness. Vivien still had the lovely shimmering green dress she'd worn that night.

'But damn-all chance to wear it back home,' she muttered as she sat at the dressing table, brushing her frothy blonde hair. She was stalling; her hair was already free of knots and gleaming like silk. Little darts of electricity were causing it to fly about rather than settle, but she hoped Vern would give up and go down to meet the ship without her. Surely she was entitled to some time to herself!

'How men change,' she sighed. Before they were married, Vern was happy to escort her wherever she wanted to go ... the theatre, parties, balls, picnics ... Brisbane was never dull. But now he had no time for social life, no interest at all. Vivien considered she'd been snared. Tricked.

It had been almost mandatory for girls like her, dreaming of wealth and social standing, to set their caps at the graziers or their sons, and she had made one of the best catches of the season.

Or so it seemed at the time, she mused crankily.

After all, Vern was wealthy, wildly rich, and very handsome. Distinguished was a better word, tall and straight-backed from his years in the military, and quite charming. He was fifteen years older than her, but as everyone said, that was all to the better. Young men were too unpredictable, their characters not properly formed.

Not that Vivien had quibbled. He could have been thirty years older for all she cared. Because at twenty-five, she'd worried that she'd been left on the shelf.

Then, when Vern proposed, she'd been beside herself with excitement. And glee! She was to be *the* Mrs Vern Holloway, mistress of Fairlea Station, forty miles west of Toowoomba. She knew he ran cattle but Fairlea was also famous as a horse stud.

When she'd heard that, Vivien had made a point of riding with Vern as often as possible, and it didn't take him long to notice that she was an excellent rider. One of her few talents, she had to admit, but the right one where he was concerned.

Her friends had also said that marrying an older man was sensible, because he'd already sown his wild oats and she wouldn't have to worry about him straying.

'They can say that again,' she muttered darkly. Vern didn't stray. No chance of that, because from the day they'd married and gone to live at Fairlea Station their social life came to a dead stop, except when they went to visit his mother in Toowoomba. He settled down with a vengeance, putting all that behind them.

He came back from the hotel bathroom in his dressing gown, washbag in his hand. 'Aren't you ready yet?'

Fiddling with her hair, Vivien ignored him. They'd only been in Brisbane two days, and she'd noticed a new fashion. Women were wearing their hair massed in curls over their foreheads and swept up at the back. Her hair, being so light and curly, was ideal for that style, but it was difficult to arrange. She kept ending up with a gap on the crown. She should really call in a hairdresser, but then he'd complain. He was in a hurry.

She sighed. To think that their wedding reception had been held in this very hotel, the best in Brisbane and the most expensive, and they'd had a wonderful time. Her parents couldn't afford such extravagance but Vern had brushed aside their concern. 'It is my pleasure. This is Vivien's day and we must see she has the very best.'

'He didn't say the very last too,' she grumbled.

They never entertained at Fairlea. Only boring local people and horse breeders or buyers, except for their yearly race meeting, which was held on the Fairlea racetrack. And then it was more business than fun. And they rarely came to Brisbane any more.

When she'd complained, he'd been angry with her. 'Vivien, if you'd only take more interest in the place it wouldn't be boring. There's more to life than parties.'

'I enjoy parties.'

'You enjoy flirting, my dear. That's more to the point. You're a married woman now, it's time you grew up.'

'Oh! I see. We don't have any social life because you're afraid other men might find me attractive.'

'Not at all. You are attractive. You're very pretty. I don't mind that other men appreciate you, but I do mind when you overreact to their flatteries. And besides, we do have a social life, but because it's not Brisbane, you won't make any effort to enjoy yourself. You have to realise that Brisbane, really, is a rather dull place. You seem to think it's some mecca of society just because you grew up there. We can have just as much fun in the country. You must try a little harder to mix with people, our own people.'

How many times had she heard that lecture? Even his patience and rationale bored her.

By the time he was ready to leave she was still fiddling with pins and combs. 'You go on without me.'

He sat down in a chair by the door. 'I can wait.'

'Vern!' she exploded. 'You're only going down to meet the ship and see if your horses have arrived. You don't need me!'

'Delaney has sent me two of the best thoroughbreds that I have ever been able to import. One would have thought you'd be interested.'

'Of course I'm interested. But I don't see why I should have to meet them too. I doubt a horse will care.'

35

'Probably not, but you can't stay here.'

'Why not?' As soon as Vern left, his wife had planned to dress quickly and go downstairs to the tea room, a favourite meeting place for the social set in Brisbane.

'Because I've paid the bill.' His fair moustache quivered in a small teasing smile. 'I daresay someone else will require the rooms.'

She whirled about. 'What did you do that for?'

'Because we're catching the train to Toowoomba this afternoon.'

'We've only just got here!'

'Two days isn't only just. The ship has berthed. That's what we came for. Now I have to get home.'

'What if your horses aren't on the ship?'

'Then I shall weep all the way back to Fairlea because it will mean that some disaster has struck. Now be a good girl and pack up, and I shall wait for you downstairs. Do you need a maid to assist you?'

'No!' She flung her hairbrush across the room and stormed over to the wardrobe, knowing he'd won. Again.

To annoy him she chose a flamboyant outfit of coral-pink silk that would be as out of place on the Brisbane wharves as fancy dress at Sunday chapel. In truth, she'd never worn it before, although it had cost a mint. She'd bought it from a catalogue, and pretty though it was, the occasion to wear it hadn't eventuated.

For that matter, she thought grimly as she threw clothes willy-nilly into the trunk, one could say the same thing about most of her good clothes.

She left the trunk and his suitcase half packed – the maids could do the rest – and turned to the mirror. The pink suit was nipped into the waist with a neat peplum. The low-cut lapels were faced in rose satin which gave a glow to her face, and the rose-silk skirt swung almost to her ankles in the latest fashion. For a minute there, Vivien thought it might look a bit common now that she had a better look at it, but who cared? It was gorgeous on her. She added a double row of pearls at the neckline and after trying several hats from her large square hatbox chose a wide, sheer leno, trimmed in pink and white satin. It messed up the hairstyle she'd been attempting but Vivien compensated by pulling her fair hair forward under the hat to frame her face with ringlets.

Who cared if she looked as if she were on her way to a garden party?

Vern was waiting in his tweeds and wide countryman hat as she descended the stairs into the lobby with exaggerated grace.

'Very becoming, my dear,' he smiled, taking her arm, and she didn't know whether or not he was being sarcastic.

When they arrived at the wharf, travellers were still milling about in a confusion of luggage. A dreary lot, she observed disdainfully, aware that quite a few turned to stare at her.

Patrick, their trainer, was waiting for them.

'I've been aboard,' he cried, 'and they're fine! They've come through it well. Wait till you see them, sir! Mr Delaney has done us proud!'

'Thank God for that!' Vern said. 'Are they bringing them off now?'

'Any minute, with people out of the way first. The groom seems to have everything under control.'

When Brodie heard that the ship was nearing the end of this long and wearisome voyage, he almost wept.

'Ah, bless my heart and soul,' he said to his shipmate, Lester O'Dowd. 'We're delivered at long last!'

'We were lucky,' Lester said. 'A good ship and fair winds.'

'Easy for you to say. You've got a stomach of cast iron. I won't be happy until I'm standing on firm ground again.'

For the first week or so he'd been horribly seasick, and even after that he'd never lost the uncomfortable queasiness that threatened to lay him low again.

The only bright spot in those miserable weeks was provided by the captain. With more care for the horses than the groom, Brodie suspected, the Captain permitted him to go up to the breezy deck inhabited by the first-class passengers whenever the foul air of the hold became too much for him.

'We can't have you collapsing on us, Brodie,' he'd said.

He didn't know that the real carer for the two expensive horses travelling in his ship was Lester.

Taking full advantage of the privilege, Brodie enjoyed talking to the first-class passengers, who were solicitous of his health and who daily enquired after the condition of the poor horses.

The fillies, Grandee Lass and Bella Rose, had become the ship's pets, known to all as Lassie and Rosie, and their welfare was of constant interest, a break from the monotony of the voyage. Brodie cashed in on his new-found popularity by listening to the first-class passengers' manner of speech to improve his own, since he was determined to better himself in every way he could.

He gave daily accounts of the horses – their good days and bad. Telling stories, often invented, of their idiosyncrasies as if they were two naughty children.

'Never you fear, though,' he told his audience proudly. 'They're in good hands.'

That was true. But the hands were those of Lester O'Dowd, who'd come across the horses in a filthy state, both lurching about unsteadily with their groom too seasick to care.

O'Dowd, now in his late twenties, had worked in the Curragh stables as long as he could recall, and his father before him, but he was now on his way to seek his fortune in the Queensland gold fields.

Shocked at the condition of the horses, he bullied Brodie to his feet, telling him that the seasickness was all in his mind, and forcing him to make the horses more comfortable.

Together they cleaned out the narrow stalls, washed the horses, curry-combed them to quieten them and brushed them until they gleamed again. Lester then cadged canvas from the crew and rolled it into thick bolsters which he affixed to the sides of the stalls to prevent injury. And it was Lester, rather than Brodie, who petted and babied his charges, insisting that they needed all this extra care because they often became depressed.

'And who wouldn't?' he asked Brodie. 'It's not natural for the poor things to be stuck in boxes all this time with no chance to stretch their legs, and wondering what's going on.'

'It's not natural for me either,' Brodie groaned. Lester was a hard taskmaster and it turned Brodie's stomach having to rake up the stinking straw every day and carry it to the stern of the ship to be hurled overboard. On rough days Brodie contemplated throwing himself into the crystal-clear wake instead, but he persevered as O'Dowd's lackey.

Steerage was a raucous, rollicking place during the first few weeks and Brodie, suffering, wished them all to hell. But eventually his fellow passengers settled into a kind of stupor, interspersed with fights and arguments, which were inevitable in such a small space. Flirting women were sweet to him but he had more of an eye for the ladies up top, and if his stomach hadn't been perpetually unsettled he was sure he'd have enjoyed himself much more with them. He was mortally afraid of throwing up in their presence.

But at last it was all over. Holloway's trainer came aboard, delighted to find the horses hale and hearty, shaking Brodie's hand over and over.

With the crew helping and the trainer hovering about, almost in a panic, Brodie led the wobbly pair down the gangway into the waiting arms of Mr Vern Holloway, where to his dismay the two horses promptly sat down like a couple of donkeys.

'What's the matter with them?' Holloway demanded, glaring at Brodie as if he'd treated them ill.

'I'm feeling much the same myself,' he said quickly. 'A man's terrible giddy, standing on steady ground after the chop and sway of the ship. Give them a few minutes, sir, to believe it's safe to stand.'

He hoped he was right. As it was, he was astonished that all vestiges of his seasickness had miraculously disappeared, and he longed to be free of the horses and their owner, so that he could dive into a pot of Guinness and a decent meal.

But still the dopey-looking nags hadn't budged. Brodie felt like kicking them but he remembered they were accustomed to Lester's petting.

'Would you get a bucket of water?' he asked Patrick, and soon he was cupping water, with his hands, to Rosie's fat lips.

'Come on, my darling,' he said. 'Nothing to be nervous about now. You'll soon be galloping about like mad things.'

As he stroked and patted them, they climbed gingerly up, shook themselves, looked about, and whinnied, as if in relief.

'There!' Brodie said triumphantly. 'I'd walk them real slow for a start, sir; they'll be tanglefoot, I'd reckon.'

Holloway examined each horse carefully, while a beautiful

woman – his wife, Brodie guessed – stood back, watching. She smiled at Brodie and his heart gave a bump. She had the face of an angel, so fair, with big blue eyes and a pretty little pink mouth. He hoped there were more like her in this strange country.

With an effort, he tore his eyes from her to gaze over at the township beyond the wharf, surprised by the newness of it all. The buildings were white, immaculate in the starched sunlight, looking as if they'd been built only last week.

He experienced a sudden flutter of nerves. The sense of space here was intimidating, as if he'd been flung into the vast and empty heavens, for there was not one wisp of a cloud in that great sky. For a minute he wondered what the hell he was doing here, a lad from a tiny closeted village where he knew every rock and burrow. Brodie Court was completely disorientated, not realising that the confines of the ship had added to his discomfort.

'Are you all right?' the woman asked him.

Brodie pulled himself together. He couldn't have her thinking he was a weak fellow.

'Oh, sure I am, ma'am,' he said. 'I was just getting my bearings.'

Holloway turned back to him. 'Well, they seem to be in good condition. You're Mr Brodie Court, I believe?'

'That I am, sir.'

'Well now, Brodie, I'm very grateful to you.' He took out his wallet and handed over a crisp pound note. 'Thank you for your good work.'

Brodie stared. 'If you don't mind my saying sir, Mr Delaney back there in Dublin, he promised me ten pounds if I delivered your horses in good order.'

Holloway laughed. 'He did? That'd be Jack! He thinks money grows on trees. Well, I'd better honour his promise.'

He gave Brodie the ten pounds without hesitation.

Unaccustomed to such easy largesse, Brodie thanked him profusely.

'I understand you'd like a job,' Holloway said.

Brodie nodded.

'That can be arranged. I think these poor horses have had enough of transport. They can be walked out to my property

40

and you can come along with them if you wish. Would that suit you?'

'Yes, sir.' Brodie was impressed by his new employer's good manners. 'How do I go about it?'

'Patrick will look after you.'

When Holloway departed with his wife, Patrick turned to Brodie. 'We'll let these beauties rest for a couple of days, then we'll be on our way. We'll ride and lead them. I suppose you wouldn't mind a couple of days off either.'

With more cash in hand, Brodie agreed.

'Righto,' Patrick said. 'Be at the Charlotte Street stables at five on Saturday morning. Anyone will point you to them.'

'What day is it today? I've lost count.'

'Thursday.' Patrick took the halters to lead the horses away.

'Just a minute,' Brodie called to him. 'Where are we going? Where is this farm?'

'It's called Fairlea Station. On past Wirra Creek, that's the nearest excuse for a village.'

'How far is it?'

'Let's see. It's about ninety miles to Toowoomba, and Fairlea is another forty miles on from there. The boss says you'll be working in the stables.'

'What does he pay?'

'Two quid a week with bed and board. It's a good place to work and he's a good boss. You won't do much better being a new chum.'

'Jesus wept,' Brodie muttered as Patrick marched away, proudly leading the new racehorses.

Where the hell was this place? He didn't fancy riding more than a hundred miles to end up nursemaiding horses again. And a hundred miles! Patrick made it sound as if it were only a few villages away.

I don't know about this, he said to himself. I didn't come all this way to be a stablehand. I'm a farmer.

Still, he had money, and a few days to make up his mind.

Rather than have Lester hanging about to share the glory, Brodie had sent him on ahead to the Albion Hotel. Sailors had told them this was the nearest pub, just past the immigration sheds.

He remembered he had to report to the authorities before

leaving the wharf, and rushed in to sign the forms that officials thrust at him, answering questions impatiently. Then he sprinted down the sandy road to the pub. Brodie had a great thirst!

Lester was already settled in a corner with their luggage – and, Brodie frowned, two blowsy women. They all seemed to be having a great time.

'The party's started,' Lester called. 'This is Pearly and that one's Lucy. Say hello to the girls, Brodie!'

Rather than give offence, he acknowledged the women, thinking that it was a long time since they'd been girls, and pulled up a heavy wooden chair.

For a pub it was bright and airy, windows wide open lending a cooling breeze, and there was a fine smell of cooking, but the drinking time came first.

Lester dissuaded him from ordering Guinness, it being too dear in this land. 'Have the local beer,' he urged.

Although the beer was too cold, it was a fine drop, and in no time Brodie was relaxed and happy, not noticing that they were also paying for the women since Lester, in magnanimous mood, had instructed the barman to keep totting up their drinks 'on our bill'. Brodie thought this was a very civilised way of paying, better than scrabbling about for coins all the time.

Eventually the kitchen aromas were too much for him. 'I have to eat,' he announced.

Lester agreed. 'We'll all eat.'

It was a meal Brodie would long remember: big steaks with eggs and mashed potatoes and gravy and a dish of fried onions, and cobs of hot bread served with slabs of yellow butter.

The women bogged in too, he noticed, beginning to worry about who was paying for them. They ate like whales!

'Did the toff pay you?' Lester asked.

'No,' Brodie lied. That was his own business.

'And you let him get away! You said they promised you ten quid for delivering the horses.'

'I didn't let him get away. I'm going to work for him. I told you I had a job lined up.'

'You're bloody mad! You should have asked for the cash and come with me. We'll find gold and never have to work again.' He put his arm about Pearly. 'It's true, isn't it?'

he asked her. 'There's gold to be found in your country-side.'

'Sure. Mountains of it. You just have to find the right mountain.'

'I'll find it,' Lester assured them.

After the meal Lester disappeared outside, where he met one of the sailors from their ship.

'Did you watch him, Johnny?' he asked.

'Ah yes.'

'And did any money change hands?'

'Yes. The squatter gent gave him a tenner.'

'The mean bastard! I did Brodie's job for him all the way and now he's trying to pretend he didn't get paid so he doesn't have to give me a share.'

'Bloody mean,' the sailor agreed. 'Get some more grog in him and we'll roll him.'

'It could take a year to get him that drunk, and he's too big to be any easy mark.'

'Then try another tack. There's an old bloke in the bar, a genius, fingers like silk. He'll do the job for you but there has to be something in it for him. His name's Henty. I'll have a word with him.'

'He won't take off with the lot?'

'No. You've given him the tip. Where does Brodie keep his cash?'

'In a flat leather wallet, not a purse, so it's easy to miss. It's in his coat pocket, a deep pocket.'

'Leave it to me. We'll teach Brodie a little lesson. Meet Henty back here in the morning.'

Returning to their corner, Lester told Brodie that there was a boarding house in the next street where they could stay.

'Why don't you take our luggage down there and get us a room. We don't want to be wandering the streets at closing time.'

'Why don't you?' Brodie argued. He was very comfortable, for the first time in months.

'Because I carried your bloody suitcase here. It's your turn.'

'Fair enough,' Brodie admitted. He hurried away, found the boarding house and deposited their luggage in a seedy room, then locked the door and made his way back to the pub, only to find that Lester and Pearly had gone.

'Never mind, dearie,' Lucy said drunkenly. 'I'll keep you company.'

Brodie was furious, knowing he was stuck with the bill. And with Lucy, who was the uglier of the two, if a man had to compare.

She moved closer to him, clinging to his arm, and the smell of her made him queasy again.

'You'd better run along,' he said. 'I'll wait here for Lester.'

'I could have gone with Lester,' she whined, 'but I chose you. And now you're turning me down!'

'Then if you hurry you'll catch Lester. He really fancied you. He was talking of taking you to the gold fields with him.'

'He was?' She lurched to her feet.

'Sure. Don't you be letting Pearly edge into your place. I'm only a farm boy, I don't know nothing about gold. Lester's the money man.'

'Oh, Jeez,' she said, stumbling about. 'That bloody Pearly!' She threw her arms round Brodie, almost smothering him. 'You're a handsome fellow and a nice lad, Brodie. But I've got to go.'

She got halfway to the door, and stumbled back. 'You aren't cross with me, are you?' she asked, slurring her words.

'Not at all. You go find Lester. You're the girl for him.'

To Brodie, the bill, for the four of them, was a tragedy. More than six pounds!

'You had a long session, mate,' the publican said, taking his cash. 'Here, have a drink on the house.'

He passed Brodie a nip of whiskey and moved on down the crowded bar.

With nothing better to do, Brodie stayed on until closing time, and then, patting his wallet, spilled reluctantly into the busy street with the mob. He shouldered his way through the crowd making for the boarding house, raging against Lester and hoping he was heading in the right direction because he was as drunk as he'd ever been.

He made it, though and almost fell into their room after struggling with the lock, determined to wait up for Lester.

But that was difficult. He managed to undress and sit on one of the beds but he was too tired to stay awake. He reached for his jacket, the one that Abe had sold him, to find his wallet and put it under his pillow. But it was gone!

He searched his jacket again, then his pants and shirt, and the floor, panicking. No wallet. He'd lost his wallet!

The shock sobered him and he almost wept. He thought of rushing back to the pub but it was closed. And he knew he'd had his wallet when he left there. He must have dropped it in the street.

Once again he searched the room, cursing his drunken state. He must have shoved the wallet somewhere, being extra careful, that's what it was! And now he couldn't recall where he'd hid it. He turned up the mattress, pulled out drawers in the cheap dresser, crawled under the bed, searched and searched. Even, in desperation, checking his jacket again.

Then he saw it! Not the wallet, but the fine slit in his good jacket. A knife cut. Someone in that crowd outside the pub or on the street had robbed him. He'd known of this sort of thief in Dublin, the real experts who could slit cloth or bags in a flash and make off with whatever they had a mind to take.

And the bastards were here too!

He sat morosely on his bed, working it out. The thief must have watched where he put his wallet and gone to work in the street. The bastard! What a welcome to Brisbane. He'd been cleaned out.

Then Lester came bundling in, complaining. 'I didn't know which room. I had to wake the landlady and she bawled me out . . .'

Brodie grabbed him by the lapels of his coat and shook him angrily. 'You left me with that bloody bill, you rat!'

'Get away. I'll pay my share! Jesus! What's got in to everyone? I go down to Pearly's place for a bit of fun, and we're just getting started and what happens? Lucy comes blazing in, screaming like a banshee, and attacks Pearly, punching her and kicking her and yelling that she's taken her man. I don't know what she's talking about and Pearly doesn't wait to find out. She clubs Lucy with a hairbrush and then there's a real tearing brawl. So I beat it. Except I got lost turning this way and that up bloody streets, and then I couldn't find this place . . .'

Another time Brodie would have thought that funny. Not tonight. 'I've been robbed,' he said, not interested in the rest

45

of Lester's story. 'My wallet's gone. Some thieving bastard lifted it after I left the pub. You owe me three quid. More than that. I never invited those floosies and I had to pay for them too.'

'Fair go. We were having a good time.' Lester delved into his waistcoat pocket and threw Brodie four pounds. 'There's my half and some, though I wouldn't see you stuck. Did they get all your cash?'

'Every bloody penny,' Brodie moaned.

'How much did you lose?'

'I didn't lose it. I told you, I was robbed. More than twenty pounds!'

'Cripes! A bloody fortune. But look on the bright side. If you hadn't paid my half of the bill you'd be short that four quid too.'

The look Brodie gave him showed that he had no intention of looking on the bright side, so Lester flung himself down on the far bed. 'Put out the lamp, Brodie, I'm tired.'

In the morning Lester was up and about when Brodie woke. 'Where are you going?' Brodie asked suspiciously.

'To the Mines Department. I have to find out where this gold is. Get me some maps. They're the fellers with all the information. Why don't you have a look round the town?'

'I've decided to take that job. I leave on Saturday.'

'Suit yourself. I'll see you later.'

The clerk at the Mines Office was a talkative bloke so Lester let him have his head, but after hearing of all the fabulous gold finds he still had no definite destination.

'What's happening right now?' he asked. 'Where's the best field?'

'Kalgoorlie. Any amount of gold there.'

'Good. How long will it take me to walk there?'

The clerk grinned. 'About two years, across the desert. It's in Western Australia.'

'Haven't you got anything closer?'

The clerk roared with laughter. 'I'm not selling houses.' He pushed a map of Queensland across the counter. 'There's still gold here in Queensland. At Mount Morgan.' He sighed. 'I should have gone there myself. It turned out to be a mountain of gold.'

'Where's this place?'

'Here!' He ringed a spot on the map. 'North of Brisbane. About five hundred miles. You can go halfway by train, then get a coach.'

'And what's the catch?'

'The syndicates are taking over. There's still time to stake a claim if you get a move on. In the end they'll buy you out but if you strike colour you can't lose either way.'

Lester slid him a shilling. 'I'll need your help to figure out how to go about this.'

He left the office with a handful of papers, including maps, regulations, advice on mining leases and a dog-eared pamphlet that explained some of the intricacies of gold prospecting.

His next stop was the Albion Hotel, where he downed a pint before meeting Henty in the back lane.

'How much did you get?' he asked the old man.

'Ten pounds, mister. Nine for you, one for me.'

'And the rest,' Lester growled. He took hold of Henty's ear and twisted it viciously. 'You can have two quid for the job and give me the real take.' He shoved Henty against the wall and searched his shabby clothes, dragging notes from various pockets. 'That's more like it.'

By the time he left the pub, Henty was already settling down in the bar to drink his earnings.

Lester was busy that day. He bought a ticket to Gympie, the halfway town, and rushed back to the boarding house to collect his belongings. He left four shillings for his board and a note for Brodie explaining that he was off to the gold fields at Mount Morgan. Remembering where Brodie had said he'd be working, Lester promised to write to him.

Relieved that Brodie was out somewhere, he signed his name with a flourish. It wouldn't do for his room-mate to discover he was suddenly cashed up.

At three o'clock that afternoon, Lester was happily seated on the train, on his way to make his fortune.

As for Brodie, still smarting from his loss, his first thought had been to charge down to the pub and complain, but he knew it would be pointless. They'd only laugh at him for being such a tomfool as to let himself get robbed.

If he hadn't soaked up so much grog he'd probably still have the wallet.

Resigned to his misfortune, he strolled along the river front until he came to a fine sandstone building with a green dome. He discovered that this was the Customs House, and peering in was greatly impressed. Then a large tree further down caught his eye. It was covered in blue-purple flowers. Never had he seen a tree as splendid as this, so he enquired of a gentleman passing by what it was.

'Jacaranda,' he was told. 'They're in bloom all over now, telling us it's spring.'

After that Brodie saw a lot more of these spectacular trees and they cheered him, helped him to accept that he really was on the other side of the world. For here it was October, and the cold should be setting in, and yet it was spring. The explanation was too deep for him to be wrestling with right now.

He ploughed on, looking about him in wonder. He discovered that the streets were named after kings in one direction and queens in another, including Charlotte Street, where he spotted the stables but kept on going.

Back in the busy main street, Brodie was a mite disappointed. He'd expected to see blackfellows and kangaroos, since he'd heard so much about them on the ship, but this was just a big country town, with nothing unusual about it except for the colour. The light was very sharp, making shadows look like cut-outs, and the glare was hard on the eyes.

Standing amid cheering crowds he watched a parade of cavalry trotting down the street. Though uniformed and bearing rifles, they looked a jolly lot, waving to all, and Brodie was envious of their confidence. They made him feel very much alone, just a stranger wandering their streets, filling in time.

Following them, on the sidelines, he almost toppled over a counter draped with banners that was set up in the street.

A giant of a man, decked out in the same drab uniform, grabbed Brodie's arm. 'Here's a likely lad. What about you, sir? You should join the bush contingent.'

'What's that you say?' Brodie stuttered.

Enthusiastic young ladies gathered about him, smiling,

urging him on. They were all wearing red, white and blue ribbons on their pretty white dresses.

'We're recruiting,' the soldier boomed. 'We need volunteers. You can sign up right here, lad. Join our best and bravest.'

Brodie was bewildered. 'What for?'

'They're off to fight the war.'

'What war?' The only one he knew about was the fight going on in South Africa. The ship had called in there for half a day but no one was permitted ashore.

'The Boer War, lad!'

'Ah yes, that's the one.' He nodded and the recruiter seemed to take this as acceptance.

'What's your name?'

'Brodie Court, sir.'

He was already writing. 'And can you sit a horse?'

'Sure I can. But whose side are you fighting on?'

'Need you ask? The side of right!' He seemed rather miffed. 'We're soldiers of the Queen, my lad. Off to do our duty and destroy those filthy Boers. Now, how old are you?'

Brodie stiffened. The English army! Jesus, Michael would throw a fit. Anyway, what did it have to do with these people, oceans away? They must be mad.

'I only got here yesterday,' he apologised, backing away. 'Let me think about it.'

'Nothing to think about!' the recruiter roared at him as, embarrassed, Brodie shuffled back and lost himself in the crowd.

He rounded a corner, away from all the fuss, and sat down on a bench facing the shops to have a smoke and decide what to do next.

Across from him was a jeweller's shop, and Brodie contemplated the display window for a while, then ambled over to take a better look. A necklace resting on black velvet in the very middle of the window had taken his eye.

He stared at it and gasped. The centrepiece was a large diamond, but it was linked by a dazzling array of the prettiest stones he'd ever seen, and more hung from below the piece like teardrops. With their colours dancing all about, pinpoints of red and blue and violet on beds of milky soft colour, these stones outshone the diamond, making it look very plain.

Sensing a customer, the jeweller came out to join him.

'A dazzling necklace, isn't it, sir?'

'It's marvellous! What are those stones round the diamond?'

'Opals. And the setting is gold.'

'You don't say. I never heard of them before.'

'They're known as the queen of gems. In fact, our dear lady Queen is very fond of them.'

'So she would be.' Brodie nodded enthusiastically. 'Where do they come from?'

'Right here in Queensland. There are other opal fields at White Cliffs in New South Wales but these are just as good.'

'They'd be worth a bit?'

'Indeed. Would you like me to take it out for you? In the sunlight the colours really blaze.'

'Ah no, they're too rich for me. Do they come out of the ground like that or are they painted?'

'Good Lord! Painted! Of course not! They're just as God made them, the only one of all the gems that only needs to be shaped.'

Realising he was wasting his time, the jeweller retreated to his shop, leaving Brodie staring, thunderstruck. It was the colour that kept him there; he loved colour and those opals, each one different in pattern, held all the glorious shades of the rainbow.

'Happy stones,' he said, beaming at them. 'Beautiful stones. I'll have to tell Lester about them. We should go prospecting for opals, not gold.'

There were several rows of gold rings lower down in the window and Brodie glanced at them disdainfully. 'Not a patch on the opals,' he grinned.

It was well past noon, so he found a tavern where for a shilling he bought a pint and a feed of fish and boiled potatoes, taking his time, still contemplating those opals. Who could afford to buy such a grand necklace? he wondered.

They'd said on the ship that Lester had the gold fever. In which case, Brodie mused, he'd caught the opal fever, and not sorry about it at all. He imagined himself picking up handfuls of the gems, placing them in a velvet bag and taking them to a jeweller. But then he guessed it wouldn't be as easy as that or they'd come cheap, and they certainly wouldn't be bordering diamonds. He walked back to have another look in the jeweller's window in case he was already exaggerating their beauty, but no. They were there, and truly fit for a queen.

Since he didn't have the confidence to try opal seeking on his own, he decided that he'd have to talk Lester into it. But when he found his way back to the boarding house, Lester had gone.

Brodie sat down with a bump. Nothing seemed to be going right. 'Oh well,' he conceded. 'I'll take Holloway's job for the time being, but one day I'll go seeking them opals, and by God, I'll find them.'

Even though she couldn't stand her mother-in-law, Vivien adored staying over at Christiana's house in Toowoomba. It was set at the top of the range, with a fabulous view of the vast plains below. The lovely grounds, extending right to the edge of the escarpment with an almost sheer drop to the base, lent an air of grace and seclusion to this elegant residence.

Not that Christiana Holloway, a widow, was a recluse. The large house, beautifully furnished, had three reception rooms which were often in use because Christiana loved to entertain in the grand manner. Although she was a short, bustling woman, her wealth and her air of authority stamped her as a leading light in Toowoomba society.

When people gushed to her about Christiana being such a fine woman, Vivien smiled sweetly. She enjoyed her status as the young Mrs Holloway. But right from the start her mother-in-law had made it clear that she didn't think Vivien was good enough for her only son. Refusing to be intimidated by this formidable woman with her upper-class accent, Vivien retaliated with thinly veiled sniping at her whenever she could find an opportunity. All of which went over Vern's head. He was a good-natured man, intent on his own affairs.

Vivien, too, was an only child. Her parents owned a draper's store in suburban Brisbane. They adored their daughter, thrilled that she was such a pretty girl, and although they couldn't afford to send her to one of the 'good' ladies' colleges, her mother compensated by seeing to it that Vivien was always well dressed and insisting she take dancing and riding lessons.

Looking back now, Vivien realised that her mother had been very pushy, to an embarrassing degree, although her efforts, she supposed, had paid off.

It was only when they met Christiana Holloway that Vivien saw the gulf between her parents and her new status. Her father was bumbling and shy and her mother was the absolute end. Affecting a phoney accent, she clung on to Christiana like a limpet, boasting that her family was descended from some obscure aristocrat.

'And what of your family?' she'd asked Christiana while Vivien squirmed.

'Only in shipping, I'm afraid,' Christiana had replied wearily.

'Oh well, never mind,' her stupid mother had gushed.

Vivien didn't see much of her parents these days, with the fortunate excuse of distance. She hadn't bothered to contact them while she was in Brisbane this time.

Recalling all this, Vivien sighed. Now, after only two days in Brisbane, they were on their way to Christiana's Toowoomba house, their usual stopover before setting out for Fairlea Station.

As the gig spun along, driven by one of Christiana's flunkeys, Vivien decided to enlist her mother-in-law's support in persuading Vern to stay on for a while. Anything to delay their return home.

It still angered her to remember the moment when, as a bride, she'd first sighted the Fairlea homestead. She'd expected her new home to be the same standard as the Holloway house in Toowoomba. Maybe a bit smaller. But certainly not the plain sandstone farmhouse that confronted her, with the bare essentials of parlour, dining room and three bedrooms. The furnishings were dreary. Sufficient, one could only say.

How Christiana must have laughed at her. Before she saw the place Vivien had been going on about how she expected to entertain at Fairlea. Thinking she could do this in the same style as the Holloways did here. To her horror, she'd realised she must have sounded like her mother.

She had refurnished the homestead but Vern had steadfastly refused to rebuild, considering it a waste of money. And now Vivien didn't care, she hated the place. It was worse than a prison, being stuck out there in the bush, missing all the fun things that happened in town. At least Toowoomba was a welcome relief, even if she did have to put up with Christiana.

And there *she* was, waiting for them on the porch, looking very elegant as usual, with her pearls and her diamonds.

She had a distant kiss for Vivien and a fond hug for Vern, whom she adored. 'I'm so pleased to see you. Were the horses all right, Vern?'

Of course she'd say the right thing, Vivien thought acidly, as Vern enthused about his new racehorses and they all moved into the long polished hallway that led through to the comfortable front sitting room with its grand view.

'How long are you staying?' Christiana asked.

'Only overnight, Mother, we're frightfully busy back home. I had to be in Brisbane to take possession of those horses. If anything had gone wrong, I wanted to be on the spot. But fortunately they're in tiptop shape. Patrick's walking them out to Fairlea.'

'Oh, Vern, surely we can stay for a few days.' Vivien looked to Christiana. 'We don't come to town very often. I'm sure your mother would love you to stay awhile.'

'Of course I would,' she said. 'But Vern knows best. It's a big job to run cattle and horses. What happened with the military, Vern?'

'They're buying as many horses as they can get. I'm bringing mobs in from the west and they're happy to have Fairlea as a staging area. A lot of them are brumbies but they're damn good work horses.'

'I hope you're charging them accordingly,' Christiana said.

Vern laughed. 'I like to do my bit but those chaps are big spenders with someone else's money. They might as well pay me as anyone else. They'll buy anything that looks like a horse.'

'You're not selling the good horses?' Vivien cried.

Christiana looked at her pityingly. 'Hardly, my dear. Vern hasn't spent years building up blood lines to let them go. What did you think of the new fillies?'

'Oh! Good stock, I'd say,' Vivien replied.

'You hardly noticed them,' Vern grumbled.

Later, when Vivien was dressing for dinner, her mother-in-law paid her a visit. 'Where's Vern?'

'He's gone for a stroll in the garden.'

'Good.' Christiana picked up shoes that Vivien had tossed aside and placed them neatly in a cupboard. 'I'm glad to have this chance to speak to you. I don't wish to be indelicate, but is there another child on the way?'

'No.' Vivien presented a wan face to her mother-in-law.

'Ah!' Christiana was clearly disappointed. 'I know two miscarriages upset you, but these things happen. You have to be more careful. Perhaps you ride too much.'

'There's nothing else to do out there.'

'My dear, women can always find something to do. Now promise me you'll stop riding. I'm sure that's the answer.'

'It might help,' Vivien admitted, with not the least intention of taking her advice. 'But you did say, when I lost the other two, that it was God's will. I think I have to wait on His will for another.'

Christiana looked at her keenly, not sure if she were being reprimanded. 'It's just that you are looking a little plump lately, Vivien. You rather raised my hopes. I'd dearly love a grandchild.'

When she left Vivien flounced over to the mirror, twisting and turning in front of it. 'The bitch! I'm not getting fat!'

She sat on the edge of the bed worrying about the conversation. That subject always made her nervous.

The last time she'd had a miscarriage, eighteen months ago, their housekeeper, Elvie Smith, had rushed her to the little bush hospital at Wirra Creek. Vern was away chasing cattle somewhere.

She had been very ill, suffering from terrible pains and fever, and she was left to the care, such as it was, of Dr Campbell. Reputed to have a drinking problem, old Campbell would never have been Vivien's first choice as her physician, but she'd been too ill to complain. She welcomed the ether.

When it was all over he came in, smelling of alcohol, and Vivien turned away to escape the fumes.

'How are you feeling?' he asked.

'Terrible. I lost the baby, didn't I?'

'There was no baby. The bleeding and discomfort were caused by problems in the Fallopian tubes.'

'Oh, God!' She sank back on the hard bed, exhausted.

He coughed. 'There's something else, I'm afraid.'

'What else can there be?' she said wearily. 'I'd like a decent cup of tea, not that slop they've brought me.'

'Yes, I'll see to it. Mrs Holloway . . .' He was sweating, wispy white hair plastered to his balding forehead. 'I have to tell you this. I'm afraid there won't be any more babies.'

She jerked up, fully awake now. 'What? You damn fool! What have you done to me?'

He stiffened. 'Let me tell you, young woman, no matter what you may think of me, no one could have done any more for you. You have an infection . . .'

'I'm infectious?' she cried.

'Good heavens, no. The infection caused the pain but you also have growths in the uterus. Lumps, let us say.'

'Can't you take them out?'

'That would require an operation and the result would be the same. As things stand now the tubes are blocked.'

'And that means I can't conceive?'

'Yes. I'm very sorry. Your husband is outside. Do you want me to break the news to him?'

'You'll do no such thing,' she snapped, panic-stricken. Vern was bad enough, looking forward to sons, but Christiana! Oh my God!

'Sit there, Doctor,' she ordered, 'until I get over this shock.'

He was only too pleased to stay and comfort her, but Vivien's mind was racing. She was barren! She needed time to think about this. In a jumble of emotions she feared being thought inadequate. She worried about Christiana and her constant harping about grandchildren. Would she somehow try to dislodge her? Find her son a better breeder? And she dreaded Vern's reaction.

'This won't affect your sex life,' Campbell was murmuring, as if that was anything to do with him. 'Don't feel bad. It happens to a lot of women.'

'Not to me!' she snapped. As it was, she and Vern had little in common these days. He had become very set in his ways; he liked nothing better of a night than to sit quietly smoking his pipe and reading the papers. Love had become lost somewhere in a haze of mutual criticism. He found her silly and immature, and she saw a man sinking into early old age. When he did make love to her Vivien knew that sons were on his mind. Sons to inherit his beloved Fairlea Station.

Oh God, she worried. The man was a horse breeder, proud of the blood lines. Proud of the day when his young wife would give him sons. Was that why he'd married a woman so much younger than himself? A hale and healthy mare?

'Oh Lord,' she said, and Campbell took her hand in his clammy paw. 'Try not to be upset, my dear.'

'Shut up, you bloody fool! You'll tell no one about this! When it suits me I'll tell my husband in my own good time.'

He smiled. 'He'll need to know.'

'No he won't. I'm staying in this hospital for another week, if I can stand it. Under observation. Have you got that?'

'Certainly, if you wish. You'd have to stay anyway, to clear up the infection.'

'And I don't want a word of this to anyone. Not to my husband and certainly not to Mrs Smith, our housekeeper. I suppose she's out there with him?'

'Yes. She's worried about you.'

'Like hell she is, the old bat. She hates me. She's been with the Holloways since Vern was a kid. She only cares about my husband.'

It was Campbell's turn to be worried. 'I think this shock has been too much for you. I should give you something to put you to sleep.'

'No you don't. I said I don't want anyone knowing about this, and I want your word on it.'

He nodded, rather grandly. 'Matters between doctor and patient are always strictly private. I have never been known to break that confidence.'

'Just as well,' Vivien said, 'because if you do I'll have you struck off. I'll lay a complaint that you were drunk when you attended me.'

'I wasn't drunk!' The doctor was appalled.

'You stink of alcohol now.'

'Only a couple of brandies while I was waiting for you to recover. This is preposterous!'

'Do you realise who I am? If Christiana Holloway gets

to hear that you were drunk attending to me, you'll be finished.'

'But it's not true!'

'Your reputation would bear me out. If I sued you, win or lose, you couldn't survive as a doctor. Mrs Holloway would see to that.'

'Perhaps you should rest,' he said, hardly believing what he was hearing.

'Perhaps nothing! You may go now, and tell my husband that I am recovering well from the miscarriage and that all is in order. I just need to remain here under observation. Are we in agreement now?'

He shrugged. 'Whatever you wish. But one day this will catch up with you, Mrs Holloway.'

'Whatever happens, it is none of your business. Remember that.'

As time went on Vivien was happy with her decision. Campbell kept his mouth shut and Vern had no idea that his wife could not conceive. He just kept hoping, as did Christiana. And the young Mrs Holloway was enormously relieved that she'd never have to suffer the misery of pregnancy again. She could survive without children.

That night she sulked. No one had been invited to join them for dinner, so it had just been the three of them again. A long, dull evening.

As soon as Christiana retired, Vivien tried again. 'We should stay in Toowoomba, there's the Bachelors' Ball on Saturday night. All your friends will be there, Vern, they'll be looking forward to seeing you.'

'They won't miss me,' he grunted, poring over the latest book he'd bought on stud management.

'Well, I should like to go!'

'It's not possible. I wish you'd stop nagging. Why don't you go to bed, I want to leave early in the morning. We're taking the gig.'

'What? I'm not going home in the gig. It takes too long.'

'Mother thinks it would be best for you. She thinks you should avoid a long ride like that.'

'I don't care what your mother thinks!' Vivien exploded. 'I like to ride! I won't have her deciding what I should and should not do. I'm entitled to some enjoyment. Tell them to have the horses ready at eight o'clock and no earlier. I shall have my breakfast in bed.'

'Very well,' he shrugged, and that annoyed her too, for no particular reason.

'I'll be asleep when you come in,' she said angrily, 'so don't disturb me.'

'I'm becoming accustomed to not disturbing my wife lately,' he retorted drily.

It crossed Vivien's mind to tell him that his lovemaking was as boring as he was, but she decided against pushing him too far with Christiana hovering about. She would hate that smug woman to hear a row between them. Instead she swept off to bed with a new plan. In a few weeks' time it would be Christiana's birthday, conveniently during Race Week, when everyone would be in town. They would have to come in for that and she would insist on staying for the whole week. Insist!

Chapter Three

The fear of another plague had passed but now the elements had turned on them. Trella couldn't recall a winter as bad as this. In the village they were saying that the flood was worse than the big one thirty years ago. Torrential rains had caused the river to break its banks and flood the valley. Fortunately, the Court farmhouse, being higher, had been spared, but their crops had been washed out.

Michael was so weakened by this that he had to stay by the fire wrapped in blankets while she and Garth picked over the crops and replanted, out there in the bitter cold.

'We have to count our blessings,' she told Garth. 'At least we didn't get water in the house like most of the others did. It takes a long time to get rid of the damp.'

But she was worried. The doctor had mentioned that it was the weather wearing Michael down. Only mentioned it, mind you, she told herself. As if in passing. Because what he really meant was that he ought to move him to a warmer climate.

Knowing their circumstances, the doctor would never recommend such a cure, he'd never be so cruel. No, he just kept offering remedies, and red flannel and potions, while he peered hopefully at the sullen skies.

Trella prayed. God, how she prayed, and all the time she kept thinking of Brodie living in that strange country with oceans of sunshine. Every day she paid a visit to the church, unable to afford to light a candle but begging the Lord to find Brodie so that she could write to him. Tell him how sick his brother was, and ask for his help. The priest had given Michael that letter from Brodie, as a comfort, and Trella had taken it down to the nuns to be shown exactly where Brisbane was on the map of the world.

'So far away!' she despaired.

'We'll say the rosary with you,' Sister Mary Joseph said.

'Pray that he'll be reminded of his family and given to write again. Brodie's been gone months now, he should be settled in his new job by this.'

But then, on Christmas Eve, her mother died. Trella found her face down in the mud outside the cowshed.

'Poor Maisie,' she wept. 'What a lonely, miserable way to go.'

Trella's patience with the Lord gave out.

Father Daly took up a collection for the burial and Trella sat through the service, silently railing at God for his lack of compassion. Her mother, a fastidious woman, hadn't deserved to die like that, sprawled out in deep, hoof-pocked mud.

'And there's Michael!' she went on. 'He's a good man, always true to you, God, with never a complaint on his lips at the way you treat him, wearing down his fine body with the consumption. You're too cruel for me and that's a fact.'

Bitterness accompanied her on the cold, grey march along the road to the cemetery, heavy fog turning shapeless the straggling mourners.

It was a matter of honour with Michael that he should walk the pace as head of the family, shunning the offer to ride on the hearse, with Garth striding manfully beside him for fear he might stumble. This was one of Michael's good days, so Trella made no objection, believing the effort to be a boost to his spirits. Although others said it was foolhardy.

Later she mused that giving God that shake-up had done no harm, since, only a few weeks after the funeral, Father Daly came chirping to the door, waving the long-awaited letter from Brodie.

'Does he not know our address?' Trella remarked caustically, but Michael took no offence. 'At least we know where he is and that he's made the crossing without mishap. What a relief it is to hear from him.'

'He says he has a job on a farm that raises cattle and horses, far out in the countryside,' Father Daly said, as excited as they were. 'And the farm is so big Mr Hadley-Jones' estate would fit in the corner without being noticed.'

Michael's eyes widened as he took the letter. 'You don't say?'

Daly laughed. 'Brodie was always given to exaggeration. But it still sounds like a fine place.'

'He's earning good money,' Michael told Trella. 'Living in bachelor quarters with eight other men, all good fellows. And they have a Chinaman to cook for them.' He shook his head. 'Did you ever hear the like?'

'Why a Chinaman?' Garth asked.

'He doesn't say. He writes that they raise thousands of cattle . . .' Michael spared the priest a wink, thinking this another exaggeration. 'And fine horses. Some for the turf and cross-breeds for the military. Mainly the offspring of wild horses.'

'Wild horses!' Garth was intrigued. 'We can't even afford one horse. Do they have them running free there? Could Uncle Brodie get some for us?'

'I doubt that. It's a long way to swim,' his father smiled.

'Then we should go there.'

The two men hardly heard him, too busy concentrating on Brodie's news. But Trella did.

'What do they grow on that farm?' she asked.

'Horses and cattle,' Daly said. 'I doubt they'd have time for spuds.'

'That'd suit me,' Garth said. 'It'd be a lot easier.'

'Nothin's easy,' Daly admonished.

'Did he put an address on this letter?' Trella wanted to know.

'Yes, here it is,' Michael beamed. 'Fairlea Station via Toowoomba, Queensland.'

'A railway station for an address!'

'As long as it finds him,' Michael admonished.

The priest explained. 'I have it on good authority, from one of the visiting priests, that out there they call their farms stations.'

'Why would they do that?' Michael asked.

'I think it's the name for big farms as against small farms. That's the best I can make of it anyway.'

Trella waited to hear the rest of the letter. For Brodie's greetings to his family, but there was only a cheerful: *Say a hulloo to everyone for me.*

'Not a word for us,' she snapped. 'Too wrapped up in himself, he is.'

'He couldn't mention everyone by name,' Michael said gently. 'It would take all night, wouldn't it, Father?'

'That it would,' Daly agreed.

But when he left, Michael turned on her. 'Don't be criticising my brother in front of the priest.'

'Why not? The man's not stupid. He sees what we see.'

'You never understood Brodie. That's your trouble. In writing to the priest he's reaching out to us in the best way his pride will allow.'

'Damn his pride! He knows our circumstances. If he's making so much money why doesn't he send you a few pounds? That was the arrangement.'

'There was never such an arrangement. We never got to that. Brodie did what you wanted. He left. We can ask no more of him.'

'So now I'm to blame for sending him off?'

Michael sat back in his chair. 'Blame's not a word to be using. It's a miserable thing. We all do our best and we should be thanking God that my brother is safe and well.'

That night he wrote a long letter to Brodie, congratulating him on his good fortune, telling him of the family and Maisie's death, and of the flood and news of the village, but never a word of their worries.

In the morning, while Michael was resting, Trella wrote her own page to slip in with the others before she mailed it.

She told Brodie the truth. That Michael was suffering badly from the consumption, that they were now so poor they were living hand to mouth and she could see no end to it. Without hesitation she asked Brodie to send Michael money, whatever he could spare.

Hadn't Brodie said that he was living in a sunny place with spring more like summer, a warm, comfortable place? Wasn't this exactly what Michael needed to throw off that debilitating sickness? She added extra lines, begging for the money to bring Michael back to health in Australia. To save his life.

If you care for your brother at all, she wrote, *you'll not deny him the only chance doctors can give him.*

Easter had well passed by the time their letters reached him, and Brodie was furious with Trella for putting him on the spot like that.

'If you care for your brother,' she'd said. What a bloody

cheek she had! Of course he cared about Michael and he was sorrier than he could say that he was sick.

Brodie shuddered. Hadn't the parents been taken off with the same thing? But how could he help? It was just her cheek to tell him he ought to send the money to bring Michael out here. A man who wouldn't leave his family. They'd all have to come, and who would support them? Michael would be too sick to work and Brodie would have the lot of them round his neck. Had she thought of that? A bloody leech, that was what she was. And what money? Here at Fairlea he was earning his keep and a fair wage, but he was saving every penny. The other blokes here ragged him about it, claiming he was more Scot than Irish, but Brodie didn't mind. He had his dream. He needed a stake to set out in search of opals.

They all said that was a mug's game. Opals weren't worth the trouble. But it excited Brodie that they knew they were out there, somewhere way out west, so it wasn't just a myth.

With the letters in the box by his bunk, nagging at him, Brodie had trouble sleeping. He had no money to spare for them. But if he didn't help, his name would be mud in Tullymore. He could hear them now, calling him a callous man, for Michael was much loved; or worse, that he was a liar and just as poor in this country as he'd been back home. Even thinking about that criticism upset him.

There was no comparing his life here with the dark drudgery back home. The ride out to Fairlea Station with Patrick and the two horses had been a breeze, taking it in easy stages, stopping at inns on the way.

They'd travelled due west, up the ranges and on across this great district Patrick called the Downs, and Brodie had been full of wonderment at what he saw. Here at last were the kangaroos, and all manner of strange animals, none of them dangerous, he was relieved to hear. The land was so vast and seemingly empty that he wouldn't have been surprised to find lions or tigers lurking in the high grass or poised on the ancient tawny rocks that occasionally lorded it over the landscape.

From a distance the forests seemed rich and green, but on closer inspection he found them strangely humble. The trees were tall and straggly, white as ghosts at night. At first glance, they seemed so sparsely set that a man might think he could see right through to the other side, but that was only an illusion. They stretched on endlessly, creating a difficult passage for riders.

'We're taking a short cut,' Patrick said, 'through to cleared land, but be warned, Brodie, if you don't know the country, stick to the tracks. It's too easy to get lost in the bush, even as close to civilisation as we are now.'

Brodie wondered what the rest of the country must be like if this was considered close to civilisation. It was near to noon and they hadn't encountered a soul. Not like home, where there was always someone on the roads.

'The sameness you see,' Patrick explained, 'that's what gets you. You might pick out a decrepit old tree, like that fallen one back there, as a landmark, but there are hundreds more. It's all more of the same in the scrub. The only way to protect yourself, if you're not sure, is to blaze markers on the trees. Otherwise you could be in real trouble.'

'Not me,' Brodie said. 'Wild horses wouldn't get me off the beaten tracks. I'd be for the long way round.'

So he worried, from the safety of his bunk, 'What could Michael do in wild country like this?'

How dare Trella question his feelings for his brother? He loved Michael. They might have had their differences, the latest caused by herself, but they were still close. He did care about him, but dragging him all the way out here to sit in the sun seemed ludicrous to Brodie. He'd already discovered that the sun could be more of an enemy. For the last few months the heat had been atrocious, daily well up over the hundred, with no let-up. He'd love to see Trella stuck on a horse all day in the blazing heat, as he had to do in his new job as a stockman. She mightn't be so smart, making all these fancy plans.

Not that Brodie himself had any complaints. At first he'd worked as a groom in the stables, but then it had been Patrick who'd spoken to Mr Holloway.

'I told him that a big strong feller like you shouldn't be mucking round here, and he agreed, so you grab yourself a saddle and front up to Taffy, the foreman. He'll show you the ropes.'

Proud of his promotion, and anxious to learn, Brodie listened carefully to everything Taffy told him, but the first week was sheer hell. A stockman earned his keep the hard way. 'Rough riding' was taken for granted, since they had to cover a great deal of country, checking the cattle or riding the boundaries, and Brodie suffered. He was sunburned, sore and sorry by the end of each day, when he was also the butt of jokes from the other men, who knew it had become agony for him to sit down.

To Brodie it was the longest week of his life, but he gained respect by refusing to give in and refusing to complain. Because he had nowhere else to go, he was determined to fit in, to be accepted by these hard-riding men, and soon they stopped noticing him. That was the best part. He didn't expect to be great mates with them at this early stage, but at least he was taken for granted. He was just another one of the blokes working the station, sharing their lives, their constant jokes and arguments and their tough, swaggering attitudes as they pitted their skills against each other.

Taffy was a ringer, a skilled stockman and a top rough rider, which Brodie discovered was entirely different from his own idea of rough riding. Rough riders took on wild horses or bucking steers.

They all laughed uproariously when Brodie told them about Mr Hadley-Jones and his guests, who rode out to the hunt in their formal attire, with hounds, chasing foxes, calling tally-ho. For hadn't he watched them often enough?

His new friends loved that yarn, not sure if it was true, but then plenty of campfire tales were stretched a bit. They were accepted just the same, for entertainment, and Brodie's story about the fox hunts was a favourite. Time and again he had to repeat it, in the most minute detail, right down to the outfits, and the men who earned their living on horses as tough as they were, listened, entranced.

Brodie, always good with words, became popular with his yarns, about the ship and the oceans he'd crossed, about the sinister battle raging in Ireland, even about the cattle sales held in the main street of Tullymore . . . difficult to explain to men when one of their wild herds would have trampled the whole village. Even Taffy was fascinated, for he wasn't a real Welshman, just born of Welsh parents. Brodie was touched by their interest; they so much wanted to learn about other lands, just as he had much to learn about their country.

They couldn't guess what a thrill it was for him, once the

pain of an aching back and red-raw thighs had subsided, to ride wild and free with them on the bony horses. They thought nothing of the distances they travelled at such a pace, it was just a question of getting from here to there as soon as possible. But to Brodie it was a childhood dream come true, a mad relief from the confines of the village. A wild way to earn a living, but he tucked his knees in, shortened his stirrups the way they did and streaked out after them, armed with a water bag and a rifle. Always the rifle, for protection, for signals, for whatever, he wasn't too sure. But he liked to see it there, holstered by his saddle.

On Sundays, their day off, they liked to watch the good horses put through their paces on the private track, and Brodie's former charges, Lassie and Rosie, were proving their worth. Sure bets in the near future, everyone agreed, rubbing their hands gleefully. For horses, racehorses and work horses, took precedence over everything at Fairlea.

For fear of being thought weak, Brodie never made any comment about the cattle. He was wary of the great beasts, known to be a menace to horses at times. Brodie considered them a menace to himself too. Some of the ferocious bullocks looked at if they weighed a ton, and when they took umbrage and charged, he was well out of the way. He'd just as soon be chased by a rhinoceros. There were accidents . . . thrills and spills, the stockmen called them, nonchalantly.

How could Michael cope in a place like this? Brodie had already decided that he himself wouldn't be waiting about for an accident to happen to him. Fairlea Station was a breathing space. It was giving him time to save some money and get a feel for the country before he set out on his real mission, to find those opals.

He moved restlessly about in his bunk, the problem of Michael gnawing at him.

Why not let Michael have the farm? He could sell it and use the proceeds to buy a warmer house somewhere, away from the damp of the valley. A place that wasn't thatched; he needed a proper roof. Brodie had never seen a thatched house in this country. And here women worked. Trella could get a job, a paying job, while Michael recuperated. Then when he was better, they could both work. Michael knew people everywhere, he'd never be short of work.

66

As this glowing scene unfolded before his eyes, Brodie breathed a sigh of relief. This was the answer. Tomorrow he'd write to Father Daly with his generous offer, enclosing a separate page signing his share of the farm over to his brother. He'd even get Patrick to witness it for him.

Hardly had he closed his eyes for a restful sleep, now that the decision was made, than the Chinese cook came yelling into the bunkhouse, whanging on the triangle he used to call them to meals.

'Out!' he shouted. 'All up. Out!'

'It's Sunday, you mug!' someone shouted, as the little cook ran out dodging boots and insults.

'Is there a fire?' Brodie cried fuzzily, and the mention of fire had them all stumbling for the door.

There was no fire. Instead the boss was outside, already mounted, and Taffy was handing out extra ammunition for their rifles.

Some time during the night, Holloway shouted, thieves had smashed down the fence of the outer paddock, near the creek, and made off with thirty horses. He wanted them back. Army men would be calling to collect them next week. Now the thieves had got a good start, knowing the station slept in on Sundays, but they could easily track a mob that size.

There was a mad scramble as the stockmen ran back to dress and then out again to grab equipment from the shed and rush down to the paddock where Patrick was rounding up the stock horses.

Holloway waited for them to join him. 'If you see any of the bastards,' he called angrily, 'shoot! Don't waste time thinking about it. But be careful of my horses.'

Bewildered by this sudden turn of events, Brodie managed to get himself mounted and out of the paddock, shoving cartridges into his pocket, in time to hear the boss's instructions, and then he was riding with the mob away from the homestead.

His comrades, grim-faced, were eager for the chase. Some, showing off, he thought, were loading their rifles on the run. As his own horse, an ungainly beast, pounded along, he wondered if any of them had spared a thought for the danger. If they were instructed to fire, then it seemed to him that the horse thieves would be aware of this reaction. They too would be armed, and very likely return fire.

He'd refused to join up and fight for the English and now he'd been catapulted into a private army owned by an Australian. His situation, he worried as he galloped along, didn't make a lot of sense, but he couldn't drop out. Holloway and Taffy were up front, hurtling forward at a pace that would make them an even bet for the Dublin Cup, so a man had to try to keep up.

As they splashed through the creek, Brodie had time to see where the wire fence had been cut before they all wheeled away to the right and hurtled on through light scrub.

The horse that had been shoved at him was a feisty old chestnut with a white blaze. He hadn't come across him before. He was fast, but it was like riding rocks, the thin stockman's saddle no match for the nag's bony back. Too late he realised that this was one of the old brumbies that was used now only for the less arduous tasks round the homestead. Still, the nag knew his business.

His heavy shoulders heaving, he hit the scrub with a steady, experienced eye, swerving among the trees and sailing over the traps of forest litter without a blink, until Brodie found himself, reluctantly, up there among the front runners.

They rode for miles, emerging into open country and then plunging into heavy scrub that bordered the river. They were well out of Fairlea land by this, Brodie guessed, because the river flowed quite close to the homestead, and he'd never seen this area before. He hoped they would give up confronted by the river, believing they were on the wrong trail, but no such luck.

'The bastards!' Taffy shouted to the horsemen gathered about him. 'They've split up.' He pointed to the tracks. 'They've taken one mob downriver and the rest up that way. An each-way bet. Patrick, you take some men and go upriver, I'll go after them downstream. I know where they'll cross this way.'

Patrick chose four men and they were away in seconds. Just as Brodie was preparing to follow Taffy, the boss wheeled his horse about and pointed to the nearest of his employees:

'You. You stay with me.'

'Yes, sir,' Brodie said smartly, congratulating himself on being ordered to remain at headquarters with the boss.

When Holloway went down to stare across the river, bemoaning the loss of thirty hard-won steeds, Brodie waited patiently.

'Down here!' Holloway shouted at length, and Brodie kneed his horse down the sandy bank.

The boss was excited. 'If we cross here, we can save miles and head them off.'

'Here?' Brodie was so startled he forgot whom he was addressing. 'That river's flowing fast and it looks bloody deep to me!'

'Of course,' Holloway enthused. 'They couldn't take a mob over, they wouldn't even try. The horses would go in all directions. But we could swim a horse across, with the rider guiding.'

'Is that right?' Brodie said, refusing to volunteer.

'Yes. You and I could easily make it. The thieves would have to go east to sell the horses. If we cross here we'd be saving hours.'

As Brodie watched, stunned, Holloway charged into the river. 'Follow me! Just let your horse strike for the other side. He'll manage.'

'If you don't mind me saying,' Brodie called, 'I don't think this is a very good idea.'

Jesus, he thought. The man's a bloody millionaire. What are a few bloody horses?

In the noise of the rushing waters, Holloway didn't hear Brodie's caution. 'Come on!' he shouted as he headed out into the stream. 'Don't waste time, you damn fool! They'll get away on us!'

With a sigh Brodie surveyed the scene. That river didn't look too promising to him. Holloway was riding a grey with a pedigree as long as your arm, and it was taller than Brodie's mount. But then again, this old brumby was strong, and bush-wise. It was on the cards that he'd taken on many a river in his heyday. Holloway knew what he was doing. So if the grey could make it, then so could the brumby. Brodie steered his horse into the shallows, irritated that the beast twisted aside to choose its own path through the scattered rocks.

Ahead of him, the other horse was plunging on, as game

69

as its rider, but his own horse wasn't so keen. It snorted and stalled as they headed into deeper water, with Brodie desperately urging it on in case the boss looked back and thought him a shirker.

All of a sudden, the brumby made a decision. It dropped forward almost to its knees, throwing Brodie forward, and then, like a camel, it just as suddenly straightened, bucking with more strength than Brodie would have given it credit for, its hind legs lashing the air. Brodie had no hope of staying in the saddle. He landed in the water with a thud.

Having divested itself of its rider, the brumby bolted up the ridge to stand and stare glumly at a wide stretch of water that obviously had no appeal for it.

'You bloody mongrel!' Brodie shouted as he clambered out of the water.

Only then did he remember the other stockmen talking about such brumby tricks. Hadn't he seen the drop-and-throw trick his own self, when the horse breakers were at work? Never thinking he'd need the skill to stay aboard. And with the boss so near at hand. Mortified, and drenched, he scaled the sandy ridge to grab the horse and start again.

But the brumby dug in. Nodding and snorting, it clenched its teeth on the bridle, refusing to budge as Brodie tried to drag it back on the job.

Afraid that the boss might be witness to his humiliation, Brodie glanced back at the river, but there was no sign of Holloway.

'Oh God,' he groaned. 'He's already over!'

He scanned the far bank, still unable to see him, and confused now, in time to see Holloway's mount struggling back to the shore, and beyond him, the boss himself being swept downstream.

Brodie ran! He charged along the bank, shouting, trying to catch up.

At a bend in the river, the current swung towards his side, and Brodie plunged in to try to grab Holloway but he was too far out. Ahead, a breakwater of rocks jutted out into the stream and Brodie shouted at him to swim for this.

Too late he realised that the end boulders right out there were a danger in themselves. Holloway was trying to extricate himself from the strong current, attempting to reach the shelter of the breakwater. Brodie heard him scream as he was slammed against the boulders!

'Hang on!' he shouted, relieved to see that although the boss had been injured in some way, he had managed to remain wedged there, precariously, with the waters pounding around him.

He waited a few minutes, staring at the limp figure, hoping that the boss could pull himself free, then he waded into the water, calling to him. When there was no response he tore off his heavy boots and jacket and struck out into the river, needing all his strength now to forge across the current.

Holloway was battered but alive, and blood was washing from a gash on his head. 'I can't swim,' he said. 'I've broken my arm.'

'Jesus!' Brodie said, swallowing water as he tried to gain a foothold on the slippery rocks. But there were none to be had, and he was having trouble keeping afloat himself.

'We can't stay here,' he gulped, 'or we'll both go.'

Frantically he looked to the shore, praying that some of the other men might appear but knowing that was not possible.

'Ah well, here we go,' he said. 'Let me get you out of there.'

Brodie gritted his teeth. He could feel the pain he was inflicting on Holloway as he dislodged him and got his arm across the man's chest, while the torrent bounced and bumped them against the unyielding lumps of granite.

He felt half drowned himself now, but he knew that he only had to drag Holloway forty yards or so to get out of the current; after that it would be easier as the main flow surged off round the bend. Fortunately, Holloway didn't struggle, and Brodie pushed them free with his feet. Swimming sidestroke, grasping the limp man, he worked his way towards the shore. He was very strong, and bigger than Holloway, and it didn't occur to him that he might not make it until he pulled the boss into the shallows and looked back at the distance he'd covered, from the centre of the wide brown river.

'Bloody hell!' he snorted. 'That brumby knew his onions.'

Holloway seemed to be in and out of consciousness, and when he did rally his first thought was for his horse.

'He's fine, the rascal,' Brodie said. 'He must have dumped you and run.'

'No! No!' Holloway wouldn't have that. 'A snag,' he breathed. 'He got caught on a snag out there, a big tree or something, underwater. He was stuck. I thought he would drown. I tried to pull him free and I lost my grip. You're sure he's clear?'

'Yes. Look at him up there! Good as gold.'

Exhausted, Holloway passed out again, and Brodie kneeled beside him on the grass. Now what?

Brodie bound the broken arm close to Holloway's body with strips from his saddle blanket. 'That will have to do for the minute, but how do I get you home?'

Holloway heard him and struggled up. 'I'm all right. I can ride.'

'I'm not so sure of that, sir. You don't look too good to me.'

'The arm hurts and my head aches, that's all,' Holloway retorted weakly. 'If you can help me on to my horse . . .'

'We'll do that, all in good time. But there's no rush. You need to rest awhile. Get your strength.'

Holloway sagged. 'Yes.' He looked up at Brodie. 'I'm sorry. I can't think of your name.'

'Brodie, sir.'

'Ah, yes. Thank you, Brodie. I won't forget you.'

'That's all right now.' But he knew it wasn't all right. The man was shivering from shock. They were both soaked. The winter sun was shining there in the blue, but it lacked the blessed drying heat of summer, at last appreciated. He had to get him home.

He'd see if Holloway could sit his horse. If not, then one of the horses would have to carry them both.

Holloway seemed better. He was dazed but with Brodie's help sat his horse. 'I'll just hang on, Brodie. Don't look so worried. We'll be home for breakfast. You lead.'

Brodie stared at him. It was mid-morn.

He mounted the brumby and took the reins of Holloway's horse, and then panic set in. He didn't know the way. Where the hell were they after all that riding? He wondered if they should follow the river, but it meandered in all directions, having carved a route through softer rock at flood times over the centuries. That route could add hours to the journey.

His own horse was impatient to be away, and Brodie looked

down. 'It wasn't the river, was it?' he said, fondling its stringy ears. 'Did you know there was a dirty big snag out there to trap us?'

The neat thoroughbred, unharmed, and with his master aboard, was waiting patiently for instructions, but not so the brumby. He snorted and set off away from the river, and the grey fell in behind him.

Brodie leaned over and whispered to him, 'I reckon you know the way. Home, boy! For Christ's sake get us home.'

In the end, Vivien wept.

On this Sunday they were expected at a luncheon in honour of Governor Charles Baillie, at Mountjoy Station, which was thirty miles away, out the other side of the Wirra Creek hamlet. She'd been looking forward to this grand occasion for weeks. Everyone who was anyone in the district had been invited, and Vivien had bought a dream of a dress. It was figured organza in blush shades of peach and apricot over a soft cream slip. The neat bodice with its full sleeves balanced the lavish full skirt, and the overall effect was so romantic, Vivien was thrilled.

The dressmaker had trimmed a wide leghorn hat with the organza, finishing off the picture beautifully.

They had both been up early this morning, to be away by nine o'clock and before Vivien went in to breakfast with Vern, she laid out her complete ensemble on the bed. Shoes, stockings, gloves, handkerchiefs and reticule were all in readiness by the hat and dress.

And then trouble struck. Taffy came stamping into her house with the news that some horses had been stolen.

Vern leapt up and rushed off to grab his riding boots and rifle. 'We'll go after them, Taffy. Call out the men!'

'What are you doing?' Vivien cried. 'You can't go. There isn't time. The horses have probably only wandered. Taffy will see to it.'

'They haven't wandered,' he said grimly, pushing past her.

Still arguing, she followed him through the kitchen and out into the yard. 'You're crazy! The men know what to do. We have to go to Mountjoy this morning! You seem to forget the Governor is there. We mustn't be late.'

'This is more important.'

As he raced over to the stables she shouted after him: 'How long will you be?' But there was no reply.

'Damn and damnation!' Fuming, she retreated to the house. 'Damn the horses! How will they find them? Why does Taffy have to come running to Vern every time something goes wrong? This is so stupid!'

At ten thirty, with the homestead area ominously quiet, even for a Sunday, Vivien stared miserably down the long drive to the gate. They should be halfway to Mountjoy by this!

She decided to dress. They'd be late, but people would understand there'd been a crisis.

Resplendent in the lovely new dress, she twirled in front of the mirror before taking out a white linen dustcoat which she often wore to protect her good clothes. Then she placed her hat carefully in a hatbox. Searching in a drawer, she found a long muslin scarf that would keep the dust from her hair until they reached the gates of Mountjoy.

'Elvie,' she called to the housekeeper. 'Come in here, please!'

The tall, grey-haired woman hurried into the bedroom. 'Oh, madam! You look lovely! What a pretty dress! It suits you so beautifully!'

'Yes, it does.' Vivien preened. 'The organza is French, you know.'

'It would have to be! I've never seen such lovely material.'

'We're so late,' Vivien said. 'I want you to lay out Vern's good suit. Put out all he needs so that he doesn't waste more time looking for things. Then I want you to tell Patrick to bring the buggy round the front, but make sure there's not a speck of dust on it.'

'Patrick's gone with Mr Vern to find the horses, madam.'

'There must be someone there.'

'Only the young stable boy, the Abo lad.'

'Surely he can hitch up a horse by this. I want it out front right away.'

'Very well, madam.'

When Vivien left, Elvie began to set out Mr Vern's clothes. 'I don't know why she couldn't do this herself,' she muttered.

'She puts on such airs and graces! Just as well that lad is there or she'd have me hitching up the horse myself.'

Elvie had been with Christiana Holloway since she was a young girl, starting at the Toowoomba house as a scullery maid and gradually rising to housekeeper and trusted friend. When Mr Vern bought Fairlea Station many years ago, she had agreed to come out here as his housekeeper, at his mother's request. Christiana wanted to make sure that his home was kept in order so that he could concentrate on the business side of the station, and Mr Vern had been delighted by the arrangement.

As she'd expected, he was a kind and thoughtful employer and Elvie loved the station. She'd enjoyed working for Christiana but this was far more interesting, Elvie had never regretted her decision, even when he brought home his giddy bride. Elvie had never liked Vivien but she soon learned to cope with her.

Young Mrs Holloway was bone lazy. She might enjoy giving orders, when she could think of something, but on the whole she preferred to leave the running of the house to Elvie. In the beginning she'd dithered around suggesting menus, since Elvie was also the cook, but eventually she gave up on that too. So Elvie simply continued as before. Keeping her distance, as much as she could, from the lady of the house.

Instead of settling down to enjoy country living, the boss's wife had become more and more petulant and tiresome, until Elvie began to wonder how much longer she could put up with her. But she was loyal to Mr Vern and could easily imagine the chaos that Vivien would inflict on him if it were left to her to run the household, or even to train a new housekeeper. These days cooks were very uppity. Even though they only had to cook for two people, few would agree to take on the rest of the chores. Some of the tales of hopeless staff she'd heard from station women would make your hair stand on end.

Elvie sighed. Admittedly Vivien was very pretty, but apart from that she wondered what Mr Vern had seen in her. These days, she had a sneaking feeling that he wondered the same thing. He was still very polite to her, but a marriage needed more than that. Elvie had heard gossip that young Mrs Holloway was an outrageous flirt, and she'd swiftly put a stop to that sort of talk, but she'd seen it herself, right here in the house. Why, even when the two army officers were here recently, she'd been all over the younger one, giggling and batting her big blue eyes at him like a real hussy. Elvie had been hurt to see Mr Vern's embarrassment and wondered how this would all end.

She prayed that God would intervene and give madam a baby to keep her busy and put a stop to her shenanigans. Preferably triplets! she grinned.

Shrugging, she finished putting out Mr Vern's clothes, piece by piece, although she knew it was pointless. The horse thieves could have struck any time last night and be miles away by this. The Fairlea men would track them for days if they had to. Cattle duffers were one thing. Horse thieves were the lowest. Elvie shuddered. She wouldn't want to be in their shoes if they were caught.

She shook her head. Unfortunate though it was, because madam, and Mr Vern himself, had been looking forward to this outing, she doubted they'd be going to Mountjoy Station today.

Vivien wandered aimlessly about the house in her lovely dress. The buggy was out front, all spick and span, and she'd put her hatbox under the seat in case she forgot it.

The gilt-edged invitation was on the mantel shelf in the parlour, under the big mirror. She primped her hair again before she picked it up.

They were invited to attend a luncheon in the presence of His Excellency, The Right Honourable Charles Wallace Alexander Napier Cochrane Baillie, Baron Lamington. She read his name aloud with a giggle. What a mouthful!

'And he's a baron,' she wailed. 'I've never met a baron! And I'll never forgive Vern if he doesn't get home this very minute.'

When the grandfather clock chimed twelve, she threw herself on the couch and wept.

A little later Elvie burst in on her: 'Mr Vern's home, madam, but you'd better come and see to him.'

'I'll see to him all right,' she retorted angrily. 'He probably took his time from spite. He just doesn't like me to meet people.'

She swept out to the back veranda in time to see Vern

being helped across the yard by Elvie and the Irishman, the one who'd brought the horses out from Ireland. He was a big chap, at least six foot two, and rather attractive, but right now the pair of them looked a mess. Both were covered in dried mud, and the Irishman was barefoot.

'Take them to the laundry,' she instructed Elvie, who disregarded the order. 'Mr Vern is hurt.'

Vivien stared. He did look all in, with an arm obviously out of action. 'What's wrong with him?'

'He has a broken arm,' the Irishman said. 'Can we get a doctor?'

Vivien stood back crossly as they brought her husband into the kitchen. 'I might have known something like this would happen,' she snapped at him. 'You would have to go bounding off at your age instead of leaving jobs like this to your men! Now what do we do with you?'

He slumped into a chair. 'I'm sorry.'

'He needs a doctor,' the Irishman insisted.

'Send for one then,' Vivien said to Elvie.

'It would be quicker to take Mr Vern straight to the Wirra Creek hospital, rather than wait for Dr Campbell to come out here,' Elvie said. 'That's what we usually do with breaks.'

At the mention of Campbell's name, Vivien shuddered, but she steeled herself. She didn't want him hanging about her house. Better to pay a quick visit to the hospital.

'Very well. The buggy's ready, if the horse hasn't fallen asleep.' She glanced at Vern. Elvie was swabbing his face with a damp cloth, to refresh him. 'What happened? Did you fall from your horse?'

'In a manner of speaking,' the Irishman said. 'He fell in the river and hurt his head too.'

'He's got a nasty gash over his temple,' Elvie said. 'I'll clean it and put on some disinfectant.'

'You're pretty shaky, sir, after that ride,' the Irishman said. 'Do you feel up to travelling to Wirra Creek?'

'I think I should,' Vern muttered, leaning heavily over the kitchen table.

'Of course he should,' Vivien said, a plan forming. Mountjoy Station was only a few miles on from Wirra Creek. No one could complain if she and Vern arrived later in the afternoon. And Vern an invalid with a broken arm. She could say it was too hard on him to ask him to travel all the way back to Fairlea, so she'd turned to their friends at the nearest station.

It was a delicious idea! They'd be asked to stay. It would be insisted upon. With the Governor in residence! It was the most marvellous excuse, added to the drama of Vern out there chasing horse thieves. All the others would have gone home and she and Vern would be able to enjoy the privilege of the Governor's company without all the hangers-on.

But this grubby Irish upstart was standing in her kitchen disagreeing. 'Mr Holloway had a bad time trying to sit his horse all the way back from the river. He's worn out. I reckon better he rests and waits for the doctor.'

'You could be right,' Elvie said, concerned.

Vivien turned on her. 'Didn't you just say it would be quicker to take him to hospital? And Vern himself agrees. His arm has to be set. How long do you think it would take that old fool Campbell to get out here?'

Elvie nodded. 'He's not very reliable,' she said to Brodie.

'Then let's get a move on,' Vivien insisted. 'Where's Patrick? He can drive us.'

'He's not here,' Elvie reminded her. 'They're all out.'

'Oh God!' Vivien exploded.

'We could take him,' Elvie said. 'I can drive the buggy.'

Like hell you can, Vivien thought. I won't have you interfering. 'There's no need, thank you, Elvie,' she said sweetly. 'He can drive us.'

'Who? Brodie?' Elvie turned to him. 'Do you know the way to Wirra Creek?'

'Sure I do. I'd be glad to help.'

'Good.' Vivien was in charge now. 'I think you'd better go and clean up first, Mr Brodie. A few more minutes won't make any difference, and that river mud smells.'

The Irishman took himself off.

Elvie turned to the boss: 'I think we should clean you up too, Mr Vern. We can hardly send you to hospital in that state. You look as if you've had a mud bath.'

Drowsily he agreed.

'I think the dear man is in a lot of pain,' she whispered to Vivien. 'We have to be gentle with him.'

Vivien noticed that Elvie had bypassed Vern's good suit and helped him into clean everyday clothes, with the arm of his shirt hanging loose and a tweed jacket half on, but she supposed it wouldn't matter when they arrived at Mountjoy. After all, these were exceptional circumstances.

The Irishman came back, spruced up, looking rather handsome, in fact. She studied him as they waited for Elvie to bring her husband out. He had blue eyes too, though much darker than hers, and they were perfect with his dark curly hair.

As if he were aware of her scrutiny, he turned away, uncomfortably, to speak to the lad who was still waiting by the buggy, but not before Vivien had taken in his fine strong physique. She wondered why she hadn't noticed him before.

When Vern finally emerged, she was aghast. 'You haven't shaved! You can't go to the hospital looking like that.'

'I don't think they'll worry,' Elvie said, but Vivien ignored her. 'Really, Vern! You must go back and shave.'

He shook his head numbly. 'I don't feel up to it.'

'Then Elvie will shave you!'

The Irishman stepped forward. 'If this is necessary, sir, I'll shave you.'

Vivien caught the note of criticism in his voice and reacted angrily. 'It is necessary! Elvie, take them through to the bathroom, and since we now have to wait, you could make us up a hamper. We haven't had any lunch and Mr Holloway can't be expected to eat the mush they serve at that awful hospital.'

She went through to watch as Elvie packed ham sandwiches, scones and cake. 'Don't forget the linen. And put in a bottle of the good red wine. And some biscuits.'

Eventually they were on the road, with Brodie driving and the boss and his wife seated behind him.

After he'd shaved Holloway, Brodie suggested that his head should be bandaged. 'It's not bleeding, sir, but perhaps it should be covered.'

'No. No fuss, please. Elvie wanted to bandage it too. Just leave it.'

Brodie managed a few words on the quiet with Elvie. 'Do you think he might have concussion?'

'Yes. He gave me a fright a while ago. He didn't seem to know where he was. It is probably best to get him to hospital.'

Brodie had been to Wirra Creek with the other men several times, on Saturday nights. He never thought he'd see the day when he'd be glad to ride twenty miles to the nearest pub, but he went along as willing as the rest. There were usually a few girls there to brighten up the night. He grinned. Never enough to go around, since stockmen from various properties liked to congregate there, but he usually managed to claim one. That led to plenty of chiacking from the other men . . .

Mrs Holloway interrupted his thoughts. 'There's no need to drive so slowly,' she called.

'I'm trying to avoid the dips and bumps,' he replied.

'And I'd like to get my husband to hospital before midnight! Get a move on!'

The hospital was an extended cottage set in a dusty, sun-baked clearing across the road from the pub. There wasn't much more of Wirra Creek, just a tiny general store and a few houses.

As Brodie reined in the horse he noticed, disappointed, that the pub was closed, and then he remembered it was Sunday. The village was deserted except for a few people gathered on the veranda of the hospital.

What a country for verandas, he mused. There must be a law here that you couldn't build anything without them.

He helped the missus down and she divested herself of her white coat while he assisted the boss.

Mrs Holloway created quite a stir among the hospital visitors as she walked in through the gate, and Brodie smiled. She looked smashing in that pretty dress, out of place in this one-horse town. It seemed to Brodie she was dressed more for a garden party than a hospital, but he supposed she'd know best.

Vivien walked ahead of the men and addressed the nearest woman on the veranda. 'Could you direct me to Dr Campbell please?'

They all gaped at her, then the woman replied, 'Don't you know? Dr Campbell's dead. He died three days ago. Heart gave out.'

Vivien turned back to Vern. 'Did you hear that? Campbell's dead. Now what do we do?'

'I'm sure he's sorry to put you out!' the same woman snapped, and a man beside her laughed. 'Yeah. Inconsiderate of him, wasn't it?'

Brodie intervened. 'We're sorry to hear about the doctor but this gentleman is hurt. Is there no one can attend to him?'

'Mrs Campbell's here. His widow. She'll know what to do.'

They trooped inside to be met by an elderly woman in black. 'Oh, Mr Holloway!' she cried. 'What's happened to you?'

'He has broken his arm,' Vivien replied shortly. 'Is there another doctor here?'

'I'm afraid not, Mrs Holloway. But I could look at it.' She smiled wanly. 'I've had experience with breaks.'

'But can you set it, Mrs Campbell?'

'Yes. The nurse is here. We'll fix you up in no time, Mr Holloway.'

Hoping they knew what they were doing, Brodie left them to it and departed the hospital to move the buggy across the road to the shade of a row of trees. He unhitched the horse and led it to a horse trough, where it drank greedily, then he sat down to wait.

Vivien didn't want to watch. This hospital gave her the creeps. She followed as the women took Vern along the familiar passageway towards the operating theatre, unnerved by the imagined presence of old Dr Campbell. Guilt accompanied her. Guilt that the news of his death had been a relief to her. He'd kept his promise, and even though she'd had to stay in hospital longer than a week Vern hadn't twigged. He'd been too busy apologising that he had to go to Brisbane to attend the annual yearling sales, promising he would bring her back a nice present. He'd been genuinely upset at having to leave her languishing in a bush hospital, but his wife had been so sweet about it, he'd rewarded her with a superb sapphire ring.

Only Elvie had been suspicious. She hadn't visited. It wasn't her place to do so. But when Vern finally brought her home, the housekeeper, in that sniffy way of hers, had intimated that there was no need for young women to drag out long stays in hospital for minor ailments. Vivien was delighted. The stupid woman had thought she'd been malingering, miscarriages not considered serious problems.

Vern was very pale and listless as they assisted him to a

chair, but when the nurse, a large, buxom woman, examined his arm and mentioned anaesthetic, Vivien froze. She couldn't stand the smell of ether.

'I'll wait outside,' she said, backing away.

The little hospital, she knew, didn't have a waiting room, so she went back to the veranda, ignoring the stares of the drab lot milling about there, and took herself to a cane chair down at the far end. She looked at her gold fob watch. Damn! It was nearly two o'clock. But they could still be away from here before three. Mountjoy was only a half-hour from here. She could still throw herself on the mercy of the Harringtons. Bill Harrington, the owner of Mountjoy, was one of Vern's best friends. She could say they were both so exhausted, Vern especially, they couldn't face the buggy ride home just yet. The Harringtons would understand.

She gazed across at the ugly timber pub over the road and on to the silent store, and shuddered. It would be just as bad living here as at Fairlea. She felt as if they were on a small cleared island surrounded by a sea of green. On all sides the tall bush hovered, shutting out the rest of the world. Insects buzzed, a sizzling sound in the still of the afternoon, reminding her that the day was a lot hotter than she'd expected it to be.

The organza dress was uncomfortable now, becoming horribly crushed, she was sure, but she knew she'd look a fool if she decided to take a walk dressed up like this. Vivien was well aware that she was wildly overdressed for this company, but she had her reasons and she didn't have to explain herself.

Gradually the small crowd on the veranda began to drift away, and two young girls in white muslin dresses and cheap boater hats came out of the hospital. They looked at Vivien and giggled, nudging each other, then walked towards the gate where they hesitated, sniggering.

Vivien soon saw who had caught their attention. It was Brodie, her driver. He was standing by the dray, smoking, the horse hitched nearby in the shade, and he was obviously the subject of their conversation now.

Pair of brats, Vivien thought with haughty disdain, making eyes at him as bold as you like.

He seemed to feel their eyes on him. He looked up and flashed them a dazzling smile.

That was all they needed; they opened the gate and strolled over to talk to him.

Vivien felt a stab of jealousy. How dare he flirt with them? Deliberately she looked away but she could still see that smile. It had transformed him from a rather gruff, servile person into a confident man, no stranger to admiration from women, and the knowledge unsettled her.

She was hungry but she could hardly sit out here eating from a picnic hamper in full view of anyone who passed by. Mrs Campbell could at least have offered her tea. And biscuits. She was very partial to biscuits. The time she'd spent, suffered, in the front room of this very hospital had introduced her to butternut biscuits. Small recompense for their vile food.

After an age, with Vivien almost dozing off, Mrs Campbell emerged. 'You can see him now, Mrs Holloway.'

Vivien was stunned to find Vern, undressed, in bed! He too had the front room. His lower right arm was bound in splints.

'It was a nasty break,' the nurse said, 'but I think we've got it right. I'm sure we have. He'll just have to take care.'

'Then why is he in bed, for God's sake?'

'He's not well,' she replied. 'That blow to his head. He's concussed.'

'Nonsense! He was quite all right before he came in here.'

'I don't think he was,' Mrs Campbell said. 'In fact, he was quite disorientated.'

'And what do you think you can do to help him? You're not doctors!' She rushed over and looked down at Vern, who was barely awake. 'How are you feeling, darling?'

He gazed at her but made no reply.

'You've given him too much ether, that's what's wrong. I insist you wake him. We have to go.'

'I wouldn't recommend it,' Mrs Campbell said quietly. 'He doesn't seem too good to me at all. He should stay at least overnight.'

'Why? Is there another doctor coming tomorrow?'

'No,' the nurse admitted. 'It will take a while to find a replacement for Dr Campbell but we're hoping a Toowoomba doctor will pay us a visit within the next day or so. We do have other patients.'

'Then attend to them. My husband is only dopey from the ether. He has no need to stay.'

They were still arguing when Brodie appeared in the doorway. For a while he stood listening to them before intervening. 'Mrs Holloway, I think it would be best for him to be staying.'

'Who asked you?' she snapped. 'I want my husband out of here. I'm taking him on to Mountjoy Station. That's closer than Fairlea so he'll be quite all right.'

Mrs Campbell was determined. 'He shouldn't be moved at all.'

'How would you know?' Vivien barked at her.

The nurse was angry. 'Mrs Campbell is in mourning; we only buried her husband yesterday and yet she's been a tower of strength helping me here. I should appreciate it if you'd give her some consideration.'

'I am! I'm relieving you of a patient. I'm very grateful that you have set my husband's arm but there's no need for him to remain and add to your workload. Now wake him up and our man here will take him out to the buggy.'

All eyes were on Brodie. He wished he'd stayed outside. But he didn't fancy trying to convey the boss anywhere. Enough was enough. 'Mrs Holloway,' he said, 'you don't seem to know what he's been through.' In fact, he recalled, she hadn't enquired. Only Elvie had wanted to know the gist of it. 'He near to drowned, then he had to cling to the horse all the way back to your house. Then he had to get on here. You ought to let him rest.'

She was furious with him. She turned and stormed out of the room, the billowy skirts swishing about her.

'Is it not just his arm?' he asked the nurse.

She was troubled. 'I don't think so. He seemed lucid at first but when we were preparing to fix the break he was not. He was talking to Mrs Campbell, whom he knows quite well, calling her Hannah.'

'I don't know much about these things,' Mrs Campbell added. 'Few people do. My husband might have been able to tell us more, but from what Mrs Holloway said – that he was all right – I think he has been fighting for consciousness all along. Could you tell us exactly what happened?'

Brodie glanced nervously over his shoulder. Any minute

he expected the boss's wife to come blazing back to tell him he was fired. From what he'd heard of her at Fairlea, she was quite capable of getting herself home. But he took the time to explain, and these two very nice women listened quietly.

'I think he's in trouble,' the nurse said at length. 'But I'll sit with him. Often concussed patients rave on a bit and afterwards they don't recall.'

'Can he hear us?' Brodie asked, even though they were all whispering now.

'No, he's asleep again,' she said. 'Sheer exhaustion. He stayed awake as long as he could before he arrived here. That's what's given his wife the wrong impression. Could you explain to her? Mr Holloway is a very important man, we don't want any trouble.'

'I'll try.'

Mrs Campbell took his arm. 'Just a minute, young man. What's your name?'

'Court, ma'am. Brodie Court.'

'Well then, I'm sure everyone will be very grateful to you for what you did.'

'Begging your pardon?'

'I know that country. You swam that river and rescued Mr Holloway. People don't forget things like that.'

'Oh dear God,' he blinked. 'There was no other way.'

She was standing by the buggy in a high old rage, pulling on the white dustcoat.

'How dare you contradict me?'

Brodie smiled. 'Was I doing that now? And there I thought I was helping you.'

'You sided with those women!'

'Only because you were so distraught. It's been a terrible day for you, what with the shock and all. We could take Mr Holloway to Mountjoy, but what if he gets worse on the way? I hear the Governor's there. Would they be thanking you for rolling up with a sick man?'

'He'd be better there than here!' she snapped.

'Then they'll come for him, won't they? In a proper vehicle. You can't prop him up on a buggy seat, Mrs Holloway. What sort of state would you be in by the time we got there?

85

You're looking so pretty now it would be a shame to arrive all mussed up.'

He saw the anger fade. Amazing what a little flattery could do. 'I'll hitch up the horse and take you on to Mountjoy then,' he said, to take her mind off the arguments.

'No. We'll go home,' she said, resigned. 'It's really too late to go out there now and I can't go without Vern. You and Taffy can come back for him tomorrow. Go back and tell the nurse we're leaving.'

Mrs Campbell watched them drive away. 'I can't stand that woman.'

'She is a peculiar person,' the nurse agreed. 'She didn't even bother to come back to say goodbye to her husband.'

'Typical of her. She's a nasty piece of work. She threatened my husband, you know. Poor Eddie, he was most upset.'

'What about? What did she threaten him over?'

'Oh, it doesn't matter,' the widow sighed. 'She's just one of those jumped-up wives who think they own the world. Throwing her weight around like she was doing today. That's why I was so determined not to give in. Poor Mr Holloway. He's a pet of a man, a real gentleman. I don't know what he's done to deserve her.'

'Who's Hannah?' the nurse asked. 'He was still mumbling her name a minute ago, in his sleep. Is she one of the family?'

'No, but I've got a pretty good idea who he means.' She closed the curtain. 'Hannah died many years ago. My husband delivered her babies. That was when we lived in Toowoomba. How things go round. I'll have to give up the doctor's residence here now, so I'll be moving back there. Just as well we kept the old house.'

Once they were out on the road, Vivien tapped him on the shoulder. 'There's a picnic spot over the crest of the next hill. Pull up there. I intend to stop and eat. I'm starving.'

'Righto,' he said.

She felt better now. This Brodie fellow was right. More than he knew. To him she probably did look pretty, but the organza had lost its stiffness and hung on her now like a limp rag. And even if they had woken Vern, what if he'd fainted on the way? She'd look the most dreadful fool! She glanced up at the driver. He had very wide shoulders. Vivien liked men with wide shoulders.

As soon as the buggy stopped, she jumped down, without waiting for his assistance, caught her dress on a side rail and ripped it.

'Damn!' she said, yanking it free.

He was appalled. 'Oh no! Look at that! You've torn your skirt. Can it be sewn up?'

'I don't know and I don't care! I won't wear it again, it's bad luck. Get the basket. And the rug too. I don't want to be sitting on ants.'

He stared at her. 'Don't you ever say please?'

Vivien gaped. 'I beg your pardon?' she snapped.

'That's better,' he grinned, deliberately misinterpreting. 'I'm not too good in the ways of a servant.'

'Are you making fun of me? If so, you'll regret it.'

He spread the rug and placed the hamper on it. 'There you are now, and what a grand view you've got here, looking right out over the countryside.'

'I asked you a question!'

'So you did. But you'd be better to sit down there and enjoy yourself.'

She wished now she'd dug into the hamper as they drove along, but it had seemed unbecoming to sit there behind the driver, munching away. Now the situation was even more unbecoming. What was she to do with him?

'Have you eaten?' she asked.

'I have not.'

'Then you might as well join me. Can you open the wine? I'm thirsty.'

He knew she wasn't inviting him by choice, but he couldn't leave well alone. 'I'd be happy to join you, ma'am, but I don't want to inconvenience you.'

'I'm inconvenienced out of my bloody brain today,' she cried, 'so don't make it any worse. If you want to eat, sit down.'

She dropped to her knees, the lovely skirt spread about her, and began searching the hamper. Unceremoniously she unwrapped the food and dumped it on the rug, using the neatly embroidered tablecloth as a throwover, protection from

87

the flies. 'You have to ferret under there for something to eat,' she announced. 'I hate flies!'

Brodie was amused. She really was a little minx. He didn't sit, as instructed. Instead he took the bottle of wine she handed him, waited for her to find the corkscrew and then retreated to open it.

She was already eating. 'These are ham sandwiches,' she said, in an attempt at conversation. 'They're quite good. She usually oversalts the ham.'

'Do we have glasses?' he asked.

'Just a minute,' Vivien said. 'Here they are. Oh God, trust her to put in these horrible kitchen glasses. If I'd packed I'd have put in decent wine glasses.'

'Maybe Elvie worried that your good glasses might get broken,' he offered.

'Who cares?'

'It's a matter of relevance,' he said easily as he poured the wine and handed her a glass. 'Now I myself would have packed these glasses, but to you I suppose the cost is not relevant.'

'Working for us, she should know better,' Vivien countered.

'Ah yes, but the habits of economy die hard,' he smiled, settling himself on the grass, on the other side of the rug. 'May I?' He looked to the spread hidden under the fine cloth.

'Yes, go ahead.'

They ate the late lunch in silence and Vivien tried not to stare at him; after all, he was only a stockman. But it was hard; he really was quite charming, and so good-looking he almost took her breath away. In the end she capitulated.

'You came from Ireland, Brodie?'

'Yes.'

Her eyes twinkled mischievously. 'Is that why you're not accustomed to the ways of servants?'

'Could be,' he laughed, picking up another scone. 'I must say your cook does a better job than the Chinaman.'

'What did you do in Ireland?'

'I have a farm there. A fine farm in a lovely green valley.'

'What do you raise there?'

'Crops and dairy cattle.' He decided that a little exaggeration here would even up the odds. 'You could say I'm an absentee landlord right now.'

'Why did you leave?'

'To see the world. When Mr Delaney asked me to bring out the horses I thought I might as well.'

'And you're happy to work as a stockman?'

'Well now, to tell you the truth, the first week was hell. I thought I'd made a terrible mistake. I ached and pained in all the wrong places. Your horses have a sense of humour; they picked me as a new chum right off and sent me flying a couple of times.'

They'd found common ground. Vivien hadn't laughed so much in ages, as he related his experiences as a total newcomer to station work. She appreciated, too, that this man could laugh at himself. He was vastly entertaining. The wine gave her a warm glow. She forgot about Vern, and about the Governor, and settled back lazily to enjoy Brodie's company. His voice, that soft Irish brogue, was so melodious. Sensual even.

'Do you plan on staying long at Fairlea?'

'For a while. You never know.'

She wished he'd find an excuse to move closer to her, but when that didn't happen she began packing up.

This time she took his arm, leaning against him, hungry for the closeness of him, as she climbed up into the buggy, but he still didn't react. He shook out the rug and tucked it round her knees. 'Comfortable?'

'Yes thank you, Brodie.' Her eyes searched his face, her lips inviting him to kiss her, but he observed the proprieties. After all, she said to herself, I suppose he is much too aware that I am the boss's wife.

It was just on dusk when they drove up to her house, and Elvie was waiting anxiously.

Vivien told her that Vern's arm had been set and he had to remain in hospital for observation, and swept inside without a backward glance.

'Is he all right?' Elvie asked Brodie.

'I'm sure he will be. A nurse and Mrs Campbell are looking after him. The doctor died a few days ago, so there was some confusion.'

89

'Campbell's dead! Oh dear, what next?'

'I thought Taffy and I could go back for Mr Holloway tomorrow. What do you say about that?'

'Oh yes, good. Talk to Taffy about it, please, Brodie. He'll be upset.'

'Did they find the horses?'

'No. Most of the men are back. They're sending out another search party first thing in the morning. Joining up with men from stations out that way to keep after them.'

Taffy *was* upset. About the boss. About the horses. He'd sent a rider off to notify the police so the search could be widened.

'What's wrong with the boss that he had to stay over?' he asked Brodie.

'I didn't want to worry Elvie, but I think he's got trouble with the bang on the head. I'd be pleased if you'd take over now. The missus is confused; the two women are doing their best but with no doctor I don't want this responsibility.'

'You've done a good job up to now. That was no mean effort to rescue the boss from the river, Brodie. None of us could have done more. You're all right,' he grinned, 'for a new chum.'

Acting on Brodie's advice, the next morning Taffy had Patrick bring out the dray. 'Line it with canvas and some rugs,' he said, 'enough to make the boss comfortable, if necessary. And we'd better have a tarp, in case of rain. Brodie and I will go on ahead, we'll meet you at the hospital.'

They made good time. In his concern for the boss, Patrick had insisted they take two of his thoroughbreds: 'This pair will get you to Wirra Creek fast. You can't keep the boss waiting.'

Brodie was delighted. This was the first time he'd ever mounted a horse of this class for such a long ride, and given their heads, the swift beasts made short work of the journey.

As soon as they arrived at the hospital, Taffy found the nurse, and Brodie was relieved to see he was more diplomatic than Mrs Holloway.

'We're all very sorry to hear of the death of Dr Campbell. Will you give our condolences to Mrs Campbell?'

'Yes, thank you, you're very kind.'

'And how is Mr Holloway?'

She shook her head. 'I don't know what to suggest. He's still very drowsy. It could be from the ether. Or concussion.'

Holloway was the only patient in the dim front room. He was in bed, his face wan and grey against the white sheets.

'How are you?' Taffy asked him. 'You gave us all quite a turn.'

Holloway nodded listlessly but gave no indication that he recognised his foreman.

Taffy walked over to the windows and let up the blinds. 'Let's have some light here.' He lifted the covers to check on Holloway's arm and then replaced them. Gently he removed the pillow and laid the patient out flat on the bed, leaning over to peer into his face.

'His eyes are out of whack,' he said to the nurse.

'Are they?' she said. 'I'm sorry, I didn't notice.'

'Don't worry about it. I think we'd better take him. We've got a dray coming along.'

'Don't you think you ought to wait for a doctor to see him?'

'That's just the point. I reckon he needs a doctor as soon as possible. We'll take him on to the Toowoomba hospital.'

She was nervous. 'I have no objections at all, I think you're doing the right thing. But what will Mrs Holloway say?'

'Mrs Holloway's not here,' he said grimly. 'But his mother is in town. She'll see he gets the best.'

Even though the boss was still in hospital and his wife was with him in Toowoomba, work went on as usual under Taffy's strong hand. Winter had set in and Brodie marvelled. The days were warm under the endless sweep of blue skies, but when the sun went down it seemed to suck the heat with it and the nights were cold. Not that Brodie minded. He welcomed the chill after those months of red-hot nights when he lay on his bunk, sweating, sleep coming only from exhaustion.

The stockmen still turned out at dawn, rugged up in heavy jackets, with frost hard on the ground, and ranged about the fire complaining bitterly about their lot, stamping their feet and blowing on their hard, lean hands. Brodie had acquired one of the jackets from the station store, and it seemed to be made of the same material as the rough horse rugs, but it kept him as warm as he need be. He was wise enough not to tell the others he didn't find the mornings too cold at all, compared with the winters in Tullymore, with their sleet and rain and freezing winds. His companions were never at their best humours in the early morn.

He had sent the letter off to Father Daly, handing the farm over to Michael, relieved that he was able to offer some assistance. Proud of himself, in fact, because it had not been an easy decision. He felt as if he were giving away his identity. Only occasionally did a jab of conscience remind him that the farm was hardly worth much, but he dismissed it angrily.

I've done my best, he would argue, and that was that. He was settled at this job for the time being, but he had his mind firmly on those opals and was eager for more information.

The men yarned of a night round the campfire. The missing horses were never located and it was accepted that the gang of thieves must have been well organised, with plans of when and where to sell them well in place. As a result Taffy put riders on four-hour shifts through the night to guard the hundred or more mounts kept in the paddocks for sale to the military. It wasn't a duty anyone relished but Taffy deemed it necessary until the war ended, when horses wouldn't be bringing such high prices.

And they all worried about the boss. Brodie heard that a special doctor had come up from Brisbane to examine Holloway, who was still in the Toowoomba hospital and so far hadn't shown any improvement.

'They say he's mental,' one of the men said.

'He's not mental,' Brodie objected. 'He just got dazed. You bash your head agin a block of granite, you'd be bloody dazed too.'

But Patrick was very concerned. 'It's been weeks. He should have come round by this. His arm's good as gold, Elvie says, but he's just not responding. Most of the time he doesn't know who he is or where he is.'

'How does she know?'

'The old lady writes to her all the time. They always bin good friends. It's a real worry, I can tell you. I saw a jockey go down once. Banged his head and hardly a mark on him but he was out to it altogether. A good jockey he was too. I sat by his bed for weeks but he never woke up at all. Just slipped away one night, died on us.'

'The boss isn't that bad,' Brodie said.

'He's not that good either.'

A few days later Elvie had news for them. 'Another specialist, from Sydney this time, has been to see Mr Holloway,' she said, waving a letter from Christiana. 'He bored a hole in his head.'

Taffy was shocked. 'What the hell for?'

'To release the pressure,' Elvie said anxiously.

'Ah, the poor bugger! Maybe I should have brung him home after all. Keep him away from them sawbones.'

At the end of that week Taffy decided to go to town to see for himself. 'I'll only be gone a day or two. You buggers know what to do, and keep up the night patrols. We can't afford to lose more horses. And look out for dingoes. There are a lot around lately.'

'Not much we can do about dingoes,' one of the men muttered.

'You can shoot the bastards,' Taffy retorted.

That night Brodie sat yarning with Patrick by the campfire, drinking beef tea laced with rum. It was a strange mixture to him, but hot and satisfying and very welcome. Patrick was in a mood to talk and Brodie always found his tales interesting, but now he took the opportunity to ask him about opals.

'Sure I know them,' Patrick said. 'Seen some beauties in my day too.'

'I'd like to go prospecting for opals.'

'So would a lot of blokes, but it's tough work. Some fellers dig for years and never sight a glimmer.'

'Others must find them.'

'Yes. They say there's a band of opal country from White Cliffs down in New South Wales that runs far up here into Queensland and on.'

'That's what I heard, that there are opals right here in Queensland. Where would that opal country be? Exactly from here?'

Patrick sucked on his teeth. 'From here? I dunno. Maybe five or six hundred miles as the crow flies. Maybe more.'

Brodie was incredulous. 'That can't be right!'

'You could go further, on to the edge of the deserts. Where once was the inland sea, a million years ago. They say that's the clue to opals. Where water got trapped in little pockets, before it all dried up, and mixed up with minerals.'

'Is that how they were formed?'

'Only a guess. Nobody seems to know, not even the geologists. But you can forget about the desert country. It's as hot as Hades and there's no water.'

'Have you been out there?'

'Not on your life!'

Brodie persisted. 'If I went out to that country you spoke of in the first place, not the desert, I'd be sure to find opals?'

'Listen, mate. If you keep going east from here you'd get to the sea. And in the sea you'd find oysters, but there's no guarantee you'd find pearls in them.'

'I get your point, but by God, I'd love to have a go at digging for opals.'

'Then take my advice. Never try that country on your own. You need back-up in case of an accident. And you need someone with prospecting experience to get you properly equipped. I wouldn't recommend that life to my worst enemy.'

Far from turning him aside, Patrick had only fired up Brodie's enthusiasm. Now he knew for sure that opals were out there! The distance worried him, but if other men could get there, so could he. Somehow. But he had to find a partner. He wished he knew where Lester was. They'd lost touch. By now Lester would have experience in prospecting for gold. Maybe he'd already made his fortune! That thought annoyed Brodie. What a fool that would make of him for not going after gold too. He tried not to think about it.

Taffy was back, and Mrs Holloway was riding with him.

Fears and rumours grew as the men waited for Taffy to give them the news.

'What's she doing home?'

'How's the boss?'

'Mrs Holloway is back to collect some things so she can stay on in town,' the foreman told them. 'I'm sorry to say the boss is no better. His head is bandaged after the operation but I can't see that it helped. He didn't even recognise me.'

'That does it,' Patrick said miserably. 'If he don't know Taffy there's little hope for him.'

94

'They're hoping he'll snap out of it,' Taffy said, but he looked so depressed, few disagreed with Patrick.

Shaking their heads, the men filed into the cookhouse for their dinner.

'Hey, Brodie!' Taffy called. 'I want a word with you.'

'Don't tell me there's worse news,' Brodie said, turning back.

'No, but I've been meaning to ask you. How come the boss lost his mount in the river and you didn't?'

Brodie sighed. 'I knew you'd get round to that sooner or later. The boss charged into that river like he was leading the cavalry and I pushed my horse in after him. To tell you the truth I wasn't all that keen but I dared not hang back. Next thing my bloody horse went down and up like he was on springs and I ended up in the water with him heading back up the bank.'

'What horse did you have?'

'An old nag. Patrick said he's called Snare.'

Taffy's lean face broke into a grin. 'That mongrel! He's always been trouble, but he's so bloody smart we never had the heart to get rid of him.'

'Just as well you didn't.'

'That's true. I've got a message for you from the old lady, the boss's mother. She wants you to come to town.'

'Me? What for?'

'She wants to thank you for rescuing Vern. But there's more to it. The boss was asking for you. I suppose not really asking, but a few times he mentioned your name.'

Brodie felt sorry for the foreman; he seemed disappointed that Holloway hadn't recognised him but could recall the name of a stockman.

'He asked me my name when we got clear of the river,' Brodie explained sadly. 'And he said he wouldn't forget me. Ah Jesus, the poor feller! The name must have stuck. But what can I do?'

'God knows, but Mrs Holloway, Christiana that is, she's desperate. She thinks that if he can remember you, that might trigger him to recalling more. I didn't want to say too much to the lads, but Patrick's right. The boss is right out of it, he's as close as you can get to a vegetable and still be walking about. He can't even feed himself.'

95

'God save us!' Brodie said.

'Now you'd better get yourself cleaned up. Mrs Holloway wants to see you at the house.'

'This Mrs Holloway, the wife?'

'Yes. Right now.'

'I haven't had my dinner.'

'That won't bother her,' Taffy said crossly. 'Tell Elvie, she'll find something for you. The missus probably wants to thank you herself, but while you're there, do me a favour. She seems to think this place runs itself. It's payday next Friday, a month's pay due to everyone. See if you can find out what she intends to do. I rode all the way out here with her from Toowoomba and not once did she ask how things were going here. Not that it matters much, I suppose, except for payday. The boss handled the payroll. Will she?'

Two dogs hurled into a yelping fight by the gate. Taffy gave a sharp whistle through his front teeth and his dog broke loose instantly. It loped over to settle at his feet, still growling menacingly.

'Then there are the sheep,' Taffy said.

'What sheep? We don't run sheep.'

'No, but they used to here, years ago, and we've still got that big old woolshed. With the strike on, shearers aren't working, so the boss had agreed to let some of his mates sneak their sheep in here in early spring, and bring in scab labour to get the job done. There'll be more than five hundred sheep coming in, for starters, as far as I know. I have to let those squatters know if they can still bring the sheep here.'

'Why don't they bring scab labour into their own sheds?'

'Because the shearers will find out and burn them down. It won't be the first time.'

'And you want me to explain all this to her?'

Taffy was exasperated. 'Just start with the pay. That's the priority.'

'She mightn't like me interfering.'

'Who cares? You're the white-haired boy at the minute with both of his women, so give it a go.'

As he stood under the shower, one of a series of taps rigged up in a corrugated-iron shed, Brodie wasn't too sure about Taffy's requests, but he was far from unsure about the lady herself. She wanted to see him, to thank him. The hell she did! On that Sunday she'd had plenty of opportunity to do that.

His skin tingled under the rush of cold water. He was willing to bet that young Mrs Holloway was up to mischief, and given half a chance he'd oblige her. Was there a man in the world who could resist a beauty like her? Deliberately he took his time, remembering her lovely face and fair hair soft as down, and those full breasts when she leaned forward. Could he be that lucky? Interesting to find out.

Obviously Taffy had no idea how to deal with her, because she always kept her distance from the staff. He didn't seem to realise that in his position he ought to tell her, not ask. But her youth and good looks, and that hoity-toity attitude, intimidated him. It was only then that Brodie took stock of the difference in age between the boss and his wife. Back home, he recalled as he shaved in front of an old mirror in the bunkhouse, it was normal for an older man to marry a young woman, because it took time for the men to be able to afford a wife, by which time the young ones were ripe for the picking.

The only catch to that, he grinned, was if the bride had a roving eye. Wild oats not yet sown.

When he arrived she was standing on the veranda, all pink and powdered in a clinging wool top and a long skirt belted tight at the waist. Elvie was with her, and both women welcomed him warmly.

'We can't thank you enough for what you did for my husband,' she said, as if they were perfect strangers, ushering him inside. 'I'm afraid that on Sunday I was too distraught about Vern to take in what exactly had happened.'

'It was nothing,' he muttered.

'Go on with you,' Elvie cried. 'Isn't it just like him to be keeping so quiet? You were a tower of strength to us, Brodie.'

'Can we offer you a drink?' Mrs Holloway asked.

'If it's not too much trouble.'

'What would you like?' Elvie was anxious to please. 'We have a good whisky.'

'That would be fine.'

So there he was, sitting on the homestead veranda with Mrs

Holloway in a genial mood. Elvie delivered the drinks on a silver tray: whisky for him and red wine for the lady of the house. Crystal decanters were set on a low table nearby for replenishment.

'I do enjoy a good red wine,' Mrs Holloway said, her blue eyes twinkling, as the housekeeper left them to it. 'Don't you, Brodie?'

'I am not a connoisseur, ma'am.'

They discussed her husband's health. She seemed to think the operation would cure him, and so Brodie agreed with her. He was uncomfortable now, in these strained circumstances, but she was quite at ease.

As darkness settled, flashy parrots in nearby trees stopped their squabbling and settled down, leaving a sudden silence.

'It's very pleasant here,' Brodie offered, for something to say.

'I suppose so,' she admitted. 'But I find it rather boring. I grew up in Brisbane; life in town is much more fun.'

'And Brisbane's an interesting town, is it? I was only there a day or so. What did you do there?'

At least he'd found a subject to set her talking, and he listened attentively to a recounting of her social life; the theatre, the balls and parties, and summers spent by the seaside.

'Most of our friends have seaside houses, the country people mainly, and they retire there during the hot months. It's much cooler on the coast.'

'And do you do the same?'

'Not now. If we had just a sheep or a cattle station we could take the time off, but having the horse stud as well makes it more difficult. Vern is entirely wrapped up in his horses, he hates to leave them for an instant. I really envy people who can just pick up and go at the end of the year. Of course, we go into Toowoomba quite a bit, his mother has a lovely home there, but that town is dreadfully hot too . . .'

Brodie's mind began to drift as she chatted on. He was thinking about opals. Wondering if this town of Toowoomba, that he and Patrick had only passed through, had a Mines Department. He remembered that Lester had headed for such a place, seeking information on gold prospecting. So he ought to try it. Why not? He could ask Taffy to give him a few days off to attend to private business.

As it turned out, luck was on his side; he didn't have to ask for leave.

When Elvie came out to announce that dinner was ready, Brodie jumped to his feet. 'I'm sorry, ma'am. I shouldn't be keeping you. I'll run along.'

The housekeeper laughed. 'Dear me, we wouldn't do that to you. The Chinaman will be finished serving by this. Mrs Holloway thought you might like to have dinner with us.'

Taken aback, he looked to Mrs Holloway, who smiled sweetly. 'There's method here, Brodie. We should like you to join us for dinner but we also want to talk to you about something that has come up.'

'What would that be?'

'We'll discuss it inside. You will stay?'

'Thank you.' He felt awkward but could hardly refuse; besides, he was hungry.

It was a fine dining room that smelled of polish, lamplight giving a tender glow to the panelled walls. He felt he'd really come up in the world to be seated at this splendid table, with its crisp linen and shining silver. And Elvie's cooking was sheer pleasure.

She served a rich mulligatawny soup, surprised to hear that his mother used to make the same. Then a succulent roast beef with all the vegetable trimmings, and Mrs Holloway insisted on a bottle of red wine.

Brodie knew she was teasing him when she picked up her crystal glass. 'I do like these glasses, Elvie, wine tastes so much better in fine glasses.' But he was more concerned with the reason for his presence. He couldn't imagine what they wanted to talk to him about.

Finally, the main course over, he was permitted to know.

'Did Taffy tell you that my husband was asking for you?' Mrs Holloway asked.

'Sort of. I believe he did mention my name.'

'It's the same thing,' she said. 'Now my mother-in-law, Mrs Christiana Holloway, is very impressed with what you did to help Vern, and even more so to think he remembers you when he hardly knows anyone else. Even me.'

'I suppose so,' Brodie said lamely.

'Well, it's like this. She's taking Vern from the hospital to her home, so that he'll be close to the doctors. He can't come back here yet. The trouble is, we'll need help with him. To put it delicately, we need a man to help him. As yet he is simply not capable of caring for himself in many ways.'

'In the matter of dressing and bathroom arrangements,' Elvie added.

'And he'll need exercise, someone to take him for good long walks, things like that.'

Elvie explained: 'His mother thinks that if you are with him, he might place his confidence in you, he might rally. So far he isn't responding at all.'

Mrs Holloway was encouraging. 'She wants you to come and stay at her house for a while – she has staff quarters – and be a sort of companion to him. I know it's a lot to ask of you, Brodie, but she's willing to pay you double what you earn here.'

'You'd be doing us all a great kindness,' Elvie said.

Brodie looked from one to the other. 'I don't know if I could do any good for him.' But he'd already made up his mind. Double the pay and a chance to spend time in Toowoomba and make his enquiries about opal mining, an opportunity too good to miss.

'We'd appreciate it if you'd try,' the boss's wife said. 'Please don't say no.'

'All right,' he said. 'When do you want me to go?'

'Tomorrow,' Mrs Holloway said. 'I've come back to pack. I left in such a hurry when Vern was moved to town I hardly had anything with me. I'll be staying in town too, of course. My luggage will be brought on, Elvie will see to that, and I'm riding to town in the morning. If you could accompany me, that would save Taffy having to take more days off.'

Brodie wondered how much she'd had to do with all this; he didn't want to end up in the middle of family arguments.

He turned to Elvie. 'You're sure Mrs Holloway Senior wants me at her place?'

'Oh yes. I have a letter from her. She realises it's an unusual request and hoped I would be able to persuade you. Now, would you like some plum pudding?'

Mrs Holloway took him through to the parlour as Elvie cleared the table, and poured two glasses of port. The room was warm and cosy, a fire burning in the large hearth, the furnishings of luxurious soft leather with a rolltop desk in the corner – and that reminded him of Taffy's problems.

'There's something I have to ask you,' he said. 'Apparently some of the sheep men here want to use your big shed, on the quiet. Is that all right with you?'

'They can do what they like,' she shrugged. 'I'm glad you're coming to town. You'll find it much more interesting than this place.'

Now there was no mistaking her smile. She took a sip of port and ran her tongue along her lips, but moved to the other side of the fire.

'Another thing,' Brodie said evenly. 'Did you know it's payday on Friday?'

'Oh God! So it is. I don't know what I'm supposed to do. I hate all this worry.' She went to the corner and flung open the desk. 'The paybook's in here somewhere. Help me find it.'

Brodie knew the book. Hadn't he signed it several times himself? He liked the idea of monthly pay, it helped him save money.

He pointed it out to her and she flipped over the pages, running a polished fingernail down names and figures with exaggerated intent. He had the feeling she was stalling and soon found out the reason. Elvie came in to bid them good night.

'Is there anything else, Mrs Holloway?' she asked.

'No, you can go off now,' the mistress said absently, not looking up from the important book.

'I'll be off too then,' Brodie said. 'And I have to thank you ladies for the finest dinner I've had since I left home.' In many a year, he added to himself. It had been a long time since the Court family had seen a meal like that.

'It was a pleasure,' Elvie smiled, walking him to the front door.

He was halfway to the gate when Mrs Holloway came running after him. 'Wait. Here's the paybook. Give it to Taffy.'

Brodie laughed. 'It's not much use without the money.'

'Oh damn! Tell him to come over and see me in the morning.' She looked back. 'Thank God she's gone! That woman's as bad as my mother-in-law, hovering about me all the time.'

'She seems very nice, Mrs Holloway.'

'Call me Vivien,' she pouted. 'Don't tell me you're going to take sides against me too.'

'Now why would I do that?'

She stood on tiptoe and gave him a kiss on the cheek. 'You are a dear.' The invitation was clear. She made no attempt to move away from him.

Brodie slipped an arm about her waist and drew her to him. 'You shouldn't have done that,' he whispered.

'Done what?' she challenged softly.

'Kissed me,' he murmured. 'All night the loveliness of you has been a trial for me.'

'And is it still a trial?'

'Yes.' He kissed her and she responded so passionately he could hardly contain the excitement in him. They moved into the shadows, where he crushed her to him, feeling the lovely breasts and the curve of her and those sweet, sweet lips.

'Say my name,' she said breathlessly. 'I want you to say my name.'

Over and over he said her name, to keep her with him.

'Oh, Brodie,' she moaned, 'you're the most beautiful man. Do you love me?'

'Yes,' he replied. A reaction. He hadn't time to give love a thought, but who wouldn't love a woman like this?

'I knew it,' she exulted. 'I knew it by the way you looked at me when we had lunch coming back from Wirra Creek. It's true, isn't it?'

'Sure it is.' He was more sure that this was a giving woman, by no means just a tease, but this was not the place. Sadly.

'Kiss me again, Brodie,' she whispered, 'and then you'll have to go. I'll see you tomorrow.'

Taffy was waiting for him. 'Did you get invited for dinner?'

'I sure did. Elvie can cook rings round the Chink.'

'Your lucky day. Did you ask the missus about the shearers?'

'Yes. She doesn't mind. And if you go over in the morning she'll fix things up with you. Did you know they want me to go to town and take care of the boss?'

'They did mention it but I didn't know if it was definite.'

'Well it is. What do you reckon about a job like that?'

102

Taffy sucked on his pipe and leaned against the wall of the bunkhouse. Inside a noisy game of cards was in progress. 'Put it this way. There are only the two women. No one else in the family. It's probably not a job a man would go looking for, but they need help. And the boss needs help. I wouldn't think any the less of you if you did them this favour, if only for a while. You could always come back here, whenever you want.'

'The missus is heading back to town tomorrow,' Brodie said. 'She wants me to go too, and start right away.'

'She does?' Taffy brightened up. 'That's a relief. You can take her to town. I thought she'd have me wasting more time playing escort.'

'You don't like her?'

'No. She's trouble, that one. And you watch yourself, Brodie, she's a God-awful flirt.'

'With stockmen?' he asked innocently.

'You wouldn't be the first.'

Brodie looked at the long, lean foreman. Taffy was about thirty years old. He had a strong, craggy face and the steady gaze of a countryman. The Irishman had the impression that Taffy could be speaking from personal experience, and if that had happened, the loyal foreman would not have been impressed.

Ah well, he said to himself as he wandered off to see if Patrick was still up. We'll see what happens.

The next day Vivien was all business. Brodie packed his gear and walked over to the house with Taffy. He waited in the kitchen as she hurried about giving orders to Elvie on what to pack and what to leave of both her and her husband's effects. Insisting the luggage be forwarded to Toowoomba as soon as possible. Then she took Taffy into the parlour to discuss the running of the station in her absence.

When Taffy joined Brodie in the kitchen for a cup of tea, he was pleased. 'I've got a free hand now. At least I can keep things going until the boss comes back.' Realising what he had said, he frowned. 'Jesus! I hope he does come back.'

At last, Vivien appeared, in a dark-blue riding habit with a velvet collar, looking gorgeous.

'You may have to wait a while,' Elvie said to her. 'There's a storm coming.'

'A bit of rain won't hurt,' Vivien retorted. 'Where's my coat?'

The housekeeper brought her a heavy oilcloth coat and hat, and Vivien put them on carelessly. 'Are the horses ready, Brodie?'

'Yes, ma'am,' he said.

As she strode out the front, Elvie following, the foreman winked at Brodie. 'Poor old Elvie will be here on her own now. I get to enjoy her cooking when this happens.'

'It's an ill wind,' Brodie replied.

A real wind blew up soon after he and Vivien left Fairlea, bringing with it the promised rain. Riding beside her, Brodie suggested they look for shelter, but she seemed to be enjoying herself. 'No! Keep going!'

She sat the horse well, water streaming from the floppy hat on to her face, the big coat protecting her like a tent, keeping a good steady pace, rarely looking back. Brodie's coat gave him no such protection and he was soaked, but he had caught her enthusiasm for the ride and was content to stay with her.

Brodie's letter from Fairlea Station did upset Michael this time. 'Have I offended him that bad that he must use you as a go-between, Father?'

'It must be just habit, would you say? I wrote to him my own self, mentioning the matter, once we had an address, but he may not have received it as yet.'

'He got my letter.'

Trella kissed Michael on his damp forehead. 'Don't be bothering yourself now. Father Daly's letter could have gone on the next ship.'

'And it could have sunk,' Garth suggested enthusiastically. 'I've read all about shipwrecks.'

'Never to mind,' Father Daly admonished him. 'It's easily seen that Brodie's heart's in the right place, deeding the farm over to you, Michael. There's a generous thing for him to do.'

'Who told him I was sick?'

'I did,' Trella said. 'I sent my own news too. He's entitled to know you're not well. We should take his advice and sell the farm now, while we can.'

'There'd be a pity,' the priest frowned. 'This farm has been in the Court family for generations.'

Sure, Trella thought. A hundred years ago the Courts owned the whole valley, but bad times and the drink whittled it down to this small corner, leaving Michael and Brodie to struggle. 'No use living in the past,' she said. 'The past won't feed us.'

'Where would we go?' Michael asked. He peered down at the letter. 'Here's Brodie saying we should move to a warmer house. What could I do there but sit by the fire until I get better? I'm not seeing the point.'

'It's just a suggestion,' Trella said gently. 'Perhaps he means we should move to Dublin.'

'The weather would be no better there,' Father Daly said. 'Nor the houses.'

Garth agreed. 'I don't want to go to Dublin. I hate the place.'

'You've never been there,' Trella smiled. They were playing into her hands now. 'But I suppose that's true enough. Dublin is a miserable place. Have you not thought of following your brother's lead, Michael?'

'And what would that be?'

'We should go to Australia too.'

'Brodie said nought of that.'

'Do we need an invitation? Did he? Think on this, Michael. His letters are all about the fine weather and the abundance of good food. Does that not appeal to you?'

'Ah, 'tis a big decision,' the priest warned, and Trella was wise enough to leave the subject for now. It was important for Michael to make the decisions, and she prayed he'd see the sense in it.

She went back to the wash-house to resume the chores interrupted by the priest's visit.

Generous of Brodie was it? she thought. Oh yes. Generous when it cost him nought. But not a word about sending his sick brother a little cash. Just boastful talk about how well he was doing.

Tonight she'd work this out with Michael and in the morning she'd have a quiet word with the land agent. In her own mind Trella was already on her way, working out what they'd need to take and what they could sell to the neighbours. A lovely sea voyage and sunshine at the end of it would be the cure for Michael; he couldn't refuse. It broke her heart to see him failing as he was now, hiding the spits of blood brought up by the coughing. They had to go. And soon.

Chapter Four

Lester and his mate Gus Kriedemann shoved their way into a second-class carriage of the crowded train and threw their swags up to the overhead baskets.

'What is this?' he growled. 'A bloody gold rush?'

'They're shearers,' Gus said. He looked down at two men who had their gear stacked on the seats beside them. 'Shift your swags, mates. Give us room.'

The man he spoke to ignored him, the other one ran a cigarette paper along his bottom lip. 'Piss off!'

Lester didn't like the look of this weaselly lot. Scab labour, he'd bet. He'd seen their type before, when the coal miners went on strike. Some of them desperate for work, some plain mean, none strangers to a fight. 'We'll go further down,' he murmured.

Gus tipped his cap back on his thatch of white-blond hair. 'There's room for us if these gents would shift their stuff.'

'Yeah. But we're not about to do that,' the nearest bloke snarled.

'Then I'll do it for you.' Gus grabbed a bedroll and hurled it out the open window.

'Jesus!' The two men came to life. 'Look what you've done. Are you bloody mad or something?'

'Shift this stuff or it goes too,' Gus warned, and Lester stood back nervously. Gus was a big, brawny bloke, normally placid, but he didn't like to be pushed around. He was also too smart to get into a fight that he couldn't win. Now, though, Lester worried that they were outnumbered by this mob of shearers. He quaked, seeing both of them being pitched off the train.

However, the other men in the carriage seemed to be watching with nothing but mild interest.

The crisis passed. The two men, thinking twice about taking on a heavyweight like Gus, had also noticed that no support was forthcoming. Grudgingly they transferred their gear to the

107

aisle and Gus and Lester were seated for the long journey up the range from Brisbane to Toowoomba.

Lester had palled up with Gus at Mount Morgan, where they'd taken out mining leases. To Lester's delight, their first lease had shown colour and they'd earned more than a hundred pounds, which they'd invested in a celebration and better equipment. Recalling the excitement of that first strike, Lester grinned. It had been the most marvellous feeling in the world to strike gold, and no one could ever take that away from him. He'd done it!

After that, their luck had run out, and broke, they'd taken jobs working for a big mining company, sending up ore that could contain gold for someone else.

In the end they'd become bored with the job, bored with the ugly little mining town run by the bosses, where their weekly pay went into the local pub.

'We're getting nowhere here,' Gus announced. 'I'm going home for a while.'

Lester knew that Gus came from a place called Toowoomba where his parents had a bakehouse.

'I've got a mate there,' Lester said. 'I'll come with you.'

He'd had a couple of letters from Brodie, the latest from a new address in the town, but he'd never bothered to answer. He decided he might as well look him up. He chortled, remembering how he'd bagged Brodie's stake. They were the sort of tales he was careful not to tell Gus, who wouldn't see the joke. He would not approve.

As the train pulled into a station, Gus nudged him. 'This is Ipswich. If the worst comes to the worst we could always get jobs here in the coal mines. I worked here years ago.'

'I'd have to be bloody hard up,' Lester growled.

The train toiled and strained up a steep mountain, and Lester shifted impatiently. 'It'd be quicker to walk.'

'Take it easy,' Gus said. 'You'll like Toowoomba, it's a quiet town but very nice. Beautiful gardens.'

'What about the women?'

'They're all right too.'

Lester sat back and closed his eyes. Scenery didn't impress him. Brodie had said, in that last letter, that he was now interested in mining too. He hoped it wasn't coal mining.

*   *   *

Now that he was living in the nice quiet town, Brodie wouldn't disagree with Gus's description. Especially about the women. One in particular.

The old lady had been very pleased to meet him, thanking him profusely for coming to her son's aid once again. 'We'll be able to bring Mr Holloway home now. I'm sure he'll be greatly cheered to see you.'

As it happened, the patient was having a bad day and didn't seem to know anyone. He was dressed ready to leave when they arrived, and Brodie was surprised that he was quite able to walk without assistance. His face was pale, from being indoors so long, but if it weren't for the bandage on his head there didn't appear to be anything wrong with him at all.

'Some days he knows people, some days he doesn't,' Mrs Holloway Senior whispered to Brodie.

To their great delight, it was the house that cheered her son. He gave a sigh of relief and strode ahead of them up the front steps to stand on the veranda, looking out with a smile on his face. For a moment there it seemed he was cured.

His mother hurried after him, stayed talking to him for a few minutes, then turned to look back at Brodie, shaking her head sadly.

Vivien hadn't come to the hospital, for reasons best known to the women, and now she hurried out the front door.

'How is he?'

'Much the same,' her mother-in-law said. 'We'll take him in now.'

As Vivien rushed forward to take her husband's arm Mrs Holloway went back to Brodie. 'We won't need you this evening. I'll just let Vern take his own time, whatever he wants to do. I think it's important that he makes decisions of his own, even about little things: where to sit, when to eat, what to do. A hospital is too regimented. Don't you agree?'

Brodie nodded. 'Is that how you want me to look after him? A sort of wait-and-see business?'

'Yes. It's entirely possible his head could clear at any time, but we have to try to keep his brain working. Now, are you quite settled?'

'Yes, ma'am.'

'If there's anything you need, just ask Cook. She'll serve

you breakfast at seven and I'd like you to wait in the kitchen after that and we'll see what to do. I'm afraid this will be a case of one day at a time, Brodie. I don't have any instructions for you just yet.' She adjusted her glasses, surreptitiously brushing away a tear. 'Pray for him, Brodie.'

He walked through the grounds to his neat room above the coach house, feeling sorry for her. He liked the woman. She was obviously a fine lady, and judging by the way the staff at the hospital had dashed about to please her, a person of note in this town, and yet there was a gentleness about her that he appreciated. He wasn't surprised that Vivien didn't get along with her. He guessed they had little in common except for Vern Holloway. And that would be a big problem now.

The next few days were almost as confusing for him as they were for the boss.

Holloway awoke upset and disorientated, and as Brodie was soon to discover, that often made the patient angry.

A maid came flying into the kitchen. 'Sir, come quick, Mr Vern's up and he's real cranky, chucking clothes about, and the ladies don't know what to do with him.'

Brodie followed her through to the bedroom, taking the opportunity to glance about this big house. It was large and rambling, single-storeyed, but truly the most beautiful house he'd ever seen. It oozed comfort and luxury. And it intimidated him. He wondered what he was doing in a grand place like this.

Fortunately there was no time for him to be shy.

Vivien met him in the passage. 'He's in there!' she said, exasperated. 'She shouldn't have brought him home. I didn't know we'd have to put up with this.'

He entered a huge bedroom, bigger than their whole farmhouse back home, with a grand four-poster bed in the centre and elegant chairs and sofas set near the open french windows. This too was very grand, but now it was untidy, with dresser drawers hanging open and bits and pieces of clothes strewn about.

Mrs Holloway was picking things up and remonstrating gently with Vern at the same time, but he was ignoring her, ferreting about in the bottom of a wardrobe. She appealed to Brodie: 'I don't know what he wants.'

110

Brodie went over and squatted on his heels beside Holloway. 'What are we looking for now?'

To his surprise Holloway stopped what he was doing and turned to him. 'Brodie! My journals! They're gone.'

'Ah yes, Taffy needed them back at Fairlea, you see. So there's no need to worry.'

'Damn nuisance,' he muttered.

Brodie looked to the open doors. 'What's out there?'

When Holloway didn't reply Brodie took his arm and stood him up. 'I'd like to see this garden. Why don't we go for a bit of a walk, sir?'

Mrs Holloway rushed forward with a dressing gown to put over Vern's pyjamas, and he allowed himself to be guided out on to the veranda, down the steps and into the garden, slipping back into mute acceptance.

Of what? Brodie wondered as they strolled along, leaving Mrs Holloway at the house. Is he thinking? Are jumbled thoughts rolling round? Or is he walking in this awful sleep? He talked as they walked, about anything and everything, since that seemed to be his role, but at the same time, having seen the bedroom, he wondered if Vivien slept in there.

The following day was bumpier. Vern suddenly became angry, shouting and cursing and fighting off an invisible demon, and it took Brodie more than an hour to completely calm him.

You poor bugger, he said to himself. I reckon you're trying to fight your way out of hell.

So he settled down to being companion to Vern Holloway, helping him to dress when needed, shaving him when Vern would allow it, and taking him for walks. He didn't take meals with the family, which was a relief, because he was already finding this job as a nurse unbearably dreary, despite his consideration for the boss. And when Vern took his nap after lunch, Brodie was free for a few hours, so he spent his time at the Agricultural Offices wherein he'd located a mining section.

The clerks here seemed to be more involved with the business of coal mining, but they gladly dug about in shelves and cupboards to give him as much information as they could about opal mining. They directed him to the public library, which was an awesome place dominated by walls of books

111

and a threatening silence. He tiptoed about nervously, having no idea where to start, until a woman took pity on him and offered to help. When she heard where he lived, she even allowed him to borrow books that had chapters pertaining to opals. Brodie had the impression that if he didn't return them in ten days, nothing less than death would be his punishment, so he backed away, nursing the precious books, promising on his mother's grave that he'd comply.

Some nights he went to the nearest pub after dinner, drinking with the locals in a back room, but he didn't stay long. He was determined to save every penny he could to set himself on the road to those opal fields. Another reason to remain with the Holloways as long as he could.

He rarely saw Vivien, and when he did, she addressed him formally. Brodie accepted that, under the circumstances, but he still got immense pleasure just looking at her. Remembering how she'd kissed him that night, knowing that sooner or later they'd get together again. For a woman like her, he could wait.

And then that time came. She didn't knock. She just slipped into his room in the early hours of the morning, and woke him by trailing a finger down his face.

Brodie awoke, startled. He couldn't believe she was standing there, all in white, like a ghost. 'Vivien! What are you doing here? What's wrong? Is it Mr Holloway?'

She sat on the bed. 'No, it's not, silly. It's me. I thought you might be getting lonely over here, all on your own.'

He sat up. 'What time is it?'

'I don't know,' she shrugged. 'Nearly two, I think. I couldn't sleep.'

'Won't they miss you?'

'Why would they? I have my own room now, I can't sleep in the same room as our patient. So I just slipped away into the night like a little elf.'

Brodie laughed. Moonlight was streaming in through the window and he could see now that she was only wearing a billowing frothy nightdress. 'And did the little elf get lonely too?'

'Yes,' she whispered, slipping into the bed beside him.

This was a woman of rare abandon, excitable, voluptuous,

and Brodie was overwhelmed by the joy of her. Vivien was well worth the wait.

When it was time for her to leave, he begged her to stay a little longer, but she was firm. 'I must go now. My bedroom doors open out on this side of the house, fortunately, but I can't take any chances.' She kissed him. 'Darling, you are my love and my lover.'

'Will you come back tonight?'

'You mean tomorrow morning,' she giggled. 'Do you want me to?'

'Every night. Every single night.'

'If I can. You just be sure you're here.'

The days were no longer dreary, they were only hours to be filled in. He gave no thought to her husband, not even trying to justify their actions by telling himself that Holloway was no longer husband to her anyway. His daily life was placid, not connected in any way with the excitement of those nights with Vivien. Their lovemaking had become more passionate than ever in those stolen hours, and Vivien was becoming restless.

'I really hate living here under Christiana's thumb all the time,' she complained.

'You could move back to Fairlea. I don't think Vern will get any better. He'd be well looked after out there.'

'And what about us? I wouldn't be able to see you there. You'd have to live in the bunkhouse. I couldn't stand that. Besides, I never liked living out at Fairlea.'

Brodie smiled. 'You don't like living here and you don't like living there. What do you want to do?'

'I don't know,' she moaned.

Then one night, lying with him in the narrow bed, she whispered: 'Why don't we run away?'

He kissed her lazily. 'Sure. Whatever you say.'

'Don't joke, I mean it.'

Brodie sighed. 'And where would we go, my darling? I'd have no job. I wouldn't be able to support you.'

'If you loved me you'd find a way. Do you really love me?'

He ran his hand down the smooth curves of her body. 'Sure I do.' He loved every minute he spent with her in this room. During the day, the very sight of her aroused him, and he spent restless nights waiting for her. If that was love, he supposed he did. Besotted, he was.

'You have to find a way,' she insisted.

'These people are very wealthy,' he said quietly. 'It'd be a comedown for you to leave all this. And I'd be miserable, unable to offer you much.'

'Oh, don't I know that!' she snapped. 'I was just thinking that if you hadn't rescued Vern, if he'd drowned, he'd be a damn sight better off than he is now. And I'd have inherited all his property.'

Taken aback Brodie corrected her. 'Ah, but I wouldn't have met you.'

'That's true. But would you leave me chained to an invalid for the rest of my life?'

He wrapped his arms about her. 'Don't be upsetting yourself, love. We've got time, I'll think of something.'

He was uncomfortable with the way she was thinking, as if she'd be glad to have her husband turn his face to the wall and die, or have someone hasten his demise. She'd almost been critical of him for saving Vern.

Leave me out of that, he said to himself, wishing he hadn't offered to think of something, in case she got the wrong idea. Brodie knew well enough that there'd have to be an end to this affair, sooner rather than later, because he had to move on. It would be up to him to make the break, but he just couldn't get around to it.

Then, as usually happened with him, other elements stepped in to send him on his way.

It began with Mrs Christiana Holloway. 'Brodie, could you do me a favour, please? I have a letter from a friend of mine who is expecting a gang of shearers to arrive in Toowoomba today. He doesn't want them to go to his property because the striking shearers are picketing the place. They are to go to Fairlea instead and the sheep will be taken there.'

'Oh yes, I heard about that.'

'Good. Now, I want you to go to the station, wait for the train and find a Mr Preston. He's the boss of the gang. I've no idea how many there are. Redirect him to Fairlea, please. That will save a great deal of bother.'

As Brodie walked down the drive, having no objection to attending to this simple matter, he remembered telling

114

Vivien on that first day that he wasn't too good in the ways of a servant, and that amused him now. 'You're learning, lad!' he told himself. 'For this job is close enough to being a servant as ever was. Teach me to be smart!' He hoped she didn't remember.

'God Almighty,' he breathed as he neared the railway station. Shearers were picketing the place, about forty of them, holding up placards, most of which read: 'Scabs go home'. They also looked as if they meant business, with their sleeves rolled up and heavy shillelaghs to hand.

The stationmaster stood outside remonstrating with them. 'Now, lads, you can make your protest out here, but stay back from the platform. There are other passengers coming in, women and children among them I've no doubt, so I don't want any trouble. You mind your business and I'll mind mine.'

A crowd had gathered to watch, and Brodie stood among them assessing the situation. The strike had been dragging on for ages, as far as he could make out, during which time the union shearers kept demanding that the squatters pay union rates. He shook his head, not understanding. It seemed a peculiar way to go about making more money. But he had to admit that the workers out here were a new breed to him. They were an independent mob and fiercely loyal to each other, and yet there were no ties of home and hearth. Back home, he mused, you earned the best you could, and it was the man who took the lowest pay who got the jobs.

Brodie smiled to himself. What sport it would be to send some of these hell-raisers back to work for Mr Hadley-Jones! Jesus! He'd choke on his whiskers at their cheek!

But he had a job to do, and he decided he'd better get on with it. This wasn't his fight. He slipped back along the station fence, and doubled round the end to climb up on to the platform and hurry down to the waiting room. Pleased with himself, Brodie lurked in the dim, windowless room, waiting for the train. As soon as it pulled in, he intended to run out, find this bloke and his gang, and send them away across the tracks, avoiding the picketers.

In theory the plan sounded fine but it didn't work out that way. As the train steamed into the station, the first-class carriages swept past, so Brodie began to walk towards the rear. But the union men were ready. They weren't about to let the scabs off the train, let alone bolt away in the other direction.

They burst past the stationmaster and came shouting and yelling down the platform. At the same time the scabs leapt from the train, ready for the fight, and Brodie was in the middle of it, under attack from both sides.

A whack from a stick that felt like iron landed across his shoulders, and he stumbled. Then someone punched him, and Brodie began to retaliate, fighting only to get out of this full-scale brawl, but still he was taking a battering.

Gus had held back. 'There could be trouble here,' he said to Lester. 'When the train stops let these mongrels get off first, while we see how the land lies.'

Sure enough they were witness to a real battle as the scabs tried to burst through and the shearers were equally determined to put them out of action.

Watching through the open window, Lester was enjoying the show. It was the best fight he'd seen in years, without even the shrill of a policeman's whistle. The police seemed to be keeping their noses out of this one.

Then he saw Brodie!

'Hey! Cripes!' he called to Gus. 'That's my mate out there, and he's taking a hiding!'

Blood was streaming down Brodie's face; he was under attack from several men.

'We have to get him out of there!' Lester yelled.

Gus leapt from the train, with Lester following, and shoved into the mêlée like a battering ram, to grab hold of Brodie.

'Back on the train,' Lester shouted.

'No,' Gus cried. 'It puts us on the wrong team. Keep going!'

With the two men supporting him, Brodie was dragged clear of the platform and out the gate, where more fights and snarling arguments were causing a row of tethered horses to act up. Suddenly one of them broke free and bolted down the middle of the street, scattering contenders and onlookers.

'Come on,' Gus said, taking advantage of the lull. They

116

marched Brodie across to the Railway Hotel where the publican stood in his doorway, barring their way.

'What are you up to, Gus?' he asked suspiciously.

'Coming home. A fine welcome this is.'

The publican peered at Brodie. 'He's not a shearer, he's a scab.'

'No he's not,' Gus said. 'He's a mate of mine. He was just coming to meet us.'

'Ah well, bring him in. No bones broken?'

'Doesn't look like it.'

They took Brodie through the hotel to the laundry, where Gus swabbed the blood from his face.

'Holy hell,' Brodie moaned. 'I feel as if me back's broke! And me nose is numb. I think it's stopped bleeding now.'

'You'll live,' Lester said. 'What were you doing there anyway?'

'I had to meet the shearers going out to Fairlea Station.'

'The scabs, you mean?' Lester snapped. 'You'd better shut up about that so we can have a drink in peace. This is Gus Kriedemann, he lives here in Toowoomba.'

'Pleased to meet you,' Brodie said. He winced as they emerged from the laundry into the white heat of the sandy yard. 'Those madmen could have killed me,' he groaned. 'What do I do now?'

Gus shrugged. 'You can forget your shearers. Let them look after themselves. What's it to be? I'm for a cold pint.'

Their mission completed, some of the union shearers congregated in the crowded bar and a hat was passed round to pay for their drinks.

Lester saw Brodie hesitate as the hat came to him. He sighed. Nothing changes, he thought. Brodie's still as tight-fisted as ever. 'Dig in,' he said as he and Gus dropped coins into the hat, 'or they'll string you up.'

The three men stayed in the bar, yarning about their travels, and despite his cuts and bruises, Brodie was feeling better. A hell of a lot better. He was enjoying himself and was in no rush to go back to the house. The riots had provided him with a perfect excuse.

When he told Lester and Gus about his new job they laughed, making it sound pathetic.

'Now there's a cushy number,' Lester grinned, poking him

in the ribs. 'I thought you'd put on a few pounds! And I bet they've got some pretty little servant girls working there too. Brodie was always one for the ladies, Gus. He did well for himself on the ship.'

Brodie hadn't intended to mention Vivien, but now, his tongue loosened, he used her to restore his dignity.

'Better than that,' he said loftily, and gave them an account of his affair with Mrs Vern Holloway.

Gus looked uncomfortable but Lester was fascinated. 'By God, Brodie. Trust you! She sounds heaven-sent, and she's got money too.' He turned to Gus. 'Do you know her?'

'I know of the family but not her. She's not a local lady.'

Lester smirked. 'That's no lady. Taking up with a servant.'

'I'm not a bloody servant,' Brodie said angrily.

'You're not a stockman either,' Lester retorted. 'But I wouldn't be complaining. Give the word and I'll change places with you.'

'As a matter of fact,' Brodie announced, 'I'm thinking of moving on. I just haven't figured out how to go about it.'

'About what?' Gus asked.

'Opals. I want to go prospecting for opals. I'm told there are plenty in the far west of this land.'

Lester shook his head. 'If you're talking prospecting, gold's the only thing. Kalgoorlie's the place now, in Western Australia.'

But Gus disagreed. 'Don't start that again, Lester. We'd have to go by ship all the way to Perth and then overland for hundreds of miles. If you think about it, opals mightn't be a bad idea. There are opal fields in this state without having to go any further, and they're getting more popular now. That means more expensive.'

Brodie told them about the opal necklace he'd seen in the Brisbane jeweller's window. 'I never saw such colours,' he enthused. 'They've really got me in, I can tell you.'

'How are they valued?' Lester asked. 'By the colour?'

'By the carat,' Gus said, 'but the colours and designs make a big difference.'

'Well, why don't we give it a go?' Brodie asked them.

Gus thought about it. 'We'd need a stake to go that far out west. Enough to buy supplies and equipment to last us for months. It wouldn't be just a jaunt up the coast, where we've come from.'

'We haven't got much cash,' Lester said, 'but you must have some, Brodie.'

Brodie was torn. He did have money in the bank but he didn't see why he should stake his partners. What if they didn't find any gemstones? They'd be no worse off and he'd be broke.

On the other hand, Lester was a friend, and Gus was the first person he'd met who hadn't brushed aside his idea. He was sure a fellow like Gus would know what to do to get their expedition on the road. Here were ready-made, ideal partners, with mining experience. Still he hesitated.

'I've only got a few quid myself. I don't know where the money goes.'

'I do,' Lester said. 'Grog, gambling and women.' He turned to stare at Brodie. 'Women! What about your rich lady friend? She'll give you a stake. Ask her.'

'Who? Vivien?'

'Yes, Vivien. Tickle her a bit more.'

'I don't know about that.'

'Go on! You've got the gift of the gab, Brodie. Tell her she's in for a share or whatever.'

Brodie looked to Gus, who shrugged. 'If she's prepared to lend you the money, nothing wrong with that. It'd be her choice.'

'There you go,' Lester grinned. 'No harm in asking.'

'How much would we need?' Brodie asked weakly.

'To do it properly,' Gus warned, 'to cover the three of us, a couple of hundred pounds. There's nothing much out west. Anyway, I have to go. I can't turn up on my parents drunk. You coming, Lester?'

'Yes.' Lester scrambled up.

Brodie frowned, disappointed that they were breaking up the party and that all-important discussion. But he left the pub with them and they parted at the next corner.

As he trudged down the long road that came up from the escarpment and barrelled through the town, he saw a silvery mirage in the distance, and wondered if this opal chasing wasn't a mirage too. Stockmen had told him that the far west was hard and perilous country; should he be pushing to go out there?

But opportunity was there, and he'd made the first move by finding men willing to give it a go. He couldn't give up now, he might never find another chance like this. In his mind's eye the colours of opals dazzled him. He could see himself prising precious gems from rock walls, reaching out for fortunes as easily as taking stores from a shelf. And yet he was worrying about a few hundred pounds. That was all it would take to see them on their way! He'd find the money. Somewhere.

Days passed, though, before he plucked up the courage to mention his problem to Vivien.

'I love you so much, Brodie,' she was saying, clinging to their last minutes together that night. 'It's terrible for me to have to sneak out like this. I want to be with you all the time. We have such fun together.'

'If only we could, my darling,' he sighed. 'But even if you were free, I couldn't ask you to marry me on my poor earnings. You know,' he added, 'just the other day I had an offer that might lead me to the path of good fortune.'

'You're not going away?' she cried anxiously.

'No.' The lie came swiftly, fetching with it a tale more likely to please. 'I met some friends of mine who have discovered an opal field and they're setting out to mine it.'

'What friends?'

Brodie smiled. 'What's this? You sound as if it would be strange for me to have friends.'

'I'm sorry. I didn't mean it that way. I was just wondering . . .'

'Wonder no more then. There's a friend who came out on the ship with me, and the other is a local chap, Gus Kriedemann. His folks have the baker shop in town.'

'Good Lord. You haven't told him about us?'

'Sure. I told him I'm madly in love with you!'

'Don't tease me, Brodie. If they're mining opal, what has it to do with you?'

'They're forming a syndicate and they need a third, to put their grub stake together. They haven't enough cash to rig up an expedition on their own.'

'Where's the mine?'

'Out west. They haven't told me yet.'

Vivien laughed. 'You wouldn't fall for that old dodge, surely?'

'I said they were friends,' he rebuked her. 'But give me credit for some sense. No one goes round telling the world where they've found gold, or silver, or even opal. The only people who need to know are the investors. They're on to a good thing, believe me, Vivien, but there's no use my thinking about it. I told them I couldn't afford to invest, but it was kind of them to think of me.'

'If you did invest, would that mean you are entitled to one third of all the opal they find?'

'It would, more's the pity. I hate to see a chance like this go past, and have them come back wealthy men, with another man in my shoes.' He kissed her on the cheek. 'But don't you be bothering your pretty head. Something else will come along one day.'

Vivien slid away from him. 'Vern's mother has a superb opal ring. I believe it is worth a lot of money. Are your friends sure about this opal mine?'

'Very sure. But they'll have found someone else by now.'

'They may not,' she said quietly.

Brodie watched while she dressed, not daring to say another word, not yet anyway. He picked up her cashmere shawl and wrapped it about her. 'Good night, my love.'

'How much would you have to pay for your third share?' she asked.

'Too much to be thinking about. Three hundred pounds.' He heard himself say three, instead of two, in a quick shift of pace. An extra hundred for himself would be handy.

'What?' Vivien stood very still, disappointing him. 'Three hundred?'

'Yes.' He shrugged as if indifferent.

'Is that all?' she cried incredulously. 'I thought they'd be asking a lot more with so few people involved. Brodie, what if they bring back bucketfuls? I've seen single opals in fine settings for more than fifty pounds. Oh my stars! If they do know where to find opal, you're missing out on a fortune!'

His shiver was real. He closed his eyes. That had become his personal nightmare. He was afraid that Gus and Lester would go off without him.

'Listen to me,' she said, becoming her bossy self again,

'I'll lend you the money. I hope to God it isn't too late. You should have told me about this before. I'll bring you the money tomorrow night, but in the meantime, tell your friends you're in.'

The longest day of his life groaned on. He went into town and wandered about but didn't look up Gus to tell him the good news for fear she'd change her mind. Three hundred was to him an enormous amount of money, but obviously not to her.

She'd said she'd lend it to him. Lend! She could afford to give it to him! What was the use of scoring that extra hundred from her, for himself, if he had to give it back? But then, once loaned to him she'd probably forget about it. The main thing was to get the cash.

Just on dusk, with the high-pitched buzz of cicadas overwhelming the heavy trees about the coach house, Vivien slipped over to see him.

'I can't stay,' she whispered, 'but here's the money.'

Brodie almost dropped the roll of notes, held together by a rubber band. 'Thank you, darling, you'll not be sorry.'

'Good, but be quick. Write me an IOU. I have to get back. You can take the money to your friends right away, and you get a receipt in writing too.' She laughed, delighted with the plan now. 'I should have said take it to *our* partners.'

Her request for an IOU startled and irritated him. God Almighty! He was her lover! Had the woman no decency?

Nevertheless he soon found a pencil and scribbled out the IOU.

When she left, he didn't bother going in search of Gus and Lester. They'd be in a pub somewhere by this and Brodie preferred not to join them with his good news. He hadn't forgotten how free Lester could be with money when he had a few drinks in him. Besides, he had this extra hundred to think about. He could place it in the bank with his growing nest egg, he supposed. What else to do with it?

The next afternoon it teemed with rain so he took time off to go into town, striding out the gate with the cash safely in his pocket. Soon he'd be on his way, he rejoiced, and he'd find opal if it killed him.

122

When he turned up a leafy side street he saw a For Sale sign on a fence outside a small cottage.

Brodie stood and stared at it, wondering how much a house cost. Wondering if he dared ask.

The garden was overgrown with waist-high weeds, and the wooden louvres on the front windows were missing several rungs.

A gentleman came to the door and shook out a mat.

'Sir!' Brodie called to him, but he was ignored, so he called again.

'What do you want?' The response was testy.

Brodie wasn't sure what he wanted. 'The garden there, it's in need of a clean-up,' he said, to make conversation.

The man glared at him, taking in his wet clothes. 'No jobs here. Get out with you!'

'Did you hear me ask for work?' Brodie retorted angrily. 'I was looking at this here sign. Are you the owner of this poor neglected house?'

The man, a stumpy fellow with a round, plump face, spared Brodie but a second. 'It's a deceased estate,' he snapped, before retreating into the house.

Brodie felt a fool now, standing there in the drizzling rain. He knew he ought to move off, to take no notice, but the deliberate snub could not be tolerated. He opened the gate and squelched up to bang on the timber wall. 'Do you want to sell this house or not?' he shouted.

His man was an agent, a Mr Clem Patchett, and he was asking forty-three pounds for the house and the very large block of land on which it was set.

To prove that he was no penniless oaf, Brodie flashed the roll of notes and demanded to be shown every corner of the furnished dwelling, finding fault wherever he could think to remark. Finally, after exacting a promise that the garden and yard be tidied up, he beat the price down to forty pounds and bought himself a house.

Although he maintained a stern face, Brodie had never been so excited in all his life. He owned a house! A real house with four rooms and a washroom that sported a tin bath. It even had a sitting room separate from the kitchen. And comfortable furniture thrown in. What a great day!

Brodie almost swooned with glee when Patchett called him 'sir'. 'I'll fix up the title deeds for you, sir. And will you be living here, sir?'

'No. I'll not be doing that. Can you rent it for me?'

'Certainly. I have a waiting list. I'll get people in there as soon as possible.'

They retired to Patchett's office, where it was arranged that the agent should collect the rent and bank it for him, and by the time all this business was completed, Brodie was walking on air. He dashed over to his bank to deposit the other sixty pounds, then made for the bakery.

'She gave it to you! Just like that!' Lester was astonished. 'The whole two hundred quid!'

'She lent it to us,' Brodie corrected him. 'It has to be paid back. The first time we make money, you each give me a third, so that I can repay her.'

'That's fair,' Gus said firmly. 'Let's hope we do well enough to cover it. I don't like debts.'

Brodie clapped him on the shoulder. 'None of that talk. We'll do good. I can feel it in me bones.'

They held a meeting in the Kriedemanns' kitchen at the back of the shop, poring over Brodie's maps.

'Where is this place?' Lester asked.

Gus ran a finger along the map. 'This is opal country.'

'Bloody hell!' Lester yelped. 'It would take us a month of Sundays to get to a place like that. How far is it?'

'As the crow flies,' Brodie said sagely, borrowing Patrick's words, 'about six hundred miles west.'

'You're bloody mad! I'm for jumping on a ship and heading to Perth and then on to Kalgoorlie.'

'It's just as far inland to Kalgoorlie, and terrible country.'

'Ha! But they've got a train!'

Gus nodded. 'They've got a train all right. Why? There's nothing there but gold.'

'Listen to him!' Lester yelled. 'Nothing but bloody gold! Why are we waiting?'

'Think about it,' Gus said. 'How many prospectors do you reckon are pouring into Kalgoorlie to warrant a special railway line out to the middle of nowhere? I think Brodie's on the right track. Every man and his dog are chasing gold. We should go after opal; there's hardly any competition so far. Not in Queensland anyway.'

'We can get a train halfway,' Brodie said. 'I've got it all worked out. The line stops here at Charleville and we strike west from there.'

'How? Shanks's pony?'

'No,' Gus said. 'That's where we buy our equipment. A horse and wagon, for a start. It won't be like Mount Morgan, with everything we need on tap. We might find a few miners but we'll be on our own out there. If we camp near a store we'll be lucky.'

Lester still wasn't convinced. 'It sounds too bloody hit and miss to me.' He stabbed his finger at the map. 'This is where you say there are opals. Along this line of country running north–south. That's hundreds and hundreds of miles. What do you want to do? Stick a pin in the map, push a wagon two hundred miles west of Charleville, jump out and start digging? You're bloody mad!'

'No we're not,' Brodie said angrily. 'Once we get to Charleville we ask about. That's what they tell me here, anyway. We rely on local information. We're not the first to go prospecting for opal. We'd soon hear where the fields are being worked.'

'You hope!' Lester snorted.

Gus folded the maps. 'Forget it, Lester. This show isn't for you. I'll take Brodie out there. I'd like to try for opals.'

Lester brooded on this for a while, and then he muttered, 'I didn't say I wouldn't go.'

'Well, quit your grizzling. You might as well know now, it won't be a picnic. It's tough country, we'll have to watch our supplies, keep near water and look out for blacks. Some of the tribes are friendly. Some aren't.'

'How the hell will we know the difference?' Lester was apprehensive now.

'The hard way, I suppose. Are you still keen, Brodie?'

'Try and stop me,' Brodie laughed.

Mrs Kriedemann came in. 'You boys,' she said, shaking her head, 'you make so much noise. If you can't agree, better you forget this foolish idea. And you, Gus! Always running off after dreams! What have you got to show? Nothing. Better you stay and help your father in the bakehouse.'

Gus got up from the table, stretched his arms and kissed his mother on the cheek. 'I'm too big to be a baker's boy. Wouldn't you like me to bring you back a nice opal?'

'And what would I do with it?'

'You could wear it to church on Sundays.'

'Oh, go on with you! Set the table for your friends! You haven't even offered them supper.'

Brodie felt he was smiling like a mad fool now, unable to stop. They were going! He was really setting out on his search for opals. He was pleased, too, that his new friend Gus seemed to be taking charge of the expedition. It was good to have a local lad in the lead. Brodie knew he had a lot to learn about the vagaries of that far west land. Fairlea Station had only given him a glimpse. Six hundred miles further west would probably be as much of a challenge as the search itself.

The stables that served the Holloway household were also owned by Christiana but were in a side street outside the fenced grounds, and that was where Brodie waited for Vivien to come in from her morning ride. 'I have to talk to you.'

'Not here,' she hissed, dismounting and leading her horse into the flagged courtyard.

'There's no one about.'

'Well, there should be.' She handed him the reins and walked away, not trusting that they wouldn't be observed, but Brodie tethered the horse and strode after her. 'I missed you last night.'

'I was tired. We had guests to all hours. You can't expect me every night.'

'I know that, but I had something to tell you.'

'What?'

'I'm going away. Just for a little while.'

'What do you mean? You can't! Where are you going?'

'Opal mining. I have to go with them.'

She stopped, stunned. 'You do not! I won't have it!'

Brodie had known this would be difficult but there was no way in the world he would allow anyone to turn him aside now. Not even Vivien. He tried to soften the blow. 'Listen to me. I've made the investment. I'm a third partner now with Gus Kriedemann and another chap. They're experienced miners. But I've been thinking about it and I have to go with them.' He began to improvise. 'I've decided it's important to know the exact locations of the mines.'

She was furious. She banged her whip against her heavy skirt. 'You told me these men were trustworthy.'

'And so they are, but a man has to be careful. You must see this is for the best. I can keep an eye on my investments myself.'

'Forget the money! An investment is just that. If it succeeds, well and good, if not, it was worth the try.'

Brodie was astonished. 'Forget the money?'

She pulled off her hat, fluffing out her fair hair. 'My husband invests in all sorts of things. He doesn't go galloping about the countryside to check on everything. That's not the job of investors. Really, Brodie, you are naive.'

Only then did Brodie begin to grasp the wealth of these people. He thought of Fairlea Station and remembered that one of the locals in the pub had said it was more of a hobby for the likes of Vern Holloway, who could afford not to work at all. At the time Brodie had passed that off as another local yarn. Now he looked towards the imposing house, with all its expensive furnishings. And here was Vivien telling him to forget the money, as if three hundred pounds wasn't worth bothering about. Jesus wept!

Now she was telling him he couldn't go about his business because he had to stay here and keep her happy like a trained monkey. His voice hardened. 'I've told them I'll be joining them. Today.'

'You're leaving here today?'

'That's what I said.'

'Thanks for nothing! I'm sorry I lent you that money. You never told me you'd be going. Anyway, you can't leave, you're here to look after Vern.'

'I can't look after him forever. Mrs Holloway will understand.'

'And I don't matter?' She moved from the path into the shadows of heavy trees, taking him with her. 'Darling, what about us? How can you think of leaving me?' She kissed him, smoothing his face with soft fingers. 'Hold me close, you've really upset me.'

Brodie couldn't resist her. He held her to him, kissing her passionately, but it was still goodbye.

127

Finally Vivien accepted his decision. 'I'll miss you terribly. When will you be back?'

'I'm not sure.'

'But you will keep in touch with me. You will come back to me, won't you? Promise!'

'I promise, darling, I promise.' And at that moment he did mean what he said. He would miss her too.

The doctors had admitted, finally, that there was nothing more they could do for Vern. Brain damage. Irreversible. He would remain in his half-world for the rest of his days, unless a miracle intervened.

Even though she'd expected this verdict, the pronouncement shook Christiana. When she looked at her son, such a fine, good man, she was overwhelmed by pity for him. He'd kept his looks too. Now into his forties, he was still handsome, if one set aside his listless eyes and the sad tilt of his head.

What was to become of him? He could no longer manage Fairlea Station. That would have to be sold.

Christiana had sent a book-keeper out to the station to relieve Taffy of that duty, and the two men were managing well, but she was of the opinion that owners should take an active interest in their properties. Vern would never be able to do that again.

As for Vivien, she had no interest in the place at all. She never had. She hadn't volunteered any suggestions as to how the station might operate in Vern's absence. As Elvie had said, she seemed to think a complicated business like that ran itself. No, Vivien was only interested in spending the money. She gave Vern as little of her time as possible and daily went into town shopping or strolling about filling in time.

Christiana knew that her daughter-in-law was unhappy living here. She was a difficult young woman, incredibly selfish, but she was Vern's wife and they had to make the best of this situation. For her part, Christiana found her presence irksome, yet another burden, but she dreaded leaving Vern to the uncaring hands of his wife. She had considered suggesting that Vivien buy a house in Toowoomba so that she and Vern could live there, close enough for his mother to help, but she soon vetoed that idea. Vivien would sit him in a room and leave him to rot.

They couldn't even agree on what was best for Vern. His wife believed rest was the thing, while Christiana fought that attitude. Determined not to allow her son to deteriorate further, she had put her mind to various activities to keep him busy and entertained. Card games were a good start.

She had also bought bowls, footballs and weight-lifting apparatus to keep up his strength, and Brodie could nearly always talk him into making the effort. It was heartening to see the two men kicking a ball backwards and forwards across the lawns as if nothing at all were wrong.

Christiana was grateful to Brodie for his persistence. Nothing was any trouble, he was patient with Vern, and, thank God, not patronising like everyone else. Even Vivien. He still called Vern 'boss', giving the man the respect he so desperately needed in his lucid times. It was during these times that Christiana worried even more, because Vern would become frustrated and often weep, realising he was trapped with a brain that was not functioning as it should.

She sighed. And yet Brodie himself was causing her concern. Christiana had seen the way Vivien looked at him, in unguarded moments, and she wondered what might be going on there. The Irishman was several years younger than Vivien but he was a good-looking fellow. He was always bland and respectful in the presence of Vern's wife but that didn't allay Christiana's suspicions by any means.

But it was time for Vern's card games. She sat him at a card table on the veranda and gave him the pack. 'You set them out, Vern.'

While he laboured at the small task, Christiana waited patiently.

He wasn't up to the more difficult games, so Christiana had resurrected a game he used to play as a child. The cards were all spread out face down on the table so the players could choose and find pairs. Since it was a memory game, she hoped it could assist him in some way, and often she allowed him to win, to boost his confidence.

'Good,' she said to him, when the cards were more or less in place. 'I'll go first since you won yesterday. Ah, look! I have a four. Let's see if I can find another? No. Bad luck.' She replaced the cards.

'My turn,' he said, swooping on a card. He turned it over 'It's a . . . a . . .'

Christiana's heart ached for him but she wouldn't prompt him unless it was necessary.

'An ace!' he burst out in childish triumph, uninhibited by the delay.

While they were playing, she saw Brodie coming towards them.

Strangely enough, despite those suspicions, she didn't bear Brodie any ill-will, which she acknowledged was rather unfair since she was prepared to be very angry with Vivien if they were true. But then, Brodie redeemed himself in her eyes by trying to help Vern, while Vivien did nothing to help anyone but herself.

'You set up again, Vern,' she said, 'while I see what Brodie wants.'

She walked round to the steps at the side of the house. 'Vern enjoyed his walk this morning, Brodie. He told me you watched the children at the pony club.'

'He remembered? That's good. How are the cards going?'

'Not bad at all. He sleeps better if he doesn't have a nap in the afternoon now, so I try to keep him busy. Did you want to see me about something?'

'Yes, ma'am.' He shuffled uncomfortably. 'I'm sorry to have to tell you this at such short notice, but I have to leave.'

'Oh.' She was nonplussed for a moment but then she recovered. 'I suppose I shouldn't be surprised. This isn't the best job for a young man. Do you want to go back to the station?'

'No, ma'am. I'm going opal mining with some friends.'

'Opal mining? That will be quite an adventure.'

'I hope so.'

She smiled. 'I like opals. They have more soul to them than the harder stones. More depth.'

'That's why I want to try for them,' he said enthusiastically. 'They're the prettiest stones I ever saw.'

'When do you want to finish up?'

'I hope you don't mind, I don't want to be an inconvenience but my partners are packing up now. I have to leave right away.'

She nodded, resigned. 'We'll miss you, but I wish you well. Perhaps you might like to say goodbye to Vern while I get your pay.'

'Thank you, I wouldn't want to leave without a word to the boss.'

She walked into the small sitting room which doubled as her office. The desk was neat, everything in its place, the way she liked it, but the drawers were always kept locked, away from the prying eyes of maids. Christiana unlocked a drawer and took out a cashbox. She checked in a ledger the amount due to Brodie and was counting out the cash when Vivien appeared.

'Where's Vern?'

'On the side veranda. Brodie's with him. He's leaving us.'

'So now who's going to mind Vern?'

Christiana took her time placing the notes and coins in a pay envelope, as she contemplated Vivien's reaction. Not a skerrick of surprise. She already knew! Christiana would have taken a wager on it. The inflection had been all wrong too, as if Vivien had already been trying to think of a replacement.

And how did she know? Unless she was friendlier with Brodie than she pretended. It was just as well that Brodie was leaving. Vern had suffered enough; she wouldn't permit his wretched wife to make a fool of him in this house.

'Brodie served the purpose for the present,' she replied. 'I'll find someone older now; a retired gentleman would be more appropriate.'

Vivien disappeared into the house, obviously not keen to bid farewell to the man who'd been such a help to her husband. Maybe she had already said goodbye to him.

When Christiana handed Brodie his pay, Vern pushed back his chair and stood to shake hands with him, and she felt tears sting her eyes at the gesture. Vern, her beloved son, could still summon his manners when he was able.

Even the Irishman was affected. He smiled gently and took the proffered hand. Christiana was glad Vivien wasn't there to mar the scene.

'I'll come back to see you, sir,' Brodie said, the lilting Irish brogue somehow soothing the parting, and Vern nodded, pleased. Then he sat down and returned to the mechanical process of spreading the cards.

*   *   *

131

Brodie walked sedately down the drive, his boots crunching on the white gravel. He opened the imposing wrought-iron gate, stepped out and closed it carefully behind him. Then, in a burst of exuberance, he ran, throwing his cap in the air and catching it again. This was the first day of his new life, his real life!

He made a point of walking down Berry Street, to stand and look across at number eight. His house. A man was already busy cleaning up the overgrown garden and Brodie, in his pride, was tempted to go over and chat to him, to pass the time of day, so to speak. But he decided against it. He did not wish to be discussing his business with anyone. Except the agent, of course. And that was his next stop.

It was a grand feeling to be able to leave the money to pay a carpenter, on completion of his work. To sign documents and instruct that the title deeds be sent to *his* bank, the Bank of Queensland, for safe keeping, and to sign more papers giving the agent permission to arrange a tenant and collect the rents on his behalf.

'A pleasure to do business with you, sir,' said Clem Patchett, *his* agent. 'You can rely on me. I keep proper accounts and I'll pay your rent money into your bank each month, if that is suitable.'

'See that you do,' Brodie said sternly. 'I'll be away for a while but when I come back I'll expect everything to be in order.'

'It will be, I can assure you.'

'Good, because I have in mind to invest in more houses yet.'

Patchett even escorted him out into the street, keen to discuss other houses that were available, but Brodie had to move on. This was his day. He stopped at a pub for a quiet drink on his own, savouring the heady experience of being a landlord.

The small baker shop was flush to the footpath, with the Kriedemann name in large letters above the awning that protected pedestrians from the sun and rain. Their living quarters were at the rear of the shop and the bakehouse was next door, though on the same large block.

Mrs Kriedemann led Brodie through to the sleep-out, which

was an enclosed section of the back veranda. 'Lester is sharing the room inside with Gus. You are welcome to sleep here tonight, Brodie.'

''Tis very kind of you,' he said, placing his canvas pack on an old sea chest that doubled as a table. The suitcase that Abe had given him had long been replaced by a pack, at Patrick's insistence. In fact, Brodie recalled now, Patrick had doubled up laughing at this emigrant arriving at his stables carrying a suitcase. 'Which end of the horse are you going to hang that on? Dump it!'

Mrs Kriedemann was in no hurry to leave him. She seemed to be in a mood to talk. 'That sea chest,' she said, 'was all that Jakob and I had when we arrived in this country. That and just a few shillings.'

'So you opened the bakery,' he replied.

'Ah, no. We never did have it that easy. We took jobs on farms, working hard for many years, saving our pennies. We never turned our noses up at any work.'

As she explained how they saved to buy this block of land and then kept working as farmhands until they could afford to build the bakehouse where they lived and worked for more years, Brodie guessed what was coming.

'Later came the shop and the house,' she added. 'This is the way people like us get on, Brodie. You too are an emigrant. It is fortunate here that there are plenty of jobs, and people are free from interference of governments and military and great lords. Yours is a poor country, I know this, where peasants are kept poor. Isn't that why you came here?'

'Yes,' he admitted.

'Then why must you chase the dream also? You're a strong lad, you'd always have work. You could save your money too and get a farm of your own. Gus said you were a farmer . . .'

Brodie nodded. 'I'm not saying you're wrong, but I have to try for these opals. Men are finding them, straight from the earth to money in the bank.'

'Only some men, very few.'

'I want to be one of those men,' he said firmly.

She shook her head. 'I don't understand. Gus is not lucky with these things. I hope you are.'

He was relieved to hear Gus and Lester come into the house

133

to put an end to the conversation, because he wasn't able to explain to her, or to anyone else, that the sheer beauty of opals still had him spellbound. His dream was to see them for himself, in their natural state, glittering in some dark underground hollow like the pot of gold with rainbow colours streaming in.

Gus had made out a list of the equipment they'd need, and Brodie stared. 'What's this? Why do we need all this?'

'I told you so,' Lester grinned. 'He hates to spend.'

'When you left to go gold mining you didn't have any of this stuff!' Brodie retorted.

'Because I went up the coast by train and coach. And I bunked in with other miners. That's where I met Gus. This time we're starting from scratch.'

But Gus was anxious to explain. 'Opal mining takes extra care. We need three different types of picks. And spares. And shovels, hammers, spikes, tomahawks, ropes, buckets, candles . . .'

'Hold on,' Brodie said, unconvinced. 'You'd need that stuff gold mining too . . .'

Lester interrupted. 'We're trying to tell you that miners were coming and going all the time at Mount Morgan. There were always tools about. We didn't even bother carting our gear home. We sold it for a few bob, same as we bought it. Out west, we might be lucky enough to find a store, and *if* it carried the tools we needed you can bet they'd charge a fortune. We'd look fools trying to dig shafts without the right shovels and buckets and stuff. Would you feel like trekking back a hundred miles for them? Wake up, Brodie, this is an expedition, not a jaunt.' He turned to Gus. 'Make sure we've got good tents and lanterns too, I like a roof over my head. Everyone says it can get bloody cold out there at night.'

'Then there's the horse and dray,' Gus continued, 'and we'll still have to make sure we've got enough cash to keep us going for at least three months. When we run out of supplies we will have to buy them somewhere. The big stations out there have stores.'

Brodie knew that, at least, but he didn't comment. He supposed Gus was right, and after going over the list with him once again, gave his approval.

The familiar rush of excitement was on him again. 'That's all settled then,' he said. 'Let's go over to the pub and celebrate our partnership. I'll buy the first round.'

'Wonders will never cease,' Lester muttered, but he was first on his feet.

As the three men were leaving the house by way of the back door, so as not to intrude in the shop, Mrs Kriedemann called to Brodie. 'Could you wait just a minute, there's someone here to see you.'

His first thought was of Vivien. Surely she wouldn't have come here? Was it the loan? That could be awkward; they were all ready to leave in the morning.

'It's Father Monaghan from St Peter's Church,' she called. 'He wants a word with you.'

Lester dug him in the ribs. 'Ha! They've caught up with you, my lad. I'm off before he ropes me in too. Come on, Gus.'

'You go ahead, I'll meet you at the pub,' Brodie told them as he turned back to greet the priest with a smile of relief. He was happy to see anyone but Vivien.

The priest was a young fellow with gingery hair and freckles, not too long out of the seminary, Brodie guessed, because he was looking uncomfortable when they were introduced.

'Could I have a word with you in private?' he asked Brodie, who agreed cheerfully. He liked the look of this chap, an improvement on the old warhorses who inflicted their opinions on families back home.

'Sure,' he said, as Mrs Kriedemann hastily withdrew. 'What can I do for you?'

'I had some trouble finding you,' Father Monaghan began. 'We were told you were out at Fairlea Station but they said at the post office that you were in town, and Gus is a friend of yours, so I thought I'd try here first. I believe you're off on a mining venture.'

'That's true. Why were you looking for me?'

'We had a request from a Father Daly in Tullymore, Ireland, to locate you. Do you know him?'

'Yes, what did he want?'

'The message came by telegram.'

Brodie watched nervously as the priest took a piece of paper from his pocket. 'Something's wrong.'

135

'I'm afraid it is.' The priest wavered, not sure whether to read the telegram or hand it on. 'I have some bad news for you. Obviously Father Daly thought it best coming from us. He's very sorry to have to inform you that your brother Michael Court passed away quietly last Saturday. God rest his soul.'

'Michael?' Brodie whispered, stunned. 'He hasn't! Me brother Michael?' It didn't seem possible. Sure he'd been sick but he was too young to be dying. 'Let me see!' he demanded, as if he could find a mistake on that telegram.

But there it was, in ink, in a clear, precise hand. 'Michael Court . . . passed away . . .'

He shook his head, desolate. Guilt creeping over him that he'd not patched up the row. That he'd deliberately snubbed his brother ever since. Seeing Father Daly's name on the telegram added to the hurt, reminding him, and now it was too late.

'I never meant him any harm,' he said bleakly.

'I'm sure you didn't,' the priest said, misunderstanding. 'Let's kneel and say a prayer for the repose of his soul.'

Still in shock, Brodie could only think how strange it was to be kneeling here on the bottom step of a strange house in a strange country, mumbling with a priest, while a million miles away Michael was deep in a cold grave. His brother Michael who was always there for him, who'd stood by him all his growing years. It just didn't seem possible.

When the priest left he shut himself in his sleep-out, not ready to face anyone, his eyes blurred with tears.

He thought how odd it was that things came round again as inevitably as the horses on the carousel. When his father died a woman and her sons were left, and now it had happened again. Trella was left alone with Garth.

She'd have no need to sell the farm now. With himself, her mother and now her husband gone, it would support the two of them.

She can't complain any longer, he thought bitterly.

And what of her wild scheme to bring Michael out here? She must have known how bad he was; no sunshine would have cured him if he was that far gone!

At least, he thought, poor Michael had died in his own bed, at home and among friends. Not in the heaving third-class quarters of a stinking ship. What was the woman thinking of?

136

Sure, a sea voyage was oft said to be curative, but that was only for the swells. Hadn't he seen for himself the charmed lives they led up in first class, swanning about in the ocean-fresh air, taking the sun? No such luxury for poor men like Michael; three months down below in packed quarters would only have caused him more suffering.

Brodie shuddered. For the first time in his life he felt desperately alone, his parents and Michael gone now. Buried side by side in the little Tullymore cemetery. Some of the shine had gone out of his dreams of making a fortune. 'Michael, you dear old fool,' he said, 'I wanted you to be there to see it.'

He looked out at the sky and the softening of the sunset pinks, as if there was regret out there too as another day died.

'Will Uncle Brodie come home now?' Garth asked his mother.

'He will not. It's too far away he is.'

'They're saying if you hadn't made Dadda sell the farm he'd still be alive today,' he accused.

'Let them,' Trella said wearily.

'They say it fair broke his heart,' Garth insisted.

Trella sat down and put an arm about him. 'Don't be underestimating your father. He was a sensible man. You wouldn't say he was stupid, would you?'

'No! Never.'

'Then listen to me, not them out there. Michael knew what he was doing. If he hadn't wanted to sell the farm, it would not be sold. He wanted to take us to where we'd find better living, not just for himself but for you too. You remember that. But time ran out on him. The Lord called him to his house instead. And you should be thankful that your dadda got a good price for this poor farm. Didn't he go himself to see Mr Hadley-Jones?'

'He did.'

'And didn't you go with him, Garth?'

'I did.'

'And you heard your father strike a good bargain with Mr Hadley-Jones, for cash up. This and all despite your father being a sick man. He made a big effort to do that, and you remember he came home, pleased as punch. And we had a celebration, the three of us, for the way was clear for us to go. Are you forgetting that?'

'No.'

'Then go to bed now and say your prayers. Dadda knows where we're going, he'll always be with us.' She kissed him. 'Don't be feared, my love. Tomorrow is a big day; we'll go together to Dublin, and then we'll find that big ship to take us to Australia. I'm glad I've got my fine big son to take care of me. You're such a comfort to me, your dadda would be proud.'

Garth looked about him and shivered. 'It's a lonely house now, isn't it?'

'That's only because the fire's out. Everything will be better in the morning. You'll see.'

She hoped it would be. Embarking on the journey ahead held many a fear for her too, and she went to bed wondering if she was doing the right thing, taking Garth away from his village, from everyone and everything that he knew so well, so soon after the death of his father. But the farm was sold. They had to leave, so they might as well keep to the original plan. What else was there to do?

Chapter Five

While Brodie was there, Vivien had been able to cope with living in Christiana's household, but now it was impossible. She was shocked at how much she did miss him, and realised that she was madly in love for the first time in her life. She had told him that she loved him, but that had been more in the heat of the moment, and perhaps he hadn't believed her. She wished she could see him, if only for a few minutes, to tell him again and this time make him listen.

She soon worked out who Brodie's partner was, one of them at least, and every time she was in town she made a point of calling at the Kriedemann bakery, hoping to hear something of them, but she dared not enquire.

And it seemed that, with Brodie's withdrawal, the last vestige of civility between her and Christiana had been removed. They were constantly at loggerheads, with Vern's mother fanatical about caring for him, completely insensitive to Vivien's needs. She had no hesitation in making it clear to Vivien that her duty now was to wait hand and foot on her husband, to make him happy. If that were at all possible.

'I think I'll go down to Brisbane for a while,' she told Christiana.

'An excellent idea. I'll come with you. I really think it would do Vern the world of good to have a change of air.'

The visit to Brisbane wasn't mentioned again. Vivien had no intention of turning up there with a mental husband and a mother-in-law who behaved like a warder.

By this, too, she was short of cash. Vern had always been generous, allowing her to have her own bank account so that she could buy personal effects without having 'ladies' bills', as he called them, arriving in the mail. Nevertheless, he kept an eye on her account, topping it up with a few hundred pounds when her funds were low. Had he been well, though, she'd never have been able to draw that money for Brodie. Her husband would have noticed such a large withdrawal and demanded an explanation. She had nothing to show for it but the IOU from Brodie, and that would hardly do.

Vivien giggled. Some things worked in her favour.

Today she would call at Vern's bank and have them transfer a sizeable sum to her account, then she would tell Christiana she was going to Brisbane for a few days. On her own! To hell with Christiana. Once there, she'd take her time about coming back. She was entitled to have a little fun in her life.

Vivien was discovering that invitations to mixed company had ceased since she no longer had a husband to escort her, and she was furious with local hostesses. Jealous bitches, she fumed. They're frightened I might pinch their husbands or their boyfriends. I'm too good-looking for that frowsy lot. As if anyone would want their dull men! None of them are a patch on Brodie.

She sighed. If they only knew! She already had a man with the physique of a Greek god. A man who loved her dearly . . .

Her visit to the bank was sheer humiliation. The men there treated her as if she were a complete idiot. First the teller, and then someone else, and then the manager himself refused to give her any money.

'Mrs Christiana Holloway still holds a small share in Fairlea Station,' the manager told her for the umpteenth time.

'Will you stop repeating yourself!' Vivien snapped. 'I know that and it's beside the point. Do as I ask and stop wasting my time.'

'As I said, Mrs Holloway,' he insisted, 'there's the matter of the power of attorney.'

'I don't want to hear any more about the stupid power of attorney.'

'But you agreed to it, since your husband is not in a fit state to handle his own affairs. You signed it.'

'So I did. But that was only to facilitate the running of Fairlea Station.'

'And Mrs Christiana Holloway has the power of attorney.'

'So what? That's only to pay the bills out there and keep an eye on Taffy's expenditure.' Christiana had suggested that she oversee the Fairlea operations until the station was sold, and

Vivien had agreed. The old chook was so mean with money, she'd keep a tight hold on those finances until the property was off their hands. Besides, Vivien recalled, she hadn't wanted to be bothered with all the stock sheets and that rubbish. The sooner it was sold the better.

'You don't seem to understand,' the manager said stiffly. 'I'm trying to explain to you, madam, that a power of attorney gives the holder complete control. In other words, we cannot draw from your husband's account without that lady's consent. Now, if you run along home I'm sure Mrs Holloway will attend to your needs. She's a very fine woman and is doing her best for you.'

Vivien drew herself up in the chair. 'How dare you tell me to run along home, you damned halfwit! This is my husband's money we're talking about, not hers. You are deliberately withholding my entitlements for your own use. Stealing my money, you robbers!'

In the end she had to leave. But she made straight for the offices of Stanley Wickham, a young lawyer who had recently opened a practice in Toowoomba and therefore would not be likely to be in her mother-in-law's set of crooks.

He listened to her tearful tale and sympathised, but he could not help. Not right away.

'By the sounds of things,' he told her, 'that power of attorney is legal or the bank wouldn't have had a bar of it.'

'They're crooks!' she exploded. 'And I told them so.'

'Please be careful, Mrs Holloway. You don't need to be sued for libel.'

'Let them sue! Then the whole world will find out they're crooks. I'm his wife! Where's my money in all this? I've got nothing! I won't have anything until they sell Fairlea Station.'

He gulped. 'Even then, I'm not too sure. You see, your husband is still alive.'

'Of course he's still alive! What do you think this is all about?'

'I mean, it's not as if you can inherit. As next of kin no one could deny your inheritance. Has your husband made a will?'

'Yes.'

'And do you know the contents?'

141

'No, it's in the lawyer's office. But I'm his wife, I'd have to inherit, there's no one else.'

'You have no children?'

'No,' she whispered demurely.

'And his mother?'

'Oh yes. She'd be paid out for her teeny share. The rest is mine. But why are you bothering with the will?'

Stanley made notes on the page before him. 'If I'm to represent you, Mrs Holloway – and I hope I shall continue to be of service to you – I need to know your circumstances.'

'The way I'm going,' she grumbled, 'I won't even be able to pay you.'

'One thing at a time,' he said mildly. 'At this point – now don't get upset – even when the station is sold, your mother-in-law will still hold the power of attorney.'

'Meaning?'

'She holds the reins.'

'And if I want money I have to ask her?'

'Yes.'

'The bitch! I won't let her get away with it. You sue her, Stanley! You don't mind me calling you Stanley?' She mopped tears from dry eyes. 'You're the only person I can turn to.'

Stanley Wickham grinned. He liked this woman. He liked her spunk. And she was a real actress. He couldn't wait to get home and tell his wife that he'd snared one of the famous Holloways as a client.

'Do you really want to take your mother-in-law to court over this power of attorney while you're living in her house?' he asked.

'Yes. What do I care?'

'In all probability you'd lose, Mrs Holloway. Trust me. Obviously her lawyers have drawn it up, and I'd say it is watertight.'

'It can't be! You're as bad as those fools at the bank. I won't have it. Do you hear me?'

Stanley sat back in his chair toying with a pencil. 'There is another way.'

'Like what?'

He settled his steel-rimmed glasses carefully on his nose and peered at her. 'You go home. To Fairlea Station.'

'I will not! I hate the place! It's lonely and miserable and the house is a dump. Vern spends more on the horses than he spends on our home. I swear those stables are more comfortable.'

'But if you were in charge?'

'What?'

'Are you in a hurry?'

'Why would I be in a hurry? Of course not. I can't even go shopping.'

'Then let's talk about this.'

Vivien saw the intelligence in Stanley's pale-blue eyes and sat very quietly, realising that she'd stumbled on a jewel here, a man who could, given his head, get her out of this mess. Not once did she interrupt, until he had finished outlining her problems and the possible solutions. And beyond! Stanley Wickham, she decided, though hardly an attractive fellow, with his skinny little frame and sallow countenance, was a man after her own heart. Smart!

'You mean to say,' she said slowly, 'that if I go home and take Vern with me, and refuse to sell the property, you can have that power of attorney revoked?'

'Oh yes. Possession is still nine-tenths of the law. Unless Mrs Holloway goes too . . .'

'She won't,' Vivien said quickly. 'She wouldn't leave her grand house.'

'Then the power of attorney becomes pointless. You and your husband are running your own property. I could have it revoked on several grounds, including inconvenience, but you don't want to do that. At all costs, remembering what I just told you about inheriting, you must avoid confrontation. You are simply taking your husband where he can live a happy and possibly involved lifestyle, surrounded by staff and by the horses that he loves, in the hopes of achieving a cure.'

'Where do you fit in?'

'Don't mention me, Mrs Holloway. We'll talk further. I'll advise you on what to do and what to say. Under no circumstances admit you're taking legal advice. I'm banking on the fact that if you do this, and your mother-in-law sees that you are prepared to take on such a responsibility, she will relinquish that power of attorney. She can be forced to do so, once you're installed, of course, but I don't think that will be necessary. Common sense and sheer necessity would have to prevail.'

Vivien smiled. 'I won't force her. By the time I'm finished with the old bitch she'll think I'm a reborn saint.'

'Yes. Well, just don't get too clever. Go quietly home and eventually admit that this is no life for your husband, that he should be out on the property where he can be cared for in a busy, familiar environment, better than the stultified existence in a suburban house, no matter how luxurious. Tell her he needs life, not coddling.'

I can do it, Vivien told herself as she strolled down the busy street, twirling her umbrella. I'll be so sweet the old bat won't know what struck her. We're going home, Vern, my love. And as soon as I get our entitlements back, we'll be changing banks. And then I will run that place to suit myself until I'm ready to get rid of it. Vern doesn't count any more. I own it.

She bumped someone aside at the door of the bakery.

'Yes, madam?' Mrs Kriedemann was looking at her over a neat pile of hot loaves, her plump pink skin as floury as the bread.

'I'll take a high tin, please,' Vivien said, producing the coins. 'Would you be Mrs Kriedemann?'

'Yes?'

'Ah, good. I'm so pleased to meet you. I'm Mrs Vern Holloway. I believe Mr Brodie Court has gone prospecting with your son.'

'That is so.'

'Then I must tell you. My husband is an invalid. He relied on Brodie to assist him and now that he is gone, Vern, my husband, misses him dreadfully.'

'Ah, that is sad. Your poor man. Here, you take him some of my fairy cakes.' She placed some iced cakes in a paper bag and handed them to Vivien. 'The men, they like these best,' she beamed.

'Thank you. It's very kind of you. I'm sure he'll enjoy them, Mrs Kriedemann.' Other women were crowding the counter but Vivien persisted. 'When he comes back, will you tell Brodie that I am taking my husband out to our station, Fairlea Station, and Vern would like him to visit.'

'Yes, dear.' Mrs Kriedemann was busy serving by this, so

having delivered her message Vivien made for the fly-wire door with its tinkling bell. Preoccupied with the plan to outwit Christiana, she didn't hear the baker's wife call to her: 'When they come back. They will be a long time . . .' Her voice drifted away in the buzz of customers as she saw that the lady had left the shop.

As the train chugged west, Gus sat by an open window and stared morosely at the open country with its line of dim blue hills in the distance. There wasn't much to see on this route, just mile after mile of scattered trees, as if the same scene were being repeated over and over again with the rhythm of the clacketing wheels. Occasionally he saw kangaroos fleeing the sudden charge of the engine, and languid horsemen with their huge mobs of sheep and sharp dogs loping determinedly on the wings, but little else to break the monotony.

Brodie was asleep, stretched right across a seat in the half-empty carriage. Further down, a woman was trying to keep two active boys in their seats, although why she bothered Gus couldn't imagine. No one was taking any notice of them. Lester was playing cards with three men, using a suitcase for a table. Gus preferred not to play, nor even to watch. He didn't want to be involved, knowing that, given half a chance, Lester would cheat. Lester's attitude amazed him. He was only a little bloke, and it was risky playing the card-sharp in this sort of company, but he was incorrigible.

Still, he shrugged, at worst he and Brodie could keep their mate from getting a few bones broken if he got too smart on this trip.

Gus wasn't all that impressed with his two companions, if the truth were known. Lester was a bit shifty, and Brodie had more enthusiasm than sense. And he was untried in the hard yakka of mining, although he had the brawn for it. Give him his due, Lester could work; there was strength in those sinewy muscles, and he was a master with the pick and shovel.

Then again, Gus mused, brushing soot from his face as the train rounded a wide curve, who am I to be looking down on them? What am I? Just another footloose tramp wandering the bare land like so many others, looking for luck. This expedition was chancy but he'd agreed to go along because he had nothing else to do. And that was his trouble, what else to do anyway? Gus knew that his parents were right, that he should find a job in Toowoomba – if not the bakery, then another occupation – but he couldn't find anything that appealed to him. Nor was it his ambition to be a miner for the rest of his days, whether at coal, gold or, now, opal. He'd seen too much of it. A terrible life that became obsessive to so many, win or lose. Sometimes he thought he'd like to go to Germany, he'd heard so much about it from the old people, but he supposed that wandering about a country where he couldn't even speak the language would be more depressing than his present situation.

That reminded him. His father had, eventually, given him the name of an old friend, Willi Schluter, who lived somewhere near Charleville.

'If you must,' he'd said, 'you find Willi. He's been prospecting for opals in the bush for years. I don't see him filling the bank with cash. You talk to him, then I reckon you'll be back pretty damn quick.'

It was a start. The old-timers were the best source of infor-mation, and they'd need all the advice they could get. Deter-mined as they all seemed, Gus thought it was probable that they could locate opal, but whether they could find enough to cover expenses was another matter. Still, he told himself once again as he dozed, mesmerised by flitting trees, it was something to do, and a glimpse of colour in those rocky walls could set the heart pounding. That put a spark into life.

After twenty-four hours on the train, Brodie felt in need of a shave but Gus warned him against it. 'You'll both be better off letting beards grow, as some protection against the weather.' He fingered his own clipped blond beard. 'I won't have to bother about keeping this neat for a while, so that's one less chore.'

He sent Lester down to collect their swags from the goods van at the rear. 'Guard them with your life, especially the guns and ammo; everything that can be lifted is fair game in these parts.' He turned back to Brodie. 'Except horses. Steal a horse out this way and you're dead.'

'Thieves stole a mob of horses from Fairlea Station,' Brodie commented as they pushed through the crowd on the platform, heading, tickets in hand, for the gate.

146

'So you said. But they were for the military so no one would care about them. Except the squatter, of course. Out here it's different.'

About the only thing this town of Charleville had in common with Toowoomba was the tree-lined main street. A hot wind, coarse with sand, buffeted them as they set off down the main thoroughfare, past drab shops and pubs, stepping round goods spilling on to the footpath, such as it was. Only long hitching rails with their hosts of weary, drooping horses, separated pedestrians from the constant traffic of riders and lumbering wagons. Local men stood silently in weathered groups, eyeing them with suspicion as they passed, and Brodie nudged Gus.

'Did you see? A lot of those blokes are wearing handguns!'

Gus laughed. 'Yeah. Just try not to stand on their toes.'

After tramping the town, following up leads, for the best part of an hour, they managed to buy a horse and dray and returned to collect Lester.

'Jesus wept!' he said crankily. 'I thought you two had left town. Let's get a feed before we do anything else.'

They found Willi Schluter living in a shack out on the banks of the Warrego, well away from any signs of civilisation.

Two cattle dogs snapped and snarled as the three men approached, but drew back when the old man emerged from the hut.

'Who the hell are you?' he growled at them.

As Gus introduced them, Brodie's heart sank. He had expected a businessman, a jeweller maybe, and here was a withered old bloke with matted grey hair and a long beard, wearing nothing but a laplap over scraggy brown hips. And the place stunk. The clearing in front of the hut was a rubbish dump of tins, bottles and piles of junk which seemed to match the hut, a shamble of corrugated iron and hessian.

'Jakob Kriedemann's son, eh?' Willi cackled, inspecting Gus with keen blue eyes. 'Come to think of it, you're the spitting image of me old mate. Should have known you. You got any tobacco?'

'Yes.' Hastily Gus produced a pack and handed it over.

'Good lad. I've run out. What about a cuppa tea?'

Gus ignored Lester's almost imperceptible shake of the head. 'Thank you. Yes.'

147

Willi banged on the iron wall, so hard it seemed the whole hut would collapse, but it survived, and a smiling black gin stuck her head out.

'This is Lena,' Willi told them. 'My missus.'

Not deeming it necessary to introduce the three men, he instructed his wife to put the billy on.

She came out, standing a head taller than him, tugging a loose cotton shift into place, and made for a rough brick fireplace beside a pile of rusting pots and pans.

'Come inside,' Willi said. 'The mossies will eat you alive out here.'

As they followed him in, a worse smell assailed them, and Willi laughed. 'Emu oil,' he explained. 'You get used to it. Keep that burning and the mossies bolt. Can't stand mossies, I swear they'll give you the fever. I keep telling folks that but no one believes me. The blacks know, though. She,' he nodded towards the woman outside, 'smears it all over her. Says it keeps her skin healthy too, and I reckon it does. She's going on forty, I'd guess, and got the soft skin of a young girl.' He licked his pale lips with smug satisfaction. 'But don't you young bucks go getting any ideas about her. She'd break your skull if you put a hand on her.'

Brodie stared back at the unkempt woman. Lester grinned. Gus nodded politely.

The hut had a dirt floor, a hessian bunk at one end and a timber work ledge at the other, under a window shutter held open by a stick. Directly in front of the door was a table with benches for seats. It carried the remains of a meal on tin plates. Overhead, the iron roof seemed to pulse with the heat, turning the room into an oven. Reluctantly they took their seats at the table as Willi plonked tin mugs in front of them.

'What do you want?' he asked Gus, taking it for granted that they wouldn't be calling on him without a reason.

'We're going prospecting for opal. My dad thought you might be able to give us a tip or two.'

'Spare me!' Willi cried. 'Bloody amachers, I bet. Nothing I can tell you.'

Brodie was sitting with his back to the door, and as his eyes became accustomed to the dim room he began to take note of the rows of shelves facing him on the far wall. He blinked and stared at the collection of tins and jars of all shapes and sizes lined up before him. The glass jars had caught his attention; they were packed with stones, coloured stones, beautiful stones, mostly bluish-pink, some darker, edged with white, stunning in contrast with their miserable surrounds.

'What are they?' he gasped.

All eyes turned to the shelves.

'My collection,' Willi said vaguely. 'Some of them just potch. Some good stuff there when I get round to cleaning them, and snip them a bit. You got to be bloody careful with opal, she's a gentle lady, you've got to treat her right.'

Lena padded in with a billy of strong tea and poured it into the grimy mugs which Brodie guessed hadn't seen a wash for a while. Then she retreated.

'You wouldn't have any sugar with you, I suppose?' Willi asked.

'I'm sorry,' Gus said. 'We haven't bought our supplies yet. We only got to Charleville this morning.'

'Never mind, I forget what it tastes like,' Willi commented, and drank greedily from his steaming mug.

'Could you show us some of your collection,' Brodie asked. 'I've only ever seen opals in Brisbane and they fair took my breath away.'

Willi roared with laughter. 'I knew it! Pack of amachers! You'd have to be joking talking about prospecting for opal, you lot. Wet behind the ears, the three of you. What sort of opal did you see, lad?'

'Just opals. They were in a necklace. Light opals, but come to think of it now, the middle one was darker than the rest.'

Expecting to be laughed at again, Brodie was surprised when Willi plonked down his mug and leaned across the table, his voice a whisper. 'Where from? Where did the dark one come from?'

'I don't know. I never thought to ask.'

'Oh, you bloody fool! I've been looking for black opals all my life. I know they're out there somewhere. He rolled himself a smoke, that thought seeming to comfort him. 'But I'll tell you this, lads. Our opals are better quality than the ones you get from South America or from the Balkans, so it stands to reason that if we ever strike black opal they'll be top of the heap.'

'We'll be happy if we find good-quality opal,' Lester put in.

149

'Never mind looking for something that mightn't exist. One thing at a time, I say.'

'And so you might,' Willi agreed. Too nonchalantly, Brodie thought. He knew he'd found a kindred spirit in this eccentric old man, another person who had come under the spell of the beautiful stones. God forbid, he thought, I should ever end up like this.

'How long have you been prospecting?' he asked kindly.

'Thirty years,' Willi said. 'Don't do much now. Come to think of it, haven't been out there in a long while. I was doing good at Coolaminka, me and half a dozen other blokes, but the drought drove us out. Terrible country, on the edge of the desert. We ran out of water and had to make a run for it. Every man for himself. If it hadn't been for Lena – she and her mob found me staggering about like a kangaroo without a tail – I'd have been done for.' He shuddered. 'Keep meaning to go back, but the days get away on you.'

'What do you do now?' Gus asked.

'I'm a cutter, opal classer. The best in the bloody business too, but there are too many smartarses out there now, all wanting their stuff upgraded, won't accept my opinions, so I tell 'em to go to hell. I won't never let 'em pass off poor-grade opal, she's too beautiful to be sold short.' He pointed at Brodie. 'He's got it, I can see it in his eyes, the way he looks at my collection there.'

'Got what?' Lester asked, almost as an aside, more interested in the array of opals on the shelves behind their host.

'The opal bug.' Willi smiled. 'It's like falling in love with the most beautiful woman in the world, but she's always beyond your reach. And she sings! When your pick hits opal it tinkles. Like glass, they say, but not to me.' Willi seemed transformed; his tired old face shone with fervour. 'I swear it's the sweetest song in the world.'

Lester broke the mood. 'Can we see your collection?'

Willi sat back and studied him. 'Sure you can, mate,' he said, his voice hard. He slipped a hand under the table and drew out a revolver. 'This is my other mate,' he told them. 'I call him the General, and he's always loaded.'

'There's no need for that,' Gus said quietly.

'You'll learn,' Willi grinned. 'Trust no one. And I'll give you another tip, since you seem set on heading west. If you

150

ever do strike opal, shut up about it. Don't come screamin' back tellin' the world, keep it quiet as long as you can.'

'What world?' Brodie asked. 'Would there be many prospectors out this way? We're heading directly west.'

Willi reached behind him for three of the jars. 'You don't think you're the only ones on the search, do you? Now look here.' He emptied a jar of small white-edged stones on the table. 'This is crystal opal, not enough colour, but find that and you're on the right track.'

Brodie fingered the jagged stones, handing them on to the others as Willi produced other samples. 'This lot are whiskery,' he told them, 'got fine cracks. No good at all. That's why you have to be careful gouging opal. Treat it like butter.'

The lesson seemed interminable as Willi produced sample after sample of rough stones that were worthless. Brodie had the impression that the old man was teasing them, testing their patience, but they all maintained their interest. The table was covered in small mounds of uncut stones, some with the white sandy exteriors, others like lumps of coloured glass.

Suddenly Willi began to laugh. 'Cripes, you blokes! You've got so used to looking at all them pieces you're not really lookin' any more.' He picked up one of the uncut stones. 'Take it outside, Gus, and tell me what you see.'

From the sunlight Gus gave a shout of delight. 'Come and see this!'

Brodie and Lester dived outside to stare in wonder at the beautiful core. The light opal shone with fluorescent green at the edge, and the centre was rose pink flushed with red and indigo and yellow. All the brilliant shades of the rainbow blazed from the tiny stone.

'That's a yowah nut,' Willi said, calling them back. 'Got a bucket of them this side of the Bulloo River. Little beauties they are.'

'Worth money?' Lester asked.

'Too right they are.'

He was amazed. 'Why don't you sell them?' He looked about the derelict camp as if good reason were evident.

'Not on your life!' Willi cried. 'They're mine. I made a lot of dough with opals and I had a bloody good time spending it, but I didn't want to end up with nothing to show for all that work. So I've got me collection, see.'

His logic bewildered them, but rather than offend the old man they sought out the other yowah nuts to admire the treasures within.

'Did you dig these out?' Brodie asked.

'Picked one up among lumps of gravel, so I knew there had to be more about. Dug out the rest.'

'By God, they're a sight to see,' Brodie enthused.

'Yeah? Well try this,' Willi said. He untied a small cloth and carefully took out an opal which he placed on the table.

'Jeez!' Lester said.

Blinking at them was a polished opal, an oval stone, softly blue and purple but carrying a preponderance of red pinpoints.

'I called it Starlight,' Willi said proudly. 'Not too many have seen that beauty. She's got all the depth and colour of the heavens at night. There's your real gem. Thirty carats. I'd never part with Starlight.'

'No wonder you're careful,' Gus said. 'But surely this opal should be in a bank?'

'Never! She might as well be buried in her earth again. No good to me in a bank. Or her.'

Gus stood up. 'I guess we'd better go. This has been a real eye-opener, Willi. We owe you thanks.'

'Oh well, lads. I wish you luck, can't say no more. Wouldn't mind one more go out there meself.'

'Then why don't you come with us?' Brodie asked impetuously. He saw Gus and Lester stop in the doorway to stare back at him as if he'd gone mad.

'Ah, the old legs aren't up to the road these days,' Willi said.

'You can ride on our dray.' Brodie wondered now what the hell had made him ask the old bloke, and he could see that his two partners were far from enthusiastic. 'But,' he countered, 'I suppose you wouldn't want to leave your collection.'

Willi remained at the table, pondering the invitation. 'Don't worry about the collection,' he said. 'I could spirit it away. Done it before. And I could farm me dogs out awhile. Wouldn't mind one more go. Us old gougers, we never learn.'

The three men waited breathlessly for his decision, hoping he'd decline.

'Sure! Why not!' Willi grinned. 'When are you leaving?'

'Tomorrow. As soon as we get all our provisions,' Gus said.

'Good. You gotta come this way. I'll be waiting out on the road there.'

As they rode the dray back to town, with Lester driving, Brodie had to defend his mad impulse. 'He's an expert. We'd never find anyone better than him to show us the ropes.'

'We don't need no more showing,' Lester argued. 'And now we've got an extra mouth to feed. I'm not paying for him. You go back and tell him he can't come, Brodie, or you're up for his keep.'

Gus clung on to the side of the dray as it rumbled along, his feet resting on a load of equipment. 'I don't know why you had to ask him, Brodie. I couldn't believe my ears. He's in no condition to even swing a pick. Lester's right. You've invited the passenger, you pay for him.'

'That I will,' Brodie snapped, unwilling to face Willi's inevitable derision if he had to back down, not to mention the old man's disappointment.

Lester snapped the reins, urging their horse to a faster pace now that was settled. 'Teach you to shut your gob,' he laughed. 'Willi's nothing to do with our arrangement. You make sure you cough up for him, Brodie.'

'I said I would! Just you keep in mind that if he finds opal he's my partner not yours.'

Gus made no comment, but he didn't like this sudden turn of events. It seemed as if they were splitting into two teams, and that bothered him. But he supposed it would all work out in time.

They stayed in town that night and were the first customers in a large store the next morning, stocking up with provisions for at least a month. Apart from the basic tea, sugar and flour, they bought salted beef and bacon, eggs in brine, bags of potatoes, onions and carrots and a good supply of tinned food. The storekeeper advised them to buy a five-gallon cask for extra water, and threw in two huge pumpkins for good measure.

'So he should,' Brodie muttered. 'We're probably the best customers he's seen all week.'

The storekeeper heard him. 'I wouldn't say that, sonny,' he scowled. 'Take a look outside.'

In the yard men were beginning to load a huge lorry drawn by ten bullocks. As they watched, the load grew and grew with supplies, until the vehicle itself seemed to groan with the weight.

'Where's that going?' Gus asked.

'To one of the outback stations,' he was told.

Gus looked about him in wonder. The store, he realised, was more like a huge warehouse. 'You've got a good business here,' he said, impressed.

'Sure is,' the storekeeper grunted.

Gus nodded, tucking that information away. Charleville was the end of the railway line, which meant that these stores had the custom of a massive district to the west. Stations, smaller stores, drovers, miners . . .

By God, he said to himself. This town has to grow as the population pushes out. I wouldn't mind a business like this. But it'd take money to set up. Maybe the opals will buy me a start.

As the other two loaded the dray, Lester fed and watered the sturdy horse that Gus had bought. He approved of the choice. The horse, called Mac, was a grey with the shoulders and shaggy fetlocks of a daddy or grand-daddy draught horse, but not too big for a dray. 'You'll do, Mac me pal,' he said, allowing the grey to nuzzle his cheek with thick wet lips. 'We're going a-prospecting, you and me. And when I make me pile, I'm off home quick-smart. Terrible country for horses this, you poor buggers, scratching for a sweet blade of grass.'

Although he'd never admit it, Lester was homesick. He longed for the perpetual green of Erin, for the soft rich grass under his feet. 'Ireland,' he told the quiet, obliging horse, 'is where all good horses go when they die. You're a good feller, Mac, you'll get there one day. In the meantime, Lester will look after you. Never mind about them other bums, they don't know nothin' about horses. You stick with me.'

As for Brodie, apart from the nervousness of having engaged a partner for himself on this expedition, he was excited again. Every time he loaded a crate and packed more goods into the dray, he felt another rush of delight. Another step

154

closer. Another step! He could hardly believe this was really happening, and was surprised that Gus and Lester were taking it all so calmly. As if they were just loading up to sell fare at the next village. This was an adventure beyond all of his dreams. Weeks it would take before they set down, before they chose a site to begin the dig, the search! Gus was checking the supplies carefully, taking his time about it, while all Brodie wanted to do was to get going. Sweet Jesus! His stomach, though well fed this morning, gurgled and writhed in nervous anticipation.

Not until they were all aboard and the dray was churning up the long sandy road could he settle down. A miracle to think everything had fallen into place so easily. The sky was solid blue and a light breeze carried the pleasant aroma of eucalypts from the surrounding bush.

'It's a grand day, lads,' he called. 'A good day to be starting off. And let me tell you, I'm feeling lucky!'

'Then we'll need some of your luck right now,' Lester growled. 'Start praying that old Willi forgets to meet us, because we're not stopping to find him.'

But another mile down the road, there was Willi, squatting on a tree stump.

He was dressed for the occasion, wearing a sleeveless flannel shirt, trousers cut off at the knees and gaping dusty boots.

'G'day, mates!' he yelled, throwing his swag on to the dray. And then he stared. 'What the hell's all this? You blokes opening a shop out there or somethin'?'

Brodie glanced at Gus, who looked a bit sheepish but said nothing. Instead, he watched as Lena came running from the bush with a bulky dillybag thrown over her shoulder.

'Get a move on, girl!' Willi shouted. 'This travelling circus don't wait for no man. Or woman.'

He pulled her on board and the two of them settled at the back with their legs dangling from the dray.

The partners stared aghast. Each one waiting for someone else to speak, to protest, until Willi broke the silence.

'Giddy-up there, Lester! No hanging about. Onward Christian soldiers!' His gleeful grin matched Lena's broad smile as they waited for the journey to commence.

Eventually Lester flicked his whip and Mac pulled away. 'Who asked this bloody comic?' he muttered, turning to glare at Brodie. 'Is that the lot?'

Brodie could only shrug helplessly. It hadn't occurred to him that Willi would bring his wife, the black gin.

From the train Brodie had found the countryside interesting, until it became monotonous and then boring and sleep came easily to him. But now, four days out and far removed from that comforting link of the railway line, he found the massive emptiness of the land unnerving. He had always considered himself a countryman, not a lover of cities, but this was different. This was a wilderness through which a man could travel on endlessly until he died in his tracks.

His distress, which he was careful not to show, was not helped by Gus's story of the famous explorers, Burke and Wills, who had perished out there somewhere, even though they'd been well equipped at the start. Brodie was now glad that Gus had gone to so much trouble with their provisions; he didn't begrudge him a penny spent, despite Willi's amusement. As they plodded on he tried to overcome this feeling of depression – or was it fear? – by reminding himself that he hadn't been concerned riding about the bush at Fairlea Station. But at least at the station he'd had a base. Now there was none. They'd even decided to by-pass the small settlement at Adavale and continue on to their destination, sandstone country as it was called; or to old-timers like Willi, the opal belt.

The journey itself, even in this early stage, wasn't the trek along country roads that Brodie had envisaged. There weren't roads, only tracks that were heavily rutted by wagons in the wet season and remained almost concreted into shape. At times the tracks, wedged through black soil plains, disappeared, overgrown by high yellow Mitchell grass, so they relied on Willi's unerring sense of direction, good practice for Gus who, maps and compass in hand, enjoyed conferring with the old man.

'Learn the country,' Willi advised them. 'Look out for landmarks, dead burnt trees, clumps of wattle, creeks, just keep watching.'

'Creeks!' Lester groaned. 'The bloody country looks flat but it's pockmarked with so many bloody creeks and dry gullies it's bloody hard going.'

And that was true. Each day seemed hotter than the

previous one, making their work harder as they urged the horse and dray down steep inclines and pushed and shoved to get them up the sides without mishap. At one fast-flowing creek they met a mob of tribal blacks who took great delight in helping them make light work of the crossing but were not so pleased when they realised that the white men were planning to camp there for the night.

The men moved forward, standing in sullen silence, spears planted firmly in front of them.

'You better learn to keep your eyes off their women,' Willi warned Lester.

'Only looking,' Lester grinned. 'What do they expect, walking about stark bollocky naked?'

Brodie knew he'd been guilty of staring too; he'd never seen so many naked women before, let alone a mob strolling about so casually. The older ones had big lolling boobies but the young girls had taut brown bodies, a joy to behold, he thought.

'Do you think we ought to move on?' Gus asked Willi nervously.

'Unless you want a spear in your bum,' Willi shrugged. He took some tins of food from the dray, punched them open with his knife and handed them to a grey-bearded native as a peace offering, then led the horse and dray on from the camp, with the others following.

Brodie noticed that Lena had made no move to associate with these blacks, keeping well away from them, so he caught up with her to ask the reason.

'Bad fellers them,' she replied.

'But they seemed all right,' he said. 'They helped us.'

'That a game. They got other games not so orright.'

Lena had proved her worth. Every night when they made camp it was she who lit the fires and cooked the meals, after which she cleaned up and repacked their stores and utensils. When Gus attempted to help her Willi stopped him.

'Leave her be. She's got a job to do and she does it. Station trained she was, she don't need you messing about.'

They covered another ten miles that day, before breaking off to spend the night sheltering from heavy frost in a clump of trees.

As usual Willi and Lena disdained a tent, preferring to take

157

their blankets and sleep somewhere in the scrub, well away from the other three.

When they'd departed, Lester pulled his overcoat about him, huddling near the campfire. 'I wouldn't mind a woman to keep me warm,' he said. 'One of them gins would have come in handy. They're all the same in the dark. I wonder if old Willi can still do it?'

'You'll never know,' Gus laughed.

'Do you reckon there'll be any women out where we're going?'

'There'd have to be some somewhere, besides the blacks. This is station land.'

Brodie had been squatting nearby, smoking his pipe. He looked up surprised. 'I thought this land was empty. Does someone own it?'

'Of course they do. According to my map we're on Boogaloor Station property.'

'But we haven't seen a bloody soul.'

'We've seen cattle. They're not strays. Most of them are branded. God knows where the homestead is, or the outstations.'

'What's an outstation?'

'That's where an assistant manager or stockmen live to help manage properties this size, sometimes a good day's ride from the main house.'

'Jesus,' Brodie said, taking in the crushing silence of the night. 'That'd be a lonely life.'

'Yes, they can have it,' Gus agreed.

The night was freezing, providing a good excuse to treat themselves to a bottle of rum and sit about talking, all three in pleasant accord after a long, tiring day. Eventually they turned in to snore peacefully in the warmth of their tent.

Willi woke them with a shout of anger. 'What the hell have you lot been doing? Throw a party, did you?'

They stumbled outside, to find their belongings scattered about the campsite. The cookpot that usually hung over the dead fire was upside down, boots were tossed into the grass, clothing hung from trees and boxes from the dray lay in battered heaps.

'We didn't do this!' Gus shouted. 'What happened?'

Willi began to laugh. 'You didn't, eh? Then I bet no one stood guard.'

'Why?' Brodie cried.

'Because you've had a visit from our mates back there!'

'The blacks?'

Lena came in leading the horse that had been hobbled nearby. She assessed the situation immediately. 'Them blackfellers play funny buggers.'

When they began sorting and repacking they found that the blacks had looted their supplies, taking only food that they recognised, salt beef, bags of flour, salt, sugar and potatoes.

To the three would-be prospectors this was a terrible blow, but Willi was philosophical. 'It could've been worse. They only took food. That's replaceable.'

'How?' Brodie said angrily.

'You've got guns. You can shoot game. You're bloody lucky they didn't take firearms or your ammo. Or for that matter if they'd chucked your prospecting gear into the bush someplace you'd have to go find it. Gouging with your fingernails ain't recommended.'

They were so angry they considered retaliation, but they knew that on foot they'd never catch the thieves, so with no other choice they had to accept that they'd lost half of their supplies and push on, with sore heads from the rum and tempers frayed.

A top-heavy Cobb and Co. mail coach drawn by five horses belted towards them in a cloud of dust. The driver shouted a greeting, passengers peered out to wave at them, and then it was gone, leaving them to the lonely road.

Suddenly the countryside changed, as if they'd turned a corner, and they were in an expanse of dry plains, broken only by the worn track that revealed an undercoat of soft black soil.

'How much further in this stuff?' Lester called angrily, halting the horse.

'It gets worse before it gets better,' Willi replied nonchalantly.

'Then we stop here,' Lester said. 'It's too hard on the horse. The soil's so soft it's heavy going for him. He needs a rest.'

Gus was worried. 'He had a rest at midday. It's only two o'clock, we can't waste half a day.'

'I don't care,' Lester said. 'Look at him sweat! This is worse than ploughing through mud.'

'It'd be quicker to walk,' Willi grinned.

'Then you bloody walk, mate! And take your missus with you,' Lester shouted. 'This isn't a passenger coach.'

Willi turned to pick up his swag and throw it to the ground. He jerked his head at Lena, who obeyed instantly, jumping from the dray clutching her dillybag.

'What are you doing?' Gus cried.

'I know when I'm not wanted,' Willi said, picking up the swag. 'You lot are so bloody smart, let's see how far you get without me.'

Lester ignored him, pouring water into his hat to give the horse a drink, but Gus tried to placate him. 'Now don't be silly,' he said. 'Get back on the dray. Everything will be all right . . .'

'Don't call me silly!' the old man shouted, and strode off into the blazing sun on his skinny legs with his wife padding behind him.

Brodie ran after him. 'Come on back. Don't take any notice of Lester. He just goes on for the sheer sake of goin' on.'

'I was never wanted from the start. I'll go me own way. But you watch out, lad, and the best of luck. Stick with the other gougers for a start. Crawl before you walk.' He turned and marched away without a backward glance.

'Good riddance,' Lester said to Gus. 'We're short on supplies and that's two less to feed.'

Gus glared at him. 'Is that right? Well, if you're so bloody smart, until we get to Sandy Ridge, you're the cook.'

Without Willi's help with directions, Gus was nervous for the next few days, confused by diverging tracks and the total lack of signs, but by good luck, he silently acknowledged, they finally reached the Barbary Creek Hotel. This was a ramshackle building perched on the high bank of a sluggish watercourse, but important as a mail change for the Cobb coaches, and to Gus as the point at which, according to Willi, they were to turn south-west.

'Where is everyone?' Lester said, staring about bewildered. 'I thought this was a town.'

'So did I,' Gus replied. The only signs of life were horses

160

grazing in a nearby paddock and the inevitable cattle dog eyeing them suspiciously from the veranda of the lonely pub.

'What does it matter?' Brodie said. 'We can have a meal here to save on supplies. And I don't know about you blokes but I've got the thirst of a camel.'

Within minutes the trio were lined up at the bar, eager to learn more about the district from the cheerful publican. There were no other customers, so their host was just as pleased to see them and willing to yarn about the gougers and the various opal mines only sixty miles away.

'A couple of weeks ago,' he told them, 'a buyer came through here with a parcel of opals worth a packet, from Sandy Ridge.'

'That's where we're going,' Brodie cried. 'Would you say we've got a chance too?'

'Why not? It's all the luck of the draw, son.'

With what the cheery publican hadn't told them, Brodie later observed, he could have written a book. And their own ignorance could have filled a second.

They soon found that Sandy Ridge wasn't a town either. It was just what it said. A ridge thirty miles long.

That information was freely given at the first mining camp they encountered, by a half-dozen hard-faced prospectors who did not welcome their intrusion.

'It's a free country,' their spokesman told Gus with a savage grin. 'You got thirty miles of broken ridge to pick yourselves a spot and dig up a fortune.'

'Like looking for a needle in the world's biggest haystack,' Lester muttered, staring at the havoc mine shafts had already created across a wide area of the lightly wooded ridge. From this distance the shafts were only black holes among hundreds of glaring white mounds of mullock.

'No different from gold mining,' Brodie countered.

'Not much it isn't. A man could cook out there in that granite.'

'We'd better move on then,' Gus said, but Brodie, remembering Willi's advice, wasn't to be pushed on so easily.

'No. This is where we start. That water hole is a spring of some sort. We have to have water. God knows how much further we'd have to be travelling to stay close to water.' He marched over to the strangers with a smile. 'What say we share a bottle of rum, mates?'

'We could do that,' the lead miner admitted, taking in the contents of the dray, 'and we could do with some spuds. And onions too,' he added, with a wink at his friends.

'How far to the nearest store?' Brodie asked him.

'Miners' store, ten miles down the track, but he ran out of fresh vegetables weeks ago. I see you've got a few bags there.'

'We've been robbed once,' Brodie said, not so casual now, 'and we wouldn't take kindly to it happenin' again, if you get my meaning. But short as we are, we could put on a good feed of fried spuds and onions if we decided to stay.'

'*If* we let you stay, you clear your own patch and cut your own timber.'

'Fair enough.' Glancing about him, Brodie saw that the prospectors' humpies were made of timber, and several heaps of timber were carefully stacked nearby, some, he guessed, for firewood and others in lengths cut for shaft supports.

'And answer to the squatter,' one of the other men laughed, but the first man shook hands with Brodie. 'Mike Ryan,' he said, introducing himself.

'Ryan,' Brodie grinned. 'Are you Irish too?'

'Oh sure,' Ryan said, unimpressed. 'Sydney Irish. Bondi Beach born and bred.'

'What was it they said about the squatter?' Gus asked Brodie as they unpacked the dray.

'I don't know.' Brodie had already walked over to examine the deep shafts and was beginning to grasp the enormity of the toil ahead of them, with tree felling as an introduction to the main effort. The other two, experienced miners, hadn't been surprised to find that the shafts led to tunnels bearing off at angles deep underground, but Brodie, who'd never dug anything deeper than a post hole, had to steel himself for the days ahead.

Chapter Six

The squatter the prospectors had referred to was none other than His Honour Judge Samuel Chiswick, owner of Plenty cattle station, a vast property that stretched beyond Sandy Ridge to the plains below and on to the natural boundary of Torrent Creek. The latter was so named as a warning to travellers: though in the dry it was a delightful rippling stream, as clear as crystal as it tumbled down its rocky meandering course, come the wet season, when the monsoonal rains in the north sent all the big rivers pounding into their tributaries, Torrent Creek lived up to its name in a sudden act of treachery, smashing its banks and flooding the surrounding countryside. This was a boon to the graziers, who knew to shift their stock in time, but a trap for the unwary.

In the early days when the Judge's grandfather had 'squatted' on the land, taking up huge tracts at a minimal cost before the law with its regulations and restrictions reached out this far, the waterway was known as Dead Man's Creek, due to a number of drownings, but the Judge had disapproved. Such a name, he felt, was undignified, and not in keeping with the proud history of the station. However, as befitted his civic duty, he chose Torrent as being descriptive enough for strangers to get the message. Not that he cared about them, if the truth be known. The Judge hated intruders on his land, deplored the fact that the road south-west cut through his property and was in the process of having it rerouted. That would stop ordinary travellers but was no hindrance to the new menace, opal miners. He hated miners worse than the Boers. They were destroyers, chopping down fine timber, turning the countryside into gaping wastelands, taking over precious water holes and turning the areas into rubbish dumps. And worst of all, whenever they were short of meat they thought nothing of butchering a steer, as if it were a right, not plain, evil theft. The bastards!

This night, as he dressed for dinner, straightening his stiff collar and bow tie, he tried not to think of the scum, as he called prospectors, because this was an important occasion, the proudest night of his life. The Barclay family had come over from their station to share Charlie's last night and all was in readiness. They were a jolly lot and the wife was a fine pianist to add a touch of gaiety to the evening, while Clover, his daughter, could be relied on to present a splendid repast.

A plain girl, Clover, big and gawky, not a patch on her mother, but she was a good housekeeper and had been a strong back-up here for her brother, in the absence of their parents.

Remembering the late Mrs Chiswick, Samuel shuddered. He would never forgive that woman, the mother of Charlie and Clover, for taking her own life! Swallowing poison just when his career was at its height, causing the worst scandal the Chiswick family had ever encountered.

The Judge took two silver brushes and thrust them through his thick grey hair as if in retaliation. Of course the woman had always been troublesome; she'd needed a firm hand to stop her mewling complaints about her imagined woes. After Clover was born she'd even tried to deny him sex but with a firm hand, and his belt, he'd soon overcome that problem. In fact, her fear of him had made those nights more exciting. He shrugged off the self-pity that always accompanied thoughts of Hannah Chiswick, and all the trouble she'd caused him.

She'd never understood him, that was the problem. With his parents well established at Plenty Station, Samuel had, at his father's insistence, gone down to the city to study law. Not his own choice by any means; he would have preferred to remain on the station. But, a good son, he had obeyed his parent in the end, as his own son Charlie was now doing.

By Jove, the old man was right too, Samuel said to himself as he searched the bottom drawer of his dresser for the leather box containing the gold watch that he intended to present to Charlie as a farewell gift.

'The Chiswicks can't be known as bushies forever,' his father had said. 'We have to strike out into the world. You're

164

going to town to be a lawyer, and don't come back without that certificate. I'll set you up in decent digs and see that you have enough cash to mix in society, but you stick with your learnin' or I'll want to know why.'

To his surprise, Samuel had not found the studies difficult. He'd always had an excellent memory, aided no doubt by the horse whip his father had wielded if his young son forgot any of his instructions, and that talent had served him well at the University of Queensland.

Hannah McRae had been his father's choice too, and as usual Samuel had taken his advice. Her family was wealthy, she was a good-looking girl and a staunch Anglican, so there was no cause for complaint at first. Not until he discovered that she was stubborn and wilful. She would not accept that her duty was to obey him without question. It appalled him that his own wife would argue with him, even contradict him, so punishments had become necessary, even routine. He shrugged. Women like her, all they understood was a decent hiding, they seemed to ask for it.

His mother had died quietly, as she'd lived, in her sleep, and several years later, Chiswick Senior had been struck by lightning while mustering out on Sandy Ridge.

Rather than cut short a promising career, Samuel had installed a manager at Plenty Station and remained in Toowoomba with his family, while still taking every opportunity he could to visit the station, keeping a firm hand on his property.

Judge Chiswick had only been four years on the bench when his wife had taken it into her head to depart this life.

'The damn woman!' he muttered. 'So much for God's laws! I hope she rots in hell!'

At the time Charlie had only been fifteen. Doing well at school, too, talking about taking up the law, but his father had other plans. Charlie was packed off to the station to learn how to run the place until he was old enough to take over, and the girl, with a governess, was sent out too. It would hardly be fitting for a man to be living alone with his daughter. People would talk.

To his delight, Samuel then found himself the gay bachelor, freed of all family encumbrances, while Charlie took to his responsibilities like a true Chiswick, born to the land. He was twenty-three now, still single, so before he settled to taking a wife and raising a family, it was time, Samuel decided, for him to strike out into the world, to make his mark too.

A patriotic man, Judge Chiswick had taken leave from the judiciary to return to his cattle station, thereby releasing his son for military duties in the war with the Boers. Before leaving Brisbane, the Judge had used his influence to secure a commission for Charlie, in the Bushmen's Corps, knowing that his lad would do his duty.

He took a little pomade, rubbed his hands together and smoothed his hair, and with a last glance in the mirror took himself downstairs to greet his guests.

'You don't have to go,' Clover said to her brother. 'Don't let him push you into this.'

'Yes I do, he'll look an awful fool if I don't. He's taken leave so that I can go. It's expected of me now. Help me pack.'

She strode over to his bed and slammed his suitcase shut. 'I won't help you! Stop this, Charlie! Let him make a fool of himself.'

He sighed. 'What am I supposed to do? Go downstairs and tell them I've changed my mind?'

'No. Tell them it wasn't your idea in the first place. Tell them he just came home and announced you were joining the army. He's using you again. This time to cover himself in glory. Skiting round Brisbane that the Chiswicks will be there to fight for England. I wouldn't care if you wanted to go, but you're not volunteering, Charlie, you're being pressed into this.'

'Please don't go on so, dear girl. Don't you see? If I back off now my reputation will be wrecked, not only in Brisbane but out here as well. It will sound as if I've funked it, and I couldn't bear that. I should hope I'm not a coward.'

'Of course you're not!' she cried. 'Good God! No one would think such a thing of you, Charlie, no one who knows you. There are men on this very station who owe you their lives! Besides, you've always said there had to be a better way of sorting out the differences between our people and the Boers than by killing each other.'

'It's no use arguing, Clover. I'm off to war and there's no dodging it. Don't worry about me, I'm a good shot and a fair devil on a horse.' He grinned. 'I ought to be able to ride myself out of trouble if all else fails, don't you reckon?'

Clover shook her head. 'This is wrong, and it's his fault. He killed Mother and now he's . . .'

'Whoa! Don't start that again. Mother took her own life.'

'Only because he made her life miserable, had her so browbeaten, and not just that. Aunt Maggie said he used to beat her.'

In her agitation Clover's tanned face was flushed and her lank brown hair had broken loose from the single plait, drooping over her face. To soothe her, Charlie lifted several strands and tucked them behind her ear.

'Aunt Maggie has never liked him,' he said quietly. 'You shouldn't listen to her.'

Clover pushed him away. 'Why would she lie? She said that after Mother died she saw the weals on her back. And she wasn't the only one who saw them. She said he must have been beating her for years and she never said a word to anyone.'

'It's not true,' Charlie said harshly. 'And I don't care if she had problems with Father. She didn't have any problems with us. We were only kids, she didn't think about us, did she? She dumped us. For all she knew, he could have married some awful woman after she died, someone who could have given us hell. But he didn't. We've had the best of everything all our lives, except a mother who deserted us.'

Clover, shocked, stared at him. 'I didn't know you felt like that.'

'Now you do,' he said sharply. 'So don't go on about past history. Dinner will be ready soon, you ought to dress.'

He walked her to the door. 'Cheer up, Clo. Don't spoil my last night.'

His outburst had put a damper on her arguments but by the time she'd taken a bath her opposition to his military service returned to worry her. Angrily she stared at her wardrobe, where her few dresses hung lopsidedly on their old hangers. Clover wasn't interested in fashion. During the day she wore shirts and dungarees, unless they had company and cotton dresses would suffice. Her evening dresses, bought off the hook on rare visits to town, were serviceable.

Still fighting her father's decision to send Charlie to war, she took out her one and only black dress.

'Good. I'll wear this,' she muttered. 'This'll show them what I think. Tonight isn't a night to celebrate. I don't care what they say.'

Then a wave of fear swept over her.

Black?

'Oh God, no. I only wear that to funerals. It might be bad luck for Charlie, putting the hex on him.'

Instead, she chose one of the other dresses, a bulky brown taffeta with puffed sleeves and a high buttoned collar. She combed her long hair back, fixed it at the nape of her neck with a rubber band and concealed that with a limp brown bow attached to a clip. Then she pulled on the black court shoes that pinched her toes.

She too glanced in the mirror before she joined the company. 'That'll do.'

Clover wasn't unlike Charlie. He stood six foot two and she was only five nine, but she had the same straight brown hair, brown eyes and clear skin. On him, though, the thick hair looked dashing; on her, Clover admitted, it was boring. She had long ago given up envying girls with curly hair and trying to figure out how to make hers look more attractive. But she did have Charlie's smile, a nice wide smile that showed good even teeth. Not that anyone noticed it on her. Charlie's smile dazzled. Hers went unnoticed.

She bared her teeth at the mirror. Maybe it wasn't done, she pondered, for girls to grin like crocodiles.

It didn't occur to Clover that in company, when these things mattered, she rarely smiled. Three years younger than Charlie, she'd loved station life right from the start. Now she was just as capable as he was, and indeed, she'd become Charlie's right-hand in running the station, even though her father still thought the kitchen was her place. But on social occasions she felt gauche and clumsy, mixing with girls who smirked and simpered and giggled and bored her stiff. As did the men, wearing their parlour manners.

Her governess, Mrs Saltman, known as Salty, had gravitated to the position of Plenty Station housekeeper when Charlie decided that his sister didn't need any more Latin

168

or European history, but she still tried to steer her charge in the way of eligible gentlemen.

'You won't be told, will you?' she railed. 'You walk like a stockman. You won't let me order nice dresses for you. You've got a figure half those plump women would kill for but you won't show it off.'

'I'm not wearing those low-cut dresses,' Clover had argued, 'as if I'm a milker at a sale. And I hate being all primped up, it's so phoney.'

'Phoney? Where did you hear such words?'

'I hear a lot more when I'm working as a stockman,' she'd grinned.

And that I do, Clover thought meanly as she made for the door, thinking of her father. If anything happens to Charlie, you bastard, watch out. I'll be coming for you. You killed my mother and if you kill my brother too . . .

Judge Chiswick was surprised when his usually glum daughter swept into the parlour, all smiles. She made the rounds of the Barclays, pecking the women on the cheek, shaking hands with the men, and then taking her place proudly beside Charlie, at the end of the room. He'd never noticed before how alike his two children were. Why! The girl was nearly as good-looking as Charlie, she had a real glow about her.

And why not? he mused happily as he ushered everyone into the dining room. Charlie was a hero. Charlie would show them what Australians were made of. No longer colonials but fighting men from a new nation out to prove their loyalty to Mother England.

'By Jove,' he said to his partner, Mrs Barclay, 'I'd give anything to be there when our lads ride into the fray.'

'Oh yes,' she gushed.

From behind him, his daughter overheard. 'Then why don't you go, Father?' she asked with a bland smile. 'You could swing it with your contacts. They'd probably make you a major. Or even a general. Commissions are up for grabs.'

Samuel cast a frown in her direction before resuming his role as the genial host, and Mrs Barclay was too busy admiring the long polished table with its glittering array of crystal and silver to be bothered with Clover's peculiar sense of humour.

*　　*　　*

169

Everyone missed Charlie. Everyone, that is, except the Judge, who brushed aside comments from the station hands that things weren't the same without Charlie taking the lead.

'Nonsense! No one's indispensable. It's the same in the military. When one man goes down, another steps forward to take his place.'

Clover loved to hear her father spouting this view, knowing it irritated the men, especially since he had now become an expert on the military as well as on the running of the station.

Most of the stockmen had been on the job for years and knew what had to be done, but the Judge seemed to think they needed daily orders, as if they'd suddenly become cavalry in his private army and the herds of cattle scattered over hundreds of square miles were the enemy. It was too early for mustering but he was ordering round-ups in all directions.

At first the men had obeyed but then they'd come to Clover with their complaints.

'I get a different job every day. Never get nothin' finished.'

'Are we mustering or just movin' them around?'

'The country's dry. We ought to leave them where they got feed.'

After two weeks of confusion Clover gave her first order. 'Take no notice of him.'

The next morning, with the brassy sun creeping up over the horizon, she sat astride her horse, a flat felt hat tipped almost to her nose, as she listened to the Judge reading out the day's schedule.

Reading! She almost choked with laughter. The men were standing about in their usual laconic way, eyes squinting impassively from their leathery faces, ropes slung over their shoulders, cigarettes drooping from dry lips, listening with wry interest. Then, when the instructions were all issued, they made for their horses without even a blink or a nudge to indicate that the Judge had been wasting his time, and Clover loved them for it. She rode over to confer with them as Charlie would have done, and serious now, was told of various trouble spots that needed attention: cattle straying into a dead-end gully; too many gathering in a patch of scrub; a troublesome bull that would have to be moved on; some sick cattle requiring immediate care . . . She nodded calmly as they rode out, not daring to reveal the excitement she felt. They really were accepting her rather than the Judge as the boss and it was a marvellous feeling. She knew she couldn't replace Charlie, but with the men's support she could keep things running smoothly until he came home. Unless the Judge found out what was happening.

Oh well, she said to herself as she headed down the track, one day at a time.

To her disgust her father cantered after her. 'Where are you going?'

'I want to check some water holes. Some of them are drying up.'

'Where?'

'Out there,' she said vaguely.

'That's no answer. Where exactly? I'll come with you.'

Clover sighed. She had told the men she'd be riding out towards Sandy Ridge, and it was considered foolish, even dangerous, to change direction without warning, in case of accident, but she didn't want to remind the Judge about the prospectors. Clover certainly didn't approve of their presence but she knew that if they made too much fuss the miners could register their claims, which were only haphazard at this point, and that would be like putting an advertisement in the papers, starting a rush. Besides, the edge of the ridge, while quite scenic, was too rocky for grazing; the watercourse that eventually fed through there was more her concern.

'The string of billabongs, west,' she mumbled, hoping he'd pull away, but he continued to ride with her, probably because he had nothing better to do. She had a long ride ahead of her but it was an easy job compared with round-ups, and he was too old and out of condition to work with the stockmen, so she was stuck with him.

There was no conversation as they rode steadily across country. Even at home they found little to talk about, since he didn't deign to discuss station affairs with his daughter, and she was wise enough not to invite a snub by broaching the subject. For her part, Clover avoided talking about Charlie, rather than engage in a futile argument.

Come home, Charlie, she prayed as the Judge took the lead, riding grandly ahead of her. It's no fun for Salty and me to have him living in the house. He's such a self-opinionated bore.

They checked the water holes. Or rather Clover did, with the Judge remaining on his horse taking notes as she, acting under his instructions, waded in, measuring depths with a stick.

'We ought to be going back now,' she said. 'Salty will be expecting you for lunch.'

'Didn't you bring anything to eat?'

'Only a couple of sandwiches.'

'Then we'll share, girl.'

'It won't be enough for you.'

'Nonsense. In the old days we didn't carry such luxuries as sandwiches. We shot game, waterbirds or 'roos, we fed ourselves on the run. None of this picnic stuff.'

Like hell you did, she thought. Half the damn day would be gone while you cleaned and cooked game. You're living in a bloody dream world.

True enough, they still enjoyed a tasty game meal at times but only when they were out mustering for days on end, and then they worked from a central camp with a designated cook in charge. Clover had always enjoyed the camps, sleeping out under the stars, even though the work was hard. Far from the homestead, those days were exciting, a change being as good as a holiday, as Salty often said.

The Judge lowered his bulk from the horse, and stood munching her sandwiches as he studied a sandy creek bed.

'How long has this been dry?'

'About ten years,' she said tonelessly.

'That's where you're wrong. I rode out here last time I came to visit, only eighteen months ago, and it was flowing. There's no point in you taking on these jobs when you don't know what you're talking about. I'll make a note of it. This has to be dug out. It has only silted up.'

'You'd be better off sinking more wells,' she commented.

'Ah yes, the simple answer. Typical of a woman. Spend money hiring well-diggers instead of using the manpower already working on the station to keep these creeks clear.'

Idly, she listened to him expounding on the subject, thinking how she'd hate to be a woman brought before this judge. A chill wind rustled through the parched trees, and Clover was surprised.

'Where did that come from?' she asked him.

'What?'

'I suddenly felt a cold wind.'

'On a day like this? You're imagining it. Mount up, we'll go that way.'

Clover's heart sank. He was headed for the ridge. He'd probably known all along that it was not a difficult route for her to cover on her own. She had been out there several times with Charlie and they had managed to strike up an amicable arrangement with Mike Ryan, who worked at the Ten Mile, the nearest gem field. He was a black-bearded man in his fifties, she'd guessed, a dedicated prospector who didn't seem to have much luck, except as the boss of the dozen or so men who worked their claims there.

The conditions Charlie had imposed, after lengthy arguments with the miners, were not always adhered to, but they were aimed at preserving the water holes and the good timber, and some miners, like Ryan, were prepared to compromise.

Ten Mile, so named because it was ten miles from the first opal diggings, was about the best of the mine sites, which wasn't saying much, she thought glumly, but at least Ryan tried to keep some order. She hoped the Judge wouldn't cause trouble there as he had at the other diggings. Ryan was a prickly character, well aware of his rights.

She had to urge her horse on now to keep in sight of her father, who was definitely riding with a purpose, his wide hat firmly in place, his white dustcoat flapping in sharp contrast with the polished gleam of his black boots and leggings.

As they topped a rise that looked over the diggings, the Judge let out a bellow that Clover thought could surely be heard for miles.

'God help us!' he shouted. 'Look at that! Those mongrels have turned the place into a bloody battlefield. There's not a tree left standing for a mile.'

Clover had to admit that the pockmarked landscape, with huge white heaps burrowed out in all directions, was an eyesore, and there seemed to be more miners here than the last time she'd visited. Or maybe just more mines.

'They're keeping to their side of the water hole,' she said

lamely. 'They promised Charlie they'd do that so as not to cut it off from any cattle that wandered this way.'

'Promises! What bloody rot! They don't give a damn! Charlie was too soft on them. I'll see about this!' He plunged his horse down the gravelly hillside and set off at a canter.

Brodie yearned for rain. For teeming, thundering rain to give him a break from the searing heat and dust of this godforsaken place. Far off to the west he thought he could see a dark-greenish hue on the horizon but decided it was his eyes playing tricks on him again. A man developed a permanent squint working in this place, caught between the hard glare of the sun and the white heat of exposed rocks.

'Get a move on!' Gus shouted from down below, and Brodie wiped the sweat from his face with his bare arm as he wound the handle of the windlass, dragging up yet another heavy bucket of rubble. This was their second shaft. After weeks of hard work, the first one they'd sunk had shown not even an inch of colour, and on seeking the advice of other miners they'd been forced to give up and sink another. This was the hardest part, and they were taking it in turns to dig a new shaft, five foot by four, into the hard sandstone.

At least, Brodie consoled himself as he hurled yet another bucketload into the heap, once we have the shaft timbered up and can start tunnelling it's cooler down there. And more interesting. He grinned. Despite the fact that they'd had no luck in the other mine, gouging away at the rock in search of elusive patches of opal, it had been exciting. You never knew, you just never knew what was there. Last week one of the other gougers had struck opal at thirty feet, and Brodie had begged to be allowed to go down and see it.

He was still overcome with wonder at the spectacle that had confronted him. The whole wall danced with glittering blue-green light, ribbed throughout with fine black crevices that accentuated the blaze of shimmering treasure. He'd tapped a small pick against it to hear the magical tinkle of opal, and was even allowed to gouge out a lump. So careful was he on his first attempt that his hands shook, and the owner of this wonderland laughed with glee. But Brodie had seen opal, had seen it for himself, and nothing would turn him back. He'd sink a hundred shafts if he had to, he'd never give up.

'Do you want a break?' he called.

'No, I can go a bit longer,' Gus replied.

All Brodie could see of him now was his head and shoulders, grey-coated with dust. They were a wild-looking trio by this, hair and beards untrimmed, skin caked with dust, their clothes ragged from the digs but their spirits still high, boosted by the good fortune of one of their neighbours.

'How's Lester going?' Gus called.

'He's splittin' logs, the darlin' lad.' Brodie laughed. His friend never seemed to mind digging – he was like a mole, burrowing away at a fast pace – but he hated the other essential chores. At least in the shaft, at any level, there was always a chance of finding traces of opal, and Lester was busting to be the one to find it first. The other chores bored him, especially when his turn came to wield the axe.

As if he knew they were talking about him, Lester, from over at the tree line, trimmed the last log, slammed his axe into the fresh tree stump and turned to raise his cap to Brodie with a theatrical bow, indicating work completed.

'And that's that for a while,' Lester muttered, reaching for the water bag. Parched, he gulped down the water. It tasted marvellous, better he was sure than any champagne. Not that he'd ever had champagne but he planned to, bottles of it, when he hit a town again, carting a swag of opals.

He and Gus had been equally impressed by Ginger Croft's strike of light opal that showed tinges of precious red when brought to the surface, but Brodie had gone crazy with excitement, providing them with extra entertainment. He'd stayed up half the night, badgering Ginger with questions and more questions until the weary gouger had yelled at Gus to take him away and bury him.

As soon as they'd heard of the strike, Lester had tried to mark out a claim adjacent to Ginger's in the hope that the opal ledge ran beyond his patch, but he'd been too late. The old stagers had kept the strike quiet until they had the adjacent area pegged out among their mates.

'Fair enough,' Lester had shrugged. It was no different on the gold fields; reefs had to be followed, explored. He'd remember to do the same when they had a strike. The trouble with this business, though, he pondered, was that opal ran from potch to precious, whereas gold was gold. Nevertheless, he still intended to stick with Brodie Court, the man had a lucky streak. Look at the way he'd been given free passage out here, and he'd fallen on his feet with the job at Fairlea Station, to say nothing of the rich woman who'd loaned him the cash. He laughed, watching a flock of pink and grey galahs scratching for grass seeds in the nearby scrub. Fat chance she had of getting Lester's part of the loan back, even if the other two, Brodie and Gus, coughed up. Brodie should regard the money as payment for services rendered, he chortled. Forget about it.

Hundreds of white cockatoos screeched from the trees bordering the water hole, and Lester watched them, dazzled by the display. After horses, he loved birds, and birds in this dreary country made up for the lack of colour, for grass that was more like straw than green, and trees that made you thirsty to look at them. No such thing as sweet little birds hopping about here; they travelled in their thousands, massive flocks of green and yellow fellers, and the bigger ones, all colours of the rainbow, lit up drab trees like glowing blossoms, perched on every single branch.

Then he saw why the cockatoos had flung into the sky. Two riders had disturbed them, cutting across the high banks of the water hole, and were coming towards him.

'A woman, by God,' he said, noting the second rider. 'Things are looking up.'

He took off his cap and smiled a welcome as best he could, since the old bloke in front came charging at him like he was riding an elephant.

'What the hell are you doing?' he shouted at Lester.

'And good day to you,' Lester replied. 'Good afternoon, miss.' The girl nodded quietly and jerked her head at the old man as if warning him to take care.

'I asked you a question!' the gent yelled.

'And who might you be?' Lester asked calmly.

'I'll tell you who I am. I own this property.'

'You do?' That surprised Lester, who'd heard that the owner was a young bloke and not a bad sport. 'Then I can say I'm not doing much at all. Just sitting here having a think.'

'Who cut this timber?'

'I have to say I did. It's needed, you see.'

'That's cedar!' the squatter spluttered.

Lester studied the logs. 'Well it might be. Good stuff, it seems, solid for shaft supports. But if it's worryin' you, we don't burn it. Ryan over there says there's rules, you see.'

'By Christ, you'll pay for this! I want you and all the rest of this scum off my land.'

Lester shook his head. 'Hang on. Who are you anyway? Do you have a name?'

'I am Judge Samuel Chiswick, and you are trespassing.'

'Not under mining laws, mate.'

'Have you got a miner's permit?'

'Sure I have,' Lester lied. 'Back there at our camp.'

'Show it to me.'

'I don't have to show you anything. That's for the Mines Inspector. Now why don't you run along.' Lester could see Brodie helping Gus from the shaft. Brodie would have to have heard the old man's raised voice, and they were coming over to investigate. Beyond them, further out against the white hillocks, dark figures were pausing.

He stalled. 'Pleased to make your acquaintance, miss,' he said, walking over to stroke the silky neck of her chestnut mount. 'I'm Lester O'Dowd. Who might you be?'

'Clover Chiswick,' she replied, but Lester was hardly listening. His action in addressing the girl had slowed down the old bloke, who was obviously her father, giving Gus and Brodie time to stride over to them.

'I was just telling Mr Chiswick here, who says he owns the land,' he told them, 'that we have a permit to mine here.'

'That's right,' Gus said quickly. 'Is there a problem, Mr Chiswick?'

'Judge Chiswick to you! And you're a pack of liars.' He took the rope notched on his saddle and charged forward, making for their shaft.

'Look out!' Brodie shouted, afraid the horse would tumble into the shaft, but at the last minute, guided by its rider, it swerved, and the Judge roped the windlass as if it were a calf, dragging it, smashing it, back to them.

'That's what I think of your permit,' he roared. 'Now you get off my land, the whole bang lot of you, or I'll have my men back here tomorrow and they'll make as much of a mess of your camps as you've made of this ridge.'

'Who says so?' Mike Ryan, backed by other miners, confronted him, but the Judge was not to be intimidated. Still on horseback, and with his daughter behind him, also armed, he wrenched his rifle from its holster and pointed it at Ryan. 'I do! Now back off, the lot of you.'

Ryan stared at him, stunned. 'Where's Charlie?' he called to Clover.

'He's gone to war,' she said flatly. 'This is my father.'

'Well, for Christ's sake, tell the bloody old fool he can't shoot us all.'

'No, but I can shoot you for trespassing,' the Judge said, enjoying his mastery of the situation. 'Look what you've done here, you and all the others fossicking on this ridge, destroying everything in your path! You have no care for the land, you're just scum. I'll have you out of here, and the sooner the better.'

'Now see here,' Ryan said, 'it's only a matter of time. We can get permits . . .'

'I knew it!' the Judge crowed. 'No damned permits. And I'll see to it that you never get them.'

'You and what army?' Ryan shouted, advancing on him. 'Shoot me, you old bastard! Have a go! And if you do, the lads will string you up right here and bloody now.'

Clover was appalled at the situation now developing. Her father was behaving with dangerous arrogance but the smarmy little fellow, O'Dowd, whom they'd first met, had disappeared when her father had wrecked the windlass and was now emerging from the bush, obviously from their camp, carrying a rifle. Several of the other men at the back of the group had also ducked away and Clover knew she didn't have to be a genius to guess where they'd gone.

'Father,' she said quietly, 'I think it would be best if we talked this over with Mr Ryan.'

'You keep your mouth shut,' he snapped over his shoulder. 'Mind your own bloody business. Now sir,' he addressed Ryan as the leader of the pack, 'I want your word you'll be out of here tomorrow, you and all these no-hopers.' He looked with disgust at the dirty, dust-caked men. 'I'm ordering you to leave!'

'You'll get no such thing from me,' Ryan said scornfully. 'Nor from my mates.'

'Then I'm taking you in!' the Judge shouted, knowing he had the force of the law. 'You, sir, are under arrest. Stand back, the rest of you,' he called, urging his horse forward, only a few feet from Ryan, the gun squarely trained on him, 'or you will be the cause of a very unfortunate incident. March out, sir,' he said to Ryan, 'you're coming back with us.'

He glanced back at Clover. 'Rope him.'

'What?'

'You heard me. Rope him!'

'You're mad!'

To Brodie this confrontation was a new twist. He'd heard it said at Fairlea Station that the law way out west didn't count for much, but here were people spouting law and using arms to back up their arguments. Shades of the troubles back home that he and poor Michael had tried so hard to avoid for the sake of the family. Hadn't Dadda's brother been shot and their uncle on the mater's side dragged from his cottage by the law, such as it was, never to be heard of again? Except that here it was out in the open.

'Now see here,' he cried, stepping forward as the girl reached for the coiled rope at her knee.

But the girl didn't pick up the rope; her hands emerged holding her rifle.

Faced with another gun, Brodie jumped back.

He heard a click as she lifted her rifle. 'Put the gun down,' she said with a voice of granite.

There was a hush. Eyes swerved. In the background Lester heard her without actually seeing and he dropped his rifle with a clang. He hadn't, in his rush, known where to find the ammunition. It wasn't loaded.

'You heard me, Father,' she insisted. 'Drop that gun.'

He wrenched about in his saddle, forgetting Ryan. 'What are you doing?'

'I'm telling you to drop that gun.'

He gave a harsh laugh. 'Or what, Clover?'

'Or you're up against worse odds than Charlie.'

'You're out of your mind!'

'That makes two of us.'

'You wouldn't shoot me, you stupid girl. I'm trying to get some order here.'

BANG!

In the stillness of the afternoon the rifle shot sounded like a cannon.

Everyone dived for cover as Chiswick's hat fluttered into the air like a wounded pigeon and, caught off guard, he toppled from his horse.

'Jesus Christ!' Brodie shouted, leaping forward to catch the Judge before he hit the ground.

Ryan was just as fast. He had the rifle that Chiswick had dropped before the old man was back on his feet screaming abuse at his daughter.

She ignored the Judge. 'I suggest, Mr Ryan,' she said, 'that you people get your permits as soon as possible.'

'Looks like we'll have to,' he grinned.

'You wait until I get you home, you Jezebel!' Samuel shouted at her. 'You'll be sorry you were ever born. Get yourself moving, we're going home.

'Give me my gun,' he yelled at Ryan, who shook his head. 'Send for it, Mr Chiswick. Send for it.'

Brodie was concerned for the girl. 'Will you be all right then?' he asked her.

But Clover had used up all her courage. She shook her head numbly. 'I don't think so. There's a storm coming.'

He nodded. 'That could easily be, miss, with what you've just done.'

'No. Look out there, I think it's a sandstorm.'

'A what?'

'Just a minute.' She rode over to her father, who was waiting for her, flushed and furious. 'I'm sorry about that but you left me no choice.'

'You threatened me!'

'They were bringing up guns. You could have been shot.'

'Oh no! I saw that look in your eye. Given half a chance you'd have shot me, you wretch of a girl. You're on your own now. Don't you ever set foot in my house again.'

'Oh, don't talk rot!' she exploded. 'What are you going to do? Shoot me? That would be bad for your image. There won't be any more trouble here now. For the time being, anyway. We have to stay. There's a sandstorm coming in from the west.'

He looked up and saw the ink-black stain spreading across the sky, but even that couldn't calm his fury. 'You stay with the scum. Where you belong. By God, if Charlie had been here today he'd have knocked you down!'

'But Charlie's not here and you're not God. And you keep in mind that I'm not Hannah Chiswick, to be belted and bullied by you. For your own sake, though, I'm telling you to wait. You won't make it home before the storm hits.'

'You're such a bloody know-all!' he snarled. He wheeled his horse and rode away, hatless, at a furious pace, heading home.

Brodie couldn't hear the exchange but he could guess the rage. He was waiting for her as she rode back and dismounted. 'Will we have some rain at last?' he asked, to try to restore a semblance of normalcy for her.

'I don't think so,' she said. 'You people ought to batten down, you should tell them. That's not a rainstorm.'

At her insistence the miners began to prepare for the storm, with the dark menace moving swiftly towards them, completely blotting out the horizon.

Lester hurried over, leading his horse. 'Sand, you say?' he asked incredulously, and she nodded, untying the scarf at her neck.

'Well then,' he said, 'the horses will need shelter. There's a ditch back there, more of a wide crevice. We can get them down there, I reckon.'

Clover wasn't sure. 'But can we get them out?'

'Yes, it runs shallow at the far end. Slopes with the lie of the land.'

'Good. Some blankets would come in handy too.'

'Hey, Gus!' Lester shouted, already feeling the sting of the sand-laden wind. 'Bring some blankets!'

They ran with the horses, away from the camp, to a rock-strewn clearing that gave no hint of shelter until they were almost on top of the gaping hole overgrown with brush.

'A trap for a careless rider, this one,' Lester grinned as he urged Mac down the gritty slope with a rush, to trample on through the undergrowth. 'Come on,' he called, noticing the girl's hesitation. 'It's all right. There's plenty of room.'

Clover could see that, but she was more nervous of snakes in an ideal nesting place like this white-walled ditch. Under

181

normal circumstances nothing would have induced her to go down there.

The wind had gathered strength and the blackness had almost blotted out the sky. Taking a deep breath, she plunged down the side, pulling her unwilling horse after her.

Within minutes the one called Brodie and another man, a tall, blond fellow, leapt down too, handing them blankets.

They covered the horses' heads and wrapped themselves in the blankets, huddling low as the wind blasted over them.

Clover tied the scarf about her face to protect herself from the tons of sand that whirled about them, and squinted back through the gloom to see that Lester was manfully crouched in front of the two horses, holding their bridles, pacifying them. She was sorry then that her first impression of the man had been critical.

In the open cut they were at least sheltered from the full fury of the wind that howled overhead, but not from the constant rain of sand, so she pressed closer to the wall, hardly able to breathe in the stifling, sand-laden air. The other two men had positioned themselves either side of her and she could hear their muffled uncomplimentary remarks about the chaotic world about them.

'Hey, Gus!' Brodie yelled. 'How long does this go on?'

'I don't know!' he replied, coughing.

Clover could have answered for him. A couple of hours. A couple of days. But she was suddenly shy, realising she was stuck down here with three strangers, and out there more strange men. And of all people, the dreaded miners! She became nervous, remembering that these men had a very nasty reputation in the district, and she wished now she had gone home with her father. Or tried to. It was pitch dark now and it would be easy to get lost out there.

She found herself worrying about him, hoping he'd had the sense to take cover before the worst hit. The silly old fool, behaving like an old-time bosso, a throwback from the days when the squatters were a law unto themselves. She'd heard some hair-raising stories about her own grandfather, who'd thought nothing of shooting blacks and taking the whip to any of the white stockmen who crossed him. The Judge didn't understand that times had changed since he was a young man growing up on the station.

Clover sighed, forgetting the storm, and was rewarded with a mouthful of fine dust that penetrated her cloth mask. She spat out the dust and, desperately thirsty, thought of the water bag slung on her saddle, right there, only a few yards away. If she asked, the men could probably find it and bring it to her, but she didn't like to bother them.

Who were they anyway? Where had they come from? Two of them, Lester and Brodie, had Irish brogues, and the quiet one, Gus, they'd called him, had a faint German accent. Her legs were becoming cramped, so she changed position, trying to stretch them, loosening her blanket to be greeted by blasts of sand that whirled mercilessly into their shelter. Far from abating, the storm was worse now, tearing at the land. A huge leafy branch crashed through the gloom, landing with a thump further down the ditch. The horses whinnied and shuffled nervously, and Clover decided that snakes were the least of her worries. No self-respecting snake would emerge in this racket.

The Judge tied his dustcoat round his horse's head and pushed on across the plains, trying for a short cut home, but as the storm worsened he climbed down to lead the animal, afraid that it would stumble in the gathering darkness. He veered off, heading for scrub that he could see in the distance, but when the full blast of the storm struck, sand as vicious as a thousand knives, the horse screamed, reared and bolted, throwing him aside.

'Dammit!' he yelled, grappling against the searing wind to retain his balance.

In seconds the horse had disappeared and he was left to stagger on alone without the weight of the beast to anchor him. He considered lying flat on the ground, allowing the storm to pass over him, but he had no idea how long it would last, and he had no water. Already a terrible thirst was upon him in this choking field of flying sand.

'Make for those water holes,' he told himself as, head down, he set out. 'You're a countryman, not some chum from the city. You can show them!'

The wind battered him and his boots were like lead as he trudged through whirling sand, forgetting that his original course had taken him away from those water holes. Nor did he realise, in his determination to prove to everyone at Plenty Station that he could survive the hazards of the bush, that he was not master of his route. The wind was in control. Samuel was experiencing an irrational glee that in the midst of this dark and dreadful storm, he, old Judge Chiswick, was making good time.

'I'll show 'em,' he laughed, spitting grit. 'I can probably make it right home at this rate.'

With the wind at his back and no sun to give directions, he was being swept on a haphazard trek towards the ridge again, towards the driest corner of station land. Completely disorientated, he failed to notice that this massive whirlwind, that had sucked up thousands of tons of sand from the deserts beyond, was no respecter of compass points. It reared and ranted and circled and charged within itself; only the sheer size of it, twenty, maybe forty miles across, gave it the power to forge on east where the last of its load, cloying red dust, would be dumped on an unsuspecting coastal town.

He took his jacket off and wound that round his head. He was hot anyway, he told himself, and sweating from these exertions, despite an atmosphere devoid of moisture. He'd forgotten the bushman's greatest fear, dehydration, because he'd become immersed in his own thoughts.

The Judge blamed Clover for this situation. It was all her fault. Stumbling along, he convinced himself that if she hadn't caused trouble he'd be home by this. He was still shocked that his daughter would not only defy him but bail him up in front of the scum, so he concentrated on her punishment. He would change his will, leaving everything to Charlie. No. He'd already done that. He could order her off the station. By God, he recalled, he'd already done that too and she'd defied him again. How could he order her off if she refused to go? She'd lived there since she was a kid. Salty, the housekeeper, and the long-term stockmen, who all liked her, not knowing what an ingrate she was, could easily buck at that prospect.

Tears of frustration coursed down his dust-caked cheeks. The wretch had him beaten for the present. There wasn't much he could do without providing her with an opportunity to make a fool of him again. Like she had at the Ten Mile, in front of the scum.

Exhausted, he stumbled, but this time his legs were wobbling and when he tried to climb up again he fell to his knees, swathed in sand.

Judge Chiswick was crying and he didn't know why. He was certain the precious water hole was only a few yards away, so there was no need to be distressed. Or was there? Clover had defied him just like her mother had that last night. When he'd taken the belt to her and she'd turned on him, screaming at him. Telling him that atrocious story.

'Not your child!' she'd yelled in manic delight. 'Not your child. What do you think of that?'

'You're lying, you crazy bitch. Where did this tale come from?'

She'd wept. She'd climbed into the far corner of the bed. 'You think you're so grand. You're nothing! You never were. You don't know what love is!' She was becoming hysterical. 'You're the epitome of the worst kind of lover. I found that out very smartly, didn't I? God, I hate you.'

He laughed. 'Who else would take you on, you've no more sex in you than the mattress you're sitting on. Haven't I told you that a hundred times!'

She scrambled across the bed in her cumbersome nightdress and grabbed the glass of sherry wine that he'd always allowed her for a nightcap, even though he was well aware she kept bottles hidden about the house. Hannah was a drinker. She was often tiddly. He could always tell; she became ever so proper in her cups, mouthing her words with exaggerated care. It infuriated him and he was certain she only drank to annoy him. What other reason could there be? She had the best of everything.

She gulped down the sherry. It seemed to give her courage this night. Dutch courage.

'A mattress, am I?' she sneered at him, pushing back the cloud of soft brown hair that had fallen over her face. She was a fine-looking woman but her long hair with its natural waves was her best feature. It was magnificent hair, falling almost to her waist.

'I'd say so,' he remarked, never averse to an argument before the inevitable. She always gave in, in the end.

But not this night.

To his surprise, she walked over to the wardrobe and,

185

scrounging among clothes in the base, yanked out a bottle. Half empty. Or half full, he reflected, at the same time amused by this performance. She was a lot drunker than he'd thought, but that didn't dismay him. It would be easier to get that nightdress off. And the rest of the paraphernalia. Her naked body was still in good nick for a woman of her age.

The night was hot and humid, rain thudding down outside the open casement windows. Samuel hung the belt over the brass bed end, unbuttoned his trousers, let them drop and kicked them aside as she poured herself another drink.

'I wasn't always,' she said, waving the crystal glass at him, and then she swallowed the contents with a sigh. 'You were the failure. You sickened me! A young girl full of romantic dreams. You hurt me and humiliated me. And you ridiculed me every time I had anything to say. I didn't know any better. And I thought if that was married life I didn't want any part of it.'

'But you soon learned,' he said patiently, there being no hurry.

'You'd be surprised what I did learn,' she said. 'Before the children came along you used to leave me here in Toowoomba and go off to see your country clients for weeks on end. It was a relief to be free of you. So I used to go to the tea dances at the Colonial Hotel.'

'On your own?' he frowned.

Hannah smiled gently. 'It's gone now, it burned down. So sad, it was a lovely hotel, with the prettiest gardens.'

'So?'

'Don't rush me,' she said, slurring her words a little. 'This is important. You have to know how unimportant you are, Samuel. Married to you I was in despair, knowing I was stuck with you, and I was such a pretty girl.' She shook her head sadly, turning back to the bottle.

'Then I found romance. Me. Could you believe it?'

'No, I don't,' he said sourly.

'Oh yes, I did.' Hannah swanned about the room, humming a little tune, nursing the bottle. 'Yes I did, and he was beautiful, he showed me what love is all about. He taught me what marriage should have been . . .'

Samuel grasped her arm, pulling her to a halt. 'Are you saying you committed adultery?'

'It was the most wonderful time, that's what it was,' she cried defiantly, wrenching away from him.

'You're drunk!'

'I am not drunk!' she said, flopping to the edge of the bed. 'A person does not have to be intoxicated to tell the truth, do they? You thought I was your very own bedmate, didn't you? But you were wrong. And after that I didn't care what you did. I had my dreams.'

Samuel picked up the belt. 'After what?'

'After that child was born, silly. I was petrified you'd find out. Or work it out, whatever comes first.' She grinned foolishly. 'But of course you never did.'

'I don't know what you're talking about. Get into bed.'

'But you have to know,' she persisted. 'We can't go on forever with you not knowing. That child isn't yours.'

'Which child?' he demanded. 'Clover?'

'No, silly!' She was laughing hysterically. 'Charlie! Charlie is *his* son. Not your child! What do you think of that?'

He grabbed the bottle from her. 'You're lying. You're making this up.'

'Oh no I'm not,' she said groggily. 'That shook you up, didn't it? Now go away, I'm tired.'

'You swear to that?'

'On a Bible, my dear!'

The belt slapped across her back but she hardly felt it.

'Who was the man?' he demanded.

She looked up at him. 'You shouldn't have done that. I was going to tell you. You should know. But now I won't.'

She managed to push herself up to confront him. 'Listen to me, Samuel Chiswick! If you ever beat me again I'll tell the whole world, so go away.'

He stood staring stupidly at the rain. Was it true or was she just baiting him in a fit of drunkenness? Frantically he tried to remember the time she was referring to, but it was years ago. Fifteen years ago. More. Charlie was fifteen. His son. He was his son and none of her wild talk could take him away.

Thunder cracked, shaking the foundations of the house, and the rain intensified, splattering on to the carpet from the window ledge.

The Judge, huddling in the sand, beaten by savage winds, could still taste that rain, the sweetness of it. He licked his

187

dry lips, watching it flow along the window ledge that was cracked from the sun and could do with a coat of paint. He was lying under it, looking up at the swaying damp curtains, catching every precious drop in his mouth, rejoicing in the swift-flowing flood with his wife asleep there on the white counterpane.

In the morning Hannah Chiswick awoke, petrified with remorse. After a bout of drinking, morning remorse was no stranger, but this time, for some reason, it was worse, a thousand times worse.

She lifted her head a few inches from the pillow and a wave of nausea conspired with a thudding headache to force it back.

Oh God, why do I drink? Why do I do this to myself? I don't even like the taste. And it leaves such a vileness in my mouth.

There was fresh water in a crystal decanter on the dresser and she longed for its cleansing, thirst-quenching goodness, but she didn't dare move. Not until she had summoned up remembrances of last night. He was asleep beside her, his back to her, taking up most of the bed, as usual, while she clung to the edge.

She shuddered. There was something ominous about those motionless shoulders, and she prayed he wouldn't wake. Not yet. Not till she'd had time to think.

She felt her torso. No new hurt from the belt, just a general ache, a weariness in her whole body.

They'd had a row. She could remember that. But they often had rows. Nothing unusual.

Then why am I feeling so terrible? So terribly afraid?

The room was hot, even though it was only about five o'clock. At this hour, at this time of the year, the summer sun began pouring heat into the room through the open windows as it lifted overhead.

Hannah put her hand over her eyes; the white glare had to be suffered for a least twenty minutes since he wouldn't allow the curtains to be drawn across. Requiring fresh air. He didn't have to face the glare.

At least it had stopped raining. The window ledge was still wet. And there was a damp patch on the carpet beside the sherry bottle. What had happened?

Confused, she pulled her hand away from her eyes to stare fuzzily at the floor.

How did I know that? Did I see it earlier and not register? The sherry bottle was lying untidily under the window, and there was a red stain on the rose-patterned carpet.

For a minute Hannah was cheered. She'd always hated that carpet, but he'd chosen it for their 'boudoir'. The pretentious fool. As he had chosen every stick of furniture in this ugly old house.

The presence of that bottle frightened her. She always managed to keep her tipples well hidden.

How could I have left that out there? He must have seen it. Why hasn't he picked it up? Why didn't he make me pick it up? It looks shocking lying there. Disreputable. I know! He wants me to see it this morning. To bear down on me with his accusations and proof of my sins. We've been through all this before. But how did I come to produce the bottle? He must have found it.

She stole a glance at the Judge's thick neck and bull head. He wasn't ageing gracefully, he was just growing thicker. Everywhere. And more set in his ways, so much so that life with him was intolerable. The belt was still hanging on the bed end.

The belt. That's what set me off!

Doing what? What did I do?

She had a vague recollection of standing somewhere near the window, a dampness on her back, waving the bottle about. Pouring herself a drink in front of him.

Oh God, no!

Seeing him with the belt again. Preparing to punish her. But he was the one who needed punishment. Not her. She despised herself for her secret life. Ashamed of her tippling. Ashamed that her husband beat her. Gradually, the awful remorse pressed in on her, forcing her into recall, forcing her to face the sordid events of the night.

The row had been about punishment. Unspoken. But that was the root of it. And she'd defied him. Was that so bad? About time, some would say if they knew. No one knew. But she'd gone too far. She'd gone too far, wanting to punish him. Trying to think of the words, savage in drunken determination to hurt him as he'd hurt her all these years. And then he had

189

used the belt. But it hadn't hurt. That was curious. She hadn't even felt it. She couldn't feel the result of the leather even now.

Anaesthetised by alcohol?

Hannah smiled grimly, a small respite.

I don't think so. I was too excited at the shock on his face. He went white, and then green. All blotchy. And I kept talking. Telling him. Cutting him down to size once and for all as I've never done before. Punishing the Judge. Handing him a life sentence. A triumph. I even felt gay. Usually I'm maudlin tippling. How did I do that? I wish I could remember.

Mercifully the sun moved on. The room steamed. The heat from his body was unbearable. The sheets were damp, crumpled. Outside in the hall the grandfather clock struck six. The housekeeper would be up, lighting the fire in the kitchen, putting on the kettle, rousing the children. He'd be up soon.

Hannah quaked. He'd be up soon.

Perspiration chilled her forehead and dribbled between her breasts. The bottle was still on the floor, mocking her.

Charlie is his son! Not yours!

She sat bolt upright in the bed. Pain slammed through her head. Fear, real heart-pumping fear, sent her rushing for her dressing gown, down the passage to the bathroom, where she was sick in the new internal water closet, clutching at the chain to wash away the horror.

He'd struck her once. Just once. Only once because he knew and she knew that in that final act of defiance she wouldn't care if he flayed her alive. His oft-uttered threat.

Charlie knocked on the bathroom door. 'Should I go down the back, Mother?'

'Yes, dear.'

Hannah rested on the floor beside the wooden box that enclosed the porcelain bowl, feeling that this was where she belonged, hopeless depression draining the life from her.

Wearily she staggered up the passage to the spare room, the best room, kept for guests, with its walnut bedroom suite and pink lace curtains. Where the Mayor of Brisbane had slept when he came to visit.

She locked the door, afraid to face him, remembering it all

now, all too clearly, and climbed into the bed between the fresh white sheets without bothering to remove the expensive puce silk bedspread.

The morning was interminable. She couldn't sleep. She waited until he'd gone to work, the children had gone to school, and the housekeeper went on her morning rounds. No one had disturbed her. No one knocked. She knew they'd be acting under his instructions. He was saving the next confrontation for himself. To call her to account like the criminal she was. And then what? She'd no one to blame but herself for the repercussions that were bound to follow. And it was all too much. Far too much.

Charlie's dog, a lonely soul in the silent house, whimpered at the door. She let him in and he followed her gratefully to her bedroom, where she dressed slowly and painfully in her good crêpe suit. Every move was now an effort, time tick-tocking down in concert with that ever-watchful clock out there.

She went into the study and wrote a short note, addressing the envelope to Charlie, propping it on the table by his bed.

Then she thought better of it. If the Judge found it, Charlie would never be allowed to read it. Better to make sure.

She put on a hat without bothering to dress her hair – it felt good to allow it to stream free as if she were young again – and ran out into the street clutching her purse.

The archdeacon was surprised to see her cutting across the lawns from the church to his front door in such haste. Even so, he reflected, as he stepped out on to the porch, even if one must hurry, the paths are there to be used. He winced as she jumped a flower bed, disturbing a fine ornamental border of scarlet salvia. The bishop would be here on Sunday and the floral displays had been specially planted for the occasion.

Patience, he told himself.

Then: 'Ah, good morning, my dear Mrs Chiswick. What brings you here this sultry morn?'

She didn't look well. Her face was pale and drawn and she was almost out of breath from the rush to his door. 'I'm so glad you're here,' she said, bypassing the morning greeting. 'I was so worried that you'd be not home. I mean out. Charlie's being confirmed on Sunday.'

'Yes. Charlie and several other young people. Is there

something you wanted to discuss about the confirmation? Would you like to come inside?'

'No. I mean, there's no need.' She fished in her purse and, trembling, handed him an envelope addressed to Charles Chiswick. 'I want you to give this to him, to Charlie, on Sunday.'

The archdeacon stared. 'You want me to give him this letter? Is it a surprise?'

'Please. Will you do this for me? It's important.'

He relented. 'Well, of course, it is an important day for all of us. I gather the words contained herein are very special.' A blessing of some sort, he imagined. From mother to son. And it would probably have more impact coming from me.

'If that is your wish, I shall be pleased to oblige. Should I hand it to the boy before or after the service?'

'Oh!' Curiously, that hadn't seemed to occur to her. 'After, I suppose. Yes, after. Thank you.'

Before he could stop her she turned on her heel and dashed away down the gravel path towards the gate.

'Good heavens!' he said, peering after her. 'Good heavens!'

The weather cleared that afternoon and the gardener came to work, hoping the Judge would pay him for a few hours' labour. He'd earned little enough this week with the rain, and there was always plenty to do in the long, wet summers, everything grew like crazy. He decided to cut back drooping, overgrown shrubs by the front fence, to make sure the boss saw him when he came home.

He marched down the back to the tool shed, to collect the shears, and that was where he found her. The missus! Dead as a doornail, lying in her own vomit.

Fred Follett was an old man. Too old and world-weary to be thrown into a panic even by such an encounter as this. She was dead all right but he had to make sure. He crouched beside her, ignoring the smell, to feel her pulse, put a hand to her heart, and in a gesture of pity took his handkerchief and wiped the bile from her lips. Shaking his head, he looked about him.

'What have you done lady?' he said quietly.

Two brown bottles, kept on the top shelf out of reach of the kids, were now lying on the stone floor, their corks missing, phenyl spilling white from one.

'Don't suppose it matters which one you drank,' he said to the still figure. 'But it was a hard way to go. You must have badly wanted to end it, God rest ye.'

Gently he took the soft grey skirt that was scrunched about her waist from the convulsions and stretched it to her ankles to give her some dignity, then he found a bucket of water and cleaned up the mess. 'I'll be the one have to do it anyway,' he reasoned. 'Might as well do the best I can for you.'

That done, he locked the tool shed and went in search of the housekeeper.

The archdeacon visited the bereaved family on Saturday morning as part of his pastoral duty and found a chance to speak to Judge Chiswick in private.

After reiterating his condolences to the shocked husband, he made mention of the late Mrs Chiswick's visit.

'In hindsight,' he said mournfully, 'it would have been an opportunity for me to counsel the poor woman. I have to tell you, Judge, that she did seem flustered. Confused, one might say. Had I known how distressed she was I might have been able to stem the shattering of her mind.'

'You weren't to know. I blame myself. She was rather peculiar lately,' the Judge lied. 'Forgetful. Always losing things. I asked her if anything was bothering her, but she said not.'

'Good heavens. What could be bothering a lady in her position? You mustn't carry a burden of blame, Samuel, that would be a cruelty unto yourself. Obviously the poor woman was suffering a delirium of the brain that came upon her like a heart attack. She wouldn't have known what she was doing. The pain in her head was probably excruciating.'

The Judge nodded. 'You're a comfort, sir. That does seem the only explanation for such a pointless act.'

'I'm sure it is. The bishop asked me to extend his condolences. He will be staying over for the funeral on Monday, as you know. And there's another matter.' He took the letter from his pocket. 'Mrs Chiswick asked me to give this to Charlie . . .'

Samuel's eyes bulged. 'When?'

'After his confirmation.'

'No. When did she give it to you?' He held his breath.

'Yesterday morning. I think she was coming from the church. Dear, oh dear, what a state she must have been in. I feel quite faint myself thinking about it.'

'The letter. What does it say?' As he spoke, Samuel felt a chill of fear.

'I'm not aware of the contents. I'm inclined to think now that it's a last farewell to her son, poor child, and she wanted me present to comfort him.'

Samuel wished he could snatch the letter from the fool. 'There's nothing anyone can do to comfort the children,' he said gruffly. 'Their mother has chosen to desert them. They'll have to live with it, as I shall have to. No one can understand this grief unless they've been through it themselves. It's far worse than natural death. I'll give the letter to Charlie when I think he's up to it.'

The archdeacon loosened his stiff collar with a thin finger, tugged at the lapels of his shiny black coat, the letter still in his hand. He moved uncomfortably in the leather chair, damp cloth clinging to the upholstery. 'Mrs Chiswick did ask me to give this letter to Charlie. Personally. On Sunday.'

'Ah, yes. I quite understand. But Charlie's confirmation will have to be postponed. We are in mourning. I may take the children out to Plenty Station for a while. It's too upsetting for them to be here. In the house. Where it happened.'

'Very sensible of you, Samuel. But that still leaves me with my obligation to your late wife. Perhaps you could bring Charlie to see me tomorrow evening, then I'd at least be keeping to the letter of the law, so to speak. I wouldn't want to let her down.'

The Judge stood up, towering over the cleric. 'My wife relinquished her rights when she took her own life. I won't have my son upset any further. As I said, this it not the time to be suddenly confronting him with words from the grave. Give me the letter, Archdeacon, and allow me to choose the right time to broach the subject with my son.'

The letter safely in his hand, Samuel wasted no time getting rid of the cleric, then he went back to the parlour, closing the door behind him. With a sigh of relief he leant against the door, sweat coursing from every pore.

'What the hell did she write?' he charged the empty room.

He lit a cigar to steady his nerves. For a while there he'd thought he might have to resort to the force of law to prise this pathetic scrap of paper in its fancy envelope from that bumptious stickynose. And thank God the archdeacon hadn't opened it.

But why would he need to? He'd have been there hovering over Charlie, taking in every word.

The Judge took an ivory letter opener from the inlaid bureau by the window and slit open the envelope.

'What have you got to say?' he demanded of her. 'A-bleating about your terrible life, eh? About how bloody hard done by you were? What a horrible husband you had? Cuts no ice with me. Do you know how many of these whinings I've heard in the courts?'

In control now, he puffed on the cigar, almost able to prophesy what she'd written.

'And do you know what?' he said. 'When suicide notes are read, people say: "Poor thing." And then they go away and forget. They forget, Hannah! They'll forget you. They'll be too busy enjoying the scandal. Is that what you wanted to do? Cause a scandal?'

The first lines of her hastily scribbled note to Charlie were expected. They ran true to form.

My darling Charlie.

This is to tell you that your mother loves you and Clover very much.

'Of course you do, Hannah,' he sneered. 'That's why you left them.'

I have to go away, but please believe I'll always be with you.

The Judge scanned the next line and fell back with a bump into a hard chair. 'The bloody bitch! No wonder she tried to get this to Charlie before I saw it.'

Every person, Charlie, is entitled to know their heritage, so this is why, while I can, I have to tell you that your father is Vern Holloway of Fairlea Station via Toowoomba. And ask your forgiveness.

Vern Holloway? That overbred dandy! So he was the nigger in the woodpile!

He'd thought she was just baiting him with that story in her drunken state. The bloody bitch! Holloway probably didn't even know. Or care.

'How dare she tell Charlie!' the Judge fumed. 'He's my son! He's mine!'

The rest of the letter spoke of her love for them again, of dear, sweet Clover. Maudlin rubbish.

He lit a match and burned the letter and the envelope, allowing the ash to gather in a black marble ashtray.

'Charlie's my son,' he said again. 'Foiled, Hannah! He's my son and no one can take him away from me. You can go to hell by your own hand.'

Nevertheless, he was feeling shaky at his narrow escape. What if Charlie had read this? Would he have gone in search of Holloway? Would he have preferred the company of a wealthy squatter to Samuel's own? And would that archdeacon have kept his mouth shut? Samuel doubted it.

That would have been Hannah's revenge. Scandal heaped upon scandal. But it hadn't worked.

He unlocked the door and pushed a button set in the panelled wall.

A maid looked in. 'Did you want something, sir?'

'Yes. I'd like tea. Where are the children?'

'They're over at Mrs MacReadie's house. She says they can stay tonight, too. If that's all right with you, sir?'

'Yes, let them stay, the poor bairns,' he said sadly, and she gave an understanding nod before ducking away.

Chapter Seven

The main storm had passed, leaving the countryside swathed in an eerie orange glow, the sun invisible beyond an atmosphere choked with dust.

Gus checked his watch. Six o'clock. But it could be noon or late afternoon for all a man could tell. Only a few hours ago the sand had thinned out, but the wind was still strong as dawn approached and they climbed out of the ditch to make for the scrub. While the trees were still taking a battering from the wind, swishing and swirling about them, anything was better than the discomfort and monotony of the long sleepless night. They emerged, dust-caked, to examine their mine. The first priority.

'We should have covered it,' Brodie said angrily. 'It's filled with sand now.'

Lester shrugged. 'Wouldn't have done any good. Some of the blokes thought of that, but the timber blew away and canvas only filled with sand and caved in.'

Gus stared about him, more out of curiosity than interest, because he had a new plan. Excitement was bubbling within him but he gave no hint of it. 'The field looks different now,' he said. 'It's all changed. Amazing!'

Windlasses had blown away, giving no indication now of the shafts. Mullock heaps were flattened or rearranged, and layers of sand were banked against new heaps. The tiny tent town far over to the edge of the scrub, close to the water hole, had been wrecked and a sheet of canvas hung wantonly from a high branch.

Their dray, at their own camp on the northern side of the open field, had stood its ground, and though covered in sand, the contents were intact.

'Well, let's clean up,' Brodie said. 'I swear I'm wearing a ton of sand meself.'

'Hang on.' Gus stopped him. 'We can't take Miss Chiswick down there. The men will be stripped. It's no place for a woman.'

She heard him. 'Don't worry, Gus. I'm used to this. If you'd bring me a bucket of water, that's all I need to wash up. Then I have to go. I'm worried about my father.'

'Wouldn't he have made it home?' Brodie asked her.

'Only with a lot of luck. The men from the station will already be out looking for us and they won't know we're over this way.'

'I don't think you'll be very popular with your father this morning,' Brodie said. 'Are you sure you'll be all right?'

'He'll get over it.'

She didn't sound too convinced, so Brodie offered to ride back with her. 'I'll apologise for the trouble here,' he added. 'Give him a chance to save face.'

Gus laughed. 'Take him with you, Miss Chiswick. He's a great persuader, is Brodie. He can talk the leg off an iron pot.'

'He'll be going some to get through to my father,' she said, 'but I would appreciate company in case he got caught in the storm. He could have had an accident.'

Gus thought it was very fine of her even to be caring about the old rascal, but then family bonds were strong. She would never have shot her father, he mused, but the bluff had worked because the Judge had mistaken her attitude for his own. Gus had no doubt that if push had come to shove the old man would have fired and they'd have had an ugly scene on their hands.

'We're grateful to you for intervening yesterday,' he said. 'The least we can do is have someone escort you home.'

He fetched her a bucket of water and placed it the other side of the dray, with a towel and soap and a large comb.

'The amenities aren't much,' he told her with a smile. 'But I'll leave you to it.'

He joined the others, swimming strongly across the wide water hole, and then back again when he saw some cattle trundling down to the water's edge. Why old Judge Chiswick made such a fuss was beyond him. The prospectors kept to the rules, leaving this side to his cattle. They never approached from the other direction anyway; the boulder-strewn incline to the ridge in this area was too much of a hazard. Besides, cattle could smell water. They wouldn't bypass it to climb the ridge where there was no water at all. He found the squatter's attitude dog-in-the-manger. Chiswick had no use for that land and didn't want anyone else there.

Gus smiled as he trod water, soaking away the dust. 'You won't get rid of me, Mr Chiswick,' he murmured smugly. 'Not now anyway.'

From his vantage point he could see either end of the water hole, about a half-mile long. It was obviously the remnants of a river that had once meandered through here, a long time ago, forcing channels through the sandstone until it made its escape over the ridge.

And that, of course, was why the prospectors were here. For opal to form, way back in time, there had to be water. The old hands had told him that this ridge had probably been pushed up by a convulsion in the earth's crust. Rivers didn't flow uphill. This water hole had collected its supply because it was sitting in a saddle of granite that had resisted centuries of erosion that had worn the ridge down to a low plateau. One of the men, who seemed to have studied geology, explained to Gus that long before the river was reduced to channels it had probably coursed strongly across this land towards the inland sea that no longer existed.

Looking to the north Gus realised that the ditch that had sheltered them through the night was probably a part of one of those ancient channels.

He found Lester lazing in the shallows, in no hurry to start work on this gloomy day.

'After breakfast, Brodie's taking Miss Chiswick back to her house,' he said.

Lester sat up. 'What do you mean? Can't she take herself back? We've got work to do. We've got to shovel out that bloody shaft.'

'Don't worry about that now.'

'Why not? Do you think it will empty itself out? And Brodie? He won't be going out of the goodness of his heart. He'll be trying to get into her pants.'

That had occurred to Gus but he wasn't concerned. 'That girl is streets in front of Brodie. She's lived out here in the bush surrounded by men all her life. Those women don't take any nonsense. You saw her in action yesterday.'

'So! She can get herself home.'

'No. I want Brodie out of the way. We're not reopening that shaft. I want to try somewhere else, but for the time being, just look as if we're only pottering about. Since we can afford to spare Brodie, no one is going to pay much attention to us.'

'Why would they?'

'Because I heard something. Last night. Not once, but several times. It's a wonder you blokes didn't hear it too.'

'I only heard the bloody wind screaming at me.'

'No. There was a definite clink. The same sound they've all been talking about. I heard it down that mine when Ginger Croft hit opal. That clinking sound. Like glass.'

'You're imagining things. Sand's got into your brain.'

'Maybe, but we have to make sure. We'll fossick quietly round there while they all think we're waiting for Brodie to come back.'

'Are you going to tell Brodie?'

'No fear. You know him. He'll be down there going berserk within minutes. He'll give the game away. I wasn't sure in the dark where the clinks came from . . .'

Lester still wasn't impressed. 'I'm putting in three months here and no longer. You probably heard the ring of a bridle and bit. We ought to stick to the job we've got.'

'Give me a day. We'll dust the walls and base of the ditch, then if we can't find anything I'll work there in my own time.'

'You won't find anything. We have to stay up on the ridge like everyone else. If we have to, I'd rather dig further out than down here.'

'A day,' Gus insisted.

In deference to the slow old horse that Brodie was riding, Clover took her time, keeping an eye out for her father.

The Irishman was charming, no doubt about that, and tidied up was also wildly handsome, with those keen blue eyes and the nicest smile. Nevertheless, she was suspicious. Miners, to her, were still vagrants. Ne'er-do-wells.

The three men had been kind to her during the night, trying to keep her as comfortable as possible, but she knew what a risk she'd taken. Charlie would have said she was stark staring mad to have bundled down with strangers. Clover, though, considered herself a good judge of men, and they'd seemed reliable, especially Gus.

Wait till I tell Salty, she thought as they headed across the plains. I met two handsome men in the one day! Chalk that up!

But she wouldn't tell Salty that for the first hour, stuck down there with three strange men, she'd been ready to bolt at any hint of a problem. Storm or no storm. She had an instinct for that sort of trouble, from experience. Like the time she'd found herself left with two new stockmen towards the end of a big muster, when there was a muck-up of shifts.

She'd been only seventeen. She'd seen no change in their attitude to her and she'd heard no remarks at all, but she'd known something was amiss. Known enough to stay on her side of the campfire with a loaded gun at her side. Known enough to disappear for a few minutes and remove the hobbles from her mount.

Then it had started.

'The girlie's got a gun,' one of them had laughed, moving towards her. 'You don't have to be scared of us. Do you want a drink? We've got a bottle here.'

'She's got to be the prettiest little filly in this neck of the woods,' the other man grinned. 'And not so little neither. We've plenty of time, we have. We can have a nice party here.'

'Keep away from me,' she warned. 'My brother will hear about this.'

'Oh, look out!' They seemed to find this hilarious. 'She's gonna tell on us!'

Clover couldn't recall the rest of the insulting, menacing conversation, just that she'd fired the gun from the ground and it had hit the billy of tea hanging over the campfire and made the most awful clanging noise, and one of the men had screamed. But she hadn't waited to find out why. She'd sprinted into the bush and was on that horse, riding bareback away from there as fast as she could go.

The stockmen disappeared and good riddance. Curly, a Plenty Station black tracker, examined the site and assured

Clover that she hadn't shot anyone. There were no signs of blood.

He'd grinned at her, bringing in the smashed billy. 'More like you burn 'em wid the hot water, missy.'

Oh yes. Clover was aware of men, but she'd learned to be more aware of situations.

She wasn't worried about this fellow Brodie. Only suspicious. He asked a lot of questions. About the station. How big it was. How many cattle. How many people lived there. And were there any more stations further west.

When she heard that question Clover was ashamed of herself. He really didn't know anything about these western properties and was obviously intrigued.

He'd said he'd worked at Fairlea Station, outside Toowoomba, and did she know it?

'I know of the station, and the Holloways. But I don't know them personally.'

When she realised he'd only been in Australia for such a short time she began to understand his curiosity.

'Are you truly telling me that there are more stations hundreds of miles on from here?'

'Until they run out of pasture,' she said. 'Then they hit the Simpson Desert but I've no idea how far that extends. I should know but I've forgotten.'

'And what's the other side?'

'Of the desert? The other side of Australia, I guess.'

'God Almighty! We're so far out now I thought we must be nearing another shore. They say it takes days to cross England. I always thought that was a fair way to travel.'

'Oh, now you're teasing me, Brodie. England's a big place.'

'So I thought, too. But I still don't know how people came to get land way out here and yonder. Who was selling it?'

'No one. The pioneers just got on their horses and their wagons and kept going until they found land no one had claimed, and then squatted on it for years, free of taxes, until the government surveyors turned up and made their claims legal. They got squillions of acres though, being first, and that's why our graziers are still called squatters.'

'Well, I'll be blowed! Is there any left? Land, I mean.'

'None worth the taking,' she laughed. 'I'm afraid you've missed the boat, Mr Court.'

'More than likely,' he said. 'But I won't do that with opal.'

'I don't know why you persist out there. Opal isn't worth all that hard work and deprivation.'

'That's where you're wrong. Ginger Croft, one of the miners there at the Ten Mile, had a strike recently.'

'I know. The buyer stayed overnight at our homestead. He said he paid fifteen quid for the lot and Croft went off all pleased with himself.'

'What did you say?' Brodie reined in his horse with a jerk. 'Fifteen pounds?'

'Yes.'

'Are you sure?'

'Of course I am. The buyer showed us the opal chunks. He had them in a sugar bag. They're very pretty but not valuable.'

Brodie was silent.

She glanced over at him. His dark features were well defined against this orange light, the beard jutting out over bony shoulders. For his size, he wasn't carrying any weight; he could do with some condition. But she supposed that hard work and poor rations on the opal fields would fine a man down.

She saw something odd in the distance and veered off to inspect it, but it was only an old saddle. Too old to have belonged to her father. Where was he?

A mob of cattle were gathered near a clump of trees, still head in for protection. Not trusting this strange light as yet.

Brodie caught up with her. 'Croft was a fool,' he muttered. 'His opal had plenty of colour.'

'The buyer said he'd given him a good price.'

'So he would. But you have to understand that fifteen quid is a lot to a man who's got nothing. Over a year that's six bob a week, and more than some earn. I know him. He'll be off blowing it all now, then he'll be back, broke, to start again.'

'Is that what all miners do?' Clover asked politely. Checking. The Judge had said they were hopeless spendthrifts.

'Not me! I'm not in this for fun. I'm a man of property.'

'You are?' she grinned. His sudden burst of arrogance had

surprised her, contrasting with his former amiability, but he seemed to think her reaction had been disbelief.

'I own a farm in Ireland,' he said, cross now, 'and a house in Toowoomba, which is bringin' me rent. So don't be thinkin' we're all no-hopers. I know what I'm doing.'

'Don't be so touchy! I didn't mean to offend you.'

When he didn't reply she shrugged and galloped on ahead. Men! she thought. No sense of humour. Always getting on their high horses about something. But she wouldn't pander to them. Never had. 'And I'm not about to start with Mr Court,' she said to herself. 'Let him stew.'

As they climbed the low hill leading to the home valley, two of the Plenty stockmen spotted them and galloped over.

'Where's the Judge?' the first man called, obviously disconcerted that the rider with her was a stranger.

'Isn't he home yet?'

'No. We've been out looking for you since sun-up.'

'Damn! I haven't seen him either. We were out at the ridge. I took shelter when the storm hit but he insisted on going home.'

'We thought you were out the other way,' he said, accusation in his voice.

'My father insisted we go to the ridge,' she countered. 'And he would have come home this way, or tried to. He probably ended up riding round in circles.'

Brodie interrupted them. 'I doubt it. Look over there.'

'Where?' they all seemed to ask in unison.

'Far along the hillside. There's a horse cutting down towards your fences. It's saddled.'

'Jesus!' the stockman yelled. He wheeled his horse and took off to collect the riderless animal.

Clover watched as he returned. 'It's my father's horse. So where is he?' She was suddenly very tired. 'I'll take this horse home,' she told the stockmen. 'You alert the rest of the men to cover that area. The horse would have made a beeline for home, so the Judge has to be out that way somewhere.'

'Let's go,' she said to Brodie, taking it for granted that he'd accompany her all the way to the house. It crossed her mind that she hadn't introduced him to the men, who would probably be curious about the stranger, but she couldn't be bothered about that now, she was too worried about her father. Guilt nagged. She kept telling herself that his own pig-headedness had placed him in this predicament, but she knew he'd blame her.

Brodie had expected yet another Queensland country homestead, the long, low, laid-back buildings of the west, seen even in town, that combined the comforts of large cottages with the necessity to bow to the climate, but this place was a disappointment.

It was a big house, as befitting the owners of this huge property, two storeys, built of sandstone, but it was ugly. The verandas and high balconies were laced with fussy wrought-iron railings; even the stone steps leading up to the open front door boasted unnecessary wrought-iron banisters. The roof was decorated with small blocks of sandstone, as if atop a fort. He had the impression that someone had gone to great lengths to impress, sparing no expense, but the overall result was, to him, most peculiar.

He sighed. The sandstone, what he could see of it, was beautiful, especially in the prevailing bright ochre light. It glowed.

But the house itself gave him an uneasy feeling. Set among drab trees, it had an air of tragedy, as if mysteries lurked behind the skirts of the frilly façade.

An elderly woman met them at the door, throwing her arms about Clover, relieved to see her and at the same time firing questions about her father.

Brodie learned, as Clover answered, that this was Salty, the housekeeper. He was shown into a dim, crowded parlour.

'Mr Court has to get back,' Clover said, putting a stop to the questions. 'Do you think you could put us up something to eat?'

'Yes, dear, of course.' She bustled away.

'Don't mind me,' Brodie said. 'I can go on my way. You'll be busy now. And there's your father to worry about.'

Clover threw herself into a chair, dragging off her riding boots to reveal that she was wearing men's socks.

She seemed to treat Brodie as if she'd known him all her life. He remembered, smarting a little, her rebuke: 'Don't be so touchy!' That had startled him. He wasn't accustomed to strange women telling him off. For that

205

matter, he wasn't accustomed to women being so chilly with him at all.

Clover put her feet up on a low table. 'Do you want a drink? I'm dying of thirst. Over there on the sideboard, Brodie. Do me a favour and pour the drinks. Whisky in the decanter and water in that silver jug.'

He obeyed, the thought of a fine whisky, which it was, overcoming his bewilderment.

She gulped half the drink. 'Oh! That's good. Thank you for delivering me home, Brodie. I really do appreciate the thought. Until now I didn't realise how tired I was. We didn't get any sleep last night, did we?'

Suddenly she laughed, glancing at the door. 'Just as well Salty didn't hear that; she'd think the worst!'

Brodie was feeling out of place in this big house. He'd seen his reflection in the glass of a cabinet, and that was no boost to his confidence. His black hair was too long and his beard was an untidy thatch. Here in company, he knew he looked like a wild man. No wonder the housekeeper had frowned at the sight of him.

'You must be worried about your father,' he offered, for something to say.

She sighed. 'To tell you the truth, I don't know. I'll be so damned unpopular when he does get home I'll be wishing they'd left him there. On the other hand, he is my father.'

In her boots, Brodie mused, having pulled a gun on the formidable old coot, he'd be happier if they brought him home feet first. He wondered then who'd own this great estate.

'Your men will find him, though, won't they?'

'Oh yes. Dead or alive, they'll bring him in now that the horse has turned up. We use black trackers.'

At that blatant remark Brodie choked on his drink. Some of the liquid must have gone down the wrong way.

'Is it just today?' he asked, deciding to go with her far from formal ways. 'Or do you not get along with your father?'

He studied her while she considered her reply. She was no beauty, with that lank brown hair and tanned skin, and the rough shirt and trousers didn't help, but her long legs clamped, ankle over, on the table had a certain appeal. And she had a nice mouth, but the brown eyes were cool and direct.

In all, he decided, though too tall for a woman, she was built to scale.

'It's not a matter of getting along with him,' she said at length. 'I could if I wanted to. But the trouble is, I dislike him.'

'Ah. I see.'

'No you don't. You're just being cautious. You don't want to back the wrong horse, do you?'

'It's none of my business,' he said, checking her.

'I suppose not. Well, I'm not riding out again today. The men know what they're doing. Why don't you stay the night? You must be tired too. If you leave at daybreak you'll feel better.'

Brodie allowed himself to be persuaded. He couldn't pass up the offer of a decent meal and a comfortable bed for a change, and then there was Clover herself. He wondered about her, hoping that she might be another Vivien and make the first move. And by God she'd be welcome.

The housekeeper showed him to his room, Charlie's room, she said, having accepted that the stranger had protected Clover during that storm. She showed him to the bathroom, where he found scissors to trim his beetling eyebrows and beard, even his hair, in a rough attempt to appear neat. He savoured a long hot bath, looking forward to dining, in state, with Clover.

They ate in the large, well-appointed kitchen with Salty. Good food but no fuss. No soft lights and no liquor.

Men came in and out, unabashed that Clover Chiswick was dining, to report on the search, to ask Salty for more oil for their lanterns, to request blankets in case they found the boss on this chilly night, and to hear from Clover how she'd dodged the storm. It was like eating in the village square, except that no one seemed to notice him.

Brodie offered to stay up to wait for news of the Judge, but Clover sent him off to bed. 'There's nothing you can do. I'm not going out myself, I'd only get in the way. We'll be up very early, so get some sleep.'

Never had he slept in a bed as comfortable as this. All his life Brodie had been relegated to the single bunk, at home and out here, not to mention the hard lines of tent living.

Charlie's bed was wide and firm. And long enough for

a man to stretch his legs without his feet hanging over the edge. Heaven on earth, it was! Though he tried to stay awake in the forlorn hope that Clover might put her head round the door, just to make sure he was comfortable – and provide him with a chance to take matters a little further – he could not. For once, opportunity had let him down. But there was time enough yet, he smiled benignly. He would find reasons to call here again. Clover lacked the beauty and the exciting sexuality of Vivien, but she was an intriguing girl. And single. No complications here.

Clover would have laughed had she heard the visitor's thoughts on her situation. Now that their father had descended on them, she considered that her life had become very complicated. She wished she could get away from the Judge, but she loved the station and was determined to stay. She'd been hoping that, at the last minute, Charlie would do what he wanted, rather than trying to please Samuel, and renege on his promise to join up.

But that hadn't happened. And worse. After perfunctory drills, his regiment of eager volunteers had sailed for South Africa, where, he'd written, they'd undergo further training before going into battle.

Battle! The word terrified her. She tried not to think about it.

Had Brodie given the matter more thought, not his strong suit, he'd have realised that Clover and Vivien had much in common. Both were from moneyed families, but neither of them was in control of the wealth unless something happened to their menfolk.

The housekeeper woke Brodie in the morning with a cup of tea and hot buttered toast.

'Miss Chiswick said to let you sleep,' Salty said. 'She was up and out at first light. They're still searching for the Judge, poor man. It's a terrible worry.'

But to Brodie it was simply an anticlimax.

He'd expected to see Clover this morning, and now he had to ride back to the ridge without so much as a fare-thee-well. And no invitation to return.

As he rode away from the almost deserted station buildings, he hoped the old man had come to grief falling off his horse, so that the prospectors would have no more trouble from him. But even that was not to be.

He met some riders on the trail who informed him that the boss had been found.

'Is he well?' he asked, feigning anxiety.

'Well enough,' they laughed. 'Cranky as all get out. We thought he'd been thrown but the horse just got away on him. He's dried out, and got a few bumps and bruises from falling about, but otherwise he'll live. Tough as old boots, he is.'

Disappointed, Brodie set out on the two-hour journey back to the ridge.

'What the hell's going on?' he asked, finding that Gus and Lester had marked off a claim site, fifteen yards by eight, round the ditch where they'd spent the night.

'Easier to dig here than where we were,' Lester replied casually.

'You're mad!' Brodie exploded. 'Can't I turn my back without having you slack off?'

Two men, passing by, nodded sympathetically.

'What about our mine over there?' Brodie continued. 'Have you just left it?'

'Full of sand.'

'And the others aren't? You should have dug it out.'

'While you were having a good time?' Lester grinned. 'I bet you'd stay the night. Was she too much of a temptation, lad?'

'She was nothing of the sort! Nothing like that.'

Furious, he swung down from the horse and tramped over to their camp, where Gus was making tea.

'Have you lost your senses, leaving our mine?' he demanded.

Gus handed him a mug of black tea. 'Well done, Brodie. You've given us just the reaction we needed. We don't want anyone snooping round just yet. Now calm down while I tell you. We've struck colour.'

'What? Where?'

'In the wall of that ditch.'

'I don't believe you.'

'We don't want to give any hint yet. Not until we see which way it's running.'

Brodie was confused, still not believing him. 'Show me where.'

209

'No need. This ought to be a start.' He placed some lumps of opal set in whitened clay on the grass beside him.

'Oh my God!' Brodie almost shouted, trying to keep his voice down. He picked them up. 'They're beautiful. Bloody beautiful! There's scarlet in them, too, and patterns. Jesus!'

Gus smiled. 'I heard it the other night. Lester found it. They say opal is the only precious stone with its beauty intact in its natural state, and I've taken that for granted. Until now.' He jumped up and shook Brodie's hand. 'But when it's your own, it's the most marvellous thing in the world.' He shed his cool manner and leapt about, wild with excitement.

'We've done it, Brodie! We've done it! We've only found a patch so far, but it's looking good.'

The walk from the camp back to the ditch seemed to have stretched by miles as Brodie forced himself to stroll over, every step stiff, one foot after the other, but at last he plunged down with them, astonished to see the fiery glow deep in the rock above a shallow ledge. It was true. They had an opal mine!

For a week the Judge was confined to his room by Salty, who demanded he rest properly. He was suffering from exposure and his face was peeling from the onslaught of sand, but it was his eyes that concerned her. Eye infections were common out here – even the Aborigines had no defence against this blight – and sandstorms such as the one they'd just experienced were dreaded. Sand and dust being generally accepted as the cause.

She'd sent for the doctor, who could only leave eye drops and ointment and recommend that the Judge keep his eyes bandaged. It had been a job to keep him in bed, but he finally accepted her warnings that he could be blinded and remained in the darkened room, shouting orders and instructions at the top of his voice.

Clover had said they'd had some sort of a row at the Ten Mile, in front of the miners, and had passed it off as unimportant, but it wasn't so with the Judge. Salty hated having to sponge those mucus-ridden eyes every hour that he was awake, because she was forced to listen to his furious denunciation of his daughter and 'the scum', threatening all sorts of vengeance when he was on his feet again. She hoped that he'd cool down by the end of the week, when his eyes cleared up, but there was no sign of that.

She suggested to Clover that she might go into Charleville to visit friends for a little while, but the stubborn girl refused to budge. 'He'll get over it,' she said.

But he didn't. He refused to have anything to do with his daughter, refusing to allow her to take her meals with him in the dining room.

'That's no loss,' she shrugged. 'I'd rather eat in the kitchen anyway.'

Finally, after avoiding each other for the following week, a terrible row erupted.

'Get out of my house!' he shouted at Clover. 'You're not fit to bear the name of Chiswick!'

'Oh, shut up, you old fool! If I hadn't stopped you, someone could have been killed. Threatening armed men with a gun! You're lucky you didn't get shot, you were deliberately provoking them.'

'I'll have them off my property too,' he yelled.

'All you've done is push them to register the claims, to make mining legal.'

Salty was listening outside. She heard him slap Clover and rushed in.

Clover was standing by the piano, a hand to her face and still defiant. 'I'm not my mother,' she spat at him. 'You do that again and I will shoot you. Self-defence, Judge,' she taunted him. 'That'd go down even in your court. So you back off.'

'Oh, Clover, please!' Salty wailed. 'You mustn't talk like that. She didn't mean it, Judge. She's just overwrought.'

Clover flung out of the room with a parting shot. 'You ought to put him back to bed, Salty. He's a screw loose.'

She was too much for the Judge, who was accustomed to obedience from all about him. He sank into a chair. 'Did you hear that, Salty?' he wailed. 'My own daughter speaking to me like that! I don't know what I'm going to do with her.'

From what Salty had heard, it seemed that Clover had somehow put a stop to a nasty situation out there, so she had little sympathy for the old man. He was genuinely shocked. Clover had stood up to him and beaten him! It seemed to Salty that he was more upset by the reversal of roles – that anyone had defied him – than by what was actually said, and she smiled grimly. Time someone got your measure, you old bully, she thought.

'You just sit quietly, I'll get you a cup of tea,' she told him. 'Clover's just a chip off the old block. She doesn't like to be bossed any more than you do. She'll cool down.'

He sulked for the rest of the day, but the next morning he was up early and left the homestead with a party of stockmen to round up more cattle.

Frank Dobson, stockman, and a horseman of note in the district, was anxious to please. He was a rangily built man, long legs, long arms and a long face to match. 'Horseface', the other men called him, behind his back, because Frank was a mean and sour character totally lacking in the humour that sustained them on the lonely outback station.

There was a rumour afoot that Slim McLure, foreman of Plenty Station, was considering joining up to do his bit in the war against the Boers.

This was the best news Frank had ever heard. He'd been working on Plenty Station for five years and he reckoned that when Slim left he was the best man to take over his job. And do it better! Of that he had no doubt. Slim, he thought, was too easy-going, too soft on all the blokes who worked this station. They needed a strong hand to keep them in line and he was just the lad to see to it. He'd even go so far as to say, were he asked, that the motley mob of station hands, including the layabout blacks, would be glad to see someone like him in charge. A real leader of men.

His first move was to fall into step beside the Judge as he headed for the stables after the morning call.

'Good to see you up and about again, Judge!'

'Eh? Yes,' the boss replied, unused to such a hearty greeting.

'By God, that was a smart move, holing up in that storm and sending the horse on home. The boys all say it takes a real bushman to know the tricks.'

It didn't bother Frank that all of them, himself included, had really thought the Judge was a bloody fool. He should have taken shelter on the ridge, as his daughter had. From the way he'd been raving about Clover's ingratitude on the way home, everyone was curious as to what had happened

212

out there, but Clover hadn't said a word. Slim figured that they'd had a row about whether or not to make for home, and she'd stayed put while her father went off on his own.

'I was born out here,' the Judge was saying, pleased by the compliment. 'Born and bred. Just because I have been pursuing my legal practice in Toowoomba doesn't mean I can't handle station work. One doesn't forget these things. I've seen many a storm. Fire and flood too. Experience, that's what counts when the chips are down.'

Frank was right beside him when the Judge chose four men to ride with him and was the first to be given the honour.

They set off on the same route that had seen them bring the Judge in from his sandstorm tribulations.

'Where are we going?' one of the men growled.

'Probably going back for his hat,' another grinned.

'He was out this way . . .' Frank began.

'I'll say he was. Bloody lost!' came the comment, and the others laughed.

Frank scowled. 'The boss saw a lot of cleanskins in a herd when he was out this way, so today we cut them out and bring them in. Save a lot of time later.'

'And later we have to go back for the rest!'

Frank knew that the stockman did have a point, but the Judge was boss and he was determined to make a good impression. He would do exactly as he was told and no arguments. He didn't care if they had to muster the same cattle fifty times; he was sticking by the Judge from now on.

Chiswick set a fast pace, and within an hour they were ploughing through the bush in search of unbranded cattle.

As they expected, there were mobs of cattle in this area but not too many unbranded, only the usual number of calves whose mothers weren't too keen on this interference.

The men grumbled. 'He said there were strays here, full grown; we'll be lucky if we can find a half-dozen.'

Frank reported to the Judge. 'The cleanskins you saw must have moved further west.' That was easier than telling him he must have made a mistake.

His boss rode among the trees, peering at the scattered herd, the huge lumbering beasts twitching nervously. One bull pawed the ground angrily and then galloped away.

213

'They're in good nick,' he said to Frank, seemingly unconcerned that they were wasting their time.

'They certainly are,' Frank agreed.

'We'll bring them all in, then.'

For a second Frank hesitated. There were more than two hundred cattle here. Even if they did drive them back, calves and all, what would they do with them then?

'Where are we taking them?' he asked, giving the Judge a chance to think again.

'Leave that to me,' the Judge snapped. 'Round them up and bring them out this way.'

'Righto!' Frank wheeled away, his whip cracking to get the rest of the men on the job.

He could hear them shouting and swearing as they crashed through the scrub, rousing the quieter cattle and chasing after the tougher beasts that tried to dodge out of their way. Eventually they had a herd moving. Frank knew that quite a few cattle had escaped the round-up because the men were only half-hearted about this job, but since the Judge hadn't noticed it wasn't his problem.

'Which way?' he asked the boss.

'We'll take them right over to the Gurelbah ponds.'

'Right!' Frank said, and dropped back to ask one of the old hands. 'Where the hell are the Gurelbah ponds?'

The old stockman pushed his hat back on his head and spat. 'That's what the Ten Mile water hole used to be called. What are we taking them there for? They'll have water but not much feed. As soon as we leave them they'll turn about and come back here.'

'I just do as I'm told.'

'Yeah. Well, keep it slow or the calves will get tangled up.'

The pointless drive continued, with the Judge riding up front near the lead.

After a while it seemed to Frank that the boss was pushing the cattle off course, and eventually he had to say something or wear the blame.

'Watch what you're doing,' he shouted at one of the stockmen, rather than criticise Chiswick. 'Keep off the high ground.'

Immediately the Judge countermanded his order. 'Stay on course. I'm running this show, Dobson.'

'Yes, but the water hole is down that way. It's getting a bit rocky up here.'

Then he was sorry he'd spoken. The Judge turned on him. 'Kindly mind your own business. It's quicker this way. A water hole has two sides, some several, in fact. It is my water hole and there's no reason why my cattle should be confined to one side. If there is, Dobson, I'd like to hear it.'

Frank had no further comment to make. He dropped back to tail the heaving, shoving herd as the Judge pushed it relentlessly along the great sandy ridge.

The sandstorm had come and gone. The sky had resumed its hard blue and the leaves on the sparse trees seemed to crackle in the dry heat. Rock wallabies leapt for their lives on to high, jutting rocks and then stopped to turn and survey the moving mass of cattle as they pushed past.

They were moving faster now, and Frank shouted to a stockman on the right flank to slow up, but no one heard him. He spurred his horse to the outskirts of the mob, cursing the rough terrain, and had almost caught up to the Judge when he saw him raise his rifle.

A sixth sense told him what was about to happen, and forgetting his resolve to pander to the boss he screamed: 'No!'

Too late. The shot spooked the lead cattle into a run, and the rest of the herd took off after them, forging forward, stampeding. Out of control!

They called their mine the Firefly, for its twinkling beauty under candlelight.

The seam was almost four inches wide and spread into the rock like a wash of molten colour, as indeed it must have been eons ago – water washing into a crevice, crystallising, coloured by minerals and forming this wonder of gems.

Carefully they gouged away the surrounding rock to follow the narrow, uneven seam, finding that it sloped gently to the right.

As soon as they altered their outside claim-markers, the other men came running. 'What have you found?'

Brodie couldn't contain himself any more. 'Opal!' he shouted. 'The prettiest you ever saw! I knew it! I always knew I'd find it.'

'Except you didn't,' Lester grinned, working happily for a

change. 'Gus and me found it. We did, while he was away romancin' the squatter's daughter.'

Soon they were displaying their treasures, sunning themselves in the congratulations and envy of their friends.

'You can be lucky,' Mike Ryan said to Lester. 'I've been on this dunghill for nearly six months and haven't struck anything but potch.'

'Luck?' Lester pondered. 'Some men are born bloody lucky. I wouldn't say it to his face, give him a swelled head, but Brodie's got the touch. I swear the bugger's got a four-leafed clover in his pocket.'

'How come?'

'He keeps falling on his feet, takes no effort on his part. Things just go his way, jobs, women, money . . . That's why I decided to stick with him, so some can rub off on me.'

'Well, it has paid off.'

'Sure has. Listen, though . . . Brodie said that Ginger only got fifteen quid for his opal. Looked to me to be worth more than that.'

'He was eager for the cash. To get more you have to take them to an expert to have them shaped and polished. And to really cash in it's better to send them to England or Germany, where they outclass everything in sight.'

'Is that so?'

Lester didn't bother to pass this information on to Brodie and Gus. One day he would have his own mine, his own supply of opals, and there'd be nothing to stop him taking his stones to England himself. He smiled smugly. Why invite competition?

Work on the Firefly mine was slow but sure, as they dug deeper and deeper under the seam, keeping pace with it, gouging from the roof above them. The seam of colour was thinning out, but that only made them more careful, picking quietly to prise loose the precious gems.

They sat for hours sorting the whitened chunks of stone, arguing over the relative values of the various pieces. There were no large lumps of opal as they'd hoped, it had come away in small pieces, as if the earth had shaken the seam at some stage. Quite a few were whiskery, feathered with fine cracks just as Willi Schluter had warned, and therefore worthless, but they had enough of the good stuff to be filling two saddlebags. Enough of the good stuff to be turning it over, night after night, by lamplight, for the sheer joy of watching the flashes of scarlet and green and gold and claiming they could see patterns. Patterned opals with good colour being the most prized of all.

Since that sandstorm had come bellowing from the dry interior of the continent, the heat had increased and the miners worked from early morn to knock off by midday. They escaped the worst of the heat by retiring to their camps for a few hours to attend to their chores or rest in the shade, gathering strength for a later stint with pick and shovel.

It was on one of these afternoons, when Brodie was stretched out, dozing, under the dray, that he heard a shot. Or thought he did. He listened for a while but no one else reacted. All was quiet at the Ten Mile, and there was no answering shot.

Then he heard a familiar noise. A rumbling. For a few minutes he wondered about that, and then, as it increased in volume, it hit him. Hadn't he worked all that time as a stockman? No wonder the thudding noise was so familiar. It was cattle.

He sat up with a jerk, banging his head, and stumbled out, cursing.

Cattle? Up here? Where?

Closer. They seemed to be crashing through the scrub behind him. But why?

'Oh Christ,' he yelled. 'The water hole!'

At the same time Gus realised what was happening. He kicked Lester awake and ran to grab Mac, but the old horse was well aware of the danger. As soon as Gus untied his halter, Mac was bolting further up the ridge.

Brodie's priority was his precious opals. He leapt on to the dray and grabbed the saddlebags from under a pile of goods, then jumped free, and was running with Lester as the herd of wild cattle, heads dipping ferociously, came lumbering madly through their camp.

The men shouted angrily as some of the cattle barged against their dray, overturning it, but their shouts turned to rage as the animals emerging from the bush spread out over the clearing, gathering speed. On the far side, amid all the dust, they could see that cattle were charging towards the Firefly mine, their mine.

Some horsemen emerged, riding like mad, desperately trying to slow the run, keeping the herd at least on the lower slope of the ridge to prevent them from falling into the shafts that pockmarked the opal field. But the low campsites were trampled, miners running for their lives, as the thirsty beasts hurtled down to the water hole, plunging in to spread out along the banks and stop, snorting and lowing in the shallows, as if wondering what that had all been about.

The rush was over in minutes and Brodie hurtled down the slope to the mine. A huge bullock, its head askew, neck broken, lay on the floor of what was once their diggings, covered by an avalanche of rocky earth. As they had dug into the wall, the trio had half filled the ditch with mullock rather than drag it to the surface, and the weight of the beasts pounding over or swerving about their mine had done the rest. What remained was a flattened dent in that patch of ground. The markers were gone. The mine was gone.

Frantically, without bothering even to glance around them, all three men grabbed shovels and began to dig, each one knowing in his heart what they would find. Each one thinking of the hours they'd spent gouging inch by inch about that precious seam, that now lay crushed somewhere down there.

Panting with fatigue at this furious effort, Gus stood back, leaning on his shovel, to mop the dirt and sweat from his face.

He saw a lone horseman waiting some distance away, just sitting there, a solitary figure, giving no indication of concern. Wiping his eyes for a clearer view, Gus recognised the man in the big hat and white dustcoat.

'By God, it's Chiswick!' he growled, and throwing aside the shovel ran back to their camp.

He ignored their trampled belongings and grabbed a rifle that was hanging from the side of the overturned dray, fossicked about for bullets and loaded the gun on the run.

He was shouting at Chiswick as he stumbled on over the rough ground. 'That was no accident, you bastard! I'll get you!'

His first shot missed, and the Judge wheeled his horse to canter out of range, stopping again as if to provoke him to try again.

Frank Dobson didn't know what to do now that the cattle were loitering quietly by the water hole. Was he supposed to move them on or leave them here? He rode quietly and carefully through the wrecked camps, pretending not to hear the angry shouts of the miners. This was what Charlie should have done a year ago. Charlie had been too soft on these trespassers, but the old man knew what to do and he didn't waste time talking!

Frank was impressed by the cunning of the old bloke, not doubting now that this had been his intent right from the start, while his men were thinking he was dotty.

Not him, Frank mused. He's the boss and he's letting them all know. And he's within his rights to drive his cattle anywhere he likes on his property. This'll shift the fossickers, and if it don't, we can always come back with another herd.

The other three stockmen had dismounted and were moving apologetically through the battered camps, picking up pots and pans and scattered goods in a haphazard manner, bearing the abuse of the owners, so Frank left them to it.

He saw one of the miners tearing down the hill towards the Judge, carrying a rifle. Instantly he spurred his horse and raced to defend the boss, running the miner down and shouldering him aside after he'd fired a shot that, fortunately, missed.

'What do you think you're doing?' he shouted.

'You bastards wrecked our mine!' the big fair-haired bloke yelled at him. 'Chiswick gave the orders, didn't he?'

'Who says so? We were mustering and something spooked the leaders. There was a run, that's all. We tried to stop it.'

'The hell you did. Someone could have been killed.'

'No one was, so quit your bleating. And put that gun down or we'll have to take it from you.'

'I'd like to see you try.'

'Suit yourself.' Frank shrugged and rode on towards the Judge, knowing he wouldn't be shot in the back.

The Judge smiled at Frank's approach, a mean, thin smile but Frank didn't care; he was in the good books.

'The cattle quiet?' asked the Judge.

'Yes, boss. Do you want us to move them on now?'

'No, leave them.'

'The miners will hunt them out.'

'I doubt it. But if so they'll be doing your job for you.

Anyway, when they've cooled off, the cattle will wander back this way for a feed. They won't go on up the ridge. Call your men; we're going home.'

Your men! Frank liked that. He rode back a short way, sitting tall in the saddle, then he put two fingers to his lips and gave a shrill whistle, summoning *his* men.

The old stockman, Barney Tait, was the last to retreat. He stopped by the two diggers who were waiting for their mate, the one toting a gun, to return.

'Sorry about this, mates,' he said, peering down at the bullock that had come to grief. 'At least you've got a free feed there.'

'We ought to shoot the bloody cattle,' one of them spat, his face and hair grey with dust.

'Don't do that,' Barney warned. 'A bad move. He'd have a good excuse to get you locked up for a long time.'

The third man strode back, fuming. 'Get out of here!' he shouted at Barney, waving the rifle about. 'Don't try to tell me that was an accident! He deliberately stampeded the cattle in our direction!'

'You're right, son, it was no accident, if knowin' that makes you feel better.'

He put the gun down. 'We'll beat the bugger. We'll get a permit.'

Barney shook his head. 'Don't bank on it. You have to get them from the local police and they won't cross the Judge. They'll bring it to him for approval, you can bet your boots on that. His land. Can't see him signing.'

'Well, what can we do?'

'I dunno,' Barney said. 'Maybe pray for the safe return of Charlie Chiswick.'

This time, the assault on their meagre possessions was too much for most of the prospectors, and a party was held to mark their departure. They all congregated round a large fire where the bullock, prime meat, was roasting on a spit. No one had any intention of leaving until he had his share of the grand feast.

The last of the liquor, mainly rum, was unearthed from hiding places and the bitter anger was soon softened as the designated cook sliced juicy cuts on to tin plates and the sizzling aroma of roasting meat filled the air.

Mike Ryan sat with the men of the now extinct Firefly mine, savouring a huge steak.

'Ah! Bloody beautiful!' he said, juices dripping into his beard. 'Best meat I've tasted in years.'

'We should have grabbed more while we had the chance,' Lester said, finishing his steak and holding his dish out for more. 'We were mad to be chewing on salt beef with a bloody butcher's shop walking all around us.'

'We'd only need to shoot one,' Brodie agreed, 'skin and butcher it, share the meat and bury the evidence. Chiswick wouldn't miss one. They've got thousands on this station.'

'Yeah. We should have thought of it before,' Lester agreed. 'And now he owes us.'

'Sure he does,' Brodie growled. 'We won't be short of meat from now on, I can tell you that. You'd be in it, wouldn't you, Mike?'

'If I was staying I'd be the first to cut one down for you, just to pay Chiswick back.'

'You're pulling out?'

'Yes. I'm not doing any good here. I'll be coming with you.'

'But we're not leaving,' Brodie said.

Mike looked from one to another. 'I thought you were.'

'No fear. He's not going to push us out. We're reopening Firefly from the east, working back to the seam.'

Gus sopped beef gravy from his dish with a hunk of fresh damper. 'No we're not,' he said quietly. 'It's no use, Brodie. We've dug all round that seam, it was just a pocket, a crevice.'

'It's finished,' Lester added.

'Don't you fellers know the old saying: where there's smoke there's fire. So where there's opal there's more.'

'Tell that to Ginger Croft. He never found any more.'

Brodie appealed to Mike. 'You know there's more opal here. There has to be!'

'Of course there is. But it's the luck of the draw. You could dig for a month of Sundays and miss a patch inches away.'

Brodie turned to the others. 'You see? We can't go!'

'We came for opal,' Gus said quietly, 'and we've got a good

swag of it. You talk as if we've failed, Brodie. Some of our pieces are worth plenty. Give over, man. This was your idea and you were right. We're going home heroes.'

'We're not going anywhere. We'll reopen Firefly and we'll go just that much further in all the shafts these blokes have deserted.'

Gus shook his head. Brodie made it sound as if the miners who were leaving were deserting their posts instead of giving up in despair. 'Lester and I have talked it over, and it's time we pulled out.'

Lester agreed. 'We've been here months, Brodie. I've had enough of this bloody mullock heap. I want out and I want my share.'

'No. We're not leaving. Don't you understand? There's money here. A fortune. Sure, we're bringing in good colour, but what have we got? Enough to keep us for a year or so. I'm after the big one. A rich shelf or a chunk of opal that will knock their eyes out. I'll find it. Just give me time.'

'You didn't even find the last lot,' Lester sneered. 'Your luck is good, I been thinking about that, but yours is catch luck. Someone throws, you catch.' Lester was becoming cranky in his determination to win this argument. 'Like the bloke in Ireland who sent you out here, the toff in Brisbane who took you to Fairlea, the woman who put up the cash, Gus and me . . . You couldn't have got out here without us. You won't get no place on your own, so give it away, Brodie. We're goin' home to Toowoomba.'

He saw the scowl on Brodie's face and added, 'There's a lot of pretty girls in Toowoomba. Me and Gus are missing them. And you've got your lady back there . . .'

'No. We stay.'

They argued with Brodie for days, as other miners packed up and left, but he wouldn't relent. They were eventually convinced that Brodie had caught the fever, well known among gold prospectors, that kept them beavering on until they joined the ranks of broken old stagers who hung about diggings.

They even mentioned this syndrome to Brodie, but he wouldn't have it. 'You're wrong. I'll make me bloody fortune and no one will stop me.'

'Think of Willi Schluter,' Gus said. 'Do you want to end up like that?'

Brodie stared at them. 'Don't you see? Willi has chosen his life. He's happy with what he does. That's not for me. I'll be rich, I tell you. I just need more time.'

'It'd be quicker and more comfortable to marry a rich woman,' Lester laughed. 'And you're just the lad for that, Brodie. We're going home with a bank, now don't be mad.'

'I'm not mad!' Brodie shouted. This argument with Lester seemed to him to be developing into the same argument he'd had with Michael. 'You two just want to cut me loose,' he yelled. 'You've had this planned from the start. You want to take everything and leave me with nothing.'

'Not at all,' Gus said. 'We're just trying to . . .'

'To do what's best!' Brodie sneered. 'Is that it? And haven't I heard that line before? You know I won't leave so you're gonna take the opal and dump me. I'm awake to you two!'

Gus was a bigger man than Michael and his punch almost split Brodie's head open. Or that was what it felt like. He lay on the patchy grass, unable to retaliate, unable to lift his head. He could feel his jaw swelling but the rest of his head was solid stone, still jarred from the impact.

Lester threw a bucket of water on to his face and squatted beside him. 'Haven't I told you not to upset Gus?' he grinned.

In the end they compromised. Mike Ryan was called in to adjudicate in the complicated process of dividing the Firefly opals into three parcels, since Brodie refused to leave.

'You'll be here on your own,' Mike warned Brodie. 'That's bad joss. You need a mate in case of accident. And you can't do much without a partner at the windlass.'

'Yes I can,' Brodie said stubbornly. 'I'll be investigating every bloody inch you blokes have left after I pick the beauties out of Firefly. And there won't be any accidents. I'm a careful man, Ryan, be sure of that.'

They fixed the wheel of the dray that had been dislodged when it was overturned by the cattle, and drove down to the miners' store to buy fresh supplies for Brodie and enough to take Gus and Lester back to Charleville. Then they spent the rest of the day yarning with other miners and travellers over welcome pints of beer.

On their return, the deserted opal fields seemed a weird place by moonlight, and Gus tried to make Brodie see sense.

'You can't stay here on your own, you haven't even got any transport. We have to take the dray; we wouldn't make it on foot.'

'Then it's a fool you think I am,' Brodie retorted. 'I've sent a message to Miss Chiswick that I wish to buy a horse. And a saddle and rig. Money's money. She'll sell.'

'You've still got money?' Gus said, surprised, knowing that their combined funds had just about given out, even though the cost of living on the opal fields had been minimal, thanks to the plethora of game.

'That's my business,' Brodie growled, still furious with them for their lack of faith in him.

'I'm sorry it's turning out this way,' Gus said. 'I like you, Brodie. You go at things like a bull at a gate all the time, and you can be a mean bastard, always making points for yourself, but you're a good man. Somewhere there. And that counts for something.'

'I don't need your preaching, Gus Kriedemann. Go back to your bakery. You'll never amount to nothing because you haven't got the guts for it, not like I have.' He strode away to stare out over the whitened ridge, with the moon riding high in a small bank of clouds.

Brodie was hurt that Gus was leaving. During their time on the ridge he'd realised that Lester, his first friend, was ratshit. Lester was a thief. When men complained that various items like picks and tobacco were missing, Brodie had been fairly certain that Lester was the light-fingered culprit, but he couldn't bring himself to mention this to Gus, remembering his desperate nights in Dublin, his short career as a footpad. Glass houses . . . he reminded himself.

He wished he had it in him to back down, to tell Gus Kriedemann that . . . what? Brodie was even embarrassed thinking about saying such things. That Gus was one of the finest men he'd ever met. Even after that concrete-like punch. For which Gus had never apologised. Nor should he. Brodie knew he'd gone too far.

All the miners had liked Gus. They'd come to him for help, to have a yarn, to share a little liquor with him. Just to be around him. Their camp had never been lonely.

224

For a minute there Brodie wondered how he would cope here on his own, but he shrugged it off, knowing he was right. It wasn't mad to stay, it was madness to leave, with this good earth a treasury of wealth. He'd made arrangements at the miners' store to expect him every Saturday so that they'd be alerted if he failed to appear. Until Clover sent the horse he'd gladly tramp the ten miles to keep to his schedule.

As Lester backed Mac into the shafts of the dray, Brodie called out to him. 'Watch that wheel. Keep it greased. It's out of whack since it got tipped over.'

'She'll be right,' Lester called, so Brodie turned to Gus.

'What'll you be doing once you get home? Where will you go next?'

'Nowhere. I'm staying in Toowoomba. I'm sick of travelling. But before I spend any of the opal sale money, what about Mrs Holloway? We have to repay our share of the loan.'

Brodie had forgotten about Vivien. He couldn't have Gus talking to her; they'd find out he'd borrowed three hundred, not two. He considered telling Gus to bank the money in his Toowoomba account, but his secretive nature couldn't allow that either.

'Hold it until I come back,' he said. 'The lady wouldn't appreciate anyone knowing she staked me. You see how it is.' He winked. 'You could embarrass her.'

'That's true. I'll give it to my father to hold. Lester's share too,' he grinned. 'Best to get the debts out of the way first. Mike says we ought to get more than a hundred pounds each if we stick to our guns. With what I have left, I was thinking of buying a business.'

Brodie was astonished. A business? He'd never thought of such a thing. In Tullymore you stayed what you were. Farmers. Shopkeepers. Even Mr Kriedemann had been a baker before he came to this country, and had continued in that occupation.

'What sort of business?'

'I probably won't have enough but I think my father will help me. There's a little pub in Station Street, the Victoria . . .'

'You'd buy a pub?'

'Why not?'

'Last chance, Brodie,' Lester yelled. 'Get aboard, you Irish lump!'

'Be careful of him,' Brodie warned Gus. 'And God go with you.'

'When are you coming back?' Gus asked him, picking up his swag.

'How do I know?'

'Make a time. I don't want to have to come searching for you. One month? Three months?'

'Three,' Brodie said. 'Give me three months.'

As the dray rattled down the hill he turned away to break out a bottle of rum from his new supplies. He poured a generous measure into a tin mug and raised a toast to himself. 'It's all yours now, Brodie Court, the Ten Mile opal is yours for the taking!'

A purple mist shrouded the dawn over the ridge, and by the time it cleared, the lone man was striding between the deserted mines, examining the shafts, determined to investigate as many as possible.

'I don't need no one,' he said, the old excitement building up in him again. 'They've made it easy for me.'

His first visitor arrived within a few days.

Brodie kept to the same routine as before, breaking from the scorching heat at noon, but he'd chosen a new spot to rest – a lookout on a high point shaded by jutting rocks. From there he had a grand view of this section of Plenty Station and took pleasure in the occasional movement on the plains below that reminded him he wasn't alone in the world. Besides the roaming cattle, kangaroos, and fleeting glimpses of mobs of emus, he was surprised to see families of tribal blacks from time to time. They intrigued him, always led by tall men with spears who strode into the distance with a purpose. He wondered who they were and where they'd come from. The blacks never came to this section of the ridge; Mike had said it was taboo for mysterious cultural reasons that they would not divulge.

This noon, he squinted into a shimmering mirage as two horsemen emerged. The figures seemed elongated, tall, thin apparitions that remained static as if etched on the horizon until suddenly they snapped into focus and he saw it was Clover, leading a horse.

'I got your message,' she said. 'One horse. Personally delivered.'

Brodie laughed. 'So you did, now. That's very kind of you. But what have we here?'

She dismounted and stood by as he stared at the fine dark bay horse.

'He's a beauty!' Brodie said, hesitating before daring to stroke his silky neck and soft fair mane. 'But what would you be asking for a horse like this?'

'His name's Jolly,' she said. 'We called him that because he's got such a happy nature. He's too good for a stock horse so I thought you might like him.'

'That I would, but what's he worth? He could be too rich for me.' Not wishing to pay too much, counting his pennies as usual, Brodie had expected to buy a stock horse on the cheap, but he doubted if he could bargain down to his price for this splendid mount.

She didn't seem ready to discuss price. 'I heard you were here on your own. The others? Have they all gone?'

'They have, thanks to your father.'

'Yes. I heard about that too, and I'm sorry. But what can I do? He's the boss.'

Brodie remembered her confrontation with the Judge. 'How did you get on?' he asked. 'After bailing up your own dad?'

'He's still not speaking to me, but that's nothing unusual. Plenty is a big station, I keep out of his way.'

'It must be unpleasant for you.'

Clover shrugged. 'I don't let it bother me. Sooner or later he'll go back to town. Salty says he's missing the social swim. He's a big noise in Toowoomba.'

'What about you? Wouldn't you rather be in town?'

'God, no. I wouldn't know what to do with myself. And what about offering a girl a cup of tea?'

'I'm sorry. Come on up to the camp. I was just having smoko before making myself a meal. Would you care to join me?'

'No, you join me. I brought lunch: chicken sandwiches, and Salty made a fruit cake for you.'

'Ah, bless her heart!'

They talked amiably over lunch, sitting by his camp which he'd moved near to the water hole since he now had his pick of the best sites, and she was intrigued that he'd remained here alone.

'Why have you stayed?'

'Because it suits me. We did find opal but we couldn't go on with that mine because the cattle squashed it. That doesn't say there isn't more here. And I don't like being pushed around. I'll leave in my own time.'

'You're a stubborn feller,' she grinned.

'Look who's talking! Do you think he'll be sending more cattle to run me down?'

'No. He had his win, he's been crowing about it ever since. One miner out here doesn't bother him.'

'He knows I'm here?'

'Of course. Even if our stockmen don't actually come this way, they see the smoke of your campfire. And the blacks keep tabs on you. They know everything that goes on.'

'Good God!' Brodie smiled. 'And here I was thinkin' I had the world to meself up here. I might as well be living in a main street.'

She got to her feet, casually tucking her shirt into sturdy moleskins. 'I'd better go. You take care out here, now, and if you need anything, come by the homestead.'

'What about the horse? What do I owe you?'

'Nothing. It's my way of apologising. I brought a stock saddle and bridle and a few other requirements for Jolly; all you have to do is look after him. He'll need exercise; don't have him standing about getting fat.'

Against his better judgement Brodie heard himself insisting on payment.

'No,' she said. 'When you leave here, you'll only be riding as far as Charleville, then you'll take the train, won't you?'

'That's true.'

'I'd hate you to sell Jolly to just anyone. You keep him until then and I'll make arrangements to bring him home.'

Brodie was delighted. ''Tis a loan, then?'

'You can keep him if you want to but it's a hell of a ride from Charleville to the coast. A loan seems more sensible.'

'That's marvellous! I'm in your debt, Clover. I promise

I'll exercise him. It'll give me a chance to look about the countryside.'

'Good. Just don't go looking too far. To strangers this country can have a terrible sameness about it. You could easily get lost.'

'Will you come back?' he asked as she was mounting up for the return journey.

'I won't be intruding on your solitary state?'

'Never. I've no desire to be a hermit.'

When she'd left, he patted the horse. 'Well! What do you know about that, Jolly? I've got you to talk to. Are you much of a conversationalist? And I've got me a friend. A country girl.'

He decided to alter his schedule, beginning on the morrow, by starting work an hour earlier so that he could exercise the horse later in the day. That was the worst time in the camp anyway, when hordes of mosquitoes took over from the flies. A good gallop before dusk would be a tonic for both of them.

When he started work again, digging an open trench round the perimeter of Firefly in the hope of picking up more of the original seam, he was still thinking of Clover. There was nothing flirtatious about that girl, nor any hint of shyness. He knew now, without putting it to the test, that if he'd made any attempt at familiarity, the lady would not have appreciated it.

He gave a snort of laughter as he jammed the pick into the hard ground. 'Lady? I reckon, Brodie me lad, if you upset Miss Chiswick, you'd find she's no lady!'

He had a sudden yearning for Vivien, to have a woman's arms about him again, and worked faster to throw off the frustration.

Often he'd thought of writing to Vivien, to make an excuse for the delay in returning, but he had no wish to compromise her. A letter could fall into the hands of her mother-in-law, or even her husband.

Never mind, he told himself. When I go back into Toowoomba with my first parcel of opal and the real find that's out here somewhere, I'll be going to her as a man of means. Then we'll see what happens. He hoped she was missing him.

That night he doused his campfire and took the lantern into

his tent to shake out his bunk. He'd fallen down on that chore lately, too exhausted to care, but there was always the worry of snakes. In the corner of the tent he noticed a glint of light and went over to investigate.

It was his compass. He'd given it to Gus for the return journey and had ordered another at the miners' store. Gus must have dropped it.

Ah well, he thought. Gus has a pretty good sense of direction. He doesn't make many mistakes.

Within minutes Brodie Court was asleep under the mosquito netting, too exhausted to dream either of opals or of Vivien.

Chapter Eight

At Fairlea Station, the boss's wife was thinking of Brodie, but not with kindness or yearning.

Thanks to the advice of her lawyer, Stanley Wickham, she'd outwitted her mother-in-law and Vern's power of attorney was safely in her hands. She was the mistress of Fairlea.

As for her other plans, regarding the management of the station, they'd gone by the board.

Living here on the boring station with a husband who was a mental case was tiresome enough, without having to be bothered arguing with Taffy about what could be done and what could not. After all, she supposed he was right. The main thing was to see that the place made money, and if that meant horses for the military, well, get on with it.

She'd been annoyed to find that Christiana had installed a bookkeeper without even consulting her, but at least she was saved the trouble. He was an elderly chap, a retired schoolmaster, and he lived in a bungalow next door to Elvie's room, so he was no bother.

In her new role, she'd thrown a big party as soon as they were settled. A welcome-home party for Vern. And everyone had come from far and wide. She'd no idea he had so many friends.

The party should have been a roaring success, despite the fact that the Fairlea homestead wasn't built for entertaining like the Holloway house in Toowoomba. Vivien had gone to enormous expense, hiring a huge marquee for the luncheon, a bush band to play for hours, and extra staff. She also had special orders of delectable hams and other delicacies sent out from town.

To set the hired trestle tables, she'd bought expensive linen and crystal and the very best silver, not to mention the cases of French champagne, and everyone had congratulated her, it was all so lovely. But that was as far as it went. The party was a dud. A day of gloom from beginning to end.

Seeing Vern, the guests were shocked. He'd sat in his chair on the veranda, sometimes tapping along to the music with a vacant smile on his face, the rest of the time staring into space, knowing no one.

Women whispered to her: 'How brave you are. We had no idea poor dear Vern was so bad.'

Men pulled up chairs. Sat with him. Talked to him, in their kindness, hoping for some response. But there was none.

They wandered about aimlessly. Some, Vivien noticed, even quit the party to go off and talk to Taffy and the men.

As soon as the luncheon was over they began to leave, claiming distance, other commitments, anything to get away, and that infuriated her. She knew that these people would stay until dawn if they were enjoying themselves. Station parties often extended to supper. And breakfast if they felt like it.

She stood stiffly at the front steps farewelling them, knowing they wouldn't return, that they were Vern's friends, not hers, and they couldn't bear to see him in this state.

There was so much food left over, she ordered it buried, but Elvie insisted on sharing it between the station hands and the blacks.

'Do what you like!' Vivien said, shutting herself in the parlour with a bottle of champagne.

Vern wandered in. 'Where did everyone go?' he asked vaguely.

'Shut up and go to bed!' she snapped at him, and Elvie came to take him away.

'Where is Brodie?' she moaned for the hundredth time. 'I'll kill him when I get my hands on him!'

Brodie would be back. Vivien was certain of that. And he'd soon find out that she'd returned to Fairlea Station.

She was so stunned by the reaction to her party, aware now that Fairlea would never be the hub of social life out here, no matter how much she spent, thanks to the handicap of a mental husband, that alternative plans began to form. She was here. She was the mistress of the station with access to all the funds, so she didn't have to answer to anyone. Brodie could come here. She could give him Taffy's job if he wanted it.

For that matter, he wouldn't have to work at all. He could

232

be a guest, and if anyone was scandalised, what the hell? Who cared? What could they do?

While she was in Toowoomba, ordering all the trappings for the party, she'd made a point of visiting the Kriedemann bakery.

'My husband wishes to know if there is any news of Mr Court.'

'Oh yes,' the woman had said. 'He's with my son and they seem to be doing well. But I ask you, Mrs Holloway, is this work for a man? Playing at lucky dips, I call it. Digging in the ground for jewels! Silly boys, the three of them. His father begs Gus to stay and work here, but will he do it? Even to help his father? No, not him.'

'Where are they?'

'Oh, somewhere beyond Charleville. Gus didn't give an address on his letter. He said they'd be home soon.'

'They will?' Vivien could hardly contain her excitement. They'd been away months. 'Would you tell Mr Court that my husband has returned to Fairlea Station and is anxious to see him. My husband is still not well and a visit from Mr Court would cheer him up, I'm sure.'

The baker's wife looked at her curiously and Vivien felt that the repeated request, purporting to be from her husband again, didn't seem so credible this time. But who cared? This woman didn't matter a fig to her.

'You will give him the message?'

'If I can, madam. If I can.'

But there was still no word from Brodie.

Taffy often came up to sit with Vern, telling him what was happening about the station, whether he understood or not.

On this day the foreman sought out Vivien.

'That was a fine party you had for the boss, Mrs Holloway. Everyone said you'd done wonders setting it all up. And ladies I spoke to said the lunch was fit for a king.'

'Did they? Good. At least that's something.'

'A great day for the boss, too, he liked seeing all his old friends, I bet.'

'He didn't recognise them. Surely you know that! His friends would have told you.' Vivien realised bitterly that most of the men had kept their distance from her, apart from desultory conversation and the endless concern for her husband, which meant that, as long as Vern was alive, she couldn't even have any fun flirting. Even old Jock Canning, a notorious lecher who had often chased her at parties, had been very circumspect with her.

Taffy was at the window, looking sadly at Vern, who was dozing in a hammock on the veranda. 'Somehow I think he does know, missus. Deep inside he'd know and take comfort from the touching and the voices. You mustn't despair, he might come good.'

'It'd take a miracle.'

'I've marked in the stud book that Irish Lass has foaled. We're leaving it to you to name her foal. By the way, have you heard from Brodie Court?'

'Why should I?' she asked sharply.

'I thought Mrs Holloway might have heard of him since he was working at her house in Toowoomba.'

'Not as far as I know. Why?'

'Because the lads tell me his wife has arrived.'

Stunned, Vivien tried to keep her voice calm. 'His wife? I didn't know he had a wife.'

'Neither did we. But she's turned up in Toowoomba with her kid, they tell me. Come all the way from Ireland.' He grinned. 'Looking for him, she is, asking about, and Brodie nowhere to be found.'

She shrugged, dismissing him. 'I wouldn't know. I'll have a look at the foal in the morning.'

The housekeeper stared at Vivien as she stormed into the kitchen. 'Is there anything wrong?'

'No,' she snapped. 'Wake Vern and give him his tea. He can't be left lying round like that all day. And where's the whisky? The decanter is empty.'

'There's a bottle in the sideboard in the parlour. I'll fill the decanter shortly.'

'Don't bother! I'll do it myself!'

'Will you have your tea in the dining room with Mr Vern?'

'No! I'll tell you when I'm ready for tea.'

She didn't wait to fill the decanter. Tearing the wrapping from the bottle she wrenched out the cork and poured herself a glass of whisky. Furiously she slopped some water into it and took a gulp.

Married? The bastard! Oh, the rotten bastard! Not a word had he said about a wife. And kid! Why was the wife looking for him? Had he run off on her like he has on me?

She kicked the door shut and paced about the parlour, too shocked, too angry to settle.

She stayed in the parlour for hours, fluctuating between self-pity and sheer rage, comforting herself with several more whiskies, trying to think what to do.

Mrs Kriedemann had said her son had written from somewhere on past Charleville, but Vivien hadn't pressed her for an address. He must have an address of some sort, and they weren't casual about mail in the bush. Even letters to the most remote areas were delivered somehow. But she'd had the impression that the baker's wife was deliberately holding back, not keen to divulge that information. The holier-than-thou old bitch. What business of hers was it who wanted to contact Brodie Court?

'The bastard!' she added.

'And where's my money?' she asked the empty room. 'She said they were doing well. Which means they must have struck opal. Or given up and taken jobs perhaps.'

During Brodie's absence Vivien had gone cold on his fantasy of striking it rich. Now she thought she must have been crazy to have encouraged him. To have even loaned him money.

'Well, I want it back!' she snapped.

Tears began to fall. 'And I want Brodie back. What is to become of me without him?'

Eventually, before she fell asleep on the couch, drunk for the first time in her life, Vivien worked out a plan of action.

She awoke, hot and uncomfortable, with a splitting headache, still sprawled on the couch, listening to the clatter from the kitchen. The early breeze had a delicate touch and the light fragrance of frangipani was assaulted by the smell of whisky that she'd spilled.

Vivien was horrified. She jumped up, remonstrating with herself. 'A fine thing! What are you doing? Turning yourself into a drunk? Do you want to end up one of those tipsy women everyone talks about?'

She tidied the room and decanted the last of the whisky, shuddering at the low level. 'And all because of Brodie Court!

What a fool you are. So Brodie has a wife. You've got a husband. These things can be overcome.'

As she walked along the veranda to her bedroom, Vivien pondered on what she'd just said. Overcome? But why bother?

By the time she had stripped off her stale and clammy clothes she had the answer. So that I can marry Brodie. That's why.

She would write to him via that baker's shop, with *Please forward* written on the envelope. She'd seen many a letter come through Fairlea Station with that message, chasing itinerant workers. It was worth a try.

There'd be no hard words. Just a pleasant letter to let him know she was here at Fairlea again and inviting him to visit.

I won't mention the wife. She smiled grimly. Why should I? Brodie may not want to see her.

On the ship Trella Court had heard that Brisbane was known as the town of twenty-seven hills, and she could well believe it on this their third day in Australia.

She hadn't enjoyed the voyage from Liverpool, she'd simply endured, relieved that Garth loved every minute of it. They were both disappointed that they saw so little of the world with only a few ports of call, and found no difference at all in the great oceans that swept them ever onwards. So many storms had jostled and harassed them that Trella lost count, but she took refuge from her fears in the Captain's insistence that strong winds were a great benefit, helping them to make good time.

At last they stepped ashore in Brisbane on a scorching hot day, strangers in a strange new world. Garth, at an age of flux, had been quite the young man on the ship, interested in everything, but alone with her in a strange town he was suddenly the boy again. Apprehensive. 'Do we know where we are, Mother?'

'Don't be foolish,' Trella said firmly. 'We know exactly where we are. What are your maps for? Was your schooling worth nothing?'

She soon found lodgings for them and sat down to count her money. She still had seven pounds left from the sale of the farm and goods, plus the ten pounds her Uncle Paddy

236

had given her as a farewell gift. 'Let's find an ice cream shop,' she said, knowing that would cheer him. 'We'll have a real splurge.'

And then: 'Before we go on to Toowoomba we must explore this town, because it is the capital and you have to know all about it.'

For her own sake, Trella sought out this town as if it were a grand house she were entering. She needed to feel the timbers and the bricks and mortar of it; to smell its clean air and its musty cellars, to stand at windows and look out at a heat haze, like woodsmoke, that gave a greenish tinge to the sky. She was a strong woman, not easily unnerved, but to keep a grip on herself, she wanted to know this place like a native. Trella hated not knowing where she was going.

For days they explored the riverside town, puffing up hilly streets from the gardens to the terraces, peering at huge timber houses standing curiously and precariously on stilts, half hidden by voluptuous greenery. They learned the names of the streets, heard the strange accents, and occasionally familiar lilts, ran for shade, where they sat and ate sweet buns, and each night sat in a cheap café that Garth had found, to gorge on steak pies and mashed potatoes.

At every turn Trella kept her son interested to instil confidence in him, and on the last day she agreed to the extravagance of paying threepence each to enter a small private park where visitors could stroke somnolent koala bears and docile kangaroos. A fitting end to their three-day holiday.

Garth slept soundly that night, excited by the prospect of a train ride the following day. Trella tried not to worry about their future, with the reality of having to earn a living ahead of them. She'd have to find a job as soon as possible, but at least Brodie was there to advise and help her if necessary. She didn't have his exact address but was sure she'd find him, taking local gossip, familiar ground, as a benchmark.

Trella laughed as she climbed into bed. At least one of her fears had been proven baseless. Several people back in Tullymore had warned her that she'd have terrible trouble in this country. 'They don't even speak English!' she'd been told.

Although others had said this was not true, she'd not been

237

sure who to believe. What a blessed relief it had been to hear the same good old language as soon as they'd arrived! Silly of her to be taking note of the worrymongers.

The train journey up the range petrified Trella. She was sure the carriages would topple over or slide back down the mountain, but Garth found it a great adventure, hanging out the window to view their progress. When she dragged him back inside he bombarded her with questions.

'What's this town like? Will Uncle Brodie be there to meet us? Will they have kangaroos too? How long are we staying? Where will we live?'

To the last question, Trella could only say: 'I don't know yet. I'll have to ask about.'

'Ask who? We don't know anyone.'

'People. Just people.'

By dint of following that course, Trella soon found them accommodation. A woman in a shop directed her to Spring Lane, where she could find a cottage to rent.

They stood outside the cottage with their cheap suitcases, staring at a neat, white-painted house set on a large block with lawns all about, and high, shady trees at the rear.

'We can't afford this,' Trella said, disappointed. She'd expected a cottage to be the same as they were at home. More like their own thatched farmhouse.

'Why not?' Garth asked. They'd walked right across the slow, sleepy town to find Spring Lane.

'It's too big,' she said.

'I haven't seen any smaller,' he argued. 'They're all much of the same here. And it's a funny lane, more like a road it's that wide.'

'No. It won't do.' She turned to leave but an elderly woman called to her from the side of the house. 'You looking for somewhere to stay?'

Trella nodded, embarrassed, wishing they'd moved off sooner.

The woman hobbled over, using a walking stick. 'Migrants, are you?'

Trella bridled. 'You could say that.' All the way across town she'd been aware of people peering at them, at her in her best black dress and shawl and Garth in his rough trousers and jacket that were too tight now. Everyone here seemed to be dressed loose and casual, and most of the women were in light summery dresses. Trella had realised that they looked poor, but she'd told herself, stoutly, that it was no crime.

'Well now,' the woman said. 'From Ireland, are you?'

'That's true,' Garth told her, stepping forward. 'Is this house to rent, lady?'

'Half of it. I live in the other half. I'm Mrs Wilkinson. Do you want to see inside?'

'Thank you, we'll not be bothering you,' Trella said, but Garth grabbed her arm. 'Mother, didn't you hear the lady? Only half a house.' He turned to the woman. 'How much would you be asking?'

'Just the two of you?' she asked shrewdly. 'No man?'

'I'm a widow,' Trella said.

'I'm near to fourteen,' Garth offered, willing to be the man if necessary.

Mrs Wilkinson grinned. 'And a big lad for that too. What do you say to six bob a week, missus?'

'It's a nice house,' Garth urged, so Trella had to put away her umbrage and agree to inspect half of the house, which she thought was a peculiar way to be renting.

Within an hour they were installed. They had two small bedrooms that opened on to an enclosed veranda, which did as a sitting room, and the use of the kitchen and bathroom, and Trella was delighted. It was better than she ever could have imagined. And clean too. Sparkling clean.

When Garth raced outside to inspect the garden, her new landlady issued the rules. 'No men, Mrs Court. I want to make that plain. I live here on the other side and I don't need disturbances.'

'That won't happen, Mrs Wilkinson. I consider us fortunate to have found such a lovely place. We only arrived in Australia a few days ago.'

'And what brought you here?'

'My brother-in-law works hereabouts but I'm not sure where to find him. Would you know of a Mr Brodie Court?'

'Can't say as I do.'

'Oh well, I'll ask about.'

'Yes. Someone will know. How are you for money? I'll need my rent every Monday.'

'We'll find work, me and the boy.'

239

Two weeks later, thanks to enquiries made by Mrs Wilkinson, Trella and Garth were both working at a cheese factory, Trella as a cleaner, kept busy scrubbing vats and bins and endless rows of containers, while Garth worked outside as a general help. He was happy to have a paid job and took it all in his stride, so Trella didn't complain, but her work was hard. The factory workers toiled from six in the morning until five at night, six days a week. The women, and boys under sixteen, were paid fourteen shillings a week. Men earned more, and that irked Trella. The other women warned her not to make a fuss, it wouldn't earn her anything but the sack, so she kept quiet, determined to find a better job as soon as time permitted. But at least they had more than a pound a week to live on, so that was something. They wouldn't starve.

There was still no sign of Brodie. Whenever she passed a pub, knowing they were the hub of information in small towns, Trella stopped to enquire after him. Some of the men knew Brodie, had known him when he'd worked on the station out of town, but couldn't say where he was now. Others said he had worked in Toowoomba for a while but had left town. She left messages for him, with her address, in the hands of obliging publicans, and then went about her own business.

They were a day out from the Barbary Creek pub when Gus had to admit to Lester that he'd lost the compass.

'I can't find it anywhere.'

'What's it matter?' Lester said. 'Charleville's a big town. We can't miss it. Jesus! It's not as if we're looking for that fly dot on the map called Barbary Creek. We just keep going.'

'A hundred miles?' Gus said nervously. 'I had Willi to guide us on the way out.'

'We'll be right. I'm a real homin' pigeon, I am, when there's wine, women and song waiting for me at the end of the trail. Leave it to old Mac here, he'll get us home.'

Gus wasn't so sure. They could easily stray off course following these bush tracks, some of which were outdated stock routes. He began to keep a careful note of their progress through forests of tall, skinny trees and over dusty plains where tracks were hardly visible, and on the fourth day, sighting a house, he insisted they pull off the road to enquire.

They found only deserted sheds, half hidden by trees.

'It's an outstation,' he sighed, 'but it hasn't been used for a long time.' He climbed to the top of a nearby hill in the hope of seeing some sign of life, but was greeted with a panorama of ominous scrub in every direction.

'I think we're lost,' he told Lester.

'Ah, be buggered! We just keep goin' east and we fall into the bloody sea!'

'The bloody sea is about six hundred miles from here, if you remember. Charleville isn't on the coast.'

'Yeah. Well, you wanted to be in charge of this show, so you figure it out. I'm for camping here tonight.'

Gus was annoyed with Lester's simplistic approach to the problem, remembering all the fearful tales of his childhood of people being lost in the bush, even station people who might be expected to know better, but he blamed himself for their predicament. He'd lost the compass. It wasn't Lester's fault. Besides, he'd grown up in this country; Lester was new to it.

'I'll work it out,' he said. 'We're bound to come across someone soon. A house, or some blacks. And keep an eye out for cattle. Where there's cattle, there's water. We're getting low.'

They entered hilly country and Lester was jubilant. 'There you are. We came over hills. We're on the right track.'

But the tracks they followed took them into rough slopes that eventually became impassable.

Both of them were angry and frustrated as they backed the dray out of the dead end and down the hill to search for another route. As they crossed a dry gully, the dray lurched, crashing to a stop, a wheel buckled.

'Oh, Christ!' Lester yelled. 'The bloody wheel's fallen off!'

'No it hasn't,' Gus said, examining the dray. 'The axle's broken.'

'So now what do we do?'

'Hang on, I'll make sure.' Gus slid under the dray, cursing the rocky ground.

All at once he gave a scream of pain.

'What didja do?' Lester laughed, seeing this as some sort of comic relief from their troubles. 'Bust a funny bone?'

'Get me out,' Gus yelled. 'I've been bitten by a snake!'

'What did you say? Where?' Lester was confused, but as

the realisation hit, he leapt away in case he too would be bitten.

By this time Gus had dragged himself free of the dray, clutching his leg. 'Quick!' he shouted. 'Get me a tourniquet!'

'A what? Where's the snake?'

'How the hell do I know? Help me!' Gus tore at his belt. 'Get my boots off! Get my pants off!' He was taking deep breaths, trying to keep calm, vital in this situation, but the pain searing through his leg was terrifying. And Lester was so slow, fumbling with the laces on his boots, muttering frantically: 'They're knotted!'

'Cut 'em!' Gus instructed through clenched teeth, his leg now aflame and throbbing. 'Use your knife!'

As Lester pulled off the boot, Gus snatched the knife from him and ripped down his trouser leg, pushing the flap out of the way. His leg was already swollen and mottled, with two fang marks flaring on his calf. He slapped the belt round his leg, above the knee, and slid it through the buckle, pulling it tight.

'Hang on to this!' he ordered Lester. 'Don't let it go, whatever you do. Keep it as tight as you can!'

He fell back, feeling faint, whether from pain or shock he couldn't tell.

'What sort of a snake was it?' Lester asked as he hung on to the belt, at the same time glancing about him.

'I don't know.' Gus was gasping now but he fought to stay awake to give Lester his instructions. Lester knew nothing about snake bite. It seemed as if his leg would burst open with that band of leather cutting into him but he dared not ask Lester to ease up. 'It was big,' he said. 'Grey, I think. It hit me like an axe and I just saw it take off behind me.'

Confused, struggling for consciousness, he knew that talking about the snake was wasting precious time, and he tried to focus.

'Give me the belt, wrap it round my hand. I'll hold it now.'

'What do I do?' Lester was so flustered sweat was dripping from his face.

'Wash the bite. Get some water. No! Whisky. Alcohol. Pour that on it. Move!'

It took all the strength Gus could muster to hang on to that belt, to loosen for a few seconds the iron grip on his leg and then grind it tight again, the muscles of his thigh agonisingly fighting back as if they were against him.

'Cut it!' he told Lester, wondering why he hadn't already done so before pouring on the whisky. Hadn't he just told him to do that? He couldn't remember. 'Make it bleed,' he whispered. 'Wash out the poison. Dig deep!'

His leg jerked as Lester dug the knife in, and Gus welcomed the new pain. He could feel his body twitching in a horrible reaction to the poison, and though his vision was blurred he could see the horror on Lester's face at these awful spasms. But he had more to say. He forced the words out. 'Fever. Coming. Plenty water. Cool. Keep . . .' His tongue seemed too big for his mouth. 'Cool.'

He lay back, looking into the sun, wishing Lester would move him inside the house. Wondering what he was doing here on the grass beside the bakehouse on such a hot day. He wanted to ask Lester if it was true that there weren't any snakes in Ireland.

'That's where we'll go,' he muttered, his speech slurred.

'Where?' Lester asked him.

Gus had moved on, his mind racing in a kaleidoscope of pain. 'I told you. Ireland. Mind out for the snake! Keep it away from me. Thirsty.' He lapsed into muttered instructions that made no sense at all, and Lester shook his head, bewildered.

'Oh, Jesus! You're ravin'. Here. Drink some water.'

To Gus that sip tasted like icy-cold spring water but then he doubled up, vomiting. Lester seemed a monster squatting beside him. He was glad to close his eyes and shut him out.

Lester managed to get Gus into the dray, and with a lot of effort Mac dragged the fractured vehicle from the open gully into the shade.

'That's the best we can do,' he told the horse as he took it out of the shafts. 'The bloody dray's finished. You're going to have to carry us the rest of the way, Mac. But we won't be too hard on you, we'll take it in turns.'

But it wasn't that simple. Gus was sick. Bloody sick. Raving mad when he wasn't out cold.

For two days Lester tried to nurse him, giving him little

sips of water and trying to keep him cool, as he'd been told, with damp cloths, but they ate water. Gus's face was on fire. Damp cloths dried out in seconds and there wasn't that much to spare.

Finally he trekked up to the edge of a bluff and stared down at a carpet of treetops that hid any vestige of a road, and could just as easily hide a spring or creek from him.

'Bloody creepy country!' he snarled. 'Miles and miles of bloody nothing!'

The far-distant horizon was ringed with misty blue hills like vast prison walls, and Lester panicked. 'Hulloo!' he shouted. 'Hulloo! Anyone there? Can you hear me? Hulloo!'

Not even an echo responded.

A rust-coloured hawk hovered overhead and Lester glared back at it. 'Which way? You bloody know-all. Can't you make yourself useful?'

The bird sailed serenely down the bluff, free-flying in the rising airstream, and came about in a wide arc to make the run again. Lester watched it jealously, begrudging its confidence.

'We have to get out of here,' he growled. 'But which way?'

He stood up, his back to the afternoon sun. 'That has to be east,' he said, pointing ahead of him. 'All we have to do is go back aways and head east. That's what I've been telling Gus all the time.'

These hills are only bumps, he decided, from his bird's-eye view. We shouldn't have tried to go over them. If we go back now and travel along beside them on the flat, we can strike east through the bush down there.

Gus had argued that tracks twisted and turned, that few went due east, having to fit in with the terrain and natural hazards, but Lester saw no problem now. The dray was wrecked, they didn't have to worry about tracks. They could push out due east.

He hurried down the hill to tell Gus, but stopped a few yards from the dray. He'd forgotten that Gus was too sick to move. He was still fevered and sweating like a pig, and that crook leg wouldn't take him a half-mile.

'You're a bloody nuisance,' he said to his patient. 'I can't hang about here forever, and I can't be wasting more water on you. The drum's near empty and I have to keep Mac watered; we have to look after him.'

Gus turned his head, startling him. Lester hadn't meant him to hear that. 'You go,' he whispered. 'Get help.'

Lester looked at him thoughtfully. 'Yeah. That's what I ought to do. I ought to go and get help. No good hanging about here.'

Finding release at last from his impossible situation, Lester began to pack up. He went back and spoke to Gus, dribbling water on to his parched mouth, but Gus had passed out again.

Lester shook his head, not willing to voice his thoughts this time. Gus couldn't make it. He was full of poison. He could leave him some water but why waste it? Gus wouldn't have the strength to reach for it.

And then there were the opals. Gus wouldn't be needing his share.

Lester filled both canvas water bags from the drum and poured the rest into a dish to give Mac a decent drink before setting off. The horse had to get him home.

He couldn't bring himself to take a last look at Gus before he left. Better not to, he decided. Let him die in peace, because there would be no help. As soon as he found help it would be for himself. And then he'd keep right on going. With both shares, he was in the money. No need to point them to Gus; it was his fault they were lost in the bush. If anyone asked, he could say they split up days ago, when the dray broke down, and went their separate ways. He could even give them false directions, if need be. How was he supposed to know in this wild country?

Soon he was riding back down the track to turn off at the base of the hills, travelling north for the time being through rocky scrub, intent on bypassing the more difficult terrain. He wasn't about to get caught in dead ends again; no mistakes this time.

The view from the bluff had been deceptive. The dull green roof of the forest hid ridges and escarpments to bar his way, and ugly blackened logs were strewn about, evidence that a bushfire had roared through here not all that long ago. Lester cursed the mind-numbing sameness of this dry, cruel scrub as he urged the horse first one way and then another.

When he eventually broke free into open country after two full days, he found himself in a plain dotted with squat bushes. The ground was white and hard, no spring in it, tiring the horse, and fine sand blew about, adding a surface of grime to Lester's face and packing an extra shell on the clammy water bags.

Looking back, the hills were lost to him, hidden behind a wall of ragged timber, but he was certain he knew where he was going. 'We're past the hills,' he told the horse. 'We only have to turn right. It's that bloody simple.'

They plugged on, the horse treading on its shadow until Lester realised that the fierce sun was blazing on his face.

'Oh, Christ! We're going the wrong bloody way! We'll turn round and find somewhere to camp. In the morning I'll get this right.'

In the morning, though, a haze of cloud with a faint but tantalising promise of rain covered the sky, and by afternoon it hung overhead like a blanket. Lester's sun compass was obliterated, but he was more concerned with finding water than keeping to his designated course. The surface of the ground was becoming worse, worn by sand and wind to flint-hard stones that perpetually troubled his horse, but he petted Mac, telling him they'd soon be out of this, with more hills offering shelter. So he rode on.

To compensate for this miserable trek, Lester ate well. He busted open tins of peaches and beans, pleased he didn't have to share, chewed on salt beef that gave him a thirst, ate the last of the biscuits, but he worried about Mac. Feed was sparse in this country. 'More like a bloody desert,' he complained, 'than cattle country,' relieved to see that the horse had the sense to eat something, even if it was chomping leaves from those dried-out bushes.

He did see animals – kangaroos, emus and small marsupials – and he considered shooting them. Gus had said they'd never starve in this country, but what could he do with them without water?

'Nice bloody mess it'd be,' he muttered, 'trying to skin them overgrown rabbits and chooks without water.'

The horse was lame. Lester walked as much as he could,

leaving a trail of tins. Becoming disorientated, he lightened the load by dropping all non-essentials, even the gun and ammunition, but hanging on to his precious opals.

He passed a strange jutting rock, a rock shaped like a man's head, remarking that he'd seen one just like it. A while back. Maybe a day or so. He couldn't recall. Nor could he remember how long he'd been riding and marching in this direction, but suddenly those precious hills reared up in front of him. Blazing red.

Confronted by towering sand hills, he slid down from the saddle and screamed in rage.

The horse gave up first as they tried to cross, foam flecking his head and flanks, so Lester led him out again, allowing him to nuzzle in the juice of the last tin of peaches. They were out of water.

He began the retreat but Mac buckled and crumpled to the ground and Lester knew he was finished. He decided then to go back, fast, on foot and find that rifle. The horse didn't deserve a slow death. Nevertheless, he carried the packs of opals with him, in case he got lost.

Lester didn't find the rifle but he did manage to escape from the cruel plateau, stumbling, battered and beaten after days on foot, into a claypan area. In time, he knew, this parched, cracked mud, exposed to the sun now, would be awash. He tore the cakes of mud aside, hoping to find water underneath, but when that failed, he decided to wait.

'Only a matter of time,' he croaked, dragging his aching, dehydrated body into the shade of a clump of needlebush, and there he rested, gratefully, the precious pack tucked in beside him.

Gus heard him leave. He wanted to call out 'Good luck!' but the words wouldn't come. Then he thought he had. He wasn't sure. Shivering, he closed his eyes, waiting for the next attack of fever that always followed these cold spells.

When he awoke stars were glittering above him, so bright, it seemed, they were causing his head to thump with pain. He tried to move to take shelter but his body felt like lead and he slumped back, astonished, trying to unravel this mystery.

'Too tired,' an inner voice told him. 'Go back to sleep.'

'No,' he said doggedly, and fought against the terrible

weariness. He was thirsty and couldn't make out why Brodie and Lester were ignoring him. Couldn't they see he was in trouble?

Gathering his strength into one desperate effort he managed to lift his upper body, but the pain in his left leg was excruciating. That brought him to his senses. The snake!

Gus knew now what had happened and why he was lying here, helpless. He could feel the leather strap still hanging loosely above his knee. No use any more.

But was it? Slowly, grimly, he managed to free the strap and bring it to his mouth, sucking on the clammy, dew-laden leather to ease his thirst. That would suffice until daylight, when he'd be able to see where Lester had left a water bag. It had to be near him somewhere.

The night was an eternity, and creeping dawn a massive sweep of scarlet and gold. Gus had never been so glad to see daylight! His eyes scanned his makeshift bunk on the dray and the worn timbers beside him. Nothing! Frantically, he inched himself a little to the side but in the end he had to give up. Lester had forgotten to leave water near him, the bloody fool! It must be on the ground somewhere. Under the dray probably.

Exhausted, he fell back. He had to get to his water bag. But not now. Later. He was shivering again. Cold.

In his dreams he heard voices. Soft. Whispering. And he felt a cold hand touch his face but did not dare open his eyes; the sun was high and the glare would be too painful. His body was rising from the hard boards, a blessed relief, and drifting towards the sun.

The blackfellows carried the sick man down the track and turned back into the hills to follow a worn footpath through the rocks to a pass below the bluff. Once clear of the foothills, they loped steadily east, mile after mile through the scrub, until they came to their camp by a chain of lagoons.

They handed him on to their women and watched with concern as the ministering began. They knew this stranger was seriously ill from the effects of snakebite, and it would be a fight to save him. The women talked excitedly among themselves as potions and cures were produced and water was brought from their lagoon, but the rest of the camp was silent. All activity ceased as the tribal people squatted in the dust outside a woman's gunyah. Waiting.

'Well! If it ain't young Gus!'

Willi peered into his shelter. 'I heard they had a boarder,' he cackled. 'Snake got you, eh?'

Gus nodded. 'Nearly finished me. Where did you come from?'

'Me and the missus, we was on our way home. Been walkabout along the Blackwater River. Your mates here, a Dieri mob, sent me a message to come and take a gander. You all right now?'

'I'm still a bit wobbly. Give me a hand. I want to get up.'

The black women ringed them, grinning shyly, as Willi helped Gus to his feet.

'You're as skinny as a rake,' Willi said, supporting him across the camp and down to the lagoon.

'You can talk,' Gus grinned. He sank down gratefully in the low-spreading shade of a coolabah tree. 'Oh cripes! I don't seem to have any energy at all.'

'Give it time. They tell me you've been here three days. Another couple will see you fit to travel.'

Gus nodded. 'Three days? I wasn't sure. I'll never be able to thank these people enough for taking me in and looking after me. I'd never have survived without them.'

'That's for sure,' Willi agreed. 'Where are your mates?'

'Brodie's back at the Ten Mile. We did all right, Willi! We found a seam of light opal, plenty of firsts in it too. Some beautiful pieces. Wait till you see them! Brodie wouldn't leave, he wanted more, so . . .'

'Ha! I knew it. I picked him, didn't I? He's got the bug good and proper.'

'Yes, so Lester and I were heading for Charleville when the dray broke down and then I got bitten by that bloody snake.'

'So where's Lester?'

'He went for help.'

Willi raised his eyes to the heavens in exasperation. 'Lester went for help, did he? And I suppose he took all the opal?'

'I don't know.'

'The blacks had a good look round. They wouldn't leave

anything that could be used in a deserted camp. They brought back pots and pans and a few bits they could use as digging sticks but they say there was no food and no water. He didn't leave you a bloody drop of water, so don't tell me he left the opal behind, any of it.'

'He probably didn't think to.'

Willi stood up and marched away to talk to the blacks. When he returned his face was grim. 'They searched the camp. They brought in blankets too but they didn't see any bundles of opal. They know what it looks like, they're not stupid. I reckon Lester and your opal are long gone.'

Dumbfounded, Gus shook his head. 'He wouldn't do that.'

'On horseback he'd have made good time. You were a bit off course, coming from Barbary Creek, but if he'd kept going the same way, through those hills, he'd soon be in more civilised country, smaller stations. He could have found someone to come back for you.'

'Maybe he did,' Gus argued.

'And if they did, and found no one lying about, wouldn't they comb the district to find out what happened to you? Face it. Lester had the horse and all the opal, that would have put wings on his feet. You can kiss that lot goodbye.'

'Maybe he got lost?'

Willi was becoming impatient with this argument. He had never liked that Lester fellow, and he was certain he was right. He shrugged and sat back, contemplating the still waters of the lagoon. He would ask permission of the elders to hang about this camp with Lena until Gus was well enough to travel. At the Langlo River crossing he could put him on a mail coach headed for Charleville. It was obvious Gus didn't have any money, but Willi Schluter's IOUs were good currency in the south-west, Willi always paid his bills. They'd get him home to Toowoomba.

Willi was less interested in the fate of Lester O'Dowd than in the whereabouts of those opals. He decided that once he had Gus on his way he'd take a couple of black trackers into that low bank of hills and have a leisurely look round the spot where the dray broke down. Then he'd see if they could track Lester. No way in the world the opal packs would be there, even Gus had accepted that, but it would be interesting to see where the ferret-faced little Irishman had got to.

With luck they could track him right to a town. And Willi knew every opal buyer within cooee. Interesting, he nodded, sucking on his pipe.

When Gus arrived at the house behind the bakery his mother was shocked. He was so gaunt and thin. 'My God! What have you done to yourself?'

She fled to fetch her husband. 'Jakob! Come and look at your son! He's at death's door!'

'No I'm not,' Gus shouted angrily. 'I've been sick. That's all!'

'How sick?' his father asked. 'What's the matter with you?'

'Snakebite. I got bitten by a snake.'

Thoroughly depressed already after the long, humiliating ride home in the train, travelling second class with his clothes in rags and his shaggy hair and bushy beard adding to his disreputable appearance, he was in no mood for explanations, but the demands of his parents had to be met.

His father was worse than Willi Schluter. 'You struck it rich, you say, and you lost it? Is this what you're telling me? That's the finish of it! You're not going prospecting again, you'll stay home and get a decent job!'

Gus laboured over a bowl of soup, answering questions without giving too much away. 'I haven't lost my opals,' he insisted. 'Lester has them. We got separated, that's all. He'll turn up.'

His father's attitude irritated him. The old man still seemed to think his son was fifteen, a youngster, not capable of making his own way in the world, but right now Gus didn't have much of a defence. Where the hell was Lester? If he'd gone back to the dray in the hills and found it deserted he must have known someone had rescued the patient. Failing to find him, the obvious next course would be to make for Toowoomba, to check in here. Gus wouldn't voice Willi's concern, that Lester had run off with their treasure. His father would call him all sorts of a fool.

That afternoon Gus tried to rest but it was impossible. He worried about Lester. What if he had become lost out there?

251

All the way in on the train from Charleville, he'd been hoping that Lester would be here waiting for him, haranguing him in his usual manner for causing such confusion by disappearing. Willi had said he'd take some blacks to search for Lester, but he seemed to be certain that Lester had 'done a bunk', as he put it. So. Was Lester lost in the bush or a thief? Anxiety over either option brought on the headaches again.

Needing to get out of the house, he borrowed a few shillings from his mother and went for a long walk. He supposed he ought to write to Brodie and tell him what had happened, but what to say? He might as well wait until he had news of Lester. God, how he wished Brodie had come with them. He mightn't be in this mess now.

He was still thinking of Brodie when he walked into a pub. 'It'd be just my luck,' he muttered to himself, 'to have him find the world's biggest opal, adding to what he's already got, and me landing back here on my bum, flat broke.'

A few men nodded to him but Gus took his pint and retreated to the far end of the bar, not in the mood to be answering more questions.

'Hey, Gus,' the publican called to him eventually. 'Ain't you a mate of that Irishman, Brodie Court?'

'Yes. Why?'

'There was a lady looking for him. His missus, I think.'

'He's not married.'

'Well, a Mrs Court was looking for him. Fresh off the boat from the land of the leprechauns, I'd say.'

Gus was intrigued. 'Where is she now?'

'I've got the address somewhere in the desk. If you hang on I'll find it.'

Garth teased her, claiming that she always smelled of sour milk. He thought that was funny, but Trella wasn't amused because she knew he was right. By Saturday night she couldn't wait to be rid of it. As soon as she'd given him dinner she soaked in a bath, soaking her hair as well and then washing it in a rare extravagance of perfumed soap that she hid from him.

As she sat on the back step this particular night she thought how her mother would be shocked. Back home it was said to be bad for the health to wash the hair at night, inviting all sorts of dire ills. But here it was the highlight of the week, and a grand pleasure to be able to sit out on a warm night and relax after the terrible long week in that factory. She'd thought work in a cheese factory would be easy after farming, but she'd been wrong. The boss was a slave-driver, keeping them at it every minute, with only a quarter-hour for lunch.

Trella snorted. Finish at five, he'd said. That was a fairy tale.

They were lucky if they could get away by six, she and the other cleaner, Deena Hobbs. They had to have the factory spick and span each night for the next day.

'There used to be four on this job,' Deena told her, 'but this new boss, he put them off to save money.'

For the first few weeks, Trella had come home exhausted; now she was managing better but the long hours were wearing her down. At least on a farm you don't have to account for every minute, she thought as she towelled her hair. And you don't have someone standing over you and shoutin' and rolling milk cans at you, fair to knock you down.

She massaged her feet. They'd become spongy from the constant swill on the concrete floors, with no protection from the sandshoes the boss insisted his staff wore.

Don't be complainin' now, she told herself. You've got a job and a fine place to live and a kind landlady. It's a damn good start and better than you hoped for. Count your blessings.

Garth had made friends in the district, and even from here she could hear them all playing in the street, despite the failing light. It pleased her that he still had the energy for games. He'd learned to play cricket and loved to organise the other kids after work. Tomorrow, Sunday, he was taking his mother to watch a cricket match. Trella smiled. How grown-up he was to be 'taking' his mother. In her prayers she must tell Michael.

Mrs Wilkinson stuck her head out the back door. 'You've got a visitor.'

'Oh no!' Trella wailed, her hair still a tangled mass of curls. 'Who?'

'I've told him to come round the side,' she said, with a sniff that was an obvious reminder of the house rules.

Before she had time to tidy herself he came round the corner of the house, stooping under the oleander bushes.

Standing at the top of the steps, in mid-flight, Trella knew she looked like a startled hare, but it was too late to run now.

'Are you Mrs Court?'

'That I am,' she said, wondering what had gone wrong that this tall man should be looking for her. There was a wailing inside her that it had all been too easy, this settling in a strange land. Shades of her mother's dismal crowing.

'Mrs Brodie Court?'

She laughed. 'Good Lord, no! He's my brother-in-law! Who are you?'

'Gus Kriedemann. Brodie's my partner.'

'He is? I'm pleased to meet you.' She ventured down the steps and extended her hand. 'Where is he, for heaven's sake? I didn't know where to find him.'

'Out west. Working on the opal fields. But he'll come back here when he's through.'

Trella was delighted. 'What do you know about that? And me and the boy thinking to find him in this town.'

'The boy?'

'My son is with me,' she said.

'Oh yes. Forgive me. Your husband passed on. Michael. We did hear. I'm sorry. And that's why you decided to come to this country, is it?'

'Things were bad at home.'

He nodded. 'My parents came from Germany. The same reason, I believe.'

'Is that right?' Trella liked him. He had an honest face. As far as she could see in the dim light. 'Could you go a cup of tea?' she asked him.

'Thank you, yes.'

'Then would you mind waiting a minute?' She hurried into the kitchen. 'Mrs Wilkinson, I'll be bringing that gentleman into my sitting room for a cuppa. He's the partner of Brodie, the relation I've been trying to find.'

The grey-haired woman pursed her lips. 'You know my rules. No men.'

'Sure I do, but I took it to mean for purposes of forni-cation.'

'I'll thank you not to use such words in my kitchen.'

'It won't break the cups. And it's tea I'm offering him, not liquor, if it's boozing you're afraid of.'

Standing with her back to Trella, the landlady busied herself slicing bread, ignoring her.

254

'Where I come from it's pure bad manners to leave a guest standing outside a shut door, and I wouldn't want that gentleman to think badly of me. Or you. I pay for that sitting room so I'm entitled to have someone sit in it.'

After a small silence the landlady relented, with bad grace. 'Don't have him stay late.'

'Oh, never,' Trella grinned as she hurried to invite him in.

He was an easy man to talk to. Comfortable. He was as interested in her travels as she was to hear about Brodie, and an hour passed quickly. Then Garth came tramping in, surprised to find his mother had company.

Introductions over, he, in his turn, had to hear about Brodie as they munched on a supper of bread and cheese.

They walked Gus to the front gate, with Garth talking animatedly about cricket.

'I'm getting good at it now,' he told Gus.

'He's taking me to see a match tomorrow,' Trella said. 'Looks like I have to get the hang of it myself.'

'I used to play for the local team,' Gus said, 'but I've been away a lot.'

'Why don't you come tomorrow?' Garth asked him.

'Dear oh dear,' Trella laughed. 'Mr Kriedemann has better things to do.'

'No I haven't,' he said. 'I'll see you there.'

As he headed home, Gus smiled wryly. How true that was. He'd never been at such a loose end, with absolutely nothing to do and not a bean to his name. But she'd cheered him up. She was a thoroughly likeable woman, and good-looking too, with that creamy skin and unruly red hair. Funny Brodie had never mentioned her or the lad. When the brother had died, he'd taken it for granted that the late Michael Court had been a single man. However, he'd given her Brodie's address, warning that it would take time for a letter to reach him, and she'd been relieved to be able to contact him at last, so he guessed there was no problem.

Gus was impressed at the way this woman had taken the move to this country in her stride, with a job and all. Obviously she wasn't impressed with the job, but she'd been philosophical about it, claiming it would do for the while. 'The lad is happy and healthy, that's the main thing,' she'd said. 'He'll have a better life here.'

That reminded him of his own parents. How many times had he heard their story of finding work, the both of them, within a week of arriving in this country? The tale had been repeated more often over the last few years as an indictment of his own itinerant and, to them, wasted life.

They'd like Trella, he mused. She conforms to their ethics of hard work and savings, a determination to make good.

So will I, he told himself. When I get a stake.

His dream of buying that little pub had gone down the drain now, and all that remained was worry about Lester.

Gus decided he would write to Brodie. He could tell him about meeting his relations; that might encourage him to come back to Toowoomba. And on the way see if he could find out what had happened to Lester. Even if he had to call in the police. Gus had considered that option when he arrived in Charleville but he'd been hoping that Lester had gone ahead to Toowoomba. If Lester was still out in the bush, the blacks would find him faster than the police. But if, on the other hand, Lester had absconded with both parcels of opal, Gus hated the thought of putting the police on to him.

Brodie would have no such inhibitions. Gus laughed, feeling better now. Brodie Court would put in his own mother if she pinched any of his opals!

In the meantime, he decided, I'd better find a job myself. What a bloody let-down this has been.

When he arrived home, his mother remembered to tell him that she'd forwarded a letter on to Brodie at the diggings. 'I wouldn't be surprised if it was from that Mrs Holloway!' she snorted. 'Coming in here after him, trying to tell me it's for her husband she's asking. Queer friends you've got.'

Gus went through to his room. Mrs Holloway? Was she looking for Brodie or her money? The realisation that he also owed that woman money was another blow. His luck had truly run out.

Weeks later, when Brodie took his usual Saturday morning ride to the miners' store, the owner came out to greet him.

'Hey, Brodie! Is it your birthday or something? There's three letters for you.'

'For me? Good God!'

As the letters were taken from a pigeon hole and handed

to him one by one, he studied them. 'This one's from Gus. They're safe home in Toowoomba, I see by the mark. But the others . . .'

'Ladies, we reckon,' the self-styled postmaster commented, unabashed by his own nosiness.

'Could be.' Brodie winked and strolled outside. The only woman who'd be writing to him was Vivien, and he didn't need anyone peering over his shoulder. He'd been away so long she was probably furious with him.

The letter from Gus, with news of the sale of their opals, was practically burning a hole in his hand, but he postponed that excitement to open the others.

One was from Vivien, and what a surprise! A lovely surprise! She wasn't cross at all; this was the sweetest letter he'd ever received. He'd treasure it, the darlin' girl. She and Vern were back at Fairlea, Vern was worse, poor fellow, no use to himself any more, and Vivien was lonely. Dreadfully lonely. Missing her dear Brodie. Missing the sublime nights they'd spent together . . .

Brodie felt himself blushing as he read on: *I smother you in kisses, my darling, and long for you to come back and take me in your arms again. I'm waiting here for you, at Fairlea, with all my loving.*

The letter aroused him so much he groaned. He'd been managing to keep his mind off those steamy nights with Vivien, but now it was impossible. He wished she were here with him. God, how he needed her. He was almost of a mind to pack up and go straight to Fairlea, it was on the route back to Toowoomba. You'll not sleep too well tonight, he told himself.

The second letter snapped him out of his dreams of rapture.

It was from Trella! She was in Toowoomba, the bitch! What was she doing there? How dare she follow him and drag the boy with her?

Brodie was stunned. Furious. And what about the farm? Was it sold after all? Michael was dead. That farm belonged to Brodie Court now, not her. Typically, she didn't mention the farm. Hoping he'd forgotten about it, he supposed. Had she no shame? It was because of her that he'd fallen out with Michael and been able to speak no more to him before he died.

As he read her excited pages about how lovely was the new town and how happy they were, he gave a sudden yelp!

Gus! She'd met Gus, and found his friend such a nice man! His friend! Now she was moving in on his friends, no doubt to cause more trouble. He ripped up the pages and scattered the pieces in the dust, then turned to the last letter.

'Oh, Jesus!' he said, sitting back on the bench outside the store.

'What's the matter, Brodie? Bad news?' a miner standing nearby asked him.

'Terrible news,' he said, and read out Gus's tale of woe.

Other miners joined them, commiserating, offering opinions on what had become of Lester, none of them hopeful in any degree.

'That does it,' Brodie said at length. 'I'll have to fill in the shaft I'm working on and give it away for a while.'

On the way back to his camp, trying to figure out what to do for the best, he admitted to himself that it was time to leave the ridge anyway. He knew there had to be more opal there, he just couldn't put his hand on it. Besides, he had a new interest.

In fact he had them in his pocket now, but he wouldn't be showing them to anyone round here. He refused to allow himself to become excited about them until he saw Willi. He still had a lot to learn.

Keeping his promise to exercise Jolly had been a pleasure, breaking the monotony, and on one ride, as he'd traversed an ugly patch of land, more rough gravel than worthy soil, Jolly's hooves had kicked aside a couple of lumps of rock that flashed darkly. So dark he'd almost missed them.

Brodie dismounted to pick them up, surprised to find they were so heavy. He was certain they were the same marvellous black opal found in the yowah nuts that Willi had shown them, but he didn't dare hack at them for fear of spoiling what might be within. He took careful note of the site and his position, using a huge dead tree, lightning-split, as a marker, then turned back to the ridge.

That night, using the new writing pad and envelopes he'd bought at the store, Brodie sat down to answer his mail. He wrote to Gus, a short note, telling him that he was on his way home but that he'd first try to locate Willi Schluter to see if there was news of Lester. The second letter, written with more care, was a fond response to Vivien, promising that he would see her soon. He couldn't bring himself to write in such passionate terms as she had but made it clear that he was missing her by underlining 'soon'.

The next morning he packed up the camp and set out for Plenty Station homestead, where he hoped to join up with others who might be heading for Charleville or points east. Brodie had no intention of running into trouble out there as Gus and Lester had. A lone rider would be even more vulnerable.

It was possible that the Judge would be on the warpath again, but Brodie felt he could handle him. Besides, he wanted a word with that character. It was time to make the peace.

Accustomed to station life, Brodie bypassed the house and made for the stables, where he hitched the horse and washed under a tap.

A stockman ambled out. 'You Court, are you?'

'Yes.'

'Thought so. I recognised Jolly there. How's she going?'

'A beauty. I'll be sorry to leave her. Could you find me some scissors, this beard could do with a clip.'

'Bloody needs shearin',' the man grinned. 'Come on in and I'll see what I can do.'

Brodie guessed that the large scissors he produced were put to better use on the horses' manes, but they'd have to do. Working without a mirror and with the interested advice of the stockman, he hacked the straggling hair into what he hoped was a neat line, and chopped his moustache back too.

'Anyone here good at barbering?' he asked.

'Yeah. Old Barney's your man, but he's not around yet.'

'Tell him I'll be looking for him later. I'm going back to town so it's time I shaved this lot off.'

Barney was the stockman who'd not appreciated the cattle raid on the diggings. He'd come by since then with Clover on one of her visits.

'Well now,' Brodie said, standing back, running his hands through his damp hair. 'I think I'll pay the family a call.'

A lanky man stepped out, barring his way. 'Who says so?'

Brodie didn't need to be told who this one was either. The

man who'd led that raid for the Judge. Barney had identified him as Frank Dobson.

'A horrible bastard,' Barney had said. 'Sucks up to the boss all the time, looking for Slim's job.'

'What's it to you?' Brodie asked Dobson.

'We don't like no strangers here.'

'Sure you don't. But I'm no stranger. Now step aside.'

'You're one of them miners,' Dobson said. 'The Judge don't like you blokes on his property.'

'You could have fooled me,' Brodie laughed. 'I thought he loved us.' He pushed past Dobson and walked over to his horse.

'That's Jolly!' Dobson said, astonished. 'What are you doing with that horse? You can't touch any of our horses.'

Fed up, Brodie turned to him. 'I'm minding my own business, that's what I'm doing, so bugger off.'

Dobson spun about to the other stockman. 'You're supposed to be keeping an eye on the place. How come you let this scum in here?'

'What did you call me?' Brodie said ominously.

'Scum, I said! Bloody vagrants, hanging about a man's land to see what you can steal. You're not welcome . . .'

He didn't finish the sentence. Brodie had had enough aggravation lately. He punched Dobson and sent him flying, but the stockman came back at him, and to the delight of the watcher, the fight was on! Dobson was a tough opponent and as they slugged it out, Brodie saw the Judge coming.

'Bloody hell!' he muttered. So much for a quiet talk with the old bloke. He deliberately tripped Dobson and chopped him in the neck as he fell. Not the rules, but the fight was over.

The Judge didn't seem concerned. Brodie had the impression that he was disappointed that he'd missed most of the fight. Calmly the boss pushed at Dobson with a polished boot and ordered the other stockman to dump him in the horse trough.

'You don't fight fair,' he said to Brodie, who was wiping splatters of blood from his chin.

'It was a decision,' Brodie said. 'I didn't want you pulling a gun on me again while I was otherwise engaged.'

'Who are you?'

'Brodie Court's the name.'

'From where?'

'The Ten Mile.'

'You're one of those damned miners!'

'Was. I'm on my way home.'

'Then get going.'

'Hang on. I wanted a word with you.'

'Why should I be bothered talking to you?'

Brodie went over to his saddle pack. 'If you'll give me some breathing space, I want to show you something.'

The Judge pulled his hat further down on his face and squinted at him. 'Don't pull any tricks on me or you won't get off this station alive. Leave that rifle in its holster.'

'It's not the rifle I'm after.'

'And I'm not interested in anything you have, Mr Court.'

'We'll see about that,' Brodie said.

Under normal circumstances, the Judge told himself slyly, he'd have sent this rascal fleeing with buckshot in his pants, especially since he had the cheek to march on to the station and beat up one of the Plenty staff.

Chiswick didn't care about Dobson. The man was insufferable. Seeing him get a hiding had been a mild pleasure. But this fellow Court, what was he up to?

His spies had told the Judge that he'd escorted Clover back after the storm, and she'd allowed him to stay in the house. In his house! The nerve of that girl! If anything, he should have been sent to the bunkhouse with the other men. But of course she'd do anything to antagonise her father.

He also knew that she'd been out to visit Court at the Ten Mile, and even loaned him Jolly. When he first heard that, he was furious with her, but what could he do with the brat? They weren't speaking. He rarely saw her and when he did all he got from her was a defiant toss of the head. She was ignoring her father but it was interesting to note that she was paying so much attention to this Irishman.

The Judge would not invite Court into the house.

'You see to the horse,' he told him, 'then I can perhaps spare you five minutes.' He strode over to a bench under a wide jacaranda tree, mulling things over.

When Charlie came home he'd be taking a wife. Two women in the household, especially with one of them as

261

bossy as Clover, was a bad thing. Regardless of what Hannah had written before she killed herself, Samuel Chiswick loved Charlie. He didn't want to believe his wife's ravings, and as he'd often said, upbringing produced the gentleman and he'd certainly succeeded with his son, even if his daughter was a failure. Growing up surrounded by men, that was her trouble. She should have been sent to a nunnery at an early age.

He sighed. At my age I should be able to lean on my daughter; instead I have to work out how to move her on. She's a perpetual thorn in my side. And she's never taken any interest in the men until this Court fellow turned up. Not that she's had many suitors; even then she's given them short shrift, missing her chances.

It's possible, too, he worried, that Charlie has been waiting for his sister to be settled before he brings a wife home.

'That's it!' he exploded, slapping his palm on his knee. 'Charlie's too kind with her.'

Now, though, there might be a chance. He suspected that Clover had a crush on the Irishman. He was a big fellow, taller than her at least, and not bad-looking; he might just be the answer.

The Judge didn't care that Brodie Court was one of the scum, probably fit only to work anywhere else as a stockman or a rouseabout; that was her problem. Obviously Clover didn't have the sense to see she was setting her cap at a no-hoper, but she wouldn't be the first or the last to make that mistake. It would get her away from here, though, give her father a break from her irritating presence and clear the way for Charlie to marry.

Nevertheless, he mustn't make it too easy or she'd shy off on principle.

'Well, what do you want?' he growled as Court approached.

'Have a look at these,' Brodie said, handing him two of his best opal samples. His 'firsts'. They were only small, about two inches long, and dusty, just as they'd been gouged from the mine, still encased in hard sandstone which only served to emphasise the blaze of colour.

'Opal,' the Judge said, shrugging.

'I'm taking it you're not an ignorant man, sir. That's first-grade stuff, anyone can see that.'

'And not worth the trouble.'

Brodie smiled. 'So the rascals of buyers out here would have us believe, but I'll not settle for their prices. I can do a lot better.'

'What's this got to do with me?'

'This opal came from my Firefly mine, the one that was wrecked by your cattle.'

Chiswick smirked. 'Bad luck, eh?'

'Not bad luck. Stupidity. On your part.'

'Now see here,' the Judge bridled, 'if you've come to insult me . . .'

Brodie held up his hand. 'Steady on. I wanted to ask you if you're a man with so much money you don't need any more. Money that's sitting on your doorstep.'

'None of your business!' the Judge snapped, but Brodie saw the flicker of interest.

'Sure it is. Listen to me now. I'm leaving the mines for a while but I'll be back. And I'll have permits. No use saying it's your land and you'll put the ban on me, because I won't have that. I know the law.' Brodie was bluffing but he kept talking, not allowing the Judge to interrupt. 'But on the other hand, I can see your point. You don't want miners burrowing on your land unless you have control.'

'I've got control now.'

'Ah, but you have not. Once I get permits, word will be out. I'm suggesting a syndicate to mine the ridge properly. Not hit and miss, the way we're going.'

'The way you're going.'

'True, but you're not getting anything out of the mines. I am, sir. Are you with me now?'

'You want me to involve myself in mining? You're mad!'

'We form a syndicate, you and me, and we employ miners. You'll be earning from land you're not using anyway. I'll continue prospecting and working and I'll manage the mines as well.'

The Judge was silent for a while, staring at the opals. 'Where will you sell the opals, if not to local buyers?'

Brodie had already decided that if Willi's assessment of his gems was good enough he'd be selling them in England, not in this country. 'We can discuss that later,' he said cannily.

'Seems to me you're taking a risk coming here,' Chiswick said. 'I could form a syndicate without you.'

So he *was* interested! Brodie appeared unconcerned. 'Then I'd have to form another one with someone else.' Another bluff. He didn't know another soul who could finance the operation he had in mind. 'But you don't have to think on it this minute. I'll keep in touch. You can let me know. I know the area, I'd be the best mines manager you can find.'

The Judge stood up. 'How do I know I could trust you?'

'You could do a lot worse, I take it you have a poor opinion of miners?'

'With good reason,' the Judge growled. 'Walk over to the house with me. I'd have to know a lot more about this before I'd even consider it.'

When Clover rode in that afternoon and saw Jolly in the home paddock, she was delighted to know that Brodie had come to call, but she was soon dismayed when she saw him sitting on the veranda talking to her father.

'What's going on?' she asked Salty.

'I don't know. Mr Court's been talking to your father out there for nearly an hour.'

'Good Lord! What about?'

'You tell me. I wouldn't have been surprised if they'd come to blows but they look peaceful enough. Why don't you go and find out?'

Clover fumed, frustrated. 'You know I can't. The Judge and I aren't on speaking terms. He'd make a fool of me straight off. He'd love to embarrass me.'

'Then go and tidy up. We'll see what happens at dinner time.'

Samuel was enjoying this little triumph over his daughter. He'd seen her come in. Now she'd have to behave herself and address him if she wished to be part of this conversation with her boyfriend, or stay out. He knew she'd be dying of curiosity.

As for Court, his proposition was beginning to make sense. Why should he let miners take the wealth out of his land with no return to the owner?

It amused him, too, to think of Clover and Court getting

264

together. This chap probably thought that if he married Clover he'd be marrying money. A monumental mistake. She'd get nothing! Perhaps a fine wedding present like a grandfather clock to show on the day; after that she'd be reliant on her husband. As it should be.

Brodie was amazed. The old rascal was even smiling. In no hurry to send him on his way, even though he hadn't offered a drink or even a cup of tea. But it looked as if a syndicate could be worked out, and that was a giant step. He decided not to overstay his welcome.

'I'll leave you to think this over, sir. Could I put up in the bunkhouse? I'll be leaving for Charleville as soon as I can join up with some travellers. I'm prepared to pay for my food.'

The Judge shrugged, as if he couldn't be bothered with such trifles. 'Go down the side way here, that will take you directly across to the men's quarters. Report to Slim.'

Brodie didn't mind being dismissed like that. He left the house more than pleased with his plan. A syndicate could take over the whole of the Ten Mile and he could explore that other patch on his own. He figured he could trust the Judge as much as he could be trusted, and as long as Chiswick played fair with him then he'd play fair too. But look out if he tried a double-cross. Two could play at that game.

Clover had to run to catch up with him. 'I saw you up at the house. You were talking to my father! What about?'

'This and that,' he said cautiously. He couldn't have the father–daughter row intruding on his plans at this point.

'Amazing!' she laughed. 'How did you manage it?'

Brodie grinned. 'Maybe he just felt like a yarn. But how are you? You're lookin' pert and pretty. First time I've seen you in a skirt.'

She flushed. 'It's cooler than heavy trousers. What are you doing here anyway? Not that I'm not pleased to see you, I mean, I'm glad you called. Is anything wrong?'

Brodie took her by the arm. 'Let's move on a bit. There is a spot of bother but I'd as soon not mention it to your dad. I'm on my way back to town.'

'Does he know that?'

'He knows that much.'

'No wonder he's talking to you. He'll be pleased as punch that all the miners have gone now.'

'Temporarily,' Brodie said. He told her the bad news he'd received from Gus. 'It's perplexing,' he said. 'Lester's missing and I don't know what to think. Gus left an old mate of ours at a blacks' camp near a place called Red Bull Creek. Do you know the place?'

'No. But Barney would. He knows every tree and rock between here and Charleville. What's your mate doing there?'

'He's the one who put Gus back on track and went back to see if he could locate Lester. Willi's married to a gin, he's accepted by the blacks.'

'Do you mean Willi Schluter?'

'You know him?'

'Everyone knows Willi.'

'Good. I was thinking I might join up with someone riding back to Charleville, someone who could direct me to Red Bull Creek on the way. When does your mailman come through again?'

'About ten days.'

'That won't do. I have to get going. I don't suppose your father could spare me a man as escort? I'm carrying my opals, remember.'

Clover stood back and stared at him in wonder. 'You wouldn't dare ask him?'

'Why not?'

'Because he'd spit in your eye! Listen, I'll ride with you. He doesn't care what I do. And we'll take Barney with us as a guide. He can't object to me insisting on a chaperon.'

Brodie was appalled. He could see the good will he'd achieved with the Judge disintegrating into a heap. 'I couldn't ask you to do that, Clover. It's hard travel.'

'Nonsense. I've ridden to Charleville hundreds of times. The coach is too slow, it detours all over the place.'

'It wouldn't be right.'

'Of course it would. I'm not a child.'

He shook his head. 'I can't agree to this unless you get your father's approval.'

'We don't need to. We'll go at sun-up. By the time he finds out, we'll be miles away.'

'No. You check with him or you stay here.'

'All right, if you insist. But come on back with me now. You can stay in Charlie's room.'

'For God's sake, Clover. Are you set on antagonising the man when I've got him calmed down? He told me I could stay in the bunkhouse and that suits me. Leave well alone.'

She confronted the Judge as he sat comfortably on the veranda with his whisky and the *Countryman* magazine. 'I want to talk to you!'

'That's a change,' he growled, and went on reading, smugly certain that this had something to do with the Irishman.

'Mr Court is riding into Charleville tomorrow but he's not sure of the directions.'

'He found his way out here. Let him find his way back.'

'I want to go into Charleville, I need to do some shopping. I'm going with him.'

'That's his idea, I suppose.'

'No, it's not, as a matter of fact. He insists I have to get your permission. Why, I don't know.'

The Judge took his time lighting a cigar. Better still. She's doing the chasing, he mused. That Court's a smart bugger. He's got her measure.

'I won't have my daughter haring round the countryside with a stranger,' he said, determined not to make it easy for her, but as far as he was concerned she could ride off into the sunset with him right now. With luck she'd keep going. Elope with him.

'We wouldn't be alone if you're worried about talk. Barney can come with us.'

'What do you want to buy that we haven't got in our storeroom?'

'Plenty of things,' she snapped.

Deliberately he gazed out over the veranda, watching a flock of parrots skim across the sky, homeward bound.

'Well?' she said.

'Well what?'

'Can I go or not?'

'Ah, do what you like.'

They were drovers, Tom Monk and his brother Alby. The family had been drovers for generations. Their grandfather had driven great herds out west in the old days, and far north too, he'd said, to open up the monster cattle stations. Their father, reversing the route, had driven stock, when the time came, from those stations to the Brisbane markets, with his wife and kids perpetually on the road with them.

Now Tom and Alby had their own rig. They'd even driven cattle from the Centre, right down to Adelaide, through the driest country on earth, they liked to boast. But their normal runs were the thousands of miles of stock routes in Queensland.

The owners of Gilpepper Station out by Lake Yamma Yamma were restocking a run out there, so Tom and Alby were called on to deliver a thousand head from the Charleville sale yards.

That task completed after months on the road, they were rewarded with bonuses of ten pounds each for delivering the herd intact; a fitting end to the long and arduous journey.

With no cattle to bring back, the brothers dispersed their stockmen at various stations on the return trek, knowing they'd be available another time, and set their hats for a good ride east. Unhampered by slow-moving cattle on the long, lonely ride, the brothers were in high spirits. Distance, to them, did not exist as such. Their life was the road; the maze of stock routes in the outback was well known to them, and if they were washed away by flood, good drovers still knew where to go. It was said that the Monk brothers, like the Aborigines, had compasses in their heads.

So it was that this cheery pair, looking forward to kicking up their heels in town, found the remains of a horse, ravaged by dingoes, fair in the middle of a hard, dry gravel plain.

'This wasn't no brumby,' Tom said. 'Here's a saddle. The dingoes have had a chew at it too. And there's other junk here.'

'What sort of a fool would ride a horse across this country?' Alby said. 'It'd cut the poor beast's hoofs to pieces. Why didn't he ride round it?'

Carefully they retreated to a line of scrub, unwilling to risk their own mounts on that stony plateau.

'A week, I'd say,' Tom said, looking about.

'Yeah. It's been dead a week. But where's its rider?'

'Dunno. He might have had a mate with him. Another

horse. But I never saw no tracks back there where we come from. And we couldn't track them across there anyway. You wouldn't know which way they went.'

They left the mystery behind them, dodging through the scrub to choose the easier run of a wide, bone-dry watercourse.

'By Jeez,' Alby said as they cantered along, 'I remember this old creek when she were in full flood. Held us up for weeks she did.'

'She stinks now, though,' Tom said, reining in his horse. 'Take it quiet, there could still be mud lying there.'

Many a time the brothers had lost animals that raced ahead, smelling water in dried-up creeks, to sink into what was known as quicksand but more often was clinging, sucking mud.

They continued down the dry creek with its overhang of listless trees until Alby said: 'That ain't mud, that smell.'

Tom nodded, dismounting, and Alby followed, walking behind his brother.

'Oh shit!' Tom said. 'I think we've found our rider.'

The body had also been visited by dingoes, dragged about, horribly askew.

'Who is he?' Alby asked, standing back.

'How do I know?' Tom tied a handkerchief about his face and went to investigate.

He couldn't find any papers, anything to identify the dead man, only the usual pieces, a penknife, a tobacco tin, a small pick. 'See this pick! He was a gouger. He must have been coming in from the desert. A lot of gougers work along the edge of the big desert. Remember we met a pack of them when we took that herd down to Adelaide?'

'Why would he come this way?'

'Why not? It's just as far south as east from the Centre.' He took a stick to examine the corpse. 'Young enough, no grey hair. Teeth in good nick. Short bloke. Look at this, small feet.'

'You look,' Alby said, edging away. 'Let's bury him and get out of here.'

'Hang on. He could have had a camp near here.'

Methodically, Tom began beating about the undergrowth. 'Can't find no camp,' he yelled to Alby, who had retreated to the horses. 'No water bags either. I reckon the poor bugger just sat down and died of thirst.'

He continued his search until he found a heavy pack and then another. 'I got two saddlebags,' he said, bringing them back to Alby. 'The dingoes must have dragged them into the scrub.'

'Bring them upwind then,' Alby said. 'The smell's making me sick.'

When Tom opened the packs Alby stared. 'Opals!'

'That's right,' Tom said, turning each piece over. 'And good stuff too. Will you look at them! Pretty as pictures. All the colours of the bloody rainbow!'

'So what do we do now?' Alby asked.

'Finders keepers, mate. They ain't no use to this chap no more.'

'Good-oh. You've got a camp spade. You dig and we'll bury him, then let's get out of here.'

Tom looked over at the remains of the opal miner. 'No. We ought to let nature take its course. He don't know nothing about it so we can't hurt him.'

'We're not gonna bury him?'

'If we do, someone will know we've been here, won't they?'

'A good tracker would know anyway.'

'Only if they're looking. I'm bettin' that if someone comes across this body they'd see plain as day, like we did, how he died. There's no sign of violence, no bullet wounds, no cracked skull . . .'

'Oh, Jesus! Shut up! You're making me sick.'

'All I'm trying to say is that we're off. We take these packs and get the hell out of here. And we don't make straight for Charleville. We'll head south and cross the border so that we'll not be on this trail. No hurry to sell the opals. We're not starving. One fine day we'll produce them like we picked 'em up ourselves someplace. Which we did.'

'And we never saw that poor bloke back there?'

'What bloke?' Tom grinned. 'Let's go. If we really move we can cover a lot of territory before dusk.'

Sometimes Clover wished that Brodie could be less of a gentleman where she was concerned. There had been so many opportunities for him to show a romantic interest in her since they left Plenty that she'd lost count, but there hadn't been a murmur or a touch to cheer her.

'Do you think he likes me?' she asked Barney.

'Sure he does. Everyone likes you, Clover.'

'Not like that. You know what I mean.'

'Oho! You fancy him, do you? Your old man won't like that.'

'I don't care, it's my life. He's not married, but do you think he's got a girlfriend somewhere?'

'How would I know? He's never mentioned one. He seems too intent on finding this bloke Lester than talking about women.'

Late on the second day, Barney led them to the blacks' camp at Red Bull Creek, where they found that Willi had not yet returned.

Brodie was impatient. 'He could have scoured the country from here to Brisbane by this!'

'He travels on foot, remember. And they'd be thorough if they think your mate's lost in the bush. Besides, he wouldn't be expecting you, so what's the rush?'

'Maybe he won't come back this way at all.'

'Yes he will, Lena's here.'

Clover intervened. 'In that case I vote we go on to Lilly Pilly Station and put up there. We'll soon hear if there's any news.'

The owners of the station and their daughter, Elizabeth, were happy to welcome the visitors. They'd heard of a missing white man in the area but no one at this property had sighted him, even though the alarm was raised.

Clover shared Elizabeth's bedroom, since they were acquainted, but she had not counted on the girl's interest in Brodie.

'He's gorgeous, Clover. Is he your boyfriend?'

'Of course not! Barney and I are just helping him to find his way. We're all worried about his friend.'

'And there's nothing going on between you two?'

'Don't be ridiculous!'

'Then you won't care if I make up to him. He's got the most beautiful eyes.'

'Why should I?'

Clover suffered seriously from heartache as she watched Elizabeth monopolising Brodie, while Elizabeth's parents entertained Clover, delighted to hear news of their friend Judge Chiswick and, of course, of Charlie, who was now in the thick of the Boer War.

Elizabeth took Brodie on tours of the station, discouraging Clover. 'You don't want to come with us, do you?'

'No, I've had enough riding for the time being.' That was a lie, of course, but what else could she say? Furiously she wandered about the homestead, watching for their return.

At dinner, Elizabeth's father took over, talking to Brodie about cattle.

'Brodie's very interested in stations,' Elizabeth whispered to Clover. 'He says one day he'll have one of his own. So tomorrow I'm going to show him our prize bulls. Two of them won medals at the Brisbane Show last year.'

'Yes, I know,' Clover replied, pretending to be bored. If Brodie wants to know about cattle, why doesn't he ask me? she thought angrily. I know more than this silly bitch will ever know.

It was days before one of the black stockmen came to the house to tell them that Willi was back at the camp, and Clover was relieved that Brodie responded quickly.

'I'm sorry, Clover, but would you mind if we left right away? I don't want Willi wandering off again.'

'Not at all,' she said, with a smile for Elizabeth, who might have been flirting with Brodie but so far had made no headway.

In retaliation Elizabeth took Clover aside. 'He was very nice to me, but I think he's true to his girlfriend.'

'What girlfriend?' Clover asked, startled.

'I'm sure I don't know, but if he's not interested in me then he must have one somewhere.'

Looking at her, Clover was inclined to agree. Elizabeth was a pretty little thing, with those dark curls and fair skin, and she wore fetching dresses in attractive pinks and blues, buttoned tight to show off her small waist. Brodie could hardly not have noticed how pretty she was.

Clover became acutely aware of her own rough shirt and trousers, and was determined to buy some nice dresses in

Charleville and have them sent to the Plenty homestead, in the hope that Brodie might return one day.

When she rode away with the two men she was more depressed than she'd ever been in her life.

Brodie shuddered. Lester was dead. 'Died of thirst,' Willi had said with a shrug, as if this were a common occurrence.

Brodie tried not to think of Lester's death, of how he had died. It was too awful to contemplate.

'Got lost,' Willi said, 'reeling about out there in all directions. We kept crossing his tracks. He was turning back this way when he gave up. But no sign of the opals.'

'He'd not have been in any state to be carrying anything,' Brodie said. 'He must have dropped the packs.'

'Possible, but I doubt it. He even threw away his rifle and ammo, the poor fool. He could have shot game, you'd have to be blind to miss a kangaroo. Even raw they're sustenance. It's my guess he dumped everything except the opals.'

'Then where are they?'

'Dunno. We searched everywhere. Even back to the horse. But the blacks tell me two horsemen rode down that old river bed where we found him. They didn't make camp and it's difficult to tell, since there's been no rain, whether they passed that spot before or after Lester came to rest there.'

'Do you think they took the opal packs?'

'They could have. Or Lester could have hidden them even before that. Whatever . . . Gus can say goodbye to his share.'

There was consolation, however, when Willi examined Brodie's parcels of opal, delighted that they'd found such good-quality stones.

'Now try this,' Brodie said, producing the two new stones he'd picked up, with the barest glint of dark opal.

'They *are* interesting!' Willi said. 'But I haven't got the proper tools with me to check. I could split them with a tomahawk but it's a terrible risk. I might destroy a good opal.'

'A black opal?' Brodie asked breathlessly.

'We'll see. Don't get your hopes up.'

'I can wait,' Brodie said. 'And I'd like you to cut and polish all my stuff. I wouldn't trust anyone else. Would you do it for me? I'm willing to pay.'

'Righto,' Willi said. 'It's time Lena and me went home anyway. She says the rains will start soon and we don't want to get cut off out here. We'll make our own way home. You go on with your lady to Charleville.'

'She's not my lady,' Brodie said, surprised.

'You'd better tell her that.' The old man winked. 'She's got calf eyes for you, lad.'

'Clover's just a friend. She loaned me the horse and she'll be taking it home when I hand it back in Charleville.'

Willi nodded. 'A friend is what a man needs. You could do a lot worse than her, even if you do have to put up with that bastard Chiswick for a father-in-law. His wife was a lovely woman but he ill-treated her. She took her own life.'

'Good God! Is that so?'

'It is, and don't you be leading that girl on.'

'I'm not. And you're imagining things. As a matter of fact, Clover's just using me as an excuse to have a break from the old man. They don't get on.'

Once again he and Clover and Barney were on their way. Brodie was glad he hadn't mentioned to Willi that he was hoping to make a deal with the Judge. That wouldn't have gone down too well. He'd had time to give the matter more thought and he hoped to persuade the Judge, as owner, to take a ten-acre mining lease on Sandy Ridge to keep out freelance miners; then they could employ men to work the mines.

When they reached Charleville, Brodie sent a telegram to Gus advising him of Lester's death and of the loss of certain packs. He then sent another telegram, this time to Mr Vern Holloway at Fairlea Station, wishing him well and stating that he would be visiting shortly.

The latter subterfuge made him feel a little squeamish, but it was necessary. He had no qualms about making love to Mrs Holloway so he wondered why that innocuous telegram should bother him.

I must be slipping, he told himself. I'm sorry for him but I have to look out for Brodie Court.

Thinking of Lester, he realised that they'd never know whether he really had gone for help or had absconded with the loot. And poor old Gus, he'd missed out altogether. All those months of work for nothing.

His next stop was the police station, where he filled in the necessary papers relating to the death of Lester O'Dowd. He promised that Willi Schluter, the man who'd found the body and buried it, would come in and complete the paperwork. And then he reported the loss or theft of two packs of opal, describing the contents as best he could, and giving his own name as well as that of Gus Kriedemann as the rightful owners.

These chores completed, Brodie spent a pleasurable hour at the barber's shop and then made his way back to the Albert Hotel, where he'd left the other two.

Clover took one look at him and laughed. 'Oh my Lord, I didn't recognise you, Brodie! Clean-shaven you're almost a stranger.'

'Then wait until I buy some new clothes,' he joked. 'I'll cut quite a dash.'

They had persuaded Barney to take a room at the hotel at Clover's expense, but he flatly refused to join them in the dining room.

'I don't like them swell places,' he said. 'I'll go and find some of my mates.'

Clover was relieved. That meant she could dine alone with Brodie, a wonderful treat. She was sure he had no idea how handsome he looked, all spruced up, but she did, and she walked proudly in with him, acknowledging the smiles of friends and acquaintances in the crowded room. She'd only packed a skirt and blouse for town, and bundled in black shoes and stockings which were good enough for now, but in the morning she really did intend to shop. She wanted Brodie to see her at her best.

For his part, Brodie was facing yet another new experience. He'd never before dined in a hotel, and he'd have much preferred to go off with Barney, but Clover gave him no choice. He was nervous, feeling that everyone was staring at him, but he reminded himself that if he were to be a moneyed man, he'd better get used to this life.

The handwritten menu had no prices on it, and that bothered him. God knows what this is costing, he thought grimly. He still had cash but couldn't see the point in throwing it away in a place like this. Vivien's money wouldn't last forever.

275

He had to admit, though, it was a good feed: soup and steak and bread and butter custard.

Clover didn't talk much but Brodie didn't mind. He'd noticed, riding with her, that she, like Barney, could travel for hours without saying much at all. The stockmen he'd worked with at Fairlea were the same; they just rode, eyes skinned all the time, not needing conversation. He supposed that living on those lonely stations the women became as sparse with words as the men. Back in Tullymore, with so many people about, it was hard to get a word in, to beat the gossip and speculations.

'Did you enjoy your dinner?' she asked him.

'Indeed I did. You've been very patient, Clover, putting up with my sidetracking to get here. I suppose you'll be heading back tomorrow.'

'No fear,' she said. 'I've come this far, I might as well have a real holiday. This hotel's very comfortable. I'll be here a week at least.'

'Good for you,' he smiled. 'Would you care to walk outside now? We might go for a stroll up the street.'

'I'd love to.'

As they walked along the dusty main street in the soft evening light, it dawned on Brodie that his friend Willi could be right. That Clover really did fancy him. And he was worried. She was a nice girl, no arguing with that. Strong and sensible too. But she wasn't a patch on Vivien. He desperately needed to see Vivien again. If Clover hadn't been such a nice girl, he'd have had her upstairs in her hotel bedroom in a flash. When you got past that mannish stride and the strong, jutting jaw like the old man's, she was built like a statue, with her long legs and pointy breasts and no sign of a corset needed.

She walked primly beside him. It would never occur to her to take his arm, he mused. Clover was no flirt and she was probably still a virgin, but he could feel the power of her enticing him.

Jesus, he said to himself, I really must be slipping. In the old days he'd never have let an opportunity like this pass.

Still, there was the problem of Clover staying in town. It was obvious that she expected him to remain in the hotel while they waited for Willi to reach Charleville, which would take at least a week, but Brodie decided he wasn't that far gone on new ideas to be wasting money like that. He could find cheap digs with Barney for a few bob a night, bunking down with other stockmen, but she'd be offended and he didn't want to hurt her feelings. She'd been a good friend.

When she'd waltzed up and booked them into the hotel, he'd tried to back out. 'I'm not sure I can afford this.'

'Don't worry, I'll pay,' she'd said airily.

Had it been Vivien, he'd have agreed, having no inhibitions with that lady, nor she with him, but with Clover some sense of dignity had made him refuse.

'I'll pay my own way,' he'd said.

And now he was stuck with it. Brodie's hair stood on end at the thought of paying full board in a real hotel for at least a week. He did have money in the bank from the rent from his house in Toowoomba, but that money was not for spending.

As they neared the front door of the hotel, he made a decision. 'Now you have a good time here in Charleville. You look up your friends and enjoy yourself. I'll see you back at your station.'

'Why? Where are you going?'

'There's a morning train to Brisbane, I have to be on it.'

'Why? I thought you had to wait for Willi?'

'Gus will be worrying. If I catch that train I can go on to Toowoomba and attend to business there, then come back next week to find Willi. I don't have time to wait about.'

'Oh.'

That was all she could say. That was all someone like Clover could say. Brodie saw the hurt in her face, he saw the sadness, a great loneliness in her eyes, but he couldn't help. He had his own problems.

'You will be back?' she asked. 'To Plenty, I mean?'

'Sure I will. As soon as I can. I'm not finished mining.'

He was tempted, then, to tell her about the deal he was hoping to work out with her father, but decided against it. He had the feeling she'd regard him as a traitor to her cause and wanted to avoid that disruption until he had things sewn up.

'You've been very kind to me, Clover, I won't forget that. Take care of Jolly.'

Brodie surprised himself by giving her a kiss on the cheek,

finding her tanned skin soft and dewy. 'You go on up now. I think I'll have a drink in the bar.'

The worst thing about arriving back at the bakery in Toowoomba was not commiserating with Gus about the death of Lester, which, despite Brodie's doubts, Gus insisted was due to Lester's heroic efforts to find help for him.

It wasn't even that Gus was now working in a bar, determined never to set foot on a gold field or an opal field ever again.

It was that Gus was now walking out with Trella Court! And Michael scarce cold in his grave.

Brodie sat coldly in the Kriedemann kitchen that first night, hearing about his insidious sister-in-law who had wormed her way into this family. Hearing from Jakob and Lisa Kriedemann that their son was a changed man since he met this good woman. Hearing about his fine nephew and how they'd all become one big family.

One big bloody family, he fumed. Is that so? Do they know how she'd wrecked *his* family? Turning brother against brother?

Gus persuaded him to unpack his opals, and as the stones fell out on the dining room table, his parents turned them over in wonder.

'They are so beautiful,' Mrs Kriedemann said. 'You really did find gems like this, Gus?'

'I told you I did,' he replied, irritated.

'Oh, what a shame.'

'No use crying over spilt milk,' his father said, and Brodie felt guilty that he'd brought nothing but depression into this household.

In the morning, being Sunday, Gus roused Brodie from a deep sleep. 'Come on, wake up. We're going to Mass.'

'We're what? Not me. I've been sitting up on trains for two days.'

'You have to come. We're all going. Trella will be there with Garth. They'll be so excited to see you. It's a surprise.'

The last person he wanted to see was Trella, but since he was a guest in the Kriedemann household, Brodie didn't have any choice. In no time, like an unwilling penitent, he was being marched along the street with the Kriedemanns, towards the church. Towards the woman whom he hated most in the whole world and who would one day pay for what she'd done to the Court family.

As if reflecting his mood, dark, green-tinged clouds mounted the sky, and when the group turned in to the churchyard a squall of rain buffeted them.

Providential, Brodie thought, because at the same time Garth came racing down the path to throw himself at his uncle with whoops of joy.

'Uncle Brodie!' he shouted, ignoring the rain. 'Where have you been? We've been waiting for you for ages!'

Brodie grinned, pulling Garth's cap down on to his face, teasing him. 'Who is this fellow? You're not Garth Court, he was just a little squirt!'

'Yes I am,' Garth insisted. 'It's me, and I've got a job now. We came all the way on a ship and I never did get sick . . .'

As Garth talked, full of excitement, Brodie felt a twinge of regret. The lad was so like his late father, even to the necessity of having to tell him everything at once, as Michael used to do.

Garth clung to him as they joined the others in the small, crowded porch. He saw her smiling at him, and nodded to her, using the confusion as an excuse not to push through and embrace her. And then it was time to go into the church; the Mass had started.

Deliberately, Brodie chose a pew across the aisle from her and was delighted when Garth broke loose from his mother to join him. A small win, he acknowledged, but not the last.

Later, in the Kriedemanns' parlour, he was forced to address her, or rather answer her questions. She was looking presentable, he had to admit, in a brown skirt with a starched white blouse dollied up with a brown bow, and a boater hat pinned on top of rolls of that red hair. Everyone, except Brodie, was thrilled at the reunion. They drank tea and ate pastries, and to celebrate, Jakob served glasses of his home-made wine.

Eventually she managed to get him on his own. 'It's good to see you looking so well, Brodie.'

He nodded. 'Is the lad missing his father?'

279

'He'll always miss him. He was broken-hearted when Michael died, God rest his soul.'

'But you're managing,' he said meanly, with a glance at Gus.

'Is that it? I wondered why you were being so cool. Gus has been very kind to me, and the boy.'

'Does he know you're in mourning? Or is this the new colour?'

'He knows,' she said quietly, 'and I'll wear what colour I like. What I do is none of your business.'

'Is that so? Then what about my farm? What happened to it?'

She stood back apace. 'Michael sold the farm. You know that. You said he could.'

'I said Michael could. Not you. He was welcome to my half, being my only brother but I never said I'd hand it to you.'

'Listen to yourself,' she snapped. 'Michael your only brother, you say! Did you ever try to get in touch with him? Not you! You had to insult him by working through the priest, and you let him die without a word to console him. You're a bitter man, Brodie Court, and you'll end up a lonely old man if you don't mend your ways.'

'No one told me he was dying.'

'Would it have mattered? You've never cared for anyone but yourself and you haven't changed. I'll pay you back for your half of the farm if it takes all my days. In the meantime, you behave yourself, unless you want to cut yourself off from Michael's son as well.'

She stormed away, and minutes later was chatting to Mrs Kriedemann as if nothing had happened.

The following night Brodie came to visit her with Gus, and Trella was relieved that he had not ignored her warning. He brought a brand-new cricket bat for Garth, and the boy was delighted. There was no apology for his outrageous demand on the sale of the farm and she determined to save the money and give it to him.

And I hope he chokes on it!

Embarrassed by his attitude, she said not a word to Gus, who, she knew, would see her point of view. He was a fair man. But if he took these matters up with Brodie on her behalf, there could be trouble. She didn't want to cause bad blood between them.

Trella shivered. She and Gus weren't just walking out, they were deeply in love. In her prayers she often spoke to Michael of her life and of the blessings that had come upon her with him watching over. 'In due time,' she told him, 'I expect we'll be married and your family will have a good man, not to take your place but to bring up your son as you would have wished.'

All of a sudden Trella was afraid of Brodie. Afraid of what he might do to break up her relationship with Gus.

She wished she hadn't let Brodie provoke her. In future she'd be nicer to him. Go out of her way to make a fuss of him. It wouldn't be easy but she'd do anything to hold on to Gus.

Chapter Nine

The mistress of Fairlea Station smothered a scream of delight when she received Vern's mail. When she opened the telegram. How clever of Brodie! He was coming back! Ostensibly to see Vern, but she could read between the lines.

She was so excited she could hardly think straight, her head swimming with all sorts of plans, wonderful plans. She didn't care about the money he owed her. She now had control of Vern's bank accounts and investments, so a few hundred to Brodie didn't matter. Christiana hadn't even tried to hold on to the power of attorney once they were back at Fairlea, but Vivien knew that was only because she'd known she'd lose.

'Marvellous!' she laughed. Christiana must be furious. She hadn't been out to Fairlea but wrote to Vern every week, long, dreary letters that Vivien didn't even show him in case they caused a flicker in his dim brain. She wanted him to forget all about that cranky old woman and those silly games she was always suggesting. He was best left alone. Sometimes Elvie took him on a picnic and Vivien went along on those jaunts, boring though they were, to be seen as the caring wife.

She wondered if she should tell the housekeeper that Mr Court would be visiting her husband shortly . . . pave the way. But then she decided against it. The Holloways didn't have to confide in their staff.

Brodie here. With her! She luxuriated in daydreams of the joys ahead. He could stay in the house and spend every night in her bed. Vivien giggled. It will be his turn to come to my room!

But what about his wife and family?

She shrugged. He still loved her, of that she was sure, or he wouldn't be on his way to Fairlea. If Brodie had a wife in tow, and he cared about the woman, then he wouldn't have bothered to reply to her letter.

'Thank God I wrote to him!' she crowed. 'At least I can prepare for him.'

But how? They'd still be restricted here at Fairlea, having to be circumspect outside the house, and inside, too, with Elvie hovering about. Maybe she should send the housekeeper away. Give her a holiday.

No, she said to herself. I won't saddle myself with chores. I need her to cook for us. We'll have splendid meals. And she can keep Vern out of the way.

Out of the way, she pondered. She ought to divorce Vern but it probably wasn't possible. Besides, that meant handing back control of his assets to Christiana. Fat chance, she thought. I'd be lucky to get a penny a week out of the old witch.

A better idea would be to sell Fairlea Station. Get rid of it. Then she could take Vern and move to Brisbane, or even further afield where no one knew them. But she'd never shake Christiana. As it was, she kept asking for Vern to come and stay with her, requests that Vivien steadfastly ignored. Sooner or later the famous Christiana Holloway would be on her doorstep, whether here or as far away as they went.

'Oh my God!' Vivien was horrified at the thought of Christiana arriving when Brodie was here. It could happen.

'Damn,' she said aloud. 'Anything could happen unless I make up my mind to sort all this out. I ought to go to Toowoomba right away, meet Brodie there, but I wouldn't know how to contact him now. I'll just have to wait until I see him. Confront him about the wife first. Then we'll see.'

In order to make a better impression on the staff, for the next few weeks Vivien took her husband horse-riding, pacing slowly beside him along bush tracks or down by the river, and displayed much more enthusiasm about the picnics, even insisting they took some of that leftover champagne to make for more festive occasions.

Elvie was delighted. 'Mrs Holloway will be happy to hear how much Vern enjoys these outings.'

With a shock, Vivien realised that Elvie was keeping in touch with Christiana. Pimping on her! She felt like sacking her on the spot.

Bide your time, she warned herself. Find a replacement first. Then get rid of her.

* * *

Brodie had no time to waste. Although he was still staying in the sleep-out attached to the Kriedemann house, he felt no need to divulge his business affairs to any of them.

He checked on his house, finding that the tenants were keeping it in good order, inside and out, and then called on the agent, who was also the rent collector. He'd heard talk that these chaps could be slick with other men's money, so he marched into the office of Clem Patchett prepared for battle.

To his surprise, everything was in order. The rent payments, less commission, tallied to the penny with the bank deposits. Patchett even offered him a cup of tea, and Brodie sat in the office feeling very important.

'By the way, Mr Court, the cottage next door to yours is for sale too. If you bought that you'd have a fine block.'

'So I would, but a man's not made of money.'

'But you're a man who's going places, I can tell. That place is solid built too, and going cheap. The owners are moving away.'

Brodie thought about his opals. 'I'll have some spare cash soon but I've other plans for the placement.'

'You don't have to find the money,' Patchett enthused. 'It's right here. Why don't you use the rent you've accumulated as a deposit, and the rent from both houses would pay off the rest.'

'Can that be done?'

'I can arrange it for you.'

'Why would you do that?'

Patchett smiled. 'I'd be getting my commission on two rents instead of one. I'm trying to build up my rent collection business.'

'And you get commission on the sale of the second cottage?'

'You don't have to pay it. You stick with me, Mr Court. I won't see you wrong.'

Bemused by this turn of events, and not a little flattered, Brodie plunged in.

'Right you are. You buy it for me, but make it under forty pounds this time. And don't tell them who's buying or they'll want more.'

Before he left, Brodie asked his agent to direct him to a reliable lawyer, and two doors down the street he stepped into another office to introduce himself to a Stanley Wickham.

'What can I do for you sir?' Wickham asked.

This was a younger man than Brodie had expected, and the Irishman wasn't too sure about him, but he listened carefully as his client outlined a plan to form a mining syndicate with Judge Chiswick.

'Chiswick?' Stanley was impressed. 'A good name to have on your side.'

'That's what I thought. He's inclined to like the idea, but before he goes cold on it, I want you to help me draw up a proposal, and then you submit it for me. I reckon it would sound more businesslike coming from you.'

'At least with a judge you know you're dealing with an honest man,' Stanley said.

He raised his eyebrows when Brodie growled: 'I wouldn't bet on it. I have to take my chances with him because he owns the land. The way I see it, the syndicate employs miners and I'm to be paid as mines manager. We have the licence and we supply the equipment to the men.'

'What about their food and accommodation?'

'They take care of their own camps. I want to keep this as simple as possible.'

Stanley looked at him keenly. 'Mr Court, what's to stop miners from stealing opal instead of handing it over?'

'A bit of that could go on, but it'd be my job to police it. Bonuses for men who strike colour are incentives in other mines, I'm told, so we could work the same way.'

They discussed the legal arrangements between Court and Chiswick until the lawyer was clear as to his client's requirements.

'How much money will it take to set up this syndicate?' he asked Brodie.

'As little as possible,' Brodie said. 'I have to work that out. At the minute I haven't got any.'

Stanley was startled. 'Then how do you expect to start?'

'I'll find it. But I want you to put that to him first. Tell him we should start with four miners. Get the estimate from him. Let him make the running. There are other miners on Sandy Ridge, he'll soon find out what equipment costs, and a going wage, without my help. He's a wily old bird. When we get that straight, then it will be time for me to see how much I need. Can you do all that for me?'

'Certainly. We'll call it an expression of interest on your part and see what he has to say.'

'Good! I'll be out of town for a while. I'll be in to see you in a few weeks.'

'Your address, Mr Court? I don't have your address.'

'That's easy,' Brodie said. 'Make it care of you.'

Pleased with himself, Brodie visited a jeweller's shop, examining opals and their prices but buying nothing. He heard there was a race meeting that day so went along to fill in time enjoying a few drinks as he watched the races, without wasting money on bets. Finding a race book he amused himself picking horses, none of which won, so he was feeling very smug when he walked back into town, deciding to visit his nephew – though not the mother – after he'd had a meal in a cheap pub.

He took the boy a bar of chocolate and sat in the yard with him, telling him stories of Ireland.

Garth was more interested in his prospecting. 'Gus said you dug up some beautiful opals. When can I see them, Uncle Brodie?'

'I'll show them to you when I have time,' he said. 'You're a big lad now, Garth. You ought to come with me. Try your luck as a miner. You might strike it rich.'

'I can? You'd really take me? When?'

'Not for a while yet. I've got a few things to do.'

'But you'll let me know when you're going? Promise me! You wouldn't go without me. I can dig. I can handle a shovel and a pick. Gus says it's hard work but I could do it. You'll have to show me your opals so that I know what I'm looking for.'

'Hang on!' Brodie laughed. 'I'm not going tonight. For that matter I have to get home. I'm tired. You take yourself off to bed.'

Garth raced in to tell his mother. 'Uncle Brodie says I can go mining with him!'

'You'll do no such thing.'

'But he said I could.'

'Where is he? Putting such ideas in your head.' Trella rushed outside but Brodie had already left.

'I made him supper of cocoa and biscuits,' she said, 'but since he didn't bother to come in you might as well have it.'

Garth sulked as he drank his cocoa. 'Why can't I go?'

'Because you're too young.'

'I'm not too young.'

'Yes you are. I won't have you going off into the wilds with him.'

'Why not? I wouldn't be any trouble.'

'Stop your talk, you're not going and that's flat. You've got a job here.'

'But I'd make more money out there. Uncle says . . .'

'I don't care what Uncle says. It's hard enough for us to keep life and limb together here without you traipsing away after pipe dreams.'

'That's why you want me to stay! Just because you want my money. My pay. You don't care about what I want.'

She reached out to him. 'Oh my dear, it's not that at all. Mining's dangerous. I wouldn't want anything to happen to you.'

But he pulled away from her. 'Nothing would happen to me. I just have to stay here and keep giving you my pay. You're plain mean, that's what you are. I am going with Uncle Brodie. I am!' He slammed out of the kitchen.

'Blast Brodie!' she snapped.

Salty, the long-suffering housekeeper, was beginning to find Clover's bad mood even more trying than the old man's tempers. They were both getting on her nerves, and every night she prayed to the Lord to send Charlie home safe and sound. All the joy of the homestead seemed to have gone with him, leaving a terrible void.

Clover and her father were speaking again, since she'd been forced to ask him about going to Charleville, but instead of silences Salty now had to listen to them sniping at one another. She'd been delighted when Clover's new clothes arrived a few weeks after the girl's jaunt to town. At last this tomboy was taking an interest in her appearance.

They'd had fun unpacking the large boxes. Clover hadn't

stinted herself, or rather her father's accounts, going at shopping head-on, as she did everything else.

'This must have taken you days,' Salty enthused as she shook out silk dresses, taffeta skirts, pretty blouses, soft white day dresses with lace flounces, neat shoes, even hats.

'Yes, it did,' Clover said grimly, as if she'd endured torture, and Salty smiled to herself. Although Clover liked to think so, she was no different from other girls; she'd have had the time of her life on a shopping spree like this.

She unpacked the hatbox, finding some of the creations weird and wonderful, but tucked them away with care.

Clover was still miserable, staring at all the finery. 'Don't know when I'll ever get to wear any of it.'

'There'll be lots of opportunities. You won't be able to use the excuse of nothing to wear any more, my girl. These dresses are gorgeous. Try them on for me.'

'Not now. I can't be bothered.'

'Then I insist you wear this cream muslin to dinner. I want to see you in something new for a change.'

The muslin was more tailored than the other dresses, with a wide, flat collar in a neat V-line to the waist, over a ribbed bodice. The skirt, in the new slim fashion, dropped softly to the floor, weighted only by a double hem.

Despite Clover's protests the housekeeper won. She was determined to see that the girl became accustomed to wearing decent clothes. She tied the satin sash at Clover's back and stood her in front of the mirror.

'Well! Look at that! It suits you beautifully, Clover. Oh, my stars! I can't wait to see you in those formal dresses.'

Clover shrugged. 'I suppose it looks all right.'

'It looks very smart and you know it. Now don't go plaiting your hair, you'll spoil the effect.'

'Who's going to care?'

'I am. Sit down and I'll fix it for you.' She set to work back-combing Clover's brown hair until it stood out all over her head in a wild and woolly mess.

'What are you doing?' Clover exclaimed. 'I look ridiculous.'

'Be quiet.' Salty took a brush and a box of hairpins and began to lift the hair into soft rolls over the puffed-out base.

At last a style emerged as Salty brushed the last strands into place.

Clover stared at herself in the mirror. Her face was framed in a wide, smooth sweep of hair that met neat rolls on the crown.

'Cripes!' she said. 'How did you do that?'

'Ladies don't say cripes. And you saw how I did it. You have to learn to dress your own hair. You look lovely, Clover.'

Transformed into a fashionable woman, even an attractive one, Clover was suddenly shy. 'I can't go about looking like this.'

'You can, and you will. Starting right now.'

When this tall, elegant woman walked into the dining room with Salty, the Judge merely glanced at them. Then he stopped, glass in hand, to stare at his daughter. 'Good God! What's got into you?'

'She's been shopping,' Salty said proudly. 'Doesn't she look nice?'

'Mutton dressed up as lamb!' he growled.

'You would say that,' Clover retorted. 'You never have a good word for anyone.' She strolled past him, feeling superior now, knowing her appearance had surprised him. 'I think I'll have a sherry too.'

'Is the boyfriend coming to dinner?' her father asked meanly.

'What boyfriend?'

'The Irishman. I thought we must be expecting someone.'

'I don't know what you're talking about,' Clover said serenely.

'Why? What did he do? Dump you?'

Clover could feel the colour rising in her face. She ignored him, concentrating on pouring a glass of sherry from the crystal decanter as if her life depended on it.

The Judge turned to Salty, laughing. 'She went galloping off with him thinking she'd at last found a beau. Even bought enough clothes to stuff a trousseau, and what happens? Nothing.'

'That's uncalled for,' Salty protested.

'No it's not. She comes back here with a face as long as a lovelorn cow. And why? Because he dumped her. Left her hanging about Charleville on her own. And she hasn't had a word from him since.' He turned to Clover. 'I'm right, aren't I? You got dumped. He used you.'

They both jumped as Clover hurled the decanter. It narrowly missed the Judge, slamming into the fireplace, splattering sherry.

'You're a pig of a man,' Clover shouted. 'I'll eat in the kitchen.'

As she stormed out he turned back to Salty, ignoring the mess behind him. 'So much for trying to turn her into a lady. I'll have my dinner now.'

'Get it yourself,' she snapped. 'I quit. And if that girl's got any sense she'll come with me.'

The two women talked late into the night.

'You can't stay here,' Salty said. 'I'm frightened that you and your father will eventually come to violence.'

'This is my home. I won't let him push me out.'

'Don't be so stubborn. You're unhappy here, you don't enjoy Plenty Station any more. Come to Toowoomba with me. You can go to your Aunt Maggie, she has always been fond of you. Maggie's a wealthy woman, she'd never see you stuck.'

'But what about you?'

'My sister lives in Toowoomba, remember? I'll move in with her. I've got my savings, and it's time I retired anyway.'

'And I let my father win?'

'Good God, girl, have a bit of sense. You're coming with me and that's that. At least until Charlie comes home.'

Clover brightened. 'That's it! I'll just lie low until Charlie gets back and then we'll see what happens. He'll be furious at the way I've been treated.'

Two days later, with Clover driving, the wagon rolled down the road, packed with their luggage. Under instructions from the foreman, Slim McClure, two stockmen rode with them, delegated to escort them to the next station homestead, where they could stay over and proceed in stages to Charleville.

Their departure from Plenty had been a glum affair, the men standing about in quiet anger, for by this, they all knew what had happened. The Judge remained inside the house.

But once on the road, enjoying the jaunt, Clover felt better. Not only was she free of that miserable old man, but the housekeeper was leaving too. He'd never find anyone as good as Salty. Now who had won? She slapped the reins and began to sing as the two horses gathered speed.

The Kriedemanns were under the impression that Brodie's departure meant that he was on his way back to see Willi Schluter, so he hadn't volunteered the truth. Instead he was making for Fairlea Station, via that little hamlet, Wirra Creek.

He'd hired a horse, rather than wait about for the mail coach, and left at dawn, safe in the knowledge that his parcels of opal were lodged in the bank, and then had ridden swiftly out on to the familiar road.

He stopped at Wirra Creek to give the horse a rest and slake his own thirst at the old timber pub. Not interested in the locals, few though they were, Brodie walked out on to the veranda with a pot of beer and a sandwich, to sit on a bench and contemplate the bush hospital across the road.

That was where he and Vivien had taken her husband for treatment after his accident. He wondered moodily if Vern Holloway might have been better off if they had taken him all the way to the big Toowoomba hospital, instead of relying on the two women here. Could the doctors in Toowoomba have treated him somehow and saved his sanity?

'Probably not,' he muttered, munching on the wedge-like beef sandwich. 'If he hadn't insisted on riding into that bloody river like a colonel leading the charge, he'd be a well man still.'

Vivien, he recalled, had behaved like the lady of the manor, giving silly orders in all directions. But he'd met the real Vivien on the way home and that had been the beginning. Their beginning. Brodie remembered the first time he'd seen her, and taken note of her beauty even then, when he'd brought Holloway's horses ashore in Brisbane.

Never did I dream, he marvelled, that one day we'd be lovers. Meant to be, he mused, that's what it was. Fate. And I'd better get a move on.

A windmill, silhouetted against a wash of pink sky, rattled and creaked as he passed. He was cutting across country to make Fairlea homestead before dark, following the tracks he'd used as a lowly stockman, working for these people.

How times have changed, he glowed. *Mrs Holloway will be waiting for me, not the mob in the bunkhouse.*

'Who goes there?' An alert boundary rider pushed his horse down a slope to confront the stranger.

'Brodie Court. I'm a friend of the family. You new here?'

'Yes,' the rider said, surprised. 'Sorry. We don't get too many visitors. Most people stick to the road at this hour.'

Brodie refrained from mentioning that he used to work here. Unfortunately this chap would find out soon enough. 'I know the way,' he replied.

'I'll ride with you,' the stockman said, still a little suspicious, so Brodie had an escort right to the home paddocks.

He couldn't help comparing the neat white fencing with the rough logs used to contain stock on the big Plenty Station, and the few cattle they saw with the big herds that roamed that other far-flung property. Fairlea, he realised, was pint-sized against Plenty. *And to think I used to believe this was the biggest farm on God's earth,* he mused wryly.

A light mist had gathered in the valley, vaguely tinged pink by the last of the sunset, softening the dark line of trees that stood guard along the river banks over there. Everything was so still, the clopping of their horses, cantering steadily, sounded to Brodie like time ticking away, and he urged his mount into a gallop to break the tension that had begun to build in him. For no apparent reason he was feeling uneasy as they neared the gate to the homestead.

The stockman obliged him by taking charge of his horse, and Brodie swung open the gate to crunch up the sandy path towards the dimly lit house, striding firmly to boost his confidence.

Before he could reach the steps, Vivien came running. She threw herself into his arms in a burst of excitement.

'It is you! I wondered who on earth could be riding up at this hour. Oh God, Brodie! How wonderful to see you at last.'

She was hugging him, kissing him in the gloom of the garden right outside her husband's house.

Taken aback, he tried to hush her, but she brushed aside his concern. 'Don't worry! Vern's gone to bed, and the housekeeper's over in her quarters.' She pouted. 'See how lonely I am. What a lonely life I lead.'

They made love first, furtively, passionately, locked in her bedroom, making up for lost time, despairing that they'd been kept apart so long, exulting in this blissful reunion, pledging undying love.

'You've worn me out,' Brodie said eventually. 'And I could do with a bite to eat.'

'Oh, not now,' she groaned, snuggling into him.

Brodie smiled. 'All very well for you, my darlin'. I've had nought but a sandwich all day.' He slapped her bottom. 'Come along now. Do the womanly thing and feed your man.'

She managed to make him a meal of steak and eggs washed down with a bottle of beer, and while he ate they talked. Vivien was amazed and delighted to hear that he really had succeeded in finding opals. 'Did you bring one home for me?'

'Not yet. I had to take them to be polished first, then I'll have one for you.'

'Worth more than three hundred pounds, I hope,' she said slyly.

'Of course,' he replied nonchalantly. 'I did well enough but my partners struck misfortune.' He told her about Gus and Lester, and she was shocked.

'Didn't I say it was dangerous out there? It's terrible country. Promise me you'll never go back, Brodie. Promise me.'

'I can't do that. There's more opal, my love. We only scratched the surface. I'm starting a syndicate with Judge Chiswick because I've been mining on his land.'

'Judge Chiswick!' Vivien was impressed. 'My God, that family's very well known. I met him a few times in Toowoomba. They say his wife was a lot younger than him but she died. Peculiar circumstances too, if I recall. They were friends of Vern's.'

'Yes, well now you see why I have to go back. This is too good an opportunity to miss.'

'I don't want to hear about you going away again. It makes me too miserable. Why don't you stay in Toowoomba so that I can come to see you?'

'And do nothing all day? Come now, tell me about yourself, what have you been up to?'

'Nothing at all. Just wait until you see Vern, then you'll

understand how awful it is for me now. I wish I could just pick up and go with you, Brodie.'

'I've got a better idea. Why don't we pick up and go back to bed?'

Vivien waited for the tenderest moment that night to ask some very important questions.

'Where are you staying in Toowoomba?'

'At the Kriedemann house, behind the bakery. I stay in their sleep-out.'

'Have you got other friends there?'

'Only Gus and his mates. He grew up in that town.'

'No women, I hope.'

He laughed. 'My darlin', I don't have time. I've only been back a few days and I'll be off again as soon as I leave here.'

'Then you don't have a wife hidden somewhere?'

'What a question! Where did you get that idea?'

Vivien kissed him. 'Tell me. If I were free would you marry me? Be truthful now.'

'Sure I would.' He wrapped his arms about her. 'You and me, we should be married, this is no life for either of us.'

'Oh Brodie, I do love you!' Vivien was thrilled, but she still couldn't overcome her suspicions about the wife. She could never allow any man to make a fool of her. Even Brodie. She took a deep breath. 'I heard there's a woman in town claiming to be your wife, and that worried me.'

'My wife?' He was genuinely astonished. 'Ah, wait a minute. A Mrs Court there is. My sister-in-law, widow of my late brother. She turned up unexpected. But I don't want to talk about her, she's no favourite of mine.'

'That's a relief. I couldn't abide competition, it's bad enough having you away so much. Will we ever be together, Brodie?'

'When I make enough cash to be able to settle down.'

Vivien lay quietly beside him as he drifted off to sleep. Damn Christiana, she worried. I thought I could sell Fairlea but I forgot she has a share. She'd never agree while Vern's alive. The only way I can sell is to wait and inherit, but Vern could outlive me. It's not fair. It's just not fair!

At least she could be grateful to Brodie's sister-in-law, whether she was his favourite or not. If it hadn't been for Mrs Court landing in town, setting off the rumour that she was Brodie's wife, Vivien knew she wouldn't have been spurred into action. Into writing to Brodie. And bringing him here now.

In future, she decided, I'll want to know exactly where Brodie is, so that I can contact him when it suits me, instead of having to go to that nosy German woman. There's nothing to stop me taking a break from here now; I should arrange to meet him more often.

But even that idea depressed her. What would Brodie be doing in the meantime? He was a very attractive man. Sooner or later he'd meet another woman, and then where would she stand? Out of sight, out of mind!

I can't let that happen, she determined. I just can't.

Brodie enjoyed the day at Fairlea Station. He and Vivien were circumspect with so many people about; she was even rather distant and imperious, as the mistress of the station, which amused him.

He'd slept for less than an hour in the spare bedroom before coming out to surprise the housekeeper in the kitchen.

'It's you, Brodie! What are you doing here?'

'I came to see the boss but he'd gone to bed. Mrs Holloway cooked me a meal and let me stay in the house.'

'So I see. I wondered who was here.' She sniffed. 'I can't imagine why she didn't call me to prepare something for you.'

'She didn't want to bother you.'

'Really?' she said, and Brodie knew that they hadn't fooled this woman. But so what?

'Could I have a cup of tea?' he asked.

'Yes. Just sit there. I won't be a minute, I'm taking tea and toast in to Mr Vern.'

'Could I take it in for you?'

'No, thank you. Mr Vern never liked to see people before he was washed and dressed and I want to keep it that way.'

'How is he?'

'Surely Mrs Holloway told you? He's not well.'

She swept away with the tray, and when she returned, poured his tea. 'Will you be having breakfast here or in the cookhouse?' she asked, the inference clear.

'Up to you,' he said easily, 'but I surely would prefer your cooking.'

In spite of herself, she served him a fine breakfast of porridge, chops, bacon and fried potatoes, in the kitchen. Another studied insult, he knew, for a guest in the house, but it didn't bother him, he was enjoying the meal too much.

After that he escaped and strolled down to the outbuildings where some of the men were saddling up for the day's work.

They were all pleased to see him, with good-humoured digs about his altered status from stockman to guest, but they knew he'd been caring for the boss in town and didn't take his visit amiss. In fact, they were all more interested in his prospecting activities, fascinated to hear that he really had struck it rich.

'Not quite rich yet,' he said modestly, 'but on my way.'

'I knew he would,' Patrick, the stable master, crowed. 'Didn't I say that bloke had a one-track mind when it came to prospecting?'

'Where's Taffy?' Brodie asked.

'Took some horses over to Mountjoy Station,' Patrick told him. 'Run off his feet these days, is poor Taffy, what with the boss out of action. Working like a bloody Trojan. He's manager now but he needs a foreman to back him up.'

'Why doesn't he get one?'

'Because she ain't gonna pay no foreman. We're short-handed as it is; four of the blokes have gone off to that bollocky war and so far we've only got two replacements.'

'Why doesn't he tell her he has to have a foreman?'

'He did, but Mrs Skinflint won't have it. She don't mind spending on herself but when it comes to anything here she shuts down like a bank on Sunday.'

Eventually Brodie returned to the house. He found Vern and the housekeeper on the veranda.

Brodie was shocked to see Holloway. He looked grey and drawn, and his clothes hung loosely on him. He was seated in a large cane chair with a vacant expression on his face as he watched Brodie approach.

'Well now, sir!' Brodie strode over to him with a cheerfulness that he did not feel. 'How are you?'

The loud, deep voice seemed to arouse some interest, and Holloway lifted his hand to Brodie's handshake, nodding a welcome.

Brodie kept up the patter. 'My word, now, you're looking well. Do you mind if I sit here with you a while?'

The housekeeper stood back as Brodie pulled up a chair. 'You remember me,' he said. 'Old Brodie! We used to go for good rides round that place of your mother's. You know. In Toowoomba. And what a grand place that is, big trees and lawns and gardens, with the grandest view out over the plains.' He looked up at Elvie. 'It's as fine a residence as ever you'd see in Ireland, wouldn't you say?'

She realised she was being brought into the conversation for a purpose, and responded eagerly. 'So they say. It's a real showplace.'

'Indeed it is, and so too is Fairlea. It's a real treat for me to come back and see all the fine horses you've got here, sir.'

This was no act. Brodie was desperately sorry for the man. He kept talking patiently, addressing Holloway as if nothing were wrong, as if they were just talking man to man about the horses, the weather, the possibility of rain.

'We've had some falls,' the housekeeper said, keeping up her end of the conversation. 'The creeks are filling now, just like the old days.'

'Where are his cards?' Brodie asked.

She pursed her lips. 'Madam said not to bother him with them.'

'Ah, go on. We like a game of snap, I'll bet you can find them.'

He drew up a table, took the cards from her and began setting them out. Holloway seemed to have forgotten the play but he did make an effort to turn over a card here and there with his thin pale hands, without Brodie's help.

Finally, Vivien appeared in a dark riding habit, looking as smart as paint from the neat topper to her shiny boots.

Brodie grinned, thinking of Clover in her work duds. Imagine her in an elegant outfit like that! Clover wouldn't be seen dead parading about in such feminine gear. Clover was all business and no nonsense on her property.

'Good morning, all,' Vivien said, and Brodie, amused, refrained from remarking that it was nearer to noon.

'Would you care to ride with me, Mr Court?' she asked. 'I like to exercise in the mornings.'

Brodie, who had stood for her, resumed his seat, feigning an ease he did not feel. What was she thinking of? Had she forgotten that the apparent object of his visit was to see her husband? Surely she must know that Elvie, who was now seated near him brimming with disapproval, was too sharp to overlook last night's strange events?

'Mrs Holloway,' he replied, 'while I'd dearly love to have a look round again, for old times, I think I'll just stay here with the boss.'

He saw Elvie's hard, angular face soften that he still allowed Holloway his title, and that the former stockman hadn't forgotten his place, even though he was a guest in the house now.

Vivien swished her small, leather-plaited whip against her skirt in a gesture of impatience. 'I'm only riding as far as the river, Mr Court, it won't take all day.'

'I'm sure that'll be very pleasant,' he said quietly, rising again to acknowledge her departure, 'but I'll be leaving soon. I have to get back to town.'

'What?' She swung about angrily, confronting him. 'Why the rush?'

'Business, I'm sorry to say. I have a man lined up to cut and polish my opals. He should be back in Charleville by this, so I have to get out there.'

'You'll at least stay for lunch?' Elvie said, and Brodie nodded. 'Thank you, I will, if Mrs Holloway doesn't mind.'

'Do as you please!' she snapped. 'We shall have the roast beef, Elvie.'

'It's on, madam.'

Left with no other option, the mistress of Fairlea stormed away.

Vern hadn't seemed to take in any of this, so Brodie gathered up the cards. 'I think he's had enough,' he said quietly. 'Perhaps I could just take him for a little walk?'

'He'd like that,' Elvie said. 'But tell me, did you really find opal?'

'I certainly did,' Brodie replied, happy to expand on his favourite subject.

Elvie was fascinated as he outlined his adventures, and didn't interrupt him until he mentioned Plenty Station.

'Does that still belong to the Chiswicks?'

'Sure does. You know it? A huge station, more than two thousand square miles, they say.'

'I know of it. I used to know the family. A long time ago.'

Elvie prepared lunch, more dinner really. She always cooked a substantial midday meal when they had guests; the country air made them hungry. By nightfall they were all ready to saddle up again for a formal four-course meal. She didn't mind. Elvie loved to cook and these days visitors were rare, and for Vern's sake she still served a good table. Even if his guest was only an ex-station hand. She was still suspicious of them, of Brodie and that wretch of a woman, but confused by his insistence on leaving when it was obvious Vivien wanted him to stay.

But his talk of Plenty Station had been interesting. Voices from the past. The kids had grown up, Charlie and Clover. Charlie had gone to the war. The Judge was out there running the place. 'And good luck to him!' she snorted.

What a time that was! When Vern had been madly in love with a married woman!

Elvie had begun working for the Holloways at the Toowoomba house, not long after the death of Christiana's husband, and she'd been with them ever since. One of the family now, if you didn't count this one, who only tolerated her.

Hannah Chiswick! She was a beauty, no doubt about it. Half the men in Toowoomba had been in love with her but she'd married old Samuel in accordance with her father's wishes. Probably, Elvie mused, she hadn't been attracted to any of her other suitors anyway. Until she met Vernon Holloway.

Too late. She was married.

Christiana soon got wind of the affair and she was very angry, but there was no talking to Vern, he was mad about her and he didn't care who knew. He threatened to run off with her.

But Christiana was always a sensible woman; she changed tack and became his confidante, listening to him with great sadness, understanding how difficult it was for him. For them both. She was firm, though, in her resolve to head off this disastrous liaison, and was distraught when Vern broke the next news.

'Hannah is pregnant, Mother. It's my child. We'll have to go away now. London, I think would be best.'

'Impossible!' she said. 'If you won't think of yourselves, pity the child, bastard son of Vern Holloway. A scandal like that marks a family for generations.'

For days she argued with him, appealing to him as a gentleman to retire from the scene before matters became worse, since this premise did seem to have some effect on him.

Once she had him wavering, Christiana called on the young woman, taking a much firmer line, blaming neither of them but insisting that Hannah must put a stop to the affair immediately.

'If you love Vern, don't do this to him. If you love the child, have some pity for it.'

Distressed, Christiana came home to confide in Elvie. 'I think she'll listen to me. God, I hope so. I don't think either of them realises how vindictive Samuel Chiswick can be. And he's a very cunning lawyer, that's why he's doing so well. I wouldn't put it past him to claim that child as his own to save face. Then where would they be?'

'Perhaps you could send Mr Vern away for a while, to get over her?' Elvie suggested.

'I thought of that, but he won't go. Perhaps, though, it's time he had more responsibility. I'll look into it.'

Fairlea Station had been Vern's recompense for losing Hannah. She'd taken Christiana's advice and made the decision to stay with her husband, and though Vern had been broken-hearted at the time there was nothing he could do.

Christiana had purchased the Fairlea property for him and that kept him busy. Elvie had volunteered to take up the role of his housekeeper, a decision she'd never regretted. She loved the station life . . .

'Until now,' she muttered as she set the table. 'Until poor Mr Vern had his accident and *she* took over.'

More and more the lady of the house had taken to eating on her own, anywhere but in the dining room with her husband. His co-ordination was failing so Elvie sat beside him, helping him. She always cut up his food before serving him, but even then he spilled things or confused the sugar and the salt. Little things that didn't bother Elvie, but revolted his wife.

Today, when Brodie was placed next to his host, Vivien had no choice. She had to sit at the table with them.

Elvie smiled to herself. It was a glum hour, with Brodie trying to make conversation, Mr Vern concentrating on the food and madam in a very bad mood, saying little. She wasn't surprised that Vivien insisted on riding with their guest, at least as far as the crossroads, when it was time for him to leave. She had a feeling that Brodie Court would get some hurry-up for declining to go with her earlier.

And he did.

'How dare you make a fool of me?' she snapped as they rode away from the homestead.

'When did I do that?'

'I asked you to ride with me and you practically cut me dead.'

'What else could I do? I came to visit the man. Should I not see him at all?'

'You didn't have to leave so soon. You could have stayed a few more days. You just don't care about me at all.'

Brodie dismounted and handed her down from her horse. 'I do care. But it would be plain blatant for me to hang about. Your housekeeper wasn't fooled.'

'Oh, spare me! I can't be worried about her. I'll get rid of her.'

'She's not the only set of eyes at Fairlea, my love. You don't need scandal. Besides, I felt sorry for the boss.'

'Oh really! Fat lot of good that does. He didn't even know you. And what about me? Doesn't anyone feel sorry for me?'

He put an arm about her. 'Now that I see how things are, I can't tell you how sad I am for you. It's very hard for you, living like that. Wouldn't it be better if you took him back to his mother?'

'Definitely not! If I do that she can take control of his affairs again. She's a scheming witch of a woman. As long as I stay here I'm safe from her.'

'Then what about if you just left? No one knows about me, for sure. Taffy could go on running the place. They say he's doing a good job. You could just say it's all too much for you.'

'Oh yes, of course. And lose everything? I've thought of that.'

Brodie worried. He did feel sorry for her, the situation was hard on her. 'Give me a while,' he said, 'to get some cash together and we'll just have to brazen it out. You'll leave and come to live with me.'

'When will that be?'

'I don't know. It takes time. But I want you, my darling. If I can't have you as my wife then so be it, we'll live together.'

Vivien clung to him. 'I can't bear for you to leave me again. Why don't you just stay here and be damned to everyone?'

'You know we can't do that. Vern is too well liked by the men, there'd be hell to pay.' He kissed her. 'I'll miss you.'

She was in his arms again and he hated the thought of leaving her. 'I won't be coming back here again, my darling. It's too much of a problem. Can you meet me in Toowoomba next time?'

'Of course I can. I don't always have to stay with him. I'll be at a hotel. And you write to me, not to Vern. No one would dare touch my mail. Don't you ever leave me worrying like that again. Promise.'

He smiled. 'I promise. You know where I'll be. Back out at the Ten Mile opal fields.'

'I love you so much, Brodie,' she whispered, kissing him, drawing his hand down over her breast. 'You don't have to hurry. Can't you feel how much I need you.'

She was hard to resist. Even though he had that long ride ahead of him Brodie lingered, unbuttoning her shirt, feeling her soft skin, kissing her passionately, knowing, somehow, that this was a mistake. But he couldn't leave now if his life depended on it. He backed her against a tree, crushing her to him, and then, out of a corner of his eye, he saw movement.

A horseman had come down the road and stopped to stare.

'Oh, Jesus!' he said. 'That's Taffy. Your foreman.'

Hastily he pulled away from her, rearranging his clothes as best he could, but Taffy wheeled his horse and rode away. He'd seen enough.

Vivien giggled. 'It could have been worse! We were only just starting.' She looked about her. 'He's gone now. Forget about him!'

But Brodie had lost the urge. 'No. Come on, let's go. I have to get back to Toowoomba.'

'Don't be worried about him. If he gives me any trouble I'll sack him.'

'Good God, woman! If you're so unconcerned then you ought to come with me right now. The word's out; they'll all know about us now, what with Taffy and Elvie.'

'I can't.'

'Then I don't understand you. One minute you're saying you want to come with me, while it's me explaining I don't have much cash. Then when I decide it's time for you to leave, you back off. Since it has become urgent, I'm not all that broke. I've a cottage in Toowoomba, you can live there for the time being.'

Even in these circumstances Brodie couldn't bring himself to tell all the truth. His business arrangements were his own private world. As he spoke, he realised with a shudder that by offering her one of his cottages on the spur of the moment, he'd be losing rent. Money that was paying for the second one.

Women! he thought. They get you so bloody confused you don't know what you're doing!

Her reply was such a relief he loved her for it.

'You're so good,' she said sadly. 'You don't have to pretend with me. If you owned even a little cottage you wouldn't be living with that German family. I don't want you having to go to expense for me, especially when it's not necessary. The Holloways are very rich, Brodie. I'd be a fool to walk away now. Give me time to work out some arrangement.'

'What sort of arrangement?'

'Leave it with me. You can see my life here is hopeless. I'll have to come to some agreement with Christiana. She dotes on Vern, she's the best one to take care of him. We could work out a financial settlement for me.'

When they parted, Vivien rode listlessly back to the homestead. Brodie was so sweet. A simple man with a heart of gold. That was what she liked about him. Plus the fact that he was just gorgeous and a marvellous lover. He wouldn't play the heavy husband as Vern had done. He would do anything to please her. Once they had money, she and Brodie could have a wonderful life.

But how? Arrangements with Christiana? That'd be the

day! The only way she could cut loose from Vern would be a divorce. On what grounds?

Could you imagine, she asked herself, suggesting that to the old bat? She'd have a fit! Throwing over her beloved son!

Then what? Back to the same question. Nothing. Christiana would throw her out on her ear, and Vern, *non compos mentis*, would retain all his holdings. And Christiana, with no one left, would probably leave all her money to a cat and dog home.

Oh no. Despite Brodie's brave offer, the darling, we can do better than that. And if by some wild chance he does make money prospecting, all the better.

One day Mr and Mrs Brodie Court will be very rich.

Travelling in the other direction, Brodie was depressed. He was becoming convinced that his love affair with Vivien was doomed. He understood her predicament and knew full well that if she left Vern it would take more than an arrangement to have old Mrs Holloway give her the golden handshake. He couldn't, yet, support Vivien in the manner to which she was accustomed, and even his offer of one of his cottages now sounded foolish. Vivien wouldn't last ten minutes in a place like that. And why should she?

Rain began to fall. Brodie turned up his collar and pulled down his cowhide hat as the good horse cantered steadily on. It seemed to him that opals were his only luck. Nothing else seemed to be working out right. Lester was dead. Gus was deserting him for that damned Trella. He really didn't have a friend in the world except those magical, devious, tantalising, frustrating opals.

'Worse than women,' he muttered, feeling better at the very thought of them. 'But a damn sight more lucrative.' He was looking forward to returning to Willi's camp at Charleville, where they could both begin a serious examination of the two new stones that showed promise. And have Willi cut and polish his opal haul from the Ten Mile. All thoughts of Vivien and her problems were whisked away as he tried to imagine what his parcels of opal were worth. Not from the shark buyers who roamed the opal fields, or from the jewellers in Toowoomba or even Brisbane city, but in Europe.

Brodie hadn't forgotten his little Jewish friend in Dublin, Abe Rosenstein. Hadn't he said to keep him in mind if opportunities arose? Brodie was prepared to take a gamble on Abe, by sending him the very best opals that Willi could produce from the selection. Probably the piece that blazed from an iridescent blue-green background into a myriad of red and gold points. A marvellous light, bright opal the size of his thumbnail if cut right, and Willi was just the man.

Willi began work on the two stones, scouring away at the shell with his knife.

'Get outside!' he yelled at Brodie. 'You're spoiling the light hanging over me like this. Get away!'

So Brodie waited, excitement over the results of Willi's previous work making him even more nervous. His dusty stones had been transformed into the loveliest opals, flashing and gleaming on the table like nests of fire. This was the first time Brodie had seen opal being turned and polished to such perfection, and he was overwhelmed at his good fortune.

That he should own all those precious gems, carefully graded now from firsts to thirds, was such a triumph, it had been worth all that hard, back-breaking work! He couldn't wait to get back to his mines.

I knew it, he said to himself. I never doubted myself on this. Once I show them to Gus, he won't be wanting to fool about in town. He knows there's plenty more where they came from.

Gus had lost heart since Lester's death and the disappearance of his opals. He'd given up and was working as a barman, a job that'd get him nowhere. Brodie had a feeling that Trella was at the back of his refusal to return to the opal fields, keeping Gus in town to suit herself. That was typical of her. She couldn't see further than her nose, and was probably doing this to spite her brother-in-law. Causing trouble again.

'It'll be a different story once he sets eyes on my opals,' he muttered. 'She won't be in the race.'

Brodie smiled grimly. 'And Chiswick thinks he's got me beat too. We'll see about that.'

Stanley Wickham had received a reply from the Judge with regard to Brodie's plan for a syndicate, but he wasn't optimistic.

'He's a hard man, Brodie. He's demanding that the syndicate should begin with capital of two thousand pounds, at a pound a share. Can you meet him halfway on that?'

'Not a hope,' Brodie had said glumly. 'What happens now?'

'Do you really need that much as a starting point?'

'We do not, the old fool. I might have known it; he's trying to bluff me out so he can take it all for himself.'

Wickham looked at him keenly. 'Wasn't it a risk inviting him in in the first place?'

'It was, but I needed him more onside than off, you see. He's got a great opinion of himself, has the Judge, and a poor opinion of me, no doubt. So. If he wants a war he's got one.'

'What will you do?'

'Not me. You. I want you to stall him. Write back agreeing to the cash but pick holes in the agreement, anything you like, just keep him busy. If he thinks I'll be handing over a thousand quid he'll be confused . . .'

'You're calling his bluff?'

'Exactly. But he'll be smelling money now and that will keep him on my team for a while. I just need time.'

Now, as he paced outside Willi's hut, Brodie was filled with renewed confidence, thanks to his hoard of beautiful opals. That last month or so at Ten Mile had sapped his energy, leaving him unsure of himself, with no new finds and worry that being new at the game he'd overestimated the value of the Firefly opals.

'You lost faith in yourself,' he muttered, 'running to the Judge for back-up.'

But it wasn't only that, he knew. He was looking for a bigger operation to sweep that patch of the ridge once and for all. Chiswick, he'd hoped, could provide that assistance, with little expense on either side and no interference, but no, the Judge had to get smart.

'Are you stayin' out there all day?' Willi called, and Brodie rushed into the hut.

'You're finished? Show me.'

Proudly Willi pointed to two gems he'd placed on an old piece of black velvet in the centre of the table.

Brodie stared. 'Is that them?'

It was the blazing scarlet he saw first, then the multitude of colour, as if he were seeing two tiny explosions on the cloth, for the background had disappeared. Black against black!

'Black opals?' he breathed.

'Sure as hell,' Willi grinned.

'God Almighty!' Brodie sat down for a better view of them.

The smaller one was round, neat as a moulded sixpence, deep emerald floating with the red in a dreamy landscape flecked with gold. The other, oval-shaped, was twice the size, and this one took Brodie's breath away. He rushed outside with it, turning and twisting it in the sunlight.

'Some of them black depths is really blue,' he shouted. 'Look at it, Willi! Did you ever see a dark blue like that in your life? It bloody glows. And it's the paler blues that bring it up on to the greens and then bustin' out red! Oh my God! What have I got here?'

'Twenty-five carats, that one, and fourteen the other.'

'And what's this worth?'

Willi shrugged. 'Not much, I'm sorry to say. They're lovely, to my mind the best of the lot, but not saleable. Not for much anyway.'

Brodie was shocked. 'I can't believe that. Look at this opal! It's a wonder! A jewel in its own right.'

'And any gouger would say the same thing, but we're selling, not buying, and the dark opals aren't fashionable.'

'How would they know? What about the one I saw in Brisbane?'

Willi nodded. 'If I recall, you said it was set among a display of light opals, probably the best place for it, as a contrast.'

'But they're rare stones,' Brodie argued.

'Tell the buyers that and they'll agree with you. Not the sort of stones people expect. I heard that some gougers have found a few dark opals down over the border at a place called Lightning Ridge, but they're having trouble selling them.'

'So far,' Brodie growled. 'What if they find more and they become the fashion?'

'Time will tell,' Willi said.

Brodie was glad he'd remembered to bring Willi a bottle of whisky. He needed that drink to offset his disappointment, but that didn't stop him taking Willi's magnifying glass and studying his black opals. 'This bigger one,' he said, 'look into it. I can see all the colours of a fire in it. I'm going to call it Desert Fire, and the little one Sunset. What do you think?'

'Fair enough,' Willi said. 'They're bloody lovely. I knew they'd be out there somewhere. Good on you, mate! You did it!' He picked up the dark opals. 'I look at them and wonder how many millions of years it took for them to capture such colour, and what other mysteries lie deep in our earth.' He sighed. 'I never tire of looking at them. If I were you I'd never sell these gems.'

'I'll find more. I'm half inclined to head for Lightning Ridge tomorrow, but I'll stick with what I know. There's still opal on the ridge, I'm sure, and where I found the black opals, would there be more?'

'Hard to tell. They could be just the residue of the ages, of mountains or boulders worn down to scrap. Get some blacks on the job; they've got sharper eyes than we have, they'd spot a glint of colour on ground level that any of us could miss. And after that . . .' he grinned, 'you're going to have to dig. I can't see you bypassing that field whether you find any more on top or not.'

'I don't know any blacks,' Brodie said.

'Jesus. You're no different from the rest. They're there. It's their country, you're walking past them all the time, but you wouldn't think to give them the time of day.'

Brodie was embarrassed. The last thing he wanted was to offend Willi.

'Tell you what,' Willi said. 'Go back to the ridge. I'll ask Lena to send you a couple of her friends. They'll do a search for you. But you pay them, mister, and not in baccy. They're entitled to a quid like the rest of us, especially since they've lost their hunting grounds.'

'I'll pay them, don't worry. But what do I owe you for your work?'

'Twenty-five quid, but if you don't have the ready, you can pay me some other time.'

'Ten down and I'll send you the rest?'

'No. Bring it. I like to see how you're going.'

Now Brodie looked at the other opals that Willi had carefully wrapped for him, and placed them in a small skin pouch. 'How much do you reckon they're worth direct to a jeweller?'

'Nothin' under a thousand pounds.'

'What? You're joking!'

'No fear. Some of your firsts are near a hundred each.'

Brodie started to laugh. He laughed until the tears ran, and Willi chortled with him, thinking this was Brodie's reaction to such a windfall. Then Brodie told him about the Judge. About Chiswick demanding a thousand pounds that he didn't have. And now he did, but the Judge wouldn't see a penny of it.

'It wasn't such a bad idea,' Willi said. 'Granted, he's a bastard, but he could be useful. He does own the land. Offer him half.'

'If I'd had it last week I might have done that. But now I've got a better plan. Chiswick has missed his chance.' He picked up the pouch of opals. 'How do you think I'll go if I plonk them down in front of opal miners? Would I get some starters?'

'You'd get killed in the rush,' Willi grinned.

That night, when Brodie left Willi's camp and rode back into the little bush town of Charleville, it was teeming with rain and everyone seemed to be celebrating, which fitted his mood. All the pubs were crowded, and amid the noise and the singing he thought he could hear the zing of cash registers. He passed the town brothel, looking up at the flash women and their customers cavorting on the veranda, and considered joining them until he realised he was carrying a parcel of gems that he couldn't afford to lose. There was nowhere he could deposit them for safety at this hour.

Deliberately, he bypassed the Albert Hotel, thinking of Clover. Such a nice girl. She'd be shocked to hear he was even contemplating a brothel. But the Albert was too fancy for his pocket. No doubt he could sell an opal right here in the morning to tide him over, but he was taking all of them to Brisbane for the best price. Brodie considered the Albert Hotel a waste of money whether a man had the cash or not. He settled for a room and a feed at a shanty pub down the darker end of the town, and retired early.

The roof leaked and cockroaches scuttled about the floor of his room, but Brodie didn't care. From his collection of polished opals he took out his favourite. He'd know it anywhere. It was the best of the light opals, that Willi had cut into an intriguing, almost rectangular shape, so delicate and so lustrous it almost seemed as if it might be too soft to touch. But it was not, he knew. The stone was strong and true.

'You, my beauty,' he said, 'are bound for Dublin. To Abe Rosenstein. I won't be selling all of my firsts until Abe gets a look at you. Something tells me that they take opals too much for granted in this country. So why not press further afield?'

Although the very idea almost broke his heart, Brodie decided to send the smaller black opal, too. His Sunset opal. He had to assess its real value. He knew he was taking a chance on Abe, who could easily pocket both, or try to cheat him on price, but Abe would think they were only samples. He couldn't be expected to know that these exquisite stones were the best Brodie could offer. And in his accompanying letter, Brodie would give the impression that they were just that. Samples.

He nodded to himself. I think old Abe will go wild at the sight of them! Fair beats his dreary old merchandise.

It was Gus who went wild at the sight of them on the kitchen table. Shouting with delight, he hammered on the walls for his parents to come and see them too.

'They're magnificent!' he cried. 'Willi sure knows his business. Look at them, Father! Willi cut and polished them. It's magic! By God, you're a lucky man, Brodie, I'll say that for you. What do you think, Mother?'

'Can I pick one up?' she asked nervously.

'Go ahead,' Brodie said, 'they won't break.'

'But you mustn't get water on them, I hear,' she added.

'That's a fairy story, water won't hurt them.' He put several more opals in her hand and she stared at them in wonder. 'God is good to show us what beauty exists.'

'He doesn't make it easy,' Brodie laughed.

'And he can take it away just as quick,' Gus said ruefully.

Brodie patted him on the shoulder. 'Never mind that now. You're well again after that snakebite. You were lucky to be rescued. There are more opals to be had. When I come back from Brisbane we'll be on our way again.'

He saw Mrs Kriedemann frown and pretended not to notice as he replaced the gems. 'I'm off again, I've a lot to do.'

Not without some misgivings, Brodie entrusted the two opals

311

to a shipping company, then sent a telegram to Abe Rosenstein advising that a parcel of some interest was on its way to Dublin. Seated in the post office, he wrote a letter to Abe, explaining the situation and requesting that he act as his agent in finding the best possible price for his opals, since there were plenty more to follow. He suggested paying his agent five per cent commission, allowing for Rosenstein to raise that a few more points.

That done, Brodie began a search of the town for miners, beginning in the pubs and calling at addresses given to him by the publicans. By late that afternoon, he had assembled ten miners in the parlour of a corner pub.

'Opal mining, is it?' one man asked. 'I've only prospected for gold.'

'You'll soon learn,' Brodie told him.

'Where is this place?'

'The Ten Mile, on Sandy Ridge. On from Charleville.'

'It's a bloody long way on from Charleville,' another man grunted.

Brodie laughed. 'You can't expect them to be next door.'

'The Ten Mile's cleaned out,' a third man said.

Brodie shook his head. 'Don't be believing that, my friend, or you'll be missing out on the chance of a lifetime.'

He took out his opals and spread them on the table, receiving the immediate response they deserved. The men charged forward, stunned by this display.

'Plenty more where they came from. Now, who's in?'

'What's the deal?' they wanted to know.

Brodie explained that he had detailed maps of the Ten Mile. 'I'll pay for your licences if you'll come with me and register them right away. We want to cover as much ground as we can.' He winked. 'We'll take out a few dummy licences while we're about it. You'll all be working mines in your own right, but if you join this team, you have to sell to me. I'll give you a better figure than any of the rascals who prey on working men like us.'

'Why do we have to work through you? Why can't I, for one, go it alone?' the first man asked him.

'Because if we pool our expenses and work from the one camp, we're saving money,' Brodie said. 'And I have to tell you the truth. The gougers who worked out there didn't leave because the ridge was cleaned out. They left because the squatter pushed them out.'

He was pleased to hear the growl about the table.

'But he won't be pushing us out. He might own the land but we'll have licences to wave at him. None of us digging there before had the papers, and that gave him the edge. Besides, if we're there as a team, not as loners, battling the big man, he'll think twice about giving us any trouble. I'm for telling him that right from the start.'

'Who owns the land?' someone asked.

'Judge Chiswick.'

'That bastard!' Brodie's meeting deteriorated into tales of the Judge until he was forced to call them to order. 'We can't waste time. If you're in, you have to come with me to the Mines Office to register your claims, and we'll get the papers stamped at the police station to make sure we're covered. We can come back here later and make our plans.'

'What if we don't find opal?' someone asked.

'That's in the lap of the gods,' Brodie said. 'But what a question to ask prospectors. Isn't that what it's all about?'

'Nothing ventured, nothing gained,' a burly man agreed. 'I'm with Brodie. Let's go, mates.'

The following day Brodie was in Brisbane, immersed in his own affairs, tramping from jeweller's shop to jeweller's shop, haggling over every stone, one by one, determined to fight for top price. He stayed overnight and began all over again, this time with his best stones, to the surprise of the buyers. He had a base price now and they knew it, but he kept haggling, pushing up their offers as he produced each stone, walking away when negotiations broke down, to retrace his steps to other buyers.

Not once did he mention that he was dealing with several men, pretending that each retreat was simply to 'think about it'. That left the door open to return for the best offer.

As the day went on, he added his takings in a small notebook, and when he knew he had a thousand pounds in his pockets, he stopped. He still had six of his best stones left and they would be safe in a bank, with his Desert Fire opal, to wait on word from Abe Rosenstein. Hopefully they would be the first batch of his overseas sale. Only Willi knew he had the black opals, and he wanted it to remain that way.

Even though he was now in the money, Brodie saw no reason to throw cash away. He stayed overnight at the same boarding house because it was cheap, and caught the train back to Toowoomba the next morning.

It was time to talk to Gus and prise him loose from Trella's clutches. Gus was his friend, he'd suffered one loss, now he could recoup. Brodie had already taken out a mining licence for Gus Kriedemann and lodged a good claim on his behalf. They'd do well together, and with Gus keeping an eye on the Ten Mile, his partner, Brodie Court, would have a chance to investigate that rocky field. To search for black opals.

Chapter Ten

Trella had problems. Several problems. It seemed to her that everything had gone wrong from the day Brodie arrived back in town. Admittedly he wasn't the cause of it all but he didn't help matters. He was, in all, a terrible disappointment.

Being family, she'd expected a warm welcome from him, even a helping hand, never the cold shoulder as if she'd come only to be a burden to him.

Oh sure, she thought, he goes out of his road to make a fuss of Garth as if the few shillings and the few hours he spends on the lad are a great favour. And Garth, poor lad, is ever so grateful. He likes Gus, but Brodie is his uncle, his hero.

Garth was growing so fast now, busting out of his clothes, always seeming to need something new, that Trella was battling to make ends meet. It was strange, she mused grimly, that when they were in Tullymore, with little food for the table, her son, and the rest of the family of course, had accepted what was put before them. But now, in a land where food was plentiful and folks ate as much for Sunday dinner as they'd have eaten in a week back home, Garth was always hungry, always looking for seconds and cleaning out her cupboard whenever her back was turned. Worse, it wasn't just Garth; she too, confronted by shops and all the delectable displays, was buying more than she should. It all cost money, and though they both worked hard, it just wasn't stretching.

Trella had suggested to her son that they move to cheaper lodgings, to a boarding house where they could share a room, but he was shocked.

'I'm too big to be sharing a room with my mum,' he said. 'You'd be making a fool of me. I like where we are. Get the old woman to drop the rent.'

Trella had tried, but her landlady was adamant. 'I have to live too. You spoil that boy, that's your trouble. Cut back on him, not me. And if you're short of cash, ask your friend Mr Kriedemann, he visits often enough.'

Never would she ask Gus. He was kindness itself, and earning precious little in that bar. Trella kept her worries to herself.

Working in that big cheese factory was still terribly tiring, with rarely a chance for a break. Cleaners like her were needed everywhere, washing and scouring until their hands were red raw. The big milk cans had to be ready for the farmers to make the exchange when they brought in their milk, vats left too long were hell to clean, and the benches and floors had to be scrubbed. On top of that, Trella was always being called to help out at the machines when they were short, or to pack the heavy cheeses, shift them, turn them, whatever the manager required. She was at his beck and call.

It was when she was cleaning out his office that Trella saw the notice pinned to the back of his door. His white coat was usually hanging from the peg above but on this day it was missing, so, as she swept, she glanced idly at it. At first. Then she leant the broom against the wall and studied it with care.

'Well! What do you know?' she muttered as she read that this was a union notice setting out hours of work and rates of pay for all workers. For workers in this factory, she supposed. While Trella knew nothing about unions, she guessed that some organisation had set out these official-looking regulations and they were meant to be honoured.

'Or they wouldn't be here,' she said to the empty room, taking careful note of the conditions outlined, her first priority being rates of pay.

'Boys under sixteen, women and girls,' she intoned slowly, 'to receive the minimum wage of fifteen shillings and tuppence per week.'

'Fifteen and tuppence!' she echoed. 'And we only get fourteen shillings!'

Sourly she read that men were entitled to a minimum of twenty-one shillings per week, and proceeded on, furtively now, afraid that someone would come in and catch her.

'Maximum of forty-eight hours' work,' she whispered, reading aloud to impress these figures on her memory, 'for a boy under sixteen or a woman or girl! For God's sake, what's going on here?'

Silently she totted up her own work schedule. Twelve hours a day, six days a week. 'Seventy-two hours it is for us! I'll have to see about this.'

Back on the factory floor, Trella began asking about these rules.

'That's union stuff,' she was told. 'It's been there for ages. No one takes any notice.'

'But it looks like law! There's a government crest on it. And it says mimimum wage. Minimum! Us women are being done out of one and tuppence a week. That's a lot of money.'

By lunchtime Trella had rallied a few supporters. 'Think of it this way,' she told them. 'If us women should only be working forty-eight hours, then they're getting another twenty-four out of us for nothing.'

'That's the way it is,' a young girl sighed. 'They say we're lucky to have jobs.'

'No, wait!' Trella insisted they listen. 'Twenty-four is half of forty-eight. So, the extra hours we are working are worth half what we should be earning. Another seven and sixpence. So we should be getting twenty-two shillings and eightpence. Do you see now?'

A woman laughed. 'Give over, Trella. Can you see them paying us more than a pound a week?'

'Probably not, but I can see us getting fifteen shillings at least for a week of forty-eight hours.'

There was more laughter. 'Fat chance.'

'Not fat chance,' she argued angrily. 'It's there in writing for all to see. We should only be working eight hours a day, Monday to Saturday.'

'And how would we get our work done?' a grey-haired woman retorted. 'We're flat out all day as it is.'

'We couldn't,' Trella admitted. 'They'd just have to employ more people.'

'Tell that to Mr Ringrose,' the woman said grimly. 'You're a troublemaker, Mrs Court, and I don't want no part of it. What right have you got to be bringing your union talk here?'

'I never heard of a union before this,' Trella said hotly. 'I just read the rules today and I'd like to know more about them, because I think we're being cheated. That's what I think.'

317

'So would I,' another woman grinned. 'I'm going to sneak into Mr Ringrose's office and have a look at that list myself.'

It became a joke among the women in the factory. One after another they slipped into the manager's office when he was out, to see for themselves, and gradually the subject became the main topic of conversation, creating rows and arguments among the female workers. Some were all for leaving well alone, others agreed with Trella.

'But what can we do?' they asked.

'Send Trella in to tell him we want our rights,' someone suggested, but Trella was warned against that.

'You'd get sacked on the spot,' she was told, and she knew they were right.

'I'll find out more about this first,' she decided. 'There's a workers' club in town, I'll go there and ask. Someone has to know.'

'But that's a men's club,' her friend Deena told her. 'You can't go in there.'

'Watch me!' Trella laughed.

As they walked home Deena tried to talk her out of it. 'You're new here, Trella. Leave it be. I've been working in that factory for three years and I've seen this before. Some of the men tried to push for higher wages last year and they lost their jobs so fast they met themselves coming in. There's nothing anyone can do.'

But undeterred, Trella Court went to the door of the workers' club, asking if it was possible to meet a gentleman from a union. The club, she saw, peering in from the open door, was no more than a smoky billiard parlour, crowded with men who seemed intent on the game in progress. For a long while she thought she'd been forgotten, but having come this far, she waited until at last a tall, rangy fellow loomed up in the doorway.

'You lookin' for someone, missus?'

'I wanted to see a union man.'

'Will I do? Tom Gilbert. Shearers' Union.'

'Oh! Shearers' Union. I don't think so. You see, I work in the cheese factory. I wanted to ask about that.'

He nodded politely. 'You got trouble there?'

'Not really. There's just something I don't understand.'

318

'And what would that be?'

She explained about the notice in the manager's office. 'A list of rules and regulations it is. What would you call it?'

'The Factories Act, that's what it is.'

'And would it be law?'

'It sure is.'

She smiled, pleased with herself. 'Then that's all I need to know.'

'Hang on. What about these regulations?'

'They're saying one thing and our boss says another. We're working a lot longer than we should according to the notice, and we're not getting the right money. I'll have to bring this to the attention of the boss.'

'No you won't. Don't be foolish.'

'But you said it's law, did you not? Won't he have to abide by the law?'

'It's not as simple as that. You could lose your job. You keep out of it, you've done your bit. I'll tip off your man at the Trades and Labour Council and he'll pay a call on your boss. That'd be Ringrose, wouldn't it?'

'Yes, sir. You know him?'

'Not personally but I've heard of him. Listen, I've got to get back in now. You leave this to me and don't be worrying your pretty head.'

He was gone so quickly Trella was startled. Would this council really do something about matters at the cheese factory? Hard to know. But Gilbert seemed a decent man. No doubt it would be better to take his advice and wait to see what happened now.

More than a week later, when Trella, not being a patient person, had just about given up on any help from the Trades and Labour Council, there was a buzz of excitement in the factory. Word had it that the stranger talking to the men in the loading yard was a union official!

'You did it!' Deena accused her. 'You sent for them!'

'Be quiet!' Trella said. 'Let me see.' She rushed over to a window, expecting to see a man in uniform who could uphold the law, but the only stranger was a gaunt fellow with a bald head, wearing ordinary workmen's clothes.

'He won't get far with Mr Ringrose,' she said glumly. 'They could have sent someone more important.'

319

'What's he doing?' Deena asked.

'Questioning them, I think. Writing things down in his book. And he's talking to Garth now. I hope that boy minds his manners, he's getting a real handful these days.' She pulled away from the window and hurried back to the separator she'd been washing. 'Here he comes!'

Heads down, trying to look busy, they watched as he spoke to other factory workers, until it was Trella's turn.

'Name please?' He was a stern fellow, with steely blue eyes.

'Trella Court,' she replied nervously.

'And you are paid?'

'Fourteen shillings a week, sir.'

'Work six to six?'

'That's right, sir.'

He looked up from his book. 'You're Irish?'

'Yes, sir.'

'Thought it was you,' he mumbled. 'Tom sends his regards.' And with a wink he turned to Deena.

Mr Ringrose came charging down from his office to head him off. 'Who the hell are you?'

'Jock McKie, union. Just taking a look round.'

'Never heard of you! We deal with Mr Moore.'

'Ah yes. I know all about him, and I think enough said there. He's had his marching orders. I'm your man now. Here are my papers.'

Ringrose snatched the pages. 'Come into my office.'

'When I've finished here,' McKie said quietly. 'I won't be long.'

The two men argued long and hard, with a copy of the regulations on the desk between them.

'They're as plain as day,' McKie said, 'so there's no point in your twisting and turning. You've got away with this for too long now.'

'Couldn't we come to some arrangement?' Ringrose said. 'Just you and me. Split a bit here and there? All the staff are well looked after here.'

McKie leaned forward fiercely. 'Don't you ever mistake me for the likes of Moore again or I'll shut you down! Now, what's it to be?'

'You have to give me time. I can't make these decisions. I have to go to the Factory Board. They won't like you coming in here giving orders like this.'

The union man sighed. 'It's nothing to do with you or me or them! The minimum wage is set in stone. You're not paying the men right and you're bloody exploiting the women.'

Ringrose slammed his fist on the table. 'The women! I knew it! It's that Irishwoman, isn't it? She's been causing trouble from the day she started, stirring up perfectly happy folks.'

'I don't know anything about any Irishwoman, so you can stop trying to shift the blame. It's on your back, Ringrose; you have to get the hours and wages into line with other factories. Not to mention the sanitary arrangements. We'll get to them.'

Ringrose chewed on his pipe. 'We can't rush into this. All this extra expense will break us.'

'I doubt that, but I'm a reasonable man. We could negotiate terms.'

'Like what?'

'You talk to the Board. Gradual upgrade might do. Come back to me next week with a raise in pay and cutback in hours. Six months later we'll have another improvement, and in twelve months' time you'll be operating this factory exactly as stated here.' He jammed his finger down on the regulations.

'They won't listen to that. It's too soon. Don't you understand that if the factory goes broke they'll all be out of work?'

'I've seen the balance sheets, mate, don't give me that. If this place goes broke it will only be due to bad management. Think on that.'

They sat in silence for a while until Ringrose tried again. 'It's all very well for you to come here ordering me about, but the Board members are influential men in Toowoomba. You won't be so smart if you have to face them.'

'Not unless I mention a black ban,' McKie said calmly. 'No deliveries. No transport. No rail. And what's on the wharves will rot. That's for starters.'

'All right! I'll talk to them.'

'Good, now let's get down to details.'

Before he left, McKie turned back to the factory manager. 'What's the name of the Irishwoman you mentioned?'

'Trella Court,' the manager snarled.

'Right you are. Now, these negotiations are between the union and the employers, nothing to do with poor working women. If I hear she's been fired you'll have a strike on your hands before the day is out. I'm posted here permanently, Mr Ringrose, so don't think I'll be forgetting about you.'

Out of the blue everyone received a few extra shillings in their pay, and the factory hooter sounded knock-off time at four instead of five. Not that the latter made much difference; unfinished work had to be completed out of time.

The workers were happy, but Trella was confused. 'That fellow let me down,' she told Deena. 'We're still not getting our rights.'

'But it's a start,' Deena said. 'Be thankful.'

'I suppose you're right. But next time I see Mr McKie I'll be asking why.'

'If I were you I'd shut up. The boss has been looking daggers at you ever since. I think he knows.'

Trella wasn't sure about that until she was told she was in charge of cleaning the lavatories.

'But Wally does that,' she said. 'It's a man's job.'

'Not any more,' the foreman said angrily. 'He's been put off.'

All she'd achieved was a few more shillings and disfavour in the factory, since everyone believed she'd caused the sacking of the elderly handyman, a nice old fellow who'd been pottering about the factory for years.

With all of these troubles building up about her, Trella didn't know where to turn. Garth was touchy about the factory; he knew his mother was unpopular and was caught between loyalty to her and the opinions of his workmates.

She sighed. At least Ringrose hadn't sacked her. Some of the women had told her that he'd been on to her even before the union man appeared.

Garth came in for his dinner looking downcast, and sat at the table without a word.

'I've made a lamb stew,' she said. 'The way you like it. Plenty of chops and mint sauce to go with it.'

He nodded and reached for some bread. 'Where's the butter?'

'We're out. You don't need butter with stew.'

'I like butter,' he said angrily.

'Come now. That's not worth the long face. What's the matter?'

'Nothing.'

'Which means, by the look of you, there is. I can't have you moping, it makes me miserable. Tell me what's wrong.'

'Why do you have to clean the lavs?' he mumbled, staring down at his plate.

'Somebody has to do it,' she shrugged.

'The men's too,' he flared. 'You shouldn't have to do those stinking jobs. They're laughing at you.'

Trella put his stew before him and sat down. 'Is it me you're bothered about or their opinion?'

When he refused to answer, she tried to make a joke of it. 'The cowsheds back home could get pretty ripe, son. The old dunnies at the factory aren't that bad. Most of the time I just hose them out.'

'Does Uncle Brodie know?' he snapped.

Trella blinked in surprise. 'What's it got to do with him?'

'He wouldn't want one of his family doing jobs like that.'

'For God's sake. Why ever not?'

'Because he's an important man. Gus said he's got a fortune in opals and he's going back for more. Gus said there'd be no stopping Brodie now.'

Trella laughed. 'And you think Brodie would care what I do?'

'Sure he would. He's got a lot of miners working for him now.'

'How do you know?'

'I called in on Gus on the way home. He told me.'

Garth often detoured past the hotel where Gus worked and was shouted a glass of ginger beer or sarsaparilla, and Trella was pleased that the friendship had developed so well, but Brodie's plans made her nervous.

'Just because Brodie's doing well, it doesn't mean he cares a whit about me. What else did Gus say?'

'He said Brodie wants him to chuck his job and go back to the opal fields.'

Trella held her breath. 'And what did he say to that?'

'He's not going. He's mad! There's Uncle Brodie trying to do the best for all of us . . .'

'For crying out loud! Who says so?'

'Brodie did. He told me himself. And he said I should call him Brodie too. Never mind about the uncle business.'

She looked at her fine son, with his dark good looks and wide, innocent eyes, and felt sorry for him. 'Brodie's a smooth talker. You have to take what he says with a grain of salt.'

'Why should I?' he flared. 'You don't like him, that's all. You're jealous of him.'

'Don't be ridiculous. I'm not jealous of him. And I'll be waiting long before I see the day Brodie Court cares about anyone but himself.' She saw the angry disbelief in Garth's eyes and hit back.

'So Brodie's such a good fellow, is he? And what does he do? Comes back to the Kriedemanns where he has a bed and pays nothing. Plants his opals on their table, brazen as you like. Gus said they were so lovely, they'd knock your eyes out.'

'Isn't that what I just told you?'

'Be quiet! Listen to me for a change. Gus was his partner. The other man died, God rest his soul, and Gus lost his share, but he worked all that time with Brodie. He worked hard. How do you think he felt, with Brodie showing off his opals and Gus ending up owing money?'

'Gus didn't mind,' Garth said sullenly.

'That's not the point. Wouldn't you think Brodie could have given him a few stones? Just a few to help him along? But not Brodie. It wouldn't enter his stupid head.'

'He didn't have to!'

'For sure he didn't, but there's the difference between your father and your uncle. Michael would have given Gus half without a murmur. And been glad about it. Don't you be forgetting your dear father in your prayers tonight, and I'll be praying that you turn out as good as Michael Court. Now get on with your dinner.'

She knew Garth wasn't convinced, but that was the way with kids; they had their opinions and mothers ranked low in the pecking order of knowledge. She was glad Brodie was out of town. She hoped he'd stay away and, please God, leave Gus alone.

*　　*　　*

Once Brodie left, Vivien felt even more isolated. Sometimes she thought *she* was going mad. That she'd end up as crazy as her husband.

Yesterday, when she was out riding, alone as usual, she was tempted to turn her horse for the open road and bolt away from this place forever. To hell with Fairlea and the dreary staff, and Vern too! He wasn't a husband any more, and yet he had her chained to this station worse than before. She wished he were dead. That would solve everything.

Brodie was sweet, offering her a cottage, offering to take care of her, but that would be a terrible mistake, and Vivien knew she had to put aside reckless thoughts of just walking out, no matter what the strain on her.

The night was cold and she sat in the parlour reading a pile of *Ladies' Journal*s for the umpteenth time.

Her housekeeper knocked at the door. 'Mr Vern's asleep, madam. Is there anything you need before I go off?'

'No.'

'Do you need any more wood for the fire?'

'No.'

'You won't forget we promised to take Mr Vern on a picnic tomorrow?'

Vivien sighed angrily. 'I won't forget, though he probably already has!'

'Well, I'll say good night then.'

'Yes. Good night.' The woman was an absolute leech, hanging about all the time. The only time Vivien felt a small patch of freedom was when Elvie took herself off to her room.

She stared moodily into the fire. Someone should put Vern out of his misery. There were things you could give people, she thought darkly, that would put them to sleep for good, just have them nod off quietly and never wake up.

'But what things?' she muttered to herself. 'Who knows? Not me.'

The storeroom contained several bottles of stuff marked 'Poison'. Vivien had noted them, all too often, but she didn't dare touch them. She'd read lurid tales of women poisoning their husbands but they'd always been caught, and besides, she couldn't cope with such horror. Those women had to be mad. And cruel. She'd seen a horse die of poisoning, having chewed on some wild bush, and it was terrible, the poor thing had perished in agony.

Nevertheless, with the thought now firmly planted, Vivien, feeling perfectly sane, began to consider what might be. How she could put an end to the appalling situation that had been forced on her.

She poured herself a nip of brandy to raise her spirits.

Whether you like it or not, she told herself, there is only one solution. Vern wouldn't blame you. He'd welcome an escape from his hopeless life. If he, as he was before, could see what has become of him, a man devoid of dignity, he'd jump off a cliff. End it himself.'

He wets his trousers, she added. And then he stands there crying. And why would he cry if he weren't aware that he'd been reduced to this state? The poor man. He can't even undo the buttons on his fly. It's all too terrible for him.

Elvie, she'd noticed, had removed Vern's guns from the hall. Maybe she thought he might try to do away with himself. Pity she couldn't mind her own business. It would have been easy enough for Vern to have an accident fiddling with his guns. That sort of thing happened all the time.

Damn her! Vivien realised that she too had lost her chance. Vern, like a witless child, always did as he was told. Directing him to the familiarity of his guns would have been easy . . .

Depressed, Vivien finished her brandy and walked out on to the veranda to stare into the darkness.

The next morning, Elvie woke her with her breakfast tray. 'Mr Vern is looking forward to the picnic. He hasn't forgotten,' she said enthusiastically.

'We can't go,' Vivien said lazily. 'It's too wet. It was raining last night.'

'Oh no. The rain has stopped. The sun's up, it's a lovely day. We can take the trap and good thick rugs. And I've got the fishing lines. He loves to fish, and with the river up again the men are catching plenty.'

'All right, I'll be up soon,' Vivien said sourly.

When Elvie left, she nibbled on toast and marmalade. 'If the truth be known,' she told the empty room, 'it's not only Vern who likes to fish, it's her too. She's fishing mad. This is just an excuse for her to have a good time.'

She drank her tea and put the tray on the floor. Tired

after a restless night, she dozed off again, but woke trembling in fright, her sleep assailed by terrible nightmares. Chilling screams still reverberated in her head, giving credence to the fearful, chaotic dreams that still lingered, and she jumped out of bed as if to run from them.

Shakily, she stood over the washbasin, dousing her face in cold water, over and over again, until her head cleared.

'It must have been the brandy,' she decided, and turned wearily to her wardrobe to find something suitable for this day's pointless expedition.

'I didn't make that much,' Brodie told Gus, 'considering I have to repay Mrs Holloway, and pay Willi and all the other expenses.' As he spoke, he realised he'd have to tell Willi the truth, so that between them they could arrive at the real value of the stones right from the start, but he saw no reason why he should tell anyone else of his success. Not even Gus.

'If you didn't do so well, why are you so anxious to go back?'

'Because I know what I'm doing now.'

'We knew what we were doing, Brodie, or we wouldn't have found opals in the first place.'

'Faith, you're a difficult man! Don't you see that this time we're starting fresh? No bills. I don't owe anyone nothing, and I can buy equipment without having to watch the coin.'

'Why all the other blokes?'

Brodie hadn't mentioned his temporary truce with the Judge. His friend might not approve. 'Safety in numbers. They've all got miners' licences now, and they won't be taking any standover stuff from Chiswick, and there's plenty of room for them. We can't dig it all ourselves, just you and me.'

'I told you. Count me out.'

'But I need you. There has to be a camp boss, and you're the man.'

'Why a boss? They don't need a boss to dig their own claims.'

Brodie sighed. 'Because they've agreed to sell me whatever opal they produce!'

'Aha! Now we're getting to the truth of it. I thought there must be more to this. I couldn't see you inviting miners on to the Ten Mile out of the goodness of your heart.' He laughed. 'Stick with it, Brodie. It's your bag. You be the boss yourself.'

No matter how much Brodie argued, Gus was adamant.

'It's Trella, isn't it?' Brodie said angrily. 'She's got you henpecked already.'

'Leave Trella out of it. I make my own decisions.'

'Sure you do. But I bet she's pleased you're staying put at this stupid bar job. Pleased as Punch she'd be to be breaking up our partnership.'

'What partnership?' Gus retorted. 'We split up, remember? We left, you stayed. You're a man driven, Brodie, you wouldn't understand what a partner means except to be useful to yourself.'

'And Lester did, I suppose?'

'We'll never know about Lester. I prefer to give the man the benefit of the doubt since he's not here to defend himself. Now I've got work to do.' He moved down the bar to serve other customers, leaving Brodie tapping his fingers on his glass.

I suppose I'll just have to find someone else to keep an eye on things, he said to himself as he left the bar. I'll need a man in charge at the Ten Mile while I investigate that new field. Gus was so determined to stay in town, there was no point in Brodie mentioning that possible black opal field to him. And why should he? 'I found them. It's my business,' he muttered.

He stayed in town long enough to hear the Judge's reactions to amendments suggested by Brodie's lawyer.

'He's made some changes of his own, has he?'

Stanley Wickham nodded. 'Nothing any more consequential than our own. Except for one.'

'And what would that be?'

'He wants to nominate one of his station men as mines manager. He has crossed out your name and reserved the right to nominate his own man.'

Brodie pulled over a chair, reversing it to straddle the seat and face the lawyer. 'That's the crux of it all. I didn't think he'd blow out the stake like he did, but I guessed he might pull this when he thought he had me roped in.

'You know,' he said grimly, 'that was the main point we agreed on. My idea, my knowledge of the Ten Miles diggings, his land. A fair deal. We shook on it. So much for the gentleman's agreement! So now give me a couple of weeks, then write and cancel the whole thing.'

'You want me to tell him you're withdrawing from all negotiations?'

'Yes. Shut 'em down. I've made my own arrangements.' He explained that he had assembled miners to prospect at the Ten Mile, all armed with legal papers. 'This way, given we do find more opal, it won't be such a good money-spinner as my original idea, but at least I've got a fist on it.'

'How? If they're all working their own mines?'

'They've agreed to sell me their stones, and they'll keep their word.'

Stanley was surprised. 'Can you afford to do that?'

'A couple of weeks ago, no,' Brodie grinned. 'This week, yes. My ship came in, you could say.'

Brodie was on top of the world. His miners were ready to leave. Everything was in place to begin an extensive search of the Ten Mile and surrounds for the elusive opals, but one thought nagged at him. Vivien. That short visit to Fairlea had renewed his need for her, she was hardly ever out of his thoughts now. He wished he'd stayed longer.

A man has to be out of his mind to deny himself her bed, he mused, remembering that last passionate night.

He wondered if she would come halfway to meet him. He couldn't spare the time to come traipsing all the way back here to Toowoomba, but Charleville was halfway. She could take the train and stay at a hotel; she was bold enough to do it.

Delighting in the prospect of a few loving nights with Vivien as a break from the long months of male company at the Ten Mile, Brodie wrote to her with this latest plan. Neither of them would give a damn what anyone thought of them in the little country town, they could have a wonderful time.

At least he was assured now that her mail wouldn't be intercepted, so he was able to write direct to her, with all his love.

As he strode back to the bakery, he wondered if he really did love her. He wasn't too sure about marrying her, even if she were free; she was a bit flighty and damned demanding. But their love affair was different, well worth every minute he could share with her.

Garth was waiting for him outside the shop, munching on a honey bun.

'By the Lord! You get bigger every day,' Brodie said, pleased to see him. 'How's the job?'

'Boring! I hate it. Gus said you're going back to the opal fields. When do you leave?'

'Tomorrow.'

'You said you'd take me with you.'

'Ah yes, but you've got your job.'

'What difference does that make? I'll leave. I could be ready in a flash. I wouldn't hold you up.'

'But what would your mother say?'

'She says I can't go!'

'That's mothers for you.'

'But if you talk to her, she'll have to let me go. I can work, Brodie, I'm strong. I'll work at anything you want.'

'You could, there are always plenty of jobs out there. And since Gus isn't coming, I could do with an offsider, but if your mum says no, there's no use my trying to talk to her. She'd never listen to me.'

Eventually Brodie had to put an end to the arguing. He patted the lad on the shoulder. 'Some other time, when you're older,' he said. 'Now you run along home, Garth, and I'll look you up when I come back.'

He watched as his nephew departed, his shoulders drooping listlessly. There'll be a row in that house tonight, he said to himself. She'll not be bossing him like she bossed his father. That one's got more of me in him.

In anticipation of good times ahead, Brodie and his miners assembled merrily at the railway station the next morning, but there was no sign of Garth. His mother had won that round, Brodie guessed. And forgot about them.

The swerve of the river had created a small inlet on the far side. In the dry season, the water level dropped and sandbanks cut the deep hole off from the main stream, forming a billabong. Now that rains had replenished the river, the current was strong enough to overtake the sandbanks and the inlet was once again married to the wide swirling stream. More importantly, to the staff of Fairlea Station, the leafy arbour had become an excellent catchment area for fish that fed among the reedy depths of the once stagnant water.

As Vivien expected, Elvie, driving the trap, made straight for this spot.

She disdained the fine wool rugs that Elvie spread out, preferring to sit in the folding canvas chair while the other two unpacked the picnic baskets, Vern obediently placing items on the linen tablecloth as Elvie passed them to him.

As soon as the chores were completed, out came the fishing rods and tins of bait, and Elvie took Vern by the hand.

'Come along now, Mr Vern, we'll go down here, it's lovely on this low bank. We can sit here and catch some really beaut fish.'

Irritated, Vivien listened to her chatter as she baited Vern's line and put the rod in his hands, trying to make him understand what was required. 'That's right, my dear. No, no! Hold on to it. We don't want to lose the rod or we'll never catch any fish, will we?'

A bloody farce, Vivien said to herself as Elvie persevered, talking all the while to encourage him. Vern didn't seem to have any idea, from the sound of things.

She unscrewed the top of a ginger beer bottle and poured herself a long, cool drink, wishing she'd thought to tell the housekeeper to bring a bottle of wine. At least that might have made the day more bearable. It was quite pretty here, she mused. And secluded. Next time Brodie comes to visit I'll bring *him* here for a picnic, it would be wonderfully romantic.

Small, gaily coloured birds flicked among the bushes, and from afar a currawong called in ringing tones. Then it switched to that demanding whistle, as sharp as a whip, and after a pause – Vivien found herself waiting for it – the response came, closer to her this time. Recognising the double thump as the identical long-drawn-out whistle rent the air, she looked up to see the large bird sitting on a branch just above her. Unafraid, the bird eyed her curiously. Were it not for the flashes of white in his tail she'd have taken him for a crow, and chased him off, but bored and lonely, she took some comfort from his company.

'What now, bird?' she said. 'Do you think they'll catch any fish? Or could you do better?

'Probably could,' she added derisively.

Elvie called to her. 'He doesn't seem to be interested today.'

'Oh well, keep trying. There's plenty of time.'

'I think he's in one of his moods,' Elvie hissed.

Vivien took that as a hint to come down and help, so to head that off she jumped up. 'I'm going for a walk.'

Unfortunately Vern managed to grasp that piece of information. He dropped the fishing rod, causing Elvie to yelp and grab for it, and scrambled up. 'Me too!' he called like a small child.

'Oh, all right,' Vivien said angrily, making no effort to assist him. 'Just follow me.'

With Vern trailing behind her, she followed the track that led to the river and then turned along the well-used path by the river bank. I'll take him a little way and then turn him back to Elvie, she decided. This was her idea. She can mind him while I go for a walk in peace.

She lifted her skirts away from the muddy path as she climbed up the sloping high bank which gave her a really good view of the river. It was swirling along full pelt now, she noted, which should please all the local folk who were always complaining about lack of water. 'If they get much more rain,' she said idly, 'they'll end up with another flood.'

Reaching the top of the bank, she slipped on the greasy slope and squealed, grabbing for a tree branch, and missed, but Vern caught her, steadying her.

'Good God!' she said, looking down anxiously at the deep river. 'I nearly fell in.'

He smiled wanly but had nothing to say. Vivien wondered if he'd known to grab her or if it had just been a reflex action. She shrugged, unwilling to try to decipher his thought processes. 'If any,' she muttered, beckoning him on.

The next patch was downhill as they crossed the mound but Vivien took more care, treading firmly, keeping well back from the river, close to the foliage. But already she'd had enough of this tall man dogging her footsteps, as if he were now her keeper. She turned abruptly, almost bumping into him. 'We're going back now.'

Vern nodded, and suddenly his arms were about her and he was kissing her.

Embarrassed, she tried to break loose but he held her tight. 'Vivien,' he whispered, kissing her on the forehead, on the cheek, tears streaming down his face.

'Don't, Vern, don't,' she cried pushing him away. 'You mustn't.'

He stood back, looking fondly at her, lucid for a change, clearer in the head than he'd been in a long while.

'I'm sorry,' he said, startling her even more.

'That's all right. Turn round now, we're going back. Elvie will be waiting for us.'

As they climbed back up the mound Vern led, glancing back to see that she was following, and when he reached the top he stood with a soft smile on his face enjoying the view over the river.

'Keep going,' she said. 'You're in my way.'

They were the last words Vivien was ever to say to her husband. He gave her no warning. One minute they were standing there together and the next . . . he was gone!

Vivien screamed, grabbing for him, but he'd jumped, purposely, well out into the river.

He'd jumped!

She ran screaming down along the banks, trying to keep up with the current, shouting at him. She saw him for an instant, bobbing right out in the swirling brown waters, and then he was gone.

Vivien slipped and fell in the mud, still screaming, but she pulled herself up to run on, frantically hoping to get a glimpse of him. She clambered out on to some boulders with water slopping about her, calling to him . . .

'What in God's name is going on here?' Elvie demanded, puffing from exertion. 'Where's Mr Vern?'

'In the river!' Vivien screamed. 'He jumped! He's in the river!'

They both ran desperately, slipping and sliding, searching the river and the banks, calling, crying . . .

They came from everywhere for the funeral at Fairlea Station, on horseback, in jinkers and wagons. They stood quietly, obediently, in small dark groups out in the garden and beyond the fence in the long driveway, awaiting instructions.

Instructions, Vivien thought fiercely, as she watched from

the window, not from her, the grieving widow, but from Christiana Holloway, who had arrived, maids in tow, to take over.

The men had found Vern's body more than a mile downstream, and from that minute there'd been chaos, people rushing everywhere. Or so it had seemed to Vivien, who'd stood about helplessly, not knowing what to do. Not knowing what she should do.

Someone must have contacted Christiana, because she'd swept in the following afternoon, with the barest of courtesy for her daughter-in-law, to sit for hours, stony-faced, by the body of her only son.

When she emerged, things began to happen. A doctor was summoned to write the death certificate, followed quickly by a minister and an undertaker, even the police. Although Vivien couldn't imagine what business it was of theirs. Either way, she had no say in any of this. Not once was her opinion sought on any of the arrangements. Not once did any of the staff refer to her. It was as if she didn't exist.

The house was abuzz with activity. Black drapes appeared from nowhere to transform the parlour where the polished coffin lay in state, and stiff black ribbons adorned the white veranda posts. Women worked quietly and methodically in the kitchen preparing for an influx of mourners, while tables were being set up in the courtyard at the rear of the house.

Fuming, Vivien kept to her room. There was nowhere else to go. A grave was being prepared on the hill beyond the orchard and several men were clearing a track to the site. Otherwise all work on the station had ceased so the station hands were hanging about the stables. It wasn't possible for her to go for a ride, or even a walk, without bumping into someone.

Restlessly pacing her room, she began to plan her future. It was sad about Vern but he'd made the decision, and now that she was over the initial shock, there was much to consider.

When the funeral was over and Christiana out of the way, Vivien planned to do some summoning of her own. First she'd write to Brodie, telling him to come to Fairlea immediately. She would want to see Vern's lawyers and have them give her a full assessment of his assets. As his widow she'd be entitled to the lot. Christiana was already a wealthy women, she couldn't see Vern leaving much to her beyond a trinket or two.

The first move would be to sell this station, lock, stock and barrel. That would bring in a pretty penny, she mused, feeling much more cheerful now. Vern's bank account was healthy, she already knew that, and he'd had stocks and shares. They were a mystery to his widow but she'd have the lawyer sell them so that she could see the result in hard cash. That she could understand.

They began arriving from early morning and, not to be outdone, Vivien, in her best black dress and a veiled hat, planted herself on the veranda to receive them. As each one murmured their condolences, some with hugs, openly tearful, Vivien motioned them inside to her mother-in-law who was seated grandly in the darkened dining room.

What a shame she has to receive all the mourners in this house, Vivien thought meanly. The big house in Toowoomba would have been ideal for a reception like this. She'd really have been in her element there.

More and more people came, until the time for the service drew near, and Vivien retired to her room again, waiting for the signal from Christiana.

At last the horse-drawn hearse appeared at the gate and the coffin was carried out.

From the time Christiana had arrived, the two women had hardly spoken a word.

Vivien had tried. She'd touched Christiana's arm as soon as she'd had a chance, on that first day: 'I'm so sorry, Christiana.'

'Yes, you would be!' she'd retorted. Nothing else. Not a word of sympathy for the widow.

Oh well. If that's the way she wants it, Vivien had said to herself, retreating, so be it. I'm rid of her too now. She never liked me, and the feeling's mutual, so we'll get this over with and then I can forget about her.

A kind gentleman stepped forward and took Vivien's arm as she walked out to stand behind the waiting hearse. Christiana followed, flanked by two of her friends, and the procession began.

When the service commenced, Vivien stood forlornly, gloved hands clutching her hymn book, feeling the great sadness all about her and expecting pity from the crowd gathered about the grave, but glancing up, she received a shock. She caught the eye of a woman standing across from her and saw, unmistakably, anger.

Bewildered, she stared, as if caught by that venomous glare, until the white-haired, matronly person had the grace to turn away.

Standing beside the minister as he led the prayers, Vivien gradually became aware of surreptitious, suspicious glances at her. Of whispered comments. She felt perhaps that she wasn't looking suitably upset, so to placate the audience she squeezed tears and dabbed at her eyes with her handkerchief.

The hymns seemed to take an eternity. Magpies in nearby trees seemed to think this was a festive occasion, joining in to carol their soaring notes on this blue and lovely day.

The same gentleman who had escorted her, and whose name Vivien could not recall, stepped out to give the eulogy, a resounding tribute to a much-loved friend, and that brought Christiana to a bout of weeping, so, dutifully, Vivien sniffed and snuffled under her veil. But she was vaguely worried. Something was wrong.

Mercifully, the minister stayed with her for the rest of the day, for few people seemed inclined to approach the widow, although Christiana was nursed through the ordeal by a number of solicitous friends.

It's understandable, Vivien kept telling herself. She knows them better than I do. And being the mother, it would be harder to accept, I suppose. But she still thought the others very rude as she desperately tried to keep her mind on a rather stilted conversation with the minister.

But at last, with the yellowing sun heaving towards the hills, the mourners began to depart, taking their leave, politely, of the mother and the widow, and the minister went on his way.

At the request of the doctor, Vivien went into the dining room to sign papers. With suitable commiserations, he handed her the death certificate.

Vivien looked at it carefully. 'Why didn't you put suicide? That's how he died.'

'We don't put suicide on death certificates, Mrs Holloway. We have to put cause of death. And that was drowning.'

336

'Oh yes, I see. Thank you. Are you leaving now?'

'Yes.'

'Well, I'll see you out. It has been a dreadful time for us but thank you for being so kind.'

He looked uncomfortable. 'Don't worry about me. I'll see myself out. Sergeant Cleary wants a word with you.'

'What about?'

'Just a matter of form, nothing to worry about.'

There was a knock at the door and the Sergeant entered, a bulky, ginger-headed man with a plump face and a soft smile. 'Do you have time for a word with me, Mrs Holloway?'

'Certainly. Do come in.'

They were both seated at the table when he took out his notebook. 'I didn't want to bother you before, Mrs Holloway, but I need to get a few things straight. Could you tell me exactly what happened by the river there.'

She sighed. 'I've told so many people. Surely you know by this?'

'Of course I do, but I need to hear it from you. For the books, you see.'

'What books?'

'Police records. Suicide is a serious matter. Against the law, you know.'

'I didn't know.'

'Well, then . . .' He licked his pencil and the tufts of eyebrows lifted expectantly.

Slowly Vivien told her story, and he made laborious notes.

'Now, just to see I've got it right, we'll go through it again, Mrs Holloway. You say he jumped. Are you sure he didn't slip?'

'Quite sure.'

'And you just stood there while he jumped?'

'What else could I do? There was no time . . .'

'No time to stop him?'

'I just said that.'

'Why do you think he jumped?'

'Probably because he was fed up with everything.'

'But you said earlier in the piece that Elvie tried to get him to fish but he didn't know what he was doing. Couldn't understand at all what he was supposed to do.'

'That's right.'

337

'In fact that had been Mr Holloway's state for quite some time. His previous accident had left him seriously mentally injured, can I say?'

'Yes.'

'He wasn't up to making decisions?'

'Normally, no.'

'But this time he did. He upped and decided to drown himself and so he jumped?'

Under the table, Vivien wrung her hands nervously. How much longer was this to go on? He was getting her so confused. Even when she'd told him the first time what had happened, he'd interrupted her constantly, and now he still hadn't got it right. 'Yes, he jumped.'

'And you had no indication this would happen? Nothing else happened prior to this that might have given you some warning? Nothing different about him?'

'No. Unless . . .'

'Unless what?'

'Well, he tried to kiss me. I mean, he did kiss me. He hugged me . . .'

'And what did you do?'

'I think I told someone else this. I pushed him away.'

'Your husband tried to kiss you and you pushed him away?'

She was embarrassed. 'Yes. It just wasn't right. I mean, it upset me. Vern wasn't capable of knowing what he was doing.'

'But he knew to jump?'

'Not that. You don't understand. He had the mentality of a child. To have him suddenly kissing me was horrible. All wrong.'

The Sergeant took out his pipe. 'Do you mind if I smoke?'

Vivien sank lower in her chair, realising that this meant her interrogator was in no hurry. Woefully she nodded her approval.

'Now,' he said, finally sucking on the pipe, 'at the time he, er, jumped, you were angry with him?'

His hesitation at that word struck fear into her. What was going on here? 'I object to your manner of question, sir!' she said. 'My husband jumped. There should be no hesitation in your statement.'

338

'Forgive me,' he relented. 'But you were alone with him and you were angry with Mr Holloway, according to your own statement. You're making it difficult for me.'

This had to be the most stupid man she'd ever come across! How many times did she have to explain? They were just going round in circles. It was almost as if he were hinting that she'd had a hand in it.

Oh my God! she put her knuckles to her mouth to prevent those words escaping. Was that what he was thinking? Was that what all those cold faces had been about? Did they think she'd done this?

'Elvie was there,' she said desperately. 'She'll tell you.'

He turned back the notebook. New, she noticed, for the occasion, with a blue cover. 'Mrs Smith was not there. She came along later when she heard you call.'

'I didn't call! I was screaming for help.'

'Mrs Smith said that you were in a bad mood. That you were irritated with your husband all the morning.'

'That's not true.'

'She said you refused to assist her with Mr Holloway when she was trying to show him how to fish.'

'That's nonsense. I knew he couldn't cope with it.'

'Because of his mental state?'

'Yes!' she said angrily.

'And yet you watched when he made the calm decision to leap out into the river?'

'I told you, I couldn't stop him. And I refuse to go over this again. If you can't understand that, then I suggest you find someone who knows how to write a report. Now, is there anything else?'

He sat back in the chair. 'I'm sorry if I've offended you. Please bear with me. Should I ask someone to bring you a cup of tea?'

'No.'

'This is a very sad time for you, I know, and I apologise that the circumstances force me to have to put you through this, but I only have a few more questions. Would you rather continue with them later?'

'For heaven's sake, no.' Mollified by his gentle tone, Vivien's thoughts strayed to Vern. If he'd had to go drowning himself in the river, why hadn't he done it with no one

339

about? Or in front of Elvie so she'd be stuck with all these questions?

'What were your relations with your husband?' he asked her suddenly.

'I beg your pardon?'

'With your late husband. Your relations?'

'Good God! There were no relations, if I understand your meaning.'

'That's what I meant.'

'How could there be any relations between a woman and a husband who was bereft of reason?'

'I see,' he said softly. 'Now, tell me, is it true that you have a lover?'

Vivien stared at him, speechless.

'I need an answer, Mrs Holloway. I'm not here to criticise, just to look into the circumstances of Mr Holloway's death.'

'Who told you that?' she managed to snap.

'Several people.'

'It's not true.'

'Not a gentleman by the name of Brodie Court?'

'No. And I'd like to know who is spreading this vile gossip!'

'That's not important.'

'It is to me. Why should I have to suffer these lies?'

He shrugged. 'People talk. I have to follow up.'

'Well, you've done all the following up you're going to do with me. I've had enough of this. I've told you what happened with more patience than you deserve, and that is the end of it! You may leave!'

The Sergeant was taken aback. Often people, under questioning, had stormed from the room, but this time he was being ejected. He put out the pipe, closed his notebook and looked earnestly at her. 'Do you firmly and unequivocally state, Mrs Holloway, that your husband jumped into the river of his own free will?'

'I do.'

'Very well. Thank you for your assistance. And again, Mrs Holloway, I'm sorry, this must have been very trying for you.'

Once outside the door he took a deep breath, shaking his head. She was a hard nut to crack. He'd get no more out of her. And this was a dicey situation. Quite possibly Vern Holloway had jumped. On the other hand it would suit the widow well to have him out of the way. Although the Sergeant hadn't given any indication, he had to admit it was no life for a good-looking woman as young as her.

He consulted his notes. Holloway had been forty-five at the date of death. He must have been a lot older than her when he married her. Hard enough for men to keep young wives in tow without coming to a hopeless situation like that. Turning back the pages, he was surprised to see that Vivien Holloway was thirty.

'Well, I'll be blowed!' he said. 'That pretty little thing in there, with her soft fair hair and big blue eyes. I'd have taken her for no more than half-twenties.'

But back to the question in hand. As everyone else admitted, this last year must have been tough on the wife. She had any amount of motives to want Holloway out of the way, if only for release, let alone the money and the lover. Two people had insisted that this Brodie Court, who had visited recently, was her lover. Was he in on it too? Hovering in the background pulling the ropes? Could be. He'd have plenty to gain too.

Mrs Christiana Holloway was waiting for him on the veranda, her face grim. 'Well?'

This woman made him nervous. She was a power in the land, that had been spelled out to him early in the piece, and she wasn't averse to wielding the big stick.

'I've taken Mrs Holloway's statement,' he said gravely.

'And?'

'And she insists that Mr Holloway took his own life.'

She stiffened. 'I told you my son would never do that.'

'Normally I imagine you're right, madam, but it is established that he was not of sound mind.'

'Then how do you equate that with the fact that she says he knew what he was doing?'

The Sergeant leant against the veranda railing. 'I don't think any of us would be qualified to form an opinion on that, even if we had been present at the time. We have to rely only on the physical evidence according to Mrs Holloway's statement.'

'That's ridiculous! Don't you understand that he was like

a puppy. He could easily have obeyed her if she told him to jump.'

Vivien had slipped from the dining room into the parlour and was eavesdropping by the open window. She drew in her breath, her heart pounding. 'The bitch!' she whispered. 'How dare she accuse me?'

'I hardly think that's likely,' the Sergeant replied. 'It doesn't help to be surmising that such things could happen.'

'Oh, doesn't it? Then I shall cease surmising,' Christiana snapped. 'The woman is a liar. For her own reasons she wanted to be free of the marriage. She hasn't got the breeding to face up to her responsibilities. She had no pity for my son, anyone can tell you that, he had become a nuisance to her. It is my opinion that she pushed him, and it is your duty to see that she doesn't get away with it.'

The silence was excruciating. Vivien wanted to rush out, to scream at that awful woman, to tell the Sergeant that Christiana had never liked her, but she was frozen to the spot, real fear causing icy droplets of perspiration on her forehead.

'Did you hear me, sir?' Christiana persisted.

'Yes, Mrs Holloway, I heard.'

'Then what do you intend to do about it?'

He sighed audibly. 'I shall hand my report to the Inspector in due course.'

Vivien watched him stride over to the stables, the dark uniform still an ominous sight. Her first inclination was to run after him, but she decided it would be better to say no more. He hadn't agreed with Christiana. Chasing after him to plead her innocence could annoy him, even cause him to wonder about her. But until he made his report, she now had Christiana's terrible accusation hanging over her head.

She ran through to the side veranda, relieved to see him ride away. At least he wasn't making any more enquiries right now. But what if he had already made up his mind? And found her guilty? She shook her head. I mustn't think like that. I won't let them get to me, especially those two women.

With that she marched through to the kitchen. Elvie was there on her own, calmly enjoying a cup of tea.

'Mrs Holloway will be leaving in the morning,' Vivien announced.

'I don't think so,' Elvie said sullenly. 'She's not well enough to be travelling just yet.'

'As I said, Mrs Holloway will be leaving in the morning. Please inform her I want her out of my house first thing. And you can go too. You're fired!'

In the morning they were gone. Deliberately, Vivien stayed in bed, although she was dying for a cup of tea. No such morning pleasantry to be expected from Elvie on this particular day. She wouldn't give them the satisfaction of catching her peeping through the curtains, so she just remained, propped up by pillows, listening as they departed.

Mrs Vivien Holloway then leapt from the bed, waltzing about her house, which, she noted, had been left immaculate, free of the grim housekeeper, free of her lying mother-in-law. Now Vivien was the proud owner of this beautiful station.

The stove was still hot, so she stoked it up, made herself tea and toast and idly read a magazine as she breakfasted in the kitchen, feeling stronger now. The presence of Christiana and Elvie had sapped her confidence. She was sorry now that she hadn't stood up to Christiana. She could have threatened to sue her if she made any further libellous accusations about her daughter-in-law. For that matter, she still could! Through her own lawyer. Stanley would know what to do.

She dressed and made for her desk to write letters. She needed only to stay on here until Vern's lawyer arrived and she had a reply from Brodie.

Now their life together could begin, and that thought was so exciting Vivien decided to spend the day sorting her belongings prior to leaving Fairlea. At last.

Chapter Eleven

The Ten Mile had come alive again. Old shafts were reopened, new mines begun. Several of the miners had brought partners with them, and that suited Brodie.

'The more the merrier,' he said, reminding them of the agreement that he had the right to make the first offer on any opals found.

The mines were spread out for more than a half-mile along the sandstone ridge, with a central camp by the water hole, but there seemed to be constant activity all about. The air rang with the swing of picks and the creak of windlasses, as the search for the elusive gems began again. Voices, noisy with enthusiasm, pitched into the wind that gusted up over the ridge as signs were hammered into the ground. Tradition was important, so each sign carried the name of the mine, for fear of displeasing Lady Luck.

Brodie noted each carefully chosen name: the Shamrock, Four Aces, Little Beauty, Last Chance, and so on, and gave some advice on the sites when he could. He knew that it wouldn't take long for the excitement to die down and the grimmer aspects of this search to become more evident. Sweat, toil and disappointment were hard masters. Nevertheless they had seen his opals, they knew this was as good a place as any to dig, and after that the outcome was in the lap of the gods.

When, finally, they were all at work, a few disagreements over claim sites settled, Brodie decided to sink a new shaft south of his other mine, which he called Firefly Two. He invited a tough little miner, Ted Price, to partner him, and his offer was accepted with a curt nod. Ted was a man of few words, interested only in the dig. He was in his forties, balding, with a white scar across one leathery cheek, right down to his twist of a mouth, that gave him a mean expression. Some of the men warned Brodie to be careful of Price, claiming that the scar was the result of a gunfight at Bathurst where he'd killed a man.

'Done hard time, that one,' they said, but Brodie saw his strength, the ropes of muscles under his tanned skin, and that was more important to him than pedigrees.

For his part, although he'd never admit it in a thousand years, the surly miner was grateful to Brodie, proud to be chosen by the boss, as Brodie came to be known, so he worked with a will. He too had only worked in gold mines and was anxious to learn and show the boss he'd made a good choice. Come nightfall, though, he preferred his own camp; a solitary fellow, he'd built himself a humpy in the scrub down near the track.

Even though Plenty Station was a huge property, Brodie knew it was inevitable that the new diggings at the Ten Mile would be noticed sooner or later, and he looked forward, confidently this time, to hearing from the Judge.

They had broken through the hard surface and had sunk a shaft almost fifteen feet down, with good solid supports, when three stockmen rode over to investigate.

Brodie whistled up the other miners, just in case there was trouble, and they stood in a body to confront the visitors.

As luck would have it, Frank Dobson was among them.

'You'll never learn, will you?' he shouted at Brodie. 'You get this mob of tramps off our land before the Judge hears about it!'

'Who are you calling a tramp?' a miner yelled belligerently.

Brodie waved him aside. 'Don't worry, mates. There's no problem.' He turned to the riders. 'You can tell the Judge we're here, and give the gentleman our respects. We're all here legal this time and we've got the licences to prove it. So you blokes run along now.'

'What licences?' Dobson sneered. 'Show me.'

'We don't have to show you nothing. We'll show them to the landowner if he comes out here, not his lackey.'

Dobson laughed. 'Bits of paper won't help you lot. Did he tell you we got rid of the last batch, and we'll do it again?' he asked the miners.

'Ah yes,' Brodie said calmly. 'Now that's another matter. My mates are all armed, remember that. If you ever turn the cattle loose on us again we'll be ready, and we'll shoot them.'

346

'The hell you will! That's a fast road to jail.'

'We'll see about that,' Brodie retorted. 'Now you get on your way and leave us to our own affairs.'

The other stockmen, losing interest, turned their horses to leave, so Dobson had no choice but to follow them.

'I'll be back,' he shouted. 'Count on it!'

'We'll be waiting,' Brodie laughed.

The Judge had been feeling off colour the last few days. Too much strenuous riding, he supposed, what with the busiest time of the year coming up.

Not as young as I used to be, he told himself as he walked down to sit under the trees for a while. He'd taken the day off and used the time to work in the office, but even the bookwork had tired him.

Clover and Salty hadn't left him in the lurch, as they probably hoped. One of the stockmen's wives had been glad of the job as housekeeper, to be near her husband, and she was doing quite well. In fact it was damned peaceful at Plenty now, without Clover to harass him. Good riddance to her.

And he'd probably seen the end of the boyfriend too.

A letter had arrived from Court's lawyer, some little new boy upstart, advising him that Court wished to withdraw from the proposed partnership.

The Judge snorted with pleasure. 'I fixed him. Couldn't stay the pace. But he can't say I broke the agreement. I simply required a few amendments. If they didn't suit him, that's his misfortune.'

But was there any opal left at the Ten Mile? That was the burning question. Samuel had been mulling it over ever since Court had approached him on the matter. The Irishman seemed to think there was, which was why the Judge had gone along with him in the first instance. To give himself time to think this over. Court's idea had been a good one; a concerted dig by a staff of workmen could easily turn up a fortune.

On the other hand, it could come to nothing. That was another reason why the Judge had demanded a stake of a thousand pounds from Brodie Court, rather than bring anyone else into the syndicate. After all, it was his land, why should he be out of pocket if the venture failed? He'd have made damned sure they used up the Irishman's stake first,

347

and if no good seams of opal had been discovered by then, he'd have shut down the whole show and let Court jump for the rest.

But now Court was out and the final decision was left to him. He could either forget about it or take up the leases himself. Once again the fear nagged him. He'd be kicking himself if someone else got in there and walked away with a fortune.

'I'll do it!' he announced, taking a deep breath and sitting upright on the bench. 'It won't take much. I'll put one of my own men in charge and bring in some diggers from Charleville. Low pay, and a bonus for finders, would do them. Times are bad, tramps are always calling by the station looking for work. They'd work for next to nothing these days.'

He thumped his hand on his knee. 'By God! Won't Charlie get a surprise when he gets home and finds I've gone into the mining business on the side? Something Charlie should have done ages ago, instead of letting those fly-by-nights take the wealth out of our land.'

Pleased with himself, he wiped the sweat from his moustache and grinned. 'It takes an old hand to know what's what about these traps!'

He looked up and saw Frank Dobson coming in the side gate.

'Over here,' he called. 'Just the man I want to see! I've got a job for you, Dobson.'

'You have, sir? What would that be?'

'A miner,' Chiswick said jovially. 'I'm putting you out at the Ten Mile.'

'You know about it?'

'About what?'

'Court and his mates. They're back. I just come in to tell you they're back at the Ten Mile.'

The Judge felt a streak of pain in his chest, and his ruddy face flamed.

'Are you all right, Judge?' Dobson asked as Samuel clutched at the arm of the stone bench.

'Of course I'm all right!' he snapped, emitting a loud burp to ease the pain. 'Bloody indigestion is all. That woman's puddings would sink a ship. Just let me get my breath.'

Eventually, with the stockman waiting politely, he began to feel better. 'Now, what's this about the Ten Mile?'

'The miners are back. A gang of them, bloody rabbit holes dug everywhere again, and that Irishman, Court, is with them, as cheeky as all get out.'

'Did you order them off?'

'By Christ we did, but they say they've got permits now. They're carting miners' licences.'

'Did you see the licences?' the Judge fumed.

'No. They said we weren't entitled. That bloody Court even had the gall to say you had to inspect them yourself. They won't show them to anyone else.'

'Ah, good God! And you let them get away with that?'

'We didn't know what else to do.'

'I'll tell you what to do,' the Judge snarled.

'What?'

'Just shut up a minute while I think.'

So Court had double-crossed him! Pulled out of their agreement while at the same time lining up his own diggers. But how could he afford to pay them?

'How many miners has he got out there?'

'A dozen or so at least.'

It didn't occur to the Judge that Brodie might have had a change of plan. His mind was still set on the employment of diggers and so he was certain that Brodie had stolen the whole operation from under his nose. And that sent him into a rage that astonished even Dobson.

'That bastard!' he shouted. 'Do you realise that every penny that comes out of those mines will belong to him? How did he cover all those claims? That's what I want to know. Did you ask him that?'

'No.'

'That just shows what a bloody fool you are! Those diggers are no more licensed than you are. They're just his workmen!'

He was still shouting as he marched up to the house with Dobson trotting along behind him.

'They threatened us,' Dobson offered in his own defence. 'Court said if they get run down by cattle again, they'll shoot them.'

The Judge spun about at the top of his front steps. 'He said he'd shoot my cattle?' He was genuinely shocked. No one within a hundred miles of Plenty Station would dare issue such a challenge to any member of the Chiswick family. 'I'll have him up for that, you mark my words.' He slumped into his chair on the veranda. 'Get me a brandy!

'I'll get that bastard,' he muttered. 'I'll have the police out here in no time. I'll run them all off. And I'll get the Mines Inspector here too. Clear 'em out!'

But what if by some sleight of hand Court had managed licences? Legal processes, as he well knew, were slow and cumbersome. It would be possible for them to keep working until such papers as they did hold were declared invalid.

And during that time one or more of the diggers could have found opal, rich veins of opal. The very thought almost made him retch. He knew now that he'd been right all along not to trust the Irishman, with his smooth talk. The bastard had just been stringing him along. He and Clover. What did she know about this?

Suspicion raged as he downed his brandy and sent Frank for another.

Then, as it subsided, in calmer mode he turned to Frank. 'You get yourself a drink and sit down here. I want to talk to you.'

In the face of the insults handed out by Brodie Court, the Judge decided not to wait for the opinions of weak-kneed police and mines inspectors. This was Chiswick land, it had been Chiswick land for generations. And he, Judge Chiswick, was the law out here. The sooner Brodie Court learned that lesson, the better.

'I'll tell you what to do,' he told Dobson. 'Just you and one other bloke. Pick someone who can keep his mouth shut and there'll be a few quid in it for both of you.'

He outlined his instructions and Dobson grinned through broken teeth. 'That should do it,' he said, impressed by his employer's fierce reaction. 'You shouldn't have to put up with no cheek from that scum. Leave it to me.'

Ted Price heard them coming. From his camp down the slope, the thud of hoofs sounded like drum beats in the still night air. He slipped quietly into the scrub, glancing up at the sliver of moon resting mildly in a scud of clouds, for Ted was a careful man. Who would be out there at this late hour?

As they came closer the horses slowed to a walk, two he reckoned, listening intently, the occasional clip of metal on stone giving them away. Then they stopped.

Keeping to cover he moved towards them, thinking it might be troopers on a night raid to catch some poor wretch. That was how the buggers had caught him, sneaking up on his camp in the dark. This lot weren't after him, he was clear now, but any one of the blokes up there could be on the run.

He was tempted to raise the alarm, to give their quarry a chance to bolt, but when the two men came into view, tethering their horses, he was surprised to see it was only a couple of stockmen. Up to no good, he was sure. Probably a spot of thieving.

'We'll see about that,' he muttered to himself, allowing them to pass.

They were treading too quietly up the track towards the ridge, so Ted went in the other direction, down towards their horses. He spoke to the beasts gently as he removed the saddles and bridles, dropping them into a clump of bushes, and then he gave each horse a hard slap on the rump. 'Home, boys! Off you go!' he laughed, and the startled horses took off, galloping madly into the night.

'Now let's see what the lads are up to,' he said as he made for the track. 'Because as sure as hell they ain't goin' no place.'

He was only halfway back when several massive bangs split the air.

'Jesus!' he yelled, running now. 'What was that?'

But he could instantly answer his own question. The claps, like thunder on this clear night, were familiar from his gold-mining days.

'Dynamite!' he yelled. 'By Christ, they're pitching dynamite!'

Having delivered their missiles the two men were running towards him, racing for their horses. The last thing they expected was to run into what felt like a brick wall. Frank Dobson took a hard punch to his face and the other man was felled by a body blow to his stomach.

Cursing, Ted dragged Frank to his feet and punched him

again. 'Who the hell are you?' he shouted. 'What do you bloody think you're doing?'

But Frank, spitting blood and teeth, was in no state to answer, and then the rest of the men came running.

'It's all my fault,' Ted groaned. 'I never thought of dynamite. I could see they wasn't armed so I didn't think they could do any damage beyond sneaking about.'

'You did good,' Brodie said. 'There was so much confusion after the bangs they'd have got clean away if you hadn't caught them, and we'd never have been able to pin it on them.'

'But Jesus! Dynamite in opal mines! That'd shatter any good stones. Was there much damage?'

'We have to wait until daylight,' Brodie said. 'It's too dangerous to be marching about that area just yet. I think the Four Aces mine got the worst of it. But young Jacky, who owns that mine, was lucky. He and his mate have gone deep and often work down there at night. They only gave it a miss tonight because they were worn out from going at it too hard. They could have been killed.'

'Do you reckon they were acting under orders?' Ted asked.

'Sure they were. This is old Judge Chiswick on the job. And he'll pay. By God he'll pay. There'll be no more trouble here ever again.'

In the morning, while the miners were examining the damage, Dobson and the stockman remained lashed to trees, where they'd been placed the night before. They were terrified, demanding to be released, claiming they were only obeying their boss's orders.

'You shut your traps until we're ready to deal with you,' Brodie told them. 'Some of the lads are all for stringing you up, and you'd be no loss, so you'd better quieten down.'

The dynamite had been thrown randomly across the field, uprooting a couple of trees, but the only mine to sustain real damage was the Four Aces.

Several of the experienced miners investigated and pronounced it unsafe.

'Sorry, mates,' Jacky and his partner were told. 'You'll have to give this away.'

'But the supports are still standing,' they argued. 'The shaft is clear, we could go down and dig it out again.'

'They know what they're talking about,' Brodie said. 'So you take notice. It's only a miracle left the shaft intact. The stick dropped and blew out down there. The rocks would be left unsound, if you try digging you could have a cave-in.'

Seeing their disappointment he turned to the other men. 'What say we give the lads a hand to sink another shaft somewhere else? That could have been any one of our mines.'

On that matter there was unanimous agreement, but groups of men milled about the camp in sullen resentment when Brodie said they should hand their two prisoners over to the police and leave it to them.

'I tell you what,' Jacky declared angrily, dark eyes flashing in his bearded face, 'if we'd struck opal in the Four Aces I'd have hung the bastards meself.'

'The squatter's as much to blame,' another man shouted. 'I say we raid his place. Give him some of his own medicine. Blow up his storeroom and a couple of his sheds.'

'Then we'd have the police down on us,' Brodie argued.

'So what? Tit for tat. They'd look t'other way.'

One of Brodie's first volunteers strode over to him with a horse whip. 'First things first,' he grated. 'Strip them buggers and we'll give them fifty of the best before we turn them loose. Then we'll see to his lordship's sheds. We don't want no police here.'

Remembering the destruction of his paying Firefly mine, Brodie was tempted to agree. He had no sympathy for the stockmen – a flogging would be too good for them, they could have killed someone – but he was single-minded about his search for opal. Nothing should be allowed to distract the men from the work here.

'Hear me out!' he shouted as the arguments raged. Some of the men were so incensed they were even demanding they find an iron and brand the prisoners. 'Chiswick isn't just a squatter, he's a judge. If we retaliate the way you want he'll have a stronger fist with the law than us, and I'm betting we'd come off second best, lads. And then there are the other station owners out here. We're as popular on their land as the blacks. They'll back Chiswick to the hilt, and if they gang up on us, we're finished.'

Ted Price agreed. 'Brodie's right. We're here for opal. We can't afford to be mixing it with the locals. I say we take those two bastards down to the miners' store and call the police.'

'Then what?' someone shouted.

'We prefer charges against them and their boss. They're squealing already, they'll heap the blame on him.'

'He'll deny it and get off scot free.'

Brodie nodded. 'I'm having to admit you'd be right there. But it would keep him busy explainin'. And if we spread the word that we're intending to retaliate with a few thunder sticks of our own, that'll keep the Judge and his mob as jumpy as fleas. It's the best we can do.'

With a show of hands, Brodie succeeded in keeping the peace, so he called for volunteers to march the frightened stockmen down to the store without further ado. He wanted them out of the place as soon as possible, before the others changed their minds.

'You're a fair man,' Ted said to him when they started work on their mine again.

'Not me,' Brodie said, smashing his pick into the rock. 'If I thought I could get away with it I'd blow up his bloody house meself!'

The foreman at Plenty Station had to repeat himself because the Judge didn't seem to hear.

'Two men missing,' he said, again. 'I don't know where they've got to, Judge. They took off in the middle of the night.' He pushed his hat back and scratched his head. 'They haven't done a bunk. All their gear is here. Dobson wouldn't go anywhere without his good boots. They're the pride of his life.'

'Have you got drovers lined up to take in the first mob of cattle?' the Judge asked.

Slim frowned. Usually the Judge was such a stickler, there was hell to pay if the men dawdled over breakfast when he was out here playing the sergeant-major, but he didn't seem to care today. Maybe he wasn't feeling well.

'I guess they'll turn up,' Slim said. 'I'll give them the rounds of the kitchen when they do. We're mustering in the gully country near the boundary today, Judge, nearly finished there, so you needn't put yourself to the trouble of riding all that way.'

Stay home, Slim thought. Prayed. Stay home, you bloody old nuisance. A savage bullock roamed that rough, uneven terrain, convinced it was his territory, causing havoc. He was a game beast, and when he charged he seemed to come from nowhere. Two days back he'd gored a horse and the rider was lucky to escape without injury. The last thing Slim needed was this old fellow getting in the way. He'd promised Charlie he'd look after his dad but it wasn't easy dealing with a man who'd lived too long in the city. He seemed to think this great station was some sort of private park inhabited by domestic animals.

'What did you say?' the Judge asked absently.

'We're mustering cattle on the Tremayne boundary,' Slim said. 'We'll have some sorting to do, his men will be waiting. I'd better get going.'

'Yes. Don't let them get away with anything. Cleanskins are ours. I'll stay here today.'

'Right,' Slim said, relieved.

The Judge watched him leave and then led his horse back to the stables.

Where the hell was Dobson? He'd stayed up most of the night, lamps burning, waiting for them to report in. They should have been well back by sun-up. Bloody fools. What had happened to them? They were stupid enough to have blown themselves up.

He marched back to the house and stormed through the kitchen, calling to the woman, 'Bring me a cup of tea. And some currant cake.'

'I haven't got any currant cake,' she said.

'Scones then.'

'We're out of scones. You ate them yesterday.'

'I didn't eat them yesterday,' he snarled. 'I threw them out. They were stale! Make some more.'

'I haven't got ten pairs of hands!' she retorted, muttering to herself as he went through to the parlour.

He settled himself on the couch, feet up, with a velvet cushion under his head, waiting for Dobson. Soon he was sleeping, angry with the woman, angry with Dobson, his dreams befuddled with frustration.

'You didn't drink your tea,' the woman said, her voice aggrieved. 'I didn't like to wake you up. The scones are cold too.'

355

He struggled up, sweating under the heavy coat and waistcoat, trying to focus his blurry eyes.

'There are two men to see you,' she said, and the Judge was suddenly wide awake.

'About damned time,' he said testily. 'Send them in.'

Expecting Dobson and the other fellow, he didn't bother to stand. Instead he crunched his tingling feet inside his riding boots, cursing himself for not removing the boots before he'd fallen asleep. His toes were racked with pins and needles, not ready to take his weight.

When the two men entered, caps in hand, Samuel stared. He took in the smart boots, the neat riding breeches and the trim officers' uniforms. Military uniforms. With black armbands.

Slowly, his heart in his mouth, he staggered to his feet, extending a hand in welcome, inviting them to be seated, offering them a drink, calling to the woman, watching their faces, dread flooding over him like an icy river.

There was a rush of questions when the two miners returned.

'Did you hand them over?'

'What did the police say?'

'Have those bastards gone to jail?'

'Did they own up to what they did?'

'Have the police got it straight? That Chiswick was at the back of the attack?'

Several days had elapsed since the event, giving the miners time to cool off, so, with their questions answered, they were satisfied. More or less. The police had come to the store as soon as they were summoned and had taken the crime seriously. Dobson and his mate were on the way to the nearest lock-up, at the little town of Glenfrew, prior to being transferred to the central jail at Charleville.

There were still rumbles of discontent, and threats to follow up if the police didn't do their jobs, but the delegated escorts had brought mail and newspapers back with them, and that provided, for Brodie at least, a much-needed distraction.

Plus the pleasure of receiving a letter from Vivien.

He retired to a quiet corner to savour her words in private.

She must have dashed this letter off in a hurry, he mused,

glancing at the writing, which was all over the place, lines running together, lacking the neatness and precision of her last sweet pages.

But as soon as he began to read, he understood. 'Good God! Vern's dead, poor feller. Drowned. So the river got him after all.'

Vivien hadn't enlarged on how he came to drown. The rest of the letter was a large cry of woe about the shock she'd suffered, and her dreadful loneliness, interspersed with demands that Brodie return to Fairlea Station immediately. She needed him desperately, she claimed, begging him to come back and comfort her.

Irritated, Brodie stuffed the letter in his pocket. What was she thinking of? How could she expect him to saddle up and leave the Ten Mile now? He'd only just got started.

Besides, there were the proprieties. A man would have to be a cold fish to go marching into a dead man's home at a time like this. The winner by default.

He decided that Vivien's frantic letter was only a reaction to Vern's death. She was upset, naturally, but she had probably calmed down by this. The ordeal was over for her and for Vern. Now she'd have all the widow things to attend to. A lot of sorting out to be done. Brodie grinned. The Lord had stepped in and solved her problems. She'd got what she wanted. She was free, and by all accounts a wealthy woman. That station was worth a mint.

Vivien had forgotten to put a date on the letter but it would have to be a couple of weeks old, given the time it took for mail to reach this end of the world. She'd be her old self now, surely, as busy as a bee making her arrangements. He would like to see her, he missed her too, but it was not possible.

This very day he'd write to her, with proper condolences, promising to be by her side as soon as he could, but it would be months before he could return to civilisation. He would be firm about that. She had to understand that he had his own business to run, and not even the welcoming arms of a wealthy widow would turn him aside. More than ever Brodie was determined to be his own man, never a poor fellow hanging on to a woman's apron strings. No respect there, none at all.

He was searching in his pack for a notebook, a page

357

from one of them would suit his purpose, when Ted called to him.

'Hey, Brodie. Didn't you say you once worked at Fairlea Station?'

'Yes.'

'I thought so. It says in this here newspaper that the owner, a Mr Vernon Holloway, died. Did you know him?'

'Yes,' Brodie admitted with a sudden twinge of guilt, the parchment of Vivien's letter a-crackle in his pocket.

'Under mysterious circumstances,' Ted added, interested. 'It says the police are investigating.'

'Show me!' Brodie grabbed the paper, passing over the first few lines about the well-respected grazier and stud-owner to find the bit about mysterious circumstances. The story took up half of the third page, describing a small family picnic by the river where Mr Holloway was alleged to have suicided.

Suicided? Vivien hadn't mentioned that. She'd just said that he'd drowned.

However, the report continued ominously, *police sources refuse to make a statement on the matter as yet because they are still investigating Mr Holloway's untimely death. It can be stated, though, that accident has been ruled out. Naturally, his widow, Mrs Vivien Holloway, and his mother, Mrs Christiana Holloway of Toowoomba, are distraught . . .*

'Jesus!' Brodie whispered. 'What's going on there?' He'd forgotten his partner was listening.

Ted shrugged. 'Well, if it ain't accident and it ain't suicide, then the traps are investigating something more serious.'

'Like what?' Brodie gasped.

'Like someone done him in.'

Brodie read the report again. There was no mention of Vern's mental state prior to his death. Didn't they know that with a man in his condition, anything was possible?

He handed the paper back. 'No, you keep it,' Price said. 'I have to sharpen up some of our tools.'

Brodie wished he could burn it. He didn't want to think about the mysterious circumstances, because if Vern hadn't suicided, all roads seemed to lead to Vivien. She'd talked wild at times about wishing to be free of him, and she'd made no bones about the necessity to stay with him, for if she left she'd

358

get nothing. No one else at Fairlea would have harmed the poor fellow . . .

'God Almighty!' he growled. Why hadn't she told him how Vern had died?

Because she didn't want to alarm you, he realised. She just wanted you to come in and hold her hand. And get mixed up in that mess, with Taffy and her housekeeper pointing the finger at him! Maybe even tattling to the police about him being too friendly with the missus. From that angle Vern's death could even sound planned. No wonder she was distraught!

By the time he went back to work that afternoon, Brodie was thoroughly confused, not knowing what to think, but he and Ted were beginning a tunnel at right angles to the shaft, and that took his mind off the problem. He volunteered for the first shift, picking away at the solid wall by candlelight, watching all about him for the slightest semblance of glitter.

That night he burned Vivien's letter. Leave well alone, he decided. There'd be no reply, not until the air was clear. He could always pretend he hadn't received it. For both their sakes it was wiser for him to lie low. Even a letter from him could implicate them. Brodie was angry with her for not warning him of the problems, but he supposed her first thought had been to turn to him. Her one good friend.

The night was cold, with stars like glass against the deep fold of sky, but Brodie couldn't sleep. He swigged on a bottle of rum and stood staring across the pitted landscape, eerie in the moonlight. Far below, the grizzled plains stretched and stretched, grey with age. He let himself remember Vern Holloway, his first boss in this country, who'd always been kind to him. And Lester, his first friend, gone too.

'Deaths come in threes,' he said, dredging up his superstitions. 'Who's next?'

The answer was only days away.

The death of Vern Holloway was the talk of Toowoomba, and everyone had an opinion. The gossip even spread to the dance at the Mechanics' Hall.

Trella heard mention of it but she didn't know the people involved and she was having too good a time to care. This was the first dance she'd been to since she'd arrived, and with big, handsome Gus to escort her she was in heaven. Deliriously happy.

This was the annual reunion of the German community of migrant families that had settled as farmers and shopkeepers on the Darling Downs, and it was so much fun! The band was strange, jolly men oom-pah-pahing on their brass instruments, the dances easy enough to learn, mostly polkas, and the people madly carefree as the ale and wines flowed. Even Garth was enjoying himself, not unaware that shy young girls were eyeing him, although he couldn't be persuaded to dance.

'Go on, give it a go,' Trella urged.

'After supper,' he said. Stalling. Twisting away. And Trella laughed, turning to Gus. 'He's spotted the food and all those cream cakes. Meself, I never saw such a feast. I'll be asking for some recipes before I leave here tonight. I'd dearly love to know how to make those big sausages the ladies are placing with the cold collations.'

'I can make them,' Gus said. 'I'll show you. I'm a good cook.'

'The devil you are!' she laughed. Disbelieving.

'It's true. I am so. When you marry me you'll find out. You'll be sorry you laughed at me then.'

'I'll have to promise not to laugh,' she said gaily. And then she stopped. 'What was it you said?' Heart fluttering. A nervousness suddenly upon her, making her as shy as those pretty little girls. For fear she'd misunderstood. Made a fool of herself.

'You're looking very lovely tonight,' he said softly. 'That dress is beautiful, it suits you.'

'Oh, this.' She glanced down at the daringly low-cut cream silk with its ruching across the bodice and the deep flounces at the hem. 'It's store-bought.' With the last of her savings.

'It looks as if it was specially made for you.' He touched her red hair, pinned up the way the shop lady had shown her, with a band of tiny silk roses. 'Very elegant. I'm so proud of you.'

Trella's face flamed. Looking at this sweet, handsome man she didn't know how to answer. It seemed stupid to echo his words.

A woman interrupted, talking to Gus. Then turning to her. 'Aren't you Mrs Court?'

'That I am.'

'Then you'd know Vivien Holloway. What's she like?'

'Who?'

'Vern Holloway's widow.'

She looked to Gus. 'I don't know. I've met so many people tonight. Should I know her?'

'Your brother-in-law obviously does,' the woman replied, a tweak in her voice.

'They're lining up for supper,' Gus said. 'Come on, Trella, we have to find Garth.' He excused them to the woman and led her away.

'What was that about?' she asked.

'Brodie's lady friend is in a bit of strife.'

'Brodie's what? I didn't know he had a lady friend.'

'Oh well, you know Brodie. He never tells the right hand what the left hand's doing.'

'I'm beginning to think I don't know Brodie at all. Who's his lady friend?'

Despite his reluctance Trella managed to prise some of the story from Gus.

'He was having an affair with a married woman?'

'I couldn't say for sure, except that they were good friends and she staked us to prospect for opal. I still owe her my share.'

'Some good friend,' Trella grinned. 'I've heard the talk of her. She's the woman people think killed her husband.'

'That's only gossip. He was a very sick man.'

'Oh. I'm sorry. But Brodie's out west. How could he be mixed up in the gossip now?'

'He went out to see her before he left Toowoomba.'

'Did he tell you that?'

'He didn't have to. He hired a horse and was gone for a couple of days. Where else would he go but Fairlea Station?'

'What's she like?' Trella found herself repeating the woman's question. Curiosity was infectious.

'I haven't met her. My mother has.' He smiled. 'Instant dislike there. She's older than Brodie by quite a few years, but that didn't bother him. Apparently she's very attractive.'

'Is that why Brodie's name is being dragged into it?'

'Seems they haven't been very discreet. But Trella, don't let it bother you. Brodie really liked Vern Holloway . . .'

'So much he was romancing his wife?'

'These things can get complicated. What I was trying to say was . . . Brodie liked Vern Holloway. He was sorry for him. He would never have harmed him. I'd back him to the hilt on that.'

She kissed him on the cheek. 'Brodie doesn't deserve a good friend like you.'

'Ah, Brodie's all right. He hasn't figured out who he is yet. But what I wanted to know, before she bowled over to us, was, do you think I'd make you a good husband?'

Of all the mad things to do, ashamed, Trella wept. She hadn't even cried at Michael's funeral, causing scowls and sidelong nudges, but she'd been too shattered, too afeared for the future. And now . . .

'We'll go outside for a minute,' he said gently. 'Take my hand while we push through this crowd.'

Gladly she reached out to him.

The Captain stepped forward to take the Judge's arm. 'Are you all right, sir?'

'Perfectly all right.' The Judge shook him off, standing haughtily before the fireplace under the portrait of his father. Of Charlie's grandfather. He didn't need these whippersnappers to help him. This was the test. Time to show the mettle. Show what the Chiswicks were made of. Charlie had gone to war, brave and proud. And Charlie had sacrificed his life for Queen and country like so many others in the glorious service of the Empire

There was a sob inside him. But he buried it deep and jutted his chin, seeing his reflection in the glass of that portrait. Strange how much he resembled his father. He'd never noticed it before. He moved along to study Charlie's fine countenance in the smaller photo on the mantelpiece.

He cleared his throat and touched the silver frame. 'Charlie sent me this photo before he sailed for South Africa. He looked well in his uniform.'

'He did, sir. He did.' They spoke in unison, the Lieutenant and the Captain. Young fellows. Clean-shaven. Natty. Soft, slim hands. Angrily he wondered if they'd seen action or if they were desk johnnies given occasional forays like this. Breaking awful news to other fathers like himself. And he wondered how other men stood up to it.

'I will, of course, need more details,' he said at length. 'Where exactly did the action take place?'

They looked from one to the other. Nervously. Standing before him like prisoners at the dock. Obviously they would prefer to sit but this he would not permit. They had a sombre duty to perform and they would do it with dignity. The military owed Charlie that much.

Despite his efforts, the Judge was mortified to hear a quiver in his voice. 'Did he suffer? I mean, was he wounded first? I've heard poor reports of those field hospitals, and by God, if my son didn't receive the best of treatment, you'll be hearing more of me.'

The words still echoed in the dim parlour: 'My sad duty to inform you, sir, that your son Charles Barfrew Chiswick met his death in . . .' The Judge couldn't recall now which one of these fellows had made the announcement, nor the place and date of death. Just that Charlie was gone. He'd been certain that Charlie would come through. Even from a kid Charlie had no fear in him. He'd ride the roughest horses, chase wild bulls to a standstill. And smart! By Jesus, he was smart. He pointed to the silver cups and trophies in the glass-fronted cabinet, his mind wandering from the formalities.

'Charlie was a fine shot. He won all of those trophies. Best marksman in the district.'

'Yes, sir,' the Lieutenant replied, bending over a leather dispatch case to draw out some papers. 'It says so here in the records. Captain Chiswick won top honours in the regimental competition . . .'

The Judge softened. 'He did, by God? Let me see. You know, he never mentioned it in his letters. But that was Charlie, never a show-off.'

'If you would care to sit down, sir? I have papers here . . .'

'Oh, very well! You may be seated.'

They sat side by side on the couch, looking no more comfortable than before, leaning forward to hunch over the dispatch case now lying open on the low mahogany table with its bevelled edges.

The Judge took his own chair. Large. Leather. Looming

over them. Proud again now. He'd known it all along. Charlie was a fine soldier.

'He was very well thought of.'

The Judge was startled when the pair of uniforms agreed. He hadn't realised he'd said that aloud.

'No doubt about that, sir,' the Lieutenant said. 'We have any number of declarations to that effect. From his men.'

'That's kind of them.' He looked anxiously, eagerly, at those papers the pair were shuffling about. Starved for the need of them, for the boost they could give to him. Some solace. Some small solace.

The Lieutenant looked up. Fingered his collar. He had a large Adam's apple that seemed uncertain of its correct position.

'Sir,' he began. Uncertainly. 'Did you know that your son was a pacifist?'

'A what? What is that?'

'An objector. To the war.'

'Hardly. Who would object? The Boers had to be put in their place. Charlie knew that. He volunteered. A man who objected would hardly have volunteered. What is the point of that remark?'

'There is a point, sir, and I'm terribly sorry to have to mention it, but it appears that Captain Chiswick became disillusioned with the war.'

As he listened to the droning words, and the crisp comments, the Judge realised that this fellow was not just a soldier. Nor was his offsider.

'What are your qualifications?' he demanded.

'I am a barrister, sir, attached to the Army Legal Service, and Captain Connelly is with Intelligence.'

'How dare you march into my house with these accusations?'

'Under normal circumstances, sir, we should not have done so,' the Lieutenant said quietly. 'But in deference to your position we have been instructed to put all the details of the court-martial before you. I can't tell you how sorry I am to have to do this. Especially since there is absolutely no doubt that Captain Chiswick was a fine man who stuck by his principles.'

'It's a pack of lies!' the Judge shouted. 'A pack of bloody lies. Charlie wouldn't have deserted. Who defended him?'

'One of his best friends. I believe you know him. Captain Raymond Hindmarsh. A top silk. But his hands were tied.'

'Tied nothing! I'll have the bastard struck off!'

While he raged, more and more papers emerged from that vile case of damned lies and trumped-up charges.

Samuel's indigestion worsened. His chest felt like concrete, but he fought on. Examining every page of the transcript. Reading every minute hand-written note. Threatening legal action. Threatening to expose the men who had sat in judgement on Charlie Chiswick. Conspired against him.

'Bloody Englishmen!' he shouted. 'Looking for a bloody scapegoat because they can't win their bloody war.'

'Only one was English,' the Captain cautioned. 'The other two were Australian. There was no defence, sir.'

'I should have been informed!'

Judge Chiswick's heart hardened as all the legal papers came before him the second time. How could Charlie do this to him? There, in his own writing, was the damning evidence. A note to his colonel before he deserted. The bloody fool! No attempt at defence. No excuse. Just this stupid note:

Dear Sir, I regret I am unable to go along with this any more. They are all farmers just like me. I shouldn't be here. Charles Chiswick.

'And that's all?' the Judge spluttered. Irrelevant though it was to the military men, he launched into a new argument. 'What's he talking about? Farmers! We're not farmers. We're cattlemen. Generations of cattlemen. This is one of the biggest stations in the southern end of this state! Plenty Station is famous for its beef.'

'Probably just a figure of speech,' the Captain murmured.

'A figure of speech nothing!' Samuel puffed, short of breath now. 'It's a deliberate insult to me and to all that the Chiswicks stand for! And the bloody fool wrote himself straight into a firing squad. Where did they pick him up?'

'Cape Town, sir. I believe he was heading home. Signing on as a seaman.'

'He wouldn't have been bloody welcome!' the Judge shouted, hurling the papers on to the floor. He was so enraged his breath was coming in short gasps. 'Get me a brandy! Over there!'

'He's having a turn!' Connelly shouted, lurching over

to the Judge, who was slipping from the chair, clutching his chest.

There was brandy. There was the woman from the kitchen. They undid his collar, they tried to help. Trying to calm the man in what seemed the throes of apoplexy.

'Don't talk, sir,' the Lieutenant urged frantically. 'Stay quiet, we'll get a doctor.'

But the Judge wasn't finished. He grasped the Lieutenant's hand. 'Not a Chiswick,' he gritted through his pain. 'Not a Chiswick. Not my son. Never was. Do you hear me?'

'Yes, sir,' the Lieutenant said, believing that the poor old bloke was disowning Charlie, the black sheep of the family.

'Never was!' the Judge insisted as he slumped to the floor.

Two women came. Black women. Mother and daughter. Asking for Brodie. The girl was tall and skinny, with a shy smile and large, lustrous eyes. Her mother, Brodie noted as they approached, would make three of her, hefty and plump but with the same marvellous eyes. Lashes like curtains.

'What can I do for you, ladies?' he asked, ignoring the catcalls of several miners behind him.

The older woman wasted no time. 'Me Ida, this my girl Pally. She good worker too. Willi send us.'

'What for?'

'Look for rocks, boss.'

'Oh, cripes!' Brodie shook his head. 'He was supposed to send me some men.'

She spat. 'Men no good. Us station peoples. Speak good English. You hear?'

Brodie heard, but the last two words sounded more like an admonishment than a request to listen.

She folded her arms and planted her bare feet in front of him. 'Where we work?'

He scratched his head, loosening caked grime, and stared at them. They were dressed for the occasion in identical shifts of hard grey calico, so new the creases formed large square patterns.

'I don't know about this,' he said, wondering what to do with them.

'You can't pay?' she said sadly, as if sorry for him. 'No matter that. Allasame we look for rocks.'

'It's not that.' He could feel a gathering of interested eyes on him.

'You can pay?' She brightened, releasing a blinding smile in her shining black face. 'How much?'

'I don't know,' he argued awkwardly. 'I have no idea.' Realising, too late, that they now considered themselves employed.

'Ten bob!' Ida announced, clapping him on the shoulders as if to seal the deal.

He was later to learn that Ida considered ten bob a princely sum, whether for a day, a week or a year, since the blacks weren't paid at all for their work on the stations.

Stalling for time, he thought to question them. 'Where did you come from?'

She pointed. 'Missus Tremayne station.'

'You work there?'

Ida nodded. 'Me and Pally.'

'Won't they miss you?'

She looked genuinely mystified. 'We go back. 'Nother day.'

This was too much for the audience of miners. Women were women. They began shouting to Brodie to bring up the 'girls', and interspersed their calls with lewd comments. He turned angrily to shut them up but Ida moved swiftly to confront them. She raised a clenched fist at them, shouting abuse, and surprised, they backed away.

To make sure everyone was covered, she turned on Brodie. 'You doan touch my girl. You hear?'

'No. No!' he said defensively, intrigued to hear her pronounce the word girl as 'gel'. Shades of her mistress, perhaps.

In the end he agreed to employ them. Bemused to think that his first employees should be two black women. A far cry from the gang of miners he'd envisaged in partnership with the Judge.

Ah well, he told himself, a man has to start somewhere. And this somewhere was only a wild chance. He'd let the women roam about for a few days, give them ten bob and send them home.

In the meantime, what to do with them?

'Do you want to come up to my camp?' he asked. But Ida

shook her head, looking about her suspiciously. 'No fear, boss. When we start?'

'Tomorrow morning. I'll take you to another place. Not here.'

She nodded, her thick black hair wobbling like a wig, and marked a spot in the dry ground with her foot. 'This place. Termorrer?'

'Yes.'

With that Ida took her daughter by the arm and marched towards the scrub.

'Have you got tucker?' he called.

They both glanced back at him, expressionless, and disappeared.

'They're friends of friends, that's all,' he told the curious that night. 'Paying a visit. I'll take them back to Tremayne Station tomorrow.'

To be on the safe side, he packed some food for them. Salt beef, biscuits, tea, sugar, the last of his apples. Poor fare, but no one at Ten Mile ate much better by the end of the week, with fresh supplies due.

At dawn, they were standing at exactly the spot agreed when Brodie led his horse down. He was completely out of his element with these black women. With any blacks.

After wishing them good morning, which drew giggles from Pally, he tried to make conversation, to put them at their ease. Being the man he was with the ladies, he used the old tried and true.

'Nice dresses,' he said.

Unimpressed, Ida shrugged. 'For modesty, missus allus say.'

'Ah yes,' Brodie replied profoundly.

Then there was the matter of the horse. Three people and only one horse. They had a long way to go. At least fifteen miles to the place where he'd found the black opals. Brodie wasn't keen on walking all that way, it would take too long but there seemed to be no choice.

'You ladies want to ride?' he asked.

Ida's hoot of a laugh split the air, and almost as if on cue, one of the weird birds that inhabited this area joined in with its noisy gabble-cackle and poked its ugly black head from nearby foliage.

'You too slow,' she said. 'You ridem.'

So they set off, with Brodie feeling like Napoleon leading his troops, two determined women with fat dillybags instead of packs.

The pace became too much for Ida. She caught up with Brodie. 'You go!' she instructed. 'Go!'

'But you won't be able to find me!'

For the first time, Pally spoke. 'She track you, boss. Real good.'

There was no time for Brodie to argue. Ida gave his horse a whack and he was on his way across country. He remembered the direction, facing hill country; noting the landmarks again . . . a boulder-strewn gully, silvery trees with soft leaves now in full bloom, a mass of bright yellow balls. Wattle, he guessed, pushing on.

Eventually there it was, the hard, gravelly plain with the split tree, white and welcoming like an old friend.

Unable to resist the temptation, he dismounted and walked the horse forward, inch by inch, studying the ground, turning over rocks and stones with his boot, and then, more carefully, with a strong stick. He had become so involved in the search it was an effort to tear himself away, to take the horse to shade, water it and move back out again, time forgotten.

He didn't even hear the women approach.

'Jesus! You're here already.'

Ida lit a fire and Brodie sat down to drink tea with them, using his billy and his enamel mug, which they handed about.

'I'll leave the billy and mug,' he said. 'But there's no water here.' He gazed out over the lonely grey stretch, taking a better look at it now. It seemed to him that this was probably the end of Sandy Ridge, lower than the Ten Mile, worn down by time, as he supposed the ridge would be in another thousand years. He looked at the quiet, calm faces of the two women, sitting straight-legged on the other side of the dying fire. Saying nothing.

Their patience seemed integral with this land, as if time were of another dimension, and Brodie felt alien, a bumbling intruder.

'No water,' he repeated, foolishly whispering.

Ida gazed at him. 'Water here.' She pointed to the lower

end of the small plain, where a row of trees perched on the remnants of a sandstone cliff. 'Olden times water.'

Brodie nodded. Hoping she was right. 'I'll leave you this food as well as the billy and mug. You need anything, you come right back to me. Do you hear?' he added with a grin, and they laughed.

'Two days,' he said. 'I'll come back in two days. And listen, this is Plenty Station land. If you have any trouble . . .'

Ida stared. 'This not Plenty. This Missus Tremayne place now.'

'Did it belong to the Chiswicks before?'

'No. Belonga blackfeller.'

'Ah.' Brodie gulped, sorry he'd asked. Embarrassed.

Ida leaned back and spoke to her daughter in their own language, her face grave, and Brodie hoped he hadn't upset them.

'Everything all right?' he asked Pally.

The girl lowered her head and muttered, 'She say spirits all cryin' over there at Plenty. Big cryin'.'

'What for?'

'She doan know.'

That seemed to be the end of the conversation, so he turned to the business in hand. 'Did Willi tell you what to look for out here?'

'Not Willi, messenger come. Willi long ways off.'

'Did he tell you I want you to look for the pretty stones?'

'Opal,' Ida sniffed, putting him in his place. 'I seen opal. I show Pally.'

Brodie grinned. 'It'll be a great day if you do find some to show her. I'd better go now.'

As he swung on to his horse he looked back, shaking his head. They were both still sitting in the same place, gazing quietly towards the hills, lost in contemplation.

Two days later, on the Saturday morning, he was back, pleased to see the two dark figures treading the gaunt plain like field labourers. Except, in this field, there was no crop. They had a mound of stones that might be of interest but nothing that even resembled an opal.

'Ah well,' he said, ''twas worth a look.' He handed over the ten-shilling note, which he thought was outrageous pay for so little work, but he couldn't afford to offend Willi Schluter.

Ida took the note, wrapped it in a leaf and buried it deep in her dillybag.

'We'll call it a day then,' Brodie said, thanking them, but he still couldn't resist spending a few more hours there, turning over rocks, squatting to examine each piece, with the two women flanking him, equally absorbed.

Eventually he gave up. 'It's hopeless! We're wasting our time.' He made his farewells politely and headed back to the Ten Mile, irritated with himself for taking precious time off. He and Ted had not seen a glimmer of colour yet, but at least the Ten Mile was a known opal field.

There was much excitement back at camp. Two of the men had struck opal. Brodie swallowed his disappointment – he'd almost chosen that site himself – and rushed over to the Goodwill mine to congratulate the miners and see the opal seam for himself.

It was a beautiful patch of iridescent light opal, glowing in the candlelight deep below the surface, and everyone was impressed, fired up now with a new determination to work harder.

They were still celebrating when riders came back with supplies from the store, with their own news.

Ted found Brodie in the Goodwill mine, watching as the two men worked with small picks.

'Be careful,' he was saying. 'Take it easy. Gouge a little at a time! Clear away round it first! Use your fingers! Dust it away.'

'Get him out of here,' they told Ted. 'He's so jumpy, he's making us nervous.'

Reluctantly, Brodie climbed up the ladder, hoping that pair knew what they were doing. He felt like an old hand now.

'We won't have any more trouble from the Judge,' Ted said laconically. 'The bugger's dead.'

'What happened?' Brodie growled. 'Someone shoot him?'

'Worse, I'd say. His son was killed at the war. It's all the talk at the store. Too much of a shock for the old bloke. He keeled over.'

Brodie was distressed. 'Poor Clover. She thought the world of her brother. Her life seemed to be hanging on him coming home.'

'Is she the daughter?'

371

'Yes. I ought to go over to see her. She's a nice girl. Helped me out more than once.'

'No point. I heard them saying she's not there. She's in town. The station's headless. No family to run it.'

'They've got a good foreman.'

'Will he give us any trouble?'

'No.'

'What's that girl's name again?'

'Clover. Clover Chiswick.'

'Yeah, that's the one. She owns the whole spread now. They reckon all the squatters' sons from hell to high water will be lining up to marry her now.'

'I suppose so,' Brodie said absently, walking away.

Damn shame, he said to himself. Everyone spoke well of Charlie Chiswick. He found himself thinking of Michael. Why hadn't they both upped and emigrated years back? In this dry air Michael would never have got the consumption. And what a time they would have had! The two of them, partners, with their own mines. Together they'd have made a fortune by this. And Michael would still be alive.

Poor Clover. It was hard to lose your only brother.

Although Clover didn't know it yet, not only had she inherited Plenty Station, she was also in line to own Fairlea Station. When the lawyers finished their tasks.

The widow Holloway was shocked to hear from Vern's lawyers, Abercrombie and Sons, that it would be impossible for them to obey her summons to Fairlea Station, and that she should present herself at their Toowoomba offices at a date to be set. She was informed that when all procedures were completed they would advise her of the reading of the will.

'What procedures?' she stormed. 'How dare they put me off like that? My husband is dead and I shall have the will read immediately.'

At first it didn't occur to Vivien that she might need her own lawyer. To her, the reading of the will was a simple matter, and the sooner it was over the better, so that she could sell Fairlea and see to her other financial affairs.

In the meantime, however, Christiana Holloway was a frequent visitor to the Abercrombie offices.

On this visit, she too was angry. She sat impatiently

in the dingy room, frowning at the worn carpet and the ugly green-painted windows. It was just her luck to have Abercrombie away on a sea voyage to the old country when she needed him, leaving her to deal with the son. Abercrombie Senior wouldn't have tiptoed about like this. He'd have had the woman charged immediately.

She fingered the Russian mink tails draped over her shoulders, shuffled uncomfortably in her heavy black dress, and twisted the rings on her fingers until she could stand it no longer. She banged her stick on the floor and called: 'Mr Abercrombie! If you please! This minute!'

He came rushing back, wispy fair hair straggling about his stiff collar, a nervous tic in one pale eye.

'I'm so sorry to keep you waiting,' he puffed, 'but the police report has just been handed to us. These things do take a time but they assured me they have been assiduous in their enquiries, and the conclusion they have drawn . . .'

'What was the conclusion?' she asked firmly.

'They believe that Mr Holloway did indeed take his own life.'

A surge of pity for her dear son almost overwhelmed Christiana, but she remained severely upright. 'And so that woman gets off scot free?'

'Mrs Holloway,' he said nervously, 'I understand how hard this time has been for you, and still is, of course, but there is no evidence to the contrary.'

'Nor is there any evidence that Vern deliberately jumped into that river. Don't they understand that she had everything to gain by his death? Didn't they take into consideration that the woman has been blatantly conducting an illicit affair with a man well known to the staff of Fairlea.'

As young Mr Abercrombie made his excuses, Christiana was reminded with a jolt that Vern himself had conducted an affair with a married woman before he met Vivien. She sighed, remembering the sad, wistful face of Hannah Chiswick, long dead now. But Hannah had been a sweet woman, genuinely in love with Vern, and when the time came, she'd done the right thing. Not so this vixen, the daughter-in-law she'd ended up with. A heartless wretch if ever there was one.

'Nothing will ever convince me that she was not responsible for Vernon's death. Is there nothing more we can do?'

'I'm afraid not.'

'And you have the death certificate there?'

'Yes.'

'Certification of death by drowning?'

'That is correct.'

'Then I want no more talk of suicide. It is never to be mentioned again.'

He squirmed into his chair, shuffling papers. 'I'm afraid that's not possible. Newspapers, you know. They've been awfully interested in the matter.'

'What? Do you mean this is to be common knowledge?'

'It appears so.'

'We'll see about that,' she declared. 'I'm a substantial shareholder in the *Chronicle*. If they dare print that, they'll have me to answer to. I shall call on them immediately I leave here. The members of the board are personal friends of mine. Now, I have to hurry, so you may read the will. Since, I presume,' she said sarcastically, 'we have no other impediments?'

His lower jaw jerked into a grimace of anxiety. 'I shall have to advise Mrs Vivien Holloway first, so that she can be present.'

'You may advise her, but I will not sit in the same room as her, so you can forget about that procedure. I need nothing from the estate of my late son but if he has left anything at all to me, as a gesture to his mother, I am entitled to know the contents. Also, I have a small share in Fairlea Station.'

In the face of this formidable woman, Abercrombie Junior decided to take the line of least resistance.

He took the will from a drawer, coughed as he unfolded the pages and began to read, first, the items of interest to the white-haired woman under that large and formidable black hat seated the other side of his father's desk.

'To my mother, Christiana Holloway, family portraits and such-like sentimental property located at my home, Fairlea Station, via Toowoomba.'

Christiana nodded, glad that these treasured items were to be returned to her. 'When did he make this will?' she asked.

He glanced at the last page. 'Two years ago.'

'Thank you,' she said, eyes misting.

'Mr Holloway also returns to you shares that he says you

374

purchased on his behalf when he was starting up the station. They are listed and amount to twenty thousand pounds at today's rates.'

She nodded. 'Yes. I bought them for him, for a rainy day. But he didn't have to return them to me.' Silently she was pleased. That would cut down Vivien's holdings.

Abercrombie continued. 'He also left bequests to his house-keeper and to the station foreman, Taffy . . . The correct name is here someplace.'

'Let me see.' She reached out and took the will reverently. The sight of Vern's familiar signature was too much for her. Still holding the stiff pages, she fumbled for her handkerchief, tears coursing down her cheeks. 'I'm sorry,' she whispered. 'Forgive me. I'll be all right in a minute.'

'Take your time,' he said gently. 'Can I get you a cup of tea?'

'No thank you.'

When her eyes cleared, she covered her embarrassment by glancing down the first page, past all the legal rigmarole.

'Good God!' she exclaimed.

Abercrombie gulped. 'My father made out the will,' he said defensively. 'It was witnessed by two of our clerks. It is rather extraordinary. I hope this news does not upset you further, Mrs Holloway.'

'Why should it upset me?' she murmured, transfixed by the words confronting her. Vivien wouldn't be poor, according to her miserable lights. He'd left her the rest of his considerable portfolio of stocks and bonds, and the balance of accounts at two banks. But no property. Not Fairlea.

'His wife never liked that property,' she commented. 'He knew that.'

'Oh, I see,'

'No you don't. My son was a good, responsible man. There is another name here and I am sure you are curious. I want this will adhered to, to the letter. Do you understand?'

'Of course.'

'The gentleman mentioned is my grandson. I always knew that. His mother told me about it. But to avoid a scandal, and for the sake of the child, she stayed with her husband, Judge Chiswick. There was nothing Vern could do but keep his distance. And, of course, the same went for me. Vern and

I never discussed the matter again, although I can tell you now that I always watched Charlie's progress.' She smiled wanly, glad to be able to talk about it now. Even to this young fellow. 'I saw myself as his fairy godmother, you know, ready to come in with my wand if he ever needed anything. But it never happened. He was well cared for, and he's grown into a fine man. I've always been very proud of him. Silly coming from an old woman he hardly knows, except as a passing acquaintance, isn't it?'

'No. Not at all,' he said gently.

'Oh well.' She replaced her handkerchief in her polished leather handbag and snapped it shut. 'At least Fairlea Station will be in good hands. Vern must have known that. He did the right thing by his son in the end. It will cause talk but it doesn't matter to me now.'

She stood up to leave, but the young lawyer moved quickly round the desk. 'Don't go yet. Please. Sit down, Mrs Holloway. Sit down, please.'

Pressured, she resumed her seat. 'What on earth's the matter with you, sir? You look as if you've seen a ghost.'

He took her hand, a liberty, he knew, but what else to do? 'Mrs Holloway. Haven't you heard? Oh, my! I am so terribly sorry to have to tell you this. Charlie Chiswick is . . . I mean, he went to the war. He was killed. At the war. South Africa. His name was on the list released today.'

'Oh, dear God!' she cried. She wept. Never in her life had Christiana felt so terribly alone. She wept for her son, and his son, for the cruel fate of two fine young men, and the tears now flowed in long, agonising sobs.

Abercrombie Junior called for a carriage and took her home himself, handing her on to her maid. As the carriage departed the imposing house, he thought what a terrible pity it was that there was no family left here except for the old lady. Because one couldn't count the daughter-in-law. Obviously, she'd be cut loose. He didn't have any sympathy for her. There was too much talk. Besides, her letters were irritating. He wondered if they'd ever know the truth of Vern Holloway's death.

Then, as the carriage spun back into town, he remembered his own duties as executor of Vern Holloway's will. Since Charlie was dead he'd have to find his will or his next of kin. There probably was a will, since most men were advised to settle their affairs before sailing to war. His address was given as Plenty Station via Charleville, somewhere way out west. Abercrombie had already prepared a letter to Charlie Chiswick. Now he'd have to make further enquiries.

He wondered how Mrs Vivien Holloway would react to discovering that someone else now owned that station. Not too well, he guessed. Funny how wills went. One old codger had recently left his cattle station to his horse, so his nephew had marched out and shot the horse. So that settled that. And he'd had another case where the two beneficiaries were dead, but then she'd been an old woman.

'This war,' he shuddered, 'will cause more than a few complications.'

Thinking of Mrs Vivien Holloway again, he hoped she wouldn't kick up when she found out that the major share of Fairlea had been left to the late Charlie Chiswick. It wasn't his place to tell her that if she contested the will she'd lose. Her mother-in-law would see to that, not to mention the powerful Chiswick connections.

'No,' he murmured. 'You'd better go quietly, my dear.'

And that was the advice Stanley Wickham gave his client when he heard her story.

Vivien had come to town, installed herself at the best hotel and gone confidently to keep the appointment with Vern's lawyers. Apart from her irritation at the delay, she was in good spirits. Weeks had passed since her husband's death, and she hadn't heard any more from the police. Not another word. So it was clear that they had accepted suicide, despite Christiana's libellous talk. The weeks of worry were over and Vivien had never felt better in her life.

As the contents of the will were read to her, she sat stunned, and then she exploded. 'I won't have this! The man was mad. Everyone knows that. He wouldn't have known what he was doing.'

Prepared, Abercrombie pointed out that the will had been written before Mr Holloway's accident, when he was of sane mind.

'It's all a lot of rot! There's a conspiracy here. Vern never had a son. I'd have known about it.' She snatched the will, read it and hurled it across the desk. 'I'll sue! I'll sue the lot of you.'

He sat passively, more interested than bothered, hands placed together on his desk, fingertips touching, the way he'd seen his father pose, as he waited for the rage to subside so that he could get this over with. But she wasn't about to give up easily.

'Who is this Charles Chiswick anyway? If he's who I think he is, he's Judge Chiswick's son. He'll have something to say about this outrageous notion. He'll be on my side. Or is he out to get his hands on my station too? Where are these people?'

Patiently, the lawyer explained that in his efforts to carry out the instructions in the will, he'd had to make further enquiries. 'Charles Chiswick was killed at the war. News of his death was too much for his father, who had been in poor health of late. He died of a stroke. It has been necessary for us to view the will of Mr Charles. He left all of his estate to his sister. So in the course of things, Fairlea Station becomes the property of Miss Clover Chiswick.'

'The hell it does! I want to know about this so-called son.'

She sat chewing her thumb while he outlined the circumstances.

'So. You're telling me he had an illegitimate son. Does his mother know about this?'

'Mrs Holloway confirmed the details.'

'True or not, she'd have confirmed it to spite me. And what does Miss Clover Chiswick say?'

'I had a response from her aunt, who says that Miss Chiswick is too upset by the tragedies that have beset her to wish to discuss any of this at present.'

'Is she? No one seems to care that I too have suffered a tragedy, witnessing my husband's dreadful death. I don't count in this at all. I shall sue!'

'Mrs Holloway. I suggest you take a few days to think this over. According to our estimates you should have an income of approximately two thousand pounds a year. Not an inconsiderable sum. The investments are solid.'

'And no home,' she snapped.

'That amount should provide you with a comfortable home.'

'What might be comfortable for you would not be suitable for me.'

Once again Vivien turned to Stanley Wickham for help, certain that he could regain Fairlea for her.

'I want you to sue them,' she said angrily.

'We could contest, but not sue,' he replied. 'Now take it quietly, Mrs Holloway, and tell me all about it.'

When he'd ascertained all the details, he shook his head. 'In the first place, you haven't been overlooked in the will. You've done quite well. Not as well as you had expected, and I sympathise with you on that account. We might have had a chance if Charles Chiswick had been just a friend. But he was not only a blood relative, he was the son.'

'You're on their side too!'

'I resent that. I'm passing up the fees I would earn in contesting the will to give you good advice; which is that I don't believe you could win. You'd be wasting your money.'

Furious with him, furious with all of them, Vivien stormed back to the hotel to try to work out what to do next. She considered engaging another lawyer but Stanley's warning about wasting more money rang in her head. With nothing better to do she wrote an angry letter to Brodie, complaining that he had not replied, and telling him of her whereabouts.

After she posted it, she thought it possible that Brodie was already on his way to town. All the better, she shrugged. The staff at Fairlea knew where she was. They would redirect him.

The disappointment at losing a station that was worth so much money remained like a nagging pain as she waited for Abercrombie to finalise the will and carry out the disbursements, but she was lulled into a more complacent mood by the pleasure of staying at this excellent hotel. It was wonderful to be so pampered for a change, to be able to wander about the shops again and return with all her parcels to such a comfortable suite. It didn't bother her that when she entered the dining room she was the centre of attention. Vivien felt like a celebrity and dressed accordingly, as she sat at her own table by the window. At least she was free of that miserable Christiana, and could now do as she pleased.

When Brodie arrived she would insist he stay here too. She would choose new clothes for him and he could join her in the dining room. That would make eyes turn. He was so good-looking; she could already hear people remarking on the handsome couple in the corner. She was free to marry now, too. Vivien enjoyed fantasising about where they could go for their honeymoon. Sydney would be ideal.

In a daze, Clover received the two officers. She heard their commiserations on the deaths. She listened to their abject apologies in relation to the collapse of the Judge and their assurances that they had endeavoured, most assiduously and with as much tact as possible, to deliver the tragic news of Charles to her father. They hoped she would understand how stricken they were that this had happened . . .

'We understand,' her aunt said. 'You were only doing your duty. A difficult duty. There are no best of times to break such news to anyone. And no easy ways. My brother-in-law was a bombastic man, rather excitable . . .' She poured the tea and offered buttered scones to their unhappy guests, and the clink of china sounded deafening to Clover in this breathless room.

In a daze she heard them say that the manner of Charlie's death would not be made public, for the sake of his family, and for morale.

'Morale?' her aunt said quietly, ice in her voice. 'Do they mean that if other men, like Charlie, realise they would be fighting countrymen, no different in outlook from themselves, they might not volunteer?'

Clover remembered then that these two men had been here before. That they had explained the circumstances of Charlie's death but she'd absorbed nothing except that he was dead. Wasn't that enough?

Now it began to seep into her conscious mind. A firing squad. Was that it?

'He wasn't killed in battle,' she said suddenly. 'You shot him! You shot Charlie!'

'It's terribly sad,' her aunt was saying, clasping her hand. 'It wasn't these gentlemen, they're just as upset as we are, I'm sure.'

'He didn't want to go,' Clover whispered to her. 'Charlie didn't want to go but he pushed him into it. He just wanted to brag that his son had gone to war, he didn't care what Charlie thought.'

'Yes, dear,' her aunt said to quieten her.

'Don't feel bad about my father,' she said coolly. 'I'm glad he's dead. It saves me the trouble.'

'Oh dear, you don't know what you're saying.' Her aunt turned to the officers. 'This has been a dreadful shock for her.'

'Of course,' they said, hastily disposing of cups, preparing to leave. 'We're very sorry, Miss Chiswick.'

Since the Judge was buried at Plenty Station and Charlie in some far-off grave, her aunt made arrangements for memorial services for the two men to be held in Toowoomba. With difficulty she was forced to explain that they would be separate services. First for Charlie and days later for the Judge.

Clover did not attend the second service, and the excuse was given that she was too distraught. Understandable, everyone agreed.

She seemed in no hurry to return to Plenty Station, which was now her property outright, and no one made any attempt to encourage her to leave Toowoomba just yet, to give her a chance to recuperate.

'I'll go with her when she's ready,' Salty, her old house-keeper said. 'She adored Charlie, it will be hard for her out there now, knowing he's never coming back. So many memories.'

But other explanations were needed, and when Clover found she was up to mentioning Charlie again, without a flood of tears, she turned to Salty. 'Did you know that he was not Charlie's father?'

'No dear, I did not. It was a shock to me.'

'Did my father know?'

'The Judge never said a word to anyone, but according to those officers he did know. It confused them at first but when that will was published, Mr Holloway's will, they understood.'

'What did he say? How come he told them?'

'I don't know, dear. Forget about it. Maybe on his deathbed he felt he should say something.'

'And Charlie was my half-brother? I wish Mother were still alive, I'd clap her on the back for being so brave as to have an affair right under the Judge's nose.'

'Really, Clover, you shouldn't say such a thing.'

'I know, Salty, but that side of it consoles me a little. Charlie was born of a real love match; maybe that was why he was such a lovely person. Me, I'm a real Chiswick, left to battle on. No wonder I never got on with the Judge, I'm too like him.'

'No you're not! Your mother and Charlie were the best influences in your life, so don't let them down. Be yourself, that's good enough for me. Now, Abercrombies are waiting for you to come in there and sign papers.'

'About Fairlea Station? I don't want it. I feel as if it has come to me under false pretences. I didn't even know Vern Holloway.'

'You ought to call on his mother.'

'One day. Yes, I will,' Clover said. 'But right now I've got things to do.' She sighed. 'If I can stop bawling at all the wrong times.'

'Yes, my dear. You've got a lot to do. There are the lawyers to see, and the foreman from Fairlea Station is in town, waiting for your instructions. You can't hold those people up. They'll be wondering what's going on.'

'All right. Tomorrow. I'll do all that tomorrow.'

'Then we might go out and visit Fairlea Station before you go home?'

Clover crunched her hands together as if she were cold. 'No. I can't go there yet. I have to pay my respects.'

'To whom?'

'To Charlie.'

'Oh dear. What else can you do?'

'I'm going to South Africa. I'll find Charlie's grave and give him a decent burial. I'll give him a monument they won't forget in a hurry. I've been thinking about what to put on it. Something like: "Here lies a man who died for his principles." I'll get it right in time.'

'But Clover, you can't!'

'Can't what?'

'You can't go to South Africa, there's a war on.'

'Why not? All you need, to go there,' she said bitterly, 'is to be able to fire a gun, and I'm damn good at that.'

'Don't be foolish. You can't possibly go there, a woman on your own.'

'They can't stop me. I won't leave Charlie lying in some

wretched potter's field. He wasn't a deserter, he was just too honest for them.'

One month later the liner *Cathay* sailed from Sydney, bound for England, via Cape Town. Miss Clover Chiswick was on board.

Chapter Twelve

The more they cursed, the more Brodie laughed. They cursed the heat and the dust, the massive lightning blasts that tore at the sky with a savagery that made the earth quake. They cursed the sweeps of rain that followed, turning the ridge into a greasy, slippery shelf and flooding the shafts. They complained about the food, the flies and the isolation, and they fought among each other over the most trivial incidents. But they worked, and they kept on working, because three mines now were opal-bearing.

Ted had come upon a small patch of opal in Firefly Two.

'Never me,' Brodie groaned in mock disappointment. 'No matter how much time I put in I'm never the one to have the joy of uncovering. Last time it was my other partners!'

Not that he was complaining. The small amount they took out was of excellent quality, so they stored it away and went on searching for its fellows.

As promised, Brodie purchased all the opal at the Ten Mile, expending only three hundred pounds so far, and when an opal buyer, having heard of the strikes, came calling, he stood back to allow him to make an offer for the lot.

All of the miners gathered about as he made his assessment, and they gasped in relief as he offered Brodie one hundred and thirty pounds.

'Can't go any higher than that, mate,' he said. 'Not much of a market about for opal these days.'

'No sale,' Brodie replied, clapping him on the shoulder. 'You've done me a great favour, sir, so don't be worrying. Have a drink before you go.'

They took a day off to attend buck-jumping competitions that were held in a paddock by the miners' store, and arrived to find that it was a real gala occasion. Station owners, stockmen, miners and visitors came from all directions to join in the fun.

Even women. A cheerful sight for lonely men, who competed to extend to these ladies the utmost courtesy.

Brodie asked about Clover, but was told she still hadn't returned to Plenty Station.

'She'll be back though,' the stockmen said. 'When she's feeling better. Slim's managing.'

It was a great day of gambling and drinking and shouts and spills, as the fierce horses raised the dust and fought to unseat their riders.

One of his miners, a fool in the drink, Brodie observed, insisted on having a go in the ring. He lasted twelve seconds before he was thrown and broke his leg. Apart from serious hangovers, he was the only casualty from the Ten Mile.

A woman approached Brodie angrily. 'Are you Brodie Court?'

'Yes, ma'am.'

'Then you'll please send my gins back.'

'What gins?'

'I'm Mrs Tremayne. From the station adjoining Plenty. Two of my gins are missing and I'm told they're with you at the Ten Mile. You ought to be ashamed of yourself! You send them back or I'll have the police on you.'

Brodie was astonished. 'Whoa now. Wait! Are you talking about Ida and Pally?'

She shook her riding whip at him. 'So you have got them?'

'No. Believe me. Nothing like that. Willi Schluter . . . you know him?'

'Yes,' she said tersely.

'He sent them over to do a little prospecting for me, nosing about surface stones.' He was careful not to say where. 'They haven't been in our camp at all. They searched a bit of ground for me, found nothing, so I paid them after two days and called it off. I haven't seen them since.'

'You paid them?' She was incredulous.

'Willi said pay them, so I did.'

'I wish he'd mind his own business! Oh, dear God. They could be anywhere now. I'm sorry, Mr Court. I'll take your word for it that they were not harmed.'

'They were not,' he insisted. 'Definitely not. But tell me. Do you know where I could write to Miss Chiswick? I'd like to send condolences.'

'You'll have to wait to do that, Mr Court. I believe she has gone to England. Poor girl. Let's hope a good, long holiday like that will be the best medicine. They say she was absolutely distraught.'

He nodded. 'She would be.'

A hard, sharp sun was lifting in the east when the roistering miners staggered back into their camp, any thought of hammer and pick too painful to contemplate. Someone was carrying a small pack of mail that had been entrusted to him early in the day, and in his drunken state he'd forgotten it. So now it was slung carelessly by Brodie's tent. Unnoticed.

Brodie, too, was suffering. It had been an age since he'd drunk so much, and his head was thumping. He flung himself on his bunk to sleep it off.

Hours later he awoke to the unusual quiet of the camp, with everyone else still resting their weary bones. To clear his head he went down to the creek, stripped and waded into the icy water, vaguely aware that something was bothering him.

As he towelled himself dry, he laughed, remembering Vivien's wild idea, ages ago, of joining him out here. She'd throw the place into confusion, he said to himself, with men marching about here in the raw. This being our open-air bathroom.

Other opal fields, he now knew, were not as fortunate as they were at the Ten Mile. Most of them had no water at all. It had to be carted in and sold by the quart, so there was no wasting it on the luxury of bathing.

'The women!' he said suddenly. 'Ida and Pally! Where *are* they?'

Then it dawned on him as surely as if they'd been standing before him. They were still out there!

By the time he'd saddled his horse, Brodie began to have doubts, but he decided to check anyway.

Ida was standing by their ti-tree shelter. Stiffened animal skins hung from nearby trees and meat of some sort was cooking among smouldering coals.

'Where you bin?' she asked caustically.

He threw out his hands in despair. 'I'm sorry. I thought you had gone home. I mean, I meant you to go home. Have you been here all this time?'

She pointed. In the distance he could see the small figure of Pally crouched over the stony ground.

'Mrs Tremayne's looking for you, Ida. She wants you to come home. She was worried about you.'

'Us busy.'

'I know. But it's time to go home now.'

'You don't want our rocks? You don't want to see?'

Rather than disappoint her, he followed her to the small hill of stones that they'd gathered, and sat down with her to investigate.

'You have been busy,' he said, pretending to be pleased with them and wondering how much he'd have to pay them now. 'These stones are all very pretty.'

She smiled. Relieved. 'Good work, eh?'

'Indeed it is,' he said to placate her, as he turned over lumps of coloured sandstone with orange and white stripes, deciding it would be a kindness to take a few with him. Give them some satisfaction for all their work.

Gradually he began building a mound of rejects, with a couple set aside, until he came upon one small knob containing the same dark opal he'd found there earlier. The opal gleaming in the stone was only the size and shape of an almond on the face of it, but nevertheless, there it was.

Delighted, Brodie held it up to her. 'Good on you, Ida! Look at what you found.'

She spat on it and polished it on her shift. 'Good stuff, eh?'

'Sure is,' he said, knowing it really didn't mean much. So now he had three such stones and all that did was leave him back where he started. Not knowing whether this place was worth mining or not.

Even when he uncovered another one, slightly bigger, he couldn't decide. This was a hard, dry area. Mining here would be tough. He sighed as he turned over the rocks, jagged and smooth, some heavy, some light and crumbly, all gathered from the weathered furrows of this stony plain.

Among the dusty rubble, one rock was hard to shift. Altering his stance because his legs were becoming stiff, Brodie put a hand behind it to pull the wedge clear but it was bigger and heavier than he'd expected. Ironstone, he guessed wrenching it free.

The old lump of rock was about a foot wide, and he smiled at the thought of the two women lugging this into place like a pair of bower birds.

Dragging it out caused the rest of the mound to collapse, raising a small cloud of dust. Brodie sneezed, reaching for his handkerchief. The dust had been getting to him lately.

The lump of rock fell at his feet and he turned it over to examine the flat side. He stared at it. Dead centre, about eight inches across and six wide, a smooth surface of black opal glowed like fire.

'Oh, Jesus!' he shouted. 'God Almighty! What have we got here?' The blazing colours seemed three-dimensional against the dark background.

'That a beauty!' Ida said.

He nodded. 'To me it's a beauty. I don't care what they say. I reckon black opal beats all.'

Reverently he wiped the surface with the palm of his hand, turning it back and forth, watching in delight as the sun highlighted the magnificent range of colours.

'Where did you find this, Ida?' he asked.

'I show you. Over by the water.' She gave a sharp whistle to call Pally back and headed over to the edge of the low plateau, where Brodie expected to find a creek, or at least a small water hole. But there was only a thread of water seeping from the far wall of the shallow gully. The water was cold, probably from an ancient artesian spring.

'Here?' he asked, feeling about the slimy damp wall.

'No.' She tramped past him to a crumbled patch near the top of the gully, where small bushes clung precariously.

'Moon show me,' she told him. 'That stone flash pretty in the night.'

Brodie could only shake his head in wonder. Hadn't Willi told him that opals were only ever found where once water had been, way back in the ages. They needed water to form in the first place.

He found nothing more of interest in their stones, but congratulated them enthusiastically.

'How much do I owe you now?' he asked weakly. Whatever they asked, he'd be happy to pay it. Not that he had any cash on him, but he could send it to the station.

The two women stared at each other, and then burst out

laughing. 'You a mad feller,' Ida chuckled. 'You forget. You paid us plenty money.'

'We go home now?' Pally asked plaintively. Obviously she was sick of this boring job.

'Yes, you go home now. Don't tell them about our rocks, will you?'

Ida knew what he meant. 'Secret,' she told Pally. 'We doan tell whitefellers nothing. You hear?'

When they walked back with him Brodie said: 'I wish I had a present for you but I've nothing with me.'

Ida strode over to his horse. 'That good water bag you got there,' she said cannily.

'It's yours,' Brodie laughed, unstrapping the damp canvas bag. 'Now you will go home, won't you?'

He rode away with the new knobs of black opal in his pocket and the hefty piece of rock balancing on his lap. A half-mile before the camp he chose a likely spot by a flowering gum, dug a hole and buried his treasure, wrapped in his worn saddle blanket.

Ted was in a cranky mood. 'You shouldn't chuck the mail down like that, it makes folk wild if their letters get lost.'

'What mail?'

'Here in this bag. Two for you. I gave the rest out.'

Brodie was so happy he didn't care who'd thrown the mail down in the scrub. He was even happy to apologise. Accept the blame.

No one asked where he'd been. No one cared. They were all too busy getting back to work.

He took his letters, both from Vivien, he noticed, lit his pipe and settled down to read. This was a great day! He wished Gus was here. Now he'd have to come out and help him open a new mine. Black opal, Brodie was convinced, would overtake light opals in the market sooner or later. It must.

Vivien's first letter, judging from the postmark, was written from a hotel in town, and her sharp, domineering attitude annoyed the hell out of him. So she'd lost the farm, as the saying went; she wasn't the only one. Which reminded him that for all her talk, Trella hadn't paid him a penny yet. He'd have his solicitor send her a bill. See how she liked that! And Vivien had been left a fair amount of cash in the final divvy-up, she was proud to tell him, boasting that she was quite well off in contrast to the whines about Fairlea in the previous paragraph. She couldn't seem to make up her mind whether she'd won or lost the game.

But she had made up her mind about him. Demanding he return immediately. Grizzling in long, self-pitying passages about not hearing from him.

Brodie held his pipe in clenched teeth as he ripped open her second letter, expecting more of the same.

And there was, for a start. More moans and groans about being on her own, waiting for him, hurt that he hadn't come to comfort her.

Against what? he wondered. Against the pain of inheriting a boodle of cash? 'She forgets who she's talking to,' he grinned.

For the first time she gave an explanation of Vern's death, almost as an aside, writing that the police had accepted his suicide so the will could be expedited. No mention of exactly how he had suicided.

Brodie shrugged. That must have been the mysterious circumstances. He was glad they'd sorted that out.

Brodie was half inclined not to read on. Vivien's world, now centred on that hotel, seemed a lifetime away. Maybe, he mused, our little fling at Fairlea was our swan song. They say out of sight, out of mind. It seems so for me, anyway. And yet I was mad for her not so long ago.

He looked down at the pages. Or maybe here you're just getting on me nerves, darlin'. A man don't like to be ordered about like a schoolkid. Come here! Do that! And never a word here about how I am. 'Twould be all the same to her if I'd fallen down a shaft and broken my neck, just so long as I get myself back to town.

In that mood he found his place, reading dully until he came across the word 'marriage'.

'Oh, Jesus, woman,' he muttered. 'I can't get married now. I've too much to do with the new field and all. Why can't she be content with what she's got? And her a new widow.'

In a state of shock he read and reread the last sentence. The arrogance was gone. She was sweeter now. Sugary.

My dear, you must understand why I miss you so. I am with child. Your child. But I'm not worried. Soon we'll be together and happy, for I love you so. We'll leave here, move to Sydney, away from prying eyes. Everyone says it's a beautiful city. We'll have a wonderful time there.

Dawn the next morning was a canvas of blue, low-lying clouds, glowing orange and gold as if lit from within, so much like the colours of light opal that Brodie despaired at being reminded. But there was nothing for it. He'd have to go back to Toowoomba. There was no choice now, he'd have to marry her.

'She can forget Sydney,' he growled as he packed up. 'As my wife, she'll live where I say.'

Ted wasn't pleased. 'If I have to work alone, with you deserting the mine before she's cleaned out, I'd be entitled to whatever I find.'

'I'm not deserting. I've got urgent business in Toowoomba. The opal I've bought can't be lying about indefinitely anyway. I have to take it to be cut and polished so I can sell it and have enough cash to buy more.'

In the end he agreed to Ted's terms, on condition that Ted took over his buyer's role. 'Take anything they find and hold it for me until I get back. I'll only be a couple of weeks.'

'It's a long haul on your own with packs of opal.'

Brodie nodded. 'I know. But I'll take the example of them buyers. Ride to Barbary Creek and hop on a coach from there to Charleville.'

'You could wait a week or so for a coach.'

'So I'll bloody wait! I haven't got any choice! Just you keep an eye on things around here.'

Willi placed the block of black opal on his table and walked round and round it in awe.

'Bloody beautiful!' he said. 'Bloody beautiful! Worth nothing or worth a mint. Who knows?'

'I know and so do you.'

'Ah yes. But will the markets agree?'

'Never mind about that. What can you do with it?'

'I could leave it in one big lump for display or handing to some duke for his collection, or I could start cutting into the best-looking gems you ever saw.'

'Cut it,' Brodie said.

'It would be a crime . . .'

'It's not gold. I couldn't sell it in one piece, could I? Except as a specimen.'

'True.'

Brodie touched it gently. 'It's a pity, but I'm in the business to make money. What's to stop my buyer chopping it up?'

'Nothing. Once you let go it ain't your stone.'

'Then that's it.'

He also left all the uncut opal he had purchased from the miners with Willi, hating to go, desperately wanting to make sure that he hadn't made a mistake in the prices he'd paid the miners at Ten Mile. Hoping that buyer was wrong. This was his first foray into opal buying and he was still unsure of himself. But Willi's opinions would give him a firmer base for the next lot.

'Get going!' Willi urged. 'Standing about like a knot on a log! You make me nervous.'

'Righto. I'll be in Toowoomba for a few days . . . maybe more, I don't know.' His voice trailed off. He didn't know how long he'd have to stay in Toowoomba. Nor what was to happen next. The thought of being caught in a shotgun marriage, with Vivien wielding the weapon, depressed him. It took the shine off the other news he had for Gus. He couldn't wait to show him the black opals that Willi would produce.

He stepped from the train tired and dusty from the long journey. The coach trip had been tedious enough, bumping and rattling over bush roads, but it was an interesting experience. Brodie had preferred to sit up beside the driver, listening to his yarns as the four horses pounded steadily on. After that, the train was plain boring. He'd tried to sleep through the night but the worry of Vivien kept him awake. He tried to tell himself he should be pleased. There was a child coming. A son for him, perhaps. But nothing seemed to be able to compensate for the looming disruption to his plans.

Toowoomba was crowded, the main street bustling with horse traffic and the footpaths surging with determined pedestrians. Brodie dodged ladies who were wearing hats as wide as their parasols. He stood back for gentlemen in their city suits and fell into step behind a group of soldiers swaggering along the footpath shouting hellos to passers-by.

After the quiet of the bush this was like walking into a noisy gallivant. Everyone was in such a hurry.

Easy to forget towns, he remarked to himself as he made his way to Vivien's hotel, to stand in the plush lobby while a minion was sent to fetch her.

His heart lifted as she came sedately down the staircase. Looking gorgeous in black, her blonde hair peeping from beneath one of those vast hats.

In mourning, of course, he reminded himself. But she sure did look well in black.

She came forward to him, gloved hands outstretched. 'My dear. How good of you to come.' Her sweet little face was upturned to him as she whispered: 'People are watching. We'll go outside.'

In the street her attitude changed. 'Oh, Brodie dear, I knew you'd come. Wait until I tell you what I've been through. I've had the most atrocious time and people are saying such vile things about me. The most dreadful lies! Christiana, of course. She's at the back of it. She has always hated me.'

Vivien was bubbling over with all her talk, and although he hadn't been allowed to get a word in, Brodie understood. All this while she'd desperately needed someone to talk to, and her someone had finally arrived.

She guided him towards the relative privacy of the botanic gardens and in a quiet corner put her arms about his neck. 'Thank God you're here. Have you missed me?'

Brodie was kissing her, all the passion flowing back, all of his doubts dismissed. He gathered her to him, pushing that hat out of the way, his hands firm about her fine little figure, wanting her again, all over again, as if he'd never before had the joy of making love to her.

'Yes, I've missed you, my darling. This is no good here. Let's go back to your room at the hotel and lock the door.'

'Not yet, dear,' she whispered, her tongue seducing his ear.

'Now,' he muttered urgently.

Vivien drew back. 'No, Brodie. We have to talk.'

'We've done enough talking.' He smothered her mouth with his.

As far as Brodie was concerned, from that moment on it was all downhill. Vivien had their lives worked out, with no thought for his plans.

They removed themselves, at her suggestion, to a park bench, where she began to outline the procedure, completely unaware of his growing irritation. Brodie listened politely.

He was to take a room at the hotel so that they could be together, and yet not appear to be, while she waited for the monies from Vern's will to be distributed.

'They're taking an age, but that's just lawyers. I still haven't got over the shock of losing Fairlea Station, so I've decided I simply won't think about it. I should have all of my entitlements any day now. But as for you, Brodie, I can tell you now, I nearly fainted when I saw you.'

'Why? Was I that much of a surprise?'

'No, dear. But you simply can't be walking about Toowoomba in those ugly old clothes. And you need a shave. I've never seen you looking so unkempt. And in the foyer of my hotel!'

'I've hardly slept for days.'

She trilled a laugh, and pecked him on his cheek. 'Darling. I suppose that's understandable, but now you have me to look after you. We'll go straight to a shop and buy you decent clothes. It will be fun, Brodie. Then we'll go back to the hotel. I doubt they would have let you in looking the way you do, in your baggy pants and jacket.'

Vivien was completely unaware of the ominous frown on his dusty face and the cold glare in his eyes, as she rattled on with the plans that she'd had so much time to work out. Including their move to Sydney.

'You haven't mentioned the child,' he said sullenly.

'There's no need to, darling. It will be born in Sydney.' She looked up at him. 'Don't tell me you're questioning the parentage?' Her voice had a shrill note. 'You know there was nothing between Vern and me.'

'I'm not questioning that.'

'Then what?'

'Where did you say we'll be married?'

'In Brisbane. I can't wait to leave here. For ever. I shall never come back.'

'I see.' He nodded. It had come to him, finally, that Vivien was still treating him as a servant. Her lover, maybe, but still a servant. A former stockman and minder of her late husband. She seemed to think that he was the luckiest man alive, to be swooped upon and elevated to her status. And therefore, if gratitude were not necessary, then obedience was. Brodie Court glowered. He wanted to say this to her but was unable to explain without reminding her that he had been her servant. And to bring that up seemed a blow to his pride. After all, he was a man of means.

He tried. 'Vivien. I am a businessman. I have affairs of my own to deal with. I'm trading in opals . . .'

She interrupted him with a giggle. 'Do be serious, Brodie. You don't have to be a miner any more. That's a horrible life. We don't have to worry about money for the time being. And when we get to Sydney, you can look about for a more suitable occupation. Darling, I have faith in you. Can't you see that?'

He shook his head. 'I don't think you do.'

'Oh, you're just tired. I'm so silly, forgetting about how far you've travelled. Never mind. For the next few days you're to do nothing but rest . . .'

Brodie gazed at a sumptuous bed of roses in full bloom. The colours, ranging from cream to gold to pink and on to a velvety red, were as heady as their perfume. He was no longer listening to her. Further over, dominating the green of these lovely gardens, he recognised the brilliant blue of a spreading jacaranda tree, the same as the trees that had caught his eye when he'd first arrived in Brisbane.

Colour, he mused. I'm taken by colour. It'd be a fine thing to be able to paint. Even the birds here wear gaudy plumage, all dressed up a treat.

Vivien tugged his arm. 'Come on, Brodie. We have to go.'

'Eh?' He heaved a sigh. 'Ah, yes. We'll go. But I've got a few rules of my own. I'll shop for some new clothes if that will please you, but by myself. And I won't be taking a room at your hotel. I have somewhere to stay.'

'But Brodie . . .'

He held up his hand. 'Hear me out. It's my turn. You make arrangements for the marriage here in Toowoomba; we'll have a nice quiet service. I can't spare the time to be dashing off anywhere else.'

'That's not fair to me,' she pouted. 'I want to leave here.'

'Then you can come with me to Charleville. I'll find us a house there. It's more than halfway to the opal fields, so I'll be able to come in. I can make my base there.'

They argued for an hour. Vivien tearful. Brodie trying to make her understand that he could do well at opal mining if she'd just give him time. But she wouldn't hear of it.

'Do you want to marry me or not?' he said, exasperated.

'Of course I do.'

'Then why can't you start behaving like a wife?'

'I am, darling. We could be so happy together if you'd only listen to me. We can't live in an outback town, Brodie. That's no life.' She kissed him fervently. 'Take me back to the hotel and you do what you have to do. We'll talk again later.'

He didn't want this marriage but he couldn't forsake her. Nor could he allow her to take control of his life. They'd have to come to some agreement, somehow.

It was guilt that took him to his bank, where he checked on the small box of opals he'd deposited there for safe keeping, and put two of the finest in his pocket. One was for Vivien, a peace offering. And the other was for Mrs Kriedemann, who'd been so kind to him, allowing him the use of their sleep-out.

Then he checked with his agent that his two houses were still earning money for him.

'Keep an eye out for another one,' he said. 'I might need another house.'

His next call was at the offices of Stanley Wickham, his lawyer.

Stanley was pleased to see him. 'A telegram came for you, only a few days ago. From Dublin. It's signed "Rosenstein".'

'Where is it?' Brodie was excited. 'What did he say? Did he get the parcel of opals I sent him?'

'Hang on, I'll find it. You know, of course, that Judge Chiswick died?'

'Yes.' Brodie watched eagerly as Stanley took out his file. 'No more trouble on the opal fields?'

'None at all.' He grabbed for the telegram:

Received parcel. Standard excellent. After commission have forwarded 295 pounds. Buyers eager for more. Well done. Rosenstein.

'Do you see this?' Brodie shouted. 'He sold them. The black opal too. What they say won't sell out here! Boy, oh boy! I'll show 'em.'

'What black opal?'

'Ah, you don't know the half of it!' Brodie crowed. 'Come

397

with me and I'll tell you all about it! We'll celebrate. Why didn't Abe tell me what he got for the black opal? Exactly. Now I don't know which one was worth the most.'

'It's all a mystery to me. You didn't leave me any instructions to deal with telegrams, so I kept it here and sent you a copy.'

Brodie stopped at the door. 'To tell you the truth, Stanley, I never mentioned Rosenstein to anyone for fear I'd made a fool of meself. Sending sample opals off to a bloke I hardly knew.' He grinned. 'But it's working. So far so good. Now get your hat. I want you to meet a friend of mine. He's a barman in a pub down the road.'

'For crying out loud!' Gus said. 'It's you, Brodie. I didn't expect you back so soon. Is everything all right with you?'

'Sure is. This here's Mr Stanley Wickham. He's a lawyer. He'll be handling our business affairs.'

'Our business affairs!' Gus laughed. 'You never give up, do you, Brodie?' He held out his hand to Stanley and introduced himself.

'My shout,' Brodie said, and Gus stared.

'What's it to be, Stanley? This is a rare occurrence.'

Brodie nodded amiably. 'He can mock. Wait till he hears my news. Then we'll see who's laughing.' He was glad to see Gus looking fit now, after his bad spell. He watched as his friend deftly set up the pots of beer, thinking that this man shouldn't be standing behind a bar, wearing that sissy striped shirt, his mop of blond hair plastered down and parted in the centre. God had given him a good physique, he should be out in the bush making use of those muscles.

With childish delight at the expressions on their faces, Brodie told his tale. First the good news that the Ten Mile was paying off for some of the miners and that he'd taken on the role of buyer; then, his voice lowered so that other customers in the long bar couldn't be overhearing, he announced the find of black opal.

'But you can't sell it, Brodie,' Gus said.

'Not here you can't, my lad. But I took precautions. Sent a sample off to Dublin, to a friend of mine. They'll sell there, I know that now. And we can get a heap more for light opals on that market than we could hope for here.'

Stanley was fascinated. Gus was pleased, but he had to be more than pleased. He had to be hooked back into opal mining.

'Willi's working on the stones now,' Brodie added. 'The light opals and the black. Come back with me to Charleville at least, Gus. You'll have to see what Willi's made of the big opal.'

'I don't know,' Gus said. 'I can't leave here.'

They talked and argued over several more drinks, and then Stanley had to go back to his office, but Brodie stayed.

'You've called your new mine Firefly Two. How's it going?' Gus asked.

'It's paying. Not much yet, the first patch ran out.'

'But couldn't the same thing happen at the new field? You got the one big opal but you could dig for years and not find any more.'

'If everyone thought that way there'd be no gold, no opals, no nothing ever found. Come on, Gus! We've got to try, a man can't just walk away from it. We could be rich.'

'You've got a partner now. Why don't you take him to the new site?'

'Because he doesn't act like a partner. I dug the shaft with him but he got cranky at me leaving and told me that while I'm away, any opal he finds is all his. I didn't appreciate that, I can tell you.'

Gus nodded. 'Not much you can do about it.'

'That's why I want to leave him at Ten Mile while we open up the black opal field. We mightn't have to dig too far there. The stone the black women found came loose from a shelf. That's where we have to prospect. Ah, Gus, you'd never turn down an opportunity like this?'

He sighed. 'I'm tempted. But I can't. Trella would be upset.'

'What's she got to do with it?'

'We're getting married.'

Brodie had enough self-control to pretend to be pleased. This was no time to annoy Gus. He muttered his congratulations, almost choking on the words, and then he laughed. 'So what? A married man needs money too. And don't I know it? I'm getting married myself.'

'You're what?'

A large clock on the wall chimed five and Brodie remembered he'd promised Vivien he'd come back to her hotel. After he'd decked himself out in new clothes, to measure up to her standards. But he'd forgotten that, and now the shops were closed. He shrugged. Tomorrow. He'd sort it out tomorrow.

'Who's the lucky lady?' Gus asked.

'Mrs Vivien Holloway.'

Gus was more than surprised. He seemed very concerned. 'But she's only just widowed.'

'I know that.'

There was a silence between them, which Gus covered by walking down to serve other customers. When he came back, he was embarrassed. 'I still owe her my share of the stake.'

'No you don't. I've settled that. Forget it. Vivien and I will be married as soon as we can make the arrangements, then I'm going back to the Ten Mile. Why is it such a problem for you? You're not even wed yet.'

Gus was startled. 'Did you say you're to be married in a few days' time?'

'That's true.'

'Look . . . you know your own business. But wouldn't it be better to wait a little while, Brodie? For her sake and yours. There's been an awful lot of talk. Vern Holloway suicided, jumped into a full-flowing river, but there's still talk that she pushed him. You know what people are like. Wouldn't it be wiser to wait?'

'We can't.' Brodie shrugged. 'She's in the family way.'

'Ah, then . . . well,' Gus said lamely. 'Of course. In which case, I'm sorry. I was out of line.' He shook Brodie's hand. 'Double congratulations are in order.'

The bar was becoming busier, so Brodie left, making his way to the bakery, where he presented a delighted Mrs Kriedemann with a lovely iridescent blue opal and sat down to wait for Gus.

Vivien was too nervous to be angry. She'd spent a horrible afternoon trying to arrange the marriage. From habit, she'd gone straight to the church frequented by the Holloways, where she found a young curate.

'Could I have a word with you?' she whispered.

'Certainly, madam. I'll be with you in a minute.'

While she waited, Vivien panicked. Afraid that if she looked over her shoulder, Christiana or some of her friends might be standing there, ready to cause her more trouble.

Eventually, forced to introduce herself, she shut her eyes in frustration as the curate, recognising her name, launched into condolences. He was sure that this widow had come for spiritual succour and was eager to oblige. Even inviting her to the manse for tea.

Having escaped with the excuse that she didn't have time for tea, Vivien walked towards the Catholic church, thinking that would please Brodie, but at the last minute she couldn't go in. The family was too well known; she could expect the same reaction from a Catholic priest before she had time to explain the real purpose of her visit.

Instead, she marched into the courthouse to enquire of a beady-eyed young clerk: 'Could you tell me how one goes about arranging a state marriage?'

'A what?' he asked, irritating her immediately.

'I believe it is possible for people who do not wish to be married in a church to be married here.'

'Who's getting married?' he asked, causing heads to turn.

Vivien drew herself up to stare down this insolent fellow with his pimply face and grimy collar. 'I requested information, not interrogation. Does someone here officiate at marriages?'

He nodded. 'Sometimes. Not very often. Why did you want to know?'

'There must be some forms to fill in,' she fumed.

'I'd say there would be.'

'Then get them,' she hissed.

His voice echoed about the sombre mahogany-timbered lobby as he turned to call to his colleagues. 'Anyone know about registry marriages? Where are the forms kept?'

Vivien cringed as a discussion ensued behind the counter and tall cupboards were opened and rifled.

A woman sidled up to her. 'Mrs Holloway, isn't it? I haven't seen you in such a long time. I was so sorry to hear about your husband. He was such a lovely man.'

'Thank you.' Vivien was curt, hoping she'd disappear.

'You don't remember me?'

401

'I'm afraid not.' Vivien remained facing the counter.

'Why, I'm Dorothy Campbell.'

'Oh yes, of course. Now, if you'll excuse me, I'm rather busy at the moment.' She tapped her fingers on the counter and an older man came to assist her. 'Could you please hurry them up?'

'Certainly. Now you're enquiring about a marriage licence?'

'Yes, that's it. And do I have to stand here all day?'

'Not at all,' he said kindly, opening a small gate. 'Come through here, I'll have the papers brought into my office.'

'So good of you,' she gushed, sweeping into the inner sanctum.

Dorothy Campbell watched. 'She didn't remember me at all,' she said to her friend. 'She was my late husband's patient. I was there at the Wirra Creek hospital when they brought Vern Holloway in, after his accident. And what a turn she put on!'

'She seems a real snob.'

'She's worse than that. Treats everyone like dirt. And once the husband was no good to her, she took up with a stockman.'

'Before he died?'

'That's why the police were so suspicious.'

'You don't say!'

'I do say. Now why would she be chasing a marriage licence?'

'Not for herself, surely. Not so soon.'

'Who else?' the doctor's widow retorted. 'I wouldn't put it past her. I know a thing or two about that woman.'

'Like what?'

'I'll tell you later. But I'm sure Christiana Holloway would be interested in what's going on here. We might call on her on the way home. I feel it is my duty to speak up.'

'Are we still going in to watch that court case?'

'No. That can wait. Your husband is the Clerk of the Courts. Go and find him. He knows everything that goes on here. Find out what she's up to.'

When Vivien left, greatly relieved to hear from that nice man that marriages could be conducted here without fuss, she didn't notice Dorothy Campbell sitting quietly in a corner of the lobby.

*　　*　　*

402

As the skies darkened over the country town she lit the lamps in the small sitting room that constituted part of her hotel suite. It was a dear little room, overlooking the main street, and because she'd arranged to have dinner sent up here, an intimate dinner for two, away from public scrutiny, she'd changed from the black into a delicious gown of Swiss cotton.

The dress was an absolute dream, low-cut, with bands of pink satin, appliquéd all over with tiny pink roses and with an underskirt of pink satin that turned the white cotton into a romantic blush of pink. Her hair was down, tonged blonde curls cascading to her shoulders. Every so often she strolled back into the bedroom to stand in front of the mirror, thrilled with the effect. She'd never looked better, especially with the addition of her superb diamond earrings. They gave just the right touch. How could Brodie possibly enthuse about opals compared with real gems like this?

But where was he?

Impatiently she opened the champagne and poured herself a glass, toasting herself as she stood at the window looking out over the town.

By seven o'clock there was still no sign of him.

A maid knocked at the door. 'What time did you want dinner served, madam?'

'When I tell you.'

'Dinner goes off at eight. I just thought I'd remind you.'

'Go down to the foyer and remind them that if anyone is looking for me they are to be sent up to my suite.'

The maid bobbed. 'Yes, ma'am.'

Three glasses of champagne couldn't cure her nervousness. There was still no sign of Brodie. Her fiancé. And the papers he had to sign were sitting neatly on the elaborate sideboard. Vivien was assailed with 'what-ifs?'.

What if he'd changed his mind?

Surely not. Brodie wouldn't do that to her. Or would he? She knew that she'd talked too much this morning. Far too much. But she'd been so relieved and excited, so happy that he'd agreed to marry her, everything had come out in a rush. All her plans, her ideas, her sheer joy that at last they could be wed. She would explain that. She would apologise. Tell him she was apt to prattle when she was excited. He would understand.

But what if she'd offended him?

He had sounded a little cranky. No, irritated. Making a few points of his own.

She would tell him they didn't have to argue. Everything would be all right. Because she did love him. Madly.

Oh, why did I have to go on about all that other stuff? she asked herself as she paced the room. That could have waited. All a man wants to hear is how much you love him. Brodie is so naive he hasn't the faintest idea how attractive he is. How beautiful, with those twinkling eyes and his gorgeous smile. She wilted at the thought of him here. Now. In this private room for the very first time. Without a worry in the world.

Vivien poured another glass of bubbling champagne and giggled. At least I'll be in the right mood when he does come. Maybe he won't want dinner!

What if I offended him telling him he had to get some decent clothes?

'Brodie's not a fool,' she muttered to herself. 'Surely he knows that he wouldn't get past the front desk here unless he cleaned himself up. Good God, he was lucky I even went with him to the park; he looked as if he'd walked straight out of a mine in those dirty clothes and a stubble of beard. I saw the way people stared at him downstairs.'

She sighed. Maybe he couldn't afford new clothes? Had she frightened him off?

'No,' she said to the empty room. 'He's too strong-minded to care. If he couldn't afford to buy clothes he'd have said so.'

Vivien realised that here was the Brodie she loved. He really didn't give a damn about society. He did as he pleased. He hadn't been the slightest bit interested in the gossip that had been raging about her. Hadn't even remarked on it. He just didn't care, any more than she did.

But what if he was having second thoughts about her haste to marry?

How could she explain to him that Vern's death, the loss of Fairlea Station and all that terrible gossip had crushed her? Vivien had never felt so lost and frightened. All the time she'd been in town, instead of finding herself the sad widow, courted by friends and relations, she'd been ostracised. There was no opportunity to tell people that Vern really had suicided, that his death had been a shock to her, because no one had called. Not a soul. Even in the hotel, the only people who spoke kindly to her were the staff.

Vivien began to cry. She didn't deserve this cruel treatment. She'd done nothing wrong.

And the only true friend she had was Brodie Court. He'd stuck by her. Even when she'd written to tell him she was pregnant.

Or because she'd written with that news?

What difference did it make? She thumbed the bell and when the maid peeped in the door, cancelled the dinner and ordered another bottle of iced champagne.

'He came, didn't he?' she asked, staring down at twinkling lights. Vivien knew him well. Other men might have disappeared into the outback when they received news like that, never to be heard of again. But not Brodie. For all his wild get-rich-quick schemes with those confounded mines, he did have a conscience.

Which was why she'd had to use that story. Without that, Brodie would have come back to town, eventually, in his own good time. He'd have said that she was perfectly capable of looking after herself. Which was true, up to a point.

Men like him could never understand what a shock it had been for her to be catapulted from the peak of local society to the bottom of the pile, with no one to stand by her. No one to console her.

After they were married she could have a miscarriage. Fall down a staircase or something. Pretend to. Break the news to him that she'd lost the baby. Men had no idea about these things.

When the maid arrived with the champagne, Vivien changed her mind.

'Take it away. I've decided I don't want it.'

Damn him! I won't pander to him. He could at least have sent a message. She locked the door, took off her lovely dress and hung it in the wardrobe.

All night, though, she lay awake in the double bed, hoping for the discreet tap on the door that never came.

*   *   *

Why the hell did Gus have to bring Trella home with him, tonight of all nights? How could he talk business with her hanging about, lowering the boom on his plans for Gus?

She walked in as if she owned the place. Hugs for her prospective in-laws and a cheery greeting for him.

'Where's Garth?' he asked. The woman should be home making his dinner. The lad worked as hard as she did.

'He's gone over to a friend's place.' She laughed. 'He's getting very independent these days. Quite the young man.'

Mrs Kriedemann produced her opal and everyone made a fuss, and for a while Brodie basked in their delight.

'It's a lovely stone,' Gus said. 'Very good of you, Brodie. One of these days you'll have to find me one for Trella. At cost, mate, no jumped-up prices.'

'If you'd come back with me you could give her a basketful.'

He saw Gus and Trella exchange glances, not the opposition that he'd expected but the look of love. Sweet and gentle. His heart gave a lurch as Gus kissed her on the cheek and took her hand.

Brodie was jealous. Hurting a little. He'd seen the trust in their eyes, the sort of love he'd always dreamed he'd find one day. For some reason it wasn't like that with him and Vivien. Beyond the bed, what did they have in common? Very little sentiment, he thought miserably. But maybe it would be better after they were married. There'd be no more need for the plotting and planning; they could be themselves, more at ease with each other.

As if she'd read his thoughts, Mrs Kriedemann burst in proudly. 'You know Gus and Trella are to be married?'

'Yes, Gus told me.'

'Oh, we're so happy,' she said. 'Father and I couldn't be happier with such a lovely daughter. I love weddings.'

Trella smiled. 'Not one but two. Don't be bashful, Brodie. I hear you're for the altar as well.'

He saw the warning glance that Gus gave her but it was too late. Mrs Kriedemann pounced. 'What's this? Am I the last to hear all the good news? Brodie, where is your girl? Why haven't you brought her to meet us?'

'You'll meet her soon enough.' Brodie shrugged. Thinking of Vivien back at the hotel, probably furious with him for standing her up. Wishing he was back at the Ten Mile, not sitting here like a man about to be burned at the stake.

'But who is she? A local girl? Do we know her?'

Ah, to hell with it! Brodie wondered why he'd been cringing under these questions. Vivien, a beautiful woman, was to be his bride, and that was that.

'Vivien Holloway,' he said firmly. Almost aggressively. 'I do believe you have met her, Mrs Kriedemann. In the shop.'

The silence took on the sound of a wail as surely as if the lament could be heard.

'*Mrs* Holloway?' she echoed.

'Yes.'

Trella tried to rescue the situation. 'I'm sure she's very nice. Isn't that so, Brodie?'

He nodded. 'She is that. Now, if you'll excuse me, I have to go.'

'Where are you going?' Gus asked, worried that they'd embarrassed his friend. That he had caused this by telling his fiancée Brodie's news.

Brodie forced a smile. 'Where do you think? Vivien's expecting me. I'm late as it is.'

He didn't go to the hotel. He walked to the far end of Ruthven Street, where he sat in a hotel bar, nursing whiskies. Never in his life had he felt so adrift. Not even during those mean days in Dublin, where he'd played the footpad. The short-lived life of crime that he'd prefer not to recall.

And why now? When everything was going so well for him. When he was within an angel's breath of becoming a rich man. He'd planned to talk to Jakob Kriedemann, to explain to him, with Gus present, how well he was doing. To enlist his support in taking Gus with him on the road to riches. Black opals would sell. They would! They were like nothing else on God's earth. He wished he had a sample with him to show the Kriedemanns.

But what was the use? They were all too busy with their stupid village talk about weddings. No better than the old black-garbed crones at Tullymore. Why couldn't they understand that a man had to make more of himself than that? The Kriedemanns, they'd made good. Coming out from somewhere in Germany and making a good life for themselves. But Jakob Kriedemann had a trade. He was a baker. Why couldn't they see that Brodie Court had no trade, he was just a farm labourer, so it was brawn he had to work with out there in the mines.

Why was it so bad to be trying to enlist Gus again?

And what did it have to do with them who he married?

'I'm never going back there again,' he said. 'I don't need them.'

'What did you say?' the barmaid asked. She was a thin girl with a sharp face and a cascade of curling black hair.

'You've got gypsy hair,' he said. 'Lovely hair.'

She refilled his glass. 'People do say that, but I've never met a gypsy.'

'I think they'd claim you,' he smiled. He took out the other opal and unwrapped the cloth. 'What do you think of that?'

She picked it up and studied it, turning it about. 'Beautiful. Where did this come from? White Cliffs?'

'No. Closer than that.'

'You a miner?'

'I am.'

'It must be marvellous to be able to reach out and take a jewel like that from the earth,' she said breathlessly.

'Just the greatest feeling in the whole wide world.'

'Oh.' She shuddered. 'You make me fair tingle. You a local?'

'No. I'm not a local any place.'

'You're not Lazarus,' she grinned. 'There's plenty others got left for dead. You sound as if you've been jilted.'

He drank the whisky, relieved to invite the haze of drunkenness. 'Were it so!' he exclaimed. 'I've got a woman to marry who wants to make a gentleman of me.'

'That's no sin,' she laughed. 'Put away the opal before I forget my manners.'

He shoved it back into his pocket. 'And another,' he added darkly, 'whose only calling in life is to be a thorn in me side.'

Brodie hadn't noticed she'd moved away. 'That Trella,' he mumbled, 'I would have told them in good time about Vivien. In me own time. But she had to throw it in like a firecracker. Throwing it at me face. "Don't be bashful, Brodie!" Trella, so smug, latched on to Gus like a leech, trying to make me look small in front of his parents.'

The girl was wiping down the counter. 'We're closing, sir.'

'Then I'll have one more drink.'

'Sorry, we're closing.'

'C'mon now. Don't be hard to get on with.' He scattered coins on the counter.

A hefty red-headed bruiser loomed up beside him. 'You heard what she said, mate. Out!'

'I'm having one more drink while you lock up.'

'You've had your fill. Get out!'

Brodie shook his head. That was true enough. He'd had his fill. Of people. Of this town. Of not being good enough for Vivien. And her not good enough for Gus's family. And now this lump of lard was telling him his money wasn't good enough.

He swung about and punched the bruiser. A beautiful punch, right to the jaw, that sent the varmint sailing across the bar to bang his head on a stool and leave him to sort out the stars. Brodie was wildly sober now, or so he thought. He felt better. He felt great at being able to hit back. At someone.

He danced on the lino floor, shaping up. 'Come on now! Who's next? Who's going to take on Brodie Court? A fair man in a fair fight.'

Faces appeared in doorways, dim, dull, apprehensive. The girl passed him a whisky. 'Here. Drink this and go. Quick.'

Her voice was sorrowful, and her eyes had become dark and luminous. Brodie downed the whisky in a gulp. 'Ah now. What a darlin' girl you are. I ought to marry you.'

The next morning, nursing bruises instead of whisky glasses, Brodie Court woke up in jail.

Chastened, remorseful, Brodie was rescued by Stanley Wickham, who seemed to think his escapade was no more than a lark.

'By God, Brodie, when you celebrate, you go all out!'

'I think there are better ways. Where can I go to clean up?'

'Will my house do?'

'Sure, I'd be grateful to you. And I have to buy some duds. I looked bad enough yesterday, now I'm worse.'

'You are a bit on the nose.'

It was close to noon when Brodie emerged from the emporium, properly suited as befitted a businessman. Or so he was told by the salesman, a friend of Stanley's.

Brodie had never felt less like a businessman. His suit was so new and stiff it creaked almost as much as his shiny new shoes. The black ribbon tie was almost choking him and he felt a fool in a bowler hat. He'd flatly refused to buy the grey gloves to complete the outfit. Hadn't he spent enough already? They seemed to think he was made of money.

Timidly, he knocked on her door, guilt and shame for company, trying to concoct some excuse for standing her up last night and a set of lies about where he'd spent the night.

There was no answer. Maybe she was out. He was tempted to bolt, postponing the inevitable bawling out. Vivien wasn't the most patient of women.

Suddenly the door opened and Vivien stood there, looking even more regal in rich black silk with tiny buttons dotting all the way from collar to neat, slim waist. Her hair was a mass of fair, winsome curls . . .

'Brodie!' she cried, as if surprised to see him. 'Why, Brodie! Don't you look marvellous! Oh, my dear! Come in!' She clutched his arm, hurrying him inside, closing the door. 'Let me look at you. You're so handsome. Who chose that suit? Not a woman, I hope!' She was smiling, teasing.

He wrenched the bowler hat from his head but she insisted he put it on again. 'It looks so jaunty. It suits you. Now, you naughty boy, where did you get to last night?'

'The suit,' he lied. 'It wasn't ready till this morning. I didn't want to come galloping back in my old clothes and have you shamed by me.'

'Of course, dear. I knew it was something like that. Now wait a minute while I fetch my hat, and we'll go down to lunch.'

Suddenly cured of his miseries by this reception, Brodie looked round the pleasant room. He put his arms about her. 'Now that I'm here,' he whispered, 'why waste the chance?' He nodded towards the open double doors that led to her bedroom.

Vivien giggled. 'No. Not yet, darling. We're both dressed and ready to go out. We'll go down to lunch and come back later. They serve excellent meals here.'

410

That reminded Brodie he was very hungry, although he would gladly have forsaken the meal ... but since she'd been such a brick about last night, the least he could do was agree.

He did enjoy the superb meal, roast chicken and all the trimmings, but he enjoyed the long, lazy afternoon much more. Ever so much more. Making love to Vivien in that hotel room with no time limits, with no fear of a knock on the door.

'I feel as if we're already married,' he said, watching her drift about the room in an odd sort of dressing gown, so sheer he wondered why they bothered to make it, but Vivien was a dream in it, glimpses of her lovely figure arousing him again.

They stayed together, he and his beautifully wanton woman, until the shadows came and he lit the lamps. And they talked of so many things.

Yesterday they'd got off on the wrong foot. They were both anxious to please now.

Brodie wasn't happy about a registry office wedding but when he heard of her attempts to arrange a church ceremony, he understood how difficult it was for her. Hadn't he met much the same thing at the Kriedemann house? The loud, unspoken disapproval.

'Never you mind,' he told her. 'Once we're settled, we'll have a church wedding. I have to do that, you know.'

'So do I. But for now, darling, we'll just be married with as little fuss as possible. The clerk told me it only takes a few minutes. Do you really have to go back out west?'

'I'll hate leaving you, but I must.'

Vivien was soft and demure; she really listened to him for a change when he explained about the opals and the black opals and Abe Rosenstein. So much so that he cuddled her to him with a laugh. 'Amazing what a bit of lovin' does to us. Yesterday I thought we could have ended up in fisticuffs.'

'That was my fault. I was so excited I talked my head off, got myself all mixed up. But Brodie, I don't want to live here. Not with Christiana breathing down our necks. And you know perfectly well I wouldn't fit in at Charleville. I just don't belong in a bush town.'

'Of course you don't, my darlin'. We'll find a house in

Brisbane for the time being. After all, the train goes straight to Brisbane, there'd be no changing, it'll be easier for me to get there than here.'

'Sydney is out?' she wheedled.

'Definitely. But we'll go there for holidays. And my love, don't you be worrying, I'll build you a fine house in Brisbane, a real showplace, and we'll fill it with young Court rascals. We'll have a big family all about us. High and healthy.' He reached over and slid his hand along her stomach. 'Did you note I've been gentle with you for fear of disturbing the little one? I'm saying it's a boy and we'll call it Michael.'

If ever there was a chance, Vivien thought fearfully, it's now. Tell him.

But she was afraid. Afraid of losing him. Afraid that the truth would have the same effect on any prospective husband. They all wanted scads of kids. She slipped from the bed and floated about the room in the sheer peignoir that excited him so, the flounces trailing on the carpet behind her.

'Brodie,' she said mischievously, 'why don't I ring down for some wine and have our dinner sent up? It would be so decadent. Just the two of us.'

'Can we do that?'

'Of course we can. We'll have it served in the sitting room. If you stay out of sight in here, you won't even have to dress. Does that appeal to you?'

'I think I've gone to heaven,' he laughed, stretching his long, lean body on the silky sheets.

Later that night a sedate Mr Court booked himself into the room adjoining that occupied by Mrs Holloway, impervious to the surreptitious glances of the desk clerk. Not caring about the cost. 'This is the life,' he said as he mounted the stairs, treasuring his room key.

He checked his waistcoat pocket. At least he hadn't been robbed last night. He still had the opal. Transferred this morning from the discarded jacket to this fine piece of cloth. He walked into his room, glanced about approvingly and then knocked on the door that separated his bedroom from her sitting room. An arrangement for families, he supposed. Keep them all together. Keep an eye on the kids.

'What will they think of next?' he said.

She had changed. She'd never looked so beautiful, all

412

swathed in pink satin as voluptuous to the touch as those softly moulded breasts.

'It's Brodie Court,' Christiana said, hobbling to her big leather chair with the aid of a stick, needed since the mild stroke she'd suffered after Vern's death.

'Yes,' Elvie said. 'That's the name she put on the form. He's marrying her. I knew something was going on there.'

Christiana sighed. 'You know, I quite liked the fellow. I think he genuinely cared about Vern. He never took credit for saving him that time. He spoke of it as if it were a normal reaction, something any decent man would have done.'

'But he's not a decent man.'

'That day he was. People don't change, the strain is there. But what does he see in her?'

'I wouldn't like to spell it out.'

'Yes. But compared to her he's very naive.'

'Mrs Holloway, I don't know why you're defending him. Your trouble is you always think well of people.'

'Don't you believe it,' she snapped. 'I never thought well of Vivien. And I certainly don't think well of that dreadful Mrs Campbell coming here with her tales.'

'But she was telling the truth.'

'I could have done with that truth years ago. And so could Vern. How dare Dr Campbell keep such information from a husband? I'm appalled that his damned wife knew too. So much for privacy. And all that time I was looking forward to having a grandchild to spoil.'

She gazed out over the cliffs, seeing nothing in particular. The spectacular view no longer of any interest to her.

'What a fool she must have thought me,' she said bitterly. 'I often spoke to her about grandchildren. If only she'd told me the truth, it would have been different. A woman's not to blame for what nature decrees. But no, she had to lie. It was in her nature, just like this affair with Court.'

'It's more than an affair,' Elvie sniffed. 'What a gall she has to be marrying her lover so soon after . . . I mean, so soon.'

'I can understand an affair. But why would she want to marry him? They're chalk and cheese. She's all show and parties, he's no drawing-room dandy.'

'I have to admit he's handsome,' Elvie said, 'and he's got a charm about him. I was near to be taken in myself the day he was out there at Fairlea visiting Mr Vern. Nothing patronising about him. He made me get out the cards, like you used to do. Treated Mr Vern as if nothing was wrong at all. It wasn't until Taffy came back to tell me what he'd seen on the road that I knew I was right the first time.'

Christiana held up her hand. 'Yes. I know about all that. Court's younger than her, though, isn't he?'

'Yes, by a year or so, taking the guess. But he's snared, well and truly.'

'Is he now?' Christiana sat upright in the chair, her well-preserved face stern under the soft silvery hair. She could forgive the woman the subterfuge about childbearing. She could have forgiven her affairs, given the circumstances, but Vivien was beyond that. Vivien had murdered her son. He hadn't jumped, she'd pushed him, to free herself from the burden. It had nothing to do with Court. After careful consideration, she'd told the police that. She had lived long enough to be a good judge of character. Court was a rascal but not a murderer. Her daughter-in-law was another kettle of fish, though. Cold, selfish, capable of anything.

But had they believed her? Of course not. No proof. They'd wavered for a time but had finally come out in favour of that wretch of a woman who had everything to gain by Vern's death. Now she was free to do as she liked, supported by the man she'd pushed to his death in the quiet seclusion of a river bank. A poor, gentle man, unable to defend himself against her.

So now she was preparing to marry her lover. The man she'd flouted right under Vern's nose. The young Irishman, full of the blood and fervour of his ancestors, roaring in him the zest of procreation.

Christiana hoped she was right, because if so, Vivien had just run headlong into more trouble.

'I wonder,' she said, 'what is really going on with those two.'

Elvie looked at her anxiously. 'In what way?'

'Why the haste for this marriage? That Campbell woman did say that Vivien wanted a quiet wedding, to be arranged as soon as possible, didn't she?'

'Yes, that's what she told them at the courthouse.'

'Why?'

Elvie smirked. 'Maybe she thought he might get away on her.'

'Yes, I would agree. A bird in the hand for a woman like her, and with her physical shortcomings. But what's *his* reason?'

'For what?'

'For agreeing to wed her so soon after Vern's death. And agreeing to a secular ceremony. That in itself is unusual for an Irishman. His church wouldn't recognise the marriage.'

Elvie picked up her crochet work. 'Anyone else but her and I'd say the bride might be in the family way. But not Vivien.'

'No, indeed not.' Christiana twirled the rings on her fingers. She'd lost a lot of weight recently and the rings were loose. She reminded herself to have them attended to.

'I am informed that the people who own the bakery in town are friends of Mr Court.'

'The Kriedemanns?'

Christiana nodded. 'I thought we might call in at that bakery this morning. We could do with some bought bread for a change. Cook will thank us. And we might be fortunate enough to run into Brodie Court. Order the carriage please, Elvie.'

That morning Vivien encountered another problem. She stared at her wardrobe in dismay. 'Oh my God, I can't get married in black.'

Brodie, waiting patiently in the sitting room, looked up from his newspaper. 'Then don't.'

'But I'm supposed to be in mourning. I've only got black and my little pink cotton. All my lovely clothes are stored in my trunks.'

'Then we'll have to go and fish something out.'

'That won't do at all. I forget what's there. And everything will need airing. Do I really have to wear black?'

'I told you. You please yourself what you wear.'

'Maybe I could find a dark grey, or a navy with some white on it, but I have nothing to match but all these dirge-like things. No hat, No gloves. Oh Lord, I hope I can find something. I hate having to shop at the last minute.'

He laughed. 'It's not the last minute. You've got all day, my love.'

She sighed. 'You don't understand. I might need fittings. I have to go shopping right now.' She began pulling hats from boxes, trying and discarding before she made a decision. 'I should wear something new anyway. For good luck. Pray I find a suitable gown.'

'That reminds me.' Brodie stood up and handed her the opal. 'Here's a small wedding present. There'll be plenty more where that came from.'

Vivien took it, glanced at it. 'Oh, it's sweet, Brodie.' Then she dropped it in her jewel box and took out a diamond brooch to pin on her black jacket. 'Now I really must rush.'

'Do you want me to come with you?'

'Lord, no! You mustn't see my gown before the wedding.' She grabbed handbag and gloves and hurried to the door.

Just before she left she turned back. 'Heavens above! The wedding ring! Don't forget to buy the wedding ring, Brodie. Make sure it's gold!'

'I thought we'd buy it together.'

'We might not have time. Here!' She slipped a silver ring from her finger. 'Take this so that you can get the size right.'

Brodie smiled, bemused. 'Whatever you say.'

His own chores were just as important. In the light of Abe's enthusiasm he had decided to send direct to Dublin all of the opals that Willi was working on, in several parcels, in case of loss or theft, and that left the supply he had in the bank. With all this extra expense he had no choice but to sell them to a local jeweller. A terrible waste, he said to himself, when I could get so much more for them over there.

He peered into Vivien's jewel box. The opal did look small and lonely among the heavier stuff, rings and brooches and bracelets. 'She wasn't too impressed with your offering,' he murmured. But then he realised he'd chosen a bad time to present it, with her rushing out like that. Later he'd show it to her again in a better light. He closed the box and tucked it into a deep drawer, covering it with her clothes, amazed that a woman should leave such treasures lying about.

'I'll have to do some heavy bargaining today. Maybe I

can trade an opal for a wedding ring; that could be a small saving.'

As he picked up his bowler hat, he was still cross with himself at the thought of selling his opals short. Then he remembered that Abe's payment was on its way to Stanley's office.

Cheer up, old chap, he told himself. That's only the beginning. I mustn't forget to tell Stanley to bank it for me as soon as it arrives.

He wondered how the men were faring out at the Ten Mile. Strange. With all the creature comforts here, he was missing the place. Missing the ever-present hopes and expectations of a lucky strike that made the fields such a lively place.

Brodie looked down at the bowler hat and with a snort of disgust threw it on to a chair. 'Makes a man look a fool,' he said as he left the hotel room.

The two ladies walked slowly along the street, peering in windows. Christiana hated having to use the walking stick, since it seemed to invite unwanted queries about her health from sympathetic friends and acquaintances, so she used the windows as an excuse to avoid them.

Elvie held the door open for her as she swept into the baker's shop, not missing the nervous blink of recognition from the pink-cheeked woman behind the counter.

'I always enjoy the aroma of a bakery,' Christiana commented, 'so warm and comforting.'

'Ah yes, makes me hungry,' Elvie agreed. 'I love hot bread.'

'We'll take two loaves, please,' Christiana said. 'And a half-dozen of those fairy cakes. No, make it a dozen.'

'Certainly, Mrs Holloway,' the German woman said, hurrying to fill the order.

Christiana nodded kindly. 'We do enjoy your bread. Would you be Mrs Kriedemann?'

'Yes, ma'am. Should I put these cakes in a box?'

'If you would. While we're here, Mrs Kriedemann, I was wondering if you know an acquaintance of mine. Mr Brodie Court.'

The woman's hands trembled so much, she dropped one of the cakes and had to reach for a replacement. 'Yes,' she muttered. 'I know Brodie.'

417

'Oh good. Where could I find him?'

'I couldn't say. We haven't seen him for a few days.'

'You don't have any suggestions?'

'His sister-in-law, Mrs Court. She might know.'

'Where does she live?'

Mrs Kriedemann gave her the address. 'But she wouldn't be home now. She goes to work.'

'Ah. I see. Well, never mind. If you do see Mr Court, please give him my regards.'

'I'll do that. Yes, ma'am.'

Their bread was wrapped, the cakes boxed and handed to Elvie in double-quick time, and Christiana guessed the poor woman was pleased to see the back of them.

'She knows about the marriage,' Elvie whispered as they stepped back into the street.

'Yes, I think so, and none too happy by the looks of things.' Christiana sighed. 'Since we're here we might as well do a spot of shopping. Now don't lose that bread.'

Elvie waited outside, admiring the glittering displays in the jeweller's windows, while Christiana went inside to enquire as to what might be done about her loose rings.

He didn't turn his head as the little bell over the door jangled, but Christiana knew who it was immediately. She raised her eyebrows and gave a small smile as she walked across the carpeted floor and arranged herself on a high gilt chair.

The gentleman who was serving him looked up with a smile. 'Good morning, Mrs Holloway. I'll be with you in a minute.'

Brodie swung about, pleased surprise on his face. Then he faltered, his jaw dropped and he stammered a greeting.

The wrong Mrs Holloway, she thought contemptuously, but she inclined her head. 'Good morning, Brodie.'

She waved a gloved hand at the opals spread on black velvet further down the counter. 'So you found what you were looking for?'

He glanced down at the opals, the question causing him even more discomfort. 'Yes, ma'am,' he muttered without looking up.

With a good customer now in the shop the jeweller was

trying to hurry him along. He held up a wedding ring. 'Have you decided? I'd suggest this one.'

Never had Christiana seen a man so horribly embarrassed, but she had no intention of letting him off the hook. Distasteful as it might be, this was her chance to unmask Vern's widow.

'When is the wedding, Brodie?' she asked, forcing him to turn back to her.

He blinked heavily and Christiana noticed his eyelashes in a mental aside. They were long and thick, adding to his good looks, for he certainly was a handsome man. She'd never seen him dressed other than in workman's clothes, but now he looked quite splendid.

'You know about it?' he croaked.

'Oh, yes. Vivien *was* my daughter-in-law.'

'Ah.' His mouth opened and closed almost soundlessly. He turned quickly to the jeweller. 'I'll take it, wrap it up.'

The jeweller collected the opals and the ring and hurried down to a glass-walled niche at the far end of the counter.

Slowly, Christiana removed her gloves. Steeling herself.

'I wish you well, Brodie.'

He was so grateful for that kindness he relaxed a little. 'Thank you, Mrs Holloway. You know I was terrible sorry to hear about Vern. Would it be out of order of me to be offering you my sympathies?'

'Not at all,' she said, her face grim. How dared he? 'No more than my offering you my good wishes. Under the circumstances. But I hope you have a good life.'

'Thank you.' He gulped, looking hopefully to the jeweller to rescue him, but the man was intent on his duties.

'I miss Vern,' she continued. 'It wouldn't be so bad if there were grandchildren, but since Vivien can't have children even that comfort was denied me.'

She saw the colour drain from his face, his tanned skin turn a blotchy grey. 'When did you say the wedding was?' she asked again.

'Tomorrow,' he gritted. 'I have to go now.' He touched his forehead where a cap might have been and strode down to the jeweller, tapping his foot impatiently as the man handed him his small parcel containing the wedding ring. Then notes were carefully counted out and Brodie stuffed them into his pocket.

He almost bumped into Elvie in his rush to escape, just as she was coming in the door.

'Did you see who that was?' she cried, but Christiana placed her rings on the counter and looked up at the jeweller.

'They're far too loose to wear,' she said calmly. 'Can you do something about it?'

He was waiting for her when she came gaily in, bearing a load of parcels. 'Oh, my. What a day! But I got the most superb suit, in dark blue. And a divine hat. But you mustn't see them yet.'

Brodie was in no mood for the proprieties. He followed her into the bedroom, watching as she dumped her parcels on the bed.

'Oh, do go away,' she said. 'You'll spoil everything.'

'Everything is already spoiled,' he growled.

'Whatever are you talking about?'

'It was all lies, wasn't it? All bloody lies.'

'What was all lies?'

'The babe. You're not with child at all.'

'For heaven's sake! What's brought this on?'

There were tears. Denials. More lies. More tears. Then anger. And a terrible row as the truth emerged.

In all his life Brodie had never been so furious.

'If you were a man,' he shouted, 'I'd knock you down. You're a cheat and a liar and you have no respect for me at all. Damn you!'

She pleaded with him, weeping, but when that failed, she turned on him, demanding that he marry her. 'I won't allow you to jilt me. It's too late, I've made all the arrangements.'

'Then the arrangements have all come to nought,' he said harshly. 'You couldn't wait, could you? You had to make me jump to your tune as if I'm some poor fool with no mind of me own.'

He took out the case containing the wedding ring and placed it on the dresser. 'I bought this for you, you might as well have it.'

As he strode for the door, Vivien rushed after him. 'You're not leaving? You can't! Brodie, I love you.'

She threw her arms about him but it was no use.

'I don't need your sort of love,' he snapped. 'Get away from me.'

Brodie banged the door behind him and stormed down to his own room to pack as fast as he could, to be free of her, free of this place and of the humiliation she'd heaped on him.

'The wedding's off,' he told Gus.

'Why? What happened?'

'Nothing much. We just don't agree on a few things. I'll not be seeing her again.'

'I suppose it's for the best then.'

'Yes.' Brodie was depressed. 'I don't seem to be having much luck.'

'Much luck? You? You have plenty of luck with opals.'

'True enough, they're good to me. But I've gone and wasted time and money here in town, I have to get back. Come with me. I have to call by your parents' house and pick up me things.'

Gus laughed. 'They won't know you in your fine gear.'

'Huh! More waste. I don't think I'll ever wear this stuff again.'

'You could lend it to me for my wedding. It's a very smart suit.'

'You need more than a suit for a marriage,' Brodie snapped. 'You need money, and plenty of it, to keep a woman happy! Come on. Let's go and see what Willi has done with my black opals.'

Gus wavered. 'I could take a couple of days off to come with you as far as Willi's place. I'd like to see them before you send them away.'

'It'll be your only chance,' Brodie urged. 'I'll be sending them to Dublin straight from Charleville.' He believed that if he could get Gus halfway to the opal fields, the rest would be easy.

Not so easy was his next meeting with Mrs Kriedemann, who looked at him keenly when he entered the house, thinking that he was already dressed for the wedding.

'I'll be going back out west tomorrow,' he said, trying not to catch her eye.

'Taking your bride with you?'

421

He shook his head. 'I'm sorry to be confusing you, but the wedding's off.'

'Good God! You boys! I can't say I'm too sad about that, Brodie. Will you be staying for supper?'

'If that's all right with you.'

'Of course it is.' She decided to speak no more of the matter, hoping the whole idea of that unfortunate liaison could be laid to rest as soon as possible. Nor did she deem it necessary to tell him that old Mrs Holloway had been asking after him. The less he saw of that family the better.

Brodie was glad to be able to shut himself in the quiet little sleep-out and throw off all the glad rags. He'd made a damn fool of himself all over the place and would be smarting from that for a long time.

'Bloody women!' he said, flinging himself down on the bunk. 'The bane of my bloody life! All I need now is for Trella to talk Gus out of coming with me.'

She tried. Gus called in on her on the way home from work, to break the news.

'Do you have to go?' she asked him. 'Why is it so necessary?'

'The opals Brodie found are something out of the box. Don't you understand? Cut and polished they'd be something to see. I won't be away long.'

'That's what you say. But I know Brodie, he'll be talking you into going back to that godforsaken place.'

'I have a mind of my own,' he said, irritated.

'But going all that way just to look at a few gemstones! They're not even yours. Don't be hoping he'll give you any. Brodie Court wouldn't give his grandmother a kind smile.'

'And what was it he gave my mother? One of his best opals. Or have you forgotten so soon? I wish you wouldn't be so critical of Brodie. He does his best.'

'Sure he does. And what about that farce with the Holloway woman? Was he marrying her for her money? Maybe she woke up to him.'

'He was doing no such thing.' Gus remembered that Brodie had said Vivien was pregnant. He had to marry her. So what *had* happened? He'd probably find out the answer in the next few days, when Brodie was in a better mood.

'Well, what was he up to?'

'It's not your business, nor mine,' he said crankily, unwilling to break a confidence. 'I'll be getting along now.' He kissed her. 'I'll be back in a few days.'

'I hope so,' Trella said miserably.

As the steam train pushed west, Brodie became less tense. Even cheerful. Especially when he won two pounds in a card game with some shearers.

Eventually Gus managed to broach the subject of the abandoned wedding plans, but Brodie only shrugged. 'It was a bad idea.'

'So it seems, but what about the baby?'

Brodie stared out at his reflection in the night. 'There wasn't any kid.'

'She wasn't pregnant?' Gus was startled.

'That's what I said.'

'How did you know? Did she tell you?'

'Not her. I had to hear it from someone else.'

His friend gaped. And then he began to laugh. 'Do you mean to say you were conned? You're the one that's always so smart, telling me not to be so trusting! And you got taken for a ride!'

'It's not funny.'

'I'd like to have seen your face when you found out!'

'Well, I did find out, and that's an end to it. And if you tell anyone about this I'll kill you!'

'Mum's the word,' Gus chortled, burying his face in his cap to try to sleep for a while. 'Mum's the word.'

But it was Brodie who had the last laugh when they walked into Willi's hut to find him still working on the light opals.

'They're looking good, mate,' Brodie said. 'But have you started on the black?'

'Couldn't resist it,' Willi replied. 'Feast your eyes on this lot.' He took out a wooden tray with a dazzling array of black opals, the colours flashing like fire against the dark matrix.

'These are the firsts, they're what's called boulder opals, Brodie. I've heard tell of them before but never seen them. Your rock was sandstone, a mix of iron and God knows what else, with this seam lying abed in it like in a cocoon.' He went on to discuss the various shapes he'd chosen and why, but they weren't listening.

Gus picked up one smooth, slim gem. 'Unbelievable! These'd be unique, wouldn't they?'

'For the time being,' Willi said. 'A mate of mine came out for a yarn a couple of days ago. He's heading down to Lightning Ridge, says it's more than a rumour that black opals are turning up there by the cartload.'

'Why go south when he can see they're right here in Queensland?' Gus asked.

Willi grinned. 'You don't think I'd tell him where these come from? Brodie would have my hide.'

'How many carats?' Brodie asked, picking up a fiery gem.

'Bit more than forty,' Willi said. 'This one's about twenty-three,' he added, touching another. 'It's a real picture show looking at them,' he said proudly. 'Like staring into a fire, you see all sorts of things. They're top-drawer, Brodie, if you can get buyers to see past the light opals.'

'I already have.' Brodie told them about his success with his samples in Dublin. 'They mightn't be the fashion here yet but it matters not at all to me. I've got a commission agent going for me in Dublin now. I'm sending all these opals to Dublin right away, that's where they'll find their true worth.'

Brodie produced a bottle of whisky for a celebration and another for Willi's primitive pantry. While they talked he saw Gus return time and again to gaze spellbound at the magnificent gems. He winked at Willi, who took the hint:

'So you're not even interested in looking for more, Gus? When your mate here's the only man in the world who knows where to find them?'

'He's interested,' Brodie said bleakly. 'But he's been house-trained. He's getting married. He's not allowed to go, are you Gus?'

'No one's stopping me. I've told you that before. A family man needs the weekly wage and I've got a good job now.'

'He's a barman,' Brodie said contemptuously.

Willi sucked on his pipe. 'Nothing wrong with that. Trouble with you, Gus, you're going at this from the wrong angle. I wager if your lady friend could get an eyeful of these gems she'd swoon. Women love jewels, and these are real class.'

'How much do you reckon I'll be making here?' Brodie asked, deliberately turning the knife.

'No telling, as long as your agent's an honest man and he doesn't bolt with the lot . . .'

'But going on the first samples? The light opals as well.'

'You're ahead by a thousand now. But these boulder opals, the big ones, are just about priceless.'

'Pounds?' Gus said weakly.

'Easy. Your mate here's already a rich man.'

'Ah no,' Brodie said smugly. 'This is only the beginning. I'm only getting started.'

Gus shook his head. 'Trella will never forgive me.'

'Sure she will,' Brodie laughed. 'Write her a love letter. She's not going any place. She'll be there when you get home!'

Brodie was raring to go now. He had his old partner back.

Chapter Thirteen

On a blustery Saturday afternoon the workers at the Toowoomba cheese factory lined up for their pay. As they walked away from the paymaster's window there were nudges and grins and surreptitious glances at Trella. Everyone had received pay increases ranging from one to five shillings, and everyone knew that the Irishwoman had been the instigator.

But no one actually spoke to Trella about this, not on the premises anyway, because Alf Ringrose was watching, standing sternly in the background.

'Look at the face on him,' Trella whispered to a friend. 'He looks as if he's swallowed a rat, and all over a few shillings.'

Nevertheless she tucked her pay gleefully in her pocket and turned back to her mop and buckets.

'You think you've got away with it,' Ringrose muttered to himself as she hurried across the yard. 'You've made a bloody fool of me, got me in bad with the board, and your union mates say I can't touch you. So . . . we'll see about that.'

Casually he tidied his desk, put on his hat and left the office. He marched down the wooden staircase, pausing halfway to look over the machine floor as the staff began closing down for the night, adjusting his glasses as if to home in on each and every one of them. To let them know that he was always vigilant, and he'd have no slacking. Then he turned back past the cool rooms to leave the factory by the side door.

The men were closing down the loading bays and clearing up the yard, crates stacked, swill bins battened down for collection.

'Not a word of thanks do we get,' he called with false cheerfulness. 'Didn't any of you notice your pay?'

That brought grins of relief, and voices raised in thanks, albeit far from spontaneous. A year ago the minimum wage had been cut by an average of one pound to meet the ravages of state-wide depression, and these two small wage rises had hardly made a dent in the loss to workers, so remembering the good old days these men saw no reason for gratitude. Except, as now, to please the boss.

'You'll all have to work harder now,' he said, 'to earn that pay rise. And we'll have to make a few changes.'

Other men, leaving the factory, stopped to listen.

'Yes,' he said, with a sigh. 'These days you get nothing for nothing. We have to watch our pennies too. The payroll is getting top-heavy.'

Faces were wary now. No one moved. They seemed to be holding their breath. A bird screeched in the trees behind them.

The factory whistle blew. Ringrose shrugged and turned away, freeing them. He had sighted his quarry.

As they drifted off he walked briskly towards the gate, his route intercepting young Court.

'A word with you,' he said, tugging on his left ear.

The kid, a hulking fellow already, grinned eagerly. 'Yes, sir?'

'We've got a problem here in the yard,' Ringrose said amiably. 'Too many men and not enough work.'

Garth Court looked surprised. 'I thought it would have been the other way now, what with the other factory out at Haverston closed down and us getting all their farmers coming in.'

The manager frowned. The kid had a mouth as big as his mother's. Even if that were true, he had a cheek contradicting his betters. 'Obviously you don't understand the running of a factory this size,' he snapped. 'We have to cut back. And we try to be fair. Last come, first go.'

The lad was puzzled. 'I don't get you.'

'It means you're it. You finish up.'

'I'm sacked, are you saying? When?'

'Not sacked,' Ringrose said evenly. 'Laid off. You finish up now.'

The lad stood staring at him for a minute, stunned. He looked furtively about him as if hoping no one else had heard, and then he turned and loped away. Before he reached the gate he broke into a run.

Garth was shattered. Hurt and embarrassed to find that he'd been sacked.

He made his way miserably to find Gus, but when he reached the pub he remembered that Gus had gone out west with Uncle Brodie. They had let him down too. Brodie had promised to take him out to the opal fields and once again he'd gone without him.

If only they'd waited a few days!

As he trudged along, Garth tried to make sense of his sacking. He hadn't done anything wrong. It was all so unfair.

Money jingled in his pocket. He'd got extra this week too. Extra! The pay rise! Everyone knew that his mother had put the union on to Ringrose. Hence this much-touted extra pay.

And this was Ringrose's way of paying her back! Don't sack her, sack her son. It was all her fault. If she'd shut up, he'd still have a job. Fat lot of good any pay rise was to them now.

That night Garth said not a word to her about what had happened. Nor did he mention it the next day. He went to Mass with her, and when they came back he left her to her chores, knowing she'd hear nothing of this until Monday morning. Lonely and upset, he wandered about the town, trying to work out what to do. Somewhere, he'd have to find another job. Or would he?

He made sure he was home on time for dinner, but she soon twigged that something was wrong.

'What's the matter with you? Are you sick? You've hardly said a word all day.'

'I'm not sick,' he retorted angrily.

'Then what is it?'

'Nothing.'

'It doesn't sound like nothing to me.'

'Leave me alone.'

So she did. And Garth hung about the house, suppressing his growing excitement. Now he knew what he could do.

The next morning he dived off, ostensibly for work, well ahead of her, but then doubled back, waiting for her to leave.

As soon as the coast was clear, he slipped back into the house and packed his things in his small suitcase. He went to the old tea tin where she kept the money and took out exactly the pay he'd received on Saturday, deeming himself an honest man that he hadn't taken a penny more. He raided the pantry and made himself some sandwiches, glad that the landlady wasn't up yet to be questioning him, stuck them in the case and put on his jacket.

Before he left, Garth wrote her a note:

Dear Mother. I got the sack, so I'm going opal mining. Your loving son, Garth.

Once the note was anchored on the table by a sugar pot, there was nothing more for him to do. Time to go.

At the station he bought himself a ticket to Charleville, one way, and an hour later he was on his way.

He wasn't sure how to get to the Ten Mile from that town but he'd find out. 'I've got a tongue in me head,' he told himself. 'Someone will know.'

Hungry already, he settled on the hard seats and munched on his sandwiches, reminding himself that he had to change trains at Dalby for the long haul west. Gus had talked about this journey often enough, Garth felt he almost knew the way by heart. Who cared about the stupid job now? This was a real adventure because he was undertaking it on his own, and when he got to the mines, he'd show Brodie. He'd be the best miner they ever saw.

Garth looked about the carriage and smiled benignly at the other passengers, wondering why he hadn't thought of this before.

Mondays were always busy, the factory cranking up again. Outside, lorries and drays banked up, horses stamping impatiently, farmers yarned while others plodded into the office to argue the price of milk before renewing their contracts. Heavy milk cans were rolled on to the gaping ledge and spun on to the waiting factory hands.

Trella worked, head down, no longer hearing the clash of cans and the hum of the separators as she ran the hoses deftly from can to can, her skirt hooked up above her ankles and a cotton scarf tied round her red hair. After a while she thought she could sense a difference in the atmosphere this particular morning. She looked about her, but everything seemed normal, so she went on with her work.

It wasn't until the noon bell that she heard that her son

wasn't at work. She ran outside to check, bewildered to find that none of the men had seen him.

'Taken a holiday, has he?' one of them grinned.

'I'll give him holiday,' she muttered, worrying that the boss might notice. Knowing that he would.

But Ringrose didn't come near her to enquire about Garth, so she worked quietly for the rest of the day rather than draw attention to his absence.

By the time she finished the long, anxious day, Trella had a splitting headache from the worry of it. Where could he be? Surely he couldn't have had an accident between the house and the factory? It was less than a mile's walk, the last half along the sandy road between farms. She remembered that she hadn't seen Garth on the road, but then he often took a short cut across the paddocks. Had he fallen down and hurt himself? Or been gored by that old bull in Cartwright's paddock? All sorts of demons haunted her as she hurried home with the dark setting in, causing her to be fearful one minute and angry the next.

And there was his note.

She stood and stared at it. Sacked? When was he sacked? And why? He was a good worker, everyone said he was.

And so he'd run off to join Brodie! The damn fool! How would he find his way out there? It was hundreds and hundreds of miles away. Trella stormed angrily about, checking the chest of drawers to make certain he had gone, and then slumping into a chair. She'd have this out with the manager in the morning, but in the meantime, what could she do about Garth? Nothing.

'By God,' she said, 'Brodie had better send him back damn quick or there'll be trouble.'

But would he? Brodie had been encouraging the lad all along to come out to the mines. He'd keep Garth there just to annoy her.

All night she tossed and turned, thinking of that man Lester, who'd got himself lost in the bush and perished. What chance would a lad like Garth have out there in the wilds? If only Gus were home. He'd know what to do. Damn him too! Why did he have to go gallivanting out there as well? Bad example to the lad, that was what it was.

With daylight came more trouble. It dawned on Trella that

431

without Garth's pay she'd be hard put to meet the rent. She leapt out of bed to empty the tea tin. Garth had taken his pay; at least he had some money on him, but he hadn't stopped to think how she would cope now. The few shillings of her savings were still in the purse in her drawer, but that wouldn't last long.

Tired and strained, she approached Ringrose as soon as he appeared in his office, aware that it was vitally necessary to keep her temper.

'Mr Ringrose, why did you sack my son?'

He looked at her with contempt. 'Who says I did?'

'He does.'

'I see. He went missing from work yesterday and that didn't seem to bother you. But now you reckon I sacked him. There's a good excuse if ever I heard one. Is he here today?'

'No. How could he be if you sacked him?'

'That's his tale. But you can tell him he's sacked now.'

'My son doesn't lie.'

'Are you calling me a liar?'

'No, sir, I'm just trying to sort this out.'

'Then sort it out downstairs. Unless you're thinking of quitting too?' The threat was clear. Trella retreated, afraid to antagonise him further. Upset and frustrated, she went back to work, praying that Gus could help. He was due home tomorrow, at the latest.

Garth presented himself at the office of Cobb and Co. 'I want to buy a ticket to Ten Mile. For the coach.'

'Not on our route,' a man said gruffly.

'But I was told, on the train, that I should board a coach here for Ten Mile.'

The man stuck his head out the back door. 'Anyone heard of Ten Mile?'

'It's an opal field,' a voice replied. 'Barbary Creek's the closest.'

'Yes! That's it. I heard my uncle speak of it. That's where I want to go.' Garth was delighted that this travelling was so easy.

'Righto, son, that'll be four and six.'

'Yes, sir.' Garth handed over the coins. 'What time does the coach leave?'

'You mean what day? It leaves Friday; you've got a few days to spare. Mondays and Fridays they go out that way. Be here seven o'clock sharp Friday morning.'

For a while Garth wandered aimlessly about the town, searching for a good place to sleep, not keen to pay for a room. The day was warm and sunny but his friends on the train had warned him that out here the nights could be very cold. He found himself staring in at a blacksmith's shed, and decided it was worth a try.

'Can I give you a hand here?' he asked.

The blacksmith looked up. 'You looking for a job?'

'No, sir, somewhere to sleep while I wait for the coach. I'd be willing to work, though, if you'd let me sleep in here.'

'No pay?'

'No, sir.'

'Righto, you're on. Bring in one of those draught horses outside while I fire up here.'

Friday morning saw him away at last. He sat inside the coach with four other passengers, two couples. The seats were hard and clouds of dust blew in the open windows, but it was an exciting ride, with the horses, like brave chargers, belting along the bush road. The stops, he worked out, were not chosen for distance, but the availability of water, and they provided the passengers with an excuse to stretch their legs and share billies of tea. Time didn't seem to be of any importance at these lonely inns and stores where mail was dumped and news was exchanged, and Garth was thoroughly enjoying himself since everyone was very friendly and no one bothered to enquire what he was doing out there on his own.

And why should they? he said to himself, with no little pride. I'm not a kid. He thought gleefully of the others back there in the dreary cheese factory, doing the same thing day in and day out. He'd escaped all that boredom now, and he'd never go back. This was fun.

They were taken across a wide river by ferry to where another coach was waiting, but because it was late they stayed overnight at a rough country inn. Garth was billeted in a chilly room with the other men, while the ladies had the 'good' room. That amused him; he didn't think any of the rooms here could be too good, but no one complained.

433

By noon the next day he was beginning to sag, wondering if there was any end to these roads. Even though Gus and Brodie had told him it was a long way to the Ten Mile, this seemed a powerful distance. In the end he was sure he'd missed Barbary Creek but didn't like to ask, so he just sat, swaying nervously with the coach as it rounded corners and sped on into the sun.

Another delay. At Barbary Creek the driver didn't waste too much time, anxious to get to the next stop before dark. Some bread and cheese, two rums 'for fortification', a change of horses and the other passengers were herded into the coach. They had told Garth where they were going but the strange-sounding names meant nothing to him. He stood outside the shanty inn to wave to them as the horses turned about, traces jingling, to head out on to the track again.

Garth felt bereft. It was a lonely business, this travelling. You met people, got along with them just fine. Then they were gone. It was the same with the ship. He wondered what had happened to all the friends they'd made on the ship; he'd never seen any of them since.

'Where are you off to, son?' the innkeeper's wife called to him.

'To Ten Mile, missus.' He picked up his suitcase. 'Could you be directing me?'

'You walking?'

'Yes, missus.'

'It's a fair hike. You'll get lost.'

'I'll find it. Just tell me which way.'

She sighed. 'Easy enough to get lost in the daylight, but setting off at this hour? You'll need a bell round your neck.'

Garth was confused. He'd thought this was just a mail stop and the village of Ten Mile was nearby. 'Would I need a bell to walk there?'

She was a tall, skinny woman with a long face, so her shout of laughter surprised him. 'Glory be, lad, come on inside and we'll see what we can do.'

She convinced him that walking was out of the question. 'Too far for a new chum. There's a wagon track to follow but we've had a fair bit of rain lately and it's been washed away. You couldn't tell it from a stock route, son, and if you followed one of them you could end up in the middle of nowhere.'

'What about a horse? Could you be lending me a horse?'

'Same difference, and we haven't any to spare. No. You just settle down here for a while; someone will come along. There's always the mail run.'

'When will that be?'

She massaged her neck as if easing pain. 'Any time. The coach drops the mail here and then folks come to collect their bags. Mostly from stations, so your best bet is the bloke who does the rounds of the miners' store and Plenty Station and beyond. He goes right past the Ten Mile. We don't have a special bag for them, not enough people. What are you going there for anyway?'

'To find my uncle. Brodie Court. Do you know him?'

'Sure I do. He came though here a while ago, heading east. Is he back now?'

That unnerved Garth. What would he do if he got to Ten Mile and there was no Brodie? 'I hope he is. You haven't seen him?'

'That doesn't mean anything. He could have picked up a horse and ridden out here.'

Garth's eyes rounded in awe. 'It's a long way to ride. More than a hundred miles!'

'It's quicker and for my book more comfortable than that old coach.'

Garth ended up staying with them for three days, despairing every hour, but his hosts were kind, refusing to accept payment for his board. 'You could cut some wood for us, though,' the innkeeper said. 'These cold nights we like a good fire.'

'Wouldn't you bloody know!' Brodie said to Gus. 'Every time I turn me back it happens! Just my luck!'

'Ah, get out with you! After what I've seen at Willi's place, you've got luck to burn. Let's have a look at what Ted has found.'

Gus was intrigued that the latest strike at the Ten Mile had been in Firefly Two. It made him feel more involved and helped to persuade him that he had done the right thing coming back here, even though Trella would be upset for a while. And walking about the familiar ridge was a thrill in itself. He'd caught the bug again, no doubt about that.

Even though he was disappointed that Brodie was back so

soon, to resume his share of the mine, Ted could scarcely contain his excitement. Both Gus and Brodie agreed that his opals were first grade, shimmering rainbows of colour like the stones from the original Firefly, so he was delighted that he had Court, as buyer, on the spot.

'We can't leave here now,' Brodie said. 'The black opals will just have to wait.'

Gus agreed. 'You'd be mad to stop with that Firefly now. He's only gone a few yards down that tunnel. But where do I fit in?'

Brodie called Ted over. 'No one else has had a strike since I left, but it's given them heart, so we'll all keep going. Now you've had your fun, but that patch has run out. Do you want to stay on and keep working Firefly?'

'By God I will.'

'Right, then this is what we do. Gus is coming in as a partner.

Ted frowned. 'I dunno about that.'

Brodie stood over him, glaring. 'You forget. I'm the boss here and what I say goes. My mate's in. But Gus and me, we're in a hurry.'

'Why?' Ted sulked.

'Because he's got a lady friend in town.' Brodie winked at Gus. 'So he has to get back to his wedding.'

Gus nodded, backing him up, knowing that Brodie would never mention the real reason to a miner.

'So,' Brodie added, 'we'll work round the clock. We have to use candles down there, even in daylight, so we're wasting hours sleeping. With a three-man team we can work shifts. What do you say, Gus?'

'Suits me.'

'And we get a three-way split,' Brodie said, without further reference to Ted, who had no choice but to agree.

Gus knew that this was Brodie's way of paying Ted back for breaking the partnership rules, and if Ted bucked, he'd be out on his ear. But he also knew that Brodie's idea of working through the night was feasible. Pairs of miners had tried it, only to wear themselves down from fatigue. A trio could do it.

They didn't waste any time. By ten o'clock that night Gus was deep in the narrow cave at the end of the short tunnel, with his candle set in the wall behind a small sheet of tin to gain better light. As he picked gently and lovingly at the sandstone wall, brushing with his fingers, listening for the clink of crystal, Gus was in his element. Nothing could beat this feeling of wonder, of suppressed excitement, that any minute . . .

He ignored the dust-ridden air, the musty smell of this ancient earth, the perspiration that mingled with the dust and clouded his eyes, the monotonous, mind-bending silence broken only by his constant tap-tapping against the wall of rock, and the cramps that assailed him as his muscles became reacquainted with working in a perpetual crouch. This was his joy, this was what he liked to do, to pit his skills against Mother Earth as he searched out her secrets. But all the time he was aware that the earth could fight back. She could as easily destroy the intruder as she could shower him with such beauty as his world had never seen.

His parents had taught him many ancient legends, among them that of Gaea, who was Mother Earth, and deep in her heartlands his thoughts turned to her. Man was not her province; she was guardian of this planet and if it were her decision to send earthquake, flood or fire then she had her reasons.

Strangely, he mused as he plugged on, his right arm becoming more and more painful, the Aborigines had much the same philosophy. They had spirits but no God as such. This earth was the be-all and end-all of their religion, if that was what it could be called. They saw themselves as nurturers and protectors of her property, obeying the laws of nature, her laws, with stringent and meticulous care.

Oft times, in his travels, Gus had sat down with Aborigines to listen to their talk, and their sadness, finding them the most charming of people. He wondered now why the similarity of their legends to the story of Gaea had not occurred to him before. He must ask them about it. He could take Trella with him to meet some of these people. They could go on a camping holiday, for their honeymoon, right out into the bush. She'd never seen anything of this country but two towns. She'd enjoy a change like that.

It bothered him that she had to work so hard. He didn't want his wife to have to work. If only he could strike opal again, and not lose it this time, he thought ruefully, he could buy that country hotel. And they'd live happily ever after.

He loved Garth like his own. The boy could come with them, learn the business. They would be a real family, instead of all three marching off to work in different directions, with little time to be together. They could all work so harmoniously in their family pub.

Gus was reaching up, picking at rock over his head when there was a sudden shower of rubble. He eased down from the narrow ledge, looking about him warily.

'Oh no you don't,' he said, thinking of Gaea. 'I'm not upsetting anything here, so just you be quiet.'

Gingerly he moved back, watching a small avalanche of rock disgorge and fill up the few feet of cavern where he'd been working. When it subsided, he went back to work, this time with a shovel, piling up rubble to be winched to the surface. Then he began to examine the walls.

He decided the mine needed reinforcing before they went any further, so he climbed the ladder to the surface and strode about in the grey pre-dawn to stretch his muscles. Determined to keep this enterprise moving along, he made for the wood heap, searching for logs to use as stays.

Brodie awoke to the familiar ring of the axe, surprised to find Gus hard at work.

'You're just in time,' Gus said. 'I had a little cave-in. Help me with this timber; we need more supports down there.'

'No colour yet?'

'No, Brodie,' Gus laughed. 'And yes, I'm fine, thank you.'

Her landlady was sympathetic. 'Your lad did head for Charleville. I went to see the stationmaster and he remembers seeing him.'

'Thank you,' Trella said. 'But where from there? What does he know of that wild country?'

'It's not the end of the earth, you know!'

'Ah, 'tis to me. I have a terrible fear in me.'

'Good Lord! You young women, you're spoiled. You should have more faith in your men!'

'Garth's still a kid,' Trella cried. 'A big, overgrown kid. There's no tellin' where he'll end up.'

'Get out with you! At his age I was working on a farm with my young sister at my heel, us being orphans, and no one ever worked harder, there's no let-up on dairy farms . . .'

Trella had heard that story a dozen times, so she sat numbly, staring into her tea cup as the woman droned on. She knew that Mrs Wilkinson had also been referring to Gus when she'd spoken of not having faith in the men. All along, she'd taken Gus's part, claiming that women shouldn't interfere in men's business.

'If his heart's set on the mining,' she'd clucked, 'why stand in his way? He's a good, God-fearing man, you won't lose him by letting him go his own way.'

Now that it was obvious that Gus had gone on to the Ten Mile with Brodie, Trella was discouraged. It wasn't Gus she was afraid of; it was Brodie, with all his persuading, who'd won out again. And this time he'd snared her son too. Any day she expected a letter to confirm Gus's change of plans but it would be too soon for news of Garth.

She'd kept away from the bakery. She cringed at having to tell them that both Gus and her son had deserted her. That Garth had run off without a word to her, just a cold note. Why couldn't he tell her that he'd been sacked? Not for a minute had she believed Ringrose. Was she such a poor mother that the lad couldn't face her? Did he not know how much she loved him? His hurt was her hurt. But then, the sacking had given him the perfect excuse, in his eyes, to go chasing after Brodie. His hero.

Doubts lodged. Trella worried that she'd been too rigid in her opposition to that mining. Should she have paid more attention to Gus and his dreams? But what had those dreams cost already? A man was dead, Gus himself had only survived by the grace of God. And for all his years of prospecting for gold and for opal, what did Gus have to show for it? Nothing! Why couldn't he see that? He himself had said that only the lucky few made good prospecting. Only the lucky few! It was worse than gambling, this prospecting vice. Sure, Brodie was one of the lucky ones but then that was Brodie. Did Gus hope Brodie's luck would rub off on him?

Trella doubted it. Wryly she wished she'd told Gus that her brother-in-law was such a selfish man he'd not spare an ounce of luck for another.

439

The letter came, as she'd known it would. Full of love, and apologies, and promises that this would be his very last effort. Tears came hard to Trella. She'd been battling for so long, she considered herself too strong to succumb, but the sweetness of his words were such as to draw a sob, an overwhelming love for this foolish man.

But the days dragged and the nights were long, and though she tried to be hopeful, even cheerful, fears clamoured, wild fears that invaded her dreams.

Her son had at last found transport. Shaking hands with his hosts at Barbary Creek, and promising to come back to visit, Garth boarded the dray with the mailman for the last leg of his journey.

Once again came the unexpected. The dray, laden with mailbags and parcels and an assortment of tools and implements, was headed for a place called the miners' store, which Garth had taken for granted was at the Ten Mile field, but that was not the case.

They'd ambled along a twisting bush track for hours, when suddenly his driver had pulled up. 'This is where you get out, son.'

Garth looked about him. There was nothing! Just this endless shaggy, unattractive bush on all sides. The lush green of Toowoomba with its flowering trees came back to him, taunting him, as he stared about. The sameness of this place to all the countryside he'd seen from the window of the coach made him feel as if he'd entered a massive maze, and he shuddered.

'Don't worry,' the driver said. 'See that track there? It heads up the rise. You can't go wrong now. Just keep going. It's only a mile or so, stick on it and you'll come to the ridge.'

'Is the ridge the Ten Mile?'

'That's it, son. Good luck now!' With a giddy-up to his horse, the driver turned away and Garth was left to make his own way.

As he trudged up the track, carrying his suitcase, Garth felt as if he were the only soul on the earth. A dingo emerged from the bush to stare at this tall person with a soft cap lodged on his black curly hair and his jacket buttoned tight across his waist. Garth tried to smile. A train passenger sure must look a trick tramping up this hill in his best clothes with his luggage. No wonder the wild dog stared.

It was the first time he'd seen a dingo close up. It was a pretty animal, reddish, not as big as he'd imagined, just a fair-sized dog, with sharp, inquisitive eyes.

'Here, dog!' he called, desperately needing company, his hand outstretched, but as he came closer the dingo dashed across the track and disappeared into the scrub.

Garth walked on, at every bend expecting to meet someone, but the still unyielding bush gave no such comfort. He felt as if he were in limbo, that place between heaven and hell, and he thought of his mother. Wishing now he hadn't crept out like that. He should have told her he'd been sacked. He should have said that he had decided to go to the opal fields. Faced with his determination, she couldn't have stopped him. She might have yelled a bit, she was good at that, but in the end she'd have come round. But the long, lonely road was no place to be entertaining regrets, so Garth pulled himself together, quickened his pace, looking ahead in better spirits. He'd made it to the Ten Mile, he hoped, all on his own. That was a feat in itself.

It was a time for regrets. Gus hoped that Trella would forgive him. He'd tried to buy two of Ted's opals for her, from Brodie, and was astonished when Brodie tossed them to him.

'Here! Give them to her!'

'Good God! What brought this on?'

'I'm a relation, aren't I?'

'Yes. But I've always had the impression you don't like Trella.'

'I'm not mad about her,' Brodie admitted.

'Then I'll take nothing for her for free!'

Brodie was embarrassed. He had his own problems. 'You're starting to sound like her. She's all right, I suppose. But she always rubbed me up the wrong way.'

'And you don't do that to her?'

'Not at all.'

'So you say! I'll take these opals on one condition. When we get back to town you smarten yourself up and be nicer to her.'

'Jesus! What have I got here? I'm trying to give her a

present and you're making conditions. I never heard the bloody like!'

'Would it be so hard? We're starting a new family here, my family and yours. It's a good mix. When you marry, our family will grow. I want us all to stay together, don't you understand that?'

'All right, that's enough,' Brodie muttered. 'You should have been a bloody preacher. Get back to the camp and start praying I strike it rich this time. I'm scared bloody stiff someone will beat us to that black opal field.'

He climbed down the shaft, lit a candle and went back to work. The quiet of the pit was a good place for thinking. His gift of opals had nothing to do with Trella. Try as he might, he couldn't get over Vivien. He couldn't put her out of his mind. The sudden gesture had more to do with Vivien, a peace offering to a woman in lieu of his own lady.

I was too hard on her, he told himself as he gouged away at the crumbling wall. I've never missed anyone in my life as much as I'm missing her.

So she had deceived him. What about the days prior? Had he ever been happier? Weren't they both, then, deliriously in love? She'd asked him the same question, crying by then.

But in his pride, and his anger, he'd pushed her aside. And the names he'd called her!

'Oh, Christ!' he said. 'It wasn't all that necessary. You're no saint yourself. What about your own tales about being the big landholder back in Ireland? How would she react if you'd told her she was marrying an ex-footpad? And what about the money you conned out of her? With never a thought of repaying?'

Brodie cringed at the thought of telling Gus, telling anyone, that he was still in love with Vivien. He hated to admit it to himself. But it had taken that fight, and the finality of it, to force him to reassess as he travelled far away from her. To go over it again and again, every word, every tear, every cruelty, because he couldn't get it out of his mind. No matter how he tried, she was there. Not as the wrongdoer, but as witness to his own hypocrisy.

As he worked, busy hands tapping, groping, searching, listening like a blind creature, Brodie argued, debated, defending her, defending himself, but all the time she was there, his

442

pretty little blonde love, with all her saucy ways, struck down by his pride. And the moments they'd had together that he'd never have with anyone else. Never, never again.

And all because she'd done what he'd never have dared. She'd tried to hold him with trickery. A man like him. A nobody. Vern had left her well-off. She was a beautiful woman. She wouldn't have any trouble finding another husband.

What did it matter if there were no kids? If she'd come down with consumption he'd have remained by her side, playing the hero. What did it matter if a man loved a woman and wanted to spend the rest of his life with her?

He had no doubt in his mind that the black opals would bring him home. They'd bring him the wealth that, as a farmer, back in Tullymore, he'd never have dreamed of. He'd known that right from the day that he'd been guided by some sure hand to view that opal necklace.

They could build a house. Brisbane, Sydney. Anywhere they liked. And they could travel. He'd take his lovely wife all round the world, even to Tullymore. What a scene that would create!

But he had no wife. He had no Vivien.

Brodie emerged from his pit of regrets, ill-tempered and morose. Since this wasn't unusual with men who went down those shafts brimming with hope, the other men let him be. Ted took over from him and Gus had gone in search of game, his usual afternoon pastime, so Brodie mooned over a meal of salt beef and biscuits before he came to a decision.

He found pencil and paper and wrote to Vivien.

It was a hard thing for a man to have to say he was sorry, and not an easy thing either for a man to put this in words. Even worse to have to blunder on about forgiveness, but with determination, and not a few cross-outs, it was done. And then, carefully sealed, the letter was placed inside another envelope addressed to Stanley Wickham.

Brodie knew she would have left the hotel, so he requested Stanley to find her and pass his letter on without delay. Not one to waste an opportunity, he also advised Stanley that he expected further payment for his opals to be sent to his lawyer, that being his business address, and Stanley was to bank the payments in his account.

He did remember to send his best regards, in remaining, your friend, Brodie Court, since he'd become quite fond of Wickham, who was not all that much older than himself.

That was the last time Stanley Wickham heard from his client, Brodie Court.

'What the hell are you doing here?'

Gus stared in amazement at the apparition that came towards him, stumbling over mullock hills, wearing a Sunday suit, even the spotted bow tie youths affected these days. He was almost speechless when he saw it was Garth Court, certainly not pleased. By no means the reception Garth expected.

Garth was equally surprised to see Gus. 'I thought you'd be back home by this,' he stammered.

'Well I'm not, I'm here. Now, you explain yourself.'

Garth planted his case on the rubble. 'I got sacked, so I . . .'

'What do you mean, you got sacked? What did you do?'

'Nothing. Ringrose made a speech about having to cut back, and next thing I know he's telling me I'm finished.'

'Did you get your pay?'

'Oh sure, that I did. Where's Brodie?'

'Down there.' Gus nodded at the gaping shaft behind him.

'Let me see,' Garth said eagerly, but a hand like iron gripped his arm.

'No you don't. Wait a minute. How come your mother let you come out here?'

'Let go, Gus, you're hurting me. She doesn't mind.'

Gus released him but still barred his way. 'So she gave you her blessing, did she? Kissed you on the cheek and sent you off prospecting? That doesn't sound like Trella.'

Garth stalled. He stared about the stark, ugly landscape, searching for some way to change the subject, but nothing came to mind except the knowledge that sooner or later Gus would hear the truth.

'I left her a note,' he muttered.

Gus nodded angrily. 'That's more like it! Now what am I going to do with you?'

'You don't have to do anything. I came here to work!'

'The hell you did! You're going home as soon as I can figure out how to get you there.'

'I am not! Brodie said I could join him any time. I'll work for him.'

'Oh, shut up! Bring your case and come with me.'

Garth wished he could talk to Brodie, but dutifully he followed Gus in the hope that, given a little time, he'd change his mind. Anyway, he thought, what's Gus doing here? I'm sure he promised Mum he'd be back in a few days. Wisely he decided not to press that point. Gus was cranky enough as it was.

Their camp wasn't much. Set in a clearing in the scrub, it was composed of a two-man tent and a shanty of saplings and brush that held their supplies and equipment. Nearby were the ashes of a campfire with a blackened billy hanging over it, and beside that a home-made bench. Several sturdy boxes lay about, for chairs, Garth supposed.

'I don't know where we're going to put you,' Gus grumbled. And he went on grumbling as he lit the fire, washed some potatoes in a tin tub and dropped them in the billy.

Garth took off his cap and jacket and then removed his tie as well, feeling out of place now. The few men they'd passed on the way to the camp had grinned at him. They were a grimy, bearded lot. Real miners! Garth was impressed. Even Gus, who was always so neat, looked the part now, in rough clothes, with his fair hair thick as thatch and the stubble of a beard. An excitement was building in Garth, despite Gus, and he was determined to stay.

He stood about awkwardly as Gus combined cooking with a nonstop gripe about his presence. He pretended to listen as he watched bacon being chopped into hunks to sizzle in a pan with halved onions.

'There's bread in a tin in that shed,' Gus said. 'Get it, and bring half a dozen eggs.'

It was the best meal Garth had ever had! All of the ingredients piled up on a large tin plate, to be attacked just with a fork and fingers, and the juice sopped up with the hard toasted bread. To be sitting out there under the trees, with the smell of eucalypt bracing the air, was terrific, even if the only company was a scowling man.

Gus was making tea in another billy when Brodie strode in.

'Well! Spare me days!' he shouted with a wide grin. 'Where did you spring from, young Garth?'

'Came out here on me own!'

'Good on you!' He clapped Garth on the shoulder. 'Is he feeding you proper?'

'Like a lord,' Garth enthused. 'He's a good cook.'

'Tell him what you told me,' Gus snapped as he began to chop up more bacon.

'About what?' Brodie asked.

'About his mother not knowing he's here. He just took off.'

'She wouldn't have let me come!'

Brodie peeled off his flannel shirt and shook the dust from it. 'What can I do? He's here now.'

'You can send him home.'

'To what?' Garth exploded. 'I lost my job, Brodie. It wasn't much of a job anyway, just a general dogsbody.'

'That's all you'd be here,' Gus warned.

'Ease up, Gus. If the kid wants to stay, let him. Make a man out of him.'

'What about Trella?'

Brodie grinned. 'Write her a letter, cool her down. You must be getting good at that now.'

Gus threw down the long cooking fork and confronted Brodie. 'Don't get smart with me!'

'Ah! Ease up, Gus. I haven't got time for all this fussing. Let the kid stay.'

'Only until I get a reply from his mother,' Gus said, 'and if she says send him home, I'll shove him on a coach myself.'

'That's not fair!' Garth cried.

Gus ignored him. 'And what's more, until he has Trella's permission to stay, he keeps out of the mines.'

Another man joined them, and Garth was introduced to Ted Price, who didn't seem too happy. 'You're not ringing in another partner on me, you blokes?'

'No,' Brodie said. 'He's our general dogsbody.' He was already thinking ahead. Garth couldn't have come at a better time. When they started prospecting for the black opal, they'd take the lad with them. He could be there to partner Gus while his uncle kept an eye on his Ten Mile interests. He'd been wondering all along how he could be in two places at once.

446

Later that night he took Garth aside. 'Do the right thing, son. Write to your mum yourself. I reckon, as long as Gus is here, she'll let you stay. Especially since you haven't got a job now.'

The miners called him the General, since they'd heard he was employed as a general dogsbody, which they thought was a great joke. But Garth wasn't all that impressed. He'd been permitted to go down the mines but only as a visitor. He was just dying to have a go at gouging but Gus had made the rule and no one argued with him. None of the miners would let him do anything but view the musty tunnels that hid the elusive gems. He had seen the opals that Ted had recovered from a small seam in Firefly Two, and he was dazzled by them, but it was small consolation.

There seemed to be no end to the chores, wood-chopping, cooking, washing, cleaning up the camp, exercising and caring for the horses, and anything else they could think up. Gus wouldn't even let him take a gun and go hunting for scrub turkeys on his own. The closest he got to the mine was working the windlass, hauling up heavy buckets of rubble.

Two weeks later, they still hadn't heard from Trella, but that wasn't surprising, he was told; everything took time out here. He rode with Brodie to the miners' store to collect their supplies, and that was interesting, hearing of strikes further along the ridge and listening to men from the stations exchanging yarns.

Garth decided he ought to buy himself some mining tools, and Brodie agreed. 'Have you got the cash?'

'A bit. But you owe me two weeks' wages.'

Brodie stared. 'I owe you what? No one gets paid out here until they strike opal.'

'But I've been working.'

'So has everyone else,' Brodie chortled.

'That's not fair. How can I find any opal if you won't let me near a mine?'

'Nothing's fair out here. Most of these blokes will fail. They'll work their guts out until they run out of cash, and then they'll keep searching until they're bloody starving, some of them. In the end they'll have to walk back. Not just to Charleville, but all the way back east. Do you still want to spend the last of your cash on tools?'

'Yes.'

'Righto.' He walked about the store. 'Let's see what we've got here on the cheap.' He turned back to Garth with an irritating smile. 'There's always stuff here belonging to blokes who've had to sell their equipment to get home.'

With a heavy heart, Trella gave her permission for Garth to stay out at Ten Mile. She had no faith at all in their hopes that the earth would produce wonders for them. To her mind it would be simpler to stay home and back racehorses. She remembered talk of Mr Hadley-Jones back in Tullymore. They said he was an inveterate gambler, and that his wife worried herself sick about it. But he was a rich man.

It was different with Gus, and now Garth. They were just wasting time that should be spent earning a living. They had ideas above their station. And Brodie was to blame for all of it.

Nevertheless, for fear of annoying Gus by being too much of the nagger, Trella wrote him a cheerful letter. She did not ask him to look out for Garth, clear in her mind that the lad had to take responsibility for his own actions now. From what Gus had told her, life out there was rough, with no amenities. With luck, she hoped, Garth would soon get his fill of it, the shine rubbing off the adventure.

She did not mention that her hold on her own job was precarious. Ringrose was out to get her now. He complained about her work, he set other staff against her – which wasn't hard, all of them too afraid for their own jobs – and he deliberately provoked her when he came down to the factory floor with crude jokes about her person and her red hair.

Trella knew it was only a matter of time before he went too far and she struck back.

Then what was to become of her? A burden on Gus Kriedemann, who would have lost his own job by this.

She kept telling herself to stop her worrying, that Gus was her friend as well as her lover, he would never regard her as a burden. And yet ghosts and goblins haunted her dreams, causing her to wake in the night shaking with fear.

Stanley Wickham, too, was attending to his correspondence. Brodie Court's letter had been returned swiftly, unopened by

Wickham's other client, Mrs Vivien Holloway, with a sharp note that she was now living in Brisbane and wished no further contact with Mr Court.

The cheque had arrived from Brodie's agent in Dublin, which Wickham duly banked for his client. That augured well for Brodie's next sales. While they were at the pub, talking to his friend Gus Kriedemann, he'd said that he'd be sending another parcel of opals to Dublin. In his absence, when the payment came, that too was to be banked in his account.

Court was a strange fellow. For all his bonhomie and that big Irish smile, he kept his cards close to his chest. The letter to Vivien Holloway had been interesting. Stanley would have given a year's salary to have opened it! He wasn't immune to gossip, and although Brodie hadn't mentioned her, even on his last day in town, Stanley was aware of the scandal between the two of them. And since then he'd heard that they'd planned to marry at the courthouse but neither had turned up at the appointed time.

Everyone in the building had been awaiting their arrival, it was said, with more than the usual number of locals finding business there on that day, even a reporter, but nothing happened. Since he knew no more than anyone else, Stanley had spent subsequent days in mysterious mode, as if he did know but would not be drawn on the business of his clients.

Brodie Court, he recalled now in hindsight, had been in a dark mood that last morning when he'd stormed into his lawyer's office before returning to his mines out west. He'd said he didn't expect to be back in town in an age, and arranged for Stanley to pay any bills that might come in. That was when Wickham discovered that Court owned two tenanted cottages up the older end of town, an area that was gradually being taken over by keen buyers.

Obviously Court was a man who preferred to plough along, making money in his own time, Stanley thought, using his lawyer in a secretarial capacity, and that wasn't unusual, even with squatters and graziers out west. As long as he was paid for his services, trusted by his clients to draw only his due, he was happy to oblige.

He checked the Court file carefully, smiling to himself. 'I'm in on the ground floor here,' he murmured. 'I think Mr Court and I can look forward to a long and rewarding association.'

It seemed that the young lawyer's predictions were proved right when, months later, he took receipt of a telegram from one Abe Rosenstein, advising Brodie that his opals had arrived and were so magnificent they were to be put to auction.

Another telegram arrived soon after, advising that the stones had been bought by a Mr Louis C. Tiffany of New York. A designer of exquisite jewellery. Bank draft forwarded 3729 pounds after expenses.

Stanley could almost hear the shouts of excitement from the other side of the world. Aware of Brodie's secretive nature, he said not a word in the town. Brodie might not thank him for drawing attention to the worth of his opals, especially the black that he'd raved about. Stanley had never seen a black opal.

By this he was holding letters from Mr Rosenstein, asking about further shipments. Letters from Mr George Kunz, buyer for Tiffany, New York, who had somehow ferreted out the name and address of the opal miner.

From all of this Stanley was one of the first to realise what an impact Australian opals were making on the world market. He began to study the matter, discovering that the previously most famous opals were the Mexican fire opals which failed in comparison, because although full of singular colour they were not iridescent like the Australian variety. They lacked the churning rainbow lustre, the element of surprise. But he could find nothing about black opals. And then he knew that Brodie Court had stumbled on a gem that was to take the world by storm.

All of his letters to Brodie were returned to sender but in the meantime Stanley invested heavily in the black opals from Lightning Ridge, because he never did find out whence came Court's magnificent dark opals, identified as boulder opal.

His law firm flourished but few knew that Stanley's wealth had really emanated from his sale of opals to the gem dealer Abe Rosenstein, in Dublin.

Chapter Fourteen

Another strike at the Ten Mile!

About time, Garth thought as he raced to see the buckets coming up. He'd been here for weeks and nothing interesting had happened. 'This could go on for months,' Ted had told him, only yesterday. 'No use getting impatient, there may be something down there or nothing. The only way to find out is to keep digging.'

'That's if you're allowed to dig,' Garth said angrily.

His mother had replied that he could stay for three months. No longer. So he'd raced off to find Brodie, waving his letter. 'Now where do I start?'

'You've already started.'

'I meant looking for opal. I've got the tools and all.'

'In good time,' Brodie said. 'There's no place for you here. But,' he added mysteriously, 'hang on for a while. You, me and Gus are opening up a new mine.'

'Where?' Garth was thrilled.

'It's a secret. No one's to know we're even thinkin' about it yet, so not a word. Just keep on with what you're doing.'

Which was all very well, Garth thought, as one boring day followed another, but he was wasting precious time. He should be down there now, searching for the fabulous seam of opal that he was certain he'd find. He dreamed of the day when they'd all be struck with wonder, when he, Garth Court, became a legend among miners for unearthing the most brilliant opals they'd ever seen.

If they'd ever let him at them!

The miner sat by Brodie's tent sorting his stones while Brodie watched carefully, dusting the glaze of colour with his hand as he occasionally picked up an interesting piece.

'What's it all worth?' Garth was crouched beside him.

'The real worth?' Brodie said. 'That's hard to say. It

depends on the skill of the cutter. After that we can talk in terms of size and carat but in the long run the beauty is in the eye of the beholder.'

'So how do you know what to buy now?'

Brodie nodded at the miner. 'We both know enough to grade them. I buy his firsts and seconds once we get over arguing which is which. Then I have to take a guess at it.' He turned his head to Garth and murmured, 'After I do a bit of bargaining.'

They haggled for ages so Garth wandered away. There were several closed mines along the ridge and he'd been eyeing them curiously, wondering which one Brodie intended to reopen. What a lark it would be to beat him to it.

The ridge was deserted in the mornings, or seemed to be, with most of them working underground or resting. It would be a simple matter for him to do a little prospecting on his own. How many tales had he heard of men who'd reopened abandoned mines and hit colour within a few feet? That was all part of the lore of frustration and luck.

'If only he'd given it another day or so,' voices mourned, recalling the fate of fellows at various mine sites they'd worked, 'he could have been a rich man.'

Ah yes. One such yarn led to another. Garth knew them all by heart, and they spurred him on to take a serious interest in abandoned mines without drawing attention to himself.

The first one he tried was Firefly One, but the shaft was wrecked; he only had to climb down a few yards with a lantern to see the crushed timber supports half buried under earth and rock. Other mines, though, also boarded up, had been filled in. He began to think he'd set himself an impossible task when he came to one with its name still visible on an askew plank: The Four Aces.

'Brilliant name,' he grinned. 'I'd never have thought of it myself.'

He looked about guiltily but there was no one in sight, so he pulled away the boards and peered down. The side stays were intact and it went down deep. Disappointed, Garth realised he'd need a ladder to investigate further. He'd seen the ladders the miners used, only saplings with rungs nailed across. Or some of them were. Others were stronger, built into the timbered walls of the shaft once the mine got going. But he decided he didn't need such care at this stage; he just wanted to get down there and see what was at the bottom.

While he chopped firewood, Garth set aside the pieces he would need, and soon he had his ladder.

That night he manoeuvred it through the scrub and darted across to the mine. He removed the boards, no longer nailed, and slid the ladder into the shaft. His heart dropped with his ladder. It disappeared into the depths. Frantically he felt about for it but since he couldn't risk a lantern, he had to leave it until the morning.

The three men might work shifts but they seemed to wander about at all hours. Garth was glad that Ted kept to his own camp down the slope, down past the Four Aces mine, because he only had to wait for Brodie to have his breakfast and bury himself in his tent. Gus was back at work.

The ladder wasn't too far down, not quite out of reach, but for leverage Garth drove two stakes into the ground at the surface of the mine. Holding on to them he could step down to the ladder and descend.

Some of the planks on the wall of the pit had sprung loose, but he ignored them and negotiated his ladder right to the bottom of the shaft, which went off to the right. Garth was wild with excitement! This was his mine! Without light he felt his way along the walls, collecting splinters in his hands as he met timber stays. The tunnel went in a long way, but gradually it narrowed and he came to the end. Perfect! This was where he'd start. As soon as possible.

He made his way back to the shaft, scrunching over the rubble left by miners who'd been gouging these walls, and hauled himself up to the light.

Every chance he got, Garth was down there with his candle and pick, tapping away at the walls, scraping and gouging, sure that he'd find treasure.

He failed to wonder why the slats holding back the sides of the shaft had busted loose. Rushing through to the end of the tunnel he didn't notice the ominous cracks in the ceiling or the drunken stance of the timber supports halfway along. He was too happy with his dreams. At times he became impatient with his slow progress, so he plunged his heavy pick into the wall with all his strength to widen his search, peering anxiously into the gaps for the expected glitter.

His work was interrupted for a few days by a new burst of excitement.

It was early morning, and cold, a dank mist low on the ridge. He was shuddering over the fire, thankful that Brodie himself, had gone down to fetch fresh water.

Brodie was a strange man, Garth thought. Moody. Gruff and surly most of the time, but then he could be kind too. Like now.

'You stay here and keep warm,' he'd said, picking up the bucket, taking over one of Garth's chores.

Gus came up from the mine, all smiles, but then that was Gus. He was always cheerful. Even when he was engaged in one of those endless arguments with Brodie. He could be very funny and he seemed to enjoy taking a rise out of Brodie.

'What do you think of this?' Gus asked him.

Garth turned over the stone that Gus handed him and saw a band of pearly colours across one side. 'It's opal, isn't it?'

'Bet your life it is!' Gus laughed.

'Where did it come from?'

'Just a minute. Brodie's coming. Don't say a word.' He placed the stone on the bench and moved away.

Brodie nodded to him, not in a very talkative mood this morning. He filled the billy and the water bags and meandered about the camp, everywhere but near that bench, until Gus had to manoeuvre him over there.

'Cut some bread for me, will you, Brodie?'

'Righto.' Even then he took his time. Fiddling about. Examining the knife. 'This knife's blunt,' he muttered. But at long last there was some action. He shoved the stone aside, set the loaf up, then stared.

'Where did this come from?' he asked, picking up the stone and peering at the opalised strip.

'Where do you think?' Gus said. Grinning.

'How the hell would I know?'

'What about Firefly Two?'

'Where?'

'You heard me.'

Brodie rubbed his eyes. 'This is from Firefly?'

'Just a sample! You want to see the rest?'

'Let's go!' Brodie cried.

Garth jumped up to go with them, but Brodie, always cautious, insisted he douse the fire first.

They let him come down into the mine to see the opal for himself, but they drew the line at allowing him to remove any.

'Leave Gus to it,' Brodie said. 'The gentler the better. We don't want to shatter any.'

Garth wished he could tell them he'd been practising in his own mine, practising removing plain old stones as if they were opals, but since that wasn't a very good idea, he stayed well back, watching as every precious piece came loose.

Ted was delighted. 'I knew there was more in there,' he crowed. 'God knows how far that seam goes in.'

With that, Garth realised they'd be spending even more time in this mine now, before turning to the other one that Brodie had in mind, and he groaned. More time passing before he could be a real partner.

Just as well I can do some fossicking in my own mine, he told himself.

At the weekend a violent storm struck the ridge. Wind roared over the exposed terrain, bringing with it days of relentless heavy rain, causing havoc in the camps. Brodie's tent was washed out and Garth's canvas-covered shelter didn't fare much better, with water running through as if he were sleeping in the centre of a creek. They were all miserable and cold, sloshing about in the wet, their fires steaming and hissing as they tried to burn damp logs. When finally the sun came out again it was more work to clean up the mess and dry out sodden clothes and blankets.

When at last everything was back to normal, Garth breathed a sigh of relief. He hurried down to inspect his mine, and although it was muddy inside, he was relieved to find that the water had now seeped away.

Down in the tunnel it was just as muddy, with water dripping from the roof, but he supposed that was to be expected. That rain had come down by the ton!

Ignoring the chilly discomfort, he turned up his collar and set to work again in the slippery depths.

Emerging from the storm, this day was bright and beautiful, and especially so for the three jubilant men of Firefly Two.

The blue in these opals was a perfect match for the peerless blue sky framed above the shaft. Occasionally vivid flashes of colour sped across the sky, and Brodie, noticing the swift pairs of parakeets, marvelled as he loaded the buckets.

After the intense green of Ireland, this land was, to him, colourless. Vast and drab.

'But the Lord compensates,' he murmured, 'livening things up with all those brilliant birds.' And then he grinned, as if nudging himself. 'And down here's the bonus. All the colour a man would want to see.'

He straightened up and called down the tunnel to Gus. 'How're you going?'

The seam had run out after a few feet and Gus was searching about, hoping to pick it up again.

'Nothing yet.'

Brodie yanked the rope and Ted wound the bucket up. 'Any luck yet?'

'No,' Brodie called, and climbed out. 'I'm starving. I'm going over to see what the kid's cooked up.'

'He's not there,' Ted said. 'I was over there at your camp a while ago to get some grease for this contraption, and there's no sign of him.'

'Where the hell is he?'

'Search me.' Ted shrugged, standing back to roll a smoke.

Angrily Brodie marched across the ridge to their camp, hoping that Garth would be on the job by this. At noon he was supposed to have something cooking, usually a stew, but here it was nearer to two o'clock and the fire wasn't even lit. A man couldn't even get a cup of tea! He'd become accustomed to the luxury of having their own cook, once Garth got the hang of it, and now having to forage for himself made him hungrier than ever. He decided to fall back on salt beef and stale damper, and maybe some cheese, so he made for their shanty storeroom, half expecting that Garth might be asleep in there, but all was quiet.

He bundled the food and the tea tin on to the bench and headed for the wood heap for firewood, but a shrill whistle from the top of the hill stopped him in his tracks.

It was Ted. Beckoning. Shouting!

Gus had found the seam again. Nearly two feet higher than the other, thanks to a shift in the earth. A classic line of light, like a slim, glistening stream, ran across the wall, widening into the blind end of the tunnel.

The three men crowded into the tunnel, crowing with delight, touching the opal, smoothing it with rough hands, trying to assess the depth.

'My turn,' Brodie said, spitting into his hands. 'Let me at the little darling!'

'No, I'll keep going,' Gus said.

Ted shook his head. 'Leave it, Gus. You're asleep on your feet. It's Brodie's shift.'

'Yes, you go and look for the kid,' Brodie said. 'Tell him to drop me down a sandwich and some boiled eggs.'

Back on top Gus stretched his cramped limbs. 'Where is Garth?'

'Haven't seen him.'

Gus lifted his arms wide, grateful for the warm sunlight. 'He won't be far away. Come over and have a drink, we have to celebrate.'

'I wouldn't say no to a beer.' Ted smiled happily. He had decided that this would be his swan song. He'd stay on until this mine petered out, take his money and run. For once in your life, he told himself, quit while you're in front.

They sat by the tent, toasting their good fortune with bottles of beer and discussing the quality of the new opals, until Gus started to worry about Garth.

'Where the hell is he? It's not like him to just wander off, he's got his jobs to do.'

'Maybe he's on strike. Jacking up on the housework.'

Gus laughed. 'Not before a meal. He's not one to miss a feed.' He walked over and kicked the ashes of the campfire. 'This is stone cold. It hasn't been lit since early this morning.'

'Do you reckon he's gone hunting?'

'With what? The guns are still in the shed. Bugger him! I'd better go looking for him.'

Ted remained at the camp to finish his beer, basking in his future plans, then he decided to go down to his own hut and rustle up a quick meal before returning to help Brodie.

He walked right past the Four Aces mine, lost in thought.

Garth had only intended to work for an hour. That would

457

give him time to chop up the potatoes and onions and the last of the beef flank to make the stew for their lunch. He'd also have a go at making damper in the camp oven. It looked easy enough the way Gus made it, just flour and water.

As he dug away at the hole he'd made at the end of the tunnel, he tried to remember if there were any other ingredients. Crusty damper, so like bread, was his favourite food these days, especially when it was covered in golden syrup. His mouth watered at the thought.

This patch he was working on came away easily. He'd dug a large niche in the wall at waist height, making himself a ledge to lean on as he progressed, so he worked methodically at the niche, picking at both sides as well as overhead, sweeping the rubble back to the base of the tunnel. As that built up at his feet he stamped it into a platform so that he could get further into the cavern, head and shoulders in almost, an excellent way to proceed. Eventually, he knew, he'd have to work from the ledge down, back to that cramping crouch, because he wouldn't have enough light in there, but for the time being this was fine. He was moving along well.

Except that he still hadn't found any opal. Not even the clink of crystal. There was opal on the ridge. That had been proven yet again in the Firefly mine.

'It could just as easily be in here,' he said, brushing a cloud of dust from his face. 'Just beyond these walls somewhere, waiting for me. If I could only strike colour, see a glimpse of that shimmer, what a surprise they'll all get!'

He thought he felt a shudder, as if someone had rolled a heavy cart nearby, and he stopped for a minute, listening. But there was no sound. He reached for the candle and peered back along the tunnel, staring at the dark walls.

'I must have imagined it,' he said, turning back to resume work. 'Only a few minutes more and I'll have to get going.'

There were no more warnings. The mine collapsed so fast, almost soundlessly, that Garth only had time to dive forward, hands protecting his head, into the niche that he had dug, in the hope that this small hollow might protect him. But tons of rock and sludge thumped over his body. He felt one agonising jolt of pain, and then nothing. It was over. He could lift his head and move his hands but the rest of his body was more than waist deep in earth and he couldn't move.

Terrified, in pitch darkness, he lay very still, wedged in this small air hole. He heard himself screaming, the shocking sound ricocheting from the walls. So he stopped. The darkness was the worst thing. The black all round. He began to weep but stopped that too. Only sooks cried. And began to scratch at the wall ahead of him with his hand pick, thinking perhaps he could keep going in that direction, forgetting that from his hips down he was cast in rock. But he tried, and he prayed to the Lord, and he thought how angry his mother would be, and he thought if he found opal now . . . but he was too tired to care.

Ted was content with a tin of beans and a tin of peaches for his midday meal. He finished them off quickly and crossed the track from his bush hideaway, eagerly striding up the hill to the mine to see how that opal had fared in Brodie's hands. Praying that the seam hadn't run out again. He considered he was due for a really big bag of stones this time.

He was walking towards the abandoned Four Aces mine when he stumbled on unfamiliar terrain. Looking down, he noticed the subsidence, a shallow network of rifts in the weedy ground.

'The rain,' he said with a shrug, and moved on.

He had passed the mine when something he'd noticed registered. The mine was open. The boards had been removed.

Curious, he doubled back.

He stared at the rough ladder propped against the wall of the shaft. 'Jesus! Who'd be mad enough to be squizzin' round down there?'

Then, on a rung of the ladder, he saw the old woollen scarf that he himself had given Garth only a few days ago, during that wet weather. 'Keep your chest warm,' he'd said. 'You Irish are sitting shots for chest colds.'

He was down the ladder in an instant, turning the corner to be confronted by a wall of rock. He wasted only a few seconds, shouting, hoping for a reply, before he was out of there and running.

'Cave-in at the Four Aces,' he yelled at two miners tramping past, as he looked wildly about for Gus and, failing him, Brodie.

He jumped down their own mine, shouting to Brodie. 'Come quick, I think the kid's caught in the Four Aces!'

'What?' Brodie cried, but he too dumped everything and ran.

Gus was soon located as the crowd grew. 'Have you found Garth yet?'

'No.'

'Then best we get over to the Four Aces, mate. Ted reckons he's down there and Brodie's throwing a fit.'

Brodie was already digging in the tunnel when Gus arrived, and Ted was organising a dig where he'd seen the subsidence, on the off chance that they'd break through from above.

Never in his life had Gus been so panic-stricken, but Brodie was very much in control, striking at that seemingly impenetrable wall with a heavy shovel, refusing to look up.

'How do we know he's in there?'

Brodie gritted his teeth, sweat already streaming down his face. 'How do we know he's not? Did you find him?'

'No. But surely . . .'

'Someone's opened up this mine. Ask about, quick. See if anyone knows about it.'

As he remounted the frail ladder, several of the rungs gave way under Gus's weight, but he heaved himself to the surface, frantically running to groups of men who were bringing up shovels. 'Who's been down there? Anyone? Who opened it up?'

They shook their heads grimly.

Then began a full-scale attack on the Four Aces mine from two directions. No one had to be told that the mine was a danger area; men rushed forward with reinforcing planks and stays dragged from other mines, no time to cut new timbers. Diggers worked with Ted putting down a new shaft, while others backed up Gus and Brodie as they fought to clear out the tunnel.

'Oh, Jesus!' Brodie kept saying, almost weeping. 'He can't be in here, can he? It's a complete bloody cave-in.'

'If he's gone fishing somewhere I'll kill him!' Gus retorted, but in his heart he knew this was where Garth had to be.

There was only just room for the two of them to work and they refused to allow anyone to give them a rest, shovelling fiercely as the men behind them disposed of the rubble with grim efficiency.

They unearthed the timber stays halfway along the short tunnel and hoisted them into place, the blank wall ahead of them.

'They won't hold,' Brodie said.

'Yes they will. There's not far to go now.' Gus leaned his back against an upright, forcing it into place, and with both hands gripped the horizontal log above him. 'Now keep going, Brodie.'

'Christ Almighty!' one of the men whispered to him. 'You can't keep this up. You'll kill the both of you. Wait until we get some more solid timber.'

But Gus refused to let go, as Brodie pitched in beneath his arms, shovelling like a madman.

They felt the rumble of the earth this time, and though everyone knew they should run, no one stopped working.

Word came through that the other rescue shaft had failed. 'It was that bloody rain!' a miner told them. 'On top of the dynamite. This whole place is slipping about like a bloody mud heap.'

Water still seeped from the roof of the tunnel and it was too much for one man. 'I'm getting out of here,' he said. 'We don't know if that kid's even in here, and if he is he's finished.'

Brodie was afraid of that too. His shovel was heavy as if he were moving concrete. At each thrust into that awful cruel wall he prayed for a miracle, while above him he could hear Gus grabbing short, sharp breaths, hanging on to those supports for dear life. All three lives now. Any minute Brodie expected the roof to engulf them.

'More timbers!' he shouted as he worked. 'We need more support.'

'They're bringing them,' a voice replied. 'Give over a while, Brodie.'

But Brodie couldn't stop. How long had the kid been in there? If he was still alive he could be in an air pocket. Faint hope, but there was no time to waste. The heavy stays they needed would have been lost in the other shaft but surely enough hands could dig them out.

'Get the stays out of Firefly!' he shouted. 'It doesn't matter if you wreck it. Send someone for them.'

A wail answered him. But it was coming from beyond the wall. A sound! A voice!

'Did you hear that?' he shouted. 'He's in there! Hold on, me lad, hold on there now! It's here we are, we'll be getting you out in a flash.'

He ploughed on, oblivious to what was happening about him as another man stepped forward to brace the other stay opposite Gus. And above them, on the surface, Ted refused to pass on the message to grab the stays from his precious Firefly mine. Instead he had all hands digging an ever-widening shaft to pull up and re-use the timbers buried there.

Several men were digging with Brodie now, widening the tunnel. They found Garth's boot first and then, scrabbling with their hands, unearthed the lad, to cheers of relief. He was alive.

As Brodie carried him out, more hands were needed to release the two men who were holding up the supports, and when they finally jumped away, that section of the tunnel collapsed again. Gus was so weak, every muscle in his body strained, he too had to be carried out. No easy feat with a giant like him, they all laughed, in welcome relief.

Brodie laid the poor lad gently on a strip of canvas and covered him with the blankets pushed at him. He heard someone say: 'Go for a doctor.' And minutes later the thuds as a horse raced away.

The boy's eyes were glittery. Strange.

'You'll be all right, lad,' Brodie said as he wiped his nephew's brow with his hands. 'You're a brave feller if ever I saw one.'

'I'm sorry, Uncle Brodie.' The voice was no more than a wheeze.

'They're makin' a stretcher,' someone offered.

And then Gus was there, wobbling to his knees. 'Ah, Garth,' he said, 'you had us worried there for a while.'

Garth held his hand. 'Give my love to the parents,' he said, seeming to forget that Michael was dead.

Gus moved his hand up to the boy's face, and Garth held on to it, resting his cheek against the palm. He smiled, comforted by the warmth. 'It doesn't hurt,' he said, as if to reassure Gus.

'How is he?' Gus asked anxiously, and was shocked to

see that Brodie was weeping, tears coursing down his grimy bearded face.

'He's as good as gold,' Brodie whispered, talking to Garth, not to him. 'Aren't you, lad?'

For a second there the eyes lit up in a fond expectant smile, and then they died. The light was gone.

Frantically Gus bent over him, searching for breath, for life. He lifted up his head and cradled it on his lap as the men surrounding them drew back in shock.

'His back was broke.' Brodie wept openly. 'I knew it when I carried him up. The rest of him was crushed. That's why there was no pain.'

A voice behind them began to recite the Our Father as caps were wrenched aside as a mark of respect, but still the two men crouched by the body of Garth Court, unable to give him up.

There was still the mine. While Brodie and Gus stayed in their camp, guarding the body of the lad, Ted worked nonstop. He worked until the seam ran out and he hit rock that would require nothing less than dynamite to shift it, and then he brought all the opal to Brodie Court.

By this time a doctor had been and gone, after issuing a death certificate, and they were waiting for the undertaker to come out with his hearse, for Court would have nothing else. It would cost him a fortune, Ted mused, but Brodie nearly killed the bloke who suggested a dray would do to get him as far as Charleville. Ted had never seen two men so devastated by a death, but then, being a young 'un, he supposed . . .

He was surprised when Brodie took time off from his mourning to sit with him and sort the opals into three parcels. He was as tight as ever he was but when Ted asked what Brodie would give him for his share, the Irishman simply said: 'Name your price.'

Quick as a flash, Ted doubled his original estimate, on the assumption that a man could go down but never up.

Without so much as a blink, Brodie wrote him a cheque on the Bank of Queensland, which he said could be cashed in Charleville or Toowoomba.

Never having seen a cheque before, Ted was nervous about this, but the other men assured him it was safe.

'Brodie could write it on bark and you'd get your money,' they told him.

Since he too was headed east, Ted decided to travel with Gus and Brodie and the hearse, which was a fancy affair, the horses all done up in feathers and the mahogany coffin draped in black and silver.

Gus and Brodie were leaving for good. All of the miners understood that, even though nothing was said, and Ted thought it was real nice of them to form a guard of honour down the track as the hearse prepared to leave.

At the last minute, Brodie called him aside. He handed Ted his own parcel of opal tied up in an old trouser leg, since bags were short out here.

'Gus isn't watching,' he said. 'Let me see you go over and put this in his saddlebag. I don't want no mistakes this time.'

'But these are yours,' Ted protested.

'Not any more.' Brodie's dark eyes were wet with tears that Ted was sure he wasn't meant to see, so he hurried down and shoved the opals into Gus's pack while he was shaking hands with his friends.

Not so Brodie Court. He farewelled no one.

Ted climbed up on the hearse beside the undertaker and they set off, with Gus and Brodie riding behind.

At the first turn Brodie cut away, riding to the west.

'Where are you going?' Gus shouted, but Brodie never looked back.

Gus insisted they wait a while but in the end Ted whistled to him. 'Give it up, mate. I reckon he's gone.'

'Gone where?' Gus was bewildered.

'Who knows?' Ted shrugged.

Trella's screams could be heard all along the quiet lane.

Friends gathered to comfort her. To comfort Gus Kriedemann who had brought the coffin all the way home from out west and taken it to Father Monaghan's church, where the candles were already lit in solemn vigil.

Gus was well known in the town, and word of the tragedy spread even before the mother was aware. He was waiting for her on the front steps of her house when she came home from work, preferring to break his terrible news to her in the privacy of her home.

464

She ran when she saw him and threw herself into his arms. 'Oh Gus, my darlin'! You're home! What a joy it is to see you. And me in me old working clothes looking a fright! You should have given me a chance to tidy up.'

He kissed her. 'You always look lovely to me.'

She laughed as they entered the house. 'I swear you've got the blarney in you too! Is Garth with you?'

Her question seemed to remain frozen in the chill that spread over her when she saw that his parents were there too, waiting for her, standing miserably with her landlady, their faces ashen. They reached out to her, in slow motion it seemed, with the world reeling, their words grinding, though they whispered, and someone was screaming. Trella wished it would all stop, that they'd go away and take their lies with them.

The church was a blur of faces crowding, of flowers weeping, so many flowers, and the familiar smell of incense, and that pine coffin there, so close, with its silver handles blinking. Weak and dazed, Trella was sure they had it wrong. This was Michael, not Garth, not her lovely son.

But in the end, when they laid him to rest, she knew she had lost him, lost their son. She had failed Michael. Would he forgive her?

For weeks Gus stayed by her side.

'Will she ever get over it?' he asked his mother.

'No, but she'll recover. Yesterday she was saying she'd have to get back to work. They're keeping her job open for her.'

'Too late for their kindness. She's not going back, I'll see to that.'

There was no sign of Brodie but Gus understood. A man had to do his mourning his own way. He'd found Brodie's opals in his pack eventually and guessed they were for Trella, but he'd said nothing about that yet because Trella refused to speak of Brodie. She seemed to blame him for Garth's death, bridling when his name was mentioned. Gus sighed. She'd have to get over that too; there was no fault to be found in anyone. No use to talk about what might have been. Accidents happened in every walk of life. He hadn't been able to tell her that if Garth had heeded their warnings and stuck to his own job he'd still be alive. He probably never would. Too cruel. And it would sound as if he and Brodie were making excuses.

Before he left Charleville on his sad pilgrimage, he'd sent the opals out to Willi Schluter, and now he waited anxiously for the gems to arrive. He didn't have time to send them to Dublin as Brodie would expect; his need was more urgent. As soon as they were sold he and Trella would be married. He'd insist on that in an effort to help her to begin her life again.

He was surprised to receive a letter from the manager of the Bank of Queensland, requesting he call at the bank. Gus had no dealings with that bank, and he figured it must be a mistake, but he called in anyway, to set the fellow straight.

That afternoon he summoned his father from the bakery and placed some papers on the table. 'Have a look at this.'

'What is it?' Jakob asked fearfully. Official papers bothered him.

'They are the deeds of two houses, here in Toowoomba. And the deeds are in my name.'

'How did this happen? Where did you get the money?'

'I didn't. Brodie's been in town.'

'You saw him?'

'No. It seems he just came and went.'

Jakob was shocked. 'Without even paying his respects to Trella?'

'I don't suppose he was up to it, Father.'

'Then why did he come at all?'

Gus smiled sadly. 'I think to clean the slate. He was always close, you never knew what he was up to. I had no idea that rascal owned two houses only a few blocks from here.'

'And what has that got to do with you?'

'Apparently he came to his bank and drew out some money. He still owed money on one house, so he paid that off and then signed papers transferring the deeds into my name. The manager did the rest, registering them as he requested, and then he contacted me to pick them up.'

'Two houses! God in heaven! Why would a man give away two houses? You can't keep them!'

'I can't give them back either, but I can keep them in the Court family. That's what he wanted.'

'Does he expect you to read his mind?'

'No, not him. He expects me to do as I'm told. He liked being boss.'

'Mad, the pair of you!' Jakob said.

'Maybe. But I don't want Trella to know about this. Since I'm suddenly cashed up, let her think it was from the sale of the opals.'

Gus didn't bother to mention that the bank manager, welcoming him hopefully as a new customer, since both the houses were now accruing rent payments, had confided in him that Mr Court had also entrusted him with another duty. To forward to Mrs Vivien Holloway the sum of three hundred pounds.

'I believe he was a friend of that person,' he said with a slight sniff.

'A good friend,' Gus said firmly.

He wondered what the three hundred had been about. The original loan had been two hundred pounds, but Brodie had repaid that. Had he borrowed more money at a later stage? Probably.

Gus walked out to the sleep-out that still housed some of Brodie's things, including that fine suit, and smiled. 'Thanks, mate,' he said. 'I'll take care of her. Try not to take it all so hard. You'll have to come back one day so I can thank you.'

He sat on the bunk and lit a cigarette. 'Opals. Two houses and a wedding suit. You've more than paid the debts, mate, if there were any such debts outside of your own mind. Now, where the hell are you?'

That night he took a despondent Trella in his arms. 'Are you feeling better?'

She shook her head.

'Well now, you have to be. I've had a talk to Father Monaghan and I want to set a date for the wedding.'

'What wedding?'

'Our wedding.'

She burst into tears, pushing him away. 'How can you think of such matters now?'

'Because I want you for my wife. Because you can't jilt me. And because we can afford to be married.'

'With blood money!' she cried. 'From mines!'

'No,' he said quietly. 'I won't have you putting that burden on me, Trella. I was a miner before I ever met you.'

She was silent, and Gus sat for a long time, waiting for her response. Her silence was a refusal to retract so he stood up.

'As long as you have that in your heart, there's no place for me. And no future for us.'

'You don't understand,' she wept.

'Yes I do. We can go on from here or we can call it a day.'

'I can't face a wedding.'

'I only had in mind a small family ceremony, as sweet as any big show but that's beside the point now. You don't have to face anything.'

'You're leaving?'

Out there someone was playing a mouth organ, a mournful trolling of sad events, lost chances, depressing Gus even more. He picked up his cap. 'What more can I say?'

'Don't go. I'm sorry. I shouldn't have said that. It was cruel. I didn't really mean it. But I've been wanting to talk to you, Gus. About the wedding. Everything's changed now. I can't marry you.'

'Why not?'

She turned away from him to stare out of the window at the lush blossoming of pink and white oleanders that sheltered her side of the house. 'Because I can't stay here any longer. I've made up my mind. I'm going home.'

He was bewildered. 'Home? Where?'

'To Ireland. To Tullymore. That's where I belong. I should never have left.'

No matter how much he begged, pleaded, argued, Trella was adamant. She had made her decision.

Daily they visited Garth's grave; she had a need to be there as often as possible before she left.

'Your mother said she'd keep the grave neat,' Trella told him. 'I'm grateful for that.'

Gus could only nod. What great plans he'd had for the three of them. It was too late for Garth, but surely not for two people who still loved each other.

By the time they reached her gate, he too had made a decision. 'I'll take you home, Trella.'

She stared. 'To Ireland?'

'Yes.'

'Oh no. I couldn't ask you to do that.'

'You haven't asked. I'm telling you. We'll go together.'

'You'd do that for me?'

'For us.'

'But I'm not planning to come back.'

'That's fine. I'm not planning to leave you.'

'What would you do there?'

'We could buy a pub. I've always wanted a little pub, and they say Irish pubs are never short of customers.'

'That they're not.' She smiled. Only a small, wan smile, but it was a beginning.

Gus Kriedemann and his bride sailed for Ireland in the liner *Otago*, which departed Brisbane just as the blue-purple jacaranda trees were bursting into bloom again.

Chapter Fifteen

After two long years away, Clover Chiswick was glad to be home. Her determination had eventually broken through official red tape. Even though the war was over by the time she arrived in South Africa, army despots were loath to give her any information or assistance, and when she did find Charlie's grave there was outright hostility to her plan to have his remains moved to a more fitting grave, not left in this pathetic wind-blown field.

They seemed to be under the impression that Clover wished to have him re-interred in a military cemetery, and when she pointed out that this was the last thing her brother would have wanted, they were more incensed. But she persevered, and at last she was able to stand by his grave in a small cemetery on the outskirts of Johannesburg guarded by a white stone church with a tall steeple.

Defiantly she chose the inscription, giving no indication of his military service.

Here lies a brave man was written on the polished granite tablet above his name and details.

'That's better, Charlie,' she said grimly. 'I'll put another one, exactly the same, back at the station so you can come home.'

After that she went on to London, where friends encouraged her to stay on, taking her on tours throughout England and the Continent, but all the time she was yearning for home.

Clover had had her fill of great cities and grand hotels, so one morning she went quietly into a shipping office and booked a suite for herself on the next ship scheduled for Sydney.

The clerk blinked at the tall, svelte woman. 'On your own, miss? Suites are doubles.'

'Yes. I think it would be fun to have a suite. I've a lot of fancy clothes to wear out before I get home.'

He shrugged. Some of these people made no sense at all. But she paid the full price without haggling for a reduction, so a splendid suite on A deck of the liner *Indiana* was hers.

Her aunt and Salty, her old housekeeper, were thrilled to welcome her home, but Clover didn't stay long in Toowoomba. Her first duty, as she saw it, was to visit the impressive Fairlea cattle station and stud.

It was a beautiful property and still well managed by Taffy, whom she'd met in town.

'Fairlea was meant for my brother,' she said. 'I don't know whether he would have kept it or not. I've been away from my own station for far too long; I'm going home now. I really don't like the idea of absentee owners so I have decided to sell Fairlea. I hope you don't think too badly of me.'

'Not at all, miss. It's up to you.'

'If it wasn't so far away from Plenty Station, I'd hang on to it,' she added apologetically, 'but it's two different worlds. Plenty is big and rugged, it's got sections I haven't even explored yet. I think that's the excitement.' She grinned. 'And we can run a helluva lot more cattle. If you ever decide to leave here, Taffy, look me up.'

'I'll keep that in mind, miss.'

Another duty confronted her. Not sure how she'd be received, since she'd left it so long, Clover called on Mrs Christiana Holloway.

As she rang the doorbell of this lovely house Clover looked about her curiously. She wondered if it would be possible to have real gardens round her house at Plenty instead of dry old stockyards. Some of the elegance of her travels had rubbed off on her.

A maid admitted her and led her through the house to a long drawing room with a spectacular view from the range. While she waited for Mrs Holloway she admired the serenity of this room, with its fine furnishings and the grand piano down the far end. Such good taste, she said to herself, with none of all that mad clutter that seems to be the mode overseas. The house at Plenty, she recalled, was a haphazard arrangement; rooms added on by the Chiswicks over the years and furniture purchased with more thought to necessity than comfort or appearance.

Once I settle down and see that everything's in order, why don't I build a new house? A really nice house.

She stood when Mrs Holloway entered, hoping she'd pass muster in a neat tailored suit of French silk, grey, with cream lapels. 'I'm Clover Chiswick,' she said, almost stammering.

The small, plump woman in rustling black reminded Clover of a pouter pigeon on guard.

'I know who you are,' she said. 'What can I do for you?'

'I thought it would be nice to talk to you.'

'Why? What do you want?'

Clover was taken aback. She realised she'd made the most awful gaffe. Charlie was, had been, this woman's natural grandson. Did she think that Charlie's sister had come seeking more from his inheritance than she'd already received? It seemed so from Mrs Holloway's frosty reception. Or did she resent the fact that Fairlea Station, a Holloway property, had come through Charlie to Clover?

Still standing, Clover decided that a quick, dignified exit would be the best move. Damn the woman!

Then she remembered why she had come. She grabbed her handbag and, fumbling, dragged out some photos wrapped in white muslin. 'I won't detain you,' she said, thrusting them forward. 'I thought you might like these.'

Mrs Holloway took the large flat parcel gingerly. As if they were a claim on her damn house, Clover thought angrily.

'They're photos of Charlie,' she snapped. 'But if you don't want them, give them back!'

'Oh.' Mrs Holloway softened. She untied the ribbon and began to unwrap them. 'Sit down, girl. Why have you brought them to me?'

Clover was outraged. 'They're photos of your grandson and my brother. Don't you care? I'm the only one left in my family and you're the only one left in yours. I admit that all we have in common now are those photos but I thought it would be nice to meet.'

Mrs Holloway glanced down at the large photo of Charlie in uniform and sighed. She looked up at Clover. 'Do forgive me. I've had a bad time lately. My former daughter-in-law has been bombarding me for years for more financial support and it has been wearing.'

'And you thought I was tarred with the same brush?'

'Oh no, not really.'

'Yes you did. You thought I was after the silver.' Clover was laughing. 'Go on, own up.'

The old woman sat back and peered at her. 'Something like that,' she admitted. And then she smiled. 'What a refreshing person you are.'

They pored over the photographs. 'This last one,' Clover said, 'is of Charlie's grave. In South Africa. I needed to tell you about that, I hoped you'd understand what I had to do.'

For the rest of the morning they talked. Clover heard the story of Vern and her mother. Christiana learned more about her grandson, and at the same time more about this young woman who wanted nothing from her except a remembrance of her beloved brother.

'Can't you stay for lunch?' she asked, not wanting to lose the girl so soon.

'Thank you, I'd be glad to.'

The afternoon cemented a lasting friendship.

'Will you write to me?' Clover asked.

'Of course I will. And you must promise that whenever you come to town you'll spare some time to stay here with me.'

'I promise. But if you ever need me, I'll be in sooner than that. We have to stick together, you and I. Vern and Charlie would have liked that.' Clover kissed her on the cheek as she was leaving. 'Besides, I've got a job for you. I intend to build a new homestead at Plenty Station, so I'll need your advice on the house and furnishings. Where to get things. Will you help me?'

'My dear, I'd be delighted.'

Christiana never did forget Clover Chiswick. Over the years she became the caring daughter that Christiana had always wanted. Her letters were a delight, her visits, for weeks on end, a constant joy. Christiana thanked the Lord that he'd spared someone for her to care about.

Friends and neighbours gathered at Plenty Station for a surprise party, organised by the manager, to welcome Clover home, and no one was disappointed.

She was overwhelmed by the reception, a typical two-day celebration that included horse races and barbecues and a dance in the main shed.

'I thought you'd have forgotten me by this,' she laughed.

'We thought you'd be bringing home a husband,' they countered.

Ambitious matrons were busy matchmaking, because Clover Chiswick, they knew, was now a very wealthy woman. Not only had she inherited two stations but all of the old Judge's assets, which, according to the official estimate published as usual in the paper, were considerable.

Gossip about Vern Holloway and Clover's mother surfaced again, but everyone was careful to avoid the subject in Clover's presence.

She had changed, they agreed; she was more outgoing now, mixing well with everyone, thoroughly enjoying her homecoming. But when she rode in the ladies' race and won easily, throwing her hat in the air, they laughed. The old Clover was home.

As soon as the party was over and a new day dawned, she joined forces with Slim, who'd remained on as manager, and began an inspection of the herds.

'I'm glad you're back,' he said to her. 'Plenty Station without a Chiswick in the saddle didn't seem right to me. Are you staying?'

'Yes, I can't tell you how marvellous it is to be home at last.

Clover didn't marry. There were flirtations, and 'understandings', but nothing came of them. Taking the advice of Christiana Holloway she handed her house over to Slim and his family and built a new homestead on a hill overlooking the valley, surrounding it with gardens that linked the main house with guest rooms. But the management of the station was still a priority, and she continued working closely with Slim, employing fencers, well-diggers, even a full-time veterinarian.

Clover became a familiar figure at cattle sales and meetings in Charleville, where men learned, at their cost, not to dismiss the opinions of a woman.

By the time she was in her forties, she was highly regarded as the owner of one of the finest cattle stations in the west, although some referred to her as an old maid. Clover knew, but it didn't bother her; she was too busy to care.

Then came the massive sandstorm, far worse than anything they had previously encountered. It blotted out the sun for days, invading the houses, leaving everything covered in fine dust, but more importantly causing cattle to wander off in all directions, throwing a big muster into confusion.

Clover was out with the men, searching for strays. They rode past the old worked-out mines at the Ten Mile, long abandoned, pushing on past the boundary of Plenty Station to retrieve a mob of cattle that outriders had said had stumbled this way.

Cursing, they followed the tracks of the cattle across the edge of a stony plateau, only to find that the mob had wheeled west into thick scrub.

And that was where she found him.

They spotted smoke from a campfire, and curious, Clover cut away with a stockman to investigate.

It was a primitive camp by a deep overgrown creek, just a log humpy with skins drying on sticks by a cold stone fireplace.

'An Abo?' the stockman said.

'I don't think so,' she replied thoughtfully.

A tall man with matted hair and a straggling beard emerged from the bush, rubbing at eyes that were streaming from the blight. 'What do you want?' he growled.

'What are you doing here, more like it?' the stockman retorted.

'Minding me own business, that's what.' The hermit turned away, slouching towards his hut.

'You better be careful lighting fires out here, mister.' The stockman seemed ready for a confrontation but Clover dismounted.

'You go on. I'll see to this.'

'Go on? I can't leave you here. What if he . . .'

'Never mind. I said go!'

He shrugged, wheeled his horse about and reluctantly, very slowly, headed back into the bush, glancing back over his shoulder, concerned for her.

She walked over to the fireplace and kicked at the embers. 'You might at least offer a person a cuppa tea, Brodie Court.'

He stopped. 'Who are you?'

476

'You know who I am. Let me have a look at those eyes.'

'They're all right!' he said impatiently. 'It's just since that storm.'

'The hell they are. Blight doesn't get that bad in a couple of days. I'll boil the billy.'

She could feel his irritation behind her as she lit the fire, but she took no notice of him. 'What have you been doing all these years?' she asked.

'Travelling.'

'Where to?' Clover could see that his eyes were seriously damaged and she needed to gain his confidence. He couldn't stay here.

'To the north. To the far west. And to the south,' he replied grudgingly, telling her nothing.

'You must have seen a lot of the country.'

'More than most.'

'And what brought you back this way?'

'Me feet.'

She laughed. 'Don't go cantankerous on me, mate. I've still got a short fuse.'

Clover shuddered as she saw him feel for a tree stump behind him and sit down, realising he was almost blind.

'You do know who I am?' she asked apologetically. 'I took it for granted . . .'

He held up his hand. 'You always had a bossy voice. You still at Plenty?'

'Oh yes, it's been mine for a long time now. I've made a lot of changes. You ought to come and see it.'

'I'll do that one day.'

He objected to her bathing his eyes with the hot water but she persevered, putting up with his grumbles. 'Keep your hands away from the cloth and let me do it,' she said. 'I've had practice with the blight. Have you got any ointment or boracic?'

'None of that stuff was any good. They'll get better on their own. It was that damned storm made them worse.'

So he had tried the cures, she pondered as she made tea with the powdery remains of tea leaves she found in the bottom of a tin. That was enough to tell her that Brodie had come to the end of the line.

He sat quietly with her, drinking the weak, unsweetened

477

tea, and eventually he spoke. 'I would have written to you when your brother died, I knew you cared about him. But they said you'd gone.'

'Yes,' she sighed. 'Charlie's death was a terrible blow. But I went to South Africa myself and buried him properly, with a decent headstone.'

'You did?' he said with a spark of interest for the first time, so she pressed the point.

'I'll tell you all about it one day.'

'You'd better be getting along,' he said, at length.

'I was hoping you'd come to visit me.'

The broad smile was still there behind the bush of greying black hair. 'I might, one of these days.'

'Nothing like the present.'

'Can't be done.'

'Yes it can. You're on my neighbour's property.'

'I know that. I'm not completely stupid.'

Or blind, she thought. Not yet. 'Then you know they won't appreciate fires being lit here. The bush is tinder dry, a spark could set off a bush fire.'

'So I'll move on.'

'Good. You can come over to Plenty for a while. I could do with some company.'

They argued and Clover won. They argued about who should ride her horse, since he didn't have a mount, and Brodie won. He had no belongings worth collecting, except two sugar bags of small rocks which he refused to leave behind.

'What are they?' she asked.

'Specimens.'

'Of what?'

'Rocks.'

'Do you still prospect for opal?'

'Gave that away years ago.'

'Where did these come from?' she asked, unwilling to load her horse with this rubbish.

'Round here,' he said. 'It was something to do. I'm not much use for anything else.'

Exasperated, she stared at the bulky bags. 'Are they worth the trouble of carting back, Brodie? How do you know they're any good?'

He packed one bag on the horse and slung the other one over his shoulder. 'You mean, how can I see? Well, when you've got all the time in the world, you listen for that chink of crystal. It's not the worth of them that counts, it's that music. I'd almost forgotten the fun of it.'

The stockmen stared as their boss rode into the mustering camp with the bleary old hermit loping beside her.

By the time the doctor arrived, Clover had her guest shorn and shaven, looking human again. Even though his dark hair was well-peppered with grey, he was still a handsome man, she thought, his face leaner, accentuating his strong, firm features.

When he'd finished examining the patient, which seemed to take ages, the doctor came out to report to Clover. 'He's malnourished but he's fit enough. As for his eyes,' he shook his head, 'the left eye is too far gone. Apparently he caught the sandy blight in the western desert. Your Mr Court has been quite a traveller. From all accounts he's criss-crossed the continent, investigating mines and pushing on.'

'No success?'

'That's the strangest part. He says he made all he needed to keep moving, that the joy was in the finding. But maybe that was just a boast.'

'I don't think so. He's a contrary fellow.'

'True. And that's his problem. He went to doctors in Perth and Adelaide, but he wouldn't accept their diagnoses. He says they were all no-hopers! I don't think he really understood what they were saying. There is no cure for the blight, but his other eye, his right eye, has a cataract growing over it. They probably told him they couldn't do anything until the cataract finished growing, and that's correct, but it's a shock for a man to hear he has to go blind before they can assist him.'

'Doctor, he's all but blind now.'

'I know. But that's the good news. We can remove the cataract now.'

'And the right eye will have sight?'

'It should do.'

'Good Lord! Oh, thank you, doctor. This is great news. My word, your bedside manner must be working overtime. I could hardly get a word out of him.'

The doctor smiled. 'That's not surprising. He's thoroughly shamed by his blindness. "Struck down to useless", as he put it. He is embarrassed for you to see him like that.'

Clover sighed. 'As if I'd mind! He's an old friend. Can you operate on him?'

'No. We'll bring out an eye specialist. I'm not sure Brodie believes me yet, so just make sure you keep him here.'

'That's marvellous! Now don't worry about the cost. Let me cover the bills.'

The doctor was surprised. 'He's not short of cash, Clover. He had a roll in one of his dusty old bags. He has already paid me.'

'Then what was he doing living out there like a hermit?' she said crossly.

'He says that since his eyesight started petering out he just wandered back to country he knew.'

'So that he could find his way about I suppose.'

The doctor led Clover out to the front of the house, looking out at the soft glow of sunset. 'A blind man couldn't survive in the bush, not a white man anyway. No, I think he'd have only been following his nose for the last year or so, trekking to nowhere. He'd lost interest in life since it meant living in darkness. Just as well you came along.'

'That was only chance.'

'Well, he's a lucky man. You found him just in time.'

A month after the cataract was removed, Brodie marvelled that his sight had been restored in that eye.

'Glory be to God!' he cried, 'and to the delicate hands of Mr McDowell. You will thank him for me won't you, doctor?'

'I surely will, Brodie. And he gave me this to present to you. It's a patch to cover your blind eye.'

Brodie took it and held it away from him by his fingertips as if it might bite him. 'I'll not wear a thing like that!' He turned to Clover. 'Did you ever see the like? A man would look a damn fool getting about like a drunken pirate!'

'You don't have to wear it,' the doctor said. 'It was just a thought.'

But Clover had other ideas. She took a hand mirror to Brodie. 'Take a good look here before you throw out the patch.'

The doctor was startled. 'I don't think that's necessary, Clover,' he warned.

'Yes it is,' she said firmly. 'It will help him to make up his mind.'

For the first time Brodie was able to see the ugly results of the disease on his blind eye. 'Oh, Jesus!' he said. 'What a mess! There's no colour left at all.'

'That's right,' Clover said. 'Now if you wear the patch your face will look normal.'

She grinned as Brodie wasted no time slipping the patch over his eye. 'I'm only wearing it to please you,' he growled. 'I'm not the one who has to look at the bad eye. But here,' he dug in his pocket and produced two small lumps of glittering silver. 'One for you, doctor, it's twisted like a corkscrew so don't leave it in a bar. And yours, Clover, it might do for a brooch or something.'

'Good heavens!' the doctor said, 'you don't have to do this Brodie!'

'Yes I do, for your kindnesses.'

'Where did you get them?'

'Picked them up in a silver mine in my travels.'

'Thank you,' Clover said. 'It's a fascinating piece. And as heavy as lead.'

'As heavy as silver,' Brodie corrected.

When the doctor went on his way, Brodie turned back to Clover. 'I'd best be moving on too now. It's been terribly kind of you to have me here all this time.'

'You don't have to go yet. I want to show you round the station.'

'Ah, come on! You're feeling sorry for me and you want to take me in like a lost soul!'

'Why would I feel sorry for you? There's nothing wrong with you now. I'm simply inviting you to stay awhile. I could do with the company.'

'Well I'm sorry about that but I have to go.'

'Where?'

He adjusted the patch fractiously. 'What does it matter?'

'Don't you think you're getting a bit long in the tooth to be taking to the road again?'

They argued. They always argued. But Brodie stayed the while. He was soon back on a horse, insisting on making himself useful, after first clearing his presence with the foreman.

'I didn't want to be butting in,' he told the man who appreciated the thought.

'Any friend of Clover's is a friend of mine,' he said. 'We're all glad to see you well again and, on a station this size, we can always do with an extra hand.

Some time later Clover said to him, 'I heard what happened at the Ten Mile. About your nephew. Is that why you went bush?'

'I can't remember,' he snapped.

'Christ!' she snorted. 'You're a bloody cantankerous old coot.'

'And I've noticed your language hasn't improved for all your fine airs.'

'I haven't got fine airs!'

'Not so you'd notice! And by the way, the two wells down by the widow tree have dried up. For that matter with the dry season coming on they all need checking.'

'Then why don't you go out and do it?'

Brodie laughed. 'Why don't we both go?'

The 'while' stretched on and on. Clover encouraged Brodie to stay and he never did get around to leaving. She resumed her business interests, attending district meetings, and left the station for weeks on end visiting friends in Charleville and Toowoomba but Brodie preferred to stay at Plenty Station. He still had no interest in the outside world.

On quiet nights, after dinner, they sat on the veranda looking out at the starry skies, sometimes talking, or arguing, sometimes saying little, content in their own company.

They never married. Old folks said they lived like brother and sister, as if Clover had Charlie back. Younger folks, doubting, looked askance with a wink. But then no one really knew.

When Clover Chiswick died, in her sixty-fourth year, not, as everyone had expected, from a fall from a horse, since she still rode the range as if she were twenty, but quietly in her sleep, her friend, Brodie Court, mourned her deeply.

He kept the house exactly as she'd left it, especially her neat bedroom, and although he allowed the housekeeper to remove her clothes, her collection of wide-brimmed work hats remained slung from a rack in the corner.

He ordered a gravestone that matched exactly the one already weathering in the small Plenty cemetery, that of the long-forgotten Charles Chiswick, so that sister and brother could be remembered side by side.

He made sure that the station continued to be run as Clover would have had it, keeping its proud name as a first-rate station, because Clover had left a simple will, leaving everything she owned to her dear friend, Brodie Court.

Chapter Sixteen

'Good God!' Stanley said. 'I didn't know he was still alive!'

'Obviously he's not,' Angus Wickham grinned, and his father turned on him.

'Don't get smart with me, young man! Either you're being deliberately obtuse or you haven't the capacity to grasp a simple remark. Where's his will?'

Angus frowned. 'As far as we can ascertain there is no will. He died intestate. I'll sort it out, there's no need for you to worry about it.'

Stanley Wickham, the founder of the law firm had retired years ago, much to Angus's relief, but that relief had been short lived. Whenever he felt like it the old man would bowl into his former office, which Angus now occupied, and without so much as a by your leave, scrutinise papers and files.

Stanley believed he was being helpful, that his advice was needed. His son saw it as interference but dare not say so.

'I'm not worrying about it,' his father said loftily. 'I'm just interested to know who will be the recipient of his estate.'

'There'll be someone about. We'll dig up his next of kin.'

'I would suggest you take one step at a time and begin with our own files.'

'Why would I do that?'

'Because Brodie Court was one of my first clients and quite a good friend of mine.'

'Oh, really? Well there might be something in our archives.'

'It wouldn't occur to you to ask me, I suppose?'

'Righto! When did you last see him?'

Stanley coughed, stalling. How long ago was it? Almost half a century. But he'd prefer not to admit that. 'Quite a while. I tell you what, leave this to me. I'll track down the beneficiary. It'll be an interesting exercise.'

'Father, we pay people to do that work.'

'You what? More money than sense! But if you insist you can pay me. Now let me see. Where did he die? And when? I'll get right on it.'

Angus was even further irritated when Stanley announced his intention to visit Plenty Station in search of information that could lead to Brodie's next of kin.

'Why are you bothering, father? We can advertise.'

'And get all sorts of ratbag replies. I won't hear of it. Your wife's brother, Donald, has kindly agreed to drive me, he's a stock and station agent, he can take an inventory while we're there.'

'It's a long and difficult drive,' Angus protested. But Stanley had made up his mind.

He had to admit it was a horrendous journey. The car broke down several times in the heat and dust, the radiator steaming like a kettle. Further out, past Charleville, they got bogged in deep sand several times and tyres blew on the rough roads. Eventually they had to rely on real horse power to tow them to a nearby cattle station where they stayed while repairs were undertaken. At times they wondered if the old Cobb and Co coaches, now obsolete, might not have been a faster mode of transport after all, since they were held up for days waiting for replacement parts to be sent out.

However, the hospitality of station people in this lonely countryside soothed frayed tempers and gave Stanley an opportunity to learn more about Clover Chiswick, who had been quite famous in these parts. His firm had drawn up her last will and testament, at her request, during one of her visits to Toowoomba.

'Didn't it occur to you to mention this to me?' Stanley had stormed as he began his investigation into the source of Brodie Court's wealth.

'No. Why should I? Miss Chiswick left all of her estate to one person, there was no difficulty about it. His name didn't mean a thing to me, and no one challenged it.'

'But if I'd seen it, I'd have recognised his name. Good heavens, Angus, this is an immense responsibility! Her estate was worth more than a million pounds, and by Court's death the value had increased. You speak as if they had some small farm on the Downs.'

Angus shrugged. 'It's easy enough for you to talk. What would you have done?'

'I'd have followed through as you should have done when Court was made beneficiary, and seen to it that he left a will. If that was done, we wouldn't be in this tangle now. Look at this!' He waved the list of assets at his son. 'It's not just the property, there are bank accounts and investments you can't jump over. And from what I've been told, hardly a penny of it has been touched, reinvested, or looked after since the day she died. Brodie Court was one of the wealthiest clients we ever had and you didn't even bother to contact him after the disbursement.'

'I never even met him,' Angus said defensively. 'He signed the papers related to the transfer of property and funds and returned them, and our bill was paid promptly.'

'And you didn't offer further services and advice, to keep him on our books? It beats me! I don't know what will become of this firm. You're too lackadaisical, you young people. A man like that . . . you should have gone out to visit him.'

'I didn't want to intrude. I heard he was a man who preferred to keep to himself.'

'You heard!' Stanley said angrily. 'If you'd heard that Mr Court was a big fish in the social swim you'd have been out there with knobs on! Couldn't you at least have requested that he lodge his will with you for safekeeping?'

'But he didn't leave a will.'

'God Almighty! That would have been a reminder to him to prepare one, and given you a foot in the door. Not that you needed one! Anyway, who says he died intestate?'

'Everyone! His staff, and friends from an adjoining station, they searched the house. And there's no record at the Registrar's office.'

'We'll see about that. I'll look around myself.'

Stanley hadn't been surprised to learn that Brodie had died a rich man, but not in the manner he'd expected. The Irishman had boasted that opals would make him wealthy, that they would bring him luck, and they'd certainly done that, but he'd gone far beyond being just an opal dealer.

Over the years, as a collector and investor in opals, Stanley Wickham had toured opal fields in New South Wales and in Queensland, always on the lookout for Brodie, but no one knew of him. There were now mines producing light opals in western Queensland, and Lightning Ridge was the place for the beautiful black opals. But somewhere out west, where Brodie had prospected, were those wondrous dark boulder opals. It seemed that Brodie had taken his secret to the grave.

'But they're out there,' Stanley mused. 'One day someone will stumble across them, someone with Brodie's luck.'

And so Brodie had ended up living at Plenty Station as a friend and companion to the famous Miss Chiswick.

How had that come about?

His hosts on the cattle station, en route to Plenty Station couldn't enlighten him on that subject, but gossip survived. As they talked, Fairlea Station was mentioned and Stanley sat up with a jolt. Of course! Vivien Holloway!

What had become of Vivien Holloway? She had lost Fairlea to her late husband's illegitimate son. How could he forget her rage?

The station elders could pick up the story from there, and nodding, Stanley began to piece it together.

The illegitimate son had been Charlie Chiswick, killed in the Boer War so long ago. Two world wars had almost obliterated memory of that skirmish. And so Fairlea had passed to his sister. Who else but Clover?

'You remember old Judge Chiswick?' an elderly lady asked him as they sat reminiscing over an excellent port.

'Well I do,' he laughed.

'Then who do you think inherited his estate as well? His only daughter! Clover!'

Stanley sat back. 'Ah. I see. It's all starting to make sense now.'

'And the rest,' she laughed, nudging her husband. 'Tell him the rest. They say money makes money.'

The white-haired cattle man lounged back in his chair. 'Clover and Christiana Holloway were great mates. Clover often came to town with us, for race meetings, cattle sales . . . you know. And she always stayed with Christiana at that big house at the top of the range. You know the one?'

'Yes.'

'Who owns it now?'

'I couldn't say. It has changed hands many times over the years.'

'A lovely house,' the cattle man said. 'We used to go to dances there in the early days.'

'Never mind that,' his wife interrupted. 'Get on with it.'

'I will, I will,' he said testily. 'You see the connection, Mr Wickham? It was young Charlie. He was Clover's brother and old Mrs Holloway's only grandson, though illegitimate. So the two women got together. Old and young they might have been but Clover had lost her mother when she was a kid, and Christiana had lost her only child. That made for a powerful friendship.'

'And so . . .' his wife urged.

'And so when the old lady died, she left everything, lock stock and barrel, to Clover!'

'Good Lord!' Stanley said, thinking he'd strangle his son for passing up clients like this.

'It's really quite decadent,' his wife laughed. 'Clover was the last person who needed a penny from old Mrs Holloway. It only made her richer than ever! I mean she had Fairlea *and* Plenty Station, neither of them to be sneezed at, and the Holloway wealth to boot. And to think she wasn't even one to care about money.'

'What was she like?'

'A Tartar! More interested in horses and cattle than people. And she had a tongue on her! Not the sort of person you'd want to cross.'

'Ah . . . I don't know,' her husband said dreamily. 'I remember Clover as a girl. She was a tall blonde. A fine figure of a girl. And as straight as a die. I liked her. She always called a spade a spade, but nothing wrong with that.'

'Did you meet her friend, Mr Court?'

'Oh yes. We met him. Not often though. Only at the station. He kept to himself. Never went to town or joined in anything.'

'He wore an eye-patch,' his wife said. 'He was blind in one eye.'

'He was what? I haven't heard this before.'

'The blight,' she said. 'Rumour has it that Clover took him

in out of pity in the first place, because both eyes were afflicted and he couldn't see a foot in front of him. But she called in a specialist. Who else but Clover could summon a specialist to go all the way out there from Brisbane? Anyway, the specialist saved one eye, and after that Court just stayed on.'

'Did she know him before this?'

'Some people said she did. But Clover was never one to explain her actions. Not her. Sometimes she'd laugh and say Brodie couldn't join us for lunch because he was busy with his hobby, but I think that was just a cover-up. We were all curious about him and she was probably embarrassed.'

'Clover embarrassed!' her husband snapped. 'Never! He was her guest! It was immaterial to her how long he stayed, and she didn't give a damn what anyone thought.'

As they set off the next day, Donald, Stanley's driver, peered at the dusty road ahead. 'Do you think we'll make the rest of the way in one piece?'

'I hope so,' Stanley said, settling the large goggles on his face. 'They said we're to ring them on the party line when we get to Plenty Station to let them know we've arrived safely, otherwise they'll send out riders to search for us.'

'Some consolation. At least we won't expire by the roadside. If you can call it that. You talked to those people till all hours last night. Did you learn anything?'

'Oh yes. Background information which was very interesting. Quite a story. But as for Brodie, all I have is a large gap from the time I last heard from him until the day he turned up at Plenty Station. He didn't marry Miss Chiswick and there's definitely no issue. People out here wouldn't miss that.'

'Angus said you shouldn't be dragging out here. He could have advertised to find the next of kin.'

'He would. He has no spirit of adventure! Press on, driver!'

The manager of Plenty Station could not offer any further information about Brodie Court. 'He was here when I took on the job, her previous foreman bought himself a station further north. I had been foreman here for five years when Miss Clover died. Brodie promoted me to manager. I'd have expected nothing less, but it was a bloody miserable time. We all broke our hearts. She was a woman you could be real proud of. But then, one day she's all about, and the next day she's gone! Just gone! Died in her sleep.'

'It must have been a shock!'

'I'll say it was.'

'How did Brodie react?'

'How would you expect? The poor bastard was shattered. He couldn't believe it! Then after the funeral, what does he do but pack up his gear! Said he was leaving.'

'"No rush," I told him. "I might be coming with you. The new owners of Plenty mightn't want to keep me on. If they come in with sons, like a lot of them do, a foreman has to move on." But he was hell bent on leaving, the silly old bugger.

'"Give me a horse," he said, "and I'll be on me way."

'"Where are you going?" I asked him but he just says, "Nowhere in particular. I might head west again."

'Then the next thing we heard, Clover went and left the whole show to Brodie. And didn't we cheer? Clover didn't let us down. But he was flabbergasted! Not impressed at all.'

'"What did she have to go and do that for?" he kept saying.

'But I told him he had to take a hold. We've got a big staff here and a job to do. I had to stand over him to make him sign all the papers they sent, and finally he did, grouching for days.'

'Did he take an interest in the station after that?'

'Oh sure. But he'd always done that. He knew the place backwards. He just had to resign himself to the fact that she wasn't around any more. He was a good boss, believe me, don't write him off as anything less.'

'I wouldn't do that,' Stanley said. 'I knew Brodie Court myself.'

'You did?' A warm smile spread across the manager's weather-beaten face. 'Then I don't have to preach to you.'

'Not at all. How did he die?'

The manager stared. 'You don't know? It was in the papers out here. Then I suppose our local news isn't much interest in the big towns.'

'I suppose not,' Stanley said lamely. 'The bank notified our law firm since we handled Miss Chiswick's will. Banks would have been very interested, right up the line!'

'They sure would.' Genuine grief clouded his face. 'Brodie

saved my son's life. He fell down a well. He's only two. Brodie heard the commotion and came running. I wasn't home and my wife was hysterical. That old well is deep, dried up luckily, but she couldn't get to him. She could hear him crying down there and she lowered the bucket, yelling to him to climb into it, but even if he had understood being so scared, he wouldn't have been able to reach it.'

'Did Brodie get him out?'

'Oh yes,' the manager sighed. 'He shimmied down that well like it was no trouble at all, then he yelled at them to drop the bucket. Apparently he had some trouble reaching up to get the boy in the bucket, so that took a while, but he was a very tall chap and he managed it. They pulled the boy up and dropped the rope down to Brodie.'

The manager stopped to stare helplessly about him. 'It's no use blaming anyone. There was only the women and a couple of young rouseabouts, they were frantic, trying to do their best. If Brodie had waited a bit, to tell them what to do before he went down, it would have been all right. But by the time any of the men came in it was too late.'

'What happened?'

'They put all hands to the windlass to haul the boy up, and that was fine. They were so excited that he wasn't hurt except for a few bumps and bruises they did the same thing for Brodie. My wife still hasn't got over the shock. For his weight they should have brought a horse to haul him out, but they didn't think of that, they heaved and pulled on the windlass and they nearly got him to the top. Then the windlass collapsed. He was killed in the fall.'

'Ah dear God,' Stanley whispered.

'He's buried up there in the little cemetery, and we've ordered a headstone the same as the others to keep it neat. *The Western Chronicle* had a big write-up about him. They did him proud. Said how the owner of Plenty Station gave his life to rescue a boy who had fallen down a mine . . .'

'But he fell down a well.'

'Yes. They made a mistake there but I suppose it doesn't matter. It hurts me that I never got a chance to thank him, but my family will never forget Brodie Court.'

Stanley took the manager's arm and walked with him back

to the house. 'I'm sure he wouldn't have wanted thanks. At least he knew the boy was safe.'

'I suppose you're right. He never liked a fuss.'

They opened the gate to the garden and Stanley stopped. 'There's a grand sweeping view across the valley from the house, but I noticed this morning that here in this charming garden one feels secluded. I can almost feel them here, Brodie and Miss Chiswick.'

'Oh yes, they loved this garden. Brodie did a lot of work here himself, he used to joke that he was a born farmer, just to annoy her. He'd even call her station a farm for the fun of it!'

'Blasphemy!' Stanley smiled. 'It seems to me that they must have had similar attitudes. Somewhere along the line, for reasons lost to us, the pair met and became soul mates. Independent and yet together. Both very private people. Brodie never spoke of where he came from? Apart from the obvious, Ireland.'

'No, Mr Wickham. Never.'

'And did he ever have any visitors?'

'No, sir. Is there anything else I can show you?'

'I don't think so. I've been through the office papers but I can't find anything personal. No letters, photographs, nothing. I'm no further advanced in my search for his next of kin, there are no leads at all. It's almost as if he didn't live here.'

'Except for his hobby room.'

'What's that?'

'He used to potter about in a shack at the back of the house. I reckon he was an amateur minerologist. Miss Clover called it his hobby room, he always kept it locked, didn't like anyone going in there. It's just a dusty old room with lumps of rock lying about. Nothing of value.'

Stanley was tiring, the hard dry heat proving a little too much for him, but this sounded more like the Brodie he'd known. There was a chance that Brodie had left a hint of some sort in his work room, something that might give him a lead, so he'd have to check.

The shack was musty, stifling, so the manager threw open the windows, revealing long benches covered in a residue of dust and rock chips. Even the floor crunched as they walked in.

'He wasn't the tidiest of workers,' Stanley commented, pushing aside a tall stool. 'It's more like stepping into a cave, but let's have a look here.'

He examined the lumps of rock and crystal that had been cut and polished into various shapes, and others that were still in their natural shape. 'They're quite attractive, some of them have interesting colours and patterns but they're not worth anything.'

'Poor Brodie, all that work for nothing.'

'I hardly think so,' Stanley said. 'Brodie would have known at first glance that none of this stuff had any value.' He unwrapped a folded chamois to discover gleaming gem-cutters' tools and then he stared thoughtfully at the hundreds of pieces that Brodie had been working on. 'Do you know what I think? He was practising on all this stuff! Just practising! It takes a long time for a man to become an expert gem-cutter, mistakes are costly. And it would have been even more difficult for a man with only one eye. Still,' he shrugged, 'that doesn't answer my question. Obviously he wasn't given to paperwork. There's not a note in sight. I've come to another dead end.'

As they prepared to leave the shack, Stanley took one last look around. 'What's in that drawer?'

'What drawer?'

'Under that bench in the far corner?'

'I don't know, I've never noticed it before.'

It was a wide, slim drawer, and Stanley was surprised that it slid out easily. He lifted it out and swept aside rubble to place it evenly on the bench, and then he laughed. 'Ah! Now we're talking! This is more like it!'

The drawer was stuffed with soft white muslin but on the top were several lumps of uncut opals.

'Black opal!' the manager cried.

'Yes! Look at the deep dark colour of them. But these are pieces of rare boulder opal.' He rushed over to the light with them. 'They're gorgeous! This was what he intended to work on.'

'Intended's right!' the manager called. 'Come on back and see what I've found!'

He'd removed the layers of muslin and underneath, nestling in cotton wool, were three rows of superb opals.

'Jesus wept!' he exclaimed. 'They must be worth a fortune! And look! Each one is named!'

Hardly daring to touch them Stanley gazed at the opals in delight as his companion read the names on the small stiff cards.

'This is Clover's writing,' the manager added, 'she had a real neat hand. And ah! This big opal is called *Plenty*!'

Stanley shuddered as he grabbed it and passed it to him, but then he too was fascinated by the names Brodie had chosen for his parade of gems. 'It's a fitting name for this wide and wonderful stone,' he said, replacing it. 'And here we have *Parrot*! Look into this opal, I swear I can see the shape and colour of a parrot.'

'This one,' the manager echoed, 'the red and gold one is called *Glory*.' He bent over looking along the names. 'Here's one called *Tullymore*. I bet it's the name of a station somewhere.'

'They're all of very high quality,' Stanley murmured, still overwhelmed at their find.

'Why did he leave them stuck in a drawer? Why didn't he sell them?'

'Because they were his,' Stanley said quietly. 'He loved opals, he was completely entranced by them.'

Eventually he decided he'd have to take the opals back to town to have them valued as part of the estate. 'I'll give you a receipt,' he told the manager who was happy to acquiesce.

'Suits me. I don't want the responsibility of them.'

Gently, the old man wrapped each opal and then packed them in a fold of muslin, but as he removed the last piece of cloth he looked down at the base of the wooden drawer and there it was. Just one sheet of parchment paper. The last will and testament of Brodie Court.

And it was witnessed by Clover Chiswick.

Although Brodie's statement obviously referred to the opals, his only possessions at the time, the wording was short and concise, sufficient for Stanley's purposes.

Being of good health and of sound mind, I hereby leave all my worldly goods and chattels to my sister-in-law, Trella Kriedemann, of Tullymore, Ireland.

Kriedemann! Stanley was astonished. His first meeting with Brodie Court came flooding back to him as if it were yesterday. The day Brodie had dragged him over to the pub to meet his friend, Gus Kriedemann. The name had stayed with him, because for years the Kriedemanns had owned a bakery in town, but it, and the name, had long gone.

Had Gus married Brodie's sister-in-law? How had that come about? And if so, how had he ended up in Ireland? Or had he not?

'Another mystery,' he muttered.

But by the time they left the shack, Stanley was all smiles, hugging the precious parcel.

'I can't wait to see my son's face!' he said. 'I've found the will! He wanted to advertise for the next of kin! A fat lot of good that would have done him. This will teach him to listen to his father!'

The elderly man hummed as he drove his new Morris car through the quiet streets of Limerick one Sunday afternoon. He was thoroughly enjoying himself. The search for Brodie's next of kin had brought him halfway across the world and provided him with a splendid excuse to see the Old Country.

Angus, as usual, had tried to put obstacles in his way. 'What's the point? They have solicitors in Ireland you know! I can appoint someone to represent us.'

'Can you indeed? More money wasted! And who is to say this Trella Kriedemann is still alive? And if not? Who is next in line? I'd prefer to attend to Brodie's affairs myself.'

'Good God, father! You talk as if he were your best friend! You never even kept in touch.'

'I was the first lawyer he engaged to conduct his affairs. He trusted me to open his mail and bank monies that were sent to him from his Dublin representative. I appreciated his trust, now I can repay him by seeing that this matter is dealt with efficiently. Has it ever occurred to you to wonder why Clover Chiswick came over to our firm towards the end, even to lodging her will here?'

'Should I need to?'

'One would think so, but never mind that now. I believe that Brodie had spoken to her, at some stage, of his acquaintance with me, and that's why she came here. To a firm that knew the man, since he had no friends outside of the people at her station.'

Angus shrugged. 'Conjecture.'

'But logical. Anyway, I have made up my mind. I will go to London and from thence to Ireland to find this village of Tullymore.'

'Madness! It's too soon after the war. London is devastated. It's no place to be going now. The travelling will be too much for you.'

Stanley laughed. 'Are you trying to tell me that a six weeks' sea voyage, travelling first class on a luxury liner, will be more trying than that bumpy six-hundred-mile drive out to Plenty Station? I am looking forward to the voyage, and I'm only sorry that your dear mother isn't alive to come with me. We always promised ourselves a trip to England but the war intervened and then it was too late for her.'

His son was no match for Stanley's determination and in the end, he was even enthusiastic.

'Glad to be rid of me, I fear,' Stanley muttered to himself. He had survived the journey west to Plenty Station. He had enjoyed the voyage to England, gratified that his Bridge playing was of a high enough standard to keep him busy. He had bought the car in London, very pleased to find that the sales tax was waived under the new export laws to boost trade, and his Morris was a real bargain.

Then he'd driven across England and taken the car by ferry to Ireland to continue his mission.

'Too old am I?' These adventures seemed to have given him a new lease of life, he hadn't felt so well in years. Now he was beginning to wonder why he had retired.

He booked into a small hotel, finding himself the centre of interest; the new car, even a modest car like the Morris Major, and the Australian accent, drawing curiosity. Everyone seemed to have relations in Australia and they were all keen to enquire of them. His host was astounded that he'd driven right across England, because of the distance, not, he noticed because of his age. That made him happier still. No one saw anything strange about a seventy-year-old man travelling all this way on his own.

When asked his occupation, amid all the other questions,

Stanley announced he was a solicitor. His retirement, he decided, was behind him.

The next morning he enquired of the best route to Tullymore, since he'd found it on the map but had already discovered that road signs in this land were unreliable. With hopefully a clear understanding of the route, he packed his bags in the car. He was ready to leave when a bulky middle-aged policeman came running towards him.

'Sir!' he called. 'They say you're going to Tullymore?'

'Yes.'

'Then would ye mind giving me a lift? Me bicycle's broken down once and for all. I've been tellin' them they'll have to sport me a new one.'

'Not at all,' Stanley said. 'I'd be glad of the company.'

Sergeant Jim Corrigan was a talkative chap and excellent company, pointing out ancient landmarks and giving a running commentary on local residents and their histories, but it wasn't long before Corrigan's questions began.

'You're a solicitor, Mr Wickham?'

'Yes.'

'And do you have relations in Tullymore?'

'No I don't. As a matter of fact I'm here on business.'

'You've come all this way on business?' Corrigan was understandably curious. His eyes lit up. 'What business would bring you to Tullymore?'

'I am trying to locate a woman.'

'Not a felon I'm hoping?'

'Heavens no. I just need to find this lady, if she's still alive. You could be just the man I need to help me. Would you know a lady called Trella Kriedemann?'

'Trella! Sure I do. She's well known about these parts. Getting on she is, and a bit of a battleaxe, but I could take you to their farm. It's in the valley, this side of the village.'

Stanley was delighted. 'This *is* good news.'

'Come to think of it,' Corrigan said. 'Old Gus Kriedemann is Australian too. Would you be knowing him?'

For the first time since he had landed in Ireland, Stanley was able to answer that very question in the affirmative, and he could hardly contain his excitement. He'd made it. He'd found them.

'They had a pub over in Killourn for many years,' Corrigan

continued. 'Did well too and when they retired they bought the farm in the valley. They say Trella grew up in these parts, she was a Miss Grogan, a lot of Grogans around. Me mother's related to them herself. But what would you be wanting with Trella?'

'Just a few words. Enquiries. You know.'

'Can't say I do. But you've not bad news for her?'

'I don't think so.'

'Good news, then?'

'Is that Tullymore up ahead?' Stanley asked.

'Ah yes. Turn off here. To your left, sir.'

'Where?' Stanley was flustered.

'Back a bit, we've over-run the turnoff to the valley. Be careful you don't get bogged there on the corner, it's a bit damp.'

Reversing, Stanley managed the turn into a picturesque country lane and drove slowly across a wide green valley, pondering the end of his journey, not without a pinch of disappointment. He always felt let down like this when a case was over, win or lose, and the next client was the only cure. Now he'd have to retrace his steps without any particular purpose except to return home. Maybe he should go to Scotland and search out his ancestors.

'Whoa there!' Corrigan cried, 'we've passed the gate. This is their cottage.'

Reversing again, this time along a hedge, Stanley stopped the car in front of a low gate, rousing two dogs that were noisily competing for honours as defenders of their territory.

The sergeant was out of the car in an instant, an opportunity to be centre stage in this intrigue was not to be missed. He saw the elderly woman working in the garden and called to her. 'Mrs Kriedemann, a word with you! There's a gentleman here to see you! All the way from Australia!'

She was older than Stanley had expected, but then years moved swiftly. She stood up with a keen glance at them, wiping her hands on her apron and pushing strands of grey hair from her face to tuck them in a knitted wool cap that reminded Stanley of a tea cosy. But there was nothing cosy about Trella Kriedemann.

'What do you want?' she called, no hint of welcome in the voice.

'Mr Wickham here wants to talk to you,' Corrigan called above the yapping of the dogs.

As she came towards them Stanley saw past the lines on her face to the fine bone structure, thinking she must have been a good-looking woman in her day.

'Do I know you?' she asked him, her gaze firm and direct.

'No, madam, I wanted to ask you about Mr Brodie Court.'

'Humph! What's he up to now?'

'Mrs Kriedemann, it's my sad duty to inform you that Mr Court passed away last November.'

'Oh.' She seemed to consider this for a minute. 'I'm sorry to hear that.'

'He was your brother-in-law, I believe?'

'He was that. He was brother to my first husband Michael Court who is buried here in Tullymore.'

'And he was an opal miner in the early days? Is that right?'

Her face slammed shut, the eyes cold. She turned away to shush the dogs. 'Yes,' she admitted grimly. 'Is that all you wanted to know?' The gate was still firmly closed.

'Not quite. There's a matter of his estate.'

'His estate?' she echoed. 'What's that got to do with me?'

Corrigan was practically dancing about with impatience. 'Looks to me, Trella, as if you've got an inheritance here.' He put his hand on the gate as if to take his friend in but she stood her ground.

'Ah, get out with you! I haven't seen Brodie for thirty years! Longer!'

'That doesn't make any difference,' Corrigan tried to explain. 'You have to hear Mr Wickham out. He's come far to see you.'

'What's an estate? Some cash?' she asked Stanley. 'Has he left us some cash?'

'Yes. That's why I came to see you, Mrs Kriedemann. You're his sole beneficiary.'

Trella stared at him. 'You wouldn't want to be joking with me, sir!'

'Goodness me, not at all.'

'Then what about his own family? Wouldn't they be better entitled than me?'

'Mr Court had no other family. He never married.'

Stanley breathed a sigh of relief to see a mischievous grin crease her face. 'He never married? Brodie! Are you sure? He was a ladies' man if ever there was one. Don't tell me no one caught him?'

'Not really,' he replied, tiring of this stand-off. 'Perhaps I could come in and explain the circumstances to you.'

'Mr Wickham, that's not necessary. Best you find someone else. Brodie, I have to say, gave us our start in life. We don't need any more from him. Gus and me, we've got all we need.'

Corrigan intervened quickly. 'Is Gus home? Perhaps we could talk to him.'

'He's not here, he's up at my daughter's place.'

'Then we'll go get him,' Corrigan said, but that didn't suit Stanley.

'Really, Mrs Kriedemann,' he protested. 'My business is with you. There's a lot of money involved.' He looked down helplessly at the briefcase he'd carted across the world. 'There are papers for you to sign.'

'I told you,' she said, 'wishing you no disrespect, but we don't need it.' She turned away from them, calling to the dogs, then as an afterthought, she looked back to Stanley. 'Give it to my daughter. She's the one as needs it, not me.' And she disappeared into the cottage.

Corrigan sighed. 'We'd better go and find Gus.'

They drove through the village, past the church at the crown of the hill and down a winding road towards a Georgian-style house set in a stretch of ploughed fields.

'It used to be a grand house in the old days,' Corrigan told him, 'but it's the worse for wear now, falling down about their ears. Gus is always up here making repairs. They say this old house was a great place for entertaining, very posh, ladies and gentlemen coming from far away in their carriages to skip the light fantastic at balls and parties that went on for days.' He threw his hand out expansively, almost causing Stanley to run off the road. 'This land, for miles about, was not just paddocks, not for them gentry. I've seen paintings. There were fine gardens and miniature lakes, and beyond them again the tenant farms.' He clucked his tongue sadly. 'But the family fell on hard times. Gradually lost the lot, bar the house and a few fields. They say the men were great gamblers.'

As the car approached the house, Corrigan touched Stanley's arm. 'Don't be holding out on me. When you said you were a solicitor and we've got no crimes involved, I guessed what you might be up to, and I was right, wasn't I?'

'You were right,' Stanley smiled.

'I heard they were takin' bets at the hotel last night, as to your purpose here. Some were guessing that a rich uncle had died back there in Australia and left someone in Tullymore a sheep farm. Would that be right?'

'As you've seen, not an uncle but a brother-in-law.'

'And he left Trella a sheep farm?'

'Not exactly.'

'God help us, Mr Wickham, you're close with information. You know I'll be finding out sooner or later. I'm fair busting to know! How much would it be adding up to? You didn't come all this way for a few pounds.'

Stanley opened the car door and then he hesitated. He too was busting to tell someone. Trella's reaction had been all wrong. He'd expected to be part of the joy, the excitement, and Trella's disinterest had been a monumental let down. What if the rest of the family were like her? He'd end up shoving the estate on them like a pushy hawker.

Even if it had been just the opals. Just the *boulder* opals, he reiterated, he should have expected delight, but with all the rest . . .

He turned to Corrigan. 'Have you ever heard of a cattle station?'

'A farm would it be? For cattle?'

Stanley found himself laughing. Remembering how Brodie used to tease Clover. His excitement spilled over into the ears of his avid listener. 'For about thirty thousand cattle,' he chortled. 'Or more. I forget. Trella has inherited a huge cattle station, fully equipped and in working order, with a fine homestead.'

'Oh bejasus!' Corrigan roared. 'Why didn't you tell me this when we passed the pub? We could have had a drink on it. How big is a farm that would take that many cattle?'

'About a thousand square miles. It's called Plenty Station.'

'And a fittin' name is that,' Corrigan shouted in delight.

'Then there's the rest,' Stanley added.

'What rest, man? God love us, what rest?'

But Stanley sobered. 'I'd better talk to Gus.'

'How did a lad from here make all that money?' Corrigan persisted.

'It's a long story.'

A woman in her late thirties opened the door. A woman with smooth flaxen hair and wide blue eyes.

'Is there anything wrong?' she asked nervously, taking in Corrigan's black uniform with its silver buttons.

'Not a thing, Bridie,' he said. 'We're looking for your dad.'

'I'll get him.' Unconvinced, she hurried away so Corrigan took it upon himself to escort Stanley inside. They walked across the hall past the staircase to a long room roughly furnished, but the high ceiling still showed glimpses of opulence, faded blue paint and gilt withering on the ornamental mouldings above him. He peered into adjoining rooms ignoring the state of disrepair and the economical furnishings. 'This is a beautiful house!'

'Didn't I just tell ye?' Corrigan said. 'But no one could afford to put it right. Not any more.' He slapped Stanley on the back. 'Until now. Until you turned up, eh? You're a godsend, Mr Wickham, if ever there was one. We ought to celebrate.'

Primly, the solicitor placed his briefcase on a table and waited, feeling a little guilty that he'd spilled the beans to Corrigan. Hoping this family wouldn't object because there was no chance of the sergeant keeping his mouth shut.

Then Gus Kriedemann walked in and Stanley recognised him immediately. Baldness had replaced the blond hair and his skin was a lot paler than Stanley recalled, but here in Tullymore was the big burly barman he'd met in Toowoomba.

Gus strode forward his hand outstretched as Corrigan introduced them.

'You don't remember me, I suppose,' Stanley said.

Gus replied, 'I'm sorry, Mr Wickham. I'm afraid I don't.'

Gus had no trace of an accent. No trace at all. And that surprised Stanley, among all the Irish brogues until he realised that of course there was no accent. He was listening to another Australian voice. As unique as his own in these lands.

'Brodie Court introduced us in a pub in Toowoomba,' he grinned. 'You were a barman and I had just been engaged as Brodie's lawyer.'

'Good God!' Gus peered at him. 'So you are. I'm sorry. I'm bad on names.'

'Stanley. I was introduced as Stanley. Brodie was in fine form that day.'

'He sure was. You're a real voice from the past. Bridie, do you think you could find us a drink? There's a bottle of whiskey in the kitchen, the good Irish whiskey. I know the sergeant won't mind a drop. What about you, Mr Wickham?'

'Stanley.'

'Goodoh, Stanley.'

'I'd be delighted.'

The daughter perched politely on a chair behind them as the men talked, or rather Stanley tried to talk, with excited interruptions from Corrigan while Gus listened. Astonished.

Stanley gave him the bare outline of why he'd come to Tullymore. 'Sentimental of me, I suppose,' he said, 'but Brodie introduced me to opals and I did quite well with them myself. But I liked him and I wanted to see this through to the end.'

'And so he left Trella some money,' Gus said at length, while Stanley gave Corrigan a warning glance to be quiet.

'Yes.'

'That was nice of him. Brodie was a remarkable man.'

'In what way?'

'He saw beauty in colour. He was fascinated by colour. That's why the opals got him in. He was like a bower bird. You know, they fill their nests with everything blue. Marvellous! He just loved colour, we'd be working like mad and drag out of those mines and he'd say: "Will you look at that sunset!" All we wanted was a drink and grub. Forget the sunset.'

'You're right there,' Stanley told him. 'When he died we found a drawer of the most gorgeous boulder opals you could imagine.'

'Ah no,' Gus breathed. 'You haven't sold them yet have you? I'd love to see them.'

'I can't sell them. They belong to Trella.'

'Oh Christ, he left her them too. No family?'

'No, he never married.'

'That surprises me. But on the other hand, Brodie was the most single-minded man I ever met in my life. Whatever he made up his mind to do, he did. No one could turn him aside. Not even a woman. He always did exactly what he wanted to do. Some people said he was mean, but it was only his one track mind. Others said he had the luck of the Irish but I don't see a lot of luck in this country.'

'Did you ever know a woman called Clover Chiswick?'

'Yes. From Plenty Station. We were mining on Plenty Station and ran into trouble with the boss. We had other troubles there too,' he added softly but that's another story. 'That was the last time I saw Brodie.'

'On Plenty Station?' Stanley was fascinated. 'So he did know Clover Chiswick before.'

'Before what?'

'Gus. We have a lot to talk about and a lot to unravel. But I have to tell you that Brodie died a very rich man. He owned Plenty Station.'

'You're joking?'

'Believe me, I'm not. But you have to talk to Trella. He's left her the lot.'

'Oh God,' Gus cried, 'he was still bloody mourning. Poor Brodie. It was so unnecessary.'

'What was?'

'That he leave everything to Trella. She forgave him years ago.'

'I'd like to hear about that, if it isn't intruding, but that's not the point. He did leave a will, but even if he hadn't, Trella is still his only surviving relative, and if your wife hadn't survived the next of kin would have been you, Gus, or your daughter Bridie, who has not as yet been introduced to me.'

'I'm sorry.' Gus leapt up. 'Bridie, this is an old friend of mine, Mr Stanley Wickham. This is Bridie Hadley-Jones. Her husband is not home at the moment. He works as a bookkeeper at the co-operative store.'

'He's going to have his time cut out now,' Corrigan chortled.

'I think we should have them here,' Stanley said. 'Both

505

Trella and your husband, Bridie.' He handed the keys of his car to Corrigan. 'Would you mind, Sergeant?'

'It'll be a pleasure! I can take your car?'

'Yes. As long as you come back with Mr Hadley-Jones and Mrs Kriedemann.'

'I'd better go with him,' Bridie said. 'Mum mightn't be too keen by the sounds of things.'

'Tell her I'm waiting for her,' Gus said. 'And, Jim, what about picking up a couple of bottles of Maloney's top shelf?'

'I'll get right on it, Gus.'

When they left, Gus and Stanley sat quietly, suddenly bereft of words. Where to start? Too much to talk about. Too many gaps.

'Was he happy in the end?' Gus asked.

'I think so. He had lost interest in becoming the richest man in the world and Clover had too much. All they needed was true friendship and they found it together. Eventually. He lived with her for years.'

Gus refilled their glasses. 'Trella was right. We don't need any more from Brodie but it will be a boost to Bridie and her husband and their kids.'

'It'll be some boost,' Stanley replied. 'There's a lot of money involved.'

'I realise that. There'll have to be some very careful decision-making. I don't want any great upheavals.' He smiled. 'At least we can put the Hadley-Jones family back on their feet again. That would have amused Brodie.'

'Maybe,' Stanley said.

Gus laughed. 'And maybe not.' He raised his glass. 'So here's to Brodie, he's disorganising me again. But as the Irish say: He was a fine upstandin' fella. A darlin' man.'

'And you?' Stanley asked.

'He was a good bloke.'

Stanley echoed the toast solemnly. Then when they resumed their seats he asked, 'How *did* you come to meet your wife?'